CRIME AND PUNISHMENT

This acclaimed new translation of Dostoyevsky's 'psychological record of a crime' gives his dark masterpiece of murder and pursuit a renewed vitality, expressing its jagged, staccato urgency and fevered atmosphere as never before. Raskolnikov, a destitute and desperate former student, wanders alone through the slums of St Petersburg, deliriously imagining himself above society's laws. But when he commits a random murder, only suffering ensues. Embarking on a dangerous game of cat and mouse with a suspicious police investigator, Raskolnikov is pursued by the growing voice of his conscience and finds the noose of his own guilt tightening around his neck. Only Sonya, a downtrodden prostitute, can offer the chance of redemption.

* * *

'A truly great translation . . . Sometimes new translations of old favourites are surplus to our requirements. . . . Sometimes, though, a new translation really makes us see a favourite masterpiece afresh. And this English version of *Crime and Punishment* really is better. . . . *Crime and Punishment*, as well as being an horrific story and a compelling drama, is also extremely funny. Ready brings out this quality well. . . . That knife-edge between sentimentality and farce has been so skilfully and delicately captured here. . . . Ready's version is colloquial, compellingly modern and—in so far as my amateurish knowledge of the language goes—much closer to the Russian. . . . The central scene in the book . . . is a masterpiece of translation.'
—A. N. Wilson, *The Spectator*

'This vivid, stylish, and rich rendition by Oliver Ready compels the attention of the reader in a way that none of the others I've read comes close to matching. Using a clear and forceful mid-twentieth-century idiom, Ready gives us an entirely new kind of access to Dostoyevsky's singular, self-reflexive and at times unnervingly comic text. This is the Russian writer's story of moral revolt, guilt, and possible regeneration turned into a new work of art. . . . [It] will give a jolt to the nervous system to anyone interested in the enigmatic Russian author.'
—John Gray, *New Statesman*, 'Books of the Year'

'At last we have a translation that brings out the wild humour and vitality of the original.'
—Robert Chandler, *PEN Atlas*

'A gorgeous translation . . . Inside one finds an excellent apparatus: a chronology, a terrific contextualizing introduction, a handy compendium of suggestions for further reading, and cogent notes on the translation. . . . But the best part is Ready's supple translation of the novel itself. Ready manages to cleave as closely as any prior translator to both spirit and letter, while rendering them into an English that is a relief to read.' —*The East-West Review*

'Oliver Ready's dynamic translation certainly succeeds in implicating new readers in Dostoyevsky's old novel.' —*The Times Literary Supplement*

'What a pleasure it is to see Oliver Ready's new translation bring renewed power to one of the world's greatest works of fiction. . . . Ready's work is of substantial and superb quality. . . . [His] version portrays more viscerally and vividly the contradictory nature of Raskolnikov's consciousness. . . . Ready evokes the crux of *Crime and Punishment* with more power than the previous translators have . . . with an enviably raw economy of prose.'
—*The Curator*

'Ready's new translation of *Crime and Punishment* is thoughtful and elegant [and] shows us once again why this novel is one of the most intriguing psychological studies ever written. His translation also manages to revive the disturbing humor of the original. . . . In some places, Ready's version echoes Pevear and Volokhonsky's prize-winning nineties version, but he often renders Dostoyevsky's text more lucidly while retaining its deliberately uncomfortable feel. . . . Ready's colloquial, economical use of language gives the text a new power.' —*Russia Beyond the Headlines*

'[A] five-star hit, which will make you see the original with new eyes.'
—*The Times Literary Supplement*, 'Books of the Year'

PENGUIN CLASSICS

CRIME AND PUNISHMENT

FYODOR MIKHAILOVICH DOSTOYEVSKY was born in Moscow in 1821 at the Mariinsky Hospital for the Poor, where his father worked as a doctor. His mother died in 1837 and his father two years later, rumoured to have been murdered by his serfs. From 1838 to 1843 he studied at the Academy of Military Engineers in St Petersburg. In 1844 Dostoyevsky resigned his commission and devoted himself fully to literature. His debut, the epistolary novel *Poor Folk* (1846), made his name, though *The Double*, published later that year, was greeted with much less enthusiasm, not least by Dostoyevsky's champion, Vissarion Belinsky. His epilepsy, which became increasingly severe, set in at this time. In 1849 he was arrested and sentenced to death for involvement with the politically subversive 'Petrashevsky circle'; his sentence was commuted at the last moment to penal servitude and until 1854 he lived in a convict prison in Omsk, Siberia. From this experience came *Notes from the Dead House* (1860–2), which restored his literary reputation on his return to St Petersburg. In 1861 he and his brother Mikhail launched *Time* (*Vremya*), a monthly journal of literary-political affairs. Already married, Dostoyevsky fell in love with one of his contributors, Apollinaria Suslova, eighteen years his junior, and also developed a ruinous passion for roulette. The year 1864 saw the deaths of his wife Maria Dmitrievna and brother Mikhail, and the publication of *Notes from Underground*. He set to work on *Crime and Punishment* (1866) the following year. While writing this novel he engaged a young stenographer, Anna Grigoryevna Snitkina, and married her in 1867. The major novels of his late period, written in Russia and abroad, are *The Idiot* (1868), *Demons* (1871–2) and *The Brothers Karamazov* (1879–80). He died in 1881 at the peak of his fame.

OLIVER READY is Research Fellow in Russian Society and Culture at St Antony's College, Oxford. His translations include, from contemporary fiction, *The Zero Train* (2001; 2007) and *The Prussian Bride* (2002; Rossica Translation Prize, 2005) by Yuri Buida, and *Before and During* (2014) by Vladimir Sharov. He is the general editor of the anthology *The Ties of Blood: Russian Literature from the 21st Century* (2008) and Russia and East-Central Europe editor at the *Times Literary Supplement*.

FYODOR DOSTOYEVSKY

Crime and Punishment

Translated with an Introduction and Notes by
OLIVER READY

PENGUIN BOOKS

PENGUIN BOOKS
Published by the Penguin Group
Penguin Group (USA) LLC
375 Hudson Street
New York, New York 10014

USA | Canada | UK | Ireland | Australia | New Zealand | India | South Africa | China
penguin.com
A Penguin Random House Company

Crime and Punishment first published in Russian in monthly instalments
in *Russkii Vestnik* (The Russian Messenger) 1866
This translation first published in Penguin Classics (UK) 2014
Published in Penguin Books (USA) 2015

Translation and editorial material copyright © 2014 by Oliver Ready
LIBRARY OF CONGRESS CATALOGING-IN-PUBLICATION DATA

Dostoyevsky, Fyodor, 1821–1881, author.
[Prestuplenie i nakazanie. English. (Ready)]
Crime and punishment / Fyodor Dostoyevsky; translated and with an introduction
and notes by Oliver Ready.
pages; cm
Includes bibliographical references.
ISBN 978-0-14-310763-7
I. Ready, Oliver, 1976– translator, writer of added commentary.   II. Title.
PG3326.P7 2014
891.73'3—dc23
2014033003

Printed in the United States of America
3   5   7   9   10   8   6   4

Set in Sabon LT Std

Contents

CRIME AND PUNISHMENT

Chronology

1821 (30 October)* Born Fyodor Mikhailovich Dostoyevsky in Moscow, the son of Mikhail Andreyevich, head physician at Mariinsky Hospital for the Poor, and of Maria Fyodorovna, daughter of a merchant family.

1823 Pushkin begins *Eugene Onegin*.

1825 Death of Tsar Alexander I and accession of Nicholas I, followed by the revolt of several thousand officers and soldiers in St Petersburg (the 'Decembrist Uprising').

1831 Mikhail Andreyevich, having risen to the status of nobleman, buys a small estate south of Moscow at Darovoe, where his wife and children now spend their summers. During this year he also takes his wife and elder sons to see Schiller's play *The Robbers*, which makes a great impression on the young Dostoyevsky. Pushkin finishes *Eugene Onegin*.

1834 Enrolled with his elder brother Mikhail (*b.* 1820) at Chermak's, Moscow's leading boarding school.

1837 Pushkin killed in a duel. Maria Fyodorovna dies and the brothers are sent to preparatory school in St Petersburg.

1838 Enters the St Petersburg Academy of Military Engineers (Mikhail is not admitted).

1839 Father dies, apparently murdered by serfs on his estate.

1840 Publication of Lermontov's *A Hero of Our Time*.

1841 Obtains a commission. Works on two historical plays (*Mary Stuart* and *Boris Godunov*), both lost.

1842 Promoted to second lieutenant. Publication of Gogol's *Dead Souls* and 'The Overcoat'.

1843 Graduates from the Academy. Attached to St Petersburg Army Engineering Corps.

---

* Dates are Old Style, following the Julian calendar, which was twelve days behind the Gregorian calendar and remained in force in Russia until 1918.

1844 Resigns his commission. Publication of his translation of Balzac's *Eugénie Grandet*. Also translates George Sand's *La dernière Aldini*, only to find that another translation has already appeared. Works on *Poor Folk*, his first novel.

1845 Establishes a friendship with Russia's most prominent and influential literary critic, Vissarion Belinsky, who praises *Poor Folk* and acclaims its author as Gogol's successor.

1846 *Poor Folk* and *The Double* published. While *Poor Folk* is widely praised, *The Double* is much less successful. 'Mr Prokharchin' also published.

1846–7 Nervous ailments and the onset of epileptic seizures. Begins regular consultations with Dr Stepan Yanovsky. Utopian socialist and atheist M. V. Butashevich-Petrashevsky becomes an acquaintance; begins attending the 'Petrashevsky circle'. 'A Novel in Nine Letters' and 'The Landlady' are published.

1848 Several short stories published, including 'White Nights', 'A Weak Heart', 'A Christmas Party and a Wedding' and 'An Honest Thief'.

1849 First instalments of *Netochka Nezvanova* published. Arrested along with other members of the Petrashevsky circle, convicted of political offences against the Russian state. Sentenced to death, taken out to Semyonovsky Square to be shot by firing squad, but reprieved moments before execution. Instead, sentenced to an indefinite period of exile in Siberia, to begin with eight years of penal servitude, later reduced to four years by Tsar Nicholas I.

1850 Prison and hard labour in Omsk, western Siberia.

1853 Outbreak of Crimean War.

1854 Released from prison and sent to serve in an infantry battalion at Semipalatinsk, south-western Siberia. Allowed to live in private quarters. Becomes a regular visitor at the home of Alexander Isayev, an alcoholic civil servant, and his wife Maria Dmitrievna Isayeva. Promoted to non-commissioned officer.

1855 Alexander II succeeds Nicholas I: some relaxation of state censorship.

1857 Marries the widowed Maria Isayeva after a long courtship, and soon after has a major seizure which leads to the first official confirmation of his epilepsy. Publication of 'The Little Hero', written in prison during the summer of 1849.

1858 Petitions Alexander II to be released from military service on medical grounds. Works on *The Village of Stepanchikovo and Its Inhabitants* and *Uncle's Dream*.

1859 Allowed to return to live in European Russia; in December returns with his wife and stepson Pavel to St Petersburg. First chapters of *The Village of Stepanchikovo and Its Inhabitants* and *Uncle's Dream* published.

1861 Emancipation of the serfs. Launch of *Time* (*Vremya*), a monthly journal of literature and socio-political affairs edited by Dostoyevsky and his elder brother Mikhail. In the first issues he publishes his first full-length novel, *The Insulted and the Injured*, and the first part of *Notes from the Dead House*, based on his experience in Omsk.

1862 Second part of *Notes from the Dead House* and *A Nasty Tale* published in *Time*. Makes first trip abroad, to Europe, visiting Germany, France, England, Switzerland, Italy. Gambles in Wiesbaden. Meets Alexander Herzen in London. Turgenev's *Fathers and Sons*.

1863 *Winter Notes on Summer Impressions*, based on his European travels, published in *Time*. Liaison with Apollinaria Suslova begins at about this time. After Maria Dmitrievna is taken seriously ill, he travels abroad again, gambles and visits Italy with Suslova. Publication of Nikolai Chernyshevsky's novel *What Is to Be Done?*

1864 In March launches with Mikhail the journal *Epoch* (*Epokha*) as successor to *Time*, now banned by the Russian authorities. *Notes from Underground* published in *Epoch*. In April death of Maria Dmitrievna. In July death of Mikhail. The International Workingmen's Association (the First International) founded in London.

1865 *Epoch* ceases publication owing to lack of funds. Courts Anna Korvin-Krukovskaya, a contributor to *Epoch* and future revolutionary activist; she turns down his proposal of marriage. To meet his debts, signs very unfavourable contract with the publisher Stellovsky. Gambles in Wiesbaden. Works on *Crime and Punishment*. First fragment of Tolstoy's *War and Peace*.

1866 Dmitry Karakozov attempts to assassinate Alexander II. Interrupts writing of *Crime and Punishment* to write *The Gambler*, promised to Stellovsky by 1 November. Hires young stenographer Anna Grigoryevna Snitkina (*b.* 1846), who helps him complete the novel in twenty-six days. *The Gambler* published in December. *Crime and*

Punishment serialized in eight issues of *The Russian Messenger* (*Russkii Vestnik*).

1867 Marries Anna. Hounded by creditors, they leave for Western Europe, where they will spend the next four years.

1868 Birth of daughter Sofya, who dies at three months. *The Idiot* published in serial form in *The Russian Messenger*.

1869 Birth of daughter Lyubov in Dresden. The Nechayev Affair: Ivan Ivanov is murdered by fellow members of a clandestine revolutionary cell led by Sergei Nechayev.

1870 Starts work on *Demons*. V. I. Ulyanov (later known as Lenin) is born in the town of Simbirsk on the banks of the Volga. *The Eternal Husband* published.

1871 Moves back to St Petersburg with his wife and family. Birth of son, Fyodor.

1871–2 Serial publication of *Demons*.

1873 Becomes contributing editor of conservative weekly journal *Citizen* (*Grazhdanin*), where his *A Writer's Diary* is published as a regular column. 'Bobok' published.

1875 *The Adolescent* published. Birth of son, Alexei.

1876 'The Meek One' published in *A Writer's Diary*.

1877 'The Dream of a Ridiculous Man' published in *A Writer's Diary*.

1878 Death of son Alexei after an epileptic fit. Works on *The Brothers Karamazov*.

1879 Iosif Vissarionovich Dzhugashvili (later known as Stalin) born in Gori, Georgia. First part of *The Brothers Karamazov* published.

1880 *The Brothers Karamazov* published in complete form. Speech in Moscow at the unveiling of a monument to Pushkin is greeted with wild enthusiasm.

1881 Dostoyevsky dies in St Petersburg after repeated pulmonary haemorrhage (28 January). Buried in the cemetery of the Alexander Nevsky Monastery. The funeral procession from the author's apartment numbers over 30,000. Assassination of Alexander II (1 March).

Introduction

I

A ready-made title, 'Crime and Punishment' suggests a ready-made plot. A man will commit a crime. He will be caught. He will be punished. His fate will revolve around the conflicts between freedom and conscience, the delinquent individual and the punitive state. Justice, no doubt, will be done.

In January 1866, when the first instalment of *Crime and Punishment* appeared in *The Russian Messenger* (*Russkii Vestnik*), prospective readers might have indulged in further well-reasoned speculation. Here was a title steeped in the ferment of its time, an era marked on the one hand by the ambitious reforms of Tsar Alexander II (1818–81), not least to the entire judicial process, and on the other by mounting radicalism and nascent terrorism, prompted in large part by the perceived failure of these same reforms. Serfdom may have been consigned to history five years earlier, but the harsh terms of the serfs' 'emancipation' had done little to alleviate social injustice. Would this, then, be a novel of political rebellion? Or perhaps, given the increasingly conservative leanings of the ageing Dostoyevsky (and of Mikhail Katkov, editor of *The Russian Messenger*), a satire of these revolutionary tendencies?

Inevitably, the novel would also be rooted in the bitter experience of its famous author. After all, he, too, in his free-thinking youth, had known crime and punishment at first hand. His chief 'crime' was to read out, more than once, Vissarion Belinsky's letter to Nikolai Gogol (1809–52), in which Russia's leading critic railed against Russia's leading author, whose latest book had revealed him to be a 'proponent of the knout', of Church, State and serfdom. Dostoyevsky's 'punishment' – and that of a disparate group of his associates, broadly linked by utopian-socialist sympathies – was to face the firing squad on St Petersburg's Semyonovsky Square in December 1849. The sentence was commuted by Tsar Nicholas I (1796–1855) at the last possible moment and in the most theatrical manner. Instead, Dostoyevsky endured years of hard labour in Siberia, described upon his return to St Petersburg in the lightly fictionalized *Notes from the Dead House* (1860–2), the first masterpiece of his mature period.

Finally, *Crime and Punishment* would be imbued with ideas familiar to all readers of Dostoyevsky's post-Siberian journalism: educated Russia needed to return to its roots, to the soil, to the people. Only thus could the warring tribes of Westernizers and Slavophiles, elites and commoners, be joined; only thus would the country's ancient wounds be healed.

At one level the novel we go on to read satisfies all of these conventional expectations. At another all of them are unsettled, if not thoroughly undermined. We read of murders committed by a handsome young man whom it would be difficult to identify precisely with the radicals of the 1860s (though some offended young readers contrived to do so) or with its unhandsome author. Disturbingly, this man is unsure that his gruesome acts were crimes at all; unsure at times that they even happened. For much of the book he even seems to forget one of his murders entirely. The reality of punishment also eludes him for an unreasonably long time, despite his best efforts. In his mind everything begins to merge: past and future, right and wrong, perpetrator and victim, crime and punishment. The opposition stated by the title, so familiar and in its way so comforting, begins to dissolve for the reader, too; a dark joke, perhaps – like Dostoyevsky's own 'execution'? – yet no less serious for that.

Because it was written before *The Idiot* (1868), *Demons* (1871–2) and *The Brothers Karamazov* (1879–80), and because it is so often described as a version of the murder mystery or as a novel of religious conversion, *Crime and Punishment* has an entrenched reputation as the most straightforward of Dostoyevsky's great quartet of late novels. Yet its puzzles and ambiguities, when fully entered into, allow the reader to share the same vertiginous confusion experienced by its protagonist, Rodion Romanovich Raskolnikov. In the words of Virginia Woolf: 'Against our wills we are drawn in, whirled round, blinded, suffocated, and at the same time filled with a giddy rapture. Out of Shakespeare there is no more exciting reading.'[1]

II

The sources of the novel's complexity can be traced to the opening sentences of the first detailed record we have of Dostoyevsky's plans for the book. Originally envisioned as a long story, *Crime and Punishment* was proposed to Katkov in a letter from Wiesbaden, where the recently widowed, forty-three-year-old Dostoyevsky was enduring what his most comprehensive biographer, the late Joseph Frank, aptly calls a 'period of protracted mortification'.[2] His first wife, with whom he had rarely been happy, had succumbed to tuberculosis the previous year. Mikhail – his brother and soulmate – had also died in 1864, leaving enormous debts. This moral and financial destitution was further compounded by Dostoyevsky's two uncontrollable manias: one for roulette, another (only marginally weaker) for his ex-mistress Apollinaria Suslova, a femme fatale eighteen years his junior. To top it all, he had recently signed a contract with the unscrupulous publisher Fyodor Stellovsky, requiring him, on pain of losing all rights to his own works, to complete an additional novel by 1 November 1866.

Yet for all this pressure and turmoil, the proposal for a 'psychological record of a crime' which Dostoyevsky submitted to Katkov is notable for its clarity, confidence and precision. It begins:

> A contemporary setting, this current year [1865]. A young man, excluded from student status at university, of trading class, living in extreme poverty, succumbs, through frivolity and ricketiness of thought, to certain strange, 'half-baked' ideas in the air, and makes up his mind to get out of his foul situation in a single bound.[3]

A great deal changed between the conception of this story in a German spa town and the eventual birth of the novel in Russia. It expanded not only in size, but also in perspective, which grew from the confessional mode (often favoured by Dostoyevsky in his fiction hitherto) to a third-person viewpoint of virtual omniscience and deliberate 'naivety', as Dostoyevsky himself described it in his notebooks. Very little changed, however, about the two sentences quoted above.[4] They contain in embryo the strange mixture of ingredients that will determine Raskolnikov's half-real, half-theoretical drama: poverty and social exclusion on the one hand, and frivolous, 'half-baked' thoughts

on the other. Only one element is missing – the element of psychoge-
ography, as it would now be called. This is memorably supplied by St
Petersburg, 'the most premeditated and abstract city in the world',[5]
built on a northern swamp by Western architects and Russian serfs.
Here, too, we are in the realms of the semi-real and semi-theoretical,
of rationalism and delusion – a tradition first developed in the St Petersburg texts of Alexander Pushkin (1799–1837) and Gogol and now
taken in new directions by their pupil, Dostoyevsky.

As we first see him, cooped up in his garret and barely able to rise
from his couch, Raskolnikov exists (or thinks he exists) only in his own
mind. For much of the novel that will remain the case, a sign of his
catastrophic isolation from mankind. Yet at the same time, through a
chain of spatial metaphors, Dostoyevsky makes us see how deeply his
mental disarray is tied to the city that surrounds him. Such metaphors
are characteristic of the novel's curious artistic achievement: as subtle
as the axe that Raskolnikov brings down on the head of his first victim,
they are also freighted with the exceptional weight of association that
makes us, as readers, share in the protagonist's experience of suffoca-
tion from causes both abstract and real. Thus, Raskolnikov's mental
state finds its external embodiment in his low-ceilinged, cramped garret. This garret, in turn, is a 'cupboard', a 'ship's cabin', a 'cell', and
even, as perceived by his mother, a 'coffin'.

Raskolnikov's mind also stands in metaphorical relation to the broader
topography in which his fate is to be played out: the overcrowded,
shabby area of St Petersburg's Haymarket district, with its narrow,
twisting streets, its fetid canal (or 'Ditch') and its filthy stairwells, drinking dens and connecting courtyards, through which tradesmen, girl-
prostitutes and criminals 'hurry and scurry'. Only a stone's throw from
the imperial majesty of the Neva River and Nevsky Prospect (associated
with Pushkin and Gogol respectively), this is the shadow St Petersburg,
airless and coffin-like in the height of summer, that Dostoyevsky made
his own in both literature and life. In place of the sober 'military capital'
evoked by Pushkin in *The Bronze Horseman* (1833) – with its 'severe,
elegant appearance', its perfection of form – Dostoyevsky's Haymarket is
drunken and unkempt. Here, Baltic Germans shout atrocious Russian,
villagers pour in to sub-rent 'corners', and students and officers spout
caricatured versions of Bentham and Mill. This, too, is a prison of sorts:
not the prison of Pushkin's military autocracy, nor the bureaucratic

nightmare of Gogol, but the false freedom of those torn from their roots, left with nothing but words and borrowed ideas.

The opening pages acquaint us with these borrowed ideas in the recurring themes of Raskolnikov's wretched soliloquies: how to overcome his cowardice and indecisiveness, how to utter 'a new word', to take a 'new step'; above all, how to stop talking and start doing. Before us is a Hamlet without a clearly identifiable cause, a man-child who fears the frivolity of his own thoughts (mere 'toys'), which he is unable to arrange in satisfactory order. A penchant for self-contradiction lends a rebarbative texture to his ruminations, marked by the frequency of 'but' and 'still' and tapering off in rows of dots. It is the self-lacerating language familiar from the narrator of Dostoyevsky's *Notes from Underground* (1864), but spoken now from beneath the eaves, rather than from beneath the floorboards. The masochism of the mouse-man of the Underground is replaced by Raskolnikov's 'Satanic pride'.[6]

This pride, however, is knowingly misplaced. Raskolnikov's thoughts are evidently as stale to him as they would have been to contemporary readers, for whom the anxieties of the ineffectual intellectual had long been familiar from novels set on country estates among gifted young men too weak or too comfortable to address the malign status quo. By 1865 the idle moral torments of the 'superfluous men' of Ivan Goncharov (1812–91) and Ivan Turgenev (1818–83) had filtered down to the new breed of déclassé, de-Christianized intellectuals, the most influential of whom, such as the socialist Nikolai Chernyshevsky (1828–89) and the nihilist Dmitry Pisarev (1840–68), were inspiring a generation of revolutionaries with their heavily ideological fiction and criticism. For both of these men, prison was more than a metaphor.

In this context, Raskolnikov's vacillations and ruminations are decidedly old-school, and not infrequently derivative. Thus, Pisarev, in response to Bazarov, the anti-hero of Turgenev's *Fathers and Sons* (1862), had already set out a division between the conformist masses and the select few to whom all is permitted and who may be prevented only by 'personal taste' from murder and robbery.[7] Now, three years later, this idea is plagiarized by Raskolnikov. Nor does Dostoyevsky want us to ignore, from the opening page, the belated echoes of the title of Chernyshevsky's hymn to the emancipatory power of 'rational egoism', the novel *What Is to Be Done?* (1863). Later, Raskolnikov will address the same question verbatim to his good angel, Sonya, and she, in turn, will pose it to him. Raskolnikov's answer will again be an act of plagiarism: we must break what must be broken – an almost direct quote from Pisarev, recycled many years later by Lenin. But Raskolnikov is an unlikely revolutionary. He is too much a loner to be the 'political conspirator' his friend Razumikhin mistakes him for, and he is certainly no leader of men; perhaps he is just a belated Romantic, framing his outdated, somewhat comical delusions in the language of his day?

Dostoyevsky also introduces in the early chapters a further element latent in his pitch to Katkov: the impatience of his protagonist, who 'makes up his mind to get out of his foul situation in a single bound'. This is brought to the surface by the maid and country girl Nastasya, who, endowed with the intuition that Dostoyevsky often reserves for his less educated characters, divines that Raskolnikov is too lazy to work and wants his fortune 'right now'. Unimpressed by 'eggheads' who never do a stroke of work, she nevertheless feels a rough tenderness towards him as a human being, foreshadowing the much deeper feelings and intuition that will be shown by Sonya, who similarly opposes her own unconscious wisdom (Sonya: Sophia) to the sophistry of Raskolnikov.

In the folkloric context that would have constituted Nastasya's own education, Raskolnikov might be cast as Ivan the Fool, who sits on the stove all day and waits for a pretty maiden and a crock of gold to fall into his lap. Raskolnikov, who also hails from the provinces, has himself kept one foot in the cuckoo land of magic tales, as an early, jarring reference to King Pea (*Tsar Gorokh*, associated with bygone happiness) makes plain. But St Petersburg, he will find, is no place for childish dreams.

Nor is it a place for a 'player' (*igrok*), to give the literal translation of the Russian word for 'gambler'. For Raskolnikov – like Pushkin's Hermann in 'The Queen of Spades' (1834), and like Dostoyevsky himself – is obsessed by the mirage of a winning formula, and it should be no surprise that the short novel for which Dostoyevsky had to break off work on *Crime and Punishment* bears the title *Igrok* (*The Gambler*). Produced to fulfil his contract with Stellovsky, it was dictated to a young stenographer, Anna Grigoryevna Snitkina, and completed in less than four weeks.[8] But if *The Gambler* is set in a Wiesbaden-esque 'Roulettenburg', where rich and poor throw caution to the winds, *Crime and Punishment* is set in St Petersburg, where numbers are calculated coldly and old pawnbrokers make sure to take their interest in advance. In such a city, murder, too, must be 'premeditated and abstract', and Raskolnikov's first crime, however risky, is both those things; he even counts the steps from his room to the home of his victim. Yet when the crime is actually set in motion he is barely aware of what he is doing: 'As if a scrap of his clothing had caught in the wheel of a machine that was now pulling him in.' This striking contradiction stands at the heart of the novel's innermost concerns, developed over the five hundred-odd pages that remain after Raskolnikov's murders.

III

The nature of these deepest concerns, however, is far from obvious. The unusual construction of *Crime and Punishment*, which gives so much weight to the aftermath of the crime (five parts out of six) and only an epilogue to the punishment itself, has led many to see the novel as less a whodunnit than a whydunnit. According to Joseph Frank: '*Crime and Punishment* is focused on the solution of an enigma: the mystery of Raskolnikov's motivation.'[9] We may wonder, though, whether this 'enigma' is not itself a decoy planted by this most devious of writers.

Certainly, there is no shortage of motivating factors. Raskolnikov is desperately poor and desperately proud, unable to countenance his own humiliating situation; nor can he accept the humiliations endured and imposed by his mother and sister, who send him remittances and sacrifice everything to their 'priceless Rodya'. His intended victim, the withered pawnbroker, is a 'noxious louse' who does nothing but harm; killing her would yield a net gain for humankind (the utilitarian argument). He dreams of being a good man in the future, a benefactor of humanity (the philanthropic argument). He dreams of being a great man, one of the select few, like Lycurgus, Muhammad or Napoleon, 'criminals to a man', whose evil deeds in the present will be forgotten by grateful generations in the future (the heroic argument).

All of these motivations are valid; but equally, none of them is. Raskolnikov's initial crime is both over- and under-motivated; mere 'casuistry', as he calls it himself. Not for nothing does he overhear another student telling an officer, over tea after a game of billiards, not only about the self-same pawnbroker, but about why her murder would be morally justified. The student expounds the logic of such a hypothetical crime persuasively and at great length, but the conversation ends in bathos:

'Here you are speaking and speechifying, but tell me: are you going to kill the old woman *yourself*, or aren't you?'
'Of course not! I'm talking about justice . . . It's not about me . . .'
'Well, as I see it, if you don't dare do it yourself, there's no justice to speak of! Let's have another game!'

This coincidence – brazen in its technical 'naivety' even by Dostoyevsky's standards (unless, of course, Raskolnikov is imagining the entire conversation) – serves to make a powerful point, just before Raskolnikov finally turns words into deed. A 'why' can always be found for a crime; much more difficult to explain is the 'how': how an intention becomes reality, how theory is enfleshed, how abstract reasoning ends in a sensitive, compassionate man slipping in 'sticky, warm blood'. What state of mind is needed for this to happen?

Leo Tolstoy (1828–1910) responded to this quandary in his late essay 'Why Do People Stupefy Themselves?' (1890), where he sought to explain the state of mental automatism in which Raskolnikov carried out his crime. But Tolstoy, an aggressive teetotaller by this stage in his life, was surely exaggerating when he implies that the glass of beer Raskolnikov consumes at the end of the first chapter 'silences the voice of conscience'. Raskolnikov's utter passivity, which makes him succumb to 'ideas in the air' and to gamble everything on one desperate act, reaches back far further than the glass of beer, deeper even than the question of 'conscience'. Nor can it be reduced to the verdict of insanity, as Raskolnikov himself is aware (even when others are not). This passivity is a state of spiritual death and it is this that enables the crime. Dostoyevsky shows how a man who feels as if he is not alive and not truly capable of affecting reality will affect it for precisely that reason – and with catastrophic results. In his own estranged perception, not only is his sense of his own reality attenuated, so too is his sense of the reality of his fellow human beings, of the boundaries between separate lives. The eerie astonishment that overcomes Raskolnikov throughout his crime is the eeriness of a dead man meeting and muffling life.

Where does this state of spiritual death come from, and why is this wretched man-child, Raskolnikov, buried alive in his youth? Here, perhaps, is the true 'enigma' to which Dostoyevsky applies himself in *Crime and Punishment*, both before and after the murders. In so doing, he scatters clues and red herrings to enlighten and confound us. Family pressures, societal pressures, illness, loss of faith: all of these possible explanations are deepened in the course of the novel, but also, at various times, ironized and presented as somehow dishonest. Psychoanalytic, religious, sociological and other interpretations all have much to offer us, but all are also limited, in the final analysis, by Dostoyevsky's strategy of ambivalence in both literature and life. Here was a talented actor who could ask his interrogators what proof they had that he was on the side of the critic and not the author, when he read out Belinsky's letter to Gogol, and who infused the words of his fictional characters with an exceptional ambiguity of meaning and intonation, employing humour less to lighten their arguments than to complicate them. The regrettable division of much Dostoyevsky scholarship (Soviet and post-Soviet) into secular and religious camps ignores the fact that in his fiction Dostoyevsky always thought in terms of *pro* and *contra* – not just in his final masterpiece *The Brothers Karamazov*, with its legendary dramatization of atheism versus Orthodoxy, but equally in *Crime and Punishment*. The vector of Dostoyevsky's intentions – to judge from his notebooks, letters and (arguably) the final pages of this novel – may have tended towards faith and self-abnegation, but the reality of his artistic achievement is very different. Some will be moved by Sonya's selflessness, forgiveness and acceptance of God's world, whatever its injustices, but many readers will be even more struck by the defiance shown by another woman, Katerina Ivanovna – a drunkard's widow with three children on her hands, consumption and no money – towards the priest summoned against her will at her dying hour. The fire of self-abnegating faith and the fire of injured pride blaze with equal strength from the first chapter of the novel to the last, sometimes within the same hearts, and there is no guarantee which will burn the reader more fiercely.

There is, perhaps, only one chain of clues whose validity seems beyond question in helping us approach the enigma mentioned above: the determinative role of literature itself in shaping Raskolnikov's plight. Incongruous though it may sound in the context of a novel about murder, such a claim will come as less of a surprise to readers of Dostoyevsky's earlier works, which are filled with writers or would-be writers, or of his

journalism of the early 1860s, with its recurrent concern with the effects
of *knizhnost'* (or bookishness) on Russian society.[10]

IV

Though never, to my knowledge, presented as such, *Crime and Punishment* is one of the most self-reflexive classics of pre-Modernist European literature, continuing – and developing – a line that stretches
from Cervantes's *Don Quixote* (1605) to Pushkin's *Eugene Onegin*
(1823–31). It is a novel about words and texts as much as deeds and life,
and it is correspondingly saturated with self-quotation and misquotation. The apparently simple line of Raskolnikov's destiny – crime, then
punishment – is interwoven with hints about the complicit and com-
plicating role of literature itself.

This self-reflexivity is not just a matter of the belatedness and imi-
tativeness already discussed, the possibility that Raskolnikov, like
Pushkin's Onegin, might be a 'parody' of earlier bookish types and
ideas. Nor can it be fully contained by Mikhail Bakhtin's pioneering
analysis of the 'polyphony' of Dostoyevsky's fiction, the interpenetra-
tion of characters' thoughts and speech with each other's words and
consciousness, as constantly exhibited by Raskolnikov's monologues,
which are, in fact, dialogues with the words of others.[11] Rather, it is
about the immersion of an entire society in texts and in literary dreams,
and the baneful consequences for Raskolnikov in particular.

Raskolnikov has blood on his socks and ink on his fingers. He pre-
pares for his crime not only by extensive reading, but also, we later
learn, by attempting his first literary debut – a scholarly article with
the same theme as the drama in which he plays the starring role. Published without his knowledge, this article is shown to him much later
by his proud mother, whereupon, despite the grotesque incongruity
with his current situation, he experiences 'that strange and caustically
sweet sensation which every author feels on seeing himself published
for the first time, especially at only twenty-three years of age'. Raskolnikov's achievements as an author may be modest, but his readerly
habits are unshakeable. After committing his murders he visits a tavern to hunt through a pile of recent newspapers for textual evidence
of his crime, which itself evokes dozens of other crimes from Russia
and Europe widely reported in the Russian press in the 1860s – and
especially in Dostoyevsky's own journal *Time* (*Vremya*).[12] The trail of

his crime is not only physical, but also (and much more elusively) textual, keeping Dostoyevsky scholars busy for many decades to come.

Raskolnikov is himself a textual sleuth, an inveterate literary critic. Before and after his crime he shows an uncommon analytical interest in written communications, which are shared with the reader in their entirety: a ten-page letter from his mother, a much curter missive from his sister's odious suitor. He reads between the lines (thereby encouraging us, as readers, to do the same) and judges character by style, surprising those around him by picking on apparently trivial choices of words and phrase at moments when far weightier issues seem to be at stake. For Raskolnikov, life is a text to be understood, and even, at times, a text that has already been written. At the novel's end he imagines what the future has in store for him and asks himself, 'So why live? Why? Why am I going there now, when I know myself that this is exactly how it will be, as it is writ?'

In his bookishness, as in his other characteristics, Raskolnikov is the type of eccentric who, at the deepest level, is most exemplary of his society (a paradox Dostoyevsky explicitly formulated in his prologue to his last novel, *The Brothers Karamazov*). Subtly, insistently, we are encouraged to see that Raskolnikov's addiction to the written word is a symptom of a general, albeit less pathological condition that eddies out from the hero to encompass his family and the country at large. One might not want to make too much of the fact that Raskolnikov's patronymic – Romanovich – etymologically suggests not just 'son of Roman' (a perfectly common name), but also 'son of the novel', were it not for Raskolnikov's mother telling us that his father 'when he was still alive, twice tried sending work to the journals: first some poems (I still have the notebook – I'll show it to you one day), then a whole novella (I begged him to let me copy it out for him), and you should have seen how we prayed for them to be accepted . . . They weren't!'

Frustrated literary ambition is a powerful motif in *Crime and Punishment*, displayed in one form or another by several characters across society, especially Raskolnikov's adversaries in the police and civil service. In particular, the investigator Porfiry Petrovich, who engages Raskolnikov in repeated, chapter-long verbal jousts, is a literary artist and actor manqué, who, like Dostoyevsky himself, reveres the comic genius of Gogol, citing liberally from his works. In Porfiry's extraordinary rhetoric we see the interweaving of literary and legal discourse that was such a feature of the Russian judicial system before and after the legal reforms of 1864, and which Dostoyevsky criticized in his journalism for distracting from the true purpose of the law: to discover the truth.[13] A graduate from the prestigious Imperial School of Jurisprudence, which produced an unusual quantity of eminent writers as well as lawyers, Porfiry imbues his words with Gogolian slipperiness.[14]

The saturation of Russian society in texts, furthermore, not only relates to modern, secular literature. Sonya used to meet with one of Raskolnikov's victims to read from the Bible together, and later she will read out a passage to the murderer himself about the raising of Lazarus. Indeed, in *Crime and Punishment* all believers are fervent readers. Mikolka, the country lad who first confesses to Raskolnikov's crime, 'kept reading the old, "true" books and read himself silly'. The fact that Mikolka is introduced by Porfiry to Raskolnikov as a *raskolnik* – an adherent of the 'Old Belief', which broke off from the official Orthodox Church in the seventeenth century – marks him out as one of the protagonist's many alter egos in the novel, just as his reading habits suggest that Raskolnikov, too, 'read himself silly'. This connection is further enriched if we bear in mind that the *raskolniki* were a prime target of the propaganda envisioned by the (proto-Communist) revolutionary faction into which Dostoyevsky himself was drawn in the late 1840s. The revolution this secret society had in mind was decidedly textual. With the aid of an illegal hand press, assembled shortly before the arrest of the participants in the group, they set about composing revolutionary texts in the language and stylistic register (including the use of Old Church Slavonic) that serfs and 'particularly, perhaps, the *raskolniki*' would understand.[15]

As Porfiry goes on to say however:

> 'Mikolka's not our man! What we've got here, sir, is a fantastical, dark deed, a modern deed, a deed of our time, when the heart of man has clouded over; when there's talk of "renewal" through bloodshed; when people preach about anything and everything from a position of comfort. What we have here are bookish dreams, sir, a heart stirred up by theories [. . .]'

The investigation leads (as the reader knows from the start) straight back to Raskolnikov, the modern man, who stands, from our twenty-first-century perspective, like a bridge between the advent of Russian

Christianity a thousand years before, bringing with it books and an alphabet, and the no-less literary zeal of Russian Communism. 'Bookish dreams' bore terrible fruit in Soviet Russia, whose leaders (Lenin, Stalin, Brezhnev) doubled as prolific authors and fastidious literary critics, and whose drastic changes in policy could be 'justified' by reference to one or another line in one or another of the great books in the Chernyshevskian-Marxist-Leninist canon. As the one-time Bolshevik Victor Serge wrote in Moscow in 1933, 'No real intellectual inquiry is permitted in any sphere. Everything is reduced to a casuistry nourished on quotations.'[16]

Demons is usually seen as Dostoyevsky's great prophetic novel, but *Crime and Punishment*, written half a dozen years earlier, is no less so. Analysing the sealed space of Raskolnikov's mind, Dostoyevsky shows how theory estranges life, and casuistry – wisdom; how reality becomes a game, at once trivial and fatal, in the mind of the reader (writer, artist), the domain of a self-appointed king. In this space the invisible links that hold both the individual psyche and communal life in some sort of balance dissolve. Not just the arguably relative notions of good and evil, but more seemingly fixed dichotomies collapse: here, mere words become murderous deeds, almost without the thinker's awareness; an aesthete becomes a 'louse'; subject becomes object. 'It was myself I killed,' Raskolnikov later reflects. His murders are at once a suicide, his crime is his punishment. The word 'Raskolnikov' may suggest schism (*raskol*), but the point about his modernity, his novelty, is not that he is divided – in Dostoyevsky's world everyone is divided – but that he divides himself, taking an axe to his own humanity.

V

And yet, although he commits suicide of the spirit, Raskolnikov does not commit suicide of the body; like Lazarus, he is given – or does he find? – new life. In a characteristic move that would be repeated in *The Brothers Karamazov*, Dostoyevsky argues against his novel's own pessimism, writing a book against bookishness and setting 'living life' against the coffin-life of Raskolnikov.[17] This second narrative is the novel that eventually grew from the story pitched to Katkov. It is a journey that will be negotiated not through texts, but through people – the same people whose company Raskolnikov wants to avoid from the opening page. In them, opposites do not collapse, but are held in tension, as the novel's gallery of physical and psychological portraits, riven with contradiction, often attests.

In these encounters the worlds of theory and life finally intersect, and their meeting place is the workshop of human intentions. Dostoyevsky, indeed, is the great novelist of intentions. His characters are always defined, to an unusual degree, by the futures that they, like authors, construct for themselves, whether secretly or in public, and which, like Don Quixote, they try to coax into being through language. Now, on his second journey, Raskolnikov is brought face to face with the intentions (good, evil or confused) of other living beings, who represent not so much doubles for him, as is so often stated, but possibilities: different paths between which he must choose.

It is at this intersection that the universal aspect of Raskolnikov's fate emerges most forcefully, for it is only among people that his analysis of his own fateful intentions attains a degree of clarity and honesty. He tells Sonya:

> 'Try to understand: taking that same road again, I might never have repeated the murder. There was something else I needed to find out then, something else was nudging me along: what I needed to find out, and find out quickly, was whether I was a louse, like everyone else, or a human being? Could I take that step or couldn't I? Would I dare [. . .]?'

To the end, Raskolnikov's 'Satanic pride' remains with him, but the reader can strip away the rhetoric and see that his fundamental motivation may have been little more than that of a child all along: could he 'dare'? As Raskolnikov himself is painfully aware, this would make a mockery of any claims to lofty morality, but it also renders his story universal: a story of the passage from childhood to maturity. Etymologically, a crime in Russian is a 'stepping-over' (*pre-stuplenie*), a transgression. To feel alive and free, every person must 'step over' their conscience and the limits imposed on them by themselves and by others. In this sense, everyone has their crime to commit; or, as a certain cynic tells Raskolnikov, everyone has their 'steps to take'. Punishment, too, can be measured in steps – all the way to Siberia – but it must be imposed by another to be meaningful. Here, as throughout the novel, themes, motifs and verbal echoes (whether to do with walking, with air or fire) coincide with exceptional force and complexity.

It is at this intersection, too, that autobiographical undercurrents can, if we so wish, be identified. If all people are determined by their plans for the future, then how did Dostoyevsky's own theoretical plans as a youthful revolutionary differ from Raskolnikov's? Were not the 'criminal intentions to overthrow the existing state order in Russia' with which he and his associates were charged (not without foundation) potentially even more murderous than the realized intentions of Raskolnikov?

Speculation, however, is all we have. The elusiveness that Dostoyevsky cultivated in his fiction was replicated in his life and literary persona. He left no private diaries, no memoirs, no autobiography. Instead he gave us a very public *Diary of a Writer*, in which he appears before his readers wearing a variety of masks (notably that of the 'Paradoxicalist'); letters, in which he frequently declares the impossibility of expressing his true self (his correspondence with his brother Mikhail is an important exception); and notebooks, in which his plots branch off along endless alternative paths. The author's inner life, meanwhile, largely escapes us. We know the facts but not the person, and this is in tune with Dostoyevsky's own lifelong polemic with modernity's exaggeration of the value of mere data. Whatever 'key fact' we take from his life proves – as Porfiry likes to say – 'double-edged' in its potential meaning. Even the meaning of Dostoyevsky's suffering eludes us. We might say that the sadistic charade before the firing squad on Semyonovsky Square traumatized the author for life, or we might say, with William Empson, that 'It was a reprieve / Made Dostoevsky talk out queer and clear.'[18] We might say that four years of forced labour in Siberia left him old before his time and disabused him about human nature, or we might say that it saved him as a writer and a man, removing him from the hothouse of St Petersburg literary society in which he was wilting and supplying him with a new-found maturity, as well as the trove of fresh material, linguistic and human, that he acquired by observing his fellow 'common' convicts – much of which resurfaces in the present novel. We can argue that his frequent and violent attacks of epilepsy were a curse, inflicting terror, near-madness and pain, or we can argue (following the late J. L. Rice) that they were a creative tonic.[19]

It is apt that some of the most interesting recent books on Dostoyevsky have been works of fiction. The 'master', one suspects, might well have approved of J. M. Coetzee's *Master of Petersburg* (1994), in which an invented plot sets off a compelling portrait of Dostoyevsky surrounded and oppressed by the atmosphere of his own novels. He himself needed invention as a path to understanding. Indeed, he appeared to need it to the same extent that his great rival Tolstoy – whose *War and Peace* (1865–9) was published at the same time as *Crime and Punishment*, and in the very same journal – grew to abhor it. The two works meet in their dethronement of the 'great man' theory of history, the 'Napoleon complex', but have little else in common. Tolstoy needed certainty and truth, Dostoyevsky required 'lies': that vibrant stream of invention in relation to the past, present and future that, as channelled through the rogue Masloboyev in *The Insulted and the Injured* (1861), makes even his weakest novel memorable. Perhaps, like Razumikhin, Dostoyevsky thought that 'fibbing' would bring him to the truth, or at least to a more complete picture of the truth than that provided by his tendentious writing in non-fictional genres.

Certainly, in the much-disputed epilogue to *Crime and Punishment* the 'truth' remains elusive. Some will conclude that Raskolnikov rediscovers himself in his rediscovery of his native land and native people; others will cite his own astonishment at 'the dreadful, unbridgeable gulf that lay between him and all these commoners' and his own enduring confusion about his 'crime'. Some, following one of Dostoyevsky's sharpest critics and biographers, Konstantin Mochulsky, have read the epilogue as a 'pious lie' – an unconvincing conversion to Christianity; others remain unpersuaded that any conversion takes place at all. What is beyond dispute is that these final pages, filled with a restrained joy, show Dostoyevsky at his most tender and his writing at its most delicate. Here, one would like to think, the autobiographical subtext is far from arbitrary. For as he wrote these pages Fyodor Mikhailovich Dostoyevsky was himself setting out on a new path, taking with him a new wife – his stenographer, Anna Grigoryevna – and, no doubt, the very best intentions.

NOTES

1. From Woolf's essay 'The Russian Point of View' in *The Common Reader* (1925). The quotation describes the experience of reading Dostoyevsky in general, but is especially appropriate to *Crime and Punishment*.

2. Joseph Frank, *Dostoevsky: A Writer in His Time* (Princeton: Princeton University Press, 2010), p. 460.

3. My translation from F. M. Dostoyevsky, *Polnoe sobranie sochinenii v tridtsati tomakh* (Leningrad: Nauka, 1972–90), vol. 28.2, p. 136.

4. The one exception is the protagonist's class of origin, which seems closer to impoverished gentry than trade, but which is in any case left strikingly vague – the better to emphasize his status as a 'former student'.

5. As described by the narrator of Dostoyevsky's *Notes from Underground* (1864).

6. The reference to Raskolnikov's 'Satanic pride' comes from Dostoyevsky's notebooks; Dostoyevsky, *Polnoe sobranie sochinenii*, vol. 7, p. 149.

7. See Derek Offord's article '*Crime and Punishment* and Contemporary Radical Thought', reprinted in *Fyodor Dostoevsky's Crime and Punishment: A Casebook*, ed. Richard Peace (Oxford: Oxford University Press, 2006), pp. 119–48.

8. The Soviet-era film *Twenty-Six Days in the Life of Dostoyevsky* (*Dvadtsat' shest' dnei iz zhizni Dostoevskogo*, 1980) captures all the drama of that month – October 1866.

9. Frank, *Dostoyevsky: A Writer in His Time*, p. 484.

10. This latter topic sparks some fascinating reflections on Dostoyevsky in Lesley Chamberlain's *Motherland: A Philosophical History of Russia* (London: Atlantic, 2004), pp. 173–82.

11. Mikhail Bakhtin, *Problems of Dostoevsky's Poetics*, translated and edited by Caryl Emerson (Minneapolis: University of Minnesota Press, 1984).

12. On Raskolnikov as 'media man' and the 'subsumption of the social world by the discursive reality of the press', see Konstantine Klioutchkine, 'The Rise of *Crime and Punishment* from the Air of the Media', *Slavic Review*, vol. 61, no. 1 (Spring, 2002), pp. 88–108. I would argue that in *Crime and Punishment* the social world is subsumed not only by the press, however, but by literature more broadly.

13. The literariness of Russian legal culture in this period has been superbly analysed by Kathleen Parthé in 'Who Speaks the Truth? Writers vs Lawyers', *Universals and Contrasts* (The Journal of the NY – St Petersburg Institute of Linguistics, Cognition and Culture), vol. 1, no. 1 (Spring, 2012), pp. 155–71. See also Gary Rosenshield, *Western Law, Russian Justice: Dostoevsky, the Jury Trial, and the Law* (Madison, Wisconsin: University of Wisconsin Press, 2005).

14. This matches the ambivalence of Porfiry's own position on the cusp of the reforms that were intended to create an independent judiciary. Educated under the old system, when (in the words of the historian Richard

Pipes) 'justice was a branch of the administration', he will stay on with a new title under the new dispensation, owing to a lack of well-qualified new recruits – a suitable fate for a born actor like Porfiry, as well as an ironic comment on the 'reforms' themselves.

15. See Frank, pp. 151–4.

16. Victor Serge, *Memoirs of a Revolutionary* (New York: New York Review of Books, 2012), p. 327.

17. The phrase 'living life' is taken from Dostoyevsky's later novel, *The Adolescent*, but has a longer history in Russian literature.

18. From 'Success' in William Empson, *The Complete Poems* (London: Penguin Classics, 2001), p. 80.

19. J. L. Rice, *Who Was Dostoevsky?* (Oakland, California: Berkeley Slavic Specialties, 2011), pp. 73–104, and the same author's *Dostoevsky and the Healing Art* (Ann Arbor, Michigan: Ardis, 1985).

Further Reading

Dostoyevsky's own writings are the best place to start. Among the works that cast most light on *Crime and Punishment* are the early novella *The Double* (1846, but revised in the mid-1860s), *Notes from the Dead House* (1860–2), and *Notes from Underground* (1864). See, too, *The Notebooks for Crime and Punishment*, translated and edited by Edward Wasiolek (Chicago: University of Chicago Press, 1967).

Also recommended is the long line of fiction inspired (sometimes negatively) by *Crime and Punishment* or by the Dostoyevsky of that period. Among the highlights: *Under Western Eyes* (1911) by Joseph Conrad; *Despair* (1934; English translation 1965) by Vladimir Nabokov, Dostoyevsky's most ungrateful reader; *Summer in Baden-Baden* (completed 1980; English translation 1987) by Leonid Tsypkin; *The Master of Petersburg* (1994) by J. M. Coetzee; and, in a more light-hearted vein, the untranslated *F. M.* (2006) by Boris Akunin.

In the list of secondary reading that follows, categories inevitably blur; all the biographies, for example, are also exercises in literary criticism.

BIOGRAPHY AND MEMOIR

Robert Bird, *Fyodor Dostoevsky* (London: Reaktion Books, 2012). A short and stimulating reading of the life and works, and the threads that join them.

Anna Dostoevsky, *Reminiscences*, translated and edited by Beatrice Stillman (London: Wildwood House, 1976). The memoirs of Dostoyevsky's second wife: a unique, if inevitably partisan, portrait of a loving marriage.

Joseph Frank, *Dostoevsky: A Writer in His Time* (Princeton: Princeton University Press, 2010). The condensed version (running to almost 1,000 pages) of Frank's five-volume literary biography, the fourth volume of which, *Dostoevsky: The Miraculous Years, 1865–71* (London: Robson Books, 1995), contains more detailed treatment of

Crime and Punishment and the years in which it was written. Frank pays particular attention to the intellectual and ideological context from which Dostoyevsky's fiction emerged.

Konstantin Mochulsky, *Dostoevsky: His Life and Work*, translated by Michael A. Minihan (Princeton: Princeton University Press, 1967). Focused and highly readable.

James L. Rice, *Who Was Dostoevsky?* (Oakland, California: Berkeley Slavic Specialties, 2011). A collection of articles towards a portrait of a 'secular Dostoyevsky' by one of his most contrarian interpreters.

Peter Sekirin, *The Dostoevsky Archive: Firsthand Accounts of the Novelist from Contemporaries' Memoirs and Rare Periodicals* (Jefferson, North Carolina: McFarland & Co., 1997)

CRITICISM

Carol Apollonio (ed.), *The New Russian Dostoevsky: Readings for the Twenty-First Century* (Bloomington, Indiana: Slavica, 2010)

Mikhail Bakhtin, *Problems of Dostoevsky's Poetics*, translated and edited by Caryl Emerson (Minneapolis: University of Minnesota Press, 1984)

René Girard, *Resurrection from the Underground: Feodor Dostoevsky*, translated and edited by James G. Williams (East Lansing, Michigan: Michigan State University Press, 2012)

Robert Louis Jackson, *Dostoevsky's Quest for Form: A Study of His Philosophy of Art* (New Haven: Yale University Press, 1966)

___ (ed.), *Twentieth-Century Interpretations of Crime and Punishment: A Collection of Critical Essays* (Englewood Cliffs, New Jersey: Prentice-Hall, 1974)

Malcolm V. Jones, *Dostoyevsky after Bakhtin: Readings in Dostoyevsky's Fantastic Realism* (Cambridge: Cambridge University Press, 1990)

Y. Karyakin, *Re-reading Dostoyevsky*, translated by S. Chulaki (Moscow: Novosti Press, 1971). An engaging exploration of the questions posed by *Crime and Punishment*.

W. J. Leatherbarrow (ed.), *The Cambridge Companion to Dostoevskii* (Cambridge: Cambridge University Press, 2002). An innovative, wide-ranging collection of essays.

George Pattison and Diane Oenning Thompson (eds.), *Dostoevsky and the Christian Tradition* (Cambridge: Cambridge University Press, 2001)

Richard Peace (ed.), *Fyodor Dostoevsky's Crime and Punishment: A Casebook* (Oxford: Oxford University Press, 2006)

Lev Shestov, *Dostoevsky, Tolstoy, and Nietzsche*, translated by S. Roberts (Athens, Ohio: Ohio University Press, 1969)

George Steiner, *Tolstoy or Dostoevsky: An Essay in Contrast* (London: Faber and Faber, 1960)

René Wellek (ed.), *Dostoevsky: A Collection of Critical Essays* (Englewood Cliffs, New Jersey: Prentice-Hall, 1962)

Rowan Williams, *Dostoevsky: Language, Faith and Fiction* (London: Continuum, 2008)

REFERENCE

Kenneth Lantz, *The Dostoevsky Encyclopedia* (Westport, Connecticut: Greenwood, 2004)

Boris Tikhomirov, *'Lazar'! Gryadi von': Roman F. M. Dostoevskogo 'Prestuplenie i nakazanie' v sovremennom prochtenii* ['Lazarus! Come Forth': F. M. Dostoyevsky's Novel *Crime and Punishment* Read in the Light of Its Time] (St Petersburg: Serebryanyi vek, 2006). Some extracts from this important commentary are available in translation in *The New Russian Dostoevsky*, pp. 95–122.

Note on the Translation

The troublesome question 'Why retranslate the classics?' has perhaps only one satisfactory answer: because the translator hopes to offer a closer approximation to his or her experience of the original than is otherwise available. A new interpretation of a famous symphony or play is valuable simply for being itself, for being unique; the argument is less convincing when applied to a retranslation, if only because most readers cannot be expected to read long novels in multiple versions. For this reason it seems appropriate to set out what I have tried to achieve that I found lacking in previous translations – for all their other, non-replicable virtues. Only the reader, of course, can judge the result.

The most widely read translations of *Crime and Punishment* have tended, in my view, towards a polish, and therefore tameness, absent from Dostoyevsky's text (effects gained in large part by judicious trimming or padding); or else they have clung so closely to the Russian that the spell cast by the original is periodically broken by jarring literalism, and the author's peculiarities of style, smoothed over in other translations, are made odder still. In my rendering I have sought to preserve both the novel's spell and the expressive, jagged concision palpable from the very first sentence.

Observations made fifty years ago by George Steiner about Dostoyevsky's method helped set me on my way: 'all superfluity of narrative is stripped away in order to render the conflict of personages naked and exemplary; the law of composition is one of maximum energy, released over the smallest possible extent of space and time' (*Tolstoy or Dostoevsky*). These comments are especially pertinent to the constricted setting and style of *Crime and Punishment*, where Dostoyevsky largely eschews the verbosity that is a feature and a concern of several of his earlier, and later, works. In fact, the narrative passages are notable for the narrowness of their lexical range, using verbal repetition to help evoke the psychological experience of Raskolnikov, who repeats actions almost as often as he repeats words. Lexical and thematic clusters – to do with memory or family relations or time – prove inseparable. Sometimes, idiomatic English has to be forced a little to capture these repetitions; on other occasions a single Russian word gains an accretion of reference that can be recovered in English only in part – by compensating for its untranslatability elsewhere. A salient example is the noun *delo* ('deed', 'action', 'criminal case', 'matter', 'thing', 'business'), which is repeated so often, and in so many contexts, that it comes to mimic the great obsession of Dostoyevsky's time, and of Raskolnikov himself: when will words finally become deeds?

Another aspect of the 'maximum energy' mentioned by Steiner has to do with the vitality and variety of the spoken word in Dostoyevsky's fiction. The characters of *Crime and Punishment* are defined by their language, irony and humour. To recapture their speech patterns – especially those of Porfiry Petrovich, the detective – a considerably greater licence seemed appropriate than in the compressed passages of pure narrative. Dostoyevsky's characters would, furthermore, have sounded very modern to his readers, except where they consciously invest their speech with archaism (to recall, in many cases, the fading Russia of fixed social hierarchies). The narrator's language would also have sounded fresh and alive. To replicate this vividness, while reserving scope for archaism elsewhere, I have aimed for an idiom that still sounds modern today, but is not exclusively of our time.

A related point is the translation of biblical language. Part Four of *Crime and Punishment* contains extensive extracts and quotations from the Gospels. For these, I have used the mid-twentieth-century Revised Standard Version, to reflect the fact that the Russian translation cited in the novel sounded (and still sounds) modern, in stark contrast to the much older translation done into Old Church Slavonic, strong traces of which can be heard, for example, in Part One, Chapter II, where, correspondingly, I have used the seventeenth-century King James Version.

NOTE ON THE TEXT

This translation is based on the text found in F. M. Dostoyevsky, *Polnoe sobranie sochinenii v tridtsati tomakh* (Leningrad: Nauka, 1972–90), vol. 6 (1973). Since this celebrated edition, a further Collected Works, which claims to adhere more closely to Dostoyevsky's own preferences for the visual appearance of his text and markers of emphasis, has been published in Moscow (Voskresenye, 2003–5). The differences between the editions have mainly to do with punctuation (modernized to some degree in this translation), and for most scholars of Dostoyevsky the authority of the Soviet 'Academy' edition remains unsurpassed.

ACKNOWLEDGEMENTS

As the first new translator of *Crime and Punishment* in a generation, I have had the good fortune of benefiting not only from the experience of my predecessors, recent and distant, but also from the copious scholarship that has appeared in the intervening period, both in the digital wonderland and in more traditional formats (notably, Boris Tikhomirov's Russian commentary on the novel, listed in Further Reading).

A personal debt is owed to those who have read parts of the draft at various stages: Catriona Kelly, Iain Rogers, Dmitry Shatalov, Richard Short, Adrian Tahourdin, James Womack, Sarah Young. For helping to answer intractable queries I thank Alexander Ilichevskii, Alexander Krasovitsky, Nina Kruglikova, Aleksandr Rodionov and especially Boris Tikhomirov. The Dostoyevsky reading group run in Oxford by Muireann Maguire and attended by the late Diane Oenning Thompson provided vital stimulation. For valuable comments on my Introduction and Notes I thank Malcolm Jones, Andrew Kahn, Eric Naiman and Anna and Thomas Ready. The support of Wolfson College (Oxford), St Antony's College (Oxford) and the Russkiy Mir Foundation has been essential. Without the editorial confidence of Alexis Kirschbaum, I would never have started, and without the skilled guidance of Rose Goddard, Anna Hervé and Ian Pindar, I might never have finished. Anthony Hippisley and Stephen Ryan spared no effort to improve my text.

Above all, this translation has been a family affair. It was typed up from manuscript by my mother, Marisa, the most responsive first reader one could wish for, reviewed with the greatest discernment by my father, Nigel, willed on from afar by my siblings, Natasha and Tom, graced by the births of two daughters, Isabel and Natalie, and accompanied at every step by my wife, Ania.

Note on Names

The List of Characters that follows contains the full and alternative names of all the novel's protagonists, as well as those of the most prominent secondary and episodic characters.

All Russians have three names – a first name, a patronymic and a surname. Thus: Rodion Romanovich Raskolnikov or Marfa Petrovna Svidrigailova. The patronymic is the father's given name with the ending -ovich or -evich for men, and -ovna or -evna for women.

Russian knows three main modes of address, in descending order of formality: by honorific and surname (Mr Raskolnikov), by first name and patronymic (Rodion Romanovich) and by first name alone. First names and patronymics are routinely shortened or softened in spoken Russian to suggest greater familiarity and affection: thus Rodion may become Rodya or Rodka, and Romanovich may become Romanych. Confusingly for the foreign reader, some diminutive forms of given names are quite distant from the original: Raskolnikov's sister, for example, who bears the proud and formal-sounding name Avdotya, is most commonly referred to in the text as Dunya and Dunechka.

Sudden shifts to the use of the affectionate forms of given names are typical of Dostoyevsky's style and are preserved in translation. It is not just the characters who shift freely and meaningfully between these modes, but the narrator himself, who thereby subtly registers his apparent sympathies and antipathies. A few characters, such as Svidrigailov, are most commonly mentioned by surname alone, thereby creating a sense of distance and perhaps mystery. More common in the stiflingly close-knit world of *Crime and Punishment* is the use of first name and patronymic. Indeed one central character, the investigator Porfiry Petrovich, who declares himself opposed to formality on principle, is given no surname at all; nor is the pawnbroker, Alyona Ivanovna.

Like Gogol before him, Dostoyevsky makes great play of 'speaking names' (such as Marmeladov) for various purposes, notably irony and humour. The possible referents of some surnames are explained in the list that follows. Further comments on names are included in the Notes.

List of Characters

*Characters referred to most often by their surnames
(stressed vowels are underlined)*

Lebezyatnikov, Andrei Semyonovich: Neighbour of the Marmeladovs and a 'young friend' of Luzhin. Works 'in one of the ministries'. The Russian verb *lebezit'* means 'to fawn'.

Luzhin, Pyotr Petrovich: A middle-aged 'man of business' recently arrived from the provinces to work as a lawyer in St Petersburg. *Luzha*: puddle or pool.

Marmeladov, Semyon Zakharovich: Married to Katerina Ivanovna. Father of Sonya from his first marriage. A failed civil servant. *Marmelad*: fruit jelly, from the French *marmelade*.

Raskolnikov, Rodion (Rodka, Rodya) Romanovich: The twenty-three-year-old hero, who has recently dropped out of university. *Raskolot'*: to cleave, split, chop, break. *Raskol*: a split or schism, especially in reference to the Schism within Russian Orthodoxy in the seventeenth century, though with broader metaphorical application; *raskolnik*: religious schismatic, dissenter. Raskolnikov's first name and, in particular, its associated diminutive forms (Rodya, Rodka) point to the family theme: *rod*, meaning 'family, kin, origin'.

Razumikhin, Dmitry Prokofyevich: A friend of Raskolnikov's from university. *Razum*: reason, intellect.

Svidrigailov, Arkady Ivanovich: A nobleman and country gentleman with a disreputable past.

Zametov, Alexander Grigoryevich: Head clerk at the police bureau. A friend of Razumikhin. *Zametit'*: to notice, observe.

Zosimov (only surname given): Doctor. Friend of Razumikhin.

Characters referred to most often (or always) by first name and patronymic

Alyona Ivanovna: Ageing, widowed pawnbroker.

Amalia Ivanovna Lippewechsel: The Marmeladovs' (and Lebezyatnikov's) landlady.

Avdotya (Dunechka, Dunya) Romanovna Raskolnikova: Raskolnikov's sister. Worked as a governess in the country for the Svidrigailovs.

Ilya Petrovich ('Powder Keg'): Assistant to the district superintendent
Nikodim Fomich at the police bureau. Lieutenant.

Katerina Ivanovna Marmeladova: Married to Marmeladov. Mother
from her first marriage of two girls, Polina (Polya, Polechka,
Polenka) and Lenya (first mentioned as Lida/Lidochka), and a boy,
Kolya (the common diminutive of Nikolai).

Lizaveta: Alyona Ivanovna's younger half-sister. Mends and sells clothes.
Friend of Sonya.

Luiza (Laviza) Ivanovna: A madam well known to the local police.

Marfa Petrovna Svidrigailova: The recently deceased wife of Svidrigailov, whom she saved from ruin. Distantly related to Luzhin.

Mikolai (Mikolka) Dementyev: A young man of peasant background,
from the province of Ryazan, who decorates apartments in Petersburg. Mikolka is also the name of the peasant in Raskolnikov's
dream in Part One, Chapter V. Mikolai is a fairly rare derivative of
Nikolai, which is also used in the original but is avoided here in
order to spare the English reader further confusion.

Nastasya (Nastyenka, Nastasyushka): A country girl who now works
as a cook and maid in the house where Raskolnikov lives. A diminutive form of Anastasiya. Like Sofya (see below), Anastasiya also
has a strong spiritual meaning derived from Greek: resurrection.

Nikodim Fomich: District superintendent at the police bureau. Captain.

Porfiry Petrovich: Chief investigator. Distant relative of Razumikhin.

Praskovya Pavlovna Zarnitsyna (Pashenka): Raskolnikov's widowed
landlady.

Pulkheria Alexandrovna Raskolnikova: Raskolnikov's widowed mother.

Sonya (Sonechka) Semyonovna: Marmeladov's daughter and Katerina
Ivanovna's stepdaughter. A prostitute. Though usually referred to
as Sonya, the full form of her first name Sofya (Sophia: divine wisdom) is clearly significant.

CRIME AND PUNISHMENT

PART ONE

I

In early July, in exceptional heat, towards evening, a young man left the garret he was renting in S——y Lane, stepped outside, and slowly, as if in two minds, set off towards K——n Bridge.[1]

He'd successfully avoided meeting his landlady on the stairs. His garret was right beneath the eaves of a tall, five-storey building and resembled a cupboard more than it did a room. His landlady – a tenant herself, who also provided him with dinner and a maid – occupied separate rooms on the floor below, and every time he went down he had no choice but to pass her kitchen, the door of which was nearly always wide open. And every time he passed it, the young man experienced a sickening, craven sensation that made him wince with shame. He owed his landlady a small fortune and he was scared of meeting her.

Not that he was really so very craven or browbeaten – far from it; but for some time now he'd been in an irritable, tense state of mind not unlike hypochondria.[2] He'd become so self-absorbed and so isolated that he feared meeting anyone, not just his landlady. He was being suffocated by poverty; yet lately even this had ceased to bother him. He'd entirely abandoned – and had no wish to resume – his most pressing tasks. And he couldn't really be scared of a mere landlady, whatever she might be plotting. But to stop on the stairs, to listen to her prattle on about everyday trivia that meant nothing to him, and pester him about payments, threaten and whine, while he had to squirm, apologize and lie – no, better to slink past like a cat and slip out unnoticed.

Still, as he stepped out into the street, even he was astonished by the terror that had overcome him just now at the thought of meeting his creditor.

'Here I am planning to do a thing like that and I'm scared of the merest trifle!' he thought with a strange smile. 'H'm . . . yes . . . man has the world in his hands, but he's such a coward that he can't even grab what's under his nose . . . an axiom if ever there was . . . Here's a question: what do people fear most? A new step, a new word[3] of their

own – that's what they fear most. But I'm talking too much. That's
why I never do anything. Or maybe it's because I never do anything that
I'm always talking. It's only this past month that I've learned to witter
away like this, lying in my corner for days on end and thinking . . . about
King Pea.[4] So why am I going there now? Am I really capable of *that*?
Can *that* be serious? It's not serious at all. It's just a way of keeping myself amused, a flight of fancy, a toy! That's right, a toy!'

It was dreadfully hot, not to mention the closeness of the air, the
crush of people, the mortar, scaffolding, bricks, dust, and that specific summer stench so familiar to any Petersburger too poor to rent a
dacha – all this gave a nasty jolt to the young man's already rattled
nerves. The unbearable stink from the drinking dens, of which there
are so many in this part of town, and the drunks who kept crossing
his path even though it was only a weekday, added the final touches to
this sad and revolting scene. A feeling of deepest disgust flickered
briefly across the young man's delicate features. He was, by the way,
remarkably good-looking, with beautiful dark eyes and dark brown
hair, taller than average, with a slim and elegant figure. But soon he
seemed to sink deep in thought, or even, to be more precise, into a
kind of trance, and he walked on without noticing his surroundings,
nor indeed wishing to notice them. He merely muttered something to
himself every now and then, a sign of the habit to which he'd just confessed. At such moments even he could see that his thoughts were
prone to confusion and that he was extremely weak: he'd barely eaten
a thing for the better part of two days.

He was so badly dressed that many a man, even one used to the life,
would have been ashamed to be seen in such rags in the daytime. But
then, this wasn't the sort of district where people were easily shocked.
The proximity of the Haymarket, the profusion of notorious establishments, and the local residents, mainly craftsmen and workers, all
crammed into these streets and lanes in the middle of town, often furnished the scene with such colourful characters that it would have been
strange to be shocked, whoever you met. Anyway, the young man's soul
had already stored up so much spite and scorn that, for all his sometimes
childish touchiness, his rags were the last thing he was ashamed of in
public. Running into certain acquaintances or former friends was a different matter – these were people he disliked meeting on principle . . .
Yet when a drunk, who was being carried down the street heaven knows
why or where, in an enormous empty cart pulled by an enormous dray

horse, suddenly shouted as he went by 'Oi, you in the German hat!' and started yelling at the top of his voice and pointing at him, the young man stopped in his tracks and his hand leapt to his head. It was a top hat, a Zimmerman,[5] but badly worn and now rusty in colour, riddled with holes and covered in stains, brimless and knocked hideously out of shape. It wasn't shame, though, that overcame him, but a quite different feeling, more like alarm.

'I knew it!' he muttered in his confusion. 'I just knew it! How disgusting! This is just the sort of idiocy, just the sort of vulgar, petty little detail that can wreck the whole scheme! It's far too conspicuous, this hat . . . Comic, therefore conspicuous . . . These rags need a cap, some old pancake or other, not this monstrosity. Who wears hats like this? It'll be spotted a mile off and, above all, remembered . . . a clue if ever there was. This isn't the time to be conspicuous . . . It's the petty details that matter most! . . . The petty details that always ruin everything . . .'

He hadn't far to go; he even knew how many steps it was from the gates of his building: seven hundred and thirty. He'd counted them out once, letting his dreams run wild. At the time he still didn't believe in these dreams himself, and merely tormented himself with their hideous but alluring audacity. But now, a month later, he was beginning to see things differently, and for all his taunting soliloquies about his own weakness and indecision he had somehow, without even meaning to, grown used to perceiving his 'hideous' dream as an actual venture, while still not believing his own intentions. Now, he was even on his way to carry out a *test* of his venture, and his excitement grew with each step.

Shaking with nerves, his heart in his mouth, he approached a massive great building which faced the Ditch on one side and ——a Street[6] on the other. It was broken up into small apartments inhabited by working people of every stripe – tailors, locksmiths, cooks, various Germans, girls paying their own way, petty bureaucrats, and so on. There was a constant hurry and scurry through the two arches leading into and out of the front and back courtyards.[7] Three caretakers,[8] at least, were employed there. The young man was delighted not to meet a single one of them and slipped through the arch unnoticed, turning directly right up a staircase. It was dark and narrow – these were the back stairs – but he knew that already, having studied the whole arrangement in advance and having found it to his liking: in a place as dark as this, even a curious gaze presented no danger. 'If this is how scared I am now, what on earth would it be like if somehow it ever came to the point of actually *doing* the thing?' he couldn't help thinking as he climbed up to the fourth floor. Here he found his way barred by ex-soldiers-turned-porters carrying furniture out of an apartment. He already knew who lived there – a German in the civil service and his family: 'So the German must be moving out now; so for a while only the old woman's apartment will be occupied on the fourth floor, on this staircase and this landing. That's good . . . just in case . . .' – and thinking this, he rang the bell of the old woman's apartment. It jangled weakly, as if made of tin, not brass. Small apartments like these always seem to have bells like that. He'd already forgotten the sound of this particular one, and now the ring suddenly seemed to remind him of something, bringing it clearly before him . . . He even shuddered, so weak had his nerves now become. A few moments later the tiniest of chinks appeared in the doorway: through it the occupant examined her visitor with evident mistrust, and all that could be seen of her were little eyes twinkling in the dark. But, noticing a lot of people on the landing, she took heart and opened the door fully. The young man crossed the threshold into a dark entrance hall with a partition, behind which lay a tiny kitchen. The old woman stood before him in silence, fixing him with a questioning look. She was a tiny, dry old thing of about sixty, with sharp, evil little eyes and a small sharp nose. Her head was uncovered and her whitish-blonde hair, touched by grey, was thickly greased. Her long thin neck, which resembled a chicken leg, was wrapped up in an old flannel rag, and despite the heat a fraying, fur-wadded jacket, yellow with age, hung from her shoulders. The little hag kept coughing and groaning. The young man must have glanced at her in some particular way, because the same mistrust suddenly flickered in her eyes once more.

'Raskolnikov, the student. Visited you a month ago,' he muttered with a hasty bow, making an effort to be polite.

'I remember, father,[9] I remember that very well,' said the old woman distinctly, keeping her questioning eyes fixed on his face.

'Well, ma'am . . . it's the same kind of business . . . ,' Raskolnikov continued, rather disconcerted and surprised by the old woman's mistrust.

'Maybe she's always like this, I just didn't notice that time,' he thought uneasily.

The old woman paused, as if hesitating, then stepped aside and, pointing to the main room, let her guest go first:

'Come through, father.'

The small room into which the young man stepped, with its yellow wallpaper, geraniums and muslin curtains over the windows, was brightly lit at that moment by the setting sun. 'So *then*, too, the sun will shine just like this!' The thought flashed unbidden across Raskolnikov's mind and he cast a quick glance over the entire room, so as to study and remember its layout as best he could. But there was nothing special about it. The furniture, all very old and made of yellow wood, consisted of a couch with a massive curved back, an oval table in front of the couch, a dressing-table with a little mirror between the windows, chairs along the walls, a few two-copeck prints in yellow frames depicting young German ladies with birds in their hands – and nothing else. In the corner, before a small icon, a lamp was burning. Everything was immaculate: furniture and floor had been rubbed to a shine. Everything sparkled. 'Lizaveta's work,' thought the young man. There wasn't a speck of dust to be seen in the entire apartment. 'Only nasty old widows keep everything so clean,' Raskolnikov carried on to himself, throwing a curious glance at the chintz curtain hanging in front of the door into the second, tiny room, in which the old woman had her bed and chest of drawers and into which he had never even peeked. These two rooms made up the entire apartment.

'What do you want?' the little hag asked sternly, entering the room and standing right in front of him, as before, so as to look straight into his face.

'Something to pawn: there!' – and he took out an old flat silver watch from his pocket. A globe was depicted on its reverse. The chain was of steel.

'But the last thing you brought is overdue. The month was up two days ago.'

'I'll bring you the interest for another month; be patient.'

'That's up to me, father, to be patient or to sell your thing right away.'

'How much for the watch, Alyona Ivanovna?'

'You're bringing me trifles; it's hardly worth a thing, I tell you. I gave you two nice little notes[10] for that ring of yours last time, when there are jewellers selling new ones for a rouble fifty.'

'Four roubles, then. I'll buy it back – it's my father's. I'm being paid soon.'

'One rouble fifty and the interest in advance, if you're so very keen.'

'One rouble fifty!' the young man shrieked.

'As you wish.' The old woman passed the watch back to him. The young man took it, so angry that he was on the verge of leaving; but he immediately thought better of it, remembering that there was nowhere else for him to go and that he had another reason for being there anyway.

'All right!' he said roughly.

The old woman rummaged in her pocket for her keys and went off behind the curtain into the other room. The young man was left standing in the middle of the room, straining his ears and concentrating hard. He could hear a drawer being opened. 'Must be the top one,' he thought. 'So she carries the keys in her right pocket ... All in one bunch, on a steel ring ... And one key's bigger than the rest, three times bigger, with a jagged end – can't be for the chest of drawers ... So there must be some casket or other as well, or perhaps a box ... Now that's interesting. Strongboxes always have keys like that ... But how vile this all is ...'

The old woman came back.

'Here you are, father: ten copecks a rouble each month,[11] so that's fifteen copecks from you for a rouble and a half, for a month in advance. And for the two roubles from before that's twenty copecks advance payment by the same calculation. Thirty-five copecks altogether. Leaving you with just one rouble fifteen for your watch. There you are.'

'What? So now it's a rouble fifteen copecks?'

'Exactly, sir.'

The young man took the money without arguing. He looked at the old woman and was in no hurry to leave, as though there were something else he wanted to say or do, though what that was he didn't seem to know himself ...

'I might bring you something else in a day or two, Alyona Ivanovna ... silver ... good quality ... a cigarette case ... just as soon as I get it back from a friend.'

He lost his thread and fell silent.

'So we'll talk about it then, father.'

'Well, I'll be off ... Seems you're always at home on your own – what about your sister?' he asked in as casual a tone as he could manage, stepping out into the hall.

'And what business might you have with her, father?'

'Oh, nothing much. I just asked. Really, Alyona Ivanovna, you . . . Well, goodbye!'

Raskolnikov left in a state of complete confusion. This confusion merely grew and grew. Walking down the stairs, he even stopped several times, as though suddenly struck by something. Finally, already outside, he exclaimed:

'God! How revolting it all is! And am I really? Am I really? . . . No, it's absurd. It's ridiculous!' he added with conviction. 'How could I ever think of something so awful? What filth my heart can sink to! That's the main thing: it's all so filthy, so nasty, so foul! And there was I, for a whole month . . .'

But neither words nor cries could fully express his agitation. The feeling of infinite disgust that had begun to oppress and stir up his heart even before, while walking over to the old woman's apartment, was now so much greater and so much more vivid that there seemed no escape from his anguish. He went along the pavement as if drunk, not noticing passers-by and walking straight into them, and it was only on the next street that he recovered his senses. Looking around, he noticed that he was standing by a drinking den, the entrance to which lay down a flight of steps, below ground. Two drunks were coming out that very moment; supporting and cursing one another, they staggered up onto the street. Without stopping to think, Raskolnikov immediately went down. He'd never once set foot in a drinking den, but his head was spinning and his throat was burning with thirst. A cool beer was what he wanted now, not least because his sudden debility, he thought, was also due to hunger. He sat down at a sticky table in a dark and dirty corner, ordered beer and drained the first glass. His anxiety immediately subsided and his thoughts grew clearer. 'What rubbish!' he said hopefully. 'How stupid to get so flustered! My distress was purely physical! Just one glass of beer, a piece of rusk, and there you are – in the space of a second the mind becomes stronger, thoughts clearer, intentions firmer! How petty this all is . . .' Despite this contemptuous outburst, he seemed cheerful now, as if he'd suddenly shaken off some terrible burden, and he cast a friendly gaze around the room. But even then he had a distant intuition that this rush of optimism was not entirely healthy either.

There was hardly anyone left in the den. An entire party – five men, a wench and an accordion – had left soon after the two drunks he met on the stairs. Now it felt quiet and empty. One man, only a little bit tipsy, sat at a table with a beer – a tradesman,[12] by the look of him – while his companion, a fat, hulking, grey-bearded man in a merchant's coat, dead drunk, drowsed on a bench, though every now and again, as if in his sleep, he'd click his fingers, spread out his arms and start bobbing up and down without getting up from the bench, while singing some nonsense or other to which he could barely remember the words:

> All year long I kissed my wife
> All ye-ear long I kissed my wi-ife . . .

Or suddenly, waking once more:

> Along Podyachesky I strolled
> And found my lady love of old . . .[13]

But nobody shared his happiness; his taciturn companion observed all these effusions with mistrust and even hostility. There was one other man present, a retired civil servant, perhaps, to judge by his appearance. He sat on his own with a pot of vodka, taking the occasional sip and looking about the room. He, too, seemed rather restless.

II

Raskolnikov was unused to crowds and, as has already been said, he shunned society, recently more than ever. But now, for some reason, he suddenly felt drawn to other people. Something new seemed to be stirring inside him, bringing with it a thirst for human company. A whole month of intense anguish and dismal excitement had left him so exhausted that he yearned for at least a moment's rest in another world – any world would do – and now he was only too happy to remain in the den, filthy though it was.

The landlord was upstairs somewhere, but he often came down some steps into the bar, and the first that could be seen of him were his foppish blacked boots with their big red tops. He wore a long coat and a badly soiled black satin waistcoat, with no tie, and his whole face looked as if it had been smeared with grease, like an iron lock. A boy of about fourteen stood behind the counter, and another, younger kid was on hand if anyone needed serving. There were chopped-up cucumbers, black rusks and fish cut in little pieces; the smell was awful. It was very stuffy – just sitting there soon became unbearable – and everything was so steeped in alcohol fumes that the air alone, it seemed, could make you drunk in five minutes.

It happens sometimes that we meet people – even perfect strangers – who interest us at first glance, quite suddenly and unexpectedly, before a word has been spoken. Just such an impression was made on Raskolnikov by the customer who sat off to the side and resembled a retired civil servant. Later, the young man would recall this first impression several times and even explain it to himself as a premonition. He couldn't stop looking over at him – partly, of course, because the latter kept staring at him and was clearly desperate to strike up a conversation. As for the others in the den, including the landlord, the civil servant looked at them in a familiar and even bored sort of way, though not without a hint of lofty disdain, as if they were people of lesser status and education to whom he could have nothing to say. He was already in his fifties, of average height and stocky build, greying and balding, with a yellow, almost greenish face swollen by constant drinking, and with puffy eyelids hiding a pair of reddish eyes that were as tiny as slits yet beamed with life. Even so, there was something very odd about him; a kind of rapture shone from his eyes – and perhaps even intelligence – yet madness, too, seemed to flicker there. He was dressed in an old, utterly ragged black tailcoat which had shed its buttons. Only one was still clinging on, and, clearly eager to keep up appearances, he made sure to use it. A shirt-front, all crumpled, stained and splattered, stuck out from beneath a nankeen waistcoat. His face had been shaved, civil-servant style, but not for some time, and a thick bluish-grey stubble was poking through. There was something of the respectable state official about his mannerisms, too. But he was uneasy, kept ruffling his hair, and occasionally, in anguish, propped his head in his hands, resting his tattered elbows on the bespattered, sticky table. Eventually he looked straight at Raskolnikov and said loudly and firmly:

'My good sir, may I make so bold as to engage you in polite conversation? For though you may be of indifferent appearance, my experience detects in you a man of education and one unaccustomed to drink. I myself have always respected learning, when combined with heartfelt sentiment; moreover, I hold the rank of titular counsellor.[14]

Marmeladov's the name. Titular counsellor. Dare I ask whether you have been in the service?'

'No, I'm studying . . . ,' replied the young man, somewhat surprised both by the speaker's distinctive flowery tone and at being addressed so directly and so bluntly. Despite his recent pang of desire for human company of any kind, the very first word addressed to him in reality instantly elicited his usual, unpleasant and irritable feeling of disgust towards any stranger who came into contact with him, or showed the slightest wish to do so.

'I knew it – a student or a former student!'[15] the civil servant cried. 'Experience, my good sir, long years of experience!' He put a finger to his forehead as if to congratulate himself. 'Either you were once a student or you were still walking that road! Permit me . . .' He rose, swayed, grabbed his pot and little glass, moved over to the young man and sat down next to him at a slight angle. Though drunk, he spoke with a vigorous eloquence, only occasionally tripping over his words and drawling. He threw himself on Raskolnikov almost hungrily, as if he, too, hadn't spoken to anyone for an entire month.

'My good sir,' he began almost solemnly, 'poverty is no sin – that much is true. And drunkenness is no virtue – that's even truer. But beggary, sir – yes, beggary – now that is a sin. In poverty, you still retain the nobility of your innate feelings; in beggary, nobody retains it, ever. Beggars are not driven from the fold of humanity with a stick – no, they are swept out with a broom to make the insult all the greater; and rightly so, for in beggary I am the first to insult myself. Hence the public house! My good sir, a month ago Mr Lebezyatnikov gave my spouse a thrashing – and my spouse is nothing like *me*! Do you follow, sir? Permit me further to enquire, if for no better reason than mere curiosity: have you ever had occasion to pass the night on the Neva, on the hay barges?'

'No, I haven't,' replied Raskolnikov. 'How do you mean?'

'Well, sir, that's where I've been, for the fifth night running . . .'

He refilled his glass and drank, lost in thought. Wisps of hay did indeed cling to his clothes here and there, and there was even some in his hair. It was more than likely that five days had passed since he'd last changed his clothes or washed. His hands, in particular, were filthy, greasy and red, the nails black.

His conversation appeared to arouse a general, if idle interest. The boys behind the bar began to titter. The landlord, it seemed, had come down specially from the room upstairs so as to listen to this 'entertainer', and he sat at a distance, yawning lazily and self-importantly. Marmeladov was clearly an old face here. And his penchant for flowery speech must have derived from his habit of talking to strangers in bars. For some drinkers this habit becomes a need, especially if at home they are ordered about and harshly treated. That's why, in the company of other drinkers, they always go to such lengths to be vindicated and, if possible, earn their respect.

'A right entertainer!' the landlord boomed. 'Why's you not working, then? Why, pray, d'you not serve, civil servant?'

'Why do I not serve, my dear sir?' echoed Marmeladov, addressing himself exclusively to Raskolnikov, as though it were he who had posed the question. 'Why do I not serve? Does my heart not ache to know that I bow and scrape in vain? A month ago, when Mr Lebezyatnikov thrashed my spouse with his own bare hands, while I lay tipsy, did I not suffer? Pray tell me, young man, have you ever had occasion to . . . ahem . . . well, beg for a loan, say, without hope?'

'I have . . . but what do you mean, without hope?'

'I mean, without any hope at all, sir, knowing in advance that nothing will come of it. For example, you know in advance and with complete certainty that this man, this most well-intentioned and most helpful citizen, will not give you a copeck, for, I ask you, why should he? After all, he knows full well that I shan't return it. Out of compassion? But Mr Lebezyatnikov, who keeps abreast of the latest thinking, was explaining only the other day that in our age even science has prohibited compassion, and that is how they already do things in England, where political economy[16] is all the rage. So, I ask you, why should he? And yet, knowing in advance that he will not give it to you, you set out all the same and . . .'

'So why go?' Raskolnikov put in.

'What if there is nowhere else to go and no one else to go to? After all, every man must have at least somewhere he can go. There are times when one simply has to go somewhere, anywhere! When my only-begotten daughter went off to work for the first time on a "yellow ticket",[17] I, too, went off . . . (for my daughter lives on a yellow ticket, sir . . .),' he added in parenthesis, looking at the young man with a certain unease. 'Never mind, good sir, never mind!' he hurriedly continued with apparent equanimity, when the two boys behind the bar snorted and the landlord grinned. 'Never mind, sir! The mere wagging of heads cannot embarrass me, for now everything is known to all and all that was hidden is made manifest; and I respond not with contempt, but with humility. So be it! So be it! "Behold the Man!"[18] Pray tell me, young man: can you . . . ? No, let's put it more strongly, more vividly: not *can* you, but *dare* you, gazing at me here and now, state for a fact that I am not a pig?'

The young man said nothing.

'Well, sir,' the orator continued, pausing with an imposing and even, on this occasion, exaggeratedly dignified air for the latest round of sniggering to abate. 'Well, sir, I may be a pig, but she is a lady! I may bear the likeness of a beast, but Katerina Ivanovna, my spouse, is an educated person, who was born to a field officer. I may be a scoundrel, but she is endowed with a sublime heart and feelings ennobled by good breeding. And yet . . . oh, would that my lady had pity on me! After all, kindest sir, every man must have at least one place where even he might be pitied! Katerina Ivanovna is high-minded, but unjust . . . And though I understand myself that even when she seizes me by my forelocks she does so purely from the pity of her heart (for I am not embarrassed to repeat, young man, that she seizes me by my forelocks),' he reaffirmed with redoubled dignity, after hearing sniggers once more, 'but heavens – if she could only once, just once . . . But no! No! All this is vanity! A waste of breath and nothing more! . . . For my desire has come to pass more than once and I have been pitied more than once, but . . . that's just how I am: a born brute!'

'Not half!' observed the landlord with a yawn.

Marmeladov banged his fist on the table.

'Yes, it's the mark of my character! Are you aware, good sir, that I even drank away her stockings – are you aware of that fact? Not her boots, sir, for at least that would have borne some resemblance to the order of things, but her stockings – yes, sir, her stockings! Her little mohair shawl, I drank that away too – a gift, from before, her very own, not mine; and we live in a chilly little corner,[19] and she caught cold this winter, and now she's coughing up blood. Not to mention our three little mites: Katerina Ivanovna's hard at it from dawn till dusk, scrubbing and cleaning and washing the children, for cleanliness has been a habit of hers since infancy, and she is weak of chest and prone to consumption, and I can feel it. Do I not feel? The more I drink, the more I feel. That is why I do it: imbibing, I seek compassion and feeling. It is not merriment I seek, but sorrow, only sorrow . . . I drink that I may suffer more deeply!' With that, he lowered his head onto the table, as if in despair.

'Young man,' he continued, raising himself once more, 'I read, as it were, a certain sorrow in your features. I read it there the moment you walked in, which is why I was so quick to address you. For it is not to disgrace myself before these gentlemen of leisure, who already know it all anyway, that I relate the story of my life to you; rather, I seek a man of feeling and education. You should know that my spouse attended an aristocratic school for daughters of the nobility, and at the leaving ball she danced the *pas de châle*[20] in the presence of the governor and other persons, for which she received a gold medal and a certificate of distinction. The medal . . . well, the medal was sold . . . long ago now . . . H'm! . . . But the certificate of distinction is still in her trunk, and just recently she showed it to our landlady. And though she and the landlady are in perpetual discord, the urge to show off a little before someone – anyone – and reminisce about better, happier days was too strong to resist. And I do not judge her – no, I do not – for this is what has remained in her memory, when all else has turned to dust! Yes, yes; a proud lady, proud and unbending. She scrubs the floor herself and gets by on black bread, but she will not be slighted. That is why she could not let Mr Lebezyatnikov's rudeness pass unchallenged, and when Mr Lebezyatnikov gave her a beating for it, she took to her bed less from injury to her body than from injury to her feelings. I married her when she was already a widow, with three children, three tiny little mites. She married her first husband, an infantry officer, for love, and ran away with him from her father's home. She loved him beyond measure, but he started gambling, ended up in court and promptly died. He beat her towards the end; and though she stood up to him, which I know for a fact, with papers to prove it, she remembers him to this day with tears in her eyes and reproaches me with his example, and I am glad, I am glad, for in her imagination, at least, she once was happy . . . So she was left with three infants in a far-flung, savage district, where I also happened to find myself, and she was left in such hopeless beggary that I, for all that I have seen in my life, am quite incapable of even describing it. Her relations turned

their backs on her. And she was proud, too proud ... So then, my
good sir, I, also widowed, with a fourteen-year-old daughter from my
first wife, offered my hand in marriage, for I could not bear to look on
such suffering. You may judge the depth of her plight from the fact
that she, educated, well brought up, the bearer of a famous surname,
consented to marry me! She did! Crying and sobbing and wringing
her hands – but marry me she did! For she had nowhere else to go. Do
you understand, my good sir, do you really understand what that
means, to have nowhere left to go? No! This you have yet to understand ... For an entire year I carried out my duty in godly, pious
fashion and not a drop did I touch,' (he jabbed at his pint-measure of
vodka) 'for I am a man of feeling. Yet even thus I could not please.
Then I lost my position, also through no fault of my own: a change of
personnel; and then I began to partake! ... A year and a half must
have passed now since we finally found ourselves, after lengthy wan-
derings and numerous calamities, in this magnificent capital city
graced by numerous monuments. And here, I received a position ...
Received it and lost it again. Understand, sir? This time it *was* my
own fault; the mark of my character came to the fore ... So now we
occupy a little corner of a house, and Amalia Fyodorovna Lippewechsel is our landlady, and how we get by and how we pay, I do not know.
Many others live there, too, of course ... Sodom, sir, of the foulest
kind ... H'm ... Yes ... Meanwhile, my girl from my first marriage
has grown up and the things she has had to endure from her stepmother along the way – well, the less said, the better. For although
Katerina Ivanovna's soul overflows with the noblest sentiments, she is
fiery and irritable, and quick to slap you down ... Yes sir! But what is
the use in remembering? Sonya, as you can well imagine, received no
education. I did try, some four years ago, to give her a grounding in
geography and world history; but because my own grasp of these
fields is uncertain, and due to a lack of decent primers (for what books
there were ... h'm! ... well, they are no longer even around, those
books) that was all the teaching she had. Cyrus the Great[21] was as far
as we got. Later, on reaching maturity, she read several books of a
romantic bent, and just recently, through the good offices of Mr Lebezyatnikov, she read with great interest a certain little tome, Lewes's
Physiology[22] – perhaps you know it? – and even conveyed parts of it to
us aloud: and that is the sum of her education. Now let me turn to
you, my good sir, with a private question of my own: in your view,

can a poor but honest girl earn much through honest labour? . . .
She'll not earn fifteen copecks a day, sir, if she is honest and has no
particular talents, and even then only if she works herself into the
ground! And even then Counsellor Ivan Ivanovich Klopstok – are you
familiar with the name? – not only failed to pay her for sewing half a
dozen Holland-cloth shirts, he even insulted her and showed her the
door, stamping his feet and calling her all sorts of names, claiming
that a collar she'd sewn was the wrong size and not straight. Not to
mention the little mites going hungry . . . and Katerina Ivanovna
wringing her hands and pacing the room, her cheeks coming out in
red blotches, as is always the way with this ailment: "You're spong-
ing, girl, eating and drinking and keeping yourself warm," but search
me how you can drink and eat when even the little ones don't see a
crust of bread for three days at a time! I had my feet up at the time . . .
well, all right, I was tipsy, sir, and I could hear my Sonya (as tame as
they come, with that meek little voice of hers . . . and her fair hair and
her little face, always so pale and thin), I could hear her saying: "Well
then, Katerina Ivanovna, do I really have to do *that*?" Meanwhile
Darya Frantsevna, a malicious woman well known to the police, had
already made a few enquiries through the landlady. "Well then,"
mocked Katerina Ivanovna, "what are you saving exactly? Precious
jewels?" But blame her not, my good sir, blame her not! This was said
not in soundness of mind, but in a tumult of feeling, in sickness and to
the crying of unfed children, and it was said more to offend than for
its precise meaning . . . For such is Katerina Ivanovna's character, and
the moment the children start crying, albeit from hunger, she immediately beats them. Come six o'clock, I saw Sonechka get to her feet,
cover her head, put on her little burnous and leave the apartment, and
by nine she was back again. She went straight to Katerina Ivanovna
and laid out thirty roubles on the table without saying a word. Not a
word, not even a glance. She just took our big, green *drap de dames*[23]
shawl (we have one between us, made of *drap de dames*), buried her
head and face in it and lay down on the bed, her face to the wall, her
little shoulders and body a-quivering . . . As for me, sir, I was in the
same state as before, with my feet up . . . And that, young man, was
when I saw Katerina Ivanovna walk over to Sonechka's little bed, also
without saying a word, and kneel at the foot of the bed for the rest of
the evening, kissing Sonechka's feet, not wanting to get up, and, in the
end, they both fell asleep just like that, in each other's arms . . . both

of them ... both ... yes, sir ... and as for me ... I was tipsy and had
my feet up.'

Marmeladov fell silent – his voice just seemed to break off. Then,
with sudden haste, he poured out a glass, drank it and cleared his
throat.

'And ever since then, good sir,' he went on after a pause, 'in consequence of a certain unfavourable circumstance and certain malicious
reports, in which activity Darya Frantsevna proved especially zealous, alleging that she had not been shown due respect – ever since
then my daughter, Sofya Semyonovna, has been obliged to take the
yellow ticket, on account of which she could remain with us no longer.
For our landlady, Amalia Fyodorovna, would not allow it (though she
had previously assisted Darya Frantsevna), and Mr Lebezyatnikov
himself ... H'm ... Well, it was on account of Sonya that he had that
rumpus with Katerina Ivanovna. First he tried his luck with Sonechka, then he suddenly got up on his high horse: "Am I, a man of
considerable education, to live under one roof with the likes of her?"
Well, Katerina Ivanovna didn't let that pass; she stepped in ... and
that was that ... Sonechka usually comes by at dusk now, helps out
Katerina Ivanovna and brings us what she can ... She lives at Kapernaumov's, the tailor's, rents a room there, and Kapernaumov is lame
and tongue-tied, and his entire numerous brood is also tongue-tied.
And his wife, she too is tongue-tied ... They squeeze into a single
room, while Sonya has one of her own, with a partition ... H'm,
yes ... The poorest of people and tied of tongue ... yes indeed ... So
I got up bright and early, put on my rags, raised my hands to heaven
and set off to see His Excellency Ivan Afanasyevich. Perhaps you
know His Excellency Ivan Afanasyevich? ... No? Then you do not
know a godly man! He is wax ... wax before the face of the Lord; as
wax melteth![24] He was even moved to tears after deigning to hear me
out. "Well, Marmeladov," he says, "you've already disappointed me
once ... Now I'm giving you a second chance as my personal responsibility," (those were his very words) "so remember that, and be off
with you!" I kissed the dust at his feet – in my mind, of course, for in
reality he would not have allowed it, being a dignitary and a man of
the latest thinking in matters of state and education – and when I returned home and announced that I had been taken back into the service and was drawing a salary, well, good heavens, you should have
seen what happened then! ...'

Marmeladov broke off once again in the greatest excitement. At that moment, an entire platoon of drunkards, who were already far gone, came in off the street, and the sounds of a rented barrel organ and a cracked, seven-year-old voice singing 'Little Farm'[25] carried over from the entrance. It grew noisy. The landlord and the serving boys busied themselves with the new group. Paying the latter no heed, Marmeladov went on with his story. By now, he appeared to have lost all strength, but the drunker he became the more he wanted to talk. The recollection of his recent success at work seemed to have revived him and had even marked his face with a sort of radiance. Raskolnikov listened attentively.

'All this, good sir, happened five weeks ago. Yes . . . The moment those two, Katerina Ivanovna and Sonechka, found out – goodness, I thought I'd been taken up to heaven. Before, you would lie there like a beast and abuse was all you heard! But now they're going round on tiptoe, hushing the little ones: "Semyon Zakharych is tired out from work, he's resting, shhh!" I was being served coffee before work – and hot cream! Real cream, do you hear! And how they scraped together eleven roubles and fifty copecks to fit me out so nicely, I'll never know! Boots, magnificent cotton shirt fronts, a new uniform, all tip-top, for just eleven fifty. I walked in after my first morning at work and what did I find? Katerina Ivanovna had prepared two courses – soup and corned beef with horseradish – something we'd never even heard of before then. She doesn't have a single dress . . . not a single one, sir, but now here she was, got up as if to go to a party; incredible how she does it; incredible how she makes everything from nothing: the hairdo, a nice clean collar, cuffs, and by the end she looks a completely different person – younger, prettier. Sonechka, my precious, only assisted with money. "It's not proper," she says, "for me to come over to your place too often now, not for a while anyway, maybe only at dusk, so nobody sees me." Do you hear? I came home after lunch for forty winks and just imagine what I heard then: only a week before Katerina Ivanovna had had the most almighty row with Amalia Fyodorovna, but here she was inviting her round for coffee. Two hours they sat together, whispering. "So now Semyon Zakharych is working and drawing a salary, and he presented himself before His Excellency, and His Excellency came out in person, told everybody else to wait, took Semyon Zakharych by the hand and led him past everyone to his office." Do you hear? "In view of past services, Semyon Zakharych," said His Excellency, "and though you succumbed for a time to this frivolous weakness, but as you are now making a promise, and besides we have been doing poorly without you" – do you hear? – "then I shall count on your word of honour" – and she'd made the whole thing up, I tell you, and not out of silliness or just to sing my praises! No, sir, she believes it all herself, she amuses herself with her own imaginings, by heaven! And I do not condemn it; no, this I do not condemn! . . . And when, six days ago, I brought home twenty-three roubles and forty copecks – my first salary, in its entirety – she even called me her little boy: "My clever little boy!" she says. And in private, understand? After all, I'm not much to look at and not much of a husband, am I? But no, she pinched my cheek and said, "My clever little boy!" '

Marmeladov paused as if to smile, but his chin suddenly began to quiver. Still, he held himself together. This pothouse, his depraved appearance, the five nights on the hay barges, the vodka and to top it all, this sickly love for wife and family, disorientated his listener. Raskolnikov listened intently, but with a sick feeling. How he wished he hadn't come here.

'My good sir, my good sir!' Marmeladov exclaimed, having recovered. 'Oh, sir, for you, perhaps, as for everyone else, this is all just a joke and I should really stop bothering you with all the idiotic, pathetic details of my domestic life, but it's no joke to me! For I can feel everything . . . Throughout the entire course of that one heavenly day and throughout the entire evening, I, too, was carried away by dreams: how I would arrange everything and clothe the little mites and give her some respite and bring my only-begotten daughter back from disgrace into the bosom of the family . . . And much else besides . . . Quite forgivable, sir. Well, my good man' – Marmeladov suddenly gave a kind of start, raised his head and stared straight at his listener – 'well, sir, on the very next day, after all these reveries (that is to say, precisely five days ago), towards evening, by a clever ruse, like a thief in the night,[26] I stole the key to Katerina Ivanovna's chest, took what remained of the salary (I no longer remember how much), and look at me now, sir – kaput! My fifth day away from home and the search party's out, and it's the end of my career; and the uniform, in exchange for which I received these vestments, is in a pothouse by Egypt Bridge . . . and it's the end of everything!'

Marmeladov struck his forehead with his fist, clenched his teeth, shut his eyes and planted an elbow on the table. But a minute later his face suddenly changed; glancing at Raskolnikov with an air of slyness and manufactured insolence, he laughed and said:

'Today I went to Sonya, to beg some money – you know, hair of the dog! Heh-heh-heh!'

'Don't tell me she gave it you?' shouted one of the newcomers, then roared with laughter.

'This very pint of vodka was bought with her money, sir,' Marmeladov went on, addressing himself exclusively to Raskolnikov. 'Brought me out thirty copecks, in her own hands, her very last coins; it was all she had, I saw for myself . . . Didn't say a word, just looked at me in silence . . . That's how – up there, not down here – people grieve and weep, but never a word of reproach, not a word! And that hurts even more, sir, when there's no reproach – yes, sir, that hurts more . . . Thirty copecks. She'll be needing them herself now, eh! Wouldn't you say, my dear sir? After all, she has to keep herself immaculate.[27] It costs money to be immaculate in that particular way, does it not? Does it not? Then there's lipstick to be bought, no getting away from that, sir, starched skirts, high-heeled shoes with a touch of class, to show a bit of leg when there's a puddle to be crossed. Do you see, sir, what it means to be immaculate – do you? Well, sir, and there's me, her very own father, swiping these thirty copecks to clear a sore head! And here I am spending them! In fact, I've already spent them! . . . So who could ever pity a man like me? Eh? Do you pity me now, sir, or do you not? Tell me, sir, yea or nay? Heh-heh-heh-heh!'

He was about to pour another glass, but there was nothing left. The pot was empty.

'Pity you – what the hell for?' shouted the landlord, who had come back down again.

There was more laughter and even swearing, among those who were listening and even among those who were not – the sight of the retired civil servant was quite enough for them.

'Pity me! Why pity me?' Marmeladov suddenly howled, standing up with his arm outstretched before him, in an access of inspiration, as though he had been waiting for precisely those words. 'Why pity me, you ask? Oh yes! There is nothing to pity me for! I should be crucified, I should be nailed to the cross – not pitied! So crucify, O judge, crucify, and, having crucified, take pity! Then I shall come to you myself to be nailed to the rood, for it is not merriment I crave, but sorrow and tears! . . . Do you imagine, O vendor, that this pot of yours brought me pleasure? It was sorrow I sought at its bottom, sorrow and tears, which I did taste and I did find; and He shall pity us who pitied all, who understood all men and all things, He alone, He the judge. He shall come on that day and He shall ask: "Where is the daughter who did betray herself for a wicked, consumptive stepmother and infant, alien children? Where is the daughter who did take pity on her mortal father, an obscene drunkard whose brutishness did not appal her?" And He will say: "Come! I forgave thee once . . . Yes, I forgave thee . . . Now, too, thy many sins are forgiven, for thou loved much . . ." And He will forgive my Sonya, He will, I know He will . . . I felt it just now, when I visited her, felt it in my heart! . . . He will judge and forgive all, the good and the wicked, the wise and the meek . . . And when He has finished with them He will speak unto us, too: "Come forth," He will say, "even you! Come forth the tipsy, come forth the feeble, come forth the shameless!" And we shall all come forth, without shame, and we shall stand. And He will say, "You are swine, marked with the image and the stamp of the beast; yet even so – come!" And the wise and the reasonable shall proclaim: "Lord! Why takest Thou these men?" And He will say: "I take them – O men of wisdom, O men of reason – because not one of their number did think himself worthy . . ." And He shall reach out His hands to us, and we shall fall down . . . and we shall weep . . . and we shall understand all things! All things shall we understand! . . . and all will understand . . . even Katerina Ivanovna . . . she, too, will understand . . . May Thy kingdom come,[28] O Lord!'

Exhausted, enfeebled, he lowered himself onto the bench, not looking at anyone, as though oblivious to his surroundings and deep in thought. His words made quite an impression; for a moment there was silence, but the laughter and cursing soon resumed:

'Pull the other one!'

'Load of cobblers!'

'Bureaucrat!'

And so on and so forth.

'Let us be off, sir,' said Marmeladov suddenly, raising his head and addressing Raskolnikov. 'You lead the way . . . Kozel's house, facing the courtyard. High time . . . to Katerina Ivanovna . . .'

Raskolnikov had been wanting to leave for a while, and the thought of helping had already occurred to him. Marmeladov proved far weaker on his legs than in his oratory and leant heavily on the young man. It was a walk of two hundred yards or so. The closer they drew to the house, the more troubled and fearful the drunkard became.

'It is not Katerina Ivanovna I fear now,' he muttered nervously, 'nor the fact that she will start pulling my hair. Hair! . . . Hair is nothing! I say so myself! All the better if she starts pulling it, that's not what scares me . . . It's . . . her eyes that scare me . . . yes . . . her eyes . . . The red blotches on her cheeks scare me, too . . . not to mention – her breathing . . . Have you seen how people breathe with this sickness . . . when they are all worked up? And I fear the crying of the children . . . Because if Sonya has not fed them, then . . . well, search me! Search me! But I do not fear a beating . . . Know, sir, that such beatings, far from bringing me pain, often bring me pleasure . . . I cannot live without them. It's for the best. Let her beat me, vent her feelings . . . for the best, I say . . . And here's the house. Kozel's house. A locksmith, a German, very well off . . . lead the way!'

They entered from the courtyard and went up to the fourth floor. The higher they climbed, the darker the stairwell. It was nearly eleven and although night as such never falls at this time of year in Petersburg, the head of the stairwell was very dark.

A small soot-covered door stood open at the very top of the stairs. A candle stub illuminated a wretched room, the whole of which – ten paces or so from one end to the other – was visible from the door. Children's rags and other stuff lay strewn in disarray. A sheet full of holes was stretched across the far corner. Behind it there was probably a bed. The room itself contained just two chairs and a very tattered couch covered with oilcloth, before which stood an old kitchen table made of pine, unpainted and bare. On the edge of the table a tallow candle was guttering out in its iron holder. So Marmeladov did have his own room, not just a 'corner', but it was a connecting one. The door leading into the other lodgings or cells into which Amalia Lippewechsel's apartment was divided stood ajar. It was noisy there. People were shouting and laughing, probably playing cards and drinking tea. Some choice obscenities flew out.

Raskolnikov instantly recognized Katerina Ivanovna. She was terribly thin, quite tall, with a delicate and elegant figure, still-beautiful dark-brown hair and cheeks that had indeed turned red and blotchy. She was pacing her little room with her arms folded on her chest; her lips were crusted, her breathing uneven and broken. Her eyes had a feverish gleam, but their gaze was sharp and still, and her consumptive, distressed face made a painful impression in the last, trembling light of the dying candle. To Raskolnikov she looked about thirty, and she and Marmeladov really did seem ill-matched . . . She neither heard nor noticed them enter; it was as if she were in a kind of trance, neither hearing nor seeing. It was stuffy, but she didn't open the window; there was a stink from the stairwell, but the door to the stairs wasn't closed; waves of tobacco smoke floated in from the inner rooms through the half-closed door – she kept coughing, but didn't shut it. The smallest girl, aged six or so, was asleep on the floor, half-sitting, huddled up, head buried in the couch. The boy, a bit older, was quivering and crying in a corner. He was probably fresh from a beating. The eldest girl, aged nine or so, tall and stick-thin, wearing nothing but a thin, tattered chemise and a decrepit little burnous of *drap de dames* on bare shoulders (it must have been sewn for her a couple of years before, since now it barely reached to her knees), stood in the corner by her little brother, her long arm, dry as a matchstick, draped around his neck. She seemed to be trying to soothe him; she was whispering something in his ear and doing all she could to stop him snivelling again, while following her mother fearfully with her big dark eyes, which seemed even bigger on her emaciated, frightened little face. Without entering, Marmeladov dropped to his knees right there in the doorway, shoving Raskolnikov into the room. On seeing the stranger, the woman paused absently before him, briefly coming to her senses and appearing to ask herself: what's he doing here? But she must have decided that he was going straight through, to someone else's room. Thinking this and ceasing to pay him any further attention, she made for the entrance door, so as to close it, and suddenly screamed, seeing her husband on his knees on the very threshold.

'Ha!' she yelled in sheer frenzy. 'He's back! Jailbird! Monster! . . . So where's the money? What's in your pockets? Show me! And your clothes aren't the same! Where are your clothes? Where's the money? Speak! . . .'

She set about searching him. Obediently, submissively, without the slightest delay, Marmeladov flung open his arms to assist the search of his pockets. Not a copeck was found.

'So where is the money?' she shouted. 'Lord, don't say he's gone and drunk it all! There were twelve roubles left in the trunk!' – and suddenly, in wild fury, she grabbed him by his hair and dragged him into the room. Marmeladov assisted her, crawling after her meekly on his knees.

'And I find pleasure in this! Not pain, but pleasure, pleasure, my . . . good . . . sir . . . !' he cried, while being shaken by the hair, and even knocking his forehead against the floor. The child asleep on the floor woke up and began crying. The boy in the corner couldn't stand it, started shaking and shouting, and threw himself on his sister in sheer panic, as if he were having a fit. The eldest girl, half-asleep, was trembling like a leaf.

'Drank it! All of it!' cried the poor woman in despair. 'And his clothes aren't the same! They're hungry, hungry!' (She pointed to the children, wringing her hands.) 'Oh, damn this life! And you, have you no shame?' she yelled, suddenly pouncing on Raskolnikov. 'Straight from the bar! You drank with him? You as well! Get out!'

The young man left as quickly as he could, without saying a word. Moreover, the inner door was now wide open and several curious faces were looking in. Insolent laughing heads in skullcaps, smoking papirosi[29] and pipes, poked through the doorway. There were people wearing unbuttoned dressing gowns and outfits that were seasonal to the point of indecency; a few had cards in their hands. They laughed loudest when Marmeladov, being dragged by the hair, shouted that he found it a pleasure. They even started inching into the room, until at last there came a sinister shriek: Amalia Lippewechsel was elbowing her way through to take charge of the situation after her own fashion and to terrify the poor woman for the hundredth time with a foul-mouthed demand that she vacate the premises the very next day. As he was leaving, Raskolnikov managed to dig around in his pocket for whatever small change was left from the rouble he'd spent in the drinking den and quietly placed it by the little window. No sooner was he on the stairs than he had second thoughts and almost went back.

'What a stupid thing to do,' he thought. 'They've got Sonya and I need it myself.' But after reasoning that it was too late to take it back now and that he would never have done so anyway, he wished it good riddance and set off home. 'Anyway, Sonya needs her lipstick, doesn't she?' he continued, striding down the street and smirking sarcastically. 'It costs money to be immaculate . . . H'm! And who's to say Sonechka herself won't be out of pocket by the end of the day? A risk

like that, the hunt for big game . . . mining for gold . . . by tomorrow
they could all be on their uppers, if not for my money . . . Ah, Sonya!
What a well they've managed to dig! And they draw from it! Damn
me, if they don't! They've got used to it. Had a little cry and got used
to it. There's nothing human scum can't get used to!'
    He sank into thought.
    'But if that's not true,' he suddenly exclaimed without meaning to,
'if man isn't actually a scoundrel, isn't actually scum, the whole human race, I mean, then all else is mere preconception, just fears that
have been foisted upon us, and there are no barriers, and that's exactly how it should be!'

III

He woke up late the next day, unrefreshed, after a troubled night's
sleep. He woke up sour, irritable and angry, and looked with loathing
at his garret. It was a tiny little cell, about six paces in length, and a
truly wretched sight with its dusty, yellowy, peeling wallpaper and a
ceiling low enough to terrify even the modestly tall – you could bang
your head at any moment. The furniture was no better: three old
chairs, not in the best repair; a painted table in the corner, on which
lay several books and notebooks, under a layer of dust so thick that
no hand could have touched them for many a day; and, lastly, a large
ungainly couch which took up virtually the entire length of the wall
and half the width of the room. Once upholstered in chintz, now in
tatters, it served Raskolnikov for his bed. He often slept on it without
bothering to undress and without sheets, covering himself in his old
threadbare student coat and resting his head on a small pillow, which
he bolstered by placing all the linen he had, clean or worn, beneath it.
In front of the couch stood a little table.
    One could hardly sink any lower or live more squalidly; but in his
current mood Raskolnikov barely minded – just the opposite. He had
withdrawn from people completely, like a tortoise into its shell, and
even the face of the maid, who was obliged to attend to him and sometimes looked in, was enough to make him turn yellow and shake. So
it goes with certain monomaniacs[30] who focus too much on one thing.
His landlady had ceased sending up food to him two weeks before,
but it still hadn't occurred to him to go down and have it out with her,

even though he went hungry. The tenant's mood rather suited
Nastasya – the cook and the landlady's sole maid – and she'd stopped
cleaning for him altogether, except for the occasional half-hearted
sweep every week or so. It was she who woke him up now.

'Hey, lazybones!' she yelled right over his head. 'It's gone nine! I've
brought you tea. Fancy a cup? You must be skin and bones!'

The tenant opened his eyes, gave a start and recognized Nastasya.

'Who's the tea from – the landlady?' he asked, slowly lifting himself up with a pained expression.

'As if!'

She set before him her own cracked pot, with tea made from old
leaves, and dropped in two yellow lumps of sugar.

'Here, Nastasya, take this please,' he said, fumbling in his pocket
for a handful of copper coins (he'd slept in his clothes), 'and go and
buy me a roll. Get me a bit of sausage, too, while you're at it, the
cheaper kind.'

'I'll bring you the roll right now, but how about some cabbage soup
instead of sausage? Decent soup, made it yesterday. I put some aside,
but you got in late. Decent soup it is.'

When the soup arrived and he set about eating, Nastasya sat down
next to him on the couch and began nattering. She was a village girl
and liked a good natter.

'Praskovya Pavlovna wants to complain to the p'lice about you,'
she said.

He furrowed his brow.

'The police? What does she want?'

'You never pay and you never leave your digs. Clear enough what
she wants.'

'That's all I need,' he muttered, gritting his teeth. 'Talk about bad
timing . . . She's a fool,' he added loudly. 'I'll drop by today and have
a word with her.'

''Course she's a fool, just like me, and I s'pose you're the brainy one,
lying there like a sack of spuds and never showing your face? You says
you used to teach children – so why ain't you doing nothing now?'

'I am doing things . . . ,' replied Raskolnikov, reluctantly and sternly.

'Like what?'

'Work . . .'

'What work?'

'Thinking,' he said seriously, after a pause.

Nastasya went into fits of laughter. She was the laughing sort, and when someone amused her she laughed inaudibly, her whole body swaying and shaking until she even began to feel sick.

'S'pose it pays handsome, then, thinking?' she finally managed to say.

'You can't teach children if you don't have shoes. Anyway, I've spat on the whole idea.'

'Mind you don't spit in the well.'

'Teaching kids pays copecks. What good are copecks?' he continued unwillingly, as though answering his own thoughts.

'S'pose you want your fortune right now, then?'

He threw her a strange look.

'I suppose I do,' he replied firmly, after a pause.

'Easy does it or you'll give me the creeps. What about that roll, then?'

'Up to you.'

'I nearly forgot! A letter came when you was out yesterday.'

'A letter! For me? Who from?'

'Don't ask me. I had to give the postman three copecks. Will I get 'em back?'

'Just bring it. For God's sake, bring it!' Raskolnikov shouted in great agitation.

The letter appeared a minute later. Just as he thought: from Mother, in R—— province.[31] Taking it, he even turned pale. It was a long time since he'd last received a letter; but now there was also something else suddenly squeezing his heart.

'Leave, Nastasya, for the love of God; take your three copecks and please, just go!'

The letter shook in his hands; he didn't want to open it in her presence: he felt like being *alone* with this letter. When Nastasya went out, he brought it quickly to his lips and kissed it; then he stared for a good long while at the address, at the small, sloping handwriting, so familiar and so dear, of his mother, who'd once taught him how to read and write. He delayed; he almost seemed scared. At last, he opened it: the letter was large and thick, double the standard weight; two large sheets were covered in a minuscule script.

'My dearest Rodya,' wrote his mother, 'two months and more have already passed since I last conversed with you in writing, on account of which I have suffered and even lain awake at night, thinking. But I trust you will not blame me for this involuntary silence of mine. You know how much I love you; you are all Dunya and I have, you are everything to us, our hope, our comfort. How awful it was for me to hear that several months had already passed since you left university, being unable to support yourself,[32] and that your lessons and other means of income had ceased! How was I to help with my pension of a hundred and twenty roubles a year? The fifteen roubles I sent you four months ago were borrowed, as you know yourself, on the strength of this same pension, from our local merchant Afanasy Ivanovich Vakhrushin. He's a kind man and he was also a friend to your father. But having granted him the right to take the pension in my stead, I had to wait for the debt to be paid off, and only now has that come to pass, so I had nothing to send you all this time. But now, thank God, it seems I can send you some more, and, in fact, we even have cause to boast of our good fortune, as I hasten to inform you. First of all, dearest Rodya, your sister – fancy this! – has been living with me for a month and a half already, and never again shall we be parted. Her torments, God be praised, are behind her, but I'll begin from the beginning, so that you may know how it all was and what we have kept from you until now. When you wrote to me, two months ago, that someone had told you that Dunya was suffering all manner of rudeness in the home of the Svidrigailovs and asked me for a precise explanation – well, what could I have replied? Had I written the whole truth, you might very well have dropped everything and come to see us, on foot if you had to, for I know both your character and your feelings, and I know that you would never allow your sister to be insulted. I was in despair myself, but what could I do? I didn't know the whole truth myself at the time. The main difficulty was that Dunechka, on joining their household last year as governess, accepted an advance of a full one hundred roubles on condition of a monthly deduction from her salary, and so there was really no question of her leaving the post without having first repaid the debt. She took this sum (I can tell you everything now, my priceless Rodya) chiefly in order to send you sixty roubles, which you were in such need of at the time and which you did indeed receive from us last year. We deceived you when we wrote that it came out of Dunechka's savings; that was not the case, and now I am telling you the whole truth, because now, by the will of God, everything has taken a sudden turn for the best,

and because you should know how Dunya loves you and what a priceless heart she has. Mr Svidrigailov did indeed behave very rudely towards her at first, making all sorts of unseemly and mocking remarks
to her at table . . . But I am loath to dwell on all these painful details,
for fear of upsetting you needlessly, when all this is now behind us. In
short, although Marfa Petrovna, Mr Svidrigailov's wife, treated her
kindly and honourably, as did all the household, life was very hard for
Dunya, especially when Mr Svidrigailov, lapsing into his old army
ways, succumbed to the influence of Bacchus. But can you imagine: it
later transpired that this madcap had long been nurturing a passion
for Dunya, but had concealed it under the guise of rudeness and contempt towards her. Perhaps he was even ashamed and horrified to find
himself – already advanced in years, the head of a family – entertaining
such frivolous hopes, so he ended up venting his anger on Dunya. Or
perhaps his vulgar manner and mockery were merely intended to hide
the full truth from others. But in the end he could resist no longer and
he dared to approach Dunya with an explicit and beastly proposition,
promising her various rewards and, what was more, to drop everything
and take her away with him to a different village or even a different
country. Just imagine how she suffered! Quitting her position there
and then was out of the question, not only because of her financial
debt, but also out of consideration for Marfa Petrovna, whose suspicions might suddenly have been aroused, which would inevitably have
sown discord in the family. Dunya, too, would have found herself
mired in scandal; it wouldn't have just blown over. There were plenty
of other reasons, too, and Dunya could entertain few hopes of escaping from that awful house for at least six weeks. You know Dunechka. You know how intelligent she is, how tough she is. She can put
up with a lot and, even in the most desperate situations, find within
herself enough nobility of mind to maintain her resolve. She did not
even write to me about it so as not to upset me, though we often exchanged news. The dénouement arrived quite unexpectedly. Chancing
to overhear her husband pleading with Dunechka in the garden,
Marfa Petrovna misunderstood everything and pinned the blame on
Dunya, assuming that she was the cause of it all. A terrible scene unfolded right there in the garden: Marfa Petrovna even struck Dunya a
blow, wouldn't listen to a word that was said to her, wouldn't stop
yelling herself, and eventually gave orders for Dunya to be driven off
to me in town, forthwith, on a simple peasant cart onto which all her

things were thrown – her linen, her dresses, untied and unpacked. Then the heavens opened and Dunya, insulted and disgraced, had to travel eleven long miles with a peasant in an uncovered cart. Just think: what could I have written to you in reply to the letter I received from you two months ago, and what could I have written about? I was in despair myself; I did not dare tell you the truth, for you would have been terribly unhappy, upset and indignant, and anyway, what could you have done? Merely make things worse for yourself, I imagine, and anyway, Dunechka forbade it; and filling a letter with trivialities, with such grief in my heart, was more than I could bear. The whole town was gossiping about this incident for an entire month, and it reached the point where Dunya and I could not even attend church on account of all the contemptuous glances and whispers, and some even spoke openly about it in our presence. All our acquaintances kept a wide berth and ceased even bowing to us in the street, and I learned for a fact that some salesmen and clerks had a mind to insult us by smearing the gates of our house with tar,[33] so the landlords started demanding that we vacate the apartment. The cause of it all was Marfa Petrovna, who managed to blame Dunya and sully her name in every household. She knows everyone here and visited the town incessantly that month, and being rather fond of talking – especially about her domestic affairs and in particular her husband, about whom she complains to all and sundry, which is quite wrong – she succeeded, in a short space of time, in spreading this story not just through the town, but across the whole district as well. I fell ill, but Dunechka was stronger and you should have seen how she bore it all; she even managed to console and reassure me! Such an angel! But by God's mercy our torments were curtailed: Mr Svidrigailov had second thoughts, repented and, presumably taking pity on Dunya, provided Marfa Petrovna with full and certain proof of Dunechka's complete innocence: namely, the letter which Dunya, even before Marfa Petrovna had found them together in the garden, had been obliged to write and give to him so as to avoid the trysts and tête-à-têtes he insisted on, and which, following Dunechka's departure, remained in Mr Svidrigailov's hands. In this letter, showing great fervour and the deepest indignation, she reproached him precisely for his ignoble conduct towards Marfa Petrovna, reminding him that he was a father and head of a family; and finally, how beastly it was of him to torture and render unhappy a girl who was miserable and defenceless enough already.

In a word, dearest Rodya, this letter is so noble and so touchingly written that I sobbed when I first read it and still cannot read it without tears. In addition, Dunya was vindicated by the belated testimony of the servants, who saw and knew far more than Mr Svidrigailov assumed, as is always the way. Marfa Petrovna was utterly shocked and "destroyed all over again", as she told us herself, but she no longer had the slightest doubt as to Dunechka's innocence, and the very next day, a Sunday, she came straight to the cathedral, fell to her knees and prayed tearfully to the Almighty to grant her strength to endure this fresh trial and fulfil her duty. Then, without paying a single visit along the way, she came directly to us, told us everything, wept bitterly and, utterly contrite, embraced Dunya and begged her forgiveness. The very same morning, without a moment's hesitation, she set off from ours to visit every house in town, shedding tears and speaking of Dunechka in the most flattering terms, so as to clear Dunya's name and reaffirm the nobility of her feelings and conduct. As if that wasn't enough, she showed everybody Dunechka's handwritten letter to Mr Svidrigailov, read it aloud and even permitted the making of copies (which I find a little excessive). She ended up having to spend several days in town, going from door to door, since some had begun taking offence at being overlooked, so a rota had to be established, with the result that she found people already waiting for her in every home, since everybody knew that on such-and-such a day in such-and-such a house Marfa Petrovna would be reading this letter, and at every reading there gathered even those who had heard the letter several times before, whether in their own homes or in the homes of other acquaintances, according to the rota. My own opinion is that much, if not most of this was quite unnecessary; but such is Marfa Petrovna's character. At any rate, she fully restored Dunechka's good name and this beastly business left its ineradicable stain on her husband alone, as the main culprit, to the extent that now I even feel sorry for him; this madcap didn't need to be treated quite so harshly. Dunya immediately began receiving invitations to give private lessons, but she turned them down. In general, everyone suddenly started treating her with marked respect. All this helped bring about that unexpected development through which our whole destiny, one might say, is now changing. You should know, dearest Rodya, that Dunya has a suitor and has already given her assent, as I now hasten to inform you. And although the matter was arranged without your opinion being sought, you will not, I expect, be displeased either with me or your sister; you will see for yourself, from the very facts of the matter, that it would have been impossible for us to wait and put it off until we had received your reply. In any case, you would not have been able to judge all this properly from far away. This is what happened. He, already a court counsellor, Pyotr Petrovich Luzhin by name, is a distant relative of Marfa Petrovna, who did much to bring this about. He began by indicating through her that he desired to make our acquaintance, was received in the appropriate manner, drank a cup of coffee, and sent a letter the very next day in which he set out his proposal with the greatest civility and requested a speedy and decisive reply. He is a business-like man, always on the go, and now he's rushing off to Petersburg, so for him every moment is precious. Of course, we were very shocked at first, since it all happened so very quickly and unexpectedly. We spent the whole day deliberating and thinking it over together. He is a trustworthy man and well-to-do, with two positions and already with capital of his own. He is forty-five, that is true, but he has a pleasing enough appearance and a woman might still find him attractive; he is, in fact, a most respectable and decent man, albeit a little sullen and, as it were, supercilious. But that might just be a first impression. In any case, I must warn you, dearest Rodya, that when you meet him in Petersburg, as is sure to happen in the very nearest future, do not rush to judgement, as is your wont, if at first sight there is something about him you don't quite like. I mention this just in case, although I am quite sure he will make a pleasant impression on you. Besides, when getting to know any person at all, one must take a measured and cautious approach, so as not to lapse into error and prejudice, such as may subsequently be corrected and smoothed over only with the greatest difficulty. There is much to suggest that Pyotr Petrovich is a highly estimable man. He declared to us on his very first visit that he is a positive man, but one who in many respects shares, as he put it, "the convictions of our newest generations",[34] and who is the enemy of all prejudice. He said a great deal else besides, because he is a little vain, as it were, and loves an audience, but there are worse vices than that. Most of it went over my head, of course, but Dunya explained to me that, although he is a man of modest education, he is intelligent and seems kind. You know your sister's character, Rodya. She is a tough, sensible, patient and high-minded girl, though with a fiery heart, one I have studied closely.

Of course, there is no great love here, neither on her side nor his, but Dunya is not just intelligent – she is also a noble, angelic creature and will consider it her duty to make her husband happy, just as he in his turn would see to her happiness, and we have no great reason as yet to doubt this, even if the matter was, I admit, arranged rather hastily. Moreover, he is a very calculating man and he is bound to see for himself that his own marital happiness will be all the more secure, the happier Dunechka is at his side. As for any discrepancies of character or old habits or even some divergence of opinion (which cannot be avoided even in the happiest of unions), on this score, Dunechka told me, she is counting on herself; she says that there is no need to worry and that she can endure a great deal, on condition that relations between them are honest and fair. At first, for example, he struck me, too, as a little abrupt, as it were; but that, after all, may be due pre-cisely to his frankness – in fact, that is certainly the case. On his second visit, for example, his proposal having already been accepted, he remarked in the course of conversation that even before knowing Dunya he resolved to take a girl who was honest but without a dowry, one who, above all, already knew misery at first hand; because, as he explained, a husband should not owe his wife a thing, and in fact it is far better if the wife considers the husband her benefactor. I should add that he expressed himself in somewhat gentler and more affec-tionate terms than these, for I have forgotten the actual expression and remember only the thought, and besides, the remark evidently slipped out without the slightest premeditation, in the heat of conver-sation, and he even tried to correct himself afterwards and soften his tone; but still, this struck me as a touch abrupt, as it were, and I said as much to Dunya afterwards. But Dunya replied, a little peevishly, that "Words are not deeds", and she is, of course, quite right. Before making up her mind, Dunechka stayed awake all night and, thinking I was already asleep, got out of bed and spent all night pacing the room; eventually she knelt before the icon, offered long and fervent prayers, and declared to me in the morning that she had reached a decision.

   'I've already mentioned that Pyotr Petrovich is leaving for Peters-burg. He has important business there and wants to set up chambers in the city as a private attorney.[35] He's had his hands full with various lawsuits for a long time now, and just the other day he won an impor-tant victory. Indeed, the reason he has to go to Petersburg is that he has an important case in the Senate.[36] All of which means, dearest Rodya, that he can be extremely useful to you as well, in every way, and Dunya and I have already resolved that, as of today, you can make a definitive start on your future career and consider your destiny to be clearly defined. Would that this came to pass! It would be such a boon that it should be considered nothing less than a direct expression of divine mercy towards us. Dunya dreams only of this. We have already ventured to say a few words on this score to Pyotr Petrovich. He expressed himself with caution and said that since he cannot get by without a secretary it would, of course, be better to pay a salary to a relative than to a stranger, assuming, of course, that the relative proves competent (as if you could ever be incompetent!), but he immediately proceeded to express the concern that your university work may not leave time for work in his office. We left it there, but now Dunya thinks of nothing else. She has been in a kind of fever for several days now and has already sketched everything out: how with time you may become Pyotr Petrovich's colleague and even partner, especially since you are yourself reading law. I fully agree with her, Rodya, and share all her plans and hopes, finding them entirely feasible; and despite Pyotr Petrovich's current and entirely understandable evasiveness (he does not yet know you), Dunya is absolutely confident of achieving everything through her good influence on her future husband – in fact, she's quite sure of it. Of course, we took great care not to let any of these future dreams slip out in conversation with Pyotr Petrovich, especially about your becoming his partner in his legal work. He is a positive type and might not have been best pleased, as all this would have struck him as mere dreaming. In the same way, neither I nor Dunya have breathed a word to him yet of our firm hope that he will help us in giving you financial assistance while you are still studying; we said nothing because, first, this will eventually happen of its own accord anyway and he will probably suggest it himself without wasting too many words (as if he could ever refuse Dunechka in such a matter!), especially now that you may become his right-hand man in the office and receive this assistance not as an act of kindness but as a fully merited salary. This is how Dunechka wishes to arrange things and I fully agree with her. Second, we said nothing because I was particularly keen for you to be on an equal footing with him at our forthcoming meeting. When Dunya sang your praises to him, he replied that in order to judge a man one must first examine him oneself, at close quarters, and that he would prefer to form his own opinion of you when he meets you. You know, my priceless Rodya, it seems to me that for various reasons (reasons which have nothing to do with Pyotr Petrovich, just my own, personal reasons and perhaps just the whims of an old woman) I might do best to live apart from them once they are married, just as I am living now. I am quite sure that he will be honourable and tactful enough to invite me and to propose that I never be parted again from my daughter, and if he has not said this yet then only because it goes without saying; but I shan't accept. I have observed more than once in life that husbands rarely take mothers-in-law to heart, and not only do I not wish to be the slightest burden to anybody, I also want to be quite free myself, at least for as long as I have a crust of bread to call my own, and children such as you and Dunechka. If possible I will live near both of you, because, Rodya, in this letter I have saved the best till last: know, my darling, that very soon, perhaps, we will be together once more and the three of us shall embrace after nearly three years apart! It has been decided *for a fact* that Dunya and I are leaving for Petersburg; when exactly I do not know, but in any case very, very soon, perhaps even in a week's time. Everything depends on the instructions of Pyotr Petrovich, who will let us know just as soon as he has taken his bearings in Petersburg. He is keen, for various reasons, not to waste any time and to hold the wedding at the earliest opportunity, before the next fast, if at all possible, or failing that, straight after the Feast of Our Lady.[37] How happy I will be to press you to my heart! Dunya is jumping for joy at the thought of seeing you and once she even said, for a joke, that this alone would be reason enough to marry Pyotr Petrovich. Such an angel! She is not going to add anything to this letter and merely told me to say that she has so much to speak to you about, so very much, that she is simply unable to pick up a pen, because a few lines are not enough to say anything and one merely succeeds in upsetting oneself; she simply told me to hug you tight and send you countless kisses. But despite the fact that very soon, perhaps, we will be together in person, I will still send you some money in the next day or two, as much as I can. Now that everyone knows that Dunechka is to marry Pyotr Petrovich, my credit has also suddenly increased, and I know for a fact that Afanasy Ivanovich will now trust me, on the strength of my pension, with up to as much as seventy-five roubles, so I may send you twenty-five roubles or even thirty. I would send still more, but our travelling expenses concern me;

and although Pyotr Petrovich has been good enough to stand part of the cost of our journey to the capital, by volunteering, at his own expense, to convey our luggage and a large trunk (through some acquaintance or other), we still need to put something aside for when we actually arrive, at least for the first few days, for one can hardly show up in Petersburg without a copeck. Actually, Dunechka and I have already worked it all out down to the very last detail, and the journey should not cost us too much. It is a mere sixty miles to the railway line from here and, to be on the safe side, we have already made arrangements with a peasant we know who has a cart; from there, Dunechka and I will have ourselves a jolly time in third class. So I may manage to send you not twenty-five but even thirty roubles. But enough. I've covered two sheets of paper from top to bottom and there's no space left. What a story it's been – how many adventures! But now, my priceless Rodya, till soon we meet, I embrace you and give you my maternal blessing. Rodya, love your sister Dunya; love her as she loves you and know that she loves you boundlessly, more than she loves herself. She is an angel, and you, Rodya, you are our everything – our every hope, our every comfort. It is enough for you to be happy for us to be happy, too. Do you still pray, Rodya, and do you believe in the goodness of our creator and redeemer? In my heart I fear: might you, too, have been visited by the faithlessness that is now so fashionable? If so, I pray for you. Remember, dearest, when you were still a child and your father was still with us, how you babbled out your prayers on my knee and how happy we all were! Farewell, or rather – *till soon we meet*! I hug you close and send countless kisses.

Yours to the grave,
Pulkheria Raskolnikova.'

All the time he was reading, from the very first line of the letter, Raskolnikov's face was wet with tears; but when he finished it was pale and twisted by spasms, and a dismal, bilious, angry smile snaked along his lips. Laying his head on his scraggy, worn-out pillow, he thought and thought. His heart was thumping and his mind was in turmoil. Eventually, he began to feel stifled and cramped in this yellow garret that resembled a cupboard or a trunk. His eyes and mind needed space. He grabbed his hat and went out, this time no longer fearing to meet anyone on the stairs; he'd forgotten all about that. He hurried

off in the direction of Vasilyevsky Island, via V—— Prospect,[38] as
though he had some urgent business to attend to, but he walked, as
was his habit, heedless of the way, whispering to himself and even
speaking out loud, which greatly astonished passers-by. Many took
him for a drunk.

IV

The letter from his mother had wrung him dry. But he had not a moment's doubt regarding the crucial, fundamental point, even while he
was still reading it. The crux of the matter had been resolved in his
mind and resolved for good: 'They'll get married over my dead body,
and to hell with Mr Luzhin!

'For it's all perfectly obvious,' he muttered to himself with a sneer,
relishing in advance the successful outcome of his decision. 'No,
Mama, no, Dunya, you won't fool me! . . . They even apologize for
not seeking my opinion and for arranging it all without me! I'll say!
They think it can't be undone; we'll see about that! What a splendid
excuse: "Pyotr Petrovich is such a business-like man," they say – so
terribly business-like, in fact, that he can only get married in a post-
chaise or even – why not? – in a railway carriage. No, Dunechka,
nothing escapes me and I know what it is you have to talk to me about
so very much; I also know what it was you thought about all night
long as you paced the room, and what you prayed for before the Virgin of Kazan by Mama's bed. Climbing Golgotha is no joke. H'm . . .
So, then, it's been definitively decided: you, Avdotya Romanovna,[39]
are pleased to accept the hand of a business-like and rational man
with capital of his own (*already* with capital of his own: that's so
much more respectable, so much more impressive), who has two positions, shares the convictions of our newest generations (as Mama
writes) and "*seems* kind", as Dunechka herself observes. That *seems*
tops everything! For this *seems* this Dunechka is to be wed! . . . Marvellous! Simply marvellous! . . .

'. . . I wonder, though, why Mama wrote to me about those "newest generations"? Was it simply to give me an idea of the man or was
there an ulterior motive: to soften me up for the benefit of Mr Luzhin?
Oh, sly ones! And there's another thing I'd like to get to the bottom
of: to what extent were they open with one another, in the course of
that day, that night, and all the days that followed? Was everything

expressed *in so many words* or did each of them realize that they both
had the same thing in their hearts and minds, so there was no point
saying it all out loud and saying too much. The second, I expect. It's
clear from the letter that he struck Mama as *a touch* abrupt, and
Mama in her naivety decided to share her observations with Dunya.
Naturally, Dunechka got cross and "replied a little peevishly". I'll say!
Who wouldn't get mad when it's all plain as day, without any need for
naive questions, and when it's already been decided that there's nothing more to be said. What is it she writes to me: "Rodya, love Dunya,
who loves you more than she loves herself"; mightn't this be her conscience secretly gnawing away at her for agreeing to sacrifice her
daughter for her son? "You are our comfort, our everything!" Oh,
Mama!' He was positively seething with spite, and had he met Mr
Luzhin now he might very well have killed him!

'H'm, it's true,' he continued, following the swarm of thoughts in
his head, 'it's true that "one must take a measured and cautious approach to get to know a person well"; but Mr Luzhin is transparent.
Above all, "he is business-like and *seems* kind": now we mustn't
laugh – he's taking care of the luggage and paying for the trunk!
Who's to say he isn't kind? And as for those two, *the bride* and the
mother, they're hiring some peasant, in a cart with bast matting
(that's how I used to travel, after all)! They'll manage! A mere sixty
miles, "then we'll have ourselves a jolly time in third class" for some
six hundred more. Makes perfect sense: cut your coat to suit your
cloth; but how about you, Mr Luzhin? This is your betrothed, after
all . . . Surely you must have known that Mother was borrowing for
the journey against her pension? Of course, this is a joint commercial
venture, with split profits and equal shares, so the outlay is also half-
and-half; friendship is one thing, business another. Still, here too the
business-like man has sold them short: the luggage is cheaper than
their fare and it might even travel for free. Do they really not see this
or don't they want to see it? Yet they're content, quite content! And
that's only the start of it – the best is still to come! After all, the main
point here is not the stinginess, not the avarice, but the *tone* of it all.
This is the tone of their future marriage, a sign of things to come . . .
But what's Mama doing living the fast life anyway? What will she
show up in Petersburg with? Three roubles or two "nice little notes",
as that woman likes to say . . . the old one . . . H'm! What on earth
does she expect to live on in Petersburg? After all, she's already

managed to work out, for whatever reason, that it will be *impossible* for her and Dunya to live together after the wedding, even only at the beginning. I expect that our nice chap *said too much* on this score and gave himself away, though Mama rushes to deny it: "I shan't accept," she says. What is she thinking, and who or what is she counting on: her 120-rouble pension, minus her debt to Afanasy Ivanovich? There she is knitting winter shawls, sewing cuffs, ruining her rheumy eyes. But I know for a fact that the shawls only bring in another twenty roubles a year. So they must be counting on Mr Luzhin's noble feelings after all: "He'll make the offer himself, he'll insist." Don't hold your breath! That's always the way with these beautiful souls steeped in Schiller:[40] until the very last moment they dress man up in peacock feathers, until the very last moment they count on good, not ill, and despite their creeping suspicions they won't admit anything to themselves in advance; the very thought disagrees with them and they'll rush to deny the truth until their noses are rubbed in it by the man they've so richly adorned. H'm, I wonder whether Mr Luzhin's been decorated. I bet he's got St Anna in his buttonhole[41] and that he wears it to merchants' dinners. He'll probably wear it to his own wedding! But to hell with him!

'. . . I suppose that's just how Mama is, God bless her, but what about Dunya? Dunechka, dearest, I know you! You'd already turned nineteen when we saw each other last: your character was already clear to me. Here's Mama writing that "Dunechka can put up with a lot." I was well aware of the fact. I was aware of it two and a half years ago and I've been thinking about it ever since, about the very fact that "Dunechka can put up with a lot." I mean, if she can put up with Mr Svidrigailov and all the consequences, then she really can put up with a lot. And now, with Mama's help, she's conceived the notion that she can also put up with Mr Luzhin, who likes to hold forth about the superiority of wives rescued from beggary, with benefactors for husbands, and who does so virtually on first acquaintance. Let's suppose that he did "say too much", despite his being a rational man (so perhaps, far from saying too much, he was actually in a hurry to spell everything out), but what about Dunya for heaven's sake? The man's transparent, but she'll still have to live with him. I mean, she would sooner live on black bread and water than sell her soul, let alone give up her moral freedom for a life of comfort; she wouldn't give it up for all Schleswig-Holstein,[42] never mind Mr Luzhin. No, that wasn't the Dunya I knew, and . . . well, that's not Dunya now! . . . Who can deny it? It's a hard life with the likes of Svidrigailov! A hard life traipsing from one province to another, year in, year out, in search of governess jobs paying two hundred roubles, but still, I know that my sister would sooner join Negroes on a plantation, or Latvians[43] in the pay of a Baltic German, than corrupt her spirit and her moral sense through a liaison with a man she doesn't respect and has nothing in common with – for evermore, and for no other reason than personal gain! And even if Mr Luzhin were made of the purest gold or of solid diamond, even then she would not agree to be Mr Luzhin's lawful concubine. So why does she agree now? What's it all about? Where's the key to the mystery? It's clear enough: she won't sell herself for her own interests, her own comfort, or even to save her skin, but she'll sell herself for someone else! For someone dear to her, someone she adores! That's what it's all about: her brother, her mother – that's what she'll sell herself for! Sell all she's got! Oh yes, we won't stop at anything here, we'll even stifle our sense of right and wrong; freedom, peace of mind, conscience – we'll barter them all! Life be hanged, so long as our precious loved ones are happy! We'll even indulge in some casuistry of our own, take lessons from the Jesuits,[44] and for a while we might even set our minds at rest, convince ourselves that it's all in a good cause and there's no other way. That's what we're like, and it's all clear as day. It's clear who's centre stage here: Rodion Romanovich Raskolnikov and no one else. Just think: what a chance to make him happy, to keep him in university, to make him a partner at the office, to secure his entire future; one day he might even become wealthy and respected, and end his life a famous man! And Mother? But this is Rodya, priceless Rodya, firstborn! No sacrifice is too great for such a son – not even that of a daughter like Dunya! Oh, sweet and unjust hearts! Even Sonechka's fate is not to be scorned here! Sonechka, Sonechka Marmeladova, eternal Sonechka, for as long as the world stands! But have you both weighed it carefully, this sacrifice of yours? Yes? Is it bearable? Profitable? Reasonable? Do you know, Dunechka, that Sonechka's fate is no more sordid than the fate of being with Mr Luzhin? "Love is out of the question here," writes Mama. But what if it's not just love that's out of the question, but respect as well, and what if instead of that there's disgust, contempt, loathing – what then? Well, once again it will be a case of being *"immaculate"*. Wouldn't you say? Do you understand what it means to be immaculate in this way – do you? Do you understand that being immaculate the Luzhin way is just the same as the Sonya way, but perhaps even worse, even more vile and despicable, because after all, Dunechka, you're counting on a life of comfort, while there it's simply a matter of survival or starvation! "It costs a lot to be immaculate, Dunechka, a lot!" And what if later it should all prove too much and you repent? How much sorrow and sadness, how much cursing and secret weeping, because you're no Marfa Petrovna, are you? And what will happen to Mother then? She's unsettled and anxious even now; but what then, when the scales fall from her eyes? And me? . . . Whatever must you have thought of me? I don't want your sacrifice, Dunechka, I don't want it, Mama! Over my dead body! I don't accept it! I won't accept it!'

He suddenly came to his senses and broke off.

'Over your dead body? And what will you do to stop it happening? Forbid it? What right do you have? What can you promise them in return, so as to have such a right? That you will dedicate your entire fate to them, your entire future, *when you complete your studies and receive a position*? We've heard all that, it's all ifs and buts; what about now? Something has to be done here and now, do you understand? And what are you doing now? Fleecing them. You know the money comes from a hundred-rouble pension and from the Svidrigailovs' advance! How will you protect them from the Svidrigailovs, or from Afanasy Ivanovich Vakhrushin, you millionaire of the future, you Zeus, you master of their fate? In ten years' time? But ten years will be more than enough for your mother to go blind knitting shawls, if tears alone are not enough; she'll wither away on bread and water. And your sister? Just think what may come of her in ten years or less? Worked it out yet?'

He taunted and tortured himself with such questions, and even found some pleasure in doing so. These questions were not new, though, and they didn't come from nowhere; they were old, ancient sources of pain. They had begun tearing at his heart long before and had torn it to pieces. All his current anguish had taken root in him in the far distant past, grown and accreted, until now it had ripened and distilled into the form of a dreadful, wild, fantastical question which had worn out his heart and mind, demanding to be solved. His mother's letter struck him with the sudden force of thunder. Clearly, now was not the time for agonizing and passive suffering, for mere deliberation about the fact that the questions permitted no solution; something had to be done, the sooner the better. He had to decide at all costs on something, anything, or else . . .

'Or else renounce life completely!' he suddenly cried in sheer frenzy. 'Meekly accept fate as it is, once and for all, and stifle everything inside me, renouncing any right to act, to live, to love!'

'Do you really understand, good sir, what it means to have nowhere left to go?' The question put to him yesterday by Marmeladov suddenly came to mind. 'For every man must have at least somewhere he can go . . .'

He gave a sudden start: one of yesterday's thoughts had shot through his mind once again. But it was not the speed of it that made him start. After all, he had known, he had *sensed*, that the thought would, without fail, come 'shooting through', and he was already expecting it; and this thought had hardly been born yesterday. The difference was this: a month ago, and even just yesterday, it was no more than a dream, while now . . . now it suddenly presented itself to him not as a dream, but in a new, threatening and quite unfamiliar form, and he'd suddenly realized this himself . . . It was like a blow to the head, and his eyes went dark.

He glanced about him in haste, looking for something. He felt like sitting down and looked for a bench; he was walking down K—— Boulevard[45] at the time. A bench appeared some hundred paces away. He quickened his step as best he could; but one small incident occurred along the way, absorbing all his attention for several minutes.

While looking for the bench, he noticed a woman walking twenty steps ahead of him, but at first he paid her no more heed than any of the other objects flitting before his eyes. It had occurred to him many times already to walk home, say, and have not the faintest memory of the route he had taken, and he was already used to walking like this. But there was something so very strange about the woman, something which immediately leapt out at him, that little by little she began to compel his attention – against his will at first, almost as a nuisance, but then with increasing force. He was seized by a sudden urge to understand what it was about her that was so very strange. For one thing, there she was – to all appearances, a very young girl – walking bare-headed in the sultry heat, without a parasol or gloves, waving her arms about in a somehow comical manner. She wore an airy silk dress and this, too, looked very odd, being barely fastened and with a rip by the waist at the back, at the very top of the skirt; a large scrap hung down, dangling behind her. A small shawl had been thrown round her bare neck, but it stuck out crookedly to one side. To top it all, the girl was unsteady on her feet, stumbling – even staggering – this way and that. This encounter eventually claimed Raskolnikov's full attention. He drew up with the girl right by the bench, but she collapsed at one end of it as soon as she got there, rested her head on the back of the bench and shut her eyes, as if she were utterly exhausted. On closer inspection, he immediately realized that she was dead drunk. To observe such a scene felt strange, bizarre. He even wondered if he were mistaken. Before him was the extremely young face of a girl of sixteen or perhaps only fifteen – a small, blonde, pretty enough face, but all flushed and swollen-looking. The girl no longer seemed capable of understanding much; she had one leg crossed over the other, baring far more than was proper, and clearly had very little idea that she was out in the street.

Raskolnikov didn't sit down and didn't wish to leave, so he stood before her in bewilderment. This boulevard is rarely busy, but now, between one and two o'clock on such a sultry day, there was almost no one. And yet over there, a dozen paces away, on the far side of the boulevard, a man had stopped and everything about him indicated that he, too, was very keen to approach the girl for reasons of his own. He, too, must have spotted her from a distance and wanted to catch up with her, but Raskolnikov had got in his way. He kept throwing him angry glances, while trying not to let him notice, and was impatiently waiting for this annoying tramp to clear off. The situation was perfectly clear. The gentleman was about thirty years old, thickset, fat, a picture of health, with pink lips and a moustache, and very foppishly dressed. Raskolnikov saw red: he had a sudden urge to insult this fat dandy in any way he could. He left the girl for a moment and walked up to the gentleman.

'Hey you, Svidrigailov![46] What're you after?' he shouted, clenching his fists and laughing through lips foaming with anger.

'What is the meaning of this?' the gentleman asked sternly, knitting his brows in supercilious surprise.

'Clear off, that's what I mean!'

'How dare you, you little wretch!'

With this, he flashed his whip. Raskolnikov threw himself on him, fists flailing, without even considering that the thick-set gentleman might respond with two fists of his own. But at that very moment somebody grabbed him firmly from behind: a police officer had come between them.

'That'll do, gentlemen. Have the good manners not to fight in public. What are you after? Who are you anyway?' he asked Raskolnikov sternly, after noticing the state of his clothes.

Raskolnikov looked at him attentively. Before him was a gallant soldier's face with a grey moustache, grey whiskers and an intelligent gaze.

'It's you I'm after!' he exclaimed, grabbing him by the hand. 'I'm a former student, Raskolnikov . . . You may as well know that, too,' he added, turning to the gentleman, 'and you, come along with me, I've something to show you . . .'

He dragged the policeman over to the bench.

'Just look at her – dead drunk. Just now she was walking down the boulevard: who knows what kind of family she's from, but it doesn't look like she's on the game. Much more likely that she was plied with drink somewhere and tricked . . . her first time . . . understand? And then just thrown out on the street. Look at the rip in her dress and look how it hangs on her: she can't have dressed herself. She was dressed, and clumsily so – a man's work. That's obvious. And now look over here: this dandy, who I was picking a fight with just now, is a complete stranger to me – I've never seen him before; but he also spotted her, drunk and insensible, as he was passing just now, and now he desperately wants to go up and grab her – seeing as she's in such a state – and take her off somewhere . . . I'm sure of it. Trust me. I could see myself that he was observing and following her, but I got in his way and now he's just waiting for me to leave. He's moved off a little; look at him standing there, pretending to roll a papirosa . . . How can we stop him? How can we get her home? Think of something!'

The policeman grasped the situation at once. The fat gentleman was no mystery, of course, but the girl? The officer leant over to take a better look, and sincere compassion was etched on his face.

'A crying shame!' he said, shaking his head. 'All but a child. Tricked, and no two ways about it. Listen, miss,' he addressed her, 'may I ask where you live?' The girl opened her tired, dazed eyes, looked dully at her interrogators and waved them away.

'Here,' said Raskolnikov, rummaging about in his pocket and

eventually fishing out twenty copecks. 'Here, hail a cab, and give the driver her address. The address, that's all we need to know!'

'Well, miss?' the policeman began again, taking the money. 'I'm going to hail you a cab and I'll accompany you myself. Where should we take you? Eh? Where do you reside?'

'Push off! . . . Pests!' the girl muttered, waving them away again.

'Dear oh dear! A shameful business, miss, a shameful business!' He shook his head again, in shame, pity and indignation. 'A fine pickle!' he added, turning to Raskolnikov, before looking him up and down once more. He, too, must have looked odd to him: in rags like those and handing out money!

'Did you find the young lady far from here?' he asked him.

'As I said: she was walking ahead of me, staggering, right here on the boulevard. She collapsed just as soon as she reached the bench.'

'Lord, what a world we're living in! An ordinary lass like her and already drunk! Tricked, and no two ways about it! Look, even her dress is ripped . . . Depravity, wherever you look! . . . Wouldn't surprise me if she's of gentry blood, the poorer kind . . . They're ten to a dozen nowadays. Looks a delicate sort, just like a gentry girl,' and he leant over her once more.

Perhaps he had daughters of his own who were also growing up 'just like gentry girls, delicate sorts', with all the airs of good breeding and second-hand fashion . . .

'The main thing,' Raskolnikov fussed, 'is to stop this scoundrel having his way with her! Are we going to let him abuse her as well? It's blindingly obvious what he's after; and look, he's still there!'

Raskolnikov was speaking loudly and pointing straight at him. The other man heard him and was on the point of losing his temper again, but thought better of it and restricted himself to a contemptuous glance. Then he slowly retreated a further ten paces or so and halted once more.

'We can stop him all right, sir,' replied the officer, thinking it over. 'If only the young lady can tell us where to take her . . . Eh, miss? Miss?' Again he leant over.

She suddenly opened her eyes wide, took a good hard look, as though she had finally understood something, got up from the bench and headed off in the direction from which she'd come.

'Shameless . . . pests!' she said with another flap of her arms. She walked off briskly, though staggering just as much as before. The dandy followed her, but along another alley, never taking his eyes off her.

'I'll stop him, don't you worry,' said the policeman decisively, and set off after them. 'Dear, dear – depravity, wherever you look!' he repeated with a sigh.

At that very moment Raskolnikov felt as if he'd been stung; as if, in a flash, he'd been turned inside out.

'Hey, listen!' he shouted to the man with the moustache.

The policeman turned around.

'Forget about it! What's it to you? Just drop it! Let him have his fun.' (He pointed at the dandy.) 'What's it to you, I say?'

The policeman failed to understand and stared at him wide-eyed. Raskolnikov burst out laughing.

'Good grief!' the policeman uttered with a dismissive wave of the hand, then headed off after the dandy and the girl, probably taking Raskolnikov for a madman or worse.

'He's taken my twenty copecks,' Raskolnikov, left on his own, muttered angrily. 'Well, he can take some off that man as well, leave him the girl and end of story . . . What on earth was I doing, offering to help? Me – helping? Do I even have the right? They can eat each other alive – what's it to me? And how dare I give those twenty copecks away? Were they really mine?'

Despite these strange words, he felt quite wretched. He sat down on the abandoned bench. His thoughts were in disarray . . . In fact, at that moment it was hard for him to think about anything at all. Total oblivion was what he wanted: to forget everything, then wake up and begin afresh . . .

'Poor girl!' he said, glancing at the empty corner of the bench. 'She'll come round, have a cry, then her mother will find out . . . First she'll beat her a bit, then she'll whip her, hurting her and shaming her, then she might even throw her out . . . And even if she doesn't, some Darya Frantsevna or other will sniff her out, and my girl will start doing the rounds . . . Then it's straight off to hospital (that's always the way with girls who live with very honest mothers and misbehave on the quiet) and then . . . well . . . back to hospital . . . booze . . . the pothouse . . . the hospital again . . . and within two or three years you've got yourself a cripple, her whole life over at the age of nineteen or less . . . Haven't I seen girls like that? And how did they get there?

That's how they got there, all of them . . . Pah! So be it! That's how it should be, they say. A certain percentage, they say, must go that way every year . . . Which way? . . . To the devil, I suppose, so as to freshen up the rest and not get in their way. Percentage![47] What lovely words they use: so soothing, so scholarly. You hear a word like that and wonder what on earth you were worrying about. Now if it were a different word, you might feel a little less comfortable . . . But what if Dunechka also ended up in that percentage . . . and if not that one, then another?

'But where am I going?' he suddenly wondered. 'How strange. After all, I must have gone out for a reason. I read the letter and set off right away . . . To Vasilyevsky Island, to see Razumikhin, that's where I was going . . . I remember now. But still, what was the reason? And why on earth did the thought of visiting Razumikhin enter my head now of all times? Quite astonishing.'

He marvelled at himself. Razumikhin was one of his old university friends. It was a remarkable fact that Raskolnikov had hardly made any friends at university; he kept his distance, never called on anyone and was a reluctant host. People soon gave up on him. Meetings, conversations, amusements – somehow, he avoided them all. He never spared himself in his studies, and for this he was respected; but nobody liked him. He was very poor and somehow haughty in his pride and unsociability, almost as if he were hiding something. Some of his peers had the impression that he looked down on them all as if they were children, as if he had outstripped them all in his development, knowledge and convictions, and that he viewed their convictions and interests as simply beneath him.

For some reason, though, he got along well with Razumikhin, or rather, he was more sociable, more open with him. In truth, there was no other way of responding to Razumikhin. He was an unusually cheerful and sociable lad, kind to the point of simplicity. This simplicity concealed both depth and virtue. The best of his friends understood this, and everybody liked him. He was far from stupid, if occasionally dim. His appearance was very striking – tall, thin, ill-shaven, raven-haired. He could be rowdy and was known for his strength. One night, among friends, he felled a seven-foot reactionary with a single blow. He could drink like a fish, but he could also not drink at all; he could lark about and go too far, and he could rein himself in. Razumikhin was remarkable in yet another way: no failure could ever ruffle him, just as no circumstance was ever bad enough, it seemed, to bring him down. He could pitch his tent on a roof if he had to, endure hellish hunger and the bitterest cold. He was dirt poor yet persisted in supporting himself all on his own, taking odd jobs to get by. He knew any number of sources from which he could draw (by working, of course). Once, he survived a whole winter without heating his room and claimed that he even preferred it that way, because you sleep better in the cold. Now he, too, had been forced to leave university, but not for long, and he was straining every sinew to put things right and continue his studies. Raskolnikov hadn't been to see him for a good four months, while Razumikhin didn't even know where his old friend lived. There was one occasion, some two months previously, when they had almost met in the street, but Raskolnikov turned away, even crossing to the other side to avoid being noticed. Razumikhin noticed him, but walked past, not wishing to trouble his *friend*.

V

'Yes, it wasn't so long ago that I was about to ask Razumikhin about work, see if he could find me some teaching or something . . . ,' Raskolnikov went on to himself. 'But what can he do for me now? Suppose he does find me some lessons; suppose he even shares his last copeck with me, assuming he has one, so that I might even be able to buy myself a pair of boots and patch up my clothes for teaching in . . . H'm . . . Well, what then? What use is small change to me? Is that really what I need now? How ridiculous this is – going off to Razumikhin . . .'

The question of why he'd set off to see Razumikhin troubled him more than even he was aware; he was racking his brain to find in this seemingly ordinary decision some sinister meaning.

'What, did I really expect to patch everything up through Razumikhin alone? Was Razumikhin really my answer to everything?' he asked himself in astonishment.

He was thinking and rubbing his forehead when a peculiar thing happened: suddenly, as if by chance and almost by itself, after very lengthy hesitation, an exceedingly strange thought entered his head.

'H'm . . . Razumikhin,' he suddenly said with perfect equanimity, as if reaching a final decision. 'I'll go to see Razumikhin, that's for sure . . . but – not now . . . I'll go to him . . . the day after, the day after *that*, when *that* will be over and done with and everything will begin afresh . . .'

He suddenly came to his senses.

'After *that*,' he cried out, fairly leaping from the bench. 'But will *that* really happen? Surely it can't, can it?'

He left the bench and walked off, almost running; he was about to turn back home, but the thought of doing so suddenly appalled him: it was there at home, in that horrid cupboard, that all *this* had been brewing for over a month now; and he walked on, wherever his legs should take him.

His nervous tremors had become almost feverish; he even felt shivery; in the stifling heat he was turning cold. As if by some almost unconscious effort, by some inner necessity, he began scrutinizing every object he passed, as though trying hard to distract himself, but he was having little success and kept sinking into thought. When, with a start, he raised his head again and looked about him, he would instantly forget whatever he had just been thinking about, even the route he had taken. He walked like so from one end of Vasilyevsky Island to the other, emerged on the banks of the Little Neva, crossed the bridge and turned towards the Islands.[48] His tired eyes, accustomed to the dust of the city, to the mortar and to the massive, cramping, crushing buildings, delighted at first in the greenery and the freshness. The closeness, the stench, the drinking dens – all had been left behind. But soon even these new and pleasant sensations began to sicken and irritate him. He stopped occasionally in front of dachas bedecked with greenery, peered through the fences, and saw extravagantly dressed women on distant balconies and terraces, and children running about in the gardens. He was particularly interested in the flowers and looked at them longest of all. Magnificent carriages also crossed his path, as well as men and women on horseback; he followed them with a curious gaze and forgot about them before they even disappeared from view. At one point he stopped and counted his money: thirty copecks or so. 'Twenty to the police officer, three to Nastasya for the letter – so yesterday I must have given the Marmeladovs about forty-seven copecks or even fifty,' he thought as he did his sums, but he soon forgot why he'd taken the money out of his pocket in the first place. He remembered as he was walking past an eating-house and realized he was hungry. Entering it, he had a glass of vodka and some kind of pie, which he finished off outside, continuing on his way. He hadn't drunk vodka for a very long time and it had an instant effect, even though it was only a glass. His legs suddenly grew heavy and he began to feel extremely sleepy. He headed home; but just as he was reaching Petrovsky Island he stopped in utter exhaustion, turned off the road into the bushes, collapsed on the grass and fell asleep there and then.

In morbid states dreams are often unusually palpable and vivid, bearing an exceptional resemblance to reality. The resulting picture may be quite monstrous, but the setting and the unfolding of the entire spectacle are so credible, and the details so fine and unexpected, while artistically consistent with the picture as a whole, that the very same dreamer could not invent them in his waking hours, were he even an artist of the order of Pushkin or Turgenev. Such dreams, morbid dreams, always live long in the memory and have a powerful effect on disturbed and already excited organisms.

It was a terrifying dream. Raskolnikov dreamt that he was back in his childhood, in their little town. He's about seven, it's a holiday, towards evening, and he's out walking with his father in the outskirts. A leaden, stifling day, the setting exactly as it was preserved in his memory: actually, his memory had smoothed it out a great deal compared to what he now saw in his dream. The town lies spread out before him, not a tree in sight; only far, far away, on the very edge of the sky, is the black dot of a small wood. A few yards away from the town's last vegetable patch is a tavern, a big tavern, which always made the most unpleasant impression on him and even frightened him when he passed it on walks with his father. There was always such a crowd there, so much yelling, laughing and swearing, so much hideous, raucous singing, so many fights; so many drunken, frightening types loitering around outside . . . Coming across them, he would cling to his father and shake all over. Next to the tavern is a road, a cart-track, always dusty and always black. On it goes, winding along and curving round to the right of the town cemetery some three hundred yards away. In the middle of the cemetery stands a stone church with a green cupola, where he used to go to church twice a year with his mother and father, for services held in memory of his grandmother, who was already long dead and whom he had never seen. They would always bring *kutya* on a white dish covered with a napkin, and the *kutya* would be made of sugar, rice and raisins pressed into the rice to form a cross.[49] He loved this church and its ancient icons, most of them without metal casing, and the old priest with the twitching head. Next to his grandmother's grave, which had a tombstone, was the small grave of his younger brother, who died at six months and whom he'd also never known and couldn't remember; but he'd been told he once had a little brother, and every time he visited the cemetery he made a pious, respectful sign of the cross before the little grave, bowed to it and kissed it. And now he's dreaming that he and his father are walking along the path past the tavern towards the cemetery; he's holding his father's hand and keeps glancing back at the tavern in terror. A particular circumstance attracts his attention: some kind of party is under way – there's a crowd of dressed-up townswomen with their husbands and assorted low life. Everyone's drunk, everyone's singing, and there's a cart, a rather strange one, by the entrance to the tavern. It's one of those big carts to which big draught horses are harnessed, which carry goods and wine barrels. He always liked looking at these enormous draught horses with their long manes and sturdy legs, walking along at a measured pace and pulling entire mountains of stuff, not straining in the slightest, as though they found it easier to carry a load than not to. But now, strangely enough, the horse harnessed to such a big cart is small, scrawny and yellowish-brown, a real peasant's nag, one of those which he had often seen struggling beneath a load of firewood or hay, especially if the cart had got stuck in mud or in a rut, and then the peasants always beat them so very hard with their whips, sometimes right across their muzzles and eyes, and he would feel so very sorry for them that he'd be on the verge of tears and Mummy would lead him away from the window. But now it's suddenly become terribly noisy: great strapping peasants, roaring drunk, in red and blue shirts, their heavy coats hanging loose from their shoulders, are coming out of the tavern, shouting, singing and playing balalaikas. 'Hop on, all of yer!' shouts one, still young, with a big fat neck and a pulpy, carrot-red face. 'I'll take the lot of yer, hop on!' But everyone starts laughing and yelling:

'On a nag like that!'

'Mikolka, you must be soft in the head: an old mare pulling a cart like that!'

'That sorrel must be going on twenty, lads!'

'Hop on, I'll take the lot of yer!' Mikolka shouts again. Jumping first onto the cart, he takes the reins and stands up tall on the front board. 'The bay's gone with Matvey,' he shouts from the cart, 'and this old mare just pains my heart! I've half a mind to kill 'er, brothers – she's money down the drain. Hop on, I say! I'll get 'er galloping! Galloping!' He picks up the whip, relishing the prospect of flogging the sorrel.

'Hop on, why not?' someone guffaws in the crowd. 'Galloping, eh?'

'Bet she's not galloped for ten years or more!'

'She will now!'

'Show no mercy, brothers – grab your whips, all of yer, and have 'em ready!'

'Right you are! Flog 'er!'

They clamber into Mikolka's cart, laughing and joking. Some half a dozen men have climbed aboard and there's still room for more. They've got a woman with them, fat and ruddy-cheeked. She's wearing red calico, a horned headdress[50] with beads, and little booties; she's cracking nuts and tittering. Everyone in the crowd is laughing as well, and who could blame them? This clapped-out old mare galloping with a load like that! Two lads in the cart grab a whip each, to help Mikolka. 'Gee up!' someone cries and the old nag tugs with all the strength she can muster, but she's barely capable of walking, never mind galloping; she just takes tiny little steps, groans and slumps under the blows raining down on her from the three whips. The laughter in the cart and the crowd becomes twice as loud, but Mikolka's furious and his blows land faster and faster, as if he really does believe that the old mare will start galloping.

'Brothers, wait for me!' shouts a lad from the crowd, getting into the spirit.

'Hop in! Hop in, all of yer!' shouts Mikolka. 'She'll take the lot of yer. I'll flog 'er dead!' He's lashing her and lashing her and no longer knows what to hit her with in his frenzy.

'Daddy! Daddy!' he shouts to his father. 'What are they doing, Daddy? Daddy, they're beating the poor little horse!'

'Come on, boy!' says the father. 'Just drunken idiots fooling around: off we go, boy, don't look!' – and tries to lead him away, but he breaks free of his grasp and, quite beside himself, runs to the horse. But the poor little horse is in a bad way. She's struggling for breath, stops, gives another tug and almost falls.

'Flog 'er till she drops!' shouts Mikolka. 'She's asking for it. I'll flog
'er dead!'

'Where's your fear of God, you mad beast?' yells an old man in the
crowd.

'When's a mare like that ever hauled such a load?' adds another.

'You'll do 'er in!' shouts a third.

'Stay out of it! She's my property! I'll do what I like. Hop on! All of
yer! I'll be damned if she don't gallop!'

A sudden volley of laughter drowns out everything else: the ever
more frequent blows prove too much for the old nag and she begins
feebly kicking out. Even the old man can't hold back a grin. And no
wonder: a clapped-out old mare like her and still kicking out!

Two other lads in the crowd grab a whip each and run up to the
horse to flog her from the side. They race in from opposite directions.

'Whip her on the snout – the eyes, the eyes!' shouts Mikolka.

'A song, brothers!' someone shouts from the cart and everyone in
the cart sings along with him. A boisterous song starts up, a tambou-
rine jingles and there's whistling during the refrain. The fat woman
cracks nuts and titters.

. . . He's running alongside the little horse, running ahead, watching them as they whip her across the eyes, right across the eyes! He's
crying. His heart surges, tears flow. One of the floggers catches him
on the face; he doesn't feel it, wrings his hands, shouts, rushes to the
grey old man with the grey beard, who's shaking his head in disapproval. A woman grabs his hand and tries to lead him away; but he
breaks free and again he runs to the horse. She has no strength, yet
still, she kicks out once more.

'Mad beast, eh?' screams Mikolka in wild fury. He drops the whip,
bends over the cart and pulls out from the bottom a long thick shaft;
he picks up one end with both hands and, straining every sinew, starts
swinging it over the sorrel.

'He'll smash 'er in two!' someone shouts.

'He'll kill her!'

'My property!' shouts Mikolka and brings the shaft down with all
his force. The impact is loud and heavy.

'Flog 'er! Flog 'er! Don't stop!' shout voices from the crowd.

Mikolka swings for a second time and another crashing blow lands
on the spine of the wretched nag. She falls right back on her rump, but
jerks up again and tugs, tugs every which way with her last ounce of

strength, trying to shift the cart; but six whips are lashing her from all sides, and again the shaft is raised and falls for a third time, then a fourth, steadily, with heaving swings. Mikolka is furious that one blow is not enough to kill her.

'She's a sticker!' someone shouts from the crowd.

'Now she's sure to fall, brothers, now she's had it!' yells another enthusiastic observer.

'An axe'll do it!' shouts a third.

'I'll feed yer to the flies! Out of my way!' Mikolka screams uncontrollably. He drops the shaft, leans over the cart once more and pulls out an iron crowbar. 'Look out!' he shouts, and clubs his poor mare with all his strength. A shattering blow; the mare begins to totter, slumps, tries to tug, but the bar comes crashing down on her spine once more and she falls to the ground, as if her four legs had all been hacked off at once.

'Finish 'er off!' shouts Mikolka and, quite beside himself, jumps down from the cart. Several lads, also red-faced with drink, grab whatever they can – whips, sticks, the shaft – and run over to the dying mare. Mikolka stands on one side and starts hitting her over the back with the crowbar. The nag stretches out her muzzle, sighs heavily and dies.

'Got there in the end!' comes a voice from the crowd.

'She should've galloped!'

'My property!' shouts Mikolka, standing there with the bar in his hands and bloodshot eyes. He seems sorry not to have anyone left to hit.

'You've no fear of God!' shouts the crowd, in many voices now.

But the poor boy is beside himself. He yells and squeezes his way through the crowd to the sorrel, throws his arms around her dead, bloodied muzzle and kisses her, kisses her on her eyes, her lips . . . Then he suddenly jumps up and charges at Mikolka with his little fists. At that very moment his father, who's been chasing after him in vain, finally grabs him and hauls him out of the crowd.

'Off we go now! Off we go!' he tells him. 'Home!'

'Daddy! The poor little horse . . . They've killed it . . . What for?' he sobs, but he can barely breathe and the words burst from his tightening chest like screams.

'Just drunks fooling around. Off we go! It's none of our business!' says his father. He hugs his father, but his chest feels tighter and tighter. He wants to catch his breath and scream, then wakes.

He woke in a cold sweat, his hair soaked; gasping for breath, he lifted himself up in terror.

'Thank God, just a dream!' he said, sitting up under a tree and drawing deep breaths. 'But what's happening? Hope it's not a fever coming on: what a hideous dream!'

His whole body felt broken, his soul troubled and dark. Resting his elbows on his knees, he propped his head in his hands.

'My God!' he exclaimed. 'Will I really – I mean, really – actually take an axe, start bashing her on the head, smash her skull to pieces? . . . Will I really slip in sticky, warm blood, force the lock, steal, tremble, hide, all soaked in blood . . . axe in hand? . . . Lord, will I really?'

He shook as he said this.

'But what am I saying!' he continued, raising himself up once more, as if in deep astonishment. 'After all, I knew this would be too much for me, so why have I been tormenting myself all this time? Yesterday, just yesterday, when I went to do that . . . *test*, even then I understood full well that I'd crack . . . So what is all this? How can I still be in any doubt? Only yesterday, coming down the stairs, didn't I say that all this is despicable, foul, vile . . . ? The very thought of it *in reality* made me sick with horror . . .

'No, I'll crack! I'll crack! Even supposing that all these calculations are entirely sound, that all the decisions taken during this past month are as clear as day, as sound as arithmetic. Lord! Even then I'll not dare! In the end I'll crack! I'll crack! So what on earth am I still . . . ?'

He got to his feet, looked about in surprise, as if his coming here were also a cause for wonder, and made off towards T—— Bridge. He was pale, his eyes were burning and every limb ached with exhaustion, but suddenly he seemed to be breathing more freely. He felt that he had cast off the terrible weight that had been crushing him for so long, and his soul suddenly felt light and at peace. 'Lord,' he prayed, 'show me my path, while I renounce this damned . . . dream of mine!'

Crossing the bridge, he gazed in quiet serenity at the Neva, at the bright setting of the bright red sun. Despite his weakness, he felt no tiredness. As if an abscess that had been developing all month on his heart had suddenly burst. Freedom! Freedom! He was free from this spell, from sorcery and charms, from evil delusion!

Subsequently, when he recalled this time and all that had happened to him during these days, minute by minute, point by point, mark by mark, he was always struck to a superstitious degree by a certain circumstance which, though in fact not all that extraordinary, had, he later felt, somehow predetermined his fate.

Namely: he was simply incapable of understanding or explaining to himself why he'd returned home via Haymarket Square, a place he had not the slightest reason to visit, when it would have made far more sense for him, tired and worn out as he was, to take the shortest, most direct route home. It wasn't much of a detour, but it was an unmistakable and quite unnecessary one. Of course, there had been dozens of occasions when he'd returned home without remembering the streets along which he'd walked. But why on earth, he would always wonder, should this encounter on Haymarket Square – one so important and so decisive for him and at the same time so very fortuitous (in a place he had no need to go to) – why should it have occurred right then, at such an hour, such a moment of his life, when he found himself in precisely the mood and precisely the circumstances required for this encounter to have the most decisive and most definitive effect on his entire fate? As if it had been lying in wait for him!

It was about nine when he crossed Haymarket. All the traders at the tables and stalls, and in the shops and little stores, were locking up their goods or taking them down and putting them away, and making their way home, as were their customers. In the filthy, stinking courtyards of Haymarket Square, near the eating-houses on the lower floors, and especially outside the drinking dens, thronged traffickers and rag dealers of every kind. Raskolnikov was often drawn to this square, and all the nearby streets, during his aimless wanders. Here his rags attracted no one's disdain and nobody could care less what he looked like. On the corner of K—— Lane a tradesman and his wife were selling goods at two tables: thread, tape, cotton handkerchiefs and so on. They, too, were packing up for the day, but they'd paused to chat to an acquaintance. The acquaintance was Lizaveta Ivanovna, or simply Lizaveta, as everyone called her, the younger sister of that same old woman, Alyona Ivanovna – the collegiate registrar's widow and moneylender whom Raskolnikov had visited the day before to pawn the watch and do his *test* . . . He had long known all there was to know about this Lizaveta, and she even knew him a little. She was a tall, ungainly, timid, meek spinster, thirty-five years old and all but an imbecile; she was completely enslaved to her sister, worked for her day and night, quivered in her presence and even took beatings from her. With a bundle in her hand, she stood in hesitation before the tradesman and his wife, listening to them attentively. They were heatedly trying to explain something to her. When Raskolnikov suddenly caught sight of her, he was overcome by a strange sensation resembling the deepest astonishment, even though this encounter had nothing astonishing about it.

'Lizaveta Ivanovna, my dear, why don't you decide for yourself?' the tradesman was saying in a loud voice. 'Come by tomorrow, between six and seven. That lot will come too.'

'Tomorrow?' said Lizaveta slowly and pensively, as if in two minds.

'Alyona Ivanovna's put the wind up you and no mistake!' jabbered the trader's wife, a lively sort. 'I look at you, lady, and think: a child, a mere child. And your sister's only your half-sister, but look how she's got you under her thumb!'

'No need to say anything to Alyona Ivanovna this time,' her husband broke in. 'That's my advice anyway – just come to us without asking. It's a nice bit of business, lady. Your big sister will see for herself later.'

'Maybe I should?'

'Between six and seven, tomorrow. Them lot will come too. Decide for yourself, dear.'

'We'll get the samovar going,' added his wife.

'All right, I'll come,' said Lizaveta, still thinking it over, then slowly moved off.

Raskolnikov walked past at this point and heard no more. He'd slipped by quietly, trying to catch every word. His initial astonishment had given way, little by little, to horror, like ice down his spine. He'd learned, suddenly and quite unexpectedly, that tomorrow, at precisely seven o'clock in the evening, Lizaveta, the old woman's sister and sole cohabitant, would not be in and that, as a result, the old woman, at precisely seven o'clock in the evening, *would be at home on her own*.

His room was only a few steps away. He entered like a man sentenced to death. He wasn't thinking, nor was he capable of thinking; but he suddenly felt in every fibre of his being that he no longer had the freedom of reason or will and that everything had suddenly been decided for good.

Of course, even if he'd waited years on end for a favourable opportunity, even then, with a plan in place, he could scarcely have counted on a surer step towards the successful execution of that plan than the one that had suddenly presented itself now. In any case it would have been difficult to establish just the day before, with greater precision or smaller risk, without the need for any dangerous enquiries or searches, that the very next day, at such-and-such a time, such-and-such a woman – the object of an intended murder – would be home all alone.

VI

Later, Raskolnikov happened to find out why exactly the tradesman and his wife had invited Lizaveta round. It was a perfectly run-of-the-mill affair. A newly arrived, impoverished family was selling off various things – clothing and so on, all women's stuff. It was hard to make anything much at the market, so they were looking for a dealer – Lizaveta's line: she took a commission, got around and had plenty of experience, being very honest and always naming her lowest price: there was no shifting her after that. She didn't talk much in any case and, as has already been said, she was as meek and shy as they come . . .

Recently, though, Raskolnikov had become superstitious. Traces of superstition would remain in him for a long time yet, almost indelibly. In fact, he would always be prone to find something rather strange about this whole business, something mysterious, the presence, as it were, of some special influences and coincidences. Back in winter a student he knew, Pokoryov, who was leaving for Kharkov, mentioned in passing the address of old Alyona Ivanovna, should he ever need to pawn anything. For a long time he stayed away: he had some teaching and could just about make ends meet. He'd remembered about the address six weeks or so ago; he had two things fit for pawning: his father's old silver watch and a small gold ring with three red stones, a farewell gift from his sister, to remember her by. He'd decided on the ring; and the moment he found and clapped eyes on the old woman, not yet knowing anything much about her, he felt overcome by disgust, took two 'nice little notes' off her and on his way back stopped off in a shabby little tavern. He ordered tea, took a seat and plunged deep in thought. A strange idea was tapping away in his head, like a chick in its egg, occupying him body and soul.

At another small table, very close to his, sat a student he neither knew nor remembered, and a young officer. They were drinking tea after a game of billiards. Suddenly he'd overheard the student telling

the officer about the moneylender, Alyona Ivanovna, a collegiate secretary's widow, and giving him her address. This in itself had struck
Raskolnikov as strange: he'd only just come from seeing her. Sheer
chance, of course, but there he was unable to rid himself of one highly
unusual impression only to see someone bend over backwards (or so it
seemed) to oblige him: the student suddenly started telling his friend
all manner of details about this Alyona Ivanovna.

'A splendid woman,' he said. 'You can always get money from her.
Rich as a Yid. She can hand over five thousand just like that, and she
won't turn her nose up at trifles either. Plenty of our lot have called on
her. She's a right bitch, mind . . .'

He set about describing what a nasty and capricious woman she
was, how you only had to be a day late paying and your item would
disappear. She gave four times less than the thing was worth, charged
five or even seven per cent interest a month, etcetera. Letting his
tongue run away with him, the student also mentioned that the old
woman had a sister, Lizaveta, whom she, so little and so horrid, never
stopped beating and kept in utter servitude, like a little child, when in
fact Lizaveta was a whole foot taller, at the very least . . .

'Just try explaining that!' the student exclaimed and roared with
laughter.

The conversation turned to Lizaveta. The student took particular
pleasure in talking about her and couldn't stop laughing, while the
officer listened with the keenest interest and asked the student to send
him this Lizaveta to mend his linen. Raskolnikov caught every word,
and learned everything there and then: Lizaveta was the old woman's
younger half-sister (by a different mother), and she was already thirty-
five years old. She worked for her sister day and night, doing all the
cooking and the laundry; on top of that, she sewed to order and even
washed other people's floors, handing over all the earnings to her sister. She didn't dare accept a single order or a single job without the
old woman's say-so. The latter, meanwhile, had already made her
own will, which was known to Lizaveta herself, who stood to receive
not a penny, apart from chattels, chairs and so on; the money was to
go to a certain monastery in N—— province, for the eternal remem-
brance of the old woman's soul. Lizaveta, who was born into trade,
not the civil service, was a spinster and frightful to look at: she was
remarkably tall with long, twisted-looking feet and a single pair of
down-at-heel goatskin shoes, and she always kept herself clean. But

the main thing that surprised the student and made him laugh was the fact that Lizaveta was forever pregnant . . .

'But you said she was hideous?' the officer observed.

'Well, she's swarthy-looking, like a soldier in drag, but actually far from hideous. Her face and eyes are ever so nice. Really very nice. There's proof – plenty of people like her. So quiet and meek, so tame and agreeable – she'll agree to anything. And she's got a lovely smile on her.'

'Sounds like you like her, too?' the officer laughed.

'For her strangeness. But what I really want to tell you is this: I could murder and rob this hag, and without the faintest pang of conscience, I assure you,' the student added with fervour.

The officer guffawed once more and Raskolnikov shuddered. How very strange this was!

'Let me ask you a serious question,' the student continued. 'I was joking just now, of course, but look: on the one hand a stupid, pointless, worthless, nasty, sick old hag who nobody needs and who is positively vicious to all and sundry, who doesn't know herself why she's alive and who in any case will drop dead tomorrow or the day after. Catch my drift?'

'Yes, I suppose,' answered the officer, fixing an attentive gaze on his excited friend.

'There's more. On the other hand, fresh-faced youths going to waste for lack of support – thousands of them, everywhere! A hundred, a thousand good deeds and initiatives could be arranged and assisted with the money doomed for the monastery! Hundreds, possibly thousands of lives could be set on the right path; dozens of families saved from beggary, disintegration, ruin, depravity, the venereal hospital – and all this on her money. Kill her and take her money, so as to devote yourself afterwards to the service of all humanity and the common cause. What do you reckon? Won't thousands of good deeds iron out one tiny little crime? For one life – thousands of lives saved from decay and ruin. One death and a hundred lives in return – it's basic arithmetic! And anyway, what does the life of this consumptive, stupid, nasty hag weigh on the scales of the world? No more than the life of a louse, a cockroach, and it's not even worth that, because the hag is vicious. She'll eat you alive: just the other day she bit Lizaveta's finger out of pure spite. They nearly had to cut it off!'

'Of course she doesn't deserve to live,' remarked the officer, 'but there's nature to think about.'

'Nature, my dear chap, is forever being corrected and directed, otherwise by now we'd all have drowned in our preconceptions. Otherwise, no great man would ever have been born. People talk about "duty", "conscience", and I've nothing against duty and conscience, but what do we understand by them, that's the thing? Hang on, I've another question for you. Now listen!'

'No, you hang on. I've a question for you. Now you listen!'

'Well?'

'Here you are speaking and speechifying, but tell me: are you going to kill the old woman *yourself* or aren't you?'

'Of course not! I'm talking about justice . . . It's not about me . . .'

'Well, as I see it, if you don't dare do it yourself, there's no justice to speak of! Let's have another game!'

Raskolnikov was in a state of extreme agitation. Of course, these were just the usual, everyday conversations and ideas of the young, such as he had heard many times before; only the form and topic varied. But why had it fallen to him, precisely then, to hear precisely this conversation and precisely these thoughts . . . at a time when *those very same thoughts* had just been conceived in his own mind? And why precisely then – just when he had carried away from the old woman the embryo of his idea – had he chanced on a conversation about her and no one else? The coincidence would always strike him as strange. This trivial conversation in a tavern exerted the most radical influence on him in the subsequent course of events: as if there really were something preordained in it all, some sign . . .

Getting back from Haymarket, he collapsed on his couch and sat there without moving for a whole hour. Meanwhile it grew dark. He had no candles and in any case it didn't cross his mind to light one. He could never remember: was he thinking about anything during all that time? Eventually he began to feel feverish and shivery, just like before, and realized with pleasure that the couch might also be used for lying on. A deep, leaden sleep soon descended, like some crushing weight.

He slept for an unusually long time, dreamlessly. Nastasya came into his room at ten the next morning and had to give him a forceful shake. She'd brought tea and bread. Once again she'd used old leaves, and once again it came in her own pot.

'What a sleepyhead!' she cried indignantly. 'Sleeping, sleeping, sleeping!'

He forced himself to sit up. His head ached. He tried to stand and turn around, but fell back down on the couch.

'Back to sleep, I suppose!' Nastasya cried. 'Are you sick?'

He said nothing.

'Fancy some tea?'

'Later,' he said, forcing out a reply before closing his eyes again and turning towards the wall. Nastasya stood over him a while.

'Maybe he really is sick,' she said, then turned and walked out.

She came back at two with some soup. He hadn't moved. The tea hadn't been touched. Nastasya took offence and set about shaking him furiously.

'Enough snoozing!' she cried, looking at him in disgust. He sat himself up, but said nothing and gazed at the floor.

'Are you sick or ain't you?' Nastasya asked and again received no reply.

'Get yourself out a bit,' she said after a pause. 'Blow away them cobwebs. Are you or ain't you eating?'

'Later,' he said weakly, then, 'Off you go now!' – and waved her out. She stood where she was a short while longer, looked at him with pity and went out.

A few minutes later he lifted up his eyes and stared for a long time at the tea and the soup. Then he took the bread, took the spoon and started eating.

He reluctantly, almost mechanically, ate three or four spoonfuls, no more. His headache eased a little. After his meal, he stretched out again on the couch, but he could no longer fall asleep, so he lay without moving, face down, his head buried in the pillow. One daydream followed another, all of them strange. In most of them he found himself somewhere in Africa, in Egypt, at some oasis or other. The caravan is at rest, the camels lie peaceably; palm trees grow around in a circle; everyone's eating. As for him, he drinks and drinks from a stream which flows and bubbles right there beside him. How cool it is and how wonderfully blue the water, and how cold, racing over the many-coloured stones, over the bright clean sand sparkling like gold . . . Suddenly he heard a clock strike loud and clear. He came round with a start, raised his head, looked out of the window, worked out the time and suddenly leapt to his feet, wide awake now, as though someone had yanked him off the couch. He walked up to the door on tiptoe, gently opened it a fraction and listened for noises on the stairs

below. His heart was thumping uncontrollably. But only silence came
from the stairs, as if everyone was asleep . . . How bizarre to think
that he could have slept through since the previous evening in such a
trance and still hadn't done anything, hadn't prepared anything . . .
Meanwhile, that clock was probably striking six . . . His sleepiness
and torpor suddenly gave way to an unusually feverish and confused
burst of activity. There wasn't much to prepare, though. He was doing
his utmost to think of everything and forget nothing, but his heart
thumped so hard that it became difficult to breathe. First, he had to
make a loop and sew it to his coat – a moment's work. He rummaged
beneath the pillow, where he'd stuffed his linen, and retrieved an old
unwashed shirt that had all but fallen to pieces. From it he tore a strip
about two inches wide and a good foot long. He folded this strip in
two, took off his broad, sturdy, coarse-cotton summer coat (his only
outer garment) and started sewing both ends of the strip to the inside,
just below the left armpit. His hands shook, but he still managed to
do it well enough that nothing was visible from the outside when he
put his coat back on. He'd had needle and thread to hand for a while,
inside a scrap of paper in the little table. As for the loop, that was a
crafty invention of his own: it was intended for the axe. After all, he
could hardly walk along the street brandishing an axe. Hiding it under his coat wouldn't do either – he'd have to hold it in place, which
would be conspicuous. But now that he had the loop, all he needed to
do was place the blade in it and the axe would hang nicely, under his
armpit inside the coat, all the way there. What was more, by thrusting
a hand into the side pocket of his coat he was able to hold the end of
the axe handle and stop it moving about; and since the coat was very
broad – a real sack – there was no way of noticing from the outside
that he was holding it through the pocket. The loop was another thing
he'd thought up a couple of weeks before.

     Having done this, he slid his fingers through the small gap between
his 'Turkish' couch and the floor, fumbled around near the left-hand
corner and extracted something he'd prepared and hidden there long
before – a *pledge*. Pledge was hardly the word for it, though: it was a
smoothly planed bit of wood, no bigger in size or thickness than a silver cigarette case. He'd found it by chance on one of his strolls, in a
yard containing some kind of workshop housed in an outbuilding.
Then he'd added to it a thin, smooth iron strip – a fragment of something, presumably – which he'd found in the street at the same time.

Putting together the two pieces, of which the iron strip was the smaller, he tied them tightly with thread, making a cross; then he wrapped them neatly and daintily in clean white paper, tied a thin ribbon around it, also in a cross, and fixed the knot in such a way as to make it hard to untie. The point of it all was to distract the old woman as she fussed with the knot, and thus, to seize his chance. As for the iron strip, it had been added for weight, to keep the old woman from guessing right away that the 'item' was made of wood. He'd kept it all under the couch until the time came. No sooner had he retrieved the pledge than there was a sudden yell from somewhere outside:

'It's well past six!'

'Well past! Good God!'

He rushed to the door, listened, grabbed his hat and set off down his thirteen steps, warily, noiselessly, like a cat. Ahead lay the crucial business of stealing the axe from the kitchen. That the deed was to be done with an axe had been decided by him long before. He also had a small folding gardener's knife; but he had little faith in it, still less in his own strength, so he settled definitively on the axe. Let us note, by the way, one peculiarity of all the definitive decisions already taken by him in this venture. They shared one strange quality: the more definitive they were, the more hideous and absurd they immediately became in his own eyes. Despite all his inner torment and strife, never, for a single moment, could he make himself believe in the prospect of his plans being carried out, not once in all this time.

And even if he should have reached the point some day, somehow, when everything had been analysed, down to the very last detail, and everything had been resolved, and not a single doubt remained – well then, it seemed, he would have rejected it all as an absurdity, a monstrosity, an impossibility. But unresolved details and doubts remained in abundance. As for the trivial matter of where to get an axe, this didn't worry him in the slightest: nothing could have been simpler. It so happened that Nastasya was always popping out, especially in the evenings, whether to the neighbours or to the shop, and she'd always leave the door wide open. This was the cause of all her squabbles with the landlady. So all he had to do, when the time came, was slip into the kitchen, take the axe, and then, an hour later (when it was all over), go in and put it back. But doubts crept in here, too: what if he were to come by in an hour to replace it and find Nastasya right there, back in the house? He'd have to walk past, of course, and wait for her to go out again. But suppose she noticed it was missing, started looking for it, raising a hue and cry – well, suspicions would be aroused, or at least cause for suspicion.

Still, these were trivialities which he had not even begun to think about, and had had no time to think about. He was thinking about the main thing, postponing the minor details until he himself *was fully convinced*. This prospect, however, was utterly remote. Or so, at least, it seemed to him. He simply could not imagine, for example, that at some point he would stop thinking, get up and – just go . . . Even his recent *test* (that's to say: his visit with the intention of making a definitive survey of the location) was itself no more than a test of a test and very far from the real thing, as if to say, 'I have to do something – there's no use just dreaming about it!' – and he'd immediately cracked, given it up as a bad job and run away, disgusted with himself. Meanwhile, his entire analysis, in terms of a moral solution to the question, appeared complete: his casuistry was now as sharp as a razor blade and he could no longer find within himself a single conscious objection. But he simply did not believe himself on this score and stubbornly, slavishly sought objections, groping for them and going off on tangents, as if someone were forcing him to do so, dragging him this way and that. This last day, which had arrived out of the blue and solved everything at once, had affected him in an almost entirely mechanical way: as if someone had grabbed his hand and dragged him along, irresistibly, blindly, with unnatural strength, without objections. As if a scrap of his clothing had caught in the wheel of a machine that was now pulling him in.

At first – though this was a long time ago – one particular question had absorbed him: why are almost all crimes so easy to trace and so poorly concealed, and why do almost all criminals leave such an obvious trail? The conclusions at which he had arrived, little by little, were varied and intriguing: the most important reason, in his view, lay less in the physical impossibility of concealing the crime than in the criminal himself; for criminals, almost without exception, succumb at the moment of the crime to a weakening of the faculties of reason and will, which are replaced, in stark contrast, by thoughtlessness of a childish and quite extraordinary kind, at precisely the moment when reason and caution are most essential. As he saw it, the eclipse of reason and the weakening of the will consume a person like a sickness, progressing steadily to their furthest point shortly before the crime is committed; they continue in that same form at the very moment of the crime and for a little while thereafter, depending on the individual; then they pass, like any other sickness. As to whether it is sickness that gives rise to crime or crime itself which somehow, by its special nature, is always accompanied by something akin to sickness – this was a question he did not yet feel capable of resolving.

Reaching these conclusions, he decided that morbid reversals of this kind could not befall him personally in his venture; that his reason and will would not and could not desert him at any moment during the execution of his plan, for the simple reason that his plan was 'not a crime' . . . We omit the entire process by which he arrived at this final decision; we've run too far ahead of ourselves already . . . We will merely add that the actual, material obstacles thrown up by his venture played only the most ancillary of roles in his mind. 'It is enough to preserve all my faculties of will and reason, and those obstacles, in their turn, will all be defeated when the time comes to familiarize myself with the finer details of the venture . . .' But the venture would not get started. He continued to believe in his definitive decisions least of all, and when the hour struck, nothing went to plan – there was a randomness about it all that almost took him by surprise.

He was stymied by a circumstance of the most trivial kind even before he'd reached the bottom of the stairwell. Drawing level with the landlady's kitchen, the door of which was open, as always, he cast a wary glance inside: what if the landlady were in while Nastasya was out, and, if not, were all the doors to her room well closed, lest she happened to poke her head round when he went in for the axe? But he was simply astounded when he suddenly saw that not only was Nastasya in the kitchen, she was busy working as well: taking laundry out of a basket and hanging it on washing lines! Catching sight of him, she stopped what she was doing, turned towards him and kept her eyes fixed on him until he passed. He averted his gaze and walked on, as though nothing had happened. But the game was up: no axe! He was devastated.

'And why on earth,' he thought, as he went under the arch leading out of the courtyard, 'why on earth was I so sure that at this precise moment she would definitely be out? Why, why, why was I so certain?' He felt crushed, even mortified. He wanted to laugh at himself from spite . . . Dull, brutish anger boiled up inside him.

He stopped in hesitation beneath the arch. The thought of going out for a walk, just for show, repelled him; the thought of returning home was even worse. 'Such a chance, gone forever!' he muttered as he stood aimlessly under the arch, directly opposite the caretaker's dark little lodge, the door of which was also open. Suddenly, he gave a start. In the caretaker's lodge, just a few steps away from him, something caught his eye, glinting at him from beneath a bench, to the right . . . He looked around – not a soul! He walked up to the lodge on tiptoe, went down two steps and called out to the caretaker in a weak voice. 'He's out, just as I thought! He can't have gone far, though – the door's wide open!' He made a dash for the axe (for that's what it was) and pulled it out from under the bench, where it lay between two logs; he secured it in the loop there and then, thrust both his hands into his pockets and left the lodge; no one had noticed! 'Better the devil than the best-laid plans!' he thought, grinning strangely. This chance event had cheered him up no end.

To avoid suspicion he walked along the street with soft, *measured* steps and without hurrying. He rarely glanced at passers-by; in fact, he tried not to look at anyone at all and to make himself as inconspicuous as possible. Then he remembered about his hat. 'Good God! To think I even had some money a couple of days ago and still didn't get myself a cap!' His soul let fly a curse.

Happening to glance out of the corner of his eye into a shop, he caught sight of a clock: ten past seven already. He had to get a move on, but he also had to make a detour to approach the building from the other side . . .

Previously, when he pictured all this in his mind, he sometimes imagined he'd be very afraid. But he wasn't. In fact, he wasn't afraid at all. In fact, his mind was occupied at that moment by various irrelevant thoughts, none of which lasted for long. Walking past the Yusupov Gardens, he was even getting carried away by the notion of introducing tall fountains there – how marvellously they'd freshen the air on every square. Little by little he came to the conclusion that extending the Summer Garden into the Field of Mars and even joining it to the gardens of Mikhailovsky Palace would be a wonderful and most beneficial thing for the city. He suddenly wondered why it is that in every large city, man – out of some particular inclination as much as actual need – lives and makes his home in precisely those parts of town where there are neither gardens nor fountains, where there is filth and stench and every unpleasantness. Then he remembered his wanders around Haymarket and briefly came to his senses. 'What drivel,' he thought. 'No, I'm better off not thinking at all!

'That's how it must be for men on their way to the scaffold, clinging to every object they pass.'[51] The thought flashed through him like lightning, but it was no more than a flash; he was quick to snuff it out . . . Almost there now: here was the house, here were the gates. Suddenly, somewhere, a clock struck once. 'What, half past seven already? Impossible – the clock must be fast!'

His luck held: this archway proved straightforward, too. In fact, at that very instant, as if on purpose, a massive hay cart entered the gates just in front of him, shielding him completely as he passed under the arch, and as soon as the cart emerged into the courtyard he instantly slipped off to the right. Over there, on the other side of the cart, several voices could be heard shouting and arguing, but no one noticed him and no one crossed his path. Many of the windows that looked down on this enormous square courtyard were open at that moment, but he didn't lift his head – he hadn't the strength. The old woman's staircase was close by, directly off to the right after the arch. Here he was, already on the stairs . . .

After catching his breath and pressing his hand to his thumping heart, after feeling for the axe and adjusting it one more time, he began climbing the stairs, warily and softly, constantly straining his ears. But the staircase, too, was completely deserted at that moment. All the doors were shut. He met precisely no one. True, there was one empty apartment on the second floor with the doors flung open and decorators working inside, but they didn't so much as glance in his direction. He stood still for a moment, pondered and walked on. 'Of course, it would be better if they weren't here at all, but . . . there's another two floors to go.'

And here it was: the fourth floor, the door, the apartment opposite – the empty one. To all appearances, the third-floor apartment right under the old woman's was also empty: the visiting card nailed to the door was gone – they'd moved! . . . He was struggling to breathe. 'Perhaps I should leave?' suddenly occurred to him. But he left his own question unanswered and put his ear to the door of the old woman's apartment: dead silence. Then he listened out again for noises below him, listened long and hard . . . He looked about one last time, straightened and tidied himself up, and tested the axe in the loop once more. Various thoughts crossed his mind. 'Hope I'm not too pale?

Not overexcited? She's mistrustful . . . Perhaps I should wait a bit . . .
for my heart to stop?'

But his heart did not stop. Quite the opposite: as if on purpose, it
beat harder, harder and harder . . . He couldn't resist, slowly stretched
his arm out towards the bell and rang. Half a minute later he rang
again, louder.

No reply. It was pointless ringing for the sake of it, and unseemly.
The old woman, needless to say, was in, but she was suspicious and she
was alone. He knew her habits . . . and once again he pressed his ear
flush against the door. Whether it was the keenness of his senses (which
is rather hard to imagine) or whether it really was very audible, but he
suddenly heard what sounded like a hand cautiously feathering the
lock and a dress rustling against the door itself. Someone was lurking
right by the lock and, just like him here on the outside, was listening
hard, crouching, and also, it seemed, pressing an ear to the door . . .

He made a deliberate movement and muttered something rather
too loudly, to make it clear he wasn't hiding; then he rang a third
time, but softly, calmly and without the slightest haste. Recalling this
afterwards, vividly, clearly – that moment was imprinted on him for
all time – he simply could not understand where he'd found such guile,
not least because there were moments when his mind seemed to go
dark, and as for his body, he could barely feel it . . . Seconds later,
someone could be heard lifting the latch.

VII

The tiniest of chinks appeared in the doorway, just like the last time,
and two sharp and mistrustful eyes stared out at him once again from
the dark. Here Raskolnikov became flustered and nearly made a serious mistake.

Fearing that the old woman would take fright at finding herself
alone with him, and far from confident that his appearance would
reassure her, he grabbed hold of the door and pulled it towards him,
just in case she should think of locking herself in again. Seeing this,
she did not yank the door back towards her, but nor did she let go of
the handle, and he very nearly ended up dragging her out onto the
stairs, together with the door. When he saw that she was blocking the
doorway and not letting him pass, he walked straight at her. She leapt

back in alarm and was on the point of saying something, but didn't seem able to and stared at him wide-eyed.

'Hello, Alyona Ivanovna,' he began as casually as he could, but his voice refused to obey him, broke off and began to quiver. 'I've . . . brought you . . . the thing . . . but why don't we go over here . . . towards the light . . . ?' Leaving her there, and without any invitation, he walked straight through into the main room. The old woman ran after him. She'd recovered her voice.

'Good Lord! What is it? . . . Who are you? What do you want?'

'For pity's sake, Alyona Ivanovna . . . we've met before . . . Raskolnikov . . . Here, I've brought the pledge I promised you the other day . . .' And he proffered her the pledge.

The old woman took one glance at the pledge before immediately fixing her eyes on those of her unbidden guest. She looked at him attentively, with malice and mistrust. A minute or so passed. He even thought he detected a hint of mockery in her eyes, as though she'd already worked everything out. He sensed that he was becoming flustered, that he was almost terrified, so terrified that another half-minute of her wordless stare would have been enough to send him running.

'But why are you staring like this, as if you don't recognize me?' he suddenly said, also with malice. 'If you want it, take it. If not, I'll take it elsewhere. I've no time for this.'

He hadn't meant to say this; the words just came out.

The old woman collected herself, evidently taking heart from her visitor's decisive tone.

'Why all the hurry, sir? . . . What is it?' she asked, looking at the pledge.

'A silver cigarette case: I told you last time.'

She stretched out her hand.

'Why are you so very pale? And look at those trembling hands! You've not been for a dip, have you, father?'

'Fever,' he replied curtly. 'Hard not to grow pale . . . when you've nothing to eat,' he added, barely getting the words out. His strength was deserting him once more. But the reply seemed credible; the old woman took the pledge.

'What is it?' she asked, fixing her gaze on Raskolnikov once again and weighing the pledge in her hand.

'An item . . . cigarette case . . . silver . . . take a look.'

'Funny kind of silver . . . Just look how he's wrapped it up.'

Trying to untie the string and turning towards the window, to the light (she kept all her windows shut, despite the closeness), she left him to himself for a few seconds and stood with her back to him. He unbuttoned his coat and freed the axe from the loop, but he didn't take it out fully yet, merely supporting it with his right hand beneath his clothing. His arms were terribly weak; he could feel them grow number and stiffer with each passing second. He was afraid he'd let the axe slip and fall . . . and suddenly felt his head begin to spin.

'What has he done with the thing?' the old woman cried in vexation, taking half a step towards him.

There wasn't a moment to lose. He took the axe out fully, lifted it up high with both hands, barely feeling a thing, and, almost effortlessly, almost mechanically, brought the butt down on her head. As if he were not even using his strength. But just as soon as he brought the axe down once, his strength was born.

The old woman, as always, was bare-headed. Her light, greying, thin hair, thickly greased as usual, was plaited in a pigtail and tucked up with a fragment of a tortoiseshell comb, which stuck out from the back of her head. The blow landed smack on the crown – she was very short, after all. She cried out, though very feebly, and suddenly sank to the floor, managing only to raise both hands to her head. In one hand she was still holding the 'pledge'. Then he struck again with all his strength, and again, always with the butt and always on the crown. The blood poured out, as from a toppled glass, and the body fell back. He stepped back to let it fall, and immediately bent over her face; she was already dead. The eyes goggled, as if wanting to leap out, while the forehead and entire face were furrowed and twisted by spasms.

He laid the axe on the floor, next to the dead woman, and, trying not to stain himself with the flowing blood, set about rummaging in her pocket – the same right pocket she'd taken her keys from the previous time. He had his wits about him – his mind did not go dark again, nor did his head spin – but his hands still shook. He later recalled how very meticulous and cautious he'd been, trying not to get himself dirty . . . He pulled the keys out right away; just like before, they were all in one bunch, on a single steel ring. He immediately ran off with them to the bedroom. This was a very small room with an enormous icon cabinet. By another wall stood a large bed, immaculately clean, with a silk patchwork quilt. Next to the third wall was the chest of drawers. How strange: no sooner did he try to fit the keys to the chest of drawers, and no sooner did he hear them jangle, than he felt a kind of spasm go through him. Once again he had a sudden urge to drop everything and leave. But this passed in a flash; it was too late for that. He even grinned at himself, before he was suddenly struck by another disturbing thought. He had a sudden fancy that the old woman might still be alive and might still come round. Abandoning the keys and the chest of drawers, he ran back to the body, grabbed the axe and brandished it once more over the old woman, but without bringing it down. There was no doubting that she was dead. Leaning over again and examining her at close quarters, he saw clearly that the skull had been crushed and was even slightly lop-sided. He was about to feel it with his finger, but drew back his hand. There was really no need. Meanwhile, a whole puddle of blood had now formed. Suddenly, he noticed a string around her neck and gave it a tug, but it was strong and refused to break; besides, it was soaked in blood. He had a go at pulling the string straight from her bosom, but something got in the way. Losing patience, he was on the point of raising the axe again, so as to chop through the string and the body from above and have done with it, but he didn't dare, and after struggling for two minutes and getting the axe and his hands all stained he finally cut the string, without the axe touching the body, and removed it; he was right – a purse. There were two crosses on the string, one of cypress and one of copper, and a little enamel icon as well; and right there alongside them hung a small, greasy suede purse with a steel rim and clasp. The purse was stuffed full. Raskolnikov shoved it in his pocket without looking inside, dropped the crosses on the old woman's breast and, taking the axe with him this time, rushed back to the bedroom.

In a terrible hurry, he grabbed the keys and began fiddling with them again. But he was getting nowhere: they just wouldn't go in. It wasn't so much that his hands were shaking – he just couldn't get it right: he could see, for instance, that he had the wrong key and that it didn't fit, but still he kept jabbing away with it. Suddenly he remembered and realized that the big key with the jagged notches, dangling there with the smaller ones, couldn't have been meant for the chest of drawers at all (this had occurred to him the previous time, too), but for some box or other, which was where everything might very well be hidden. He abandoned the chest of drawers and immediately crawled under the bed, knowing that that is where old women tend to keep their boxes. And there it was: a sizeable box, about three feet long, with a curved lid of red morocco leather studded with small steel nails. The jagged key went straight in and opened it. On top, beneath a white sheet, lay a red silk coat lined with rabbit fur; beneath that was a silk dress, then a shawl, while deeper in there seemed to be nothing but old rags. His first impulse was to wipe his blood-stained hands on the red silk. 'Red – well, blood on red won't show,' he calculated, before suddenly coming to his senses. 'God! Am I losing my mind?' he thought in terror.

But he'd barely touched the rags when a gold watch suddenly fell out of the fur coat. He hastily ransacked the rest. Yes, there were gold things mixed up with the rags – probably all pledges: bracelets, chains, earrings, pins and so forth. Some were in cases, others just wrapped in newspaper, but neatly and carefully, the paper folded double and tied round with tape. Without a moment's delay he set about stuffing the pockets of his trousers and coat, without sorting through or even opening the packages and boxes; but he soon ran out of time . . .

He suddenly heard someone moving about in the room where he'd left the old woman. He froze and fell silent, as if dead. But everything was quiet – he must have imagined it. Suddenly, unmistakably, there was a faint cry, or perhaps the sound of a soft, abrupt groan. Then: dead silence again, for a minute or perhaps two. He was squatting by the box, waiting, barely breathing, then he suddenly jumped up, grabbed the axe and ran out of the bedroom.

There, in the middle of the room, stood Lizaveta, holding a large bundle and gazing rigidly at her murdered sister, white as a sheet and seemingly unable to scream. Seeing him run in, she began quivering all over and her whole face went into spasm; she half-raised a hand and was about to open her mouth, but again she did not scream and slowly backed away from him into the corner, staring straight at him, but still without screaming, as if there was not enough air to scream. He rushed at her with the axe; her lips twisted as pitifully as those of very little children when something begins to scare them and they stare at the thing that's frightening them and prepare to yell. And so very simple was this poor Lizaveta, so browbeaten and eternally intimidated, that she didn't even lift her arms to protect her face, even though there could have been no more instinctive or essential gesture at that moment, for the axe was raised directly over her face. She just lifted her free left arm an inch or two, nowhere near her face, and slowly held it out towards him, as if pushing him away. The blow landed right on the skull, blade first, and smashed through the upper part of the forehead, almost as far as the crown. She collapsed there and then. In complete confusion, Raskolnikov grabbed her bundle, dropped it again, and ran out into the hall.

Fear was gripping him tighter and tighter, especially after this second, wholly unexpected killing. He wanted to flee, the sooner the better. And had he only been capable at that moment of seeing straight and thinking straight, had he only been able to grasp all the difficulties of his plight, all its hopelessness, hideousness and absurdity, and to understand how many obstacles and perhaps even acts of evil he still had to overcome and commit to get out and get home, then he might very well have dropped everything and immediately gone and given himself up, not out of fear for himself, but from pure horror and disgust at what he had done. This disgust, in particular, was rising and growing inside him minute by minute. Not for anything in the world would he have gone back to the box now or even into the rooms.

But, little by little, he felt himself become distracted, almost pensive: for minutes at a time he seemed to forget what he was doing, or rather, he would forget about the main thing and cling to trifles. Still, glancing into the kitchen and spotting a bucket half-filled with water on a bench, he had the presence of mind to wash his hands and the axe. His hands were bloody and sticky. He lowered the axe straight into the water, blade first, grabbed a sliver of soap from a cracked saucer on the windowsill, and set about washing his hands right there in the bucket. After washing them clean, he took the axe out as well, cleaned the metal and spent a good three minutes cleaning the wood where it was stained, even trying the soap on the blood. Then he wiped everything with the laundry drying right there on a clothes-line stretched across the kitchen, before making a lengthy and meticulous inspection of the axe by the window. No traces remained, though the wood was still damp. He carefully secured the axe in the loop under his coat. Then, as best he could in the dim light of the kitchen, he inspected his coat, trousers and boots. They seemed fine at first glance; only the boots were stained. He moistened a rag and wiped them. But he knew he couldn't see well and might have missed something obvious. He stood thinking in the middle of the room. An excruciating, dark thought was welling up inside him – the thought that he was out of his mind, that at this moment he was capable neither of reasoning nor of defending himself, that perhaps he was going about things in entirely the wrong way . . . 'God! I must run! Run!' he muttered, rushing out into the hall. But there a horror awaited him the like of which, needless to say, he had never known.

He stood, stared and could not believe his eyes: the door, the outer door, leading from the hall to the stairs, the same one through which he had entered, after ringing, just a short while before, stood ajar by as much as a hand's breadth: neither locked nor on the latch, all this time, all of it! The old woman hadn't closed the door behind him, perhaps as a precaution. God Almighty! He'd since seen Lizaveta, after all! How on earth had he failed to realize that she must have got in somehow! She couldn't have walked in through the wall.

He rushed to the door and fastened the latch.

'But no, that's wrong too! I must go. Go . . .'

He lifted the latch, opened the door on to the stairs and began listening.

He listened long and hard. Somewhere far away, down below, probably at the gates, two voices were shouting loud and shrill, arguing and swearing. 'What're they up to?' He waited patiently. Then, eventually, just like that, silence: they'd gone their separate ways. He was about to leave when suddenly a door opened with a great racket on to the stairs on the floor below and someone started going down, humming a tune. 'How noisy they all are!' flashed through his mind. He shut the door again and waited. Finally, everything went quiet – not a soul. He was just about to step onto the stairs when once again he suddenly heard footsteps; different ones.

These footsteps came from far away, right from the bottom of the stairwell, but he remembered very vividly and distinctly that somehow, from the very first sound, he suspected that their destination was *here* and nowhere else, the fourth floor, the old woman. Why? Were the sounds so very special, so very meaningful? The footsteps were heavy, even, unhurried. There: *he* had already reached the first floor and was carrying on up – louder and louder! Now came the sound of heavy breathing. Climbing up to the third . . . Coming here! He felt his whole body suddenly go rigid, as if this were a dream, the kind of dream where someone is chasing you, breathing down your neck, about to kill you, while you yourself seem rooted to the spot and can't even move your hands.

Only when the visitor was already on his way up to the fourth floor did he suddenly rouse himself and somehow manage to slip quickly and nimbly back into the apartment and close the door behind him. Then he grabbed the latch and quietly, soundlessly placed the hook in the eye. Instinct was coming to his aid. Then, he crouched right there by the door, holding his breath. The unbidden guest was also already at the door. They were standing opposite one another now, just like before with the old woman, when they were separated by the door and he was the one listening in.

The visitor drew several heaving breaths. 'Must be big and fat,' thought Raskolnikov, his hand gripping the axe. Yes, all this really was like a dream. The visitor grabbed the bell and gave it a good ring.

No sooner did he hear the bell's tinny sound than he had a sudden fancy that someone had stirred in the room. For a few seconds he even cocked an ear in earnest. The stranger rang once again, waited a bit more, then suddenly lost patience and began tugging on the door handle with all his strength. Horrified, Raskolnikov watched with dull terror as the hook of the latch twitched in the eye, and half-expected it to snap out at any moment. The way the handle was being tugged, it seemed more than likely. He thought of holding the latch in place, but then *he* might realize. Once again he felt his head begin to spin. 'I'll fall any moment!' – but no sooner had he thought this than the stranger began speaking, and he immediately came to his senses.

'What are they doing in there – dozing? Or has someone done them in? Damned women!' he roared, as if from a barrel. 'Oi! Alyona Ivanovna, my old witch! Lizaveta Ivanovna, my beauty! Open up! Fast asleep, are they?'

Working himself up into a frenzy, he tugged the little bell another ten times or so, as hard as he could. Evidently, he was used to getting his way around here.

At that very moment the sound of short, hurried steps suddenly carried up from close by on the stairs. Someone else was coming too. Raskolnikov hadn't even heard at first.

'Is there really no one in?' shouted the new man, loudly and cheerfully addressing the first visitor, who was still tugging the bell. 'Hello there, Kokh!'

'Very young, going by his voice,' Raskolnikov suddenly thought.

'Hell knows, but I almost broke the lock,' replied Kokh. 'And how do you know me, may I ask?'

'You having me on? Just the other day, playing billiards in "Gambrinus", I took three games off you in a row!'

'Ah . . .'

'So they're out? How strange. And how stupid. Where on earth could the old woman've got to? I've business with her.'

'And I've business too, my friend!'

'Well, what's to be done? Back down, I suppose. And there was I expecting some cash!' cried the young man.

'Down we go, then, but why fix a time? She's the one who told me to come at this time. Plus it was out of my way. And where the devil has she wandered off to? That's what I don't understand! The old witch spends the whole year stewing at home, nursing her gammy legs, and now look – out and about all of a sudden!'

'How about asking the caretaker?'

'Asking him what?'

'Where she went and when she's back.'

'H'm . . . what's the use? . . . I mean, she never goes anywhere . . .' He gave the door handle another tug. 'There's nothing for it – I'm off!'

'Wait!' the young man suddenly cried. 'Look: see the gap when you pull the door?'

'Well?'

'So it's not locked, it's latched – on the hook, I mean! Hear how it rattles?'

'Well?'

'But don't you see? It means one of them must be in. If they were both out, they'd have locked it with a key from the outside, not latched it from inside, like now. Hear it rattling? To latch it from the inside, you have to be in, don't you see? So they must be in – they're just not opening!'

'Ha – you're right!' Kokh exclaimed in astonishment. 'So what can they be doing in there?' And he began furiously tugging the handle.

'Wait!' cried the young man once again. 'Stop pulling! There's something amiss here . . . After all, you've been ringing, tugging – and they're not opening; so either they've both fainted, or . . .'

'What?'

'Here's what: we'll fetch the caretaker. Let him wake them up.'

'Agreed!'

They set off down together.

'Wait! You stay put, I'll run and get the caretaker.'

'Why should I stay?'

'Well, you never know . . .'

'I suppose . . .'

'I'm training to be an examining magistrate,[52] as it happens! And it's quite obvious – blindingly obvious – that something's amiss here!' the young man cried out enthusiastically, before tearing off down the stairs.

Kokh remained where he was and gently fiddled a bit more with the bell, which tinkled once; then, in a studious, thoughtful kind of way, he began fiddling softly with the door handle, pulling it and letting it go, so as to make doubly certain that the door was only on the hook. Puffing and panting, he bent down and began looking through the keyhole; but the key was in the lock on the other side, so there was nothing to see.

Raskolnikov stood gripping the axe. He was in a kind of delirium. He was even ready to fight when they came in. While they were knocking and conferring, the idea occurred to him more than once to have done with it all and shout something out to them from behind the door. At times he suddenly felt like arguing with them, teasing them, until they finally got it open. 'The sooner the better!' flashed through his mind.

'Where's he got to, damn it . . . ?'

Time passed, whole minutes passed – no one came. Kokh became restless.

'Damn it all!' he suddenly yelled, quitting his post in a fit of impatience and setting off down the stairs in a hurry, boots clattering. Silence.

'God, now what?'

Raskolnikov lifted the latch, opened the door a little – he couldn't hear a thing – and suddenly, without a thought in his head, stepped out, shut the door behind him as firmly as he could, and set off down the stairs.

He was already three flights down when he suddenly heard a loud noise below. Now what? There was simply nowhere to hide. He was even about to run back into the apartment.

'Oi! Wait there, you devil! Wait there!'

With a cry someone came tearing out of one of the apartments, not so much running as plummeting down the stairs and yelling at the top of his voice:

'Mitka! Mitka! Mitka! Mitka! Mitka! I'll have you, you devil!'

The cry ended in a squeal, a few last noises came in from outside, and everything went quiet. But at that very instant several men, speaking loud and fast, began tramping up the stairs. There were three or four of them. He recognized the young lad's booming voice. 'It's them!'

In total despair he made straight for them: 'What will be, will be! I'm ruined if they stop me, ruined if they let me pass: they'll remember.' They were about to meet; just one flight of stairs between them – when suddenly, salvation! A few steps away from him, to the right, an apartment stood empty and open, that same second-floor apartment which the workmen had been painting and which, as if on purpose, they'd now vacated. So that was them running out just now with such a hue and cry. The floors had just been painted; in the middle of the room stood a vat and a pot with paint and a brush. He darted through the open door in a flash and hid on the other side of the wall, in the very nick of time: they were already on the landing. Then they turned to carry on up to the fourth floor, talking loudly. He waited for them to go past, walked out on tiptoe and ran off down.

No one on the stairs! Or at the gates. He passed quickly under the arch and turned left down the street.

He knew full well that they were already in the apartment, right now, that they were astonished to find it open when it had just been closed, that they were already looking at the bodies, and that it would take no more than a minute for them to work out beyond any shadow of a doubt that the murderer had been there just moments before and had managed to hide somewhere, slip past them, run off; and they might also work out that he'd been waiting in the empty apartment as they climbed up. Still, for the life of him he dared not quicken his stride more than a little, even though it was another hundred paces or so to the next turning. 'Perhaps I should duck under one of these arches and wait it out in some stairwell? No, no good! Or chuck away the axe somewhere? Or hail a cab? No good! No good!'

At last, the lane. He turned into it more dead than alive. He was already halfway to safety and he understood this: there'd be less reason for suspicion, not to mention a bustling crowd in which to lose himself like a grain of sand. But all these agonies had left him so feeble he could barely move. Sweat was dripping off him; his neck was all wet. 'Drunk as a lord!' someone yelled out to him when he came out by the Ditch.

He was in a state of near-oblivion, and it was only getting worse.

But he did remember how frightened he was when he came out by the Ditch and saw how few people there were and how conspicuous he was, and he almost turned back into the lane. But even though he could barely stay on his feet, he still made a detour and returned home from a completely different direction.

He still hadn't recovered his wits when he passed through the gates to his building; at any rate, he was already on the stairs by the time he remembered the axe. Yet the task facing him was of the utmost importance: to put it back, and as discreetly as possible. Of course, he was in no fit state by now to realize that he might have been far better off not returning the axe to its former place at all, but sneaking it into some other courtyard, later if need be, and leaving it there.

But everything turned out well. The door of the lodge was shut but not locked, so the caretaker was probably in. Incapable by now of thinking straight about anything, he walked right up to the lodge and opened the door. Had the caretaker asked him, 'What do you want?', he might very well have simply handed over the axe. But the caretaker was out again, and he managed to put the axe back in its former place beneath the bench; he even covered it with a log, as before. He met no one, not a single soul, all the way back to his room; the landlady's door was shut. Entering his room, he threw himself on the couch, just as he was. He wasn't asleep, he was in a trance. If someone had come into his room just then, he'd have leapt to his feet at once and screamed. His mind was aswarm with shreds and scraps of thought; but try as he might, he couldn't catch hold of any of them, nor focus on a single one . . .

PART TWO

I

He lay like that for a very long time. Occasionally, he even seemed to wake up, and at such moments he noticed that night had long since fallen, but the thought of getting up did not occur to him. Eventually, he noticed it was already as bright as day. He lay supine on the couch, still dazed after his recent trance. The rasping sounds of terrible, desperate screams from the street reached his ears, the same sounds, in fact, that he listened out for beneath his window every night between two and three. It was this that had woken him up. 'Ah! The drunks are pouring out of the dens,' he thought, 'so it's gone two,' and he suddenly jumped to his feet, as though someone had yanked him off the couch. 'What? Gone two already?' He sat down on the couch – and everything came back to him! Suddenly, all at once!

For a second or two he thought he'd go mad. He felt freezing cold; but the cold came from the fever as well, which had set in while he was sleeping, some time before. Now he was suddenly struck by a fit of shivering so violent that his teeth almost leapt from his mouth and his insides were thrown this way and that. He opened the door and listened: the whole house was fast asleep. He looked at himself and everything else in the room in complete astonishment: how on earth could he have just walked in yesterday, left the door off the latch and flung himself on the couch, without even taking off his hat, never mind his clothes: the hat had slid down to the floor, not far from the pillow. 'If someone had walked in, what would they have thought? That I was drunk, but . . .' He rushed over to the little window. There was enough light and he hastily set about inspecting himself, all over, from top to toe, every item of clothing: any traces? But that was no way to do it: shaking uncontrollably, he started taking everything off and inspecting it all over again. He turned everything inside out, down to the last thread and scrap of cloth, and, not trusting himself, repeated the inspection another two or three times. But there didn't seem to be anything, not a single trace; only where his trousers were frayed at the ends did thick traces of caked blood still remain. He grabbed his big folding knife and cut off the frayed ends. That seemed to be it. Suddenly he remembered that the purse and the items from the old woman's box were still in his pockets! It hadn't even crossed his mind to take them out and hide them! He hadn't even remembered them now, while inspecting his clothes! Why on earth not? Quick as a flash, he began taking them out and flinging them down on the table. After emptying his pockets and even turning them inside out to check he hadn't missed anything, he carried the whole pile over to the corner. There, right in the corner, near the floor, the peeling wallpaper was torn in one place: he immediately started stuffing everything into this hole, behind the paper: 'Done it! Out of sight, out of mind, and the purse too!' he thought with a sense of joy, half-rising and looking dully at the corner, at the hole bulging even more than before. Suddenly, his whole body shuddered with horror: 'God,' he whispered in despair, 'what's the matter with me? Call that hidden? Call that hiding?'

True, he hadn't reckoned on the items. He'd only expected to find money, which was why he hadn't prepared anywhere in advance. 'But now what have I got to be so happy about?' he thought. 'Call that hiding? My wits really are deserting me!' He sat down on the couch in complete exhaustion and was immediately shaken by another unbearable fit of shivering. He reached without thinking for the winter coat lying next to him on the chair, his old student one, warm but now almost in shreds, covered himself with it, and sleep and delirium seized him once more. Oblivion came over him.

Less than five minutes later he was back on his feet and set about his clothes once more in a kind of frenzy. 'How could I fall asleep again, when nothing's been done? See, see: I haven't even taken the loop off the armpit! To forget a thing like that! A clue like that!' He ripped out the loop and set about hurriedly tearing it to pieces, then stuffing it under the pillow, in amongst the linen. 'Torn bits of old cloth can't arouse anyone's suspicion; surely they can't, surely they can't!' he repeated, standing in the middle of the room. In an agony of concentration, he began looking around again, on the floor and all around – anything else he might have forgotten? The conviction that everything was deserting him – even his memory, even the ability to put two and two together – was becoming an unbearable torment: 'What, is this it already, my punishment? Yes, that's it, that's it!' The frayed ends he'd cut off from his trousers really did lie strewn across the floor, in the middle of the room, for anyone to see! 'What on earth's the matter with me!' he cried out once more, as if lost.

Here, a strange thought occurred to him: what if there was blood all over his clothes, what if there were lots of stains, only he couldn't see them, didn't notice them, because his ability to think had been shot to pieces? . . . His mind had gone dark . . . Suddenly, he remembered: there was blood on the purse as well. 'Ha! So there must be blood in the pocket, too – the purse was still wet when I put it there!' In a flash, he turned out the pocket and there they were – traces and stains on the lining! 'So my wits haven't deserted me completely yet, nor my memory, and I can still put two and two together, if I caught myself in time!' he exulted, breathing a deep and joyful sigh. 'This is just weakness brought on by fever, a moment's delirium' – and he ripped out the entire lining from his left trouser pocket. At that moment a ray of sunlight fell on his left boot: the sock poking out of it seemed to have some kind of marks on it. He kicked off the boot: 'Yes, marks! Look, the toe's all soaked in blood'; he must have stepped in that puddle of blood by mistake . . . 'Now what? What do I do with this sock, the trouser ends, the pocket?'

He gathered it all up in one hand and stood in the middle of the room. 'Bung it all in the stove? But that's the first place they'll look! Burn it? What with? I haven't even got matches. No, I'm better off going out and getting rid of the whole lot somewhere. Yes! Get rid of it!' he repeated, sitting down on the couch again. 'And do it now, this very minute, without delay!' But no: once again, his head sank back onto the pillow; once again an unbearable fit of shivering turned him to ice; once again he reached for his greatcoat. And for a long time, for several hours, the words kept coming back to him in waves: 'Just go somewhere, right now, don't put it off, get rid of it all, out of sight, the sooner the better!' Several times he made as if to get up from the couch, but he was no longer able to. Not until there was a loud knock on the door did he wake up fully.

'Open up if you're still alive! Won't he ever stop snoozing?' shouted Nastasya, banging on the door with her fist. 'Snoozes all day long, like a dog! A dog – that's what he is! Open up. It's gone ten.'

'What if he's out?' came a man's voice.

('Ha! The caretaker . . . What does he want?')

He sat up with a jerk. His heart was thumping so hard it even hurt.

'Who put the door on the hook, then?' Nastasya objected. 'So he's locking himself in now, eh? Scared of being stolen, I s'pose. Open up, egghead, wakey, wakey!'

('What do they want? Why's the caretaker come? The story's out. Resist or open? Ah, to hell with it . . .')

He leant forward and lifted the hook.

The dimensions of his room were such that he could lift the hook without getting up from his bed.

Just as he thought: the caretaker and Nastasya.

There was something strange about the way Nastasya looked him up and down. He threw a defiant and desperate glance at the caretaker. The latter silently handed over a grey piece of paper folded in two and sealed with bottle wax.

'A summons, from the bureau,' he said, giving him the piece of paper.

'What bureau . . . ?'

'The police want to see you, that's what, in the bureau.[1] You know which bureau.'

'The police? . . . What for?'

'How should I know? They're asking, so you'd better go.' He looked at him closely, glanced around the room and turned to leave.

'Sick as a parrot, aren't you?' Nastasya remarked, never taking her eyes off him. The caretaker also glanced back before leaving. 'Running a fever since yesterday,' she added.

He made no reply and held the piece of paper, still sealed, in his hands.

'You'd best stay in bed,' Nastasya went on, taking pity as she watched him lower his feet to the floor. 'Stay put if you're sick: that can wait. What's that in your hand?'

He looked down: his right hand held the snipped-off trouser ends, the sock and the shreds of the ripped-out pocket. He'd slept with them like that. Later on, turning all this over in his mind, he recalled how, half-waking with fever, he'd clench it all fiercely in his hand and fall asleep again.

'A regular scrap collector – he even sleeps with 'em, like hidden treasure . . .' And Nastasya went into fits of her unhealthy, nervous laughter. Quick as a flash, he stuffed everything under his greatcoat and fastened his eyes on her. Though he could barely think straight, he sensed that this was not how a man being taken away would be treated. 'But . . . the police?'

'What about that tea, then? I can bring what's left . . .'

'No . . . I'm going. I'll go right now,' he muttered, getting to his feet.

'You'll not even get down the stairs.'

'I'll go . . .'

'Please yourself.'

She followed the caretaker out. He rushed over to the window to inspect the sock and trouser ends. 'There are stains, but not very noticeable ones; it's all mixed up with dirt, all rubbed and faded. You'd never spot anything unless you knew. So Nastasya, thank God, couldn't have seen anything from where she was!' Then, in trepidation, he unsealed the summons and began reading; he read for a long time before he could understand what he was reading. It was an ordinary summons from the local police bureau to present himself that very same day, at half past nine, to the district superintendent.

'It's unheard of! What business have I ever had with the police? And why today of all days?' he thought, racked with confusion. 'Lord, the sooner the better!' He was about to fall to his knees in prayer, only to burst out laughing – at himself, not the prayer. He began hurriedly getting dressed. 'If I'm done for, I'm done for – so be it! The sock! Put it on!' suddenly occurred to him. 'It'll get even dustier and dirtier, and the traces will vanish.' But no sooner had he put it on than he immediately pulled it off in disgust and horror. He pulled it off and then, realizing it was the only one he had, put it back on again – and again burst out laughing. 'This is all mere convention, merely relative, mere form,' came a passing thought, glimpsed at the very edge of his mind, while his whole body shook. 'Look, I still put it on! In the end, I still put it on!' But laughter instantly gave way to despair. 'No, I'm not up to it . . .' His legs were shaking. 'With fear,' he muttered to himself. His head was spinning and aching from the fever. 'It's a trick! They want to lure me in, then trip me up,' he went on to himself, walking out onto the landing. 'Too bad I'm almost raving . . . I might come out with something stupid . . .'

On the stairs he remembered he'd left all the items where they were, in the hole in the wallpaper – 'Now, when I'm out, would be just the time for a search' – remembered and stopped. But he was suddenly overwhelmed by such despair, by what one can only call the cynicism of doom, that he dismissed the thought and carried on.

'The sooner the better!'

Outside, it was unbearably hot again; all these days and not a drop of rain. Again the dust, bricks and mortar, again the stink from the shops and drinking dens, again the drunks at every corner, the Finnish pedlars, the decrepit cabs. The sun shone brightly into his eyes, to the point that it became painful to look and his head spun round and round – as usually happens when you suddenly step outside with a fever on a bright sunny day.

Reaching the turn to *yesterday's* street, he glanced down it at *that* house with excruciating anxiety . . . and immediately looked away.

'If they ask, I might just tell them,' he thought, approaching the bureau.

It was a few hundred yards from where he lived to the bureau. It had just moved to new premises, a new building, the fourth floor. He'd passed by the old premises once, but a long time ago now. Going under the arch, he noticed stairs on his right and a man walking down with a book in his hands: 'Must be the caretaker; so the bureau must be here,' and he started climbing up, following his nose. He was in no mood to ask anyone about anything.

'I'll go in, fall to my knees and tell them everything,' he thought, on reaching the fourth floor.

It was a tight, steep staircase, covered in slops. All the kitchens of all the apartments on all four floors opened on to these stairs and stayed open nearly all day long. That was why it was so terribly stuffy. Up and down the stairs went caretakers with registers tucked under their arms, police errand boys, and assorted men and women – the visitors. The door to the bureau itself was also wide open. He went in and stopped in the anteroom. Some peasant types were standing around waiting. It was exceptionally stuffy here, too, not to mention the nauseatingly strong smell from the freshly coated walls: damp paint made with rancid oil. After waiting a short while, he decided to press on to the next room. They were all so tiny and low. A terrible impatience drew him on. No one noticed him. Some clerks – a strange-looking lot, dressed only marginally better than he was – were sat writing in the second room. He turned to one of them.

'Well?'

He presented the summons from the bureau.

'You're a student?' the man asked, glancing at the summons.

'Yes, a former student.'

The clerk looked him over, though without the faintest curiosity. He was a particularly unkempt individual, with something obsessive in his gaze.

'You won't learn anything from him: he doesn't give a damn,' thought Raskolnikov.

'Go and see the head clerk,' said the unkempt man, jabbing his finger in the direction of the very last room.

He entered this room (the fourth), which was cramped and filled to bursting with a somewhat smarter crowd than the others. Among the visitors were two ladies. One, dressed in humble mourning clothes, was sitting at a table opposite the head clerk, who was dictating something to her. The other lady – a very plump, crimson, blotchy, striking woman, dressed rather too lavishly with a brooch on her chest the size of a saucer – was standing to one side, waiting for something. Raskolnikov thrust his summons at the head clerk, who took one glance at it, told him to wait and turned back to the lady in mourning.

He could breathe more freely. 'Must be something else!' Little by little he began to cheer up, exhorting himself as best he could to pull himself together.

'Say something stupid or even just a tiny bit careless and you'll give yourself away completely! H'm . . . Shame there's no air in here,' he added. 'So stuffy . . . My head's spinning even more . . . and my mind, too . . .'

Everything inside him was at sixes and sevens. He feared losing control. He tried to find something to hold on to, something to think about – something totally irrelevant – but without any success. The head clerk intrigued him greatly, though: he kept scanning his face for signs, for clues to his character. He was very young, twenty-two or so, with swarthy, mobile features that made him look older than his years, foppishly dressed, his hair parted at the back, combed and pomaded, with a great number of jewels and rings on white, brush-scrubbed fingers, and gold chains on his waistcoat. He even exchanged a few words in French – very competently, too – with a foreigner who happened to be in the room.

'Luiza Ivanovna, won't you sit down?' he said in passing to the overdressed, crimson lady, who was still standing as if she dared not sit, though there was a chair right beside her.

'*Ich danke*,' she said and, with a rustle of silk, lowered herself quietly into the chair. Her light-blue dress with white lace trimmings spread out around the chair like an air balloon, taking up nearly half the room. There was a whiff of perfume. But the lady was clearly embarrassed to be taking up half the room and to be filling it with her scent, though she was smiling, too, timidly and insolently at one and the same time, albeit with evident anxiety.

The lady in mourning finally finished and started getting up. Suddenly, somewhat noisily, rolling his shoulders at each step in a very dashing, rather emphatic way, an officer walked in, flung his service cap down on the table and sat down in an armchair. The lavish lady all but leapt from her seat on seeing him and set about curtseying with particular enthusiasm; but the officer didn't pay her the slightest attention and she dared not sit down again in his presence. He was a lieutenant, assistant to the superintendent, with a ginger moustache that stuck out horizontally on both sides and exceptionally small features that failed to express anything much other than a certain insolence. He looked askance and with some indignation at Raskolnikov: his clothes were too shabby for words, but his bearing was somehow at odds with them, for all his abjection; Raskolnikov, in his recklessness, had stared at the lieutenant so long and so hard he'd even managed to offend him.

'Well then?' shouted the lieutenant, probably amazed that this tramp had no intention of vaporizing beneath his fiery gaze.

'An order . . . a summons . . . .,' Raskolnikov half-replied.

'It's about that claim for some money, from *the student*, I mean,' the head clerk threw out, lifting his head from his papers. 'There you go, sir!' He tossed Raskolnikov a notebook, after pointing to the right place. 'Read it!'

'Money? What money?' thought Raskolnikov. 'But that means . . . it definitely can't be *that*!' And he shuddered with joy. He suddenly felt dreadfully, inexpressibly relieved. Everything simply fell from his shoulders.

'And when were you told to come, gracious sir?' shouted the lieutenant, who for some reason was taking ever greater offence. 'Nine o'clock is what's written and now it's gone eleven!'

'It was only delivered a quarter of an hour ago,' Raskolnikov replied loudly over his shoulder, suddenly getting angry as well, to his own surprise, and even taking a certain pleasure in the fact. 'It's enough that I'm here at all, with a fever like mine.'

'No need to shout!'

'I'm not shouting, I'm speaking perfectly calmly. You're the one shouting; but I am a student and I will not allow myself to be shouted at.'

The assistant was so incensed that at first he couldn't even speak and merely sputtered and spat. He leapt from his seat.

'Kindly hold your tongue, sir! You're on state premises. Watch your step, I say!'

'You, too, are on state premises,' shrieked Raskolnikov, 'and not only are you shouting, you are also smoking, thereby showing us all a distinct lack of respect!' Saying this, Raskolnikov experienced inexpressible pleasure.

The head clerk smiled at them. The fiery lieutenant was visibly flustered.

'None of your business, sir!' he yelled at last, more loudly than was natural. 'Now kindly supply the statement demanded of you. Show him, Alexander Grigoryevich. We've received a complaint about you! For not paying up! You've got some pluck, I'll give you that!'

But Raskolnikov was no longer listening and greedily snatched the document, desperate to see what it was all about. He read it once, twice, and still didn't understand.

'What is it?' he asked the head clerk.

'A demand for payment on a promissory note, a recovery claim. Either you pay up, including all the costs, fines and so on, or you submit a statement in writing, saying when you will be able to pay and undertaking not to leave the capital until that time and not to sell or conceal your property. The creditor, meanwhile, is free to sell your property and to deal with you in accordance with the law.'

'But I . . . don't owe anyone!'

'That's none of our business. What concerns us is the legitimate claim we have received for overdue payment on a promissory note made out for one hundred and fifteen roubles, issued by yourself to the collegiate assessor's widow Zarnitsyna nine months ago and transferred as payment to court counsellor Chebarov. Hence, we are inviting you to make a statement.'

'But she's my landlady!'

'And what if she is?'

The head clerk looked at him with a patronizing smile of pity mixed with a note of triumph, as if Raskolnikov were a raw recruit coming under fire for the first time: 'Now how do you feel?' he seemed to be saying. But how could any of this – promissory notes, recovery claims – matter to him now? Did it really warrant the faintest anxiety or even a moment's attention? He stood, read, listened, replied, even asked questions himself, but he did so mechanically. The triumph of survival, of deliverance from oppressive danger – this was what filled his entire being at that moment; no predictions or analysis, no speculations or deductions, no doubts or questions. It was a moment of complete, spontaneous, purely animal joy.

But at this very same moment something like thunder and lightning erupted in the bureau. The lieutenant, still badly shaken by such shocking familiarity, ablaze with indignation and clearly desperate to avenge his wounded vanity, was now directing all his thunderbolts at the unfortunate 'lavish lady', who'd been looking at him, ever since he walked in, with a perfectly stupid smile.

'And you, Mrs Whatnot,' he suddenly yelled at the top of his voice (the lady in mourning had already left), 'what was all that about over at yours last night? Eh? Bringing shame on the whole street again! More debauchery, more fights, more drunkenness. Suppose you fancy a stint in a house of correction! Ten times I've told you, Mrs Whatnot, ten times I've warned you that the eleventh will be one too many! And here you are, all over again!'

The document fell from Raskolnikov's hands and he stared wildly at the lavish lady who was being told off so unceremoniously; but he soon grasped what it was all about and immediately began to find the whole business most entertaining. He listened with such pleasure that he wanted to roar and roar with laughter . . . His nerves were all tingling inside him.

'Ilya Petrovich!' the head clerk began solicitously, before deciding to bide his time: there was no way of restraining the lieutenant once his blood was up other than by force, as he knew from his own experience.

As for the lavish lady, at first she simply quivered from the force of the thunder and lightning; but, strangely enough, the more frequent and the more abusive the insults became, the more courteous she seemed and the more charmingly she smiled at the menacing lieutenant. She danced from foot to foot, dropping one curtsey after another and impatiently waiting for the moment when she, too, would be allowed to have her say; it finally came.

'Zer vas no noise und no fighting in my haus, Herr Kapitän,' she suddenly rapped out, scattering her words like peas, in boisterous Russian, albeit with a heavy German accent, 'und zer vas no scandal, und he come back to haus drunken, und I tell you everysing, Herr Kapitän, und I not guilty . . . I haff honourable haus, Herr Kapitän, and honourable behaviour, Herr Kapitän, and alvays, alvays no scandal vant. Und he come back very drunken, und he three more pottles ask for, und zen he lifted one leg and begin play piano with foot, und zis very bad in honourable haus, und he break piano, und zis very, very vulgar, und I say so. Zen he pottle take and begin pushing everyone behind mit pottle. Und I begin call ze caretaker, und Karl come. He take Karl und black eye give him, und Genriet too, und my cheek hit five times. Zis is so rude in honourable haus, Herr Kapitän, und I begin shout. Zen he open window to Ditch and begin sqveal in vindow like small pig; vat disgrace, Herr Kapitän. Sqveal, sqveal, sqveal, like little pig! Vat disgrace! Foo-foo-foo! Und Karl grab him behind mit tails und take him from vindow, und zen – zis is true, Herr Kapitän – he tear sein tailcoat. Und zen he shout zat Karl muss fifteen roubles fine pay. Und I myself, Herr Kapitän, him five roubles for sein tailcoat pay. Und he dishonourable guest, Herr Kapitän, und great scandal making! I will have big satire in all ze papers about you gedruckt, he say.'

'A scribbler, I suppose?'

'Yes, Herr Kapitän, und such dishonourable guest, Herr Kapitän, in such honourable haus . . .'

'All right, all right! Enough! If I've told you once, I've told you . . .'

'Ilya Petrovich!' said the head clerk again with meaning. The lieutenant glanced in his direction and the head clerk gave the faintest of nods.

'. . . So here's what I'll say to you, most esteemed *Laviza* Ivanovna,[2] and I'm saying it for the very last time,' the lieutenant went on. 'One more scandal in your honourable house and I'll have your guts for garters, as ze poets say. Got it? So, you say, a scribbler, a writer, earned five roubles in an "honourable house" for a coat-tail. A fine lot, these writers!' he exclaimed, with a contemptuous glance at Raskolnikov. 'There was another scene in a tavern a couple of days ago: he'd eaten, but didn't want to pay. "I'll write you up in a satire instead," he said. Then there was that chap on a steamer last week who heaped the vilest abuse on the respected family of a state counsellor, his wife and daughter. And another who recently got himself chucked out of a pastry shop. That's what they're like, these writers, scribblers, students, town criers . . . Ugh! Well, clear off then! I'll be paying you a visit myself . . . so watch your step! Got it?'

With precipitate civility, Luiza Ivanovna set about curtseying in all directions and curtsied her way back to the door; but in the doorway, still walking backwards, she bumped into a rather striking officer with a fresh, open face and quite magnificent thick blond whiskers. This was Nikodim Fomich himself, the district superintendent. Luiza Ivanovna hastily curtsied almost to the floor and flew out of the bureau with quick, mincing, bouncing steps.

'Making a racket again, more thunder and lightning, a tornado, a hurricane!' remarked Nikodim Fomich to Ilya Petrovich in an amiable, friendly way. 'I see they've got you all worked up again, boiling over again! I could hear you from the stairs.'

'Come off it!' said Ilya Petrovich with well-bred nonchalance (and not so much 'off it' as 'orf it'), taking some documents or other over to another table and lifting his shoulders theatrically with each step. 'Please judge for yourself: Mr Writer here, or should I say Mr Student or rather former student, won't pay, having written out one promissory note after another, won't vacate the apartment, is the subject of endless complaints, yet still has the temerity to rebuke me for lighting a papirosa in his presence! His behaviour is simply disgraceful, and anyway, just take a look at him: a fine specimen!'

'Poverty is no sin, my friend, but why all the fuss? You're a powder keg, as everyone knows, and you can't take an insult. I expect he insulted you first, so you lashed out,' Nikodim Fomich went on, courteously addressing Raskolnikov, 'but you really shouldn't have done: he's the noblest of men, let me assure you, the noblest, but he's gunpowder! Flares up, sizzles away, burns out – and that's that! Finished! And all that's left is the gold in his heart! Lieutenant Powder Keg, that's what they called him in the regiment . . .'

'And what a regiment that was!' exclaimed Ilya Petrovich, delighted at being so agreeably tickled, though still in a huff.

Raskolnikov had a sudden urge to say something exceptionally nice to them all.

'Have a heart, Captain,' he began very freely, turning all of a sudden to Nikodim Fomich, 'and put yourself in my shoes for a moment . . . I'm even prepared to offer him an apology, if I've shown a lack of respect. I'm a poor, sick student, dejected' (that was his exact word: 'dejected') 'by poverty. I'm a *former* student, because I can't support myself at the moment, but I'm expecting some money . . . My mother and sister live in —— province . . . They're sending me some and I'll . . . pay. My landlady's a kind woman, but she's so angry with me for losing my teaching and not paying four months in a row that she won't even send up meals . . . And as for the promissory note – I haven't a clue what you mean! She's waving that IOU at me, but what can I pay her with? Judge for yourselves!'

'But that's none of our business . . . ,' the head clerk tried to put in again.

'Quite so, I couldn't agree more, but kindly allow me to put my side of the story,' Raskolnikov rejoined, still addressing Nikodim Fomich rather than the head clerk, while making every effort to address Ilya Petrovich at the same time, even though the latter kept up a stubborn pretence of rummaging through his papers and contemptuously ignoring him. 'Allow me to explain, for my part, that I've been living at hers for about three years now, ever since I arrived from the provinces, and before . . . before . . . well, why don't I just admit it? You see, I gave her my word right from the start that I'd marry her daughter, a verbal promise, freely undertaken . . . This girl was . . . well, I even took a fancy to her . . . though I wasn't in love with her . . . youth, in a word . . . What I mean is, my landlady lent me plenty of money at the time and the life I led was, to a certain extent . . . well, I was very frivolous . . .'

'Nobody's asking you for such intimacies, sir, and there's no time for them anyway,' Ilya Petrovich interrupted, rudely and gloatingly, but Raskolnikov rushed to cut him short, even though he was suddenly finding it terribly difficult to speak.

'But kindly allow me, if you would, to tell the whole story . . . to explain how it was . . . for my part . . . though it's quite unnecessary, I agree . . . but a year ago this young girl died of typhus, while I stayed on as a lodger, and the landlady, when she'd moved into the apartment she has now, said to me . . . in a friendly way . . . that she had every confidence in me and so on . . . but wouldn't I like to write her a promissory note for one hundred and fifteen roubles, which, according to her sums, was what I owed her? Take note, sir: she specifically said that just as soon as I gave her that document she'd once again lend me as much as I wanted and that never, never, for her part – these were her exact words – would she take advantage of this document, until I paid up myself . . . And now, just when I have lost my teaching and have nothing to eat, she goes and files a recovery claim . . . So what can I say?'

'All these sentimental details, honourable sir, do not concern us,' Ilya Petrovich insolently broke in. 'You must supply a statement and an undertaking, and as for being in love and all these tragic particulars, well, we couldn't care less.'

'Well really . . . that's a bit harsh . . . ,' muttered Nikodim Fomich, sitting down to sign some papers as well. He felt almost ashamed.

'Go on, write,' the head clerk told Raskolnikov.

'Write what?' asked the latter in a particularly rude sort of way.

'I'll dictate.'

It seemed to Raskolnikov that the head clerk had become more casual and scornful towards him after his confession, but, strangely enough, he suddenly felt utterly indifferent to anyone else's opinion, and this change had come about just like that, in a flash. Had he chosen to pause for a moment's thought, then he would of course have been amazed: how could he have spoken to them like that, just a moment ago, and even thrust his feelings upon them? And where had they come from, these feelings? Now, on the contrary, if the room had suddenly filled up not with police officers but with his bosom friends, even then, it seemed, he could have found no human words for them, so empty had his heart suddenly become. A gloomy sensation of excruciating, endless solitude and estrangement suddenly communicated itself consciously to his soul. His abject effusions before Ilya Petrovich, the lieutenant's abject gloating – it was not these that had suddenly turned his heart inside out. Oh, what did any of it matter to him now: his own despicable behaviour, all this vanity, these lieutenants, German ladies, recovery claims, bureaus, etcetera, etcetera? Had he been sentenced to the stake at this moment, even then he would not have stirred, even then he would scarcely have bothered listening to the sentence. Something entirely unfamiliar was happening to him, something new, sudden and completely unprecedented. He did not so much understand as sense, with the full force and clarity of his senses, that he no longer had anything to say to these people in the local police bureau, never mind exhibitions of sentiment, and had they all been his very own brothers and sisters and not district lieutenants, even then there would have been no point talking to them, whatever life threw in his path; never before had he experienced such a strange and dreadful sensation. And the most excruciating thing of all was that this was more a sensation than something conscious, something intellectual; a direct sensation, the most excruciating of all sensations experienced by him hitherto in his life.

The head clerk began dictating the statement, following the usual form in such cases, i.e., unable to pay, promise to do so on such-and-such a date (whenever), shan't leave town, shan't sell or give away my property, etcetera.

'But you can't even write – you keep dropping the pen,' the head clerk observed, peering curiously at Raskolnikov. 'Are you sick?'

'Yes . . . head's spinning . . . Carry on!'

'That's it. Now sign.'

The head clerk took the document and turned to the other people waiting.

Raskolnikov gave back the pen, but instead of getting up to leave he placed his elbows on the desk and gripped his head in his hands. As if a nail were being knocked into the crown of his head. A strange notion suddenly struck him: to get up right now, walk over to Nikodim Fomich and tell him all about yesterday, down to the very last detail, then go with them to his apartment and show them the items, in the corner, in the hole. The urge was so strong that he was already on his feet to carry it out. 'Perhaps I should think about it first?' flashed across his mind. 'No, best not to think and get it over and done with!' But he suddenly stopped dead in his tracks: Nikodim Fomich was having a heated exchange with Ilya Petrovich and their words carried over to him:

'Impossible! They'll release the pair of them! First off, it makes no sense: why would they call the caretaker if it was their doing? To inform against themselves? Or were they just being clever? No, that would be too clever by half! And anyway, Pestryakov, the student, was seen right at the gates by both caretakers and the tradeswoman at the very moment he walked in: he had three friends with him and he left them at the gates and asked the caretakers about accommodation while his friends were still there. You tell me: would he have started asking about accommodation if those were his intentions? And as for Kokh, before calling on the old woman he kept the silversmith company for half an hour downstairs, then went up to see her at a quarter to eight sharp. Think about it . . .'

'But wait, isn't there a glaring contradiction here: they say they knocked and the door was locked, then three minutes later, when they came back with the caretaker, it turns out to be open?'

'That's just it: the killer was inside, no doubt about it, and had locked himself in; and they would have caught him, no doubt about it, if Kokh hadn't stupidly run off to get the caretaker. And it was precisely then, during that brief interval, that *he* managed to go down the stairs and somehow slip past them. Kokh crosses himself with one hand then the other, and says, "If I'd stayed put, he'd have leapt out and killed me with the axe." Now he wants to hold a thanksgiving service in the Russian fashion, heh-heh!'

'So no one saw the killer?'

'How could they? It's like Noah's Ark, that house,' the head clerk observed, listening in from his desk.

'It's all clear as day, clear as day!' Nikodim Fomich excitedly repeated.

'Clear as mud!' snapped Ilya Petrovich.

Raskolnikov picked up his hat and made for the door, but he didn't reach it . . .

When he came to his senses, he saw that he was sitting on a chair, that there was someone supporting him to his right and someone else standing to his left, holding a yellow glass filled with yellow water, while Nikodim Fomich stood before him, staring at him. He got up from the chair.

'What is it? Are you sick?' asked Nikodim Fomich rather abruptly.

'Even when he was signing his name, he could barely hold the pen,' observed the head clerk, returning to his seat and busying himself with his papers again.

'Been sick long?' Ilya Petrovich shouted from his desk, as he, too, sorted through his papers. He, of course, had also been studying him after he fainted, but immediately moved off when he came round.

'Since yesterday . . . ,' Raskolnikov muttered in reply.

'And did you go outside yesterday?'

'Yes.'

'Sick?'

'Yes.'

'What time?'

'Evening, after seven.'

'And where to, may I ask?'

'Down the street.'

'Clear and to the point.'

Raskolnikov, pale as a handkerchief, replied abruptly and curtly, meeting Ilya Petrovich's gaze with his black, swollen eyes.

'He can barely stand, and you . . . ,' Nikodim Fomich began.

'Don't mind me!' said Ilya Petrovich in a very particular tone. Nikodim Fomich was about to say something else but, taking one glance at the head clerk, who was also staring hard at him, he fell silent. Everyone suddenly fell silent. It was strange.

'Very well, sir,' Ilya Petrovich concluded. 'We aren't keeping you.'

Raskolnikov left. But he could hear an animated conversation starting up once he'd gone, with the quizzical voice of Nikodim Fomich most audible of all . . . Outside, he came round fully.

'A search, a search – now, now!' he repeated to himself as he hurried along. 'They suspect me, the rascals!' His old terror seized him once more, from top to toe.

II

'But what if the search has already happened? What if I find them in my room right now?'

But here was his room. Nothing. No one. And no one had looked in. Even Nastasya hadn't touched it. Lord! How could he have gone and left all the items in that hole?

He rushed to the corner, thrust his hand behind the wallpaper and started fishing the things out and cramming his pockets with them. There were eight items in all: two little boxes containing earrings or similar – he didn't look closely – and four small morocco leather cases. One chain was simply wrapped in newspaper. As was something else, a medal by the look of it . . .

He stowed it all away in his various pockets – in his coat and in the remaining right pocket of his trousers – making sure that nothing stuck out too much. He took the purse as well, while he was at it. Then he went out, this time leaving the door wide open.

He walked at a fast, decisive clip, and though he felt utterly broken, he remained alert and aware. He feared pursuit, he feared that in just half an hour's time, a quarter of an hour's time, the instruction would be given to have him followed; he had to cover his tracks at all costs, before it was too late. And he had to do so while he could still call on at least some of his strength, at least some of his wits . . . But where should he go?

This had been decided long before: 'Throw everything in the Ditch, in the water. End of story.' He'd made up his mind about it the previous night, while raving, during those moments – he remembered them now – when he kept trying to get up and go: 'Quick, quick, get rid of it all!' But getting rid of everything proved extremely difficult.

He'd been wandering along the Catherine Canal for about half an hour already, perhaps even longer, and he'd glanced more than once at the steps leading down to the Ditch,[3] whenever he passed them. But there could be no question of him carrying out his intention: either there were rafts right by the steps, with washerwomen at work on them, or there were boats moored to the bank, and there were people everywhere; from anywhere on the embankments, from every side, people might see, might notice, the suspicious figure of a man purposely going down the steps, stopping and throwing something in the water. And if the cases floated instead of sinking? You could count on it. Everyone would see. He was getting strange looks as it was from everyone he passed, as if they had no care in the world but him. 'Why is that? Or am I just imagining it?' he wondered.

Finally, the thought struck him: wouldn't the Neva be a better idea? Fewer people, less chance of being noticed, easier in every way, and above all – far away from here. How astonishing that he could wander about for a whole half hour in anguish and alarm, and in such a dangerous place, and not think of this sooner! And the only reason he'd wasted a whole half hour so senselessly was a decision taken while dreaming, while raving! He was becoming extraordinarily distracted and forgetful, and he knew it. He had to get a move on!

He made for the Neva along V—— Prospect; but on the way another thought suddenly struck him: 'Why the Neva? Why water? Wouldn't it be better to go somewhere far, far away, maybe even back to the Islands again, and find some remote spot, in the woods, under a bush – to bury all this and perhaps mark a tree?' And though he could feel that he was in no fit state to weigh everything up clearly and soberly at this moment, the plan seemed flawless.

But he wasn't fated to make it to the Islands either: coming out onto a square from V—— Prospect, he suddenly spotted an entrance on his left to a courtyard framed by completely blind walls. On the right, immediately after the gates, the unwhitewashed blind wall of the adjoining four-storey house extended deep into the yard. On the left, parallel to this blind wall and also just after the gates, a wooden fence stretched some twenty yards into the yard before veering abruptly to the left. This was a desolate, cut-off spot, strewn with what looked like building materials. Further on, in the depths of the courtyard, from behind the fence, the corner of a low, sooty stone shed poked out – evidently part of some workshop or other, probably a carriage-maker's or locksmith's or some such trade; the whole yard was black with coal dust stretching almost to the gates. 'Just the place to dump everything and walk away!' he suddenly thought. Finding the yard deserted, he stepped inside and immediately spotted, very close to the gates, a gutter fixed to the fence (the usual arrangement in such courtyards, home to many factory hands, craftsmen, cabbies and the like), and above the gutter, right there on the fence, someone had scrawled the obligatory witticism in chalk: 'No toiletering.' Good: no one would suspect him for coming in and loitering there. 'Just chuck it all in a heap somewhere and leave!'

He looked around one more time and had already thrust a hand into his pocket when suddenly, right by the outer wall, between the gates and the gutter, which were separated by less than a yard, he noticed a big unhewn stone, weighing as much as fifty pounds and resting directly against the stone wall. On the other side of this wall were the street and the pavement, and he could hear the to and fro of passers-by, always plentiful hereabouts; but no one could see him this side of the gates, not unless someone came in off the street, which in fact was perfectly possible – so he had to hurry.

He stooped, grabbed the top of the stone firmly with both hands, mustered all his strength and overturned it. A small hollow had formed beneath the stone, into which he immediately began tipping the contents of his pockets. The purse ended up on the very top, but there was still some space left. Then he grabbed the stone once more and turned it back over in one go; it rested snugly in its former position, if slightly raised. He raked up some earth and packed it in round the edges with his foot. No one would notice.

He left the yard and made for the square. Once again he was over-whelmed momentarily by powerful, almost unbearable joy, as before in the bureau. 'My tracks are covered! Who would ever think of looking under there? I expect that stone's been lying there since the house was built and will remain there just as long. And even if the things were found, who would suspect me? It's over! No evidence!' – and he burst out laughing. Yes, he remembered this laughter later, nervous, shallow, inaudible laughter, and how long it had lasted – for as long as it took to cross the square. But when he set foot on K—— Boulevard, where he'd come across that girl two days before, his laughter suddenly ceased. Different thoughts crept into his mind. He also felt a terrible, sudden disgust at the prospect of walking past that bench now, the same one on which he'd sat and mused once the girl had gone, and thought how awful it would be to meet that man with the moustache again, the one he'd given a twenty-copeck coin to that time: 'To hell with him!'

He walked along, looking around him in a distracted, spiteful way. All his thoughts now circled around a certain crucial point, and he himself could feel that this really was the crucial point, and that now, precisely now, he'd been left one on one with it – for the very first time, in fact, in these whole two months.

'To hell with it all!' he suddenly thought in a spasm of unquencha-
ble spite. 'It's started, so it's started – to hell with it, to hell with new
life! God, how stupid this is! How I tricked and lied today! How sick-
eningly I fawned and flirted with that appalling Ilya Petrovich just
now! But that's all rubbish, too! What do I care about any of them, or
about my fawning and flirting! That's all neither here nor there!'

Suddenly, he stopped; a new, quite unexpected and extraordinarily
simple question had knocked him off course and filled him with bitter
astonishment:

'If this whole thing really was done consciously and not stupidly, if
you really did have a definite, fixed aim, then how is it you still haven't
taken one look inside the purse and don't even know what you've got,
the very reason you accepted all this agony and consciously set out on
something so despicable, so vile, so low? Just now you even wanted to
throw the purse in the water, along with all the items you haven't seen
yet either . . . How come?'

Yes, exactly. But he'd known that already and there was nothing new
about this question; and when he'd decided, the previous night, to throw
the stuff in the water, he'd done so without a moment's hesitation or a
single reservation, as if that was exactly how it should be, as if there could
be no other way . . . Yes, he knew all this already, remembered it all; and
what was to say it hadn't been decided yesterday, at that very moment
when he was sitting over the box and taking out the cases? . . . Exactly!

'It's because I'm so ill,' he decided at last, sullenly. 'I've tormented
myself, torn myself to pieces, and don't even know what I'm doing . . .
Yesterday, the day before, all these days – one torment after another . . .
I'll get better and . . . I won't torment myself . . . And if I don't get any
better? God! I'm just so sick of it all!' He walked without stopping. He
desperately wanted to distract himself, but he didn't know what to do,
what to undertake. A new, overwhelming sensation was taking possession of him, growing stronger almost by the minute: some sort of infinite, almost physical disgust – stubborn, spiteful, hate-filled – towards
everything that surrounded him. Everyone he met disgusted him – their
faces, their gait, their gestures. Had anyone tried to talk to him, he'd
probably have spat in his face, or bitten him . . .

He suddenly stopped when he came out on the embankment of the
Little Neva, on Vasilyevsky Island, by a bridge. 'This is where he lives,
this is the house,' he thought. 'Don't tell me I've come to Razumikhin's again! Just like then . . . Fascinating, though: did I mean to come

here or was I just walking by? Makes no odds; I did say . . . a couple of days ago . . . that I'd drop in the day after *that*, so that's what I'll do! What's to stop me . . . ?'

He went up to the fifth floor.

Razumikhin was at home, in his own little cell; he was busy working – writing – and opened the door himself. They hadn't seen each other for four months or so. Razumikhin was wearing a tattered dressing gown, and shoes on bare feet; he was unkempt, unshaven and unwashed. His face expressed surprise.

'What's happened?' he cried, inspecting his friend from top to toe; then he fell silent and whistled.

'That bad, eh? Just look at you! I feel positively underdressed,' – he added, staring at Raskolnikov's rags – 'but sit down, for heaven's sake, you look exhausted!' – and when Raskolnikov collapsed on the 'Turkish' oilcloth-covered couch, which was even shabbier than his own, Razumikhin suddenly saw that his guest was sick.

'You're seriously ill, do you know that?' He started feeling his pulse. Raskolnikov tore his hand away.

'Don't!' he said. 'I've come . . . here's what: I've no teaching at all . . . I was going to . . . though actually, I don't need any . . .'

'Know what? You're raving!' remarked Razumikhin, observing him closely.

'No I'm not . . . ,' said Raskolnikov, getting up from the couch. While climbing the stairs it hadn't occurred to him that he would, of course, end up face to face with Razumikhin. But now, in a flash, he had seen for himself that the very last thing he felt like doing, at this moment, was to come face to face with anyone at all in the whole world. He was turning yellow with bile. He'd all but choked with self-loathing the second he crossed Razumikhin's threshold.

'See you!' he suddenly said, and made for the door.

'Wait there, you mad dog!'

'Don't!' the other repeated, tearing his hand away again.

'So why the hell did you come in the first place? Are you off your head? I mean it's . . . almost insulting. I won't let you off so easily.'

'All right. I came to you because I didn't know anyone else who could help me . . . start . . . because you're kinder than all of them, I mean cleverer, and you talk sense . . . But now I see that I don't need a thing, not a thing, do you hear? . . . No one's favours, no one's concern . . . Me . . . on my own . . . That'll do! Just leave me in peace!'

'Now wait a minute, you chimneysweep! You're insane! You can
do as you like, for all I care. You see, I'm not giving any lessons either,
and so what? There's this bookseller at the flea market, Cherubimov
by name, who's a lesson in himself. I wouldn't swap him for five merchant students. You should see the sort of books he puts out, tomes on
natural science[4] and what have you – all selling like hotcakes! The titles alone are priceless! You've always said I'm stupid. I tell you, my
friend, I'm nothing compared to some! Now he's decided to go with
the tide. It's all Greek to him and I egg him on, of course. Look, here's
two and a bit printer's sheets of German text – low-grade quackery, if
you ask me. And here's the topic in a nutshell: is a woman a human
being[5] or isn't she? No prizes for guessing: it's solemnly proven that
she is. Cherubimov wants it for the debate on the Woman Question,
and I'm translating it. He'll stretch two and a half printer's sheets to
six, we'll think up some pompous title over half a page and flog it for
half a rouble. All in a day's work! I'm paid six roubles a sheet, so I'll
get fifteen for the lot, and I took six in advance. Once that's done, we'll
start translating something on whales, then there's some ultra-tedious
tittle-tattle we've marked up in the second part of the *Confessions* –
we'll translate that too. Someone's told Cherubimov that Rousseau
was the Radishchev of Geneva.[6] I didn't tell him otherwise, of course –
he can think what he likes! So, fancy translating the second sheet of
"Are Women Human?"? If so, take the text now, take some pens and
paper – I get given it all anyway – and take three roubles; my advance
was for the whole translation, the first and second sheet combined, so
your share is three roubles. Finish the thing and you'll get three more.
By the way, please don't think I'm doing you a favour: I'd already
worked out what you could do for me the moment you walked in. For
one thing, my spelling's poor, and for another, my German's diaboli-
cal. I'm making up more and more as I go along and my only consolation is that it comes out better this way. Who knows, though? Perhaps
it comes out worse . . . Well, what d'you say?'

Raskolnikov silently took the pages of German text and the three
roubles, and left without saying a word. Razumikhin watched incred-
ulously. But having already reached the First Line,[7] Raskolnikov suddenly turned back, went up to Razumikhin again and, placing both
the German pages and the three roubles on the desk, went off again
without saying a word.

'Have you got the DTs or what?' Razumikhin roared, finally

snapping. 'Why this song and dance? You've even confused *me* . . .
Why the hell did you come in the first place?'

'I don't want . . . any translations . . . ,' Raskolnikov muttered, already on his way down.

'So what do you want?' Razumikhin yelled from above. Raskolnikov carried on down in silence.

'Hey! Where do you live?'

No reply.

'To hell with you, then!'

But Raskolnikov was already outside. On Nikolayevsky Bridge he
was brought sharply to his senses once more by a nasty incident. A
carriage-driver lashed him full on the back with his whip, as punishment for Raskolnikov very nearly getting himself run over by his
horses, despite the driver shouting at him three or four times. The lash
so enraged Raskolnikov that after jumping aside towards the railings
(for some reason he'd been walking straight down the middle of the
bridge, in the thick of the traffic) he began furiously grinding and
gnashing his teeth. All around, needless to say, people laughed.

'Had it coming!'

'Con man!'

'You know the score – makes out he's drunk and gets himself run
over; and you're the one responsible.'

'That's their game, dear man, that's their game . . .'

But at that moment, as he stood by the railings and continued to
stare blankly and spitefully at the now distant carriage, rubbing his
back, he suddenly felt someone press money into his hand. He looked
round: it was an elderly merchantwoman wearing a silk headband
and goatskin shoes, accompanied by a girl in a hat, carrying a green
parasol, probably her daughter. 'Take it, father, for the love of Christ.'
He took it and they walked on. A twenty-copeck piece. His clothes
and general appearance were such that they could very easily have
taken him for a beggar, a real copeck collector, and he probably had
the lash of the whip to thank for receiving twenty copecks all at
once – they must have taken pity on him.

He clenched the coin in his fist, walked on a few yards and turned to
face the Neva, in the direction of the Palace. There wasn't a cloud in the
sky and the water was almost blue, a great rarity on the Neva. The cathedral's dome – which stands out better from here, on the bridge, some
twenty yards before the chapel,[8] than from any other spot – simply

shone, and through the pure air its every decoration was clearly discernible. The pain from the whip subsided and Raskolnikov forgot about the blow; one troubling and less than lucid thought was occupying his mind to the exclusion of all others. He stood and stared into the distance for a long while; he knew this spot particularly well. While attending university it often happened – a hundred times, perhaps, usually on his way home – that he would pause at precisely this spot, look intently at this truly magnificent panorama and every time be almost amazed by the obscure, irresolvable impression it made on him. An inexplicable chill came over him as he gazed at this magnificence; this gorgeous scene was filled for him by some dumb, deaf spirit[9] . . . He marvelled every time at this sombre, mysterious impression and, distrusting himself, put off any attempt to explain it. Now, all of a sudden, those old questions of his, that old bewilderment, came back to him sharply, and it was no accident, he felt, that they'd come back now. The simple fact that he'd stopped at the very same spot as before seemed outlandish and bizarre, as if he really had imagined that now he could think the same old thoughts as before, take an interest in the same old subjects and scenes that had interested him . . . such a short while ago. He almost found it funny, yet his chest felt so tight it hurt. In the depths, down below, somewhere just visible beneath his feet, this old past appeared to him in its entirety, those old thoughts, old problems, old subjects, old impressions, and this whole panorama, and he himself, and everything, everything . . . It was as if he were flying off somewhere, higher and higher, and everything was vanishing before his eyes . . . Making an involuntary movement with his hand, he suddenly sensed the twenty-copeck piece in his fist. He unclenched his hand, stared hard at the coin, drew back his arm and hurled the coin into the water; then he turned round and set off home. It felt as if he'd taken a pair of scissors and cut himself off from everyone and everything, there and then.

It was nearly evening when he reached his room, so he must have been walking for about six hours all told. Where he walked, how he got back – he remembered none of it. Undressing and quivering all over, like a horse ridden into the ground, he lay down on the couch, drew his greatcoat over himself and oblivion immediately followed . . .

He woke in deep twilight to a dreadful scream. God, what a scream! Such unnatural sounds, such wailing, howling, grinding, weeping, beating, swearing – never before had he known anything like it. Never could he have even imagined such brutishness, such frenzy. He sat up in his bed, frozen with horror and anguish. But the fighting, howling and swearing grew louder and louder. And now, to his utter astonishment, he could suddenly make out the voice of his landlady. She was howling, squealing, wailing, hurrying, rushing to get the words out, so that they all came out as one, begging for something – for the beating to cease, of course, for she was being beaten without mercy on the stairs. The voice of the man doing the beating had become so dreadful in its malice and fury that by now it was no more than a hoarse wheeze, but he too was saying something, he too was speaking quickly and unintelligibly, in a breathless rush. Suddenly Raskolnikov began trembling all over. He recognized this voice. It was the voice of Ilya Petrovich. Ilya Petrovich was here and he was beating the landlady! He was kicking her, banging her head against the step – that was obvious from the sounds, the howls, the blows! Was the world upside down? He could hear crowds gathering on every floor; all the way up the stairs he could hear voices, cries, footsteps, knocking, doors banging, people running over. 'But why is this happening? Why? And how is it possible?' he kept repeating, seriously thinking that he'd gone quite crazy. But no, he could hear too clearly for that! But in that case they would be coming to him too now, 'because . . . this must all be to do with that . . . yesterday . . . Lord!' He was about to reach for the hook and lock himself in, but his hand wouldn't move . . . and what was the use? Fear enveloped his soul like ice, exhausting him, numbing him . . . But now, finally, this whole racket, having lasted a good ten minutes, was gradually subsiding. The landlady groaned and sighed. Ilya Petrovich still threatened and swore . . . But now, at last he, too, seemed to quieten down; there was no sound from him at all. 'Can he really have gone? God!' Yes, and that was the landlady going too, still groaning and crying . . . and that was her door banging shut . . . And that was all the people going back into their apartments from the stairs – gasping, bickering, calling out to each other, shouting, whispering. How many there seemed to be; as if the whole building had gathered. 'God, can this really be happening? And why on earth did he come here?'

Raskolnikov collapsed onto the couch in exhaustion, but he was no longer able to close his eyes. He lay there for half an hour or so, experiencing such suffering and such boundless, unbearable horror as he had never experienced before. Suddenly, bright light poured into his room: Nastasya came in with a candle and a bowl of soup. Looking at him closely and seeing that he was not asleep, she set the candle on the table and began laying out what she'd brought: bread, salt, the bowl, a spoon.

'Expect you've not eaten since yesterday. Fancy knocking about town all day when you've got the shakes!'

'Nastasya . . . why was the landlady beaten?'

She stared at him.

'Who beat the landlady?'

'Just now . . . half an hour ago. Ilya Petrovich, the district superintendent's assistant, on the stairs . . . Why did he have to beat her like that? And . . . why did he come?'

Frowning, Nastasya studied him in silence, for a very long time. Such scrutiny began to make him very uncomfortable, even frightened.

'Nastasya, why aren't you saying anything?' he said at last in a timid, faint voice.

'That's blood,' she finally answered softly, as though speaking to herself.

'Blood! What blood?' he mumbled, turning pale and backing away towards the wall. Nastasya carried on looking at him in silence.

'No one beat the landlady,' she said again in a stern, decisive voice.

He looked at her, barely breathing.

'I heard it myself . . . I wasn't asleep . . . I was sitting up,' he said, more timidly still. 'I listened for ages . . . The superintendent's assistant came . . . Everyone gathered on the stairs, from every apartment . . .'

'No one came. That's your blood yelling inside you.[10] That's when it can't get out and clots up your insides and you start seeing things . . . So are you eating or not?'

He didn't reply. Nastasya was still standing over him, staring at him and not leaving.

'A drink, please . . . Nastasyushka.'

She went downstairs and returned a few minutes later with some water in a white earthenware jug; and that was the last he remembered. All he could recall was taking a swig of cold water from the jug and spilling some on his chest. Oblivion came over him.

III

Not that he was completely knocked out for the entire duration of his sickness: he was in a feverish state, sometimes delirious, sometimes semi-conscious. Much of it came back to him later. At one point it seemed to him that a big crowd was gathering around him, wanting to grab him and take him off somewhere, endlessly bickering and arguing about him. At another he was suddenly alone in the room, everyone had left, everyone was scared of him, and only occasionally did someone open the door a fraction to take a look at him; they were threatening him, plotting amongst themselves, laughing and teasing him. Nastasya, he recalled, was often beside him; he could also make out one other person who seemed very familiar, but who it was exactly he couldn't quite tell, and he was upset about it and even cried. Sometimes it seemed he'd been lying in bed for a month already; at others he thought it was all one and the same day. But as for *that* – well, he'd completely forgotten about *that*; yet not a minute passed without him remembering that he'd forgotten something that mustn't be forgotten – and he went through agony trying to recall it. Groaning, he would succumb to fury or to dreadful, unbearable terror. At such moments he wanted to get up and run away, but there was always someone holding him back, and once again he would lose all strength and awareness. At last, he came round fully.

This happened in the morning, at ten o'clock. At this hour, on bright days, a long shaft of sunlight would travel the length of his right wall and illuminate the corner next to the door. Nastasya was standing by his bed, along with another person, a total stranger, who was examining him with the greatest curiosity. This was a young lad wearing a peasant-style coat and a wispy beard – a messenger of some kind, by the look of him. His landlady was peering through the half-open door. Raskolnikov lifted himself up.

'Who's this, Nastasya?' he asked, pointing at the lad.

'Well I never, he's woken up!' she said.

'Indeed he has,' echoed the messenger. Realizing he had woken, the landlady, who was peeping in from the threshold, immediately drew the door to and made herself scarce. She'd always been shy and found any conversation or exchange of views very trying; she was about forty, large and fat, black-browed and black-eyed, kind-hearted from being large and lazy; and, as it happens, very easy on the eye. But needlessly coy.

'And you . . . are?' he persisted, addressing the messenger directly. But at that moment the door opened again and, stooping a little, in walked Razumikhin.

'A real ship's cabin!' he shouted on entering. 'I always bang my head; and they call it an apartment! So you've woken up, brother? Pashenka, your landlady, just told me.'

'He's just woken up now,' said Nastasya.

'Indeed he has,' the messenger repeated with a little smile.

'And who, pray, might you be?' asked Razumikhin, suddenly addressing him. 'I, you see, am Vrazumikhin;[11] not Razumikhin, as everyone calls me, but Vrazumikhin, a student, gentry by birth, and this is my friend. And who are you?'

'I'm the messenger at our office, on behalf of the merchant Shelopayev, sir, and I've come on business, sir.'

'Do sit down on this chair.' Razumikhin sat himself down on another, on the other side of the little table. 'Good job you woke up, brother,' he continued, addressing Raskolnikov. 'You've barely touched food or drink for four days. Except for the tea we gave you from a spoon. I brought Zosimov to see you twice. Remember Zosimov? He examined you closely and said straight away that it was nothing serious – a rush of blood to the head or something. Nerves playing up, he says, lousy nosh, not enough beer and horseradish, no wonder you're sick – but it's nothing, you'll be right as rain. He's a good egg, Zosimov! All the makings of a fine doctor. Well, sir, I'm not stopping you,' he said, addressing the messenger once more. 'Would you care to explain your purpose? Note, dear Rodya, that this is already the second visit from their office; only before it wasn't this chap, but another, and the two of us had a bit of a chat. Who was that man who called in before you?'

'That must have been the day before yesterday, yes indeed, sir. That would have been Alexei Semyonovich; also works in our office, sir.'

'He's probably a bit brighter than you, wouldn't you say?'

'Indeed, sir; a bit more impressive, sure enough.'

'Admirable, admirable. Carry on, then.'

'Well, sir, by way of Afanasy Ivanovich Vakhrushin, whom you will have heard of more than once, I suppose, and at the request of your mama, I have a remittance for you by way of our office,' the messenger began, addressing Raskolnikov directly. 'In the event of your already being in possession of all your faculties, sir, I have thirty-five roubles to hand over, sir, seeing as Mr Shelopayev was instructed about this by Mr Vakhrushin, at the request of your mama, as per previously. Do you happen to know him, sir?'

'Yes . . . I remember . . . Vakhrushin . . . ,' said Raskolnikov pensively.

'Hear that? He knows the merchant Vakhrushin!' cried Razumikhin.

'What was that about faculties? Still, I see that you're a bright spark, too. Well, well! It's always nice to hear clever talk.'

'That is he, sir, Vakhrushin, Afanasy Ivanovich, and at the request of your mama, who sent a remittance by way of him as per previously, he did not refuse on this occasion either and just the other day, from his location, he instructed Mr Shelopayev to transfer thirty-five roubles to you, sir, in the hope that things look up, sir.'

' "In the hope that things look up" – you've outdone yourself there; and the bit about "your mama" wasn't bad, either. So what d'you reckon? Is he or isn't he in full possession of his senses, eh?'

'Not for me to say, sir. All I need is a little signature.'

'He can manage that! What's that you've got – a book?'

'A book, sir, yes indeed, sir.'

'Give it here then. Right, Rodya, up you get. I'll support you. Just scribble Raskolnikov for him. Take the pen, brother – money's sweeter than syrup for us right now.'

'No need,' said Raskolnikov, pushing away the pen.

'No need for what?'

'I won't sign.'

'Hell's bells, man! What do you mean you won't sign?'

'No need . . . for money . . .'

'No need for money, he says! Now that's a lie, brother, as I'm your witness! Please don't be alarmed, he's just . . . wandering off again. Happens to him even when he's wide awake . . . You're a sensible man and we'll take him in hand. That's to say we'll simply take his hand and help him sign. Now, look lively . . .'

'Why don't I call another time, sir.'

'No, no, don't put yourself out. You're a sensible sort . . . Well now, Rodya, don't let's keep our guest . . . You can see he's waiting,' – and he prepared in all seriousness to guide Raskolnikov's hand.

'Leave off! I'll do it myself . . . ,' said Raskolnikov, taking the pen and signing the book. The messenger took out the money and left.

'Bravo! And now, brother, perhaps you're hungry?'

'I am,' replied Raskolnikov.

'Got any soup?'

'Yesterday's,' replied Nastasya, who had been standing right there all this time.

'Potato soup with rice?'

'Potato and rice.'

'I know it by heart. Well, let's have the soup, and some tea while you're at it.'

'Coming up.'

Raskolnikov observed all this in deep astonishment and with dull, meaningless fear. He resolved to say nothing and wait: what next? 'I don't think I'm raving,' he thought, 'this seems real enough . . .'

Two minutes later Nastasya returned with the soup and announced that tea was also on its way. Two spoons and two plates had materialized, along with a salt cellar, a pepper pot, mustard for beef, and other things besides – a spread the likes of which he hadn't seen for ages. The tablecloth was clean.

'Nastasyushka, we wouldn't say no to a couple of bottles of beer from Praskovya Pavlovna. That'd be just the thing, young lady.'

'You're a fast one!' muttered Nastasya, and went off to do his bidding.

Raskolnikov continued to stare with the same wild intensity. Meanwhile Razumikhin moved over to him on the couch, cradled his head with bear-like clumsiness in his left arm, even though Raskolnikov could very well have sat himself up, and with his right hand brought a spoonful of soup to his mouth, having first blown on it several times lest it burnt him. But the soup was barely warm. Raskolnikov hungrily swallowed one spoonful, then another, then a third. But after feeding him a few more, Razumikhin suddenly stopped and declared that he would need to consult Zosimov before continuing.

Nastasya came in, bearing two bottles of beer.

'Some tea as well?'

'Yes.'

'So bring that, too, Nastasya, quick as you can – no expert approval needed for tea, as far as I know. And here's the beer!' He sat down on his chair again, drew the soup and beef towards him and set about them as if he hadn't eaten for three days.

'You know, brother, I dine here like this every day now,' he said through a mouth full of beef, 'and it's all Pashenka's doing, your landlady, my dinner lady. Treats me like royalty. I don't insist on it, needless to say, but nor do I object. And here's Nastasya with the tea. She doesn't hang about! A drop of beer, Nastyenka?'

'Enough of your mischief!'

'A spot of tea?'

'Well, all right.'

'Help yourself. No, wait, I'll pour you a cup. You sit down here at the table.'

Without a moment's delay he poured out one cup, then another, abandoned his meal and moved over to the couch again. He cradled the patient's head in his left arm as before, lifted him up a bit and began giving him sips of tea with a little spoon, still blowing on it continuously and with particular zeal, as if the very crux of the remedy lay in this process of blowing. Raskolnikov said nothing and offered no resistance, despite feeling more than enough strength in himself to sit up on the couch unaided, enough not just to hold a spoon or cup, but even, perhaps, to walk. But some sort of strange, almost animal cunning suddenly prompted him to conceal his strength for the time being, to lie low, even to pretend that he was still not quite with it, if need be, while listening hard and trying to establish what was actually happening here. But his disgust proved too strong: after gulping down nine or ten spoonfuls of tea, he suddenly shook his head free, tetchily pushed the spoon away and fell back onto the pillows. He had real pillows beneath his head now – with feathers and clean slips; he noticed this, too, and took it into consideration.

'Let's get Pashenka to send us up some raspberry jam, today, then we can make him a drink,' said Razumikhin, taking his seat again and tucking into his soup and beer.

'And where's she going to find raspberries?' asked Nastasya, holding her tea-filled saucer on her five outspread fingers and filtering the tea into her mouth 'through the sugar lump'.[12]

'In a shop, my friend, that's where. Rodya, you've no idea what you've been missing. When, like a born swindler, you ran off that time without even telling me your address, I got so annoyed I decided to track you down and punish you. I set about it that very same day. I walked everywhere, asked everyone! I'd forgotten all about this place, your latest; not that there was anything to forget, mind you, seeing as I never knew. And as for your previous address – Kharlamov's house is all I remember, by the Five Corners. So I searched high and low for Kharlamov's house, only to discover that it wasn't Kharlamov's house at all, but Bukh's – funny how sounds can trip you up! Well then I really got mad. Got mad and headed off, come what may, to the address bureau the very next day and, just imagine, they found you in two minutes flat. You're on their books.'

'I suppose I am!'

'Too right. But General Kobelev now – no one could find him all the time I was there. But that's a long story. The second I barged in here, I immediately familiarized myself with all your affairs; all of them, brother, every last one. I know everything; ask her – she saw. I met Nikodim Fomich, had Ilya Petrovich pointed out to me, met the caretaker, met Mr Alexander Grigoryevich Zametov, head clerk in the police bureau here, and last of all I met Pashenka – the icing on the cake; ask her, she knows . . .'

'He sweetened her up,' mumbled Nastasya with a cheeky grin.

'You're sweet enough already, Nastasya Nikiforovna.'

'You old dog!' exclaimed Nastasya and burst out laughing. 'Anyway, I'm Petrovna, not Nikiforovna,' she suddenly added, once she'd stopped laughing.

'We'll bear that in mind, young lady. So, brother, to cut a long story short, my first thought was to unleash a stream of electricity[13] on this whole place, so as to eradicate every last prejudice here once and for all; but Pashenka came out on top. I would never have thought, brother, that she was so, well . . . *avenante*-ish[14] . . . eh? Wouldn't you say?'

Raskolnikov said nothing, though his troubled gaze did not leave Razumikhin for one second, and now, too, he carried on staring right at him.

'Not half,' Razumikhin went on, quite unembarrassed by the silence, as if he were echoing a reply, 'not half, in every department.'

'You beast!' shrieked Nastasya, for whom this conversation was, by all appearances, a source of sheer delight.

'It's a crying shame, brother, that you got off on the wrong foot with her right from the word go. That wasn't the way to play it. After all, she has the most, well, surprising character! But more of that anon . . . I mean, how did you let things get to the stage where she permits herself not to send up dinner? And what about the promissory note? You must be mad, signing such things! And what about the wedding that was on the cards when her girl, Natalya Yegorovna, was still alive . . . I know everything! But I see this is a delicate topic and I'm an ass. Forgive me. Talking of stupidity, Praskovya Pavlovna – Pashenka – isn't half as stupid as you might think, eh?'

'Yes . . . ,' said Raskolnikov, forcing out a reply and looking away, well aware that it was in his interests to keep the conversation going.

'Isn't that right?' cried Razumikhin, visibly delighted to have received a reply. 'But nor is she clever, eh? A thoroughly, thoroughly surprising character! You know, brother, I barely know what to make of her . . . I bet she's the wrong side of forty. Thirty-six, she says, and it's her sacred right to do so. Let me tell you, though: I judge her in a largely intellectual, purely metaphysical way: think of us as a kind of emblem – puts your algebra to shame! I don't understand the first thing about it! But enough of all this drivel. The fact of the matter is this: seeing that you were no longer a student, that you'd lost your lessons and your clothes, and that after the death of the young lady there was no point treating you like family any more, she suddenly got scared; and seeing as you, for your part, were holed up in your room and had started ignoring her, she came up with the idea of kicking you out. She'd been considering it for some time, in fact, only she wanted her money back. What's more, you'd assured her yourself that Mama would pay . . .'

'I said that because I'm a scoundrel . . . My mother is almost reduced to begging herself . . . and I lied in order to stay on here and . . . be fed,' said Raskolnikov, pronouncing the words loudly and distinctly.

'Very sensible of you, too. The only problem was this: who should show up but Mr Chebarov, court counsellor and all-round man of action. Pashenka wouldn't have come up with any of this without him – she's far too coy; but a man of action isn't coy and his first action, of course, was to ask: any hope of enforcing the promissory note? The reply: yes, thanks to a mama who's ready to dip into her hundred-and-twenty-five-rouble pension to save her Rodya, even if it means her going hungry, and thanks to a sister ready to sell herself into bondage for her brother. That was enough for Chebarov to be getting on with . . . Why are you fidgeting? I know all your secrets now, brother – that's what comes of you being so open with Pashenka when you were still part of the family – and I'm telling you all this now because I care about you . . . That's the thing, you see: a man of honesty and feeling opens his heart, while a man of action listens and whistles, then gobbles him up. So she let him have this promissory note by way of payment, and Chebarov made a formal claim without batting an eye. When I learned about this I was on the verge of unleashing an electric stream on him as well, just to clear my conscience, but that was when Pashenka and I had started getting on so well, so I called an end to the whole business, right at its source, by vouching that you would pay. I vouched for you, brother, do you hear? We called Chebarov over, stuffed ten roubles down his throat and got the bit of paper back, which I have the honour of presenting to you – your word is enough for them now. So here, take the thing, with a good rip in it from me, just like it's supposed to have.'

Razumikhin placed the promissory note on the table. Raskolnikov took one glance at it and, without saying a word, turned towards the wall. Even Razumikhin smarted.

'I see, brother,' he said after a minute, 'that I've made an idiot of myself again. Thought I might distract you with some small talk, but all I seem to have done is spoil your mood.'

'Was it you I couldn't recognize when I was raving?' asked Raskolnikov, who had also been silent for a minute or so and was still looking away.

'Me, and it drove you into a frenzy, especially when I brought Zametov round once.'

'Zametov? . . . The head clerk? . . . What for?' Raskolnikov turned round swiftly, staring straight at Razumikhin.

'Calm down now . . . No need to get excited. He wanted to get to know you. It was his idea, because we'd been talking about you . . . How else would I know so much about you? He's a good egg; quite splendid, in fact . . . in his own way, of course. We've become friends; see each other almost every day. After all, I live in that neck of the woods now. You didn't know? I've only just moved there. We visited Laviza together on a couple of occasions. Remember her, Laviza Ivanovna?'

'Did I say anything when I was raving?'

'Not half! You were quite beside yourself, sir.'

'What was I raving about?'

'Come again? What were you raving about? We all know what people rave about . . . But no time to waste, brother – there's things to do.'

He got up from the chair and grabbed his cap.

'What was I raving about?'

'Still harping on! Scared of spilling the beans, are you? Don't worry: not a word was uttered about the countess.[15] But as for a certain bulldog, and earrings, and chains of some kind, and Krestovsky Island, and a certain caretaker, and Nikodim Fomich, and Ilya Petrovich, assistant to the district superintendent – plenty was said about those. Not to mention, my dear sir, the quite exceptional interest you showed in your own sock! "Give it to me!" you kept whining. "Give it to me!" Zametov himself searched high and low for your socks and passed you that trash in his very own, bejewelled, perfume-washed hands. Only then did you calm down, clutching it all day and all night; we couldn't get it off you. You must still have it all under your blanket somewhere. Then you started asking for some trouser ends – you were even in tears about it! What trouser ends, we asked, but we couldn't make head or tail of your answer . . . Well, no time to waste! Here's thirty-five roubles. I'm taking ten and I'll be back in a couple of hours to report on how I spent them. In the meantime I'll let Zosimov know, although he should've been here ages ago anyway – it's gone eleven. As for you, Nastyenka, look in more often while I'm gone, should the gentleman desire a drink or anything else . . . As for Pashenka, I'll speak to her myself right now. Goodbye!'

'Pashenka, he calls her! The sly mug!' said Nastasya as he walked out; then she opened the door to catch what they were saying, but she couldn't bear the suspense and ran downstairs. She was simply dying to know what he was saying to the landlady; and besides, it was obvious that Razumikhin had completely bewitched her.

Barely had she closed the door behind her when the patient threw off his blanket and, like a madman, leapt out of his bed. He'd been waiting for them to leave with a burning, convulsive impatience, so that he could get the thing done immediately. But what thing? He seemed to have forgotten, now of all times, as if on purpose. 'Lord! Just tell me this: do they already know everything or don't they? What if they do and they're just pretending, just teasing me while I'm lying here, before suddenly walking in and saying they've known about it all along and they were just . . . ? What is it I have to do? There, I've forgotten, as if on purpose; suddenly forgotten, remembered and forgotten!'

He was standing in the middle of the room and looking around in an agony of bewilderment; he went over to the door, opened it, strained his ears; but that wasn't it. Suddenly, as if remembering, he rushed over to the corner where there was a hole in the wallpaper, inspected everything, thrust a hand into the hole and rummaged about, but that wasn't it either. He went over to the stove, opened it and started rummaging in the ash: yes, the scraps of trouser ends and the shredded pocket were lying there just as he'd left them – so no one had looked! Then he remembered the sock Razumikhin had just been talking about. There it was on the couch, under the blanket, but it had got so dusty and filthy since then that Zametov, needless to say, couldn't have spotted a thing.

'Ha, Zametov! . . . The police bureau! . . . But why am I being called in to the bureau? Where's my summons? Ha! . . . I'm mixing everything up: that was then! Then I also inspected my sock, but now . . . now I've been ill. And why did Zametov drop in? Why did Razumikhin bring him here?' he muttered feebly, sitting back down on the couch. 'What's happening to me? Am I still raving or is this all for real? Real enough, it seems . . . Ah, I've remembered: run! Just run, quick, run! Yes . . . but where? And where are my clothes? My boots have gone! Taken away! Hidden! I get it! Ah, here's my coat – they missed that! And the money's on the table, thank God! And here's the promissory note . . . I'll take the money and go, rent another room, they won't track me down! . . . But what about the address bureau? They'll find me! Razumikhin will find me. I should run away completely . . . far away . . . to America and to hell with them! And take the promissory note . . . I'll find a use for it there. Anything else to take? They think I'm sick! They don't even know I can walk, heh-heh-heh! . . . I could tell by their eyes they know everything! Get down the stairs, that's the main thing! But what if they've put men on guard, police? What's this, tea? Look, there's some beer left too, half a bottle, cold!'

He grabbed the bottle in which there was still enough to fill a glass and drank it in one pleasurable gulp, as though quenching a fire in his chest. But less than a minute later the beer had gone to his head and a light, even pleasant shiver ran down his spine. He lay down and drew the blanket over himself. His thoughts, sick and random enough already, became more and more muddled, and a light, pleasant sleepiness soon enveloped him. Voluptuously seeking out a place on the pillow with his head, he wrapped himself up tight in the soft quilt, which had now taken the place of his old shredded greatcoat, gave a soft sigh and sank into deep, sound, restorative sleep.

He woke on hearing someone come in, opened his eyes and saw Razumikhin, who had flung the door wide open and was standing on the threshold, wondering whether or not to go in. Raskolnikov quickly sat up on the couch and looked at him, as though striving to remember something.

'So you're awake – well, here I am! Nastasya, bring in the bundle!' Razumikhin shouted down the stairs. 'Prepare to receive my full report . . .'

'What time is it?' asked Raskolnikov, anxiously looking around.

'You slept like a king: it's evening, must be about six. So you've been asleep a good six hours . . .'

'God! How could I?'

'Nonsense, it'll do you good! What's the hurry? No one's expecting you, are they? Our time's our own now. Three hours I've been waiting; dropped in a couple of times, but you were sleeping. I called on Zosimov twice: not in – that's all they tell me! Don't worry, he'll come! . . . Must be out and about on his own little errands. I moved today, you know, moved for good, with my uncle. I've an uncle now, you see . . . Well, no time to waste, damn it! . . . Pass me that bundle, Nastyenka. And now we'll . . . But tell me, brother, how are you feeling?'

'I'm fine. I'm not sick . . . Razumikhin, how long have you been here?'

'I told you – I've been waiting three hours.'

'I mean before?'

'Before what?'

'When did you start coming here?'

'But I explained all that earlier, or don't you remember?'

Raskolnikov became pensive. The recent past felt like a dream to him. He couldn't recall it on his own and fixed Razumikhin with a questioning look.

'H'm!' said the latter. 'He's forgotten! I thought before that perhaps you still weren't quite in your . . . But the sleep's done you good . . . Really, you look a new man. Good on you! Well, no time to waste! It'll all come back to you now. Have a look at this, dear chap.'

He started untying the bundle, whose contents clearly fascinated him.

'I can hardly tell you, brother, how much I've been wanting to do this. It's about time you looked the part. Right, we'll start at the top. See this little casquette?' he began, taking from the bundle a fairly decent, if perfectly ordinary, cheap cap. 'Shall we see if it fits?'

'Later, later,' said Raskolnikov, peevishly waving it away.

'No chance, Rodya, don't resist: later will be too late; and anyway I'll be awake all night worrying – I bought it without measuring, by guess and by God. Perfect!' he exclaimed triumphantly. 'Fits perfectly! Headgear, brother, is the alpha and omega of a man's attire, his calling card, if you like. Tolstyakov, a mate of mine, has to remove his lid every time he enters a public place, while everyone else is standing around in hats and caps. Everybody thinks it's the slave in him, but he's just ashamed of the basket on his head: he's far too bashful, that man! So, Nastyenka, I present to you two types of headgear: this old Palmerston'[16] (he reached into the corner for Raskolnikov's mangled round hat, which for some reason he called a Palmerston) 'or this intricate piece of work? How much do you think I paid, Rodya? Nastasyushka?' he turned to her, getting no response from Raskolnikov.

'Maybe twenty copecks,' Nastasya replied.

'You silly girl!' he shouted, taking offence. 'Even you would fetch more than twenty copecks nowadays! Eighty copecks! And even then only because it's worn. It comes with a guarantee, mind you: wear this one out and you'll get another for free next year, by heaven! And now, sir, for the United American States, as we used to call them at school. Be warned – I'm proud of them!' – and he laid out before Raskolnikov a pair of grey summer trousers made of a light woollen material. 'No holes, no stains, perfectly acceptable, albeit a bit worn. Likewise the waistcoat, all one colour, as fashion dictates. And there's nothing wrong with second-hand: it's softer, smoother ... You see, Rodya, in order to make your way in the world it's enough, in my opinion, to observe the season at all times: don't buy asparagus in January and you'll save yourself a few roubles. Well, the same principle applies here. Now it's summer, so I've made a summer purchase; autumn calls for something warmer, I believe, so you'll have to throw them out anyway ... especially as all this will have fallen to pieces by then, if not from a natural increase in splendour, then from internal contradictions. Well, have a guess! How much? Two roubles twenty-five copecks! And with the same guarantee: wear these out and get others for free next year. At Fedyayev's the terms are always the same: pay once and you'll never pay again, 'cause you'll never want to go back. And now, sir, the boots – well? You can see they're worn, but they'll do for a month or two, seeing as it's foreign handiwork and foreign goods: a secretary at the British embassy flogged them at the flea market last week; he'd only worn them six days, but he needed the cash. Price: one rouble fifty copecks. A good deal?'

'What if they don't fit?' Nastasya remarked.

'Don't fit! So what's this?' – and he pulled from his pocket one of Raskolnikov's old, tough boots, all torn and caked in dirt. 'I went well-prepared and they used this monstrosity to establish the size. No effort spared. As for linen, your landlady and I cut a deal there. Take these for starters: three shirts – made of sackcloth, I admit, but with fashionable collars . . . To sum up, then: peaked cap eighty copecks, other garments two roubles twenty-five, making three roubles five copecks; one rouble fifty for the boots – because they're truly outstanding – making four roubles fifty-five copecks; add five roubles for all the linen – it was cheaper in bulk – and you have a grand total of nine roubles fifty-five copecks precisely. Forty-five copecks change, all in coppers. Do take them, sir. And thus, dear Rodya, your wardrobe is complete, because in my view your coat is not merely still serviceable, it even has a particular nobility about it: that's what comes of ordering from Charmeur's![17] Socks and everything else I leave to you. We still have twenty-five roubles, and don't you worry about Pashenka and paying for the room. As I said, you've got credit on tap. And now, brother, allow me to change your linen for you, because it wouldn't surprise me if the only place where your illness still lingers is your shirt . . .'

'Leave me alone! Don't!' Raskolnikov remonstrated, repelled by the strained, bantering tone of Razumikhin's communiqué about his purchases . . .

'Nothing doing, brother. I mean, what have I been wearing out my soles for?' Razumikhin insisted. 'Nastasyushka, don't be shy and give us a hand. That's it!' – and for all Raskolnikov's resistance, he changed his linen. Raskolnikov fell back onto the pillows and said not a word for a whole two minutes.

'How long will they pester me?' he thought. 'And where did you find the money for all this?' he asked at long last, staring at the wall.

'The money? I'll be damned! It's your own. Some messenger came by earlier, from Vakhrushin, sent by your mama; or have you forgotten that too?'

'I remember now . . . ,' said Raskolnikov, after a period of long, sullen reflection. Razumikhin looked at him uneasily, frowning.

The door opened and in walked a tall, thickset man, who also struck Raskolnikov as somehow familiar.

'Zosimov! At long last!' cried Razumikhin with joy.

IV

Zosimov was tall and fat, with a puffy, washed-out, smooth-shaven face, straight blond hair, glasses and a large gold ring on a puffy, fat finger. He was about twenty-seven years old. He was dressed in a loose, foppish light coat and summery trousers; in fact, everything he wore was loose, foppish and brand new. His linen was immaculate and his watch chain massive. He had a ponderous manner, at once listless and studiedly casual; try as he might, he was unable to conceal his self-esteem. Everyone who knew him found him heavy-going, but agreed that he knew what he was about.

'I've been over to yours twice, brother . . . See: he's woken up!' Razumikhin cried.

'Yes, I see. So, how are we feeling now, eh?' Zosimov addressed Raskolnikov, studying him intently and sitting down next to him at the foot of the couch, where he spread himself out as best he could.

'He's still moping,' Razumikhin continued. 'We were just changing his linen and he almost burst into tears.'

'Quite understandable. The linen could have waited, if that's how he feels . . . A lovely pulse. Still a bit of headache though, eh?'

'I'm fine, absolutely fine!' Raskolnikov insisted irritably, suddenly propping himself up on the couch, eyes flashing, before immediately falling back onto the pillow and turning to face the wall. Zosimov was observing him intently.

'Very good . . . all as it should be,' he said listlessly. 'Eaten anything?'

He was told, then asked what he would recommend.

'Anything at all . . . Soup, tea . . . No mushrooms or gherkins, of course, nor beef for that matter, nor . . . but enough of this chit-chat!' He exchanged glances with Razumikhin. 'No medicine, nothing, and tomorrow I'll take a look . . . Today would have been fine, too . . . but anyway . . .'

'Tomorrow evening I'm taking him out on the town!' Razumikhin decided. 'The Yusupov Gardens, then the "Palais de Cristal"!'

'Personally, I wouldn't move him an inch tomorrow, although . . . a bit of . . . but anyway, we'll see.'

'What a pain – I'm having my house-warming today of all days, a stone's throw from here; he could have been there. At least he'd have lain near us on the couch! You'll be there, won't you?' Razumikhin suddenly asked Zosimov. 'Mind you don't forget now – you promised.'

'All right, but I might be late. What are you organizing?'

'Nothing special – tea, vodka, herring. There'll be a pie. Good friends only.'

'Who exactly?'

'People from around here, pretty much new faces actually – apart

from an old uncle, and he's new too: only arrived in Petersburg yesterday, on some errand or other; we see each other about once every five
years.'

'Who's he, then?'

'Vegetated all his life as a district postmaster ... tiny pension,
sixty-five years old, hardly worth mentioning ... But I love him. Porfiry Petrovich will come: he's the chief investigator at the police station here ... studied law.[18] But you know who I'm ...'

'Don't tell me he's another relative of yours?'

'As distant as they come. But why are you frowning? What, you fell
out with him once, so now you won't come?'

'To hell with him ...'

'Much the best way. Well, then there's some students, a teacher, a
civil servant, a musician, an officer, Zametov ...'

'Now tell me: what can you or, for that matter, he' – Zosimov nodded in the direction of Raskolnikov – 'possibly have in common with
some Zametov or other?'

'There's no pleasing some people! Principles! ... You stand on your
principles as if you're standing on springs. You wouldn't dare turn round
of your own free will. But he's a good chap – that's my principle, and
that's all I want to know. In fact, Zametov is a quite wonderful chap.'

'With a greasy palm.'

'What do I care? So what if it's greasy!' Razumikhin suddenly
shouted, more annoyed than might have seemed natural. 'Did I praise
him to you for his palm? I merely said that he's a good chap, in his
own way! I mean, if you start looking every which way how many
good people will we be left with? In that case I myself, entrails and
all, will fetch no more than a baked onion, and only if they throw you
into the bargain too!'

'Come come. I'll give two for you ...'

'And I'll only give one for you! Aren't you the wit? Zametov's just a
kid and I can still pull him up by his hair, because, you see, he needs
to be kept close. Keep a man at arm's length and you'll never fix him,
especially a kid. With kids you have to be twice as careful. Look at
you all, you progressive, clueless numbskulls! Respect other people
and you respect yourself ... But if you really want to know – well, it
looks like we're joining forces.'

'Do tell.'

'It's that business about the painter – the decorator, I mean ...

We'll save his bacon and no mistake! Though, actually, the danger's already passed. The whole thing could hardly be plainer! We'll just give it a gentle push.'

'Decorator – what decorator?'

'You mean I didn't tell you? No? Too right, I only started telling you . . . It's about the murder of that old pawnbroker, the civil servant's widow . . . Well, now a decorator's got himself mixed up in it all as well . . .'

'I heard about the murder even before you did, and I even became quite curious about it . . . as the result of a certain . . . and I read about it in the papers! But as for . . .'

'Lizaveta was killed, too, by the way!' Nastasya suddenly blurted out, addressing Raskolnikov. She'd been in the room all the while, pressed up against the door, listening.

'Lizaveta?' muttered Raskolnikov in a barely audible voice.

'You know, Lizaveta, the clothes-dealer. Used to come by downstairs. Even mended your shirt.'

Raskolnikov turned to the wall, with its dirty yellow paper and its pattern of little white flowers. He chose an ungainly white flower with little brown marks and started studying it: how many leaves did it have, what kind of notches were there on the leaves, and how many marks? He could feel his arms and legs going numb, as if paralysed, but he didn't even try to move them and stared stubbornly at the flower.

'So what about that decorator, then?' Zosimov broke in, extremely put out by Nastasya's nattering. She sighed and fell silent.

'He's a suspect, too!' Razumikhin went on excitedly.

'So there's evidence?'

'Evidence, my foot! Though you're right: evidence, but evidence which isn't evidence, that's what needs to be proved! Just like at the beginning when they dragged in those two as suspects – what were their names again . . . ? Oh yes, Kokh and Pestryakov. Ugh! The way they go about it is so stupid it's disgusting – even if you've got nothing to do with it! Actually, Pestryakov might come round to see me later . . . None of this is news to you, Rodya. It happened before you fell sick, the day before you fainted in the office, when they were talking about it there . . .'

Zosimov looked curiously at Raskolnikov; he didn't stir.

'Know what, Razumikhin? I look at you and think: what a busybody you are,' Zosimov remarked.

'Fine, but we'll still save his bacon,' cried Razumikhin, banging his fist on the table. 'I mean, what's the worst thing about all this? It's not that they're fibbing; fibs can always be forgiven; in fact, there's something nice about fibs – they lead to the truth. No, what's really infuriating is that they bow down to their own fibs. Porfiry's a man I respect, but . . . Just think: what was it that threw them off from the very start? The door's locked, back they come with the caretaker, and look, it's open: so it's Kokh and Pestryakov what done it! That's about the sum of their logic.'

'No need to get so worked up. They were simply detained. You can't . . . By the way: I've met this Kokh before. Turns out he used to buy up the old woman's overdue items – right?'

'Yes, the man's a swindler! Buys up promissory notes, too. A regular operator. To hell with him! You know what really makes me mad? Their routine, their senile, crass, ossified routine . . . Whereas here, just in this one case, there's a whole new approach waiting to be discovered. The psychological data alone are enough to point to the real trail. "We've got facts!" they say. But facts aren't everything; knowing how to deal with the facts is at least half the battle!'

'And do you know how to deal with them?'

'But you can't just keep silent when you feel – feel in your bones – that you could be of some help, if only . . . Ah! . . . Do you know all the details?'

'I'm still waiting to hear about the decorator.'

'So you are! Well, listen to this, then. Precisely two days after the murder, in the morning, when they were all still fussing around with Kokh and Pestryakov – even though they could account for their every step: it was blindingly obvious! – the most unexpected fact was suddenly announced. Some peasant, name of Dushkin – he runs the pothouse opposite that very same building – showed up at the bureau with a jewellery case containing some gold earrings and launched into a long story: "Evening-time, day before yesterday, eight o'clock or thereabouts" – date and time, see! – "this decorator comes running in – Mikolai's the name, he's already come to see me earlier that day – well, he runs in and brings us this 'ere box with gold earrings and stones, and wants to pawn it for two roubles, and when I ask him, 'Where d'you find 'em?' he says, 'Lying on the pavement.' I don't ask him no more about that" – this is Dushkin speaking – "and bring him a nice little note" – a rouble, that is – "thinking that if he don't pawn it with me he'll only find someone else, and it'll all go on booze anyway, so it were better off with me: hide and you will find, as they say, and if something comes out or people start talking, I'll bring it out and present it to 'em." Well, this is all just an old woman's dream, of course, and he's fibbing like a horse. I know this Dushkin: he's in the pawning business himself and hides stolen goods, and he didn't filch a thirty-rouble pledge from Mikolai in order to "present it". He got cold feet, simple as that. Anyway, listen to what Dushkin said next: "I've known this 'ere peasant, Mikolai Dementyev, since we were kids, same province, Ryazan,[19] same district, Zaraisk. And Mikolai ain't what you'd call a drunkard, but he likes a drink, and I knew for a fact he was working in that there house, decorating, him and Mitrei, the two of 'em being from the same parts. That rouble burned a hole in his pocket soon enough – he poured two vodkas down the hatch, one after the other, took the change and walked off, and there was no Mitrei with him then. Come the next day, what do I hear? Alyona Ivanovna and her sister, Lizaveta Ivanovna, murdered with an axe, and I knew 'em both, sir, and I fell to wond'ring about them earrings – seeing as I knew the deceased lent money for suchlike. So I goes to their home to learn what I can, without giving myself away, and the first thing I ask is: 'Where's Mikolai?' 'Gone on a bender,' says Mitrei. 'Got home at dawn, drunk as you like, stayed ten minutes and then he was off again,' and Mitrei ain't seen him since and he's finishing the job on his own. And that job of theirs is on the same staircase as the murdered women, second floor. When I heard all that, I didn't spill the beans to no one" – that's Dushkin speaking – "but found out all I could about the murder and came home still wond'ring. Then this morning, about eight o'clock" – that's two days after, understand? – "there's Mikolai coming through my door, not sober, nor blind-drunk neither, and capable of being spoken to. Sits down on a bench, says nothing. Hardly anyone else in the pothouse at that time – one stranger, one regular, sleeping on a bench, and our two boys. 'Seen Mitrei?' I ask. 'No,' he says. 'And you ain't been back here?' 'Not for two days,' he says. 'So where've you been sleeping?' 'Over at The Sands,'[20] he says, 'with our lot from Zaraisk.' 'And where d'you get the earrings, then?' I say. 'Found 'em on the pavement,' he says, as if that weren't bloody likely, and keeping his eyes down. 'Ain't you heard,' I say, 'that such-and-such a thing happened that same evening, that same time, that same staircase?' 'No,' he says, and he listens with eyes all a-goggle and pale as chalk. So I'm telling him all this when I see him take his cap and start getting up. I try to keep him, of course. 'Hang about, Mikolai,' I say, 'have one on me.' Meanwhile, I'm winking at the boy to watch the door and I'm coming out from behind the bar when he makes a bolt for it and vanishes down a lane, and that's the last I see of him. Well, that soon put an end to my wond'ring – his sin and no mistake . . ." '

'You don't say!' Zosimov put in.

'Wait! You haven't heard how it ended! Everyone goes tearing off to look for Mikolai, of course. Dushkin is detained and a search is made, and Mitrei, too. The Zaraisk lads get raked over the coals as well – and then suddenly, two days ago, Mikolai himself is brought in: he was detained near ——aya Gate, at the coaching inn. He'd showed up there, taken off his cross, a silver one, and asked for a double in exchange. Deal. A few minutes later a peasant woman went into the cowshed and, peering through a crack, saw him in the barn next door: he'd fixed his belt to a beam and made a noose. He got up on a block of wood and was just about to put his head through the noose, when the woman let out an almighty curse and everyone came running: "So that's what you're about!" "Just take me to police station X," he said. "I'll confess everything." Well, he was presented with great pomp at police station X – here, that is. The usual rigmarole: who, what, how old? – "twenty-two" – etcetera, etcetera. Question: "While you and Mitrei were working, didn't you see anyone on the stairs at such-and-such a time?" Answer: "There was some coming and going, true enough, but we paid no mind." "But didn't you hear anything, noises and so on?" "Nothing special." "And did you know, Mikolai, on that same day, that such-and-such a widow was murdered and robbed along with her sister on such-and-such a day, at such-and-such a time?" "Hadn't a clue. First I heard was from Dushkin two days later, in the pothouse." "And the earrings, where d'you get them?" "Found 'em on the pavement." "Why didn't you show up at work the next day with Mitrei?" "'Cause I went drinking." "And where were you drinking?" "Here and there." "Why d'you run away from Dushkin?" "'Cause I was dead scared." "What were you scared of?" "Getting done." "But how could you be scared of that, if you feel you've done nothing wrong?" Believe it or not, Zosimov, that was the question they put to him, in those same words. I know this for a fact, from a good source! Just incredible!'

'Come on now – there's evidence, after all.'

'It's not evidence I'm talking about, it's the question that bothers me, their understanding of what they're about! Well, to hell with it! . . . So they put the squeeze on him until he finally came out with it: "It weren't on the pavement I found 'em – it were in the digs me and Mitrei were painting." "How so?" "How so that me and Mitrei painted all day long, till eight o'clock, and we're about to leave when Mitrei takes a brush and smears my face with paint, smears it and scarpers, and I give chase. So there am I running after him, shouting and yelling, and between the stairs and the arch I run smack into the caretaker and some gentlemen, and how many gentlemen he had with 'im I don't recall, and the caretaker curses me, and t'other caretaker curses me, and the caretaker's missus comes out and she curses us, and some gentleman comes in under the arch, with a lady, and he curses us too, 'cause me and Mitka are in the way. I've got Mitka by the hair, on the deck, and start clobbering him, and from under me Mitka grabs my hair, too, and starts clobbering me, and we're not doing this nasty-like, but loving-like, playful-like. Then Mitka shakes me off and runs out onto the street and I give chase, but I don't catch him, and go back to the digs alone – to clear up. I start tidying and waiting for Mitrei in case he shows up, and that's when I step on the little box by the front door, behind the wall, in the corner. It were lying there just wrapped in paper. I took off the paper, saw some teeny-tiny hooks, took 'em off – and there were the earrings inside the case . . ." '

'Behind the door? Lying behind the door? Behind the door?' Raskolnikov suddenly cried, looking at Razumikhin with clouded, frightened eyes and slowly lifting himself up on the couch, leaning on one arm.

'Yes . . . and? What's wrong with you? What is it?' Razumikhin also half-rose from his seat.

'Nothing!' Raskolnikov replied barely audibly, sinking onto his pillow again and again turning to face the wall. For a while nobody spoke.

'He's dozed off – must have been half-asleep,' Razumikhin eventually remarked, looking inquiringly at Zosimov, who gave a faint shake of his head.

'Well, carry on then,' said Zosimov. 'What next?'

'What next, you ask? As soon as he clapped eyes on the earrings, he forgot all about the apartment, all about Mitka, grabbed his cap and ran off to Dushkin, took a rouble off him, as we know, made up a story about finding the things on the pavement, and immediately went off boozing. As for the murder, he repeats what he said before:

"Don't ask me, I only heard about it two days later." "So why's it taken you all this time to come forward?" "I was scared." "And why did you want to hang yourself?" "To stop thinking." "About what?" "Getting done." And that's the long and short of it. Now tell me, what do you think they made of that?'

'No need to think: there's a trail, not much of one, but a trail all the same. A fact's a fact. They can hardly let this decorator run free, can they?'

'But they've got him down as the murderer, for crying out loud! They don't even have any doubts about it any more . . .'

'Nonsense. You're overexcited. But what about the earrings? Falling out of the old woman's box into Mikolai's hands on that same day, at that same time – they must have got there somehow, don't you think? And that must mean something in an investigation like this.'

'Must have got there somehow?' cried Razumikhin. 'Can you not see – you, a doctor, whose duty first and foremost is to study man and who has more opportunities than anyone else to study human nature – can you not see, from all these facts, what kind of nature we have here, in this Mikolai of ours? Isn't it blindingly obvious that all the evidence he gave under interrogation was the sacred truth? The earrings got there just as he said they did. He stepped on a box and he picked it up!'

'The sacred truth! But you admitted yourself that he lied the first time round.'

'Listen to me and listen to me carefully: the caretaker, Kokh, Pestryakov, the other caretaker, the wife of the first caretaker, the tradeswoman who was sitting with her in the caretaker's lodge, the court counsellor Kryukov, who'd just got out of a cab and was walking under the arch arm in arm with a lady – all of them, all eight or ten witnesses, unanimously testify that Mikolai had pinned Mitrei to the ground, was lying on him and clobbering him, then Mitrei got hold of Mikolai's hair and started doing the same. They were lying across the path, blocking the way; they were being shouted at from all sides, but they, "like little boys" (the witnesses' precise words), were lying on top of one another, shrieking, fighting, the pair of them roaring with laughter and pulling the most hilarious faces and, just like children, chased each other out into the street. Got it? Now take note: the bodies upstairs were still warm when they found them – still warm, I'm telling you! If they were the ones who did it, or just Mikolai on his own, and they were the ones who forced and plundered the box as well, or took any part at all in the robbery, then let me ask you this: how does such a state of mind – squeals, belly laughter, play-fighting under the arch – tally with axes, blood, villainous cunning, wariness, robbery? Here they are, fresh from a murder all of five or ten minutes before – can't be otherwise if the bodies are still warm – and suddenly, abandoning both the bodies and the open apartment, and knowing that people had just gone up there, and abandoning the loot, they roll around like little boys on the path, roar with laughter and draw everyone's attention, with ten unanimous witnesses to confirm it!'

'Of course it's strange! Impossible, no doubt, but . . .'

'No, brother, no *buts*, and if the earrings which turned up in Mikolai's hands on the same day, at the same time, really do constitute an important factual argument against him – though one directly explained by his testimony, therefore still *open to question* – then one must also take into account the facts in his favour, the more so since these facts are *incontrovertible*. What do you think, given the way the law works here: will they accept or are they even able to accept a fact based on nothing more than mere psychological impossibility, on a mere state of mind, as incontrovertible, trumping all incriminating and material evidence, whatever that might be? No, they won't accept it, not for anything, because, you know, the box was found and the man wanted to hang himself, "which could never have happened had he not felt guilty!" This is the fundamental point, this is what I'm getting so worked up about! Can't you see that?'

'Yes, I can see you're getting worked up. Wait, I forgot to ask: what proof is there that the case with the earrings really does come from the old woman's box?'

'There's proof,' Razumikhin reluctantly replied, frowning. 'Kokh recognized it and identified the pawner, who confirmed that the item was definitely his.'

'Too bad. Another thing: didn't anyone see Mikolai while Kokh and Pestryakov were upstairs, and can't this somehow be proven?'

'That's just it – nobody saw them,' replied Razumikhin with vexation. 'That's the worst thing about it. Even Kokh and Pestryakov failed to notice them when they were going up, though their evidence wouldn't count for much now. "We saw that the apartment was open," they say, "and that there were probably works going on inside, but we paid no mind when we walked past and now we can hardly remember whether or not there were any workers in there at the time."'

FIVE133

'H'm. So all we have is the defence that they were clobbering each other and roaring with laughter. Granted, that's a strong argument, but still . . . a fact's a fact, and how do you explain the whole thing? How do you explain the discovery of the earrings, if he really did find them as he says he did?'

'How do I explain it? There's nothing to explain: it's crystal clear! Or at least the path that needs to be followed is clear and proven, and it's precisely the jewellery case that's proved it. The real murderer dropped those earrings. The murderer was upstairs when Kokh and Pestryakov were knocking. He'd locked himself in with the latch. Kokh stupidly went downstairs. At this point the murderer nipped out and also ran off down, because there was no other way out for him. On the stairs he hid from Kokh, Pestryakov and the caretaker in an empty apartment, at the precise moment when Mitrei and Mikolai had just run out of it, stood behind the door while the caretaker and the others were going up, waited for the footsteps to die away, then went down, calm as you like, at the very same moment that Mitrei and Mikolai ran out into the street, and everyone had gone off home, and there was no one left beneath the arch. He may have been seen, but he wasn't noticed; there are always plenty of people about. As for the case, it fell from his pocket while he was standing behind the door and he didn't notice he'd dropped it because he had other things on his mind. The jewellery case clearly proves he was standing there and nowhere else. And that's all there is to it!'

'Clever! Really, brother, that's very clever. Exceptionally clever!'

'What on earth do you mean?'

'Because it's far too tidy the way it all comes together . . . and falls into place . . . like in the theatre.'

'You really are . . . !' but Razumikhin was cut short by the door being opened, and a new person, known to none of those present, walked in.

<h1 style="text-align:center">V</h1>

Here was a gentleman whose youth was behind him, with a finicky, imposing air and a wary, querulous face, who began by pausing in the doorway and looking around in brazen astonishment, as if to ask: 'Where on earth have I ended up?' With a great show of mistrust and even alarm – almost as if he felt affronted – he surveyed Raskolnikov's poky, low-ceilinged 'ship's cabin'. With the same astonishment, he shifted his gaze to Raskolnikov himself, who, undressed, unkempt and unwashed, was lying on his wretched, filthy couch and returning his motionless scrutiny. Then, with the same deliberation, he set about scrutinizing the dishevelled, unshaven and uncombed person of Razumikhin, who stared straight back at him with quizzical insolence, not moving an inch. This tense silence lasted a minute or so, until eventually, as was only to be expected, there was a subtle change of mood. Presumably realizing – on the basis of evidence that could hardly be ignored – that here, in this 'ship's cabin', an attitude of exaggerated severity would get him nowhere, the gentleman softened somewhat and politely, if still severely, turned to Zosimov, clearly enunciating every syllable of his question:

'Mr Rodion Romanovich Raskolnikov, the student or former student?'

Zosimov slowly stirred and might even have replied, had not Razumikhin, whose opinion nobody was seeking, leapt in first:

'There he is, lying on the couch!! What do you want?'

The familiar tone of this 'What do you want?' rocked the finicky gentleman back on his heels. He was even on the verge of turning in Razumikhin's direction, but managed to stop himself just in time and hurriedly turned back towards Zosimov.

'That's Raskolnikov!' mumbled Zosimov, nodding at the patient and then yawning; as he did so, he opened his mouth extraordinarily wide, keeping it in that position for an extraordinarily long time. Then he slowly reached into the pocket of his waistcoat, took out the most enormous bulging gold watch, lifted the lid, took a glance and just as slowly, just as lazily, put it back again.

All this time Raskolnikov had lain there in silence, on his back, gazing obstinately, if unthinkingly, at the new gentleman. His face, which he had now turned away from the intriguing flower on the wallpaper, was exceptionally pale and expressed extraordinary suffering, as though he'd just undergone an excruciating operation or had just been released from torture. But little by little the new gentleman began to arouse ever greater interest in him, then bewilderment, then mistrust, and even something approaching fear. So when Zosimov pointed at him and said, 'That's Raskolnikov,' he all but leapt up in his bed, and in a voice that was almost defiant, if halting and weak, he said:

'Yes! I'm Raskolnikov! What do you want?'

The visitor looked at him attentively and uttered, self-importantly:

'Pyotr Petrovich Luzhin. I trust that my name is not entirely un-known to you.'

But Raskolnikov, who had been expecting something else entirely, looked at him dully and pensively and said nothing in reply, as if he really were hearing the name Pyotr Petrovich for the first time.

'I beg your pardon? You mean no one has told you anything?' asked Pyotr Petrovich, buckling slightly.

In reply, Raskolnikov slowly sank back onto his pillow, put his hands beneath his head and began staring at the ceiling. Luzhin could not hide his distress. Zosimov and Razumikhin set about inspecting him with still greater curiosity, until in the end he became visibly em-barrassed.

'I had assumed and expected,' he began in a mumble, 'that the letter dispatched a good ten days ago now, in fact almost two weeks ago . . .'

'Listen, there's really no need for you to stand by the door,' Razu-mikhin suddenly broke in. 'If you've got something to say, then have a seat – you and Nastasya look squashed over there. Nastasyushka, budge over and let him through! Come over here, there's a chair for you! Go on, wriggle through!'

He moved his chair back from the table, freed up some space be-tween the table and his knees, and waited in a rather strained pose for the visitor to 'wriggle through' the small gap. He had chosen his mo-ment in such a way that refusal was out of the question, and the visi-tor hastily stumbled through the narrow space. Reaching the chair, he sat down and glanced suspiciously at Razumikhin.

'No need to be embarrassed,' blurted the latter. 'Rodya's been sick for five days now and raving for three, but he's come round and he's even got his appetite back. This chap here is his doctor, he's just ex-amined him, while I'm a friend of Rodya's, also an ex-student, and now here I am nursing him. So feel free to ignore us, don't be shy, and tell us what you're after.'

'I thank you. But will I not disturb the patient with my presence and conversation?' asked Pyotr Petrovich, turning to Zosimov.

'No, no,' mumbled Zosimov, 'you might even take his mind off things' – then gave another yawn.

'Oh, he came to this morning!' continued Razumikhin, whose fa-miliar tone sounded so artlessly sincere that Pyotr Petrovich took stock and even cheered up a bit, perhaps also because this insolent tramp had at last got round to introducing himself as a student.

'Your mama . . . ,' began Luzhin.

'H'm!' grunted Razumikhin loudly. Luzhin looked at him inquiringly.

'Oh nothing, nothing, ignore me . . .'

Luzhin shrugged.

'. . . Your mama, during the period while I was still present with her, began writing you a letter. On arriving here, I deliberately allowed several days to pass before coming to see you, in order to be entirely sure that you had received all the requisite information; but now, to my astonishment . . .'

'I know, I know!' Raskolnikov suddenly said, anger bursting from his face. 'And that's you? The fiancé? Well, I know! Enough said!'

Pyotr Petrovich was thoroughly offended, but bit his tongue. He was desperately trying to grasp the meaning of it all. The silence lasted for about a minute.

Meanwhile Raskolnikov, having half-turned in his direction to reply, suddenly set about studying him again with a particular curiosity, as if he hadn't finished doing so before or had been struck by something new in him: he even lifted himself up off his pillow for the purpose. Yes, there really did seem to be something striking about Pyotr Petrovich's general appearance, or more precisely, something that seemed to justify the title of 'fiancé', which he had just been so unceremoniously awarded. To begin with, it was evident, and even all too noticeable, that Pyotr Petrovich had hastened to exploit every opportunity offered by several days in the capital to array and groom himself in readiness for his betrothed, though, of course, one could hardly blame him. Even his own, perhaps excessively smug awareness of his gratifying change for the better might have been forgiven in the circumstances, for Pyotr Petrovich was on the path to the altar. Everything he wore was fresh from the tailor's, and it was all quite splendid, but for one thing – it was all too new and betrayed all too clearly its unmistakable purpose. Even his foppish, brand-new top hat attested to this purpose: there was something far too reverent and cautious in the way Pyotr Petrovich fingered it. Even his charming pair of genuine lilac Jouvin gloves[21] attested to the same, if only because such gloves were not for wearing, but for carrying in one's hands for show. Pyotr Petrovich's clothes, meanwhile, were dominated by light and youthful shades. He wore a smart summer jacket in beige, light-coloured summery trousers with matching waistcoat, newly purchased fine linen, a tie of the very lightest cambric with pink stripes, and best of all, this actually suited Pyotr Petrovich – not to mention the fact that his very fresh, even handsome face looked younger than his forty-five years. His dark whiskers cast pleasant shadows on both sides, like two mutton chops, and thickened ever so nicely around his shiny, clean-shaven chin. Even his hair, only barely touched with grey, all combed and curled at the barber's, did not thereby look in any way ridiculous or foolish, as always seems to happen with curled hair, which gives the face an inescapable resemblance to a German making his way up the aisle. If there really was anything genuinely unpleasant and repellent about this fairly handsome and respectable physiognomy, the cause lay elsewhere. After subjecting Mr Luzhin to unceremonious scrutiny, Raskolnikov flashed a venomous smile, sank back once more onto his pillow and resumed his inspection of the ceiling.

Mr Luzhin gritted his teeth, having apparently decided to turn a blind eye, for the time being, to these various eccentricities.

'I am most terribly, terribly sorry to find you in such a plight,' he began once more, breaking the silence with some difficulty. 'Had I but known of your infirmity, I would have called earlier. Alas, you know, I'm rushed off my feet! I have, furthermore, a terribly important case in the Senate in my legal capacity. And that's without even mentioning those concerns about which you, too, can guess. I am expecting your dear family – your mama and sister – at any moment . . .'

Raskolnikov stirred and was on the verge of saying something; his face expressed a certain agitation. Pyotr Petrovich paused and waited, but when nothing followed he continued:

'. . . at any moment. I have found them an apartment in the first instance . . .'

'Where?' asked Raskolnikov, weakly.

'Exceedingly close by, Bakaleyev's house . . .'

'That's on Voznesensky,' Razumikhin broke in. 'Two floors of rented rooms. Yushin, the merchant, lets them out. I've been there.'

'That's right, sir . . .'

'An unbelievably sordid place: filthy, stinking and generally disreputable; all sorts of things have happened there and you never know who you might meet! I went there too, once, on some disgraceful business or other. It's cheap, mind.'

'Naturally I was unable to gather so much intelligence, being new here myself,' came Pyotr Petrovich's prickly riposte, 'but they are two perfectly, perfectly clean little rooms, and since this is only for a terribly brief period of time . . . I have already found our real – I mean, future – lodgings,' he continued, addressing Raskolnikov, 'which are being done up as we speak. For the time being I myself have to make do in cramped lodgings a stone's throw from here, at Mrs Lippewechsel's, in the apartment of a young friend of mine, Andrei Semyonovich Lebezyatnikov. It was he who suggested Bakaleyev's house to me . . .'

'Lebezyatnikov?' drawled Raskolnikov, as if reminded of something.

'Yes, Andrei Semyonych Lebezyatnikov, works in one of the ministries. Are you acquainted?'

'Er . . . no . . . ,' replied Raskolnikov.

'I beg your pardon. Your question gave me the impression you were. I was once his guardian . . . A very nice young man . . . and well-informed . . . I like meeting the young: there's no better way of keeping up to date,' said Pyotr Petrovich, casting a hopeful glance around the assembled company.

'In what sense exactly?' asked Razumikhin.

'The most serious. The very heart of the matter, as it were,' replied Pyotr Petrovich, as if glad to be asked. 'You see, I haven't visited Petersburg for a full ten years. All these novelties of ours, reforms, ideas – we haven't remained untouched by them in the provinces either; but in order to have a clearer and more complete view of things, one has to be in Petersburg. So, sir, my opinion is this: that it is by observing our young generations that one notices and learns the most. And I'll admit: I was pleased . . .'

'By what exactly?'

'Your question is a very broad one. I may be mistaken, but I seem to find greater clarity of vision, more criticism, as it were; more doers . . .'

'True enough,' muttered Zosimov.

'You're lying. There are no doers,' Razumikhin leapt in. 'Doers don't just fall from the sky – it takes effort. And we've got used to not doing anything for nigh on two hundred years . . . There may be ideas in the air, I'll grant you that,' he said, turning to Pyotr Petrovich, 'and a desire to do good, however childish; and there's even some honesty about, despite the fact that nowadays we're up to our necks in swindlers, but there's still no sign of any doers! You'd spot them a mile off.'

'I simply cannot agree with you,' objected Pyotr Petrovich, with evident delight. 'Naturally there are excesses, irregularities, but one must also be charitable: the excesses are testimony to a fervour for getting things done and to the irregularities by which that task is surrounded. Little has been done, you might say – but there has been little time to do it in. I say nothing about the means. My own personal view, if you please, is that something has, in fact, been done: the spread of new, useful thoughts, the spread of certain new, useful literary works instead of the previous dreaminess and romanticism; literature is acquiring a riper hue; many pernicious prejudices are being stamped out and ridiculed ... In short, we have cut ourselves off irrevocably from the past, and this, to my mind, shows that something really is being done ...'

'He knows his lines!' said Raskolnikov suddenly.

'I'm sorry?' asked Pyotr Petrovich, unsure of what had been said. He received no reply.

'All perfectly reasonable,' Zosimov hastened to put in.

'Isn't it, though?' Pyotr Petrovich went on, glancing with satisfaction at Zosimov. 'Wouldn't you agree,' he continued, addressing Razumikhin, but with a new, triumphant note of superiority, to the point that he very nearly added 'young man', 'that prosperity, or progress, as it is now called, does exist, at least in the name of science and economic truth ... ?'

'A cliché!'

'No, not a cliché, sir! If hitherto, for example, I have been told to "love my neighbour" and I have done so, then what was the result?' Pyotr Petrovich continued, perhaps a little too hastily. 'The result was that I ripped my sheepskin in two, shared it with my neighbour and we both ended up half-naked, according to the Russian proverb, "Go after several hares at once and you won't reach a single one."[22] But science says: love yourself before loving anyone else, for everything in this world is founded on self-interest. Love yourself and your affairs will take care of themselves, and your coat will remain in one piece. Economic truth adds to this that the more people there are in society whose private affairs are well arranged, and the more sheepskins, as it were, that remain in one piece, the firmer are society's foundations and the better it will arrange its common task. Consequently, it is precisely by profiting myself and no one else that I thereby profit everyone, as it were, and enable my neighbour to receive something more than a ripped coat, and not by way of private, isolated acts of charity, as in the past, but as a result of universal prosperity. A simple thought, but one which has taken a regrettably long time to occur, obscured by enthusiasm and dreaminess, though it would hardly seem beyond the wit of man to guess . . .'

'I'm sorry, but I'm no great wit myself,' Razumikhin abruptly interrupted, 'so let's stop there. I piped up for a reason: for three years now I've been listening to all this talk and self-amusement, all these endless clichés, one after the other, over and over again, and I'm so damned sick of them that I blush to hear other people, never mind me, trotting them out. Naturally, you were desperate to flaunt your knowledge, and that can be easily forgiven on first acquaintance – I don't judge you for it. All I was trying to do was find out what kind of a man you are, because recently, you see, that "common task" has attracted such a motley crew of operators, ruining whatever they touch for their personal gain, that the whole thing stinks. Enough said, sir!'

'My good sir,' Mr Luzhin began, positively quivering with self-worth, 'surely you are not suggesting, so very unceremoniously, that I too . . . ?'

'Come come . . . How could I? . . . Enough said, sir!' snapped Razumikhin, before turning sharply towards Zosimov to resume their earlier conversation.

Pyotr Petrovich had the good sense to believe these words without hesitation. All the same, he had made up his mind to leave within the next two minutes.

'I trust that our newly initiated acquaintance,' he addressed Raskolnikov, 'will, after your recovery and in the light of the circumstances known to you, grow stronger still . . . Above all, I wish you good health . . .'

Raskolnikov did not even turn his head. Pyotr Petrovich began getting up from his chair.

'The murderer must have been one of her pawners!' Zosimov asserted.

'Must have been!' Razumikhin echoed. 'Porfiry gives nothing away, but we know he's interrogating the pawners . . .'

'Interrogating the pawners?' Raskolnikov asked loudly.

'Yes, and?'

'Nothing.'

'How does he find them?' asked Zosimov.

'Kokh put him on to some of them. The names of others were written on the paper their items were wrapped in, and some just came along themselves when they heard . . .'

'What a crafty, experienced little scoundrel! So daring! So bold!'

'That's exactly what he isn't!' Razumikhin interrupted. 'And that's exactly what trips you all up. He's neither crafty nor experienced, and I'll bet you this was his first time! Assume some calculating, crafty little scoundrel, and it hardly seems credible. Assume someone inexperienced and it seems like only chance could have saved him from disaster, and chance can do anything, can it not? He probably didn't anticipate a single obstacle! Just look how he went about it – grabbing ten- or twenty-rouble items, stuffing his pockets with them, rummaging about in the old woman's box, among the rags – and meanwhile, over in the chest of drawers, in a box in the top drawer, they found one and a half thousand in ready cash, excluding notes! He didn't even know how to rob – only to kill! His first time, I tell you, his first time. He lost his nerve! It was chance, not design, that saved him!'

'This has to do with the recent murder of that civil servant's old widow, I assume,' Pyotr Petrovich put in, addressing Zosimov. He was already on his feet, hat and gloves in hand, but he didn't want to leave without making a few more clever remarks. He was clearly anxious to make a favourable impression, and vanity prevailed over good sense.

'So you've heard?'

'How could I not, living so close . . . ?'

'Do you know the details?'

'I cannot say, but what concerns me here is something else, the problem in the round, as it were. Leaving aside the fact that crime among the lower classes has been on the rise during the last five years or so, leaving aside the ubiquitous and never-ending robberies and fires, what I find strangest of all is the fact that crime among the upper classes is on the rise in just the same way and, as it were, in parallel. First you hear that a former student robbed a mail coach on the high road; next, that people at the very forefront of society are counterfeiting banknotes; then, in Moscow, an entire gang is caught forging tickets for the latest lottery – with a lecturer in world history among the ringleaders; while abroad, one of our diplomatic secretaries is murdered[23] for financial reasons that remain obscure . . . And now, if this old moneylender has been murdered by one of her pawners, then he, too, must be a member of higher society – for peasants do not pawn their gold – so how can we explain this laxity, as it were, of the civilized part of our society?'

'All these economic changes . . . ,' responded Zosimov.

'How can we explain it?' asked Razumikhin, seizing on his words. 'I'll tell you how: by our inveterate shortage of doers.'

'I don't follow, sir.'

'Well, what did that lecturer of yours in Moscow have to say for himself when he was asked why he forged tickets: "Everyone's getting rich one way or another, so I wanted to make a quick fortune myself." I've forgotten his exact words, but that was the gist: money for nothing, quick, without breaking sweat! We're used to having everything laid on for us, to our leading-strings, to our food being chewed for us. But when the great hour struck,[24] everyone showed their true colours . . .'

'But what about morality? And, as it were, rules . . . ?'

'Why this great fuss?' Raskolnikov suddenly broke in. 'That was your theory in action!'

'What do you mean, my theory?'

'Take what you were preaching just now to its conclusions, and bumping people off is perfectly acceptable . . .'

'For heaven's sake!' cried Luzhin.

'No, that's wrong!' Zosimov put in.

Raskolnikov lay pale-faced, his upper lip twitching, breathing heavily.

'One must observe moderation in all things,' continued Luzhin, superciliously. 'The economic idea is hardly an invitation to murder, and it is enough to assume . . .'

'So is it true that you,' Raskolnikov cut in again, in a voice trembling with anger and reverberating with a kind of injured joy, 'is it true that you told your intended . . . the moment you received her consent . . . that what pleased you most of all . . . was her beggarly condition . . . because there is much to be said for taking a wife out of beggary, the better to rule over her later . . . and to reproach her with the favour you bestow?'

'My good sir!' cried Luzhin, with anger and irritation, all flushed and flustered. 'My good sir! . . . What a way to twist my words! Forgive me, but I must make it clear to you that the rumours that have come to your attention, or rather, that have been brought to your attention, are devoid of any sound foundation, and I . . . have an inkling as to who . . . in a word . . . this dart . . . in a word, your mama . . . She struck me even before as having, for all her outstanding qualities, a slightly over-enthusiastic and romantic cast of mind . . . But still, I was a million miles from presuming that she might apprehend and present the matter in a light so distorted by fantasy . . . And finally . . . finally . . .'

'Well, do you know what?' cried Raskolnikov, propping himself up on the pillow and fixing him with piercing, flashing eyes. 'Do you know what?'

'What, sir?' Luzhin paused, waiting with an offended and defiant air. The silence lasted a few seconds.

'If you dare utter . . . another word, ever again . . . about my mother . . . I'll send you flying down the stairs!'

'What's wrong with you?' shouted Razumikhin.

'So that's how it is!' said Luzhin, turning pale and biting his lip. 'Now listen to me, sir,' he began slowly and deliberately, restraining himself as best he could, but still gasping for breath. 'I discerned your animosity the moment I walked in, but I remained here on purpose, so as to find out more. There is much that I might have forgiven a sick man and a relative, but you . . . now . . . never, sir . . .'

'I'm not sick!' cried Raskolnikov.

'All the more reason . . .'

'Clear off, damn you!'

But Luzhin, without finishing what he wanted to say, was already wriggling his way out between the table and the chair; and this time, Razumikhin got up to let him through. Without glancing at anyone or even nodding in the direction of Zosimov, who had long been nodding at him to leave the sick man in peace, Luzhin went out, taking care to raise his hat to the level of his shoulder as he ducked beneath the door-frame. Even the curve of his back seemed to suggest that he was bearing away with him some deadly insult.

'How could you? Really, how could you?' Razumikhin asked in bewilderment, shaking his head.

'Leave me alone, all of you!' Raskolnikov cried in sheer frenzy. 'Can't you just leave me alone and stop tormenting me! I'm not scared of you! I'm not scared of anyone now, anyone! Get away from me! I want to be alone! Alone! Alone!'

'Let's go!' said Zosimov, nodding to Razumikhin.

'We can hardly leave him like this, for heaven's sake.'

'Let's go!' Zosimov insisted and walked out. Razumikhin thought for a moment, then ran out after him.

'It could have been even worse if we hadn't obeyed him,' said Zosimov, once they were out on the stairs. 'We mustn't irritate him . . .'

'What's wrong with him?'

'If only he could be given a beneficial shock of some kind . . . that would do it! He seemed to have picked up, earlier on . . . You know, there's something on his mind! Something immovable, something oppressing him . . . That's what scares me. Yes, that's it!'

'Perhaps it's this gentleman, this Pyotr Petrovich! It was clear from the conversation that he's marrying his sister and that Rodya received a letter about it just before he got ill . . .'

'Yes, the devil himself must have brought him here now. He may have spoiled the whole thing. By the way, did you notice how indifferent he is to everything? You can't get a word out of him, with one exception that completely unhinges him: that murder . . .'

'Yes, yes!' Razumikhin agreed. 'Too right I did! It interests him, frightens him. He got a fright the same day he fell ill, in the bureau, with the district superintendent; even fainted.'

'Tell me more this evening, then I'll tell you something. He interests me, he really does! I'll drop by in half an hour to check up on him . . . But it's not an inflammation . . .'

'Thanks! In the meantime I'll be waiting at Pashenka's, keeping an eye on things through Nastasya . . .'

Raskolnikov, left alone, shot an impatient, pained glance at Nastasya; but she was in no hurry to leave.

'P'haps you'll have some tea now?' she asked.

'Later! I want to sleep! Leave me . . .'

With a violent jerk, he turned to face the wall; Nastasya went out.

VI

But no sooner had she gone out than he got up, hooked the door, untied the bundle of clothes which Razumikhin had brought round earlier and then tied it up again, and started getting dressed. Strange: he seemed, all of a sudden, to have become perfectly calm; gone was the demented raving of before and the panicky terror of this whole recent time. This was the first instant of some strange, sudden tranquillity. His movements were precise and well-defined; a firm intention showed through them. 'Today, yes, today!' he muttered to himself. He understood, however, that he was still weak, but the most intense mental strain, having reached the point of tranquillity, of obsession, now gave him strength and confidence; even so, he hoped he wouldn't collapse in the street. All dressed up in his new things, he glanced at the money lying on the table, thought for a moment and pocketed it. Twenty-five roubles in total. He also took all the five-copeck pieces – the change from the ten roubles Razumikhin had spent on the clothes. Next, he quietly lifted the hook, left the room, went down the stairs and peeked through the wide-open door of the kitchen: Nastasya, standing with her back to him, was bending over and fanning the landlady's samovar. She didn't hear a thing. Anyway, who could have imagined that he might go out? A minute later he was already in the street.

It was about eight o'clock. The sun was going down. It was as stifling as before, but he hungrily breathed in this stinking, dusty, town-poisoned air. He felt his head begin to spin. His inflamed eyes and wasted, pallid-yellow face suddenly shone with some wild energy. He didn't know where he was going, and hadn't even given it a thought. He knew one thing only: 'All this has to end today, in one go, right now.' He wouldn't go home otherwise, because *he didn't want to live like this*. End how? By what means? He had no idea, no wish even to think about it. He chased away thought: thought tormented him. He merely felt and knew that everything had to change, one way or another. 'Any way will do,' he kept repeating, with desperate, immovable confidence and resolve.

By old habit, following the route he usually took on his walks, he made straight for Haymarket. Just before Haymarket, standing in the road in front of a general shop, was a young, raven-haired organ-grinder, turning out a heartfelt song. He was accompanying a girl standing before him on the pavement, aged fifteen or so and dressed up like a lady, wearing a crinoline, a cape, gloves and a straw hat with a feather the colour of fire, all old and worn. Her voice was cracked – the voice of a street singer – but pleasant and strong, and she was hoping for a copeck or two from the shop. Raskolnikov stopped for a moment to listen with a few others, took out a five-copeck piece and placed it in the girl's hand. She suddenly cut off her singing, as if with a knife, on the most heartfelt and high-pitched note, snapped 'Enough!' to the organ-grinder, and they shuffled off to the next shop.

'Do you like street singing?' Raskolnikov suddenly asked a passer-by, no longer young, who was standing next to him near the barrel organ and had the look of a flâneur. The latter stared at him in wild astonishment. 'I do,' Raskolnikov went on, but it was as if he were talking about something else entirely. 'I like songs sung to a barrel

organ on cold, dark, damp autumn evenings – dampness is a must –
when the faces of all the passers-by are pale, green and sick; or, even
better, when wet snow is falling down in a straight line, with no wind
at all (you know?) and the gas lamps shine through it . . .'

'I'm afraid I don't know, sir . . . ,' muttered the gentleman, frightened both by the question and by Raskolnikov's strange appearance,
and crossed to the other side of the street.

Raskolnikov continued on his way and reached the corner of Haymarket, where the tradesman and his wife, who had been talking to
Lizaveta that time, sold their goods; but they weren't there now. Recognizing the spot, he stopped, looked around and turned to a young
lad in a red shirt who was yawning by the entrance to a flour shop.

'There's a tradesman selling here on the corner, isn't there, with his
missus, his wife?'

'There's all sorts selling,' the lad replied, disdainfully looking him
up and down.

'What's his name?'

'The one he was christened with.'

'Don't tell me you're from Zaraisk, too? Your province?'

The lad took another look at Raskolnikov.

'Ours is a district, Your Excellency, not a province, and anyway
I'm far too provincial to know, sir . . . Do forgive me, Your Excellency, most graciously.'

'Is that an eating-house, up there?'

'That's a tavern, with billiards, too, and princesses,[25] come to
that . . . Ding dong!'

Raskolnikov crossed the square. There, in the corner, stood a
throng of people, all of them peasants. He made straight for the thick
of it, peering into faces. He had a strange urge to talk to everyone he
met. But the peasants paid him no attention, keeping up a constant
hubbub in their little groups. He stood for a while, pondered, and set
off to the right, along the pavement, in the direction of V——y.[26]
Leaving the square behind, he found himself in a lane . . .

Previously, too, he had often taken this short little lane,[27] which
made a dog-leg from the square to Sadovaya Street. Recently he'd even
felt the urge, whenever he felt sick, to wander around this part of
town, 'so as to feel even sicker'. Now he entered it without a thought
in his head. There's a large house here, entirely given over to drinking
dens and cheap restaurants; women run in and out, dressed as if 'to

go next door' – bare-headed, in simple frocks. They gather in bunches on the pavement, usually wherever a couple of steps lead down to various, very cheerful establishments on the lower floor. The racket coming from one of these at that moment could be heard from one end of the street to the other – a guitar was being strummed, songs were being sung and it was all very jolly. The entrance was thronged with a large group of women; some sat on the steps or the pavement, others stood and chatted. Nearby, on the road, a drunken soldier was sauntering along, smoking a papirosa and swearing loudly; he looked like he wanted to go in somewhere, only he'd forgotten where. Two tramps were having a row and someone else was sprawled, dead drunk, across the street. Raskolnikov stopped near the gaggle of women. They were chatting away in croaky voices; all wore cotton-print dresses and goatskin shoes, their heads uncovered. Some were over forty, others only seventeen or so; almost all had black eyes.

He was intrigued for some reason by the singing down below, and all that noise . . . He could hear, amid the laughter and the shrieks, someone dancing for dear life to the rollicking strains of a thin falsetto and to the strumming of a guitar, beating out the rhythm with his heels. He listened intently, dismally, pensively, stooping by the entrance and peering in.

> Please, my 'ansome bobby
> T'ain't no need to beat me!

sang the thin little voice. Raskolnikov was desperate to make out the words, as if they really were the key to it all.

'Perhaps I should go in?' he wondered. 'Listen to them laugh! Must be the drink. Well, why don't I get drunk too?'

'Won't you come in, kind master?' asked one of the women in a voice that still carried and was not yet completely hoarse. She was young and not even repulsive – unlike the rest of the group.

'Well you're a nice one!' he replied, straightening up to look at her.

She smiled, delighted by the compliment.

'You're very nice yourself, sir,' she said.

'He's skin and bones!' remarked another in a deep voice. 'Straight out of hospital, I suppose?'

'Generals' daughters and all sorts, but they've all got snub noses!' interrupted a peasant who'd suddenly approached, three sheets to the

wind, his thick coat open and his mug wrinkled up with sly laughter.
'Well this is fun!'

'Go in, since you've come!'

'Try stopping me!'

And he tumbled in.

Raskolnikov went on his way.

'Listen, master!' the girl shouted after him.

'What?'

She became embarrassed.

'Kind master, I'll always be glad to pass some time with you, but
here I am before you and I'm simply burning with shame. Won't you
spare me six copecks for a drink, my lovely?'

Raskolnikov fished out all he had: fifteen copecks.

'Oh, what a nice sweet master!'

'What's your name?'

'Just ask for Duklida.'

'Well, that's really something,' someone in the group suddenly remarked, shaking her head at Duklida. 'Search me how you can ask
like that! I'd die from the shame of it . . .'

Raskolnikov looked curiously at the speaker. She was a pockmarked
girl of about thirty, covered in bruises, with a fat lip. She made her
criticisms calmly and seriously.

'Where was it?' thought Raskolnikov, walking on. 'Where was it
I read how a man sentenced to death, an hour before he was due to
die, said or thought that if he were obliged to live somewhere very
high up, on a cliff, on a ledge with room for a pair of feet and nothing
more, while all around him were chasms, the ocean, eternal gloom,
eternal solitude and eternal tempest, and he had to stay like that,
standing on one square yard, for the rest of his life, for a thousand
years, for eternity – then he'd rather live like that than die there and
then? To live, to live, to live! No matter how – just live![28] There's truth
in that! Lord, what truth! Man is a scoundrel! And a scoundrel is he
who calls him a scoundrel,' he added a minute later.

He entered another street: 'Ha! The "Crystal Palace"! Razumikhin
was talking about the "Crystal Palace"[29] just earlier. Only, what was
it I wanted? Oh yes, to read! . . . Zosimov was saying that he'd read in
the papers . . .

'Any papers?' he asked, entering an extremely spacious, even salu-
brious tavern, which had several rooms and few customers. Two or

three were drinking tea, while in one of the far rooms there was a group of about four sitting around a table drinking champagne. Raskolnikov thought he saw Zametov among them. From a distance, though, it was hard to be sure.

'Well, so what?' he thought.

'Some vodka for you, sir?' asked a waiter.

'I'll have tea. Bring me some newspapers, too, old ones, for the last five days or so, and you'll get some drink money.'

'Yes, sir. Here are today's, sir. Some vodka with that, sir?'

The old papers arrived with the tea. Raskolnikov made himself comfortable and started searching: 'Izler – Izler – Aztecs – Aztecs – Izler – Bartola – Massimo – Aztecs – Izler[30] . . . damn it all! Ah, the titbits: woman falls from a landing – tradesman drinks himself to death – fire in Peski – fire on Petersburg Side – another fire on Petersburg Side – another fire on Petersburg Side – Izler – Izler – Izler – Izler – Massimo . . . Ah, here we are . . .'

He'd finally found what he was after and started reading; the lines seemed to jump about as he read, but he got to the end of the 'report' all the same and hungrily set about searching in subsequent issues for further additions. Flicking through them, his hands shook with convulsive impatience. Suddenly, someone sat down beside him at his table. He glanced up – Zametov, the very same, and looking just the same, with his jewels, his chains, the parting in his curly and pomaded black hair, wearing a foppish waistcoat, a somewhat shabby frock coat and somewhat grimy linen. He was in a jolly mood, or at least he was smiling in a very jolly and good-natured way. His swarthy face was a little flushed from champagne.

'What! You – here?' he began in bewilderment and in a tone that suggested a lifetime's acquaintance. 'But Razumikhin told me only yesterday that you still hadn't come to. How strange! I visited you only . . .'

Raskolnikov knew he'd walk over. He set the newspapers aside and turned towards him. A grin played on his lips, betraying some kind of new, irritable impatience.

'I know you did, sir,' he replied. 'You were searching for my sock, I hear . . . Razumikhin's mad about you, says the two of you went to see Laviza Ivanovna, the one you were putting yourself out for that time and winking to Powder Keg about, but he didn't catch your drift, remember? Quite incredible, really – it was all plain as day, eh?'

'Now there's a loose cannon, if ever there was!'

'Who, the lieutenant?'

'No, your friend Razumikhin . . .'

'Some life you have, Mr Zametov. A free pass to all the nicest places! So who's been treating you to champagne?'

'We were just . . . having a drink . . . Treating me indeed!'

'Your fee, then! It's all grist to your mill!' Raskolnikov laughed. 'That's all right, my dear sweet boy, that's all right!' he added, giving Zametov a light punch on the shoulder. 'I didn't mean it unkindly, "but loving-like, playful-like", just like that worker of yours said when he was clobbering Mitka – you know, that business with the old crone.'

'And why should you know about that?'

'I may know more than you do.'

'You're acting rather strange . . . You must still be very sick. Should have stayed at home . . .'

'So I seem strange to you?'

'Yes. Are those newspapers you're reading?'

'Yes, newspapers.'

'There's been a lot about fires . . .'

'No, I'm not reading about fires.' He gave Zametov an enigmatic look; a derisive smile twisted his lips once more. 'No, I'm not reading about fires,' he went on with a wink. 'Just admit it, my nice young man – you're desperate to know what I was reading about, aren't you?'

'Not in the least. I merely asked. What's wrong with asking? Why are you so . . . ?'

'Listen, you're an educated, literary type, are you not?'

'Six years at the gymnasium,' Zametov replied with a certain pride.

'Six years! Ah, my dear little dicky bird! With his hair parted and jewels on his fingers – a man of means! Such a sweet young boy!' Here Raskolnikov broke into peals of nervous laughter right in Zametov's face. Zametov shrank back, not so much offended as deeply astonished.

'My, you're acting strange!' Zametov repeated very seriously. 'Seems to me you're still raving.'

'Raving? You're lying, my little dicky bird! . . . So I'm strange? All right, but I intrigue you, don't I? Don't I?'

'Yes, you do.'

'I mean, what was I reading about, what was I hunting for, eh? Just look how many back issues I made the waiter lug over! Suspicious, eh?'

'Tell me, then.'

'Hanging on my lips, eh?'

'Hanging where?'

'I'll explain later, but now, my dearest, I declare to you . . . no, better: "I confess" . . . No, still not right: "I testify and you record" – that's it! I testify, then, that I read, showed interest in . . . searched for . . . hunted for . . .' – Raskolnikov screwed up his eyes and paused – 'hunted for anything at all – which is why I've come here – relating to the murder of the civil servant's old widow,' he uttered finally, almost in a whisper, bringing his face exceptionally close to Zametov's. Zametov stared straight back at him, neither twitching nor flinching. Strangest of all, Zametov later thought, was the fact that the silence between them should have lasted for precisely one minute, and that they should have looked at one another like that for precisely one minute.

'So you were reading, so what?' he suddenly cried, in impatient bewilderment. 'Why should I care?'

'It's that same old woman,' Raskolnikov went on in the same whisper, without a twitch, 'the very same one, remember, who you started talking about in the bureau when I fainted. Understand now?'

'What are you on about? Understand what?' asked Zametov, in near panic.

Raskolnikov's motionless, serious face was transformed in a flash and he suddenly broke into the same nervous guffaws as before, as if quite incapable of restraining himself. And in a twinkling there came back to him with exceptional clarity of sensation one recent moment, when he was standing behind the door, with the axe, and the latch was twitching about, and people were swearing and trying to force their way in, and he had a sudden urge to yell at them, to argue with them, stick his tongue out at them, tease them, laugh, roar, roar, roar with laughter!

'You're either mad or . . . ,' said Zametov – and stopped, as if suddenly struck by a thought that had just flashed across his mind.

'Or? Or what? Well? Go on, out with it!'

'Nothing!' Zametov replied in a huff. 'What utter nonsense!'

Both fell silent. After his sudden, convulsive burst of laughter Raskolnikov had suddenly become pensive and sad. He rested his elbow on the table and propped his head in his hand. He seemed to have entirely forgotten about Zametov. The silence lasted quite some time.

'Why aren't you drinking your tea? It'll get cold,' said Zametov.

'Eh? What? Tea? . . . Why not . . . ?' Raskolnikov took a swig, put a piece of bread in his mouth and suddenly, after a glance at Zametov, seemed to recall everything and even pull himself together: his face instantly regained its initial, derisive expression. He carried on drinking his tea.

'There are so many swindlers about just now,' said Zametov. 'Just recently I read in the *Moscow Gazette* that a gang of counterfeiters has been caught in Moscow. An entire band of them. Forging lottery tickets.'

'Oh, that's old news! I read that a month ago,' Raskolnikov calmly replied. 'So you call them swindlers, do you?' he added with a grin.

'What else can you call them?'

'Them? They're children, fledglings, not swindlers! Fifty people getting together for something like that! How's that possible? Three would already be plenty, and that's only if they trust one another more than they trust themselves! It just needs one of them to get drunk and spill the beans and that's that! Callow fledglings! Hiring unreliables to cash the tickets in at the bank: fancy trusting perfect strangers with a thing like that! Well, suppose the fledglings did pull it off, suppose each of them cashed a million, what then? Until death do us part? Tied to one another for the rest of their lives? You'd be better off hanging yourself! Even cashing in the tickets was beyond them: that chap went to the bank,[31] exchanged five thousand, then his hands started shaking. He counted out four, but took the fifth on trust – anything to make a quick getaway. Well, suspicions were raised. Everything ruined by one idiot! I mean, how's that possible?'

'That his hands shook?' Zametov rejoined. 'No, sir, that's possible. I'm quite sure. What if you can't take the strain?'

'What strain?'

'So you could, I suppose? I couldn't, not a chance! A hundred roubles reward to go and face a horror like that! To take a forged note to a bank of all places, where they've seen them a thousand times before – no, I'd become all flustered. Wouldn't you?'

Once again, Raskolnikov suddenly felt a violent urge to 'stick out his tongue'. Shivers kept running down his spine.

'I'd go about it differently,' he began in a roundabout way. 'Here's how I'd exchange the money: I'd count out the first thousand, four times or so, front to back and back to front, scrutinizing each note, then start on the next thousand; I'd start counting, get halfway, pull out a fifty-rouble note, hold it up to the light, turn it over, hold it up again – H'm, what if it's a fake? "I fear the worst," I'd say. "There's this relative of mine, well, she lost twenty-five roubles doing this the other day," and I'd tell the story. Then, once I'd made a start on the third thousand: "Very sorry, but I think I may have miscounted the seventh hundred in the second thousand, I'm really not sure" – so I'd put down the third and pick up the second again, and so on for all five. And when I'd finished, I'd pull one note from the fifth and another from the second, hold it up again, look all doubtful again, ask him to change it and so on – until I'd driven the clerk to complete distraction and he no longer knew how to get rid of me! I'd get to the end eventually, head off, open the door – "Ah, very sorry" – and go back again, ask about something, request an explanation. That's how I'd go about it!'

'My, what terrible things you're saying!' said Zametov with a laugh. 'But talk's cheap – I expect you'd trip up if it came to actually doing it. It's not just the likes of you and me, even a hardened daredevil couldn't vouch for himself here, I assure you. Just take the case of the old woman murdered in our district. A daredevil's work and no mistake: he went for broke in broad daylight and got away with it by pure miracle – but he still couldn't stop his hands shaking: he couldn't go through with the robbery, couldn't take it, it's obvious . . .'

Raskolnikov seemed almost offended.

'Obvious? See if you can catch him now then!' he shrieked, goading Zametov with malicious delight.

'Don't worry, he'll be caught.'

'Who by? You? You'll catch him, will you? You'll drop dead trying! All you care about is whether or not he's spending any money. He barely had a copeck before and now he's started spending – so it must be him! A child could dupe you if he wanted to!'

'But that's what they all do,' replied Zametov. 'They can kill cleverly enough, risking their lives in the process, only to get nabbed in the pothouse five minutes later. Spending's their downfall. They're not as clever as you are, you see. You'd steer well clear of the pothouse, needless to say.'

Raskolnikov knitted his brow and looked intently at Zametov.

'You've started enjoying this, I see, and want to know how I'd act here as well?' he asked with distaste.

'I would,' replied the other firmly and seriously. It was all a bit too serious, the way he was speaking and looking.

'Very much?'

'Very much.'

'All right. Here's how I'd act,' Raskolnikov began, suddenly bringing his face close to Zametov again, staring at him again and whispering again, but this time, Zametov couldn't help shuddering. 'Here's what I'd do: I'd take the money and the items and immediately, without stopping off anywhere, I'd make straight for some out-of-the-way spot where there was nothing but fences and barely anyone about – a vegetable garden or something of the sort. I'd have searched the place beforehand for a forty-or fifty-pound stone, somewhere in a corner, by a fence, where it had probably lain ever since the house was built; I'd lift the stone up a little – there should be a hollow underneath – and that's where I'd put all the items and the money. Put them there and cover them with the stone, back to how it was before, pack the earth round it with my foot and clear off. I wouldn't touch any of it for a year, two years, three years. Catch me if you can!'

'You're mad,' said Zametov, almost whispering as well for some reason and, for some reason, suddenly drawing back from Raskolnikov. The latter's eyes flashed; he went terribly pale; his upper lip quivered and began to twitch. He leant over to Zametov as close as he could and began moving his lips without uttering a word. This lasted half a minute or so. He realized what he was doing, but couldn't help himself. A terrible word twitched on his lips, like the latch on the door that time: it was on the verge of breaking loose, being released, being uttered!

'What if it was me who killed the old woman and Lizaveta?' he said suddenly – and came to his senses.

Zametov gave him a wild look and turned pale as a tablecloth. A smile disfigured his face.

'But how's that possible?' he said, barely audibly.

Raskolnikov threw him an angry glance.

'Admit it – you believed me. Didn't you?'

'Not for a second! And now I believe it less than ever!' said Zametov hastily.

'Got you at last! The dicky bird's been caught. So you must have believed it before, if now you "believe it less than ever"?'

'Not for one second, I say!' exclaimed Zametov, visibly flustered. 'Is that why you were frightening me – to lead up to this?'

'So you don't believe it? Then what were you all talking about after

I left the bureau that time? And why did Powder Keg grill me after my
fainting fit? Hey you!' he shouted at the servant, getting to his feet
and picking up his cap. 'How much?'

'Thirty copecks all told, sir,' the servant replied, running up.

'There, have another twenty for vodka. Just look at all this money!'
He stretched out a trembling hand full of notes to Zametov. 'Red
ones, blue ones, twenty-five roubles. Where have they come from?
And what about my new clothes? You know full well I hadn't a copeck! The landlady's already been questioned, I suppose ... Well,
enough of this! *Assez causé!*[32] Goodbye ... and *bon appétit!*'

He left, shaking all over with a kind of wild hysteria mixed with
unbearable delight – yet he was gloomy and terribly tired. His face was
disfigured, as if after a fit. His weariness was rapidly growing. Now
the merest jolt, the merest irritation, was enough to arouse and revive
his strength, which weakened just as fast, together with the sensation.

Zametov, left on his own, remained in his seat for a good while
longer, pondering. Raskolnikov, without meaning to, had turned all
his thoughts on this familiar topic upside down and definitively made
up his mind for him.

'Ilya Petrovich is a fool!' he decided, definitively.

Raskolnikov had barely opened the door onto the street when suddenly, right on the porch, he bumped into Razumikhin going the other
way. Neither noticed the other until they very nearly bumped heads.
They stood there for a while, looking each other up and down. Razumikhin was utterly astonished, but suddenly rage, real rage, flashed
menacingly in his eyes.

'So this is where you are!' he shouted at the top of his voice. 'Running from his sick bed! And I was looking for him under the couch!
We even checked the loft! I almost gave Nastasya a thrashing thanks
to you ... And look where he is! Rodya! What's the meaning of this?
Tell me the whole truth! Confess! Do you hear?'

'The meaning is that I'm sick to death of all of you and I want to be
alone,' Raskolnikov calmly replied.

'Alone? When you still can't walk, when you're still white as a sheet
and you're gasping for breath! Idiot! What were you up to in the
"Crystal Palace"? Confess immediately!'

'Let me go!' said Raskolnikov, trying to walk past. This was the
last straw and Razumikhin grabbed him firmly by the shoulder.

'Let me go? What cheek! Know what I'll do with you now? I'll gather you up, tie a knot around you, carry you off home under my arm and lock you up!'

'Listen, Razumikhin,' Raskolnikov began quietly, with a semblance of perfect calm, 'why can't you see that I don't want your good deeds? And why this urge to bestow your kindness on people who . . . spit in reply? For whom this is more than they can bear? I mean, why did you have to look me up when I fell ill? What if I were only too happy to die? Didn't I make it clear enough to you today that you're tormenting me, that I'm . . . sick and tired of you? Why this urge to torment people? It doesn't help my recovery at all, I assure you. In fact, it's a constant irritation. Didn't Zosimov leave earlier so as not to irritate me? Now you should do the same, for the love of God! Anyway, what right do you have to keep me here by force? Can't you see that I've got all my wits about me? What do I need to say to you – please, tell me – for you to stop pestering me and bestowing your goodness on me? Call me ungrateful, call me scum, but for the love of God just leave me alone, all of you! Just leave me!'

He'd begun calmly enough, relishing the prospect of pouring out so much venom, but he ended in a breathless frenzy, as earlier with Luzhin.

Razumikhin stood and thought for a minute, and let go of his hand.

'Clear off, damn you!' he said quietly and almost pensively. 'Wait!' he roared all of a sudden when Raskolnikov was already walking off, 'and listen to me. I declare that you are all, to a man, blabberers and blusterers! The first prick of pain and you'll be fussing over it like a hen over an egg! Even here you can't help stealing from foreign authors. There's not a spark of independent life in you! Spermaceti[33] is what you're made of, with whey instead of blood! I don't believe a single one of you! Your first priority, whatever the situation, is to avoid seeming human! Wait there, I say!' he shouted with redoubled fury, noticing that Raskolnikov was on the verge of leaving again. 'Hear me out! As you know, today's my house-warming, the guests might have already arrived, and I left my uncle – I was just over there now – to greet them. Now if you weren't such a fool, a second-hand fool, a triple fool, a walking translation – you see, Rodya, you're a bright spark, I'll give you that, but you're a fool! – now if you weren't such a fool, you'd come over to mine for the evening instead of wearing out your boots for no reason. You might as well, seeing as you can't stay in bed! I'll wheel in the landlord's lovely soft armchair for

you . . . A nice brew, a bit of company . . . If you're not up to it, I'll
make up the couch – at least you can lie amongst us . . . Zosimov will
be there too. So, are you coming?'

'No.'

'Rubbish!' Razumikhin cried impatiently. 'How can you know?
You can't answer for yourself! And you don't understand the first thing
about this anyway . . . A thousand times I've fallen out with someone
just like this, only to come running back . . . You'll feel ashamed and
you'll be back! Just remember, Pochinkov's house, third floor . . .'

'Carry on like this and you'll end up begging to be beaten, Mr Razumikhin, just for the satisfaction of bestowing your goodness.'

'Who – me? I'll twist their nose off just for thinking it! Pochinkov's
house, Number 47; the apartment of civil servant Babushkin . . .'

'I won't come, Razumikhin!' Raskolnikov turned and walked off.

'I bet you will!' shouted Razumikhin after him. 'Or else you . . . or
else I don't want to know you! Hey, wait! Is Zametov in there?'

'Yes.'

'You've seen him?'

'Yes.'

'And spoken to him?'

'Yes.'

'What about? Ah, to hell with you – don't bother. Pochinkov's house,
forty-seven, Babushkin's apartment. Don't forget!'

Raskolnikov reached Sadovaya Street and turned the corner. Razumikhin, deep in thought, watched him go. Finally, with a flap of his
hand, he went inside, but stopped halfway up the stairs.

'Damn it!' he continued, almost out loud. 'What he says makes
sense, but it's as if . . . But then, I'm a fool too! Who's to say madmen
can't talk sense? Isn't this precisely what Zosimov fears?' He tapped
his forehead with his finger. 'Well, in that case . . . but how could I let
him go off on his own? What if he goes and drowns himself? . . .
What a blunder! No way!' And he ran back to catch Raskolnikov, but
the trail had gone cold. He spat and hurried back with quick steps to
the "Crystal Palace", to quiz Zametov right away.

Raskolnikov went straight on to ——sky Bridge, stopped halfway
across, by the railings, rested both elbows on them and gazed out.
Since leaving Razumikhin, he'd become so weak that even getting this
far had been a struggle. He'd felt like sitting or lying down somewhere,
in the street. Leaning over the water, he gazed without thinking at the

sunset's last, pink gleam, at the row of houses darkening in the thickening dusk, at one distant little window, in an attic on the left bank, shining, as if on fire, with a last, momentary ray of sunlight, at the Ditch's darkening water, which, it seemed, he was attentively examining. In the end, red circles began spinning before his eyes, buildings swayed, and everything started spinning and dancing – passers-by, embankments, carriages. He suddenly shuddered, saved from another fainting fit, perhaps, by a wild and hideous vision. He sensed someone standing close by, to his right; he glanced round – and saw a tall woman in a shawl, with a long, yellow, drink-ravaged face and reddish, sunken eyes. She was looking straight at him, but it was obvious she wasn't seeing anything or anybody. Suddenly she leant her right arm on the railing, lifted her right leg and swung it over the bars, then the left leg, and threw herself into the Ditch. The dirty water parted and swallowed up its offering, but a minute later the drowning woman floated to the surface and was carried gently downstream by the current, her head and legs in the water, her back to the sky and her skirt puffed up to one side, like a pillow.

'Drowned herself! Drowned herself!' yelled dozens of voices. People came running, both embankments were strewn with spectators, and a crowd gathered on the bridge all around Raskolnikov, pushing him and pressing against him from behind.

'That's our Afrosinyushka, that is!' a woman wailed somewhere close by. 'Save her! Pull her out, good fathers!'

'Boat! Boat!' the crowd shouted.

But a boat was no longer required. A policeman ran down the steps to the Ditch, threw off his greatcoat and boots and dived into the water. He had an easy job of it: the woman had been carried to within a few feet of the steps. He grabbed hold of her clothing with his right hand and with his left managed to seize a pole held out to him by a colleague; the woman was pulled out there and then. She was laid on the granite-slabbed steps. She came round quickly, lifted her head, sat up and started sneezing and snorting, senselessly wiping her wet dress with her hands. She said nothing.

'Drank herself blind, fathers,' wailed that same woman's voice, next to Afrosinyushka now. 'Only t'other day she tried to do herself in, and we had to take the noose off her. I was only going to the shop just now, left my wee girl to keep an eye on 'er – and look! She's trading class, fathers – we're neighbours, second house from the end, over there . . .'

The crowd was breaking up, the policemen were still attending to the rescued woman, someone shouted something about the bureau . . . Raskolnikov watched it all with a strange mixture of indifference and detachment. It began to disgust him. 'No, it's too vile . . . water . . . not worth it,' he muttered to himself. 'Nothing's going to happen,' he added. 'No use waiting. What was that about the bureau? . . . So why's Zametov not there? It's open till ten . . .' He turned his back to the railing and looked around him.

'So what's it to be? Well, why not?' he said decisively, left the bridge and set off in the direction of the bureau. His heart felt hollow, desolate. He'd no wish to think. Even his anguish had passed, with not a trace of the energy he'd felt before when he left his room 'to put an end to it all!' Total apathy had taken its place.

'Well, it's one way out!' he thought, walking at a gentle, sluggish pace along the bank of the Ditch. 'I really will end it, because I want to . . . But is it actually a way out? Never mind! I'll have my one square yard – heh-heh! Still, a funny sort of end! And is it the end? Will I tell them or won't I? Oh . . . damn this! I'm tired. If only I could lie down or sit down somewhere! It's all so stupid, that's the most shameful thing. But so what? Ugh, such stupid thoughts . . .'

The bureau was straight ahead, second left: a stone's throw away. But on reaching the first turning he stopped, thought for a moment, turned into the lane and went the long way round, along two streets – aimlessly, perhaps, or perhaps in order to buy himself some more time, even if it was only a minute. He walked with his eyes fixed to the ground. Suddenly it was as if somebody whispered something into his ear. He raised his head and saw that he was standing by *that* house, right next to the gates. Since *that* evening,³⁴ he'd never been here or even walked past.

An irresistible, inexplicable urge was drawing him on. He turned in, went straight under the arch, took the first entrance on the right and started climbing the familiar stairs to the fourth floor. The narrow, steep stairwell was very dark. He paused on each landing and looked around curiously. On the first-floor landing the window frame had been removed entirely. 'It wasn't like that before,' he thought to himself. And here was the second-floor apartment where Mikolai and Mitka had been working. 'Locked, and the door's freshly painted; so now it's being let.' Now the third floor . . . and the fourth . . . 'Here!' Bewilderment seized him: the door to this apartment was wide open;

there were people inside; he could hear voices. It was the last thing
he'd expected. After a moment's hesitation he climbed the last steps
and entered the apartment.

It, too, was being done up; there were workmen inside; he felt almost shocked. For some reason he'd imagined finding everything just
as he'd left it, with even the corpses, perhaps, still lying in their same
positions on the floor. Instead: bare walls, no furniture. Strange! He
went over to the window and sat on the sill.

There were only two workmen, both young lads, one far younger
than the other. They were hanging up new wallpaper – white, with
lilac flowers, in place of the yellow, frayed and worn paper that had
been there before. For some reason, Raskolnikov was terribly put out
by this; he looked at the new wallpaper with hostility, as though sorry
to find everything so changed.

The lads must have dawdled after work and were now hurriedly
rolling up their paper and preparing to go home. They barely noticed
Raskolnikov's appearance. They were talking about something. Raskolnikov folded his arms and began to listen.

'So she comes to see me one morning,' the older lad was saying to
the younger one, 'bright and early, all tarted up. "And what d'you
think you're doing," I say, "meloning and lemoning[35] about in front of
me?" "What I want, Tit Vasilych," she says, "is to be at your beck and
call from this day on." Well, blow me down! And my, how she was
dressed: a magazine, if ever there was!'

'What's a magazine, ol' man?' asked the young lad. Evidently, he
was the 'ol' man's' pupil.

'A magazine, sonny, is lots of pictures, all coloured in, that get to
our tailors every Saturday in the post, from abroad, to tell people how
to dress – the male sex no less than the females. Drawings, if you like.
The male sex is nearly always shown in them fur-collar frock coats,
but in the female department – blimey, gorgeous tarts like you
wouldn't believe!'

'This city of Peter's got it all!' shouted the younger one enthusiastically. 'Excepting Mum and Dad, of course!'

'Everything, sonny, 'cept that,' decreed the other sententiously.

Raskolnikov got up and went to the other room, where the box, the
bed and the chest of drawers had been before; now the room seemed
horribly small without furniture. The wallpaper was still the same, but
the space in the corner where the icon-case had once stood was clearly

marked on it. He had a look and went back to his little window. The
older workman was studying him out of the corner of his eye.

'What are you wanting, sir?' he suddenly asked.

Instead of replying Raskolnikov stood up, went out to the landing,
grabbed hold of the little bell and tugged. The same bell, the same
tinny sound! He tugged it a second time, and a third; he listened hard,
remembering. The excruciatingly awful, hideous sensation of before
was coming back to him ever more clearly and vividly; he shuddered
with each ring, and found it ever more pleasurable.

'So what are you after? Who are you?' the workman shouted, coming out towards him. Raskolnikov went back inside.

'I want to rent an apartment,' he said. 'I'm having a look round.'

'Digs aren't rented out at night. Anyway, you should've come with
the caretaker.'

'The floor's been washed. Will it be painted?' continued Raskolnikov. 'So there's no blood?'

'What blood?'

'An old woman was murdered here, with her sister. There was a big
puddle right here.'

'What sort of man are you?' shouted the workman uneasily.

'Me?'

'Yes.'

'You'd like to know, would you? . . . Let's go to the bureau, then
I'll say.'

The workmen looked at him in bewilderment.

'It's late, sir, we should be gone by now. Come on, Alyoshka, time
to lock up,' said the older workman.

'All right, let's go!' Raskolnikov replied indifferently and went out
first, walking slowly down the stairs. 'Hey, caretaker!' he shouted
when he came out under the arch.

Several people were standing right by the building's main entrance,
gawking at passers-by: both caretakers, a woman, a tradesman in a
dressing gown and someone else. Raskolnikov went straight up to
them.

'What d'you want?' one of the caretakers asked.

'Been to the bureau?'

'Just now. What d'you want?'

'Are they at their desks?'

'Yeah.'

'And the assistant was there?'

'For a bit. Well, what d'you want?'

Raskolnikov didn't reply and stood alongside them, deep in thought.

'Came to look at the digs,' said the older workman, walking up.

'What digs?'

'Where we're working now. "Why's the blood been washed off?" he says. "There was a murder here," he says, "and I've come to rent the place." Then he starts ringing the bell, nearly tears the thing off. "Let's go to the bureau," he says. "I'll prove it all there." A right pest.'

Bewildered, the caretaker scrutinized Raskolnikov and frowned.

'So who are you?' he shouted more threateningly.

'I'm Rodion Romanych Raskolnikov, a former student, and I live in Shil's house in one of the lanes around here, apartment Number 14. Ask the caretaker . . . he knows me.' Raskolnikov said all this in a lazy and pensive kind of way, without turning round, his eyes fixed on the darkened street.

'So why did you go up to the digs?'

'To have a look.'

'A look at what?'

'Why don't we take him down to the bureau?' the tradesman suddenly butted in, and fell silent.

Raskolnikov glanced at him over his shoulder, gave him an attentive look and said just as quietly and lazily:

'Let's go!'

'Too right!' replied the tradesman, livening up. 'What did he bring *that* up for? What's on his mind, eh?'

'He don't look drunk, but God only knows,' muttered the worker.

'What do you want?' the caretaker shouted again, becoming seriously angry. 'You're a damned nuisance!'

'Too scared to go to the bureau, then?' scoffed Raskolnikov.

'Scared of what? You're a damned nuisance!'

'Con man!' shouted the woman.

'You're wasting your breath with the likes of him!' shouted the other caretaker, an enormous peasant with a wide-open coat and keys under his belt. 'Scram! . . . Con man's about right for you . . . Scram!'

Grabbing Raskolnikov by the shoulder, he hurled him into the street. Raskolnikov almost tumbled head over heels, but managed to straighten himself up just in time, cast a silent glance over all the spectators and went on his way.

'A queer fish,' said the worker.

'Like lots of folk nowadays,' said the woman.

'I'd still've taken him down to the bureau,' added the tradesman.

'Best stay out of it,' the big caretaker decided. 'Con man and no mistake! That's his game – pulls you in and you'll never pull yourself out . . . I know the score!'

'So, am I going or aren't I?' thought Raskolnikov, stopping in the middle of the crossroads and looking about him, as if he were expecting someone to utter the last word one way or another. But there was no response from anywhere; everything was desolate and dead, like the stones on which he trod, dead for him, for him alone . . . Suddenly, far off, some two hundred yards away, at the end of the street, in the thickening gloom, he made out a crowd, voices, cries . . . Amidst the crowd stood some kind of carriage . . . A light flickered in the middle of the street. 'What's this?' Raskolnikov turned right and made for the crowd. He seemed to be clutching at everything, and a cold smile crossed his face as he thought this: he'd made up his mind about the bureau now, and he was quite certain that all this was just about to end.

VII

In the middle of the street stood a fancy, grand carriage drawn by a pair of steaming grey horses; the carriage was empty and the coachman had got down from the box and was standing beside it; the horses were being held by the bridle. There was a large throng of people, with police officers at the front. One was holding a lantern with which, bending down, he was illuminating something on the road, right next to the wheels. Everyone was speaking, shouting, gasping; the coachman seemed bewildered and every so often would say:

'A terrible sin! Lord, what a sin!'

Raskolnikov squeezed his way through as best he could, and finally caught sight of the object of all this fuss and curiosity. On the ground lay a man, to all appearances unconscious, who'd just been trampled by horses; he was very shabbily – but 'nobly' – dressed and covered in blood, which streamed from his face and his head. His face was all battered, flayed, mangled. He'd been trampled badly and no mistake.

'Fathers!' the coachman wailed. 'What's a man to do? If I'd been tearing along or I hadn't yelled at him, fair enough, but I was going along nice and steady. Everyone saw: with me, what you see is what you get. A drunk can't hold a candle[36] – we all know that! I can see him crossing the street, wobbling along, nearly toppling over – I yell at him once, yell at him twice, and again, and pull up the horses; and he goes and falls right under them! Either he meant it or he's properly tight . . . The horses are only young, they scare easy; they tugged, he screamed, they tugged harder . . . and look!'

'He's telling it like it was!' came the voice of some witness in the crowd.

'He yelled at him all right – three times,' echoed another.

'Three, three – we all heard!' shouted a third.

The coachman, though, was not really so very despondent or frightened. The carriage evidently had a wealthy and important owner waiting for it somewhere – a problem which the police officers, needless to say, had not neglected. The trampled man would need to be taken to the police station and the hospital. No one knew his name.

Meanwhile Raskolnikov had squeezed through and leant forward even closer. All of a sudden the lantern lit up the face of the unfortunate man: he recognized him.

'I know him! I know him!' he shouted, pushing right through to the front. 'He's a civil servant, retired, a titular counsellor, Marmeladov! He lives around here, very close, Kozel's house . . . A doctor, quick! I'll pay, look!' He took the money out of his pocket and showed it to a policeman. He was extraordinarily agitated.

The police officers were pleased to learn who the trampled man was. Raskolnikov named himself, too, gave his address and did everything in his power – as if this were his own father – to persuade them to move the unconscious Marmeladov to the latter's apartment.

'Just here, three buildings along,' he chivvied them. 'The house belongs to Kozel, a German, a rich one . . . He must be drunk, expect he was trying to get home. I know him . . . He's a drunkard . . . He's got a family there, wife, children, a daughter. Why drag him all the way to the hospital – there's bound to be a doctor right here in his building! I'll pay for it! . . . At least he'll have his family looking after him and he'll get help straight away – he'd die before he ever got to the hospital . . .'

He even managed to slip one of them a note; but it was a perfectly straightforward and lawful business, and anyway, help was closer at hand here. The trampled man was lifted up and carried off; volunteers were quickly found. Kozel's house was some thirty yards away.

Raskolnikov walked behind, carefully supporting the head and pointing the way.

'Over here! Over here! We have to carry him up the stairs head first;
turn round . . . that's it! I'll pay for it, I'll thank you,' he muttered.

Katerina Ivanovna was pacing her little room, as she always did
whenever she had a free moment, from the window to the stove and
back again, her arms tightly folded over her chest, talking to herself
and coughing. Recently she'd taken to speaking more and more often
with her elder girl, ten-year-old Polenka, who, ignorant though she
still was of many things, understood perfectly well that her mother
needed her, so she always followed her with her big clever eyes and
did all she could to seem all-comprehending. Polenka was undressing
her little brother, who'd been poorly since the morning, before putting
him to bed. While waiting for her to change his shirt, which was to be
washed that same night, the boy sat on the chair, all serious and silent, straight-backed and stock-still, extending his little legs with his
heels thrust forward and his toes apart. He listened with pouted lips
and bulging eyes to what Mummy was telling his sister and didn't
move a muscle, just as clever little boys are supposed to sit when being
prepared for bed. A girl even smaller than him, wearing the shabbiest
rags, was standing by the screen and waiting her turn. The door to the
stairs was open, so as to offer at least some relief from the waves of
tobacco smoke that blew in from the other rooms and kept provoking
long and excruciating coughing fits in the poor consumptive. Katerina
Ivanovna seemed even thinner than a week ago and the red blotches
on her cheeks burned even brighter than before.

'Polenka, you just wouldn't believe, you can't even imagine,' she
was saying as she walked up and down the room, 'how fun and grand
life was in Daddy's house and how this drunkard ruined me and will
ruin you all! Papa was a state counsellor and very nearly governor;
one more step and he was there, so everyone paid him visits, saying:
"We already think of you like that, Ivan Mikhailych, as our governor!" When I . . . cuh . . . when I . . . cuh-cuh-cuh . . . oh, damn this
life!' she shrieked, coughing up phlegm and clutching her chest.
'When I . . . ach, when at the last ball . . . at the house of the marshal
of the nobility . . . when I was spotted by Princess Bezzemelnaya –
who later gave me her blessing when I was about to marry your papa,
Polya – she immediately asked: "Isn't that the nice girl who danced
the *pas de châle* at the leaving ball?" . . . (That rip needs sewing; you'd

better find a needle and darn it right now, the way I taught you, otherwise tomorrow . . . cuh! tomorrow . . . cuh-cuh-cuh! . . . it'll be even bigger!)' she shouted, her voice breaking. 'At the time, Prince Shchegolskoy, a *kammerjunker*,[37] had only just arrived from Petersburg . . . he danced a mazurka with me and wanted to visit me the very next day to propose; but I thanked him myself in the most flattering terms and said that my heart had long belonged to another. That other was your father, Polya. Daddy was terribly angry . . . Is the water ready? Well, give me the shirt, then. What about the stockings? . . . Lida,' she turned to her little daughter, 'you sleep as you are for tonight, without a shirt; you'll manage . . . and lay your stockings out . . . I'll wash them, too . . . What's keeping that tramp, that drunkard? He's worn his shirt to shreds, like some old cloth . . . If I wash it all now I won't have to break my back two nights running! Dear God! Cuh-cuh-cuh-cuh! Again! What's this?' she shrieked, looking over towards the crowd on the landing and the people forcing their way into her room, bearing some kind of burden. 'What's this? What are they carrying? Dear God!'

'Where should we put him?' asked a police officer, looking around once Marmeladov, blood-stained and unconscious, had been lugged into the room.

'The couch! Straight on the couch, head this way,' Raskolnikov pointed.

'Trampled in the street! Drunk!' someone yelled from the landing.

Katerina Ivanovna stood white-faced, struggling to breathe. The children were petrified. Little Lidochka shrieked, ran over to Polenka, hugged her and began shaking all over.

After laying out Marmeladov, Raskolnikov rushed over to Katerina Ivanovna:

'Calm down, for the love of God, and don't be scared!' he said in a rush. 'He was crossing the street, got trampled by a carriage. Don't worry, he'll come to . . . I told them to bring him here . . . I've been here before, remember . . . He'll come to. I'll pay!'

'Now he's done it!' Katerina Ivanovna shrieked in despair, rushing over to her husband.

Raskolnikov soon realized that this was not the type of woman to faint on the spot. In a flash a pillow appeared beneath the head of the unfortunate man, something which no one had even thought of till then. Katerina Ivanovna set about undressing him and examining him, kept busy and kept her head, forgetting about herself, biting her quivering lips and suppressing the cries ready to burst from her chest.

Meanwhile Raskolnikov had persuaded someone to run off for the doctor. The doctor, as it happened, lived in the next house but one.

'I've sent for the doctor,' he kept saying to Katerina Ivanovna. 'Don't worry, I'll pay. Got any water? . . . And bring a napkin, a towel, something, quick. Who knows how bad his injuries are? . . . He's injured, not killed, rest assured of that . . . Let's see what the doctor says!'

Katerina Ivanovna rushed over to the window; there, on a battered chair in the corner, stood a large earthenware basin filled with water, all ready for the nocturnal scrubbing of her children's and husband's clothes. Katerina Ivanovna performed this task herself twice a week, and sometimes even more often than that, for they'd got to the point of having almost no change of linen at all, with only one item of each type per family member, and Katerina Ivanovna couldn't stand dirt and would sooner slave away, in pain and exhaustion, when everyone was asleep, so that by morning the washing would have dried on a cord stretched across the room, than see filth in her home. At Raskolnikov's request she picked up the bowl and was about to bring it over, but nearly fell under her burden. But he'd already found a towel, dipped it in water and begun cleaning Marmeladov's blood-soaked face. Katerina Ivanovna stood beside them, drawing painful breaths and clutching her chest. She herself was in need of help. It began to dawn on Raskolnikov that having the trampled man brought here may have been a mistake. The policeman was also bewildered.

'Polya!' shouted Katerina Ivanovna. 'Run to Sonya, quick. If she's not in, tell them anyway that Father's been trampled by horses and she should come over immediately . . . when she returns. Quick, Polya! Here, cover yourself with a shawl!'

'Run for your life, thithter!' the boy suddenly shouted from the chair and, having done so, relapsed into silence, sitting straight-backed, eyes wide open, his heels thrust forward and his toes apart.

By now, the room had filled to bursting. The police officers had all left apart from one, who'd stayed behind for a while and was trying to drive the spectators who'd come in from the stairs back out again. At the same time, nearly all Mrs Lippewechsel's tenants were spilling out from the inner rooms. At first they seemed content merely to crowd the doorway, then they poured into the room itself. Katerina Ivanovna was beside herself.

'At least let him die in peace!' she yelled at the mob. 'A nice spectacle you've found for yourselves! While you smoke! Cuh-cuh-cuh! Where are your hats, I wonder? . . . Look, there's one! . . . Out! A dead body deserves some respect!'

Her cough was choking her, but the warning did its job. The tenants were clearly a little scared of Katerina Ivanovna. One by one they shuffled back towards the door with that strange inner sense of satisfaction that may always be observed at moments of sudden misfortune, even among people who are as close as can be, and there is not one person, without exception, who is free of it, notwithstanding even the sincerest feelings of pity and sympathy.

From the other side of the door, though, came talk of the hospital and what a pain it was to be disturbed for no reason.

'It's death that's a pain!' shouted Katerina Ivanovna, and she'd already rushed over to fling open the door and let them have it when she collided in the doorway with Mrs Lippewechsel herself, who'd only just heard about the misfortune and was hurrying over to restore order. A more cantankerous and disorderly German would be hard to imagine.

'Oh my God!' she cried, clasping her hands. 'Your husband drunken trampled by horse. To ze hospital! I – landlady!'

'Amalia Ludwigovna! Please think before you speak,' Katerina Ivanovna began haughtily (speaking to the landlady, she always took a haughty tone, so that the latter would 'know her place', and even now she could not deny herself this pleasure). 'Amalia Ludwigovna . . .'

'I told you for-once-and-for-twice: don't dare you call me Amal Ludwigovna; it's Amal-Ivan!'

'Your name is not Amal-Ivan, but Amalia Ludwigovna, and since I am not one of your vile flatterers, like Mr Lebezyatnikov, who is laughing as we speak on the other side of the door,' – laughter rang out from there as if on cue, along with the cry, 'They're at it again!' – 'I shall always call you Amalia Ludwigovna, although why you should dislike this name so much is quite beyond me. You can see what's happened to Semyon Zakharovich: he is dying. Be so kind as to close this door immediately and not let anyone in. Let him die in peace, at least! I assure you that otherwise the Governor General will be informed of your behaviour by tomorrow at the latest. The prince[38] has known me from even before my marriage and remembers Semyon Zakharovich very well, having bestowed his kindness on him on many occasions. It is widely known that

Semyon Zakharovich had many friends and patrons, whom he, in his
noble pride, forsook of his own accord, conscious of his unfortunate
weakness, but now' – she pointed to Raskolnikov – 'we are being helped
by a young and generous soul, well-off and well-connected, whom Semyon Zakharovich has known since childhood, and rest assured, Amalia Ludwigovna . . .'

All this was said at extraordinary, ever-increasing speed, but a fit
of coughing instantly put paid to Katerina Ivanovna's oratory. That
same moment, the dying man came to and groaned, and she ran over
towards him. He opened his eyes and, still not recognizing or understanding, began to stare at the man standing over him – Raskolnikov.
He was breathing heavily, deeply and sporadically; the edges of his
lips were marked with blood; his forehead was beaded with sweat.
Failing to recognize Raskolnikov, he began anxiously looking round.
Katerina Ivanovna fixed him with a sad but severe gaze, and tears ran
down her face.

'Dear God! His whole chest has been crushed! The blood, the blood!'
she despaired. 'His outer clothing has to come off, all of it! Turn a little,
Semyon Zakharovich, if you can!' she shouted at him.

Marmeladov recognized her.

'A priest!' he croaked.

Katerina Ivanovna stepped back towards the window, rested her
forehead on the frame and cried despairingly:

'Damn this life!'

'A priest!' the dying man repeated after a moment's silence.

'They've already gone!' Katerina Ivanovna yelled back. He obeyed
and fell silent. He sought her out with timid, sorrowful eyes; she returned to him and stood by his bedside. He calmed down a little, but
not for long. Soon his eyes came to rest on little Lidochka (his favourite), who was shaking in the corner as if she were having a fit and
looking at him with her surprised, childish stare.

'Ah . . . ah . . . ,' he stammered anxiously in her direction. He wanted
to say something.

'Now what?' shouted Katerina Ivanovna.

'No shoes! No shoes!' he muttered, staring wild-eyed at the little
girl's bare feet.

'Just shut up!' Katerina Ivanovna shouted with irritation. 'You
know damned well why!'

'Thank God, the doctor!' Raskolnikov rejoiced.

In came the doctor, a little, neatly dressed old German, looking around with a mistrustful air. He walked over to the patient, took his pulse, carefully felt his head and, with Katerina Ivanovna's help, undid all the buttons on the blood-soaked shirt, baring the patient's chest. It was thoroughly mangled, crumpled and mutilated; several ribs on the right side were broken. On the left, right over the heart, was a sinister, large, yellow-black mark, where a hoof had struck him hard. The doctor frowned. The police officer told him that the trampled man had got caught in the wheel and was dragged, spinning, some thirty paces along the road.

'Incredible he came round after that,' the doctor whispered softly to Raskolnikov.

'So what's your verdict?' the latter asked.

'He'll die any moment.'

'There's no hope at all?'

'None! His last gasp . . . Not to mention the terrible injury to his head . . . H'm. I suppose we could let some blood . . . but . . . it won't help. In five or ten minutes he'll be dead, I'm certain.'

'Well let some blood, then!'

'All right . . . But I warn you: it won't help.'

At that moment there came the sound of more footsteps, the crowd around the door parted and a priest, a grey old man, appeared on the threshold with the last sacraments. A police officer, one of those from before, followed him in. The doctor immediately yielded his place and gave the priest a meaningful look. Raskolnikov begged the doctor to wait a bit longer. The doctor shrugged his shoulders and stayed.

Everyone took a step back. The confession was very brief. The dying man could scarcely have taken much in; he was capable only of broken, indistinct sounds. Katerina Ivanovna grabbed Lidochka, picked the boy up off the chair, took them over towards the stove in the corner and kneeled, making the children kneel down in front of her. The girl merely shook, but the boy, kneeling on his bare little knees, steadily raised his hand, made the full sign of the cross and bowed down to the ground until he knocked his forehead, which evidently gave him particular pleasure. Katerina Ivanovna bit her lip and fought back tears; she too was praying, adjusting the boy's shirt every now and again and covering the girl's exposed shoulders with a shawl, which she'd taken from the chest of drawers while still praying on her knees. In the meantime the doors to the inner rooms were being opened again by curious residents, while by the entrance the crush of spectators – tenants from every floor – swelled and swelled, though without crossing the threshold. Just one candle stub illuminated the entire scene.

At that moment Polenka, who had run off to fetch her sister, quickly squeezed back through to the room. She was completely out of breath from sprinting, took off her shawl, sought out her mother, walked up to her and said: 'She's coming! I found her in the street.' Her mother got her to kneel down next to her. Soundlessly and timidly, a girl squeezed through the crowd, and strange was her sudden appearance in this room, amidst the beggary, rags, death and despair. She too wore rags; her get-up was cheap, but it came with all the adornments of the street, as the rules and etiquette of that special world demanded, with its shamingly flagrant purpose. Sonya stopped on the threshold; she didn't cross it and looked quite lost, as if her mind had gone blank. She'd quite forgotten about her fourth-hand, colourful silk dress, utterly out of place here with its ridiculously long train, and about her enormous crinoline obstructing the doorway, and her bright shoes and her parasol, which she'd taken with her even though it was night, and the ridiculous round straw hat with a feather the colour of fire.[39] From beneath its boyish tilt there peered a thin, pale, frightened little face with a wide-open mouth and eyes frozen in horror. Sonya, a shortish girl of eighteen or so, was a skinny but pretty enough blonde, with marvellous blue eyes. She stared at the bed, at the priest; she too was out of breath. Eventually, a whispered word or two from the crowd must have reached her ears. Eyes lowered, she took one step over the threshold and stood in the room, though still in the doorway.

Confession and communion were over. Katerina Ivanovna returned to her husband's bed. The priest stepped back and tried, as he was leaving, to offer a few words of counsel and consolation to Katerina Ivanovna.

'And what'll I do with this lot?' she broke in sharply, pointing at the little ones.

'God is kind. Trust in the help of the Almighty,' the priest began.

'Ha! Kind, just not to us!'

'That's a sin, ma'am, a sin,' the priest remarked, shaking his head.

'And this isn't a sin?' shouted Katerina Ivanovna, pointing at the dying man.

'Perhaps those who were the unwitting cause will agree to recompense you, at least for the lost income . . .'

'That's not what I mean!' Katerina Ivanovna shouted irritably with a flap of her hand. 'Recompense for what? He got himself run over when he was drunk! What income? There was no income from him, only pain. He spent whatever there was on booze. Robbed us, then straight to the pothouse, wasting their life and mine on drink! Thank God he's dying! We can cut our losses!'

'Forgiveness is called for in the hour of death, but this is a sin, ma'am; such feelings as these are truly a sin!'

Katerina Ivanovna was fussing around the patient, giving him water, wiping the sweat and blood from his head and adjusting the pillows, while talking to the priest and occasionally managing to turn in his direction. Now she suddenly pounced on him in a kind of frenzy.

'Father! These are nothing but words! "Forgive!" Take today – he'd have come home drunk if he hadn't been trampled, wearing the only shirt he's got, all tattered and worn, and he'd be sound asleep two minutes later, while I'd be slopping about till dawn, washing his rags and the children's, then drying them out by the window, and at first light I'd be sitting down to mend them – so much for my night! . . . What's forgiveness got to do with it? Haven't I forgiven him enough?'

A terrible cough from deep in her chest cut her short. She spat everything into her handkerchief and held it out for the priest to see, clutching her chest with her other hand. The handkerchief was all red with blood . . .

The priest hung his head and said nothing.

Marmeladov was in the final throes. He kept his eyes fixed on Katerina Ivanovna's face as she bent over him once more. He was trying to tell her something. He made a start, working his tongue with difficulty and mumbling a word or two, but Katerina Ivanovna, realizing he was about to ask her forgiveness, instantly shouted him down:

'Shut up! Just don't! . . . I know what you want to say!' – and he fell silent; but at that same moment his wandering gaze fell on the doorway and he saw Sonya . . .

He hadn't noticed her before; she was standing in a corner, in the shadows.

'Who's that? Who's that?' he suddenly said in a hoarse gasp, panicking and indicating with horror-filled eyes the doorway where his daughter was standing, and straining to lift himself up.

'Lie down! Lie down, I say!' shouted Katerina Ivanovna.

But somehow, making an unnatural effort, he managed to prop

himself up on one arm. For a while he looked wildly and fixedly at his daughter, as if unsure who she was. This was the first time, after all, that he'd seen her in such an outfit. Then suddenly he recognized her: abject, crushed, dressed up and ashamed, meekly waiting her turn to say farewell to her dying father. His face expressed infinite suffering.

'Sonya! Daughter! Forgive!' he cried and was about to stretch out his hand towards her but, losing his balance, tumbled from the couch face down onto the floor: he was quickly picked up and put back, but he was already slipping away. Sonya gave a weak cry, ran up, embraced him and froze in that embrace. He died in her arms.

'Well, he's done it this time!' shouted Katerina Ivanovna, seeing her husband's corpse. 'Now what? How will I bury him? And how will I feed this lot tomorrow?'

Raskolnikov walked over to her.

'Katerina Ivanovna,' he began, 'last week the deceased, your husband, told me the story of his whole life, in every detail . . . Rest assured that he spoke of you with the most exalted respect. Ever since that evening, when I learned how devoted he was to you all, and, in particular, how much he respected and loved you, Katerina Ivanovna, despite his unfortunate weakness, ever since then we've been friends . . . So permit me now . . . to assist . . . as a way of returning my debt to my late friend. Here . . . twenty roubles, I believe – and if this can be of any help to you, then . . . I . . . in a word, I'll be back – for sure . . . perhaps I'll come by tomorrow . . . Goodbye!'

With that he hurried out of the room, squeezing through the crowd to the stairs; but in the crowd he suddenly came face to face with Nikodim Fomich, who'd heard about the misfortune and wanted to take charge of the situation in person. They hadn't met since the scene at the bureau, but the district superintendent recognized him at once.

'Ah, it's you?' he asked.

'Dead,' replied Raskolnikov. 'The doctor came, the priest came, everything's fine. Don't trouble this poor, poor woman, she's consumptive as it is. Cheer her up, if you can . . . You're a kind sort, after all . . . ,' he added with a smirk, looking straight into his eyes.

'But look at you – you're soaked in blood,' Nikodim Fomich observed, noticing in the light of the lantern several fresh stains on Raskolnikov's waistcoat.

'Yes, I'm soaked . . . all red with blood!' Raskolnikov said with a peculiar air, then smiled, nodded and set off down the stairs.

He went down in no great hurry, feeling feverish all over and, though unaware of it, filled by a new, boundless sensation of life surging over him suddenly in all its strength. This sensation might have been compared to that of a man sentenced to death who's been granted a sudden and unexpected pardon. The priest, who was on his way home, caught up with him halfway down the stairs. Raskolnikov let him pass, exchanging a silent bow. But then, having almost reached the bottom, he suddenly heard rapid footsteps behind him. Someone was hurrying after him. It was Polenka. She was running and calling out to him, 'Wait! Wait!'

He turned round. She was running down the last flight and stopped right in front of him, one step above him. A dull light seeped in from outside. Raskolnikov made out the girl's thin sweet face smiling at him, looking at him with childish cheerfulness. She was clearly delighted to have been entrusted with this task.

'Wait, what's your name? . . . Oh yes, and where do you live?' she asked in a breathless little voice.

He laid both hands on her shoulders and gazed at her with a kind of happiness. It felt so nice to look at her – he himself didn't know why.

'So who sent you?'

'Sister Sonya sent me,' the girl replied, smiling even more cheerfully.

'I thought it must have been sister Sonya.'

'Mama sent me, too. When sister Sonya was telling me, Mama also came and said, "Quick as you can, Polenka!" '

'Do you love sister Sonya?'

'I love her more than anyone!' said Polenka with particular certainty, and her smile suddenly became more serious.

'And will you love me?'

Instead of a reply he saw the girl's little face coming towards him and her chubby little lips guilelessly puckering out to kiss him. Suddenly she hugged him tight in her matchstick arms, rested her head on his shoulder and sobbed softly, pressing her face tighter and tighter against him.

'I feel sorry for Daddy!' she said a minute later, lifting her wet face and wiping away the tears with her hands. 'It's one bad thing after another at the moment,' she added unexpectedly, with that particular air of gravity which children always try to assume when they suddenly want to speak 'like grown-ups'.

'And did Daddy love you?'

'He loved Lidochka best of all,' she continued, very seriously and unsmilingly, just like grown-ups speak, 'because she's little and because she's sick, and he always used to give her sweets, and he taught us to read, and taught me grammar and scripture,' she added with pride, 'and Mummy didn't say anything, but we could tell she liked it, and Daddy could, too, and Mummy wants to teach me French, because it's time for me now to receive my education.'

'What about praying – can you do that?'

'Oh, of course we can – since forever! I pray on my own as I'm big already, and Kolya and Lidochka pray aloud with Mummy. First they say "Hail Mary" and then another prayer, "Lord, forgive and bless sister Sonya", and then another, "Lord, forgive and bless our other daddy", because our older daddy has already died, and this one's our second, so we pray for the other one, too.'

'Polechka, my name's Rodion. Pray for me, too, sometimes; "and your servant Rodion" – nothing else.'

'I'll pray for you every day of my life,' said the girl ardently and suddenly burst out laughing again, threw herself on his neck and hugged him once more.

Raskolnikov told her his name, gave his address and promised to come by the very next day without fail. The little girl left, completely entranced. It was gone ten when he stepped outside. Five minutes later he was standing on the bridge, on exactly the same spot from which the woman had thrown herself earlier.

'Enough!' he uttered decisively and solemnly. 'No more mirages! No more false fears! No more phantoms! . . . There is life! Wasn't I alive just now? So my life hasn't died yet together with the old hag! May you see the kingdom of heaven – and that's your lot, old mother, your time's up! Now for the kingdom of reason and light and . . . and will, and strength . . . and now we'll see! Now we'll see how we measure up!' he added haughtily, as though addressing and challenging some force of darkness. 'Haven't I already agreed to live on one square yard?

'. . . I'm very feeble now, but . . . my sickness seems to have passed completely. I knew it would when I went out earlier. Hang on: Pochinkov's house, it's a stone's throw away. Yes, I must go to Razumikhin, even if it's more than a stone's throw . . . Let him win his bet! . . . Let him have his fun . . . So what! . . . Strength is what's needed, strength: you won't get anywhere without it. And you can only win strength with strength – that's what they're missing,' he added with arrogant pride and, scarcely able to place one foot in front of the other, left the bridge behind him. His pride and self-confidence were growing by the minute; and a minute was all it took for him to become a different man. What on earth could have happened to bring about such a change? He himself did not know; like a man clutching at a straw, he'd suddenly felt that 'even for me there is life, and life goes on, and my life hasn't died yet together with the old hag.' His conclusion was too hasty, perhaps, but he had other things to worry about.

'Still, I did request a mention for your servant Rodion' – suddenly flashed through his mind – 'but that's . . . just in case!' he added, before immediately laughing at his own childish sally. He was in a quite splendid mood.

Finding Razumikhin proved easy enough. The new tenant was already a familiar face at Pochinkov's house and the caretaker immediately pointed Raskolnikov in the right direction. Even halfway up the stairs there was no mistaking the noise and animation of a large gathering. The door to the stairs was wide open; he could hear shouting and arguing. Razumikhin's room was fairly big and some fifteen people had gathered. Raskolnikov stopped in the entrance hall. Behind a partition two of the landlord's maids were busy with two large samovars, bottles, plates and dishes bearing a pie and some *hors d'oeuvres* brought from the landlady's kitchen. Raskolnikov asked for Razumikhin, who rushed over in the greatest excitement. One glance at him was enough to see that he'd put away a quite phenomenal amount, and though Razumikhin hardly ever managed to drink enough to get drunk, this time the signs were there.

'Listen,' Raskolnikov rushed, 'I've just come to say that you've won the bet and that it really is true that no one knows what the future holds for them. I can't come in. I'm so weak I'm about to collapse. So hello and goodbye! Come and see me tomorrow . . .'

'Know what? I'll walk you home! If even you admit that you're weak . . .'

'What about your guests? Who's the one with the curly hair who just poked his head round?'

'Him? Damned if I know! Must be a mate of my uncle's, or maybe he just turned up . . . I'll leave my uncle with them, he's a priceless man. Shame you can't meet him. But to hell with them all anyway! They're doing fine without me and I could do with some fresh air – so you've come in the nick of time: another minute or two and I'd have picked a fight in there! Chronic fibbers, the lot of them . . . You've no idea how deep a man can sink in lies! Though actually, why shouldn't you? Don't we lie often enough? So let's leave them to it: lie now, and they won't lie later . . . Hang on a minute, I'll go and get Zosimov.'

Zosimov fell upon Raskolnikov almost hungrily; there was some special curiosity in him; soon his face brightened.

'Straight to bed,' he decided, after examining the patient as best he could, 'and take one of these for the night. Agreed? I prepared it earlier . . . just a little powder.'

'Fine by me,' replied Raskolnikov.

He took the powder there and then.

'A very good thing you're going with him,' Zosimov remarked to Razumikhin. 'We'll have to see what tomorrow will bring, but today's not been bad at all: a significant change for the better. You learn something new every day . . .'

'Know what Zosimov whispered to me just now when we were leaving?' Razumikhin blurted out as soon as they were outside. 'I'll be straight with you about everything, brother, seeing as they're all idiots. Zosimov told me to chat to you on the way and get you talking, too, and then tell him, because he's got a notion . . . that you're . . . mad or near enough mad. Can you imagine? First of all, you're three times cleverer than him. Secondly, if you're not crazy why should you care less about his wild ideas? And thirdly, this lump of meat – a surgeon by trade – has gone crazy about mental illness, and your chat with Zametov today made up his mind about you for good.'

'Zametov told you everything?'

'The whole lot, and a good thing too. Now I know all the ins and outs, and so does Zametov . . . Well, to cut a long story short, Rodya . . . The thing is . . . I'm a bit tipsy right now . . . But never mind . . . The thing is, this notion . . . You know? Well, it really is pecking away at them . . . I mean, none of them dare come straight out with it, 'cause it's such raving nonsense, and then, once that painter was brought in it all went up in smoke. But why do they have to be so stupid? I smacked Zametov around a bit at the time – that's between ourselves, brother, and please don't let on. I've noticed he's touchy. It happened at Laviza's – but today, today everything became clear. That Ilya Petrovich, he's the key! He took advantage of you fainting in the bureau that time, and even felt ashamed about it later; I know the whole story . . .'

Raskolnikov was all ears. Razumikhin was drunk and saying more than he should.

'The reason I fainted that time was the stuffiness and the smell of oil paint,' said Raskolnikov.

'As if you need to explain! It wasn't just the paint: you'd had an inflammation developing all month. Ask Zosimov! And what about that kid Zametov – he's simply mortified! "I'm not worth that man's little finger!" he says. Your little finger, he means. He has his kinder moments, you know. But what a lesson he was given today in the "Crystal Palace" – the peak of perfection! What a fright you gave him – turned him into a quivering wreck! You almost had him believing all that hideous nonsense again, then suddenly stuck out your tongue as if to say, "Ha! Fooled you!" Perfection! Now he's crushed, destroyed! You're a genius, damn it – that's the only way to show 'em. If only I'd been there! He was desperate for you to come just now. Porfiry also wants to meet you . . .'

'Ah . . . him as well . . . But why have they decided I'm mad?'

'Not mad exactly. I've been talking too much, brother . . . What struck them, you see, was that you only care about this one point (but now it's clear why, given the circumstances) . . . and how annoyed you got at the time and how it all got mixed up with your illness . . . I'm a bit tipsy, brother, but he's got this notion . . . I'm telling you, he's gone crazy about mental illness. Just ignore him . . .'

Both fell silent for half a minute or so.

'Listen, Razumikhin,' Raskolnikov began, 'I'll be straight with you: I've just come from a death, a civil servant . . . I gave away all my money there . . . and, what's more, I was kissed just now by a creature who, even if I really had killed someone, would also . . . to cut it short, I saw another creature there, too . . . with a feather the colour of fire . . . actually, I'm lying through my teeth. I'm very weak – help me . . . here are the stairs . . .'

'What's wrong with you? What is it?' asked Razumikhin in alarm.

'My head's started spinning, but never mind. I just feel so sad, so terribly sad! Like a woman . . . I mean it! Look, what's that? Look! Look!'

'What?'

'Can't you see? A light in my room, see? Through the crack . . .'

They were already at the bottom of the last flight of stairs, by the landlady's kitchen, and a light in Raskolnikov's garret really was visible from below.

'How strange! Might be Nastasya,' said Razumikhin.

'She's never in my room at this hour, and anyway she'll be fast asleep by now. But . . . what do I care? Goodbye!'

'Are you joking? I'll go with you – we'll go in together!'

'I know we'll go in together, but I feel like shaking your hand and saying goodbye to you here. Well, give me your hand, then, and goodbye!'

'What's wrong, Rodya?'

'Nothing. Let's go. You'll be the witness . . .'

They started climbing the stairs, and the thought flashed through Razumikhin's mind that perhaps Zosimov was right after all. 'I've gone and upset him with all my talk!' he muttered to himself. Suddenly, approaching the door, they heard voices in the room.

'What on earth's going on here?' cried Razumikhin.

Raskolnikov got to the handle first, flung open the door and stood rooted to the threshold.

His mother and sister were sitting on his couch and had already been waiting for an hour and a half. Why had he not been expecting them? Why had he not even been thinking about them, despite the reports, confirmed only today, that they were leaving, that they were on their way, arriving any moment? For an hour and a half now they'd been vying with one another to interrogate Nastasya, who was still standing there before them, having already filled them in on everything. They were beside themselves with worry on hearing that he 'ran off today' while sick and, by all accounts, delirious! 'God, what's the matter with him?' Both had been crying; both had suffered all the agonies of the cross during this one-and-a-half hour wait.

A joyful, ecstatic cry greeted Raskolnikov's appearance. Both women threw themselves upon him. But he was more dead than alive; an awareness of something struck him like thunder, with sudden, excruciating force. He couldn't even lift his arms to embrace them: they wouldn't move. Mother and sister smothered him in embraces, kissed him, laughed, cried . . . He took one step forward, swayed and crashed to the floor in a faint.

Alarm, cries of horror, groans . . . Razumikhin, who'd been standing on the threshold, flew into the room, grabbed the sick man in his mighty arms and laid him out on the couch a second later.

'It's nothing, nothing!' he shouted to the women. 'He just fainted, that's all! The doctor said just now that he's so much better, that he's right as rain! Some water please! See, he's already coming round. See, he's already come to!'

And grabbing Dunechka's hand so hard he almost twisted it, he made her bend over to see for herself that 'he's already come to'. Both mother and sister looked at Razumikhin as if he were Providence itself, with tenderness and gratitude; they'd already heard from Nastasya what this man had done for their Rodya throughout his sickness – this 'competent young man', as he'd been called that evening, in private conversation with Dunya, by Pulkheria Alexandrovna Raskolnikova herself.

PART THREE

I

Raskolnikov raised himself and sat up on the couch.

He gestured feebly to Razumikhin to put an end to the torrent of muddled, fervent reassurances he was directing at the two women, took them both by the hand and spent about two minutes silently studying one, then the other. His mother was frightened by his gaze. It betrayed the most intense emotion, even suffering, but there was also something fixed, almost insane about it. Pulkheria Alexandrovna began to cry.

Avdotya Romanovna was pale; her hand trembled in her brother's.

'Go home now . . . with him,' he said in a faltering voice, pointing towards Razumikhin. 'Till tomorrow. Tomorrow, everything . . . When did you arrive?'

'This evening, Rodya,' Pulkheria Alexandrovna replied. 'The train was terribly late. But Rodya, nothing will drag me away from you! I'll spend the night here beside you . . .'

'Don't torment me!' he said with an irritable wave of his hand.

'I'll stay with him!' cried Razumikhin. 'I won't leave him for even a minute, and all the people at my place can go to hell. They can climb the walls for all I care! I've left my uncle in charge.'

'How, how will I ever thank you?' Pulkheria Alexandrovna began, squeezing Razumikhin's hands once more, but again Raskolnikov interrupted her:

'I can't bear this, I just can't,' he repeated irritably. 'Stop tormenting me! That's enough, just leave . . . I can't bear it!'

'Let's go, Mama, let's wait outside, at least for a moment,' whispered Dunya in fright. 'This is killing him, it's obvious.'

'But can't I even look at him, after three whole years?' wept Pulkheria Alexandrovna.

'Wait!' he stopped them once more. 'You keep interrupting me and I can't think straight . . . Have you seen Luzhin?'

'No, Rodya, but he already knows we've arrived. We heard, Rodya, that Pyotr Petrovich was so kind as to pay you a visit today,' added Pulkheria Alexandrovna with a certain timidity.

'Yes ... so kind ... Dunya, I told Luzhin I'd throw him down the stairs, then I sent him packing ...'

'Rodya, how could you? You must have ... You don't mean to say ... ?' began Pulkheria Alexandrovna in alarm, but stopped after taking one look at Dunya.

Avdotya Romanovna was staring intently at her brother and waiting for him to go on. Both had been forewarned about the row by Nastasya, insofar as she could understand and explain it, and both had gone through agony waiting and wondering.

'Dunya,' Raskolnikov went on with an effort, 'I'm against this marriage, which is why the first thing you should say to Luzhin, tomorrow at the latest, is to reject him and let that be the last we see of him.'

'Good grief!' cried Pulkheria Alexandrovna.

'Brother, think what you're saying!' Avdotya Romanovna flared up, before instantly checking herself. 'Perhaps you're not up to this now. You're tired,' she continued meekly.

'I'm raving, am I? No ... You're marrying Luzhin for me. But I don't accept your sacrifice. So write a letter tonight ... turning him down ... Give it to me to read in the morning and that'll be the end of it!'

'I can't do that!' cried the offended girl. 'What right ... ?'

'Dunechka, you've got a quick temper, too. That's enough ... Tomorrow ... Can't you see?' her mother panicked, rushing towards Dunya. 'Come, we're better off leaving!'

'He's raving!' shouted Razumikhin drunkenly. 'He wouldn't dare otherwise! By tomorrow he'll be making sense again ... But today he really did send him packing. That's true enough. And that chap lost his rag ... There he was holding forth, showing off his learning, and left with his tail between his legs ...'

'So it's true?' cried Pulkheria Alexandrovna.

'Until tomorrow, brother,' said Dunya, compassionately. 'Let's go, Mama ... Goodbye, Rodya!'

'Listen, sister,' he repeated as she was leaving, summoning the last of his strength, 'I'm not raving. This is a scoundrel's marriage. I may be a scoundrel, but you shouldn't ... One or the other ... And even if I am a scoundrel, a sister like that is no sister of mine. It's me or Luzhin! Now go ...'

'You're out of your mind! You're a tyrant!' roared Razumikhin, but Raskolnikov said nothing more; perhaps he had no strength left to do so. He lay down on the couch and turned to the wall in complete exhaustion. Avdotya Romanovna glanced with interest at Razumikhin. Her black eyes flashed: it was enough to make Razumikhin flinch. Pulkheria Alexandrovna just stood there in shock.

'Nothing will drag me away!' she whispered to Razumikhin, in near despair. 'I'll stay here, somewhere . . . you accompany Dunya.'

'And you'll ruin everything!' Razumikhin whispered back, almost beside himself. 'Let's go out onto the landing, at least. Nastasya, give us some light! I swear to you,' he continued on the stairs in a half-whisper, 'that he very nearly started hitting us before, the doctor and me!! Understand? The doctor, no less! He didn't retaliate, for fear of irritating him even more, and left, while I stayed behind downstairs to keep an eye on him, but he got dressed and slipped out. He'll slip out now, too, if you irritate him, out into the night, and who knows what he might do to himself . . . ?'

'What are you saying?'

'And Avdotya Romanovna simply can't be left on her own in those rooms without you! What a place to be staying! As if that scoundrel, Pyotr Petrovich, couldn't have found you anywhere better . . . But I'm a bit drunk, you know, and that's why I was so . . . rude. Don't pay any . . .'

'But I'll go and see the landlady here,' insisted Pulkheria Alexandrovna. 'I'll beg her to find Dunya and me a corner somewhere, just for tonight. I can't leave him in this state. I just can't!'

They were standing on the stairs, on the landing, right in front of the landlady's door. Nastasya was shining a light from the bottom step. Razumikhin was extraordinarily excited. Only half an hour before, walking Raskolnikov home, he may have been talking too much, as he himself was aware, but he felt bright and almost fresh, despite the appalling amount he'd drunk that evening. But now his state of mind verged on ecstasy and it was as though everything he'd drunk had gone to his head all over again, all at once and with redoubled force. Having grabbed both ladies by the hand, he was trying to talk them round and was making his case with astonishing frankness; and as if to press his point home more vigorously, he would give both hands a very hard, painful, vice-like squeeze with almost every word, while almost devouring Avdotya Romanovna with his eyes and without the slightest hint of embarrassment. Sometimes they tried to wrest their aching hands from his enormous, bony great fists, but far from noticing that there was anything the matter, he drew them even harder towards him. Had they ordered him there and then, as a favour, to hurl himself from the stairs head first, he'd have done so immediately, without a moment's hesitation. Pulkheria Alexandrovna, worried sick about her dear Rodya, may have sensed how very eccentric the young man was and how very hard he was squeezing her hand, but for her he was Providence itself, so she had little inclination to notice all these eccentric details. While sharing the same anxiety, Avdotya Romanovna met the blazing, wild gaze of her brother's friend with astonishment and almost with fear, though she was by no means timid, and only the limitless confidence inspired by Nastasya's stories about this strange man stopped her from attempting to run away from him with her mother in tow. She also realized that it was probably too late for that now. In any case, ten minutes or so later she felt considerably calmer: Razumikhin had the habit of getting everything off his chest all at once, with the result that everyone soon learned what kind of man they were dealing with.

'Going to the landlady's out of the question – the very idea's absurd!' he cried, prevailing upon Pulkheria Alexandrovna. 'I know you're his mother, but by staying you'll only whip him up into a frenzy, and the devil knows what will happen then! Listen, here's what we'll do: Nastasya can sit with him for a bit, while I walk you home, because you mustn't be out on your own; in Petersburg that would be . . . Well, never mind! . . . Then I'll run straight back here from yours and within a quarter of an hour, word of honour, I'll bring you my report: how he's feeling, how he's sleeping, etcetera. Then (listen!) I'll dash from your place to mine (I've got guests there, all drunk) and grab Zosimov – that's the doctor who's treating him, he's at my place now, sober. He's always sober, that man, always! And I'll drag him over to Rodya and then straight on to you, so in the space of an hour you'll get two bulletins, one from the doctor – that's right, the doctor himself, so you can forget about me! If it's bad news I'll bring you here myself, I swear, and if it's good news you can just go to bed. And I'll spend the whole night here, near the door, he won't even hear, and I'll tell Zosimov to sleep at the landlady's, so as to have him on hand. Well, what's the best thing for him now, you or a doctor? A doctor and no two ways about it. So you're best going home! The landlady's out of the question; for you, I mean, not for me: she won't have you, because . . . because she's a fool. She's fond of me and jealous of Avdotya Romanovna, if you must know, and of you, too, come to that . . . But definitely Avdotya Romanovna. A quite astonishing individual! But then I'm a fool, too . . . Never mind! Let's go! Do you believe me? Well, do you believe me or don't you?'

'Let's go, Mama,' said Avdotya Romanovna. 'I'm sure he'll do as he says. He's already brought my brother back to life, and if it's true that the doctor will agree to spend the night here, then what could be better?'

'See, you . . . you . . . you understand me . . . You're an angel!' cried Razumikhin in ecstasy. 'Let's go! Nastasya! Go up, quick as you can, and sit with him, with a candle; I'll be back in a quarter of an hour . . .'

Pulkheria Alexandrovna, though not entirely convinced, offered no further resistance. Razumikhin took them both by the arm and dragged them down the stairs. Still, he worried her: 'Yes, he's competent and he's kind, but is he in any condition to do what he promises? Just look at the state of him!'

'Ah, I see what you're thinking: I mean, look at the state of me!' Razumikhin broke in, guessing her thoughts and striding with great big steps along the pavement, with both ladies struggling to keep up – not that he noticed. 'Poppycock! I mean . . . I'm as drunk as an oaf, but that's not the point. I'm not drunk from drink. It was seeing you that went to my head . . . But never mind me! Take no notice: I'm talking rubbish. I'm unworthy of you . . . I'm exceedingly unworthy of you! . . . But just as soon as I've walked you home I'll pour two tubs of water over my head right here by the Ditch and I'll be ready . . . If you only knew how much I love you both! . . . Don't laugh! Don't get angry! Get angry with everyone else, but don't get angry with me! I'm his friend, so I'm your friend too . . . I had a feeling this would happen . . . last year there was this moment . . . Actually, that's not true at all: you fell out of a clear blue sky. And now, I expect I won't sleep a wink all night . . . That Zosimov was afraid he might go mad . . . That's why he mustn't be irritated . . .'

'What are you saying?' cried Pulkheria Alexandrovna.

'Did the doctor really say that?' asked Avdotya Romanovna, frightened.

'He did, but he's completely off the mark. He even gave him some medicine, a powder, I saw him, and then you arrived . . . Dear me! You're better off coming back tomorrow! A good job we left. And in an hour's time Zosimov himself will give you a full report. Now there's a man who's not drunk! And I won't be drunk either . . . But why did I have to get so tanked? Because they picked an argument, damn them! Just when I'd vowed not to argue! . . . The rubbish they talk! I nearly got into a fight! I left my uncle in charge . . . I mean, can you believe it? A complete lack of personality,[1] that's what they're after, that's what excites them! Anything so as not to be themselves, not to resemble themselves! For them, that's the very height of progress. I mean, if only their lies were their own, at least . . .'

'Listen,' Pulkheria Alexandrovna interrupted timidly, but this merely added fuel to the flames.

'Now what are you thinking?' cried Razumikhin, raising even more. 'That it's their lies I can't stand? Nonsense! I like it when people lie. Telling lies is humanity's sole privilege over every other organism. Keep fibbing and you'll end up with the truth! I'm only human because I lie. No truth's ever been discovered without fourteen fibs along the way, if not one hundred and fourteen, and there's honour in that. But our lies aren't even our own! Lie to me by all means, but make sure it's your own, and then I'll kiss you. After all, lies of your own are almost better than someone else's truth: in the first case you're human; in the second you're just a bird! The truth won't run away, but life just might – wouldn't be the first time. I mean, just look at us now! Name anything you like: science, development, thought, inventions, ideals, desires, liberalism, rationalism, experience, anything at all, anything, anything, anything – and we are all, without exception, still stuck in the first years of preparatory school! We just love making do with other people's thoughts – we can't get enough of them! I'm right, aren't I?' shouted Razumikhin, squeezing and shaking the hands of both women. 'Aren't I?'

'Good grief, how should I know?' said poor Pulkheria Alexandrovna.

'Yes, yes . . . although I can't agree with you on every point,' Avdotya Romanovna added seriously, before immediately letting out a shriek, so hard was he gripping her hand.

'Yes? Yes, you say? Well, after this you're . . . you're . . . ,' he cried in ecstasy, 'you're the fount of goodness, purity, reason and . . . perfection! Give me your hand, your hand . . . and you give me yours as well. I want to kiss your hands, here, now, on my knees!'

With that, he fell to his knees in the middle of the pavement, which, thank goodness, was deserted.

'Stop, I beg you! What are you doing?' cried Pulkheria Alexandrovna, deeply alarmed.

'Up you get!' laughed Dunya, also somewhat concerned.

'Not on your life. Not until you give me your hands! There, that'll do. Now I'm up and we can go! I'm a miserable oaf, I'm unworthy of you, and drunk, and ashamed ... I'm unworthy of loving you, but bowing down before you is the duty of any man unless he is an utter brute! So now I have bowed down before you ... And here are the rooms, and they alone justify Rodion for throwing out that Pyotr Petrovich of yours! How dare he put you up in such a place? What a scandal! Do you know what kind of people they allow in here? And you, a bride! You are a bride, aren't you? Well then, let me tell you – your groom is a scoundrel!'

'Mr Razumikhin, you've quite forgotten yourself,' Pulkheria Alexandrovna began.

'Yes, yes, you're right, I've forgotten myself, and I'm ashamed of myself!' said Razumikhin, catching himself. 'But ... but ... you can't be angry with me for speaking like this! It's because I'm speaking my mind, and not because ... H'm! That would be vile. In a word, not because I'm in love with ... H'm! ... Well, let's leave it there. I'd better not. I won't say why, I don't dare! ... Well, we all understood the moment he walked in that he wasn't our sort of chap. Not because he walked in straight from the barber shop, not because he was in such a hurry to flaunt his intelligence, but because he's a snitch and an operator, a niggard and a charlatan – anyone can see it. You think he's clever? No, he's an idiot! An idiot! I mean, is he really any match for you? Good Lord! You see, ladies,' he suddenly stopped, when they were already climbing the stairs to the rooms, 'they may all be drunk at mine, but at least they're honest, and we may all lie, me as much as the next man, but we'll end up with the truth sooner or later, because our path is noble, while Pyotr Petrovich's path ... is not. I may have cursed them just now with every name in the book, but actually I respect them all, even Zametov – all right, I don't respect him, but I love him because he's such a puppy! Even that beast Zosimov, because he's honest and knows his job ... But enough: all is said and all is forgiven. Forgiven? Yes? So let's go. I know this corridor. I've been here before. There was a scandal right here, room Number 3 ... Which is yours? Which number? Eight? Well, lock up for the night and don't let anyone in. I'll be back in a quarter of an hour bearing news, and then half an hour later with Zosimov. You'll see! Goodbye! Must dash!'

'Good grief, Dunechka, where will this end?' said Pulkheria Alexandrovna, turning to her daughter in alarm.

'Calm yourself, Mama,' replied Dunya, taking off her hat and cape. 'God Himself sent us this gentleman, even if he is fresh from some party or other. He can be relied upon, I'm sure of it. Just think of everything he's already done for Rodya . . .'

'Oh, Dunechka, God knows whether he'll come or not! And what on earth made me decide to leave Rodya? . . . And how very different he was from how I'd imagined! How severe! As if he wasn't even happy to see us . . .'

Tears appeared in her eyes.

'No, that's not true, dear Mama. You didn't look closely enough; you were always crying. He's very disturbed by his serious illness – that's the reason behind it all.'

'Oh, this illness! There's trouble ahead! The way he talked to you, Dunya!' she said, looking timidly into her daughter's eyes so as to read all her thoughts, and already half-consoled by the fact that Dunya was actually defending Rodya, so she must have forgiven him. 'I'm convinced he'll have a change of heart tomorrow,' she added, as a final test.

'And I'm equally convinced that tomorrow he'll say exactly the same . . . about that,' snapped Avdotya Romanovna, which, of course, killed the conversation dead, for this was a subject that Pulkheria Alexandrovna was now too frightened to touch. Dunya went up to her mother and kissed her. Pulkheria Alexandrovna hugged her tight, without a word. Then she sat down to wait anxiously for Razumikhin's return and began timidly observing her daughter, who, also waiting, began pensively pacing the room, arms folded. Walking like this from corner to corner, lost in thought, was a common habit of hers, and at such moments her mother was always scared to disturb her.

Razumikhin was ridiculous, of course, in his sudden, drunken infatuation with Avdotya Romanovna; but one look at Avdotya Romanovna – especially now as she was pacing the room with her arms folded, sad and pensive – and many might have forgiven him, to say nothing of his eccentric state of mind. Avdotya Romanovna was remarkably good-looking: tall, astonishingly elegant, strong, with a confidence expressed in her every gesture, while taking nothing away from the softness and gracefulness of her movements. Her face resembled her brother's, but it would have been no exaggeration to call her a beauty. Her hair was brown and slightly lighter than her brother's; her eyes almost black, flashing, proud, yet occasionally, for minutes at a time, uncommonly kind. She was pale, but not sickly pale; her face shone with freshness and health. Her mouth was a little small, and her lower lip, fresh and crimson, protruded ever so slightly, together with her chin – the only imperfection on this beautiful face, but one which gave it its particular character and, incidentally, a kind of haughtiness. Her expression was always more serious than cheerful, always thoughtful; but how well her face was set off by a smile, by laughter, by cheerful, young, carefree laughter! Was it any wonder that ardent, candid, foolish, honest, mighty, drunken Razumikhin, having never seen anything of the kind, lost his head at first sight? What was more, chance – as if on purpose – had given him his first sight of Dunya at this sublime moment of love and joy on seeing her brother. Later, he saw her lower lip quiver indignantly in response to her brother's impudent and ungratefully cruel orders – and could resist no longer.

Still, he was telling the truth earlier on the stairs, when he let slip that drunken comment about Raskolnikov's eccentric landlady, Praskovya Pavlovna, being jealous not only of Avdotya Romanovna but, as likely as not, of Pulkheria Alexandrovna as well. Pulkheria Alexandrovna was already forty-three, but her face still retained traces of her former beauty, and, what was more, she looked far younger than her years, as is almost always the case with women who retain their lucidity of spirit, freshness of impressions and pure, honest ardour of heart into old age. Let us add in parenthesis that retaining all this is, in fact, the only way of keeping one's beauty, at whatever age. Her hair had already begun to turn grey and thin out; small wrinkles had long ago spread out around her eyes; her cheeks were sunken and dry from worry and grief; yet still this face was beautiful. It was the image of Dunechka's face, only twenty years on and without the expression given to Dunya's by her protruding lower lip. Pulkheria Alexandrovna was sensitive but not mawkish, timid and accommodating, but only up to a point: she could concede a lot, agree to a lot, even to things that went against her beliefs, but there was always a limit set by her honesty, her principles and her deepest beliefs, which no circumstances could ever force her to cross.

Precisely twenty minutes after Razumikhin's departure there were two restrained but hurried knocks at the door: he was back.

'Can't stay, must dash!' he rattled off when they opened the door. 'He's snoring away like a trooper, and God willing he'll sleep another ten hours. Nastasya's with him; I told her to stay put till I get back. Now I'll bring Zosimov over. He'll give you his full report and then you should turn in, too. You're dead on your feet, I can see.'

With that, he set off down the corridor.

'What a competent and ... devoted young man!' exclaimed Pul-kheria Alexandrovna, having completely recovered her spirits.

'Seems a very nice chap!' replied Avdotya Romanovna with feeling, beginning to pace the room once more.

Almost an hour later there were footsteps in the corridor and an-other knock at the door. This time both women had waited with com-plete confidence in Razumikhin; and, indeed, here he was already with Zosimov. Zosimov had agreed without a moment's hesitation to leave the party and take a look at Raskolnikov, but he'd come to see the ladies with great reluctance and suspicion, mistrusting Razu-mikhin in his drunken state. His vanity, though, was instantly as-suaged and even tickled: he saw that they really had been waiting for him, as if for an oracle. He stayed for precisely ten minutes, and wholly succeeded in persuading and reassuring Pulkheria Alexan-drovna. He spoke with unusual sympathy, but also with a degree of restraint and with a pronounced seriousness, just as a twenty-seven-year-old doctor ought to speak during an important consultation, and not once did he digress from the subject in hand or show the slightest desire to put his relations with both ladies on a more personal and private footing. Having noted Avdotya Romanovna's dazzling beauty the moment he walked in, he immediately set his mind to ignoring her entirely for the duration of his visit, and addressed himself solely to Pulkheria Alexandrovna. All this afforded him the profoundest inner satisfaction. Regarding the patient, he declared that he found his cur-rent condition wholly satisfactory. His own observations, meanwhile, suggested that the patient's sickness, quite apart from the wretched material circumstances of his life in recent months, also had certain moral causes, 'being the product, so to speak, of many complex moral and material influences, of anxieties, fears, cares, of certain ideas ... and so on'. Noting in passing that Avdotya Romanovna had become especially attentive, Zosimov decided to elaborate a little on this sub-ject. To Pulkheria Alexandrovna's anxious and timid query regarding 'certain suspicions, as it were, of insanity', he replied with a calm and candid smile that his words had been greatly exaggerated; that yes, of course, one could observe in the patient some sort of obsession,

something betraying monomania[2] – after all, he, Zosimov, was following this exceptionally interesting branch of medicine particularly
closely at present – but one had to bear in mind that the patient had
been delirious almost until today and . . . and, of course, the arrival of
his family would make him stronger, distract him and have a salutary
effect, 'so long as fresh shocks to the system can be avoided' – he
added meaningfully. Then he got up, took his leave in an impressive,
cordial manner, accompanied by blessings, fervent gratitude, entreaties and even, without his prompting, the outstretched hand of Avdotya
Romanovna, and walked out, exceptionally pleased with his visit and,
even more so, with himself.

'We'll talk tomorrow. Now off to bed and no dawdling!' Razumikhin said through gritted teeth as he and Zosimov were leaving.
'Tomorrow I'll be back as early as I can with the latest.'

'Now there's a delicious creature, that Avdotya Romanovna!' Zosimov observed, almost licking his lips, once the two of them were
outside.

'Delicious? Delicious, you said?' Razumikhin roared, before suddenly hurling himself at Zosimov and seizing him by the throat. 'Just
you try . . . Got it?' he shouted, shaking him by the collar and pressing
him to the wall. 'Got it?'

'Let me go, you mad drunk!' said Zosimov, fighting him off; then,
once Razumikhin had released him, he stared at him and suddenly
burst out laughing. Razumikhin stood drooped before him, lost in
gloomy, grave deliberation.

'All right, I'm an idiot,' he said, dark as a thunder cloud, 'but then . . .
so are you.'

'No, brother, just you. I'm not the one dreaming.'

They walked on without speaking, and only as they were approaching Raskolnikov's house did Razumikhin, deep in worry, break the
silence.

'Listen,' he began, 'you're a good chap, but, aside from all your
other lousy qualities, you're a letch, I know you are, and a filthy one
to boot. You're highly strung and weak-kneed and half-crazy; you've
run to fat and can't deny yourself anything, which is what I call filth,
because only filth can come of it. You've cosseted yourself so much
that I simply fail to comprehend how you also manage to be a good,
even selfless physician. A doctor who sleeps on a bed of feathers and
gets up at night to tend the sick! Give it three years and you'll stop

getting up at night . . . But that's not the point, dammit. The point is this: you sleep in the landlady's apartment tonight (I had a job convincing her!) and I'll sleep in the kitchen: it's your chance to get to know each other better! It's not what you think! There's not even a hint of that here, brother . . .'

'I wasn't thinking anything.'

'What we have here, brother, is prudery, taciturnity, bashfulness, chastity of the fiercest kind, and yet – she sighs and she melts, she melts like wax! Save me from her, for the love of every devil on earth! She's simply too *avenante*! . . . I'll be forever in your debt!'

Zosimov guffawed even louder than before.

'What on earth's got into you? And what do I want with her?'

'She's not much trouble, I assure you. Just say whatever comes into your head. Just sit with her and talk. Besides, you're a doctor: find something and start curing it. I swear you won't regret it. She's got a clavichord; I like a little tinkle, as you know. I've got a piece there, a real, Russian song: "Burning tears will I shed . . ." She loves the real ones – actually, it was the song that started it all; and you're a virtuoso on the piano, a maestro, a Rubinstein[3] . . . You won't regret it, I assure you!'

'You didn't promise her anything, did you? Or sign something? Maybe you promised to marry her . . .'

'Nothing of the kind! Absolutely not! Anyway, she's not that type at all. Chebarov had a go . . .'

'So just drop her, then!'

'I can't just drop her!'

'Why on earth not?'

'Well, I can't, simple as that! Call it magnetism.'

'So why've you been leading her on?'

'I haven't led her on in the slightest. Maybe I'm the one being led on, in my stupidity, but it won't make a blind bit of difference to her whether it's you or me, just so long as there's someone sitting beside her and sighing. What we have here, brother . . . I just can't put it into words . . . I know you're good at maths and you still keep your hand in . . . Well, start by teaching her integral calculus. I'm not joking, dammit, I'm perfectly serious – it won't make a blind bit of difference to her: she'll look at you and she'll sigh and a year will pass before you know it. You should have heard me telling her about the Prussian House of Lords[4] for two days running (what else should I talk to her about?) – she just sighed and perspired! Just don't touch the subject of love (she's hysterically bashful about that) and make it look like you'll never leave – and that'll do. It's terribly cosy, just like home – you can read, sit, lounge about, write . . . You can even steal a kiss, if you're careful . . .'

'But what good is she to me?'

'If only I could make you understand! Can't you see? You're ideally suited to one another! This isn't the first time I've thought of it . . . After all, this is where you'll end up! So what does it matter whether it's now or later? Think of it, brother, as the bed-of-feathers principle – ha! And not just feathers! It's a magnetic force, the end of the world, an anchor, a quiet haven, the earth's navel, the three fish on which the world still stands, the essence of pancakes, greasy coulibiac pies, the evening samovar, soft sighs and warm knitted jackets, heated benches by the stove – as if you've died, but you're still alive: the best of both worlds! Well, brother, enough of my fibs and nonsense, it's time for bed! You know, I sometimes wake up at night and go and take a look at him. But never mind that, everything's fine. So don't you worry, either, but if you feel like it, you take a look too. And if you notice anything at all – delirium for instance, or a temperature, or whatever – wake me up at once. Though I can't see it happening . . .'

II

It was a worried, serious Razumikhin who woke some time before eight the next morning. He found himself suddenly plagued by a multitude of new and unexpected uncertainties. Never before had he imagined waking in such a state. He remembered yesterday's events down to the very last detail and realized that something out of the ordinary had happened to him, that he had absorbed an impression the like of which he had never known or knew existed. At the same time he was all too aware that the dream that had taken fire in his mind was utterly unrealistic – so unrealistic he even felt ashamed of it and hurriedly turned his attention to the other, more pressing concerns and uncertainties bestowed on him by the previous day, 'may it be forever cursed'.

Most appalling of all was the memory of how 'loathsome and vile' he'd proved himself to be, not just because he'd been drunk but because, jealous fool that he was, he'd rushed to abuse the girl's fiancé to her face, taking advantage of her plight while knowing little not only of their mutual relations and obligations, but even about the man himself. And anyway, what right did he have to judge him so hastily and recklessly? Who'd asked him to act as judge and jury? And could such a creature as Avdotya Romanovna really give herself to an unworthy man for money? So he, too, must have his virtues. Those rooms? How could he have known what they were like? He was preparing an apartment for them, after all . . . ugh, how loathsome! And being drunk was no justification! A stupid excuse that only degraded him all the more! There's truth in wine, and now that truth had all spilled out, i.e., 'all the filth of my coarse and jealous heart'! And how could he, Razumikhin, have even permitted himself such a dream? Who was he next to a girl like that – he, a rowdy drunk, yesterday's show-off? 'Even mentioning us in the same breath is laughable, outrageous!' Thinking this, Razumikhin turned a desperate shade of red, when suddenly, right on cue, at that very same second, yesterday's words on the stairs came back to him loud and clear: that stuff about the landlady being jealous of Avdotya Romanovna . . . This really was the final straw. He struck his fist with full force against the kitchen stove, injuring his hand and dislodging a brick.

'Of course,' he muttered to himself a minute later, filled with a kind of self-abasement, 'nothing will ever be able to paper over so much filth . . . which means there's no use even thinking about it, and I should present myself in silence, and . . . discharge my duties . . . in silence and . . . and not beg for forgiveness, and not say a word and . . . and, of course, all is now lost!'

And yet, getting dressed, he inspected his attire more thoroughly than usual. He had no other clothes, and even if he had, he might not have worn them – 'just because'. Be that as it may, he couldn't carry on being so outrageous, so slovenly: he'd no right to offend other people's feelings, especially when those same people needed him and were themselves inviting him round. He gave his clothes a thorough clean with a brush. His linen was always presentable: he was very particular on that score.

His ablutions that morning were vigorous – he got some soap from Nastasya and washed his hair, his neck and especially his hands. When it came to deciding whether or not to shave (Praskovya Pavlovna had some first-rate razors left over after the death of her late husband, Mr Zarnitsyn), the question was answered fiercely in the negative: 'I'll go as I am! What if they thought I'd shaved for . . . ? They'd be bound to think that! Not on my life!

'And . . . and the main thing is I'm so coarse, so filthy, with manners fit for the tavern; and . . . and so what if I know that I'm actually half-decent, despite all this . . . well, is that anything to be so proud of? Every man should be decent. It's the least you can expect and . . . but still, I've not forgotten that I have the odd skeleton in my closet, too . . . Nothing too disgraceful, but still! . . . And as for some of the ideas I've had! H'm . . . and to set all this alongside Avdotya Romanovna! That's a good one! Well, so what? Now I'll go out of my way to be filthy, lewd, a man of the tavern! Now more than ever!'

He was interrupted in full flow by Zosimov, who'd spent the night in Praskovya Pavlovna's drawing room.

Zosimov was hurrying home and wanted to look in on the patient on his way out. Razumikhin informed him that he was sleeping like a log. Zosimov gave instructions not to wake him. He promised to call round after ten.

'That's assuming he's home,' he added. 'A devil of a business! Try being a doctor when you can't tell your patient what to do! Perhaps you can tell me: will *he* go over to them or will *they* come over to him?'

'The second, I think,' answered Razumikhin, grasping the purpose of the question, 'and they'll be talking about family matters, of course. I'll make myself scarce. Naturally, you have more right to be there than me, being a doctor.'

'I'm hardly his confessor, either. I'll arrive and I'll be gone. I've plenty else to be getting on with.'

'There's one thing bothering me,' interrupted Razumikhin, frowning. 'Yesterday, when I was drunk, I blurted out some stupid things to him on the way home . . . about this and that . . . including your fear that he might be . . . prone to insanity . . .'

'You blurted that out to the ladies, too, yesterday.'

'I know – completely idiotic! Don't mind if you punch me for it! But were you serious about that?'

'Serious? Please! You described him yourself as a monomaniac when you brought me to see him . . . And then yesterday we added more fuel to the flames, or rather you did, with those stories . . . about that painter. A fine topic of conversation when that might have been just the thing that drove him out of his mind! If I'd known the details of what happened in the bureau that time, if I'd known what that

suspicious rascal had said to offend him ... H'm ... Then I'd never
have allowed such a conversation yesterday. These monomaniacs
make mountains out of molehills; in their minds, the wildest inventions take on flesh and blood ... From what I can remember of Zametov's story yesterday, at least half of this business has now become
clear to me. And so what? I know a case of one hypochondriac, forty
years old, who couldn't put up with being mocked every day, over
dinner, by an eight-year-old boy, and killed him! And what do we
have here? A man in rags, an insolent lieutenant, incipient sickness,
and a suspicion like that! Addressed to a crazed hypochondriac![5] Who
happens to be madly, exceptionally vain! Perhaps this is where it all
began – the sickness, I mean! Too bloody right! ... That Zametov, by
the way, really is a sweet little boy, only, h'm ... shame he went and
said all that yesterday. He can never keep his mouth shut!'

'But who did he tell? Me, you, and?'

'Porfiry.'

'So he told Porfiry. So what?'

'By the way, do you have any influence with them, the mother and
sister? We'd better be careful with him today ...'

'They'll get over it!' Razumikhin reluctantly replied.

'And what's he got against this Luzhin? He's a man of means and
she doesn't seem to mind him ... and they haven't a copeck between
them, eh?'

'Why all these questions?' shouted Razumikhin irritably. 'How
should I know how many copecks they have? Ask them and maybe
they'll tell you ...'

'Ugh, what an idiot you are sometimes! That's the drink still talking ... Goodbye then; and thank Praskovya Pavlovna on my behalf for
the bed. She's locked herself in and didn't respond to my *Bonjour*, though
she got up at seven and had the samovar brought in to her straight from
the kitchen ... I wasn't granted the honour of beholding her.'

Razumikhin arrived at Bakaleyev's house at nine o'clock sharp.
The two ladies had been waiting for him for a good long time in a
state of hysterical impatience. They'd been up since seven, if not earlier. He walked in, dark as the night, and bowed awkwardly, which
immediately made him angry – with himself, needless to say. His fears
were ill-founded: Pulkheria Alexandrovna fairly threw herself at him,
seized him by both hands and all but kissed them. He glanced timidly
at Avdotya Romanovna, but at that moment even this haughty face

expressed so much gratitude and friendship, such total and unexpected respect (no mocking glances, no involuntary, ill-concealed contempt!) that he would have found it easier, in all seriousness, to have been greeted with abuse – for this was all far too embarrassing. Luckily, a topic of conversation lay ready and waiting, and he grasped it eagerly.

Hearing that Raskolnikov hadn't woken up yet, though everything was 'absolutely fine', Pulkheria Alexandrovna announced that this was a good thing, too, because she 'desperately, desperately' needed to talk everything over in advance. Razumikhin was invited to take tea with them, as they'd been waiting for him before having theirs. Avdotya Romanovna rang, a filthy ragamuffin appeared, and tea was ordered and eventually served, but in so filthy and disgraceful a manner that the ladies felt positively ashamed. Razumikhin was on the verge of laying into Bakaleyev's rooms but, remembering about Luzhin, fell into an embarrassed silence and was terribly relieved when at last Pulkheria Alexandrovna's questions began flowing thick and fast.

Responding to them, he spoke for three quarters of an hour, through continual interruption and interrogation, and managed to impart all the most crucial and essential facts known to him from the last year of Rodion Romanovich's life, concluding with a detailed account of his illness. All the same, he left out whatever needed to be left out, including the scene in the police bureau, with all its consequences. His listeners hung on his every word; but just when he thought he'd reached the end and satisfied their demands, it turned out that for them he had barely begun.

'Now tell me, tell me, what is your opinion . . . ? Oh, forgive me, I still don't know your name,' rushed Pulkheria Alexandrovna.

'Dmitry Prokofich.'

'Well then, Dmitry Prokofich, I am desperately, desperately keen to learn about how he . . . in general . . . sees things now. I mean – how should I put it, put it best? – I mean, well, what does he like and what doesn't he like? Is he always so very irritable? What does he wish for, as it were, and, as it were, dream about? What influences is he subject to right now? In a word, I would like . . .'

'Oh, Mama, how could anyone reply to all that in one go?' remarked Dunya.

'But heavens, I could never, ever have expected to find him like this, Dmitry Prokofich.'

'That's very understandable, ma'am,' replied Dmitry Prokofich. 'My mother's dead, but my uncle comes here once a year and he nearly always fails to recognize me, even physically, though he's clever enough; so just think how much must have changed in the three years that you've been apart. What can I say? I've known Rodion for a year and a half: he's sullen, gloomy, haughty, proud; recently (and perhaps much earlier, too) he's paranoid and hypochondriac. Generous and kind. Doesn't like to express his feelings and would sooner do something cruel than say what's in his heart. Sometimes, though, he's not hypochondriac at all, just cold and unfeeling to an almost inhuman degree, as if two contrasting characters were taking turns inside him. And he can be terribly untalkative! Never has time for anyone, finds everyone a nuisance, yet lounges around doing nothing. Not given to mockery, but not through lack of wit – rather, it's as if his time is too precious to waste on such trifles. Never listens to the end. Never interested in what everyone else is interested in. Terribly conceited and not, perhaps, without cause. What else? . . . If you ask me, your arrival will have a very salutary effect on him.'

'Pray God!' cried Pulkheria Alexandrovna, worried to death by Razumikhin's report about her Rodya.

Now, at long last, Razumikhin looked up at Avdotya Romanovna with a touch more confidence. He'd glanced at her often in the course of the conversation, but fleetingly, for a mere instant, before immediately looking away. One moment Avdotya Romanovna would sit down at the table and listen closely, the next she would get up again and start pacing the room, as was her habit, from one corner to the other, folding her arms, pressing her lips together and occasionally posing a question of her own, while still walking, deep in thought. She, too, had the habit of not listening to the end. She was wearing a darkish dress of thin material, with a white transparent scarf tied around her neck. It was impossible for Razumikhin not to notice at once the desperate poverty in which both women lived. Had Avdotya Romanovna been dressed like a queen, he would not, it seems, have been remotely afraid of her; but now, precisely because her clothes were so poor, perhaps, and because he could no longer ignore the meanness of her surroundings, terror took root in his heart and he began to fear his every word, his every gesture, and this, of course, was rather inhibiting for a man already lacking in confidence.

'You've said many interesting things about my brother's character and . . . you've spoken without prejudice. That's good. I thought that perhaps you revered him,' Avdotya Romanovna observed with a smile. 'It's also true, it seems, that he needs a woman at his side,' she added pensively.

'I didn't say that, though you may be right there too, only . . .'

'Only what?'

'Well, he doesn't love anyone, and perhaps he never will,' Razumikhin snapped.

'He's not capable of loving, you mean?'

'You know, Avdotya Romanovna, you're just like your brother, in every possible way!' he suddenly blurted out, surprising even himself, then immediately recalled everything he'd just told her about her brother and turned red as a lobster in his embarrassment. Avdotya Romanovna couldn't help laughing aloud at the sight of him.

'You might both be mistaken about Rodya,' Pulkheria Alexandrovna intervened, a little piqued. 'I don't mean now, Dunechka. Pyotr Petrovich may be wrong in what he writes in his letter . . . and you and I may have been wrong in our suppositions, but you can't imagine, Dmitry Prokofich, how fanciful and – how should I put it? – capricious he is. I never had much confidence in his character, even when he was only fifteen. I'm quite sure that even now he is capable of suddenly doing something to himself the like of which no one else would ever even think of . . . To take just one example, did you hear about how, a year and a half ago, he astonished and shocked me with the bright idea of marrying that girl – what's her name again? – the daughter of Zarnitsyna, his landlady? It almost finished me off.'

'Do you know about that story?' asked Avdotya Romanovna.

'Do you imagine,' Pulkheria Alexandrovna went on heatedly, 'that anything would have stopped him then – my tears, my pleas, my illness, my death, perhaps, from grief, our beggary? He'd have stepped right over every obstacle without a second thought. But does he really not love us?'

'He never said anything to me himself about this story,' replied Razumikhin warily, 'but I did hear something about it from Mrs Zarnitsyna, who's not exactly a chatterbox herself, and what I heard was, you might say, a little strange . . .'

'But what, what did you hear?' both women asked at once.

'Nothing so very extraordinary. I merely learned that this marriage, which was all set up and fell through only because of the death of the bride, was not to Mrs Zarnitsyna's liking at all . . . Besides, apparently the bride wasn't even pretty; in fact they say she was ugly . . . and very sickly and . . . and strange . . . though not, it seems, without certain qualities. There must have been some qualities or else one can't make head or tail of it . . . No dowry, either, though he wouldn't have been counting on one anyway . . . Well, it's hard to know what to make of a case like that.'

'I'm sure she was a worthy girl,' remarked Avdotya Romanovna tersely.

'Forgive me God, but I was glad when she died, though I couldn't say who would have ruined whom,' concluded Pulkheria Alexandrovna; then, hesitating and glancing again and again in the direction of Dunya, to the latter's obvious displeasure, she warily launched into another interrogation about yesterday's scene between Rodya and Luzhin. This event evidently worried her more than anything, even terrified her. Razumikhin went over it all again, in detail, but this time he added his own conclusion: he directly accused Raskolnikov of having set out to insult Pyotr Petrovich in advance, making very few allowances this time round for his sickness.

'He thought this up while he was still well,' he added.

'That's what I think, too,' said Pulkheria Alexandrovna, looking devastated. But she was very struck by the fact that Razumikhin had spoken so cautiously on this occasion about Pyotr Petrovich, almost respectfully. Avdotya Romanovna was struck by it, too.

'So that's what you think of Pyotr Petrovich?' Pulkheria Alexandrovna asked, unable to restrain herself.

'I can hold no other opinion about your daughter's husband-to-be,' Razumikhin answered firmly and with feeling, 'and it's not just vulgar courtesy that makes me say so, but because . . . because . . . well, if only because Avdotya Romanovna has herself, of her own free will, seen fit to choose him. And if I was so rude about him yesterday, then only because I was filthy drunk and . . . crazy. Yes, completely crazy, out of my mind . . . and today I'm ashamed of myself!' He reddened and said no more. Avdotya Romanovna flushed, but did not break the silence. She hadn't said a word from the moment the conversation turned to the topic of Luzhin.

Meanwhile her mother, without her support, was evidently in two minds about something. Finally, stammering and glancing again and

again at her daughter, Pulkheria Alexandrovna announced that she
was extremely concerned about one particular circumstance.

'You see, Dmitry Prokofich . . . ,' she began. 'I'll be completely
frank with Dmitry Prokofich, shall I, Dunechka?'

'Yes, of course, Mama,' Avdotya Romanovna encouraged her.

'This is how it is,' she hurried, as if suddenly liberated by this permission to share her grief. 'Today, very early this morning, we received
a note from Pyotr Petrovich in reply to our notification yesterday of
our arrival. Yesterday, you see, he was supposed to meet us, as he'd
promised, at the station. Instead, some servant or other was dispatched
there to meet us and show us the way to this address, and a message
was conveyed from Pyotr Petrovich informing us that he would visit us
here this morning. Instead, this morning we received this note from
him . . . It would be better if you read it yourself. There is one point
that worries me greatly . . . You'll see for yourself which point I mean,
and . . . please be completely frank, Dmitry Prokofich! You know Rodya's character better than anyone and are best placed to advise us. I
should warn you that Dunechka has already decided everything,
straight away, but I, well, I'm still not sure what to do and . . . and was
waiting for you.'

Razumikhin unfolded the note, which bore the previous day's date,
and read the following:

Dear Madam, Pulkheria Alexandrovna,

I have the honour of informing you that owing to the occurrence of un-
foreseen delays I was unable to greet you off the train, having dispatched
to that end a highly competent person. Equally I must forgo the honour of
meeting you tomorrow morning, owing to pressing business in the Senate
and so as not to disturb your family reunion with your son and Avdotya
Romanovna's with her brother. I shall have the honour of visiting you and
paying you my respects in your apartment on the morrow, at 8 p.m. sharp,
moreover I take the liberty of adducing an earnest and, let me add, very
firm request that Rodion Romanovich not be present at our general meeting, in light of the unprecedented and discourteous offence which he
caused me yesterday during my visit to his sickbed, and, aside from that,
having an urgent need to discuss a certain point with you personally in
depth, regarding which I desire to know your personal interpretation. I

have the honour of giving prior notification that if, contrary to my request, I should meet Rodion Romanovich, I shall be obliged to take my leave without delay – and then you'll have no one to blame but yourselves. For I write in the supposition that Rodion Romanovich, having appeared so very sick during my visit, suddenly recovered two hours later, and therefore, on leaving his premises, may present himself at yours. I have received confirmation of this with my own eyes, in the apartment of a drunk who was run over by horses and died as a result, to whose daughter, a girl of notorious conduct, he gave as much as twenty-five roubles yesterday, on the pretext of a funeral, which fact greatly astonished me, knowing how much of a struggle it was for you to assemble this sum. By these presents, with an expression of my especial respect to the esteemed Avdotya Romanovna, I ask you to accept the respectful devotion of

> your humble servant
> *P. Luzhin*

'So what should I do, Dmitry Prokofich?' began Pulkheria Alexandrovna, on the verge of tears. 'How on earth can I suggest to Rodya not to come? He was so insistent yesterday that we reject Pyotr Petrovich, and here he is under instructions not to be accepted himself! He'll come on purpose when he finds out . . . and then what?'

'Do as Avdotya Romanovna has decided,' Razumikhin answered calmly and without hesitation.

'Good grief! She says . . . she says God knows what and she doesn't explain the point of it! She says it is better, or rather not better but for some reason absolutely essential for Rodya also to come specially today at eight o'clock and for them to meet without fail . . . But I didn't even want to show him the letter – I wanted to find some cunning way, through you, of stopping him coming . . . because he's so very irritable . . . And I don't understand any of this anyway – what drunkard, what daughter, and how did he manage to give away to this daughter all the remaining money . . . which . . . ?'

'Which was obtained at such cost to yourself, Mama,' added Avdotya Romanovna.

'He wasn't himself yesterday,' said Razumikhin pensively. 'If you'd heard some of the things he was saying in the tavern yesterday, clever as they were . . . h'm! He did say something to me when we were walking home about some chap who'd died and some girl or other, but I didn't understand a word of it . . . But then I wasn't up to much yesterday, either . . .'

'We're best off going to see him ourselves, Mama. I'm sure we'll know what to do as soon as we get there. And just look at the time – goodness me! Gone ten already!' she cried, after glancing at her splendid gold, enamelled timepiece, which hung from her neck on a fine Venetian chain and was utterly out of keeping with the rest of her outfit. 'Present from the fiancé,' thought Razumikhin.

'Oh, we must go! . . . Time to go, Dunechka, time to go!' fussed Pulkheria Alexandrovna. 'He'll think we're still angry from yesterday, if it's taken us so long. Good grief!'

Saying this, she hurriedly threw on a cape and put on her hat. Dunechka also got herself ready. Her gloves were not only worn, they were in shreds, as Razumikhin noticed, yet the patent poverty of their attire gave both women an air of particular dignity, as is always the way with those who know how to dress in pauper's clothes. Razumikhin looked with reverence at Dunechka and felt proud to be accompanying her. 'The queen,' he thought to himself, 'who darned her own stockings[6] in prison must have looked every inch the part at that moment, even more so than during her most lavish public ceremonies.'

'Good grief!' exclaimed Pulkheria Alexandrovna. 'Could I ever have imagined fearing a meeting with my son, my sweet Rodya, as I fear it now? . . . I'm scared, Dmitry Prokofich!' she added, with a timid glance.

'Don't be scared, dear Mama,' said Dunya, kissing her, 'you should have faith in him. I do.'

'Good grief! I do have faith in him, but I didn't sleep a wink last night!' cried the poor woman.

They went outside.

'You know, Dunechka, just as soon as I snatched a little sleep this morning, I suddenly dreamt of Marfa Petrovna, God rest her soul . . . dressed all in white . . . She came up to me and took my hand while shaking her head at me, so very seriously, as if in disapproval . . . What am I to make of it? Good grief, Dmitry Prokofich, you still don't know: Marfa Petrovna has died!'

'No, I didn't know. Which Marfa Petrovna?'

'Quite suddenly! And just imagine . . .'

'Later, Mama,' Dunya broke in. 'After all, the gentleman still doesn't know who Marfa Petrovna is.'

'Oh, you don't? There was I thinking you already knew everything. Please forgive me, Dmitry Prokofich, I'm at my wits' end. Truly, I think of you as our Providence, and that's why I was so sure you already knew everything. I think of you as one of the family . . . Don't be angry with me for speaking like this. Good grief, what's happened to your right hand? Have you hurt it?'

'Yes, I hurt it,' muttered Razumikhin, suddenly happy.

'Sometimes I speak rather too openly and Dunya has to prod me . . . But how on earth can he live in such a tiny cell? Has he woken up, though? And that woman, his landlady, calls that a room? Listen, you say he doesn't like to display his feelings, so perhaps I'll only annoy him with my . . . foibles? . . . Can't you teach me, Dmitry Prokofich? How should I act with him? I'm all at sea.'

'Don't keep asking him about anything if you see him frowning, and in particular don't ask him too much about his health. He doesn't like it.'

'Oh, Dmitry Prokofich, how hard it is to be a mother! But here's that stairwell . . . Such a horrid stairwell!'

'Mama, you've even gone pale. Calm yourself, my dearest,' said Dunya, stroking her. 'He ought to be happy to see you, and here you are tormenting yourself,' she added, with a flash of her eyes.

'Wait, I'll go ahead to see if he's woken up yet.'

The ladies set off slowly up the stairs after Razumikhin, and when they drew level with the landlady's door on the fourth floor they noticed that it was just slightly ajar and that two quick black eyes were examining them both from the dark. When their eyes met, the door suddenly slammed shut with such a bang that Pulkheria Alexandrovna nearly screamed with fright.

III

'Better, better!' Zosimov shouted to them cheerfully as they entered. He'd arrived some ten minutes earlier and was sitting at the same end of the couch as the day before. Raskolnikov was sitting at the opposite end, all dressed up and even thoroughly scrubbed and combed, for the first time in a very long while. The room filled up at once, but Nastasya still managed to follow the visitors in and started listening.

Raskolnikov really was almost better, especially when compared to the previous day, but he was very pale, distracted and sullen. He might have been taken for a man who'd been wounded or who was in acute physical pain: his brows were knitted, his lips clenched, his eyes swollen. He spoke little and unwillingly, as though he were forcing himself or discharging a duty, and every now and again his gestures betrayed a certain anxiety.

The only thing lacking was a sling on his arm or gauze round his finger to complete his resemblance to a man with an excruciating abscess or an injured hand or something of that kind.

Still, even this pale and sullen face seemed to light up momentarily when his mother and sister walked in, though this merely lent to his features a greater intensity of torment, in place of the anguished distraction of before. The light faded quickly, but the torment remained, and Zosimov, observing and studying his patient with all the youthful enthusiasm of a doctor who has only just begun to practise, was surprised to see him react to his family's arrival not with joy but with a kind of grim, hidden resolve to endure an hour or two of torture that could be put off no longer. Later, he noticed how almost every word in the ensuing conversation seemed to touch a nerve in his patient or irritate a wound; but at the same time he was amazed by his self-control, by the new-found ability of yesterday's monomaniac to conceal his feelings, when only the day before the slightest word had been enough to drive him to the edge of fury.

'Yes, I can see myself I'm almost better,' said Raskolnikov, kissing his mother and sister warmly, which instantly made Pulkheria Alexandrovna beam, 'and that's not the me of yesterday speaking,' he added, turning to Razumikhin and offering him a friendly handshake.

'I've been quite amazed by him today, I must say,' Zosimov began, greatly relieved by their arrival: keeping up a conversation with his patient for a whole ten minutes had proved beyond him. 'In three or four days' time, if he keeps on like this, he'll be just as he was before; I mean, just as he was a month ago, or two . . . or perhaps even three? After all, this didn't just begin now . . . it's been brewing for a while, eh? Perhaps you'll admit now that you were to blame, too?' he added with a wary smile, as if still afraid of irritating him in some way.

'Quite possibly,' Raskolnikov answered coldly.

'The reason I say that,' Zosimov continued, warming to his theme, 'is that your full recovery now depends mainly and solely on you. Now that you are capable of proper conversation, I should like to impress upon you how essential it is for you to eliminate the primary and, as it were, deep-rooted causes that helped bring about your illness; only then will you be cured, while the alternative may be even worse. I don't know what these primary causes are, but you should. You're an intelligent man, after all, and you must have studied your own symptoms. It seems to me that the onset of your condition coincided at least in part with your leaving university. You need to keep yourself occupied, which is why work and a clearly defined aim could, it seems to me, help you greatly.'

'Yes, yes, how right you are . . . I'll resume my studies just as soon as I can and then everything will be . . . just dandy . . .'

Zosimov, who had delivered these pearls of wisdom partly to impress the ladies, was, of course, rather taken aback when, after finishing his speech and glancing at his listener, he noticed a look of unmistakable derision on his face. But it lasted no more than an instant. Pulkheria Alexandrovna immediately set about thanking Zosimov, especially for his visit to their rooms the night before.

'You mean he was with you last night too?' asked Raskolnikov, as if in alarm. 'So you didn't get any sleep after the journey either?'

'Oh, Rodya, that was all over by two. Even at home Dunya and I never went to bed before two.'

'I don't know how to thank him either,' Raskolnikov went on, frowning and staring at the floor. 'Setting aside the question of money – and do forgive me for mentioning it' (he remarked to Zosimov) 'I just can't imagine what I've done to deserve such special attention from you. I simply don't understand it . . . and . . . and actually, I find it rather difficult, for that same reason. I'm being frank with you.'

'Now don't get worked up,' said Zosimov with a forced laugh. 'Just imagine that you're my first patient and, well, anyone who's just started practising loves his first cases like his own children; some almost fall in love with them. As for me, I'm hardly overrun with patients.'

'And I haven't even mentioned him,' added Raskolnikov, pointing to Razumikhin. 'He's had nothing from me except insults and bother.'

'Complete drivel! Feeling sentimental, are we?' Razumikhin shouted.

He would have seen, had he been a little more perceptive, that there was nothing sentimental about Raskolnikov's mood; if anything, just the opposite. But Avdotya Romanovna had noticed. Her anxious gaze never left her brother.

'I daren't even mention you, Mama,' he went on, as though he'd memorized these lines in the morning. 'Only today could I begin to understand what you must have been through here, yesterday, waiting for me to return.' Having said this, he suddenly stretched out a hand to his sister with a wordless smile. But this time real, unfeigned emotion could be glimpsed in his smile. Dunya immediately grabbed the hand extended towards her and squeezed it tight, gladdened and grateful. It was the first time he'd spoken to her since yesterday's disagreement. His mother's face lit up with ecstatic happiness at the sight of this definitive, silent reconciliation between brother and sister.

'And that's why I love him!' whispered Razumikhin, exaggerating as always and turning round energetically in his chair. 'He has these sudden gusts!'

'And how well he carries it all off,' Pulkheria Alexandrovna thought to herself. 'What noble impulses he has, and how simply, how tactfully he put an end to yesterday's misunderstanding with his sister – merely by stretching out a hand and looking at her nicely . . . And what beautiful eyes he has, what a beautiful face in general! . . . He's even better looking than Dunechka . . . But good grief, just look at the state of his suit! Even Vasya, the errand boy in Afanasy Ivanovich's shop, is better dressed than he is! . . . If only I could run over to him and hug him and . . . cry – but I'm afraid, afraid . . . dear God, there's something about him! . . . Even when he's tender I'm afraid! What on earth am I afraid of?'

'Oh, Rodya,' she said suddenly, hurrying to reply to his comment, 'you wouldn't believe how . . . miserable Dunechka and I were yesterday! Now it's all over and we're all happy again, I can tell you more. Just imagine, we were rushing over here to embrace you, almost straight off the train, and this woman – ah, here she is! Hello, Nastasya! . . . She suddenly told us that you'd been in bed, raving deliriously, and that you'd just given your doctor the slip and gone out, still delirious, and people had run off to look for you. Can you imagine the state we were in? I couldn't help thinking of the tragic death of Lieutenant Potanchikov, an acquaintance of ours, a friend of your father's – you won't remember him, Rodya. He was delirious, too, and ran off just like you did and fell down the well in the yard – he wasn't pulled out till the next day. And, of course, that wasn't the worst we imagined. We were about to rush off to look for Pyotr Petrovich, maybe he could do something . . . because we were alone here, quite alone,' she went on plaintively, then suddenly cut herself short, remembering that it wasn't yet safe to bring up Pyotr Petrovich, despite the fact that everyone was 'already entirely happy again'.

'Yes, yes ... all very vexing, of course ...,' Raskolnikov mumbled in reply, but with such a distracted, almost inattentive air that Dunechka looked at him in astonishment.

'What was the other thing?' he continued, trying hard to remember. 'Oh yes. Please, Mama, and you, Dunechka, please don't think I didn't want to come to you first today and was just waiting for you here.'

'Whatever next, Rodya?' cried Pulkheria Alexandrovna, also surprised.

'Why's he replying like this – from a sense of duty?' Dunechka wondered. 'Making peace, asking forgiveness, as if he were going through the motions or had learned it all by rote.'

'I'd just woken up and was all ready to go, but my clothes kept me back. I forgot yesterday to tell her ... Nastasya ... to wash off that blood ... I've only just managed to get dressed now.'

'Blood! What blood?' panicked Pulkheria Alexandrovna.

'It's nothing ... don't worry. There was blood because yesterday, when I was knocking about, slightly delirious, I came across a man who'd been run over and trampled ... a civil servant ...'

'Delirious? But you remember everything,' Razumikhin broke in.

'That's true,' Raskolnikov replied with unusual solicitude, 'I remember everything down to the very last detail, but try asking me why I did this or that, went here or there, said this or that, and I'd be hard put to tell you.'

'An all too familiar phenomenon,' Zosimov intervened. 'A deed can be carried out in a consummate, highly resourceful fashion, but the subject's control over his actions, the basis of his actions, is disturbed and depends on various morbid impressions. As if he were dreaming.'

'Well, it's probably no bad thing that he thinks me half-mad,' thought Raskolnikov.

'But you could probably say exactly the same about the healthy,' observed Dunechka, looking anxiously at Zosimov.

'A quite accurate observation,' the latter replied. 'In this sense all of us are, often enough, pretty much crazy, with the one small distinction that "the sick" are that little bit crazier – one must draw a line. It's true, though, that there's almost no such thing as a well-balanced person. You might find one in a hundred, or one in several hundred thousand, and even then only a fairly weak specimen ...'

At the word 'crazy', which Zosimov, getting carried away by his favourite topic, had carelessly let slip, everyone frowned. Raskolnikov sat there as if he hadn't noticed, deep in thought and with a strange smile on his pale lips. He was still trying to work something out.

'Well, what about that man who got trampled? I interrupted you!' shouted Razumikhin in a hurry.

'What?' said Raskolnikov, as if waking up. 'Oh yes . . . well, I stained myself with blood when I helped carry him into the apartment . . . By the way, Mama, I did one unforgivable thing yesterday. I really must have been out of my mind. Yesterday I gave away all the money you sent me . . . to his wife . . . for the funeral! She's a widow now, consumptive, a pitiful woman . . . Three little orphans, all hungry . . . nothing in the house . . . and another daughter as well . . . You might have done the same if you'd seen . . . Though I had no right at all, I admit, especially knowing how you got this money in the first place. To help, one must first have the right to help, otherwise it's "*Crevez, chiens, si vous n'êtes pas contents!*"[7] He laughed. 'Isn't that right, Dunya?'

'No, it's not,' Dunya replied firmly.

'Ha! Now you, too . . . with your own intentions!' he muttered with a mocking smile, looking at her almost with hatred. 'I should have expected that . . . Well, I suppose it's commendable . . . and at some point you'll reach a mark: stop there and you'll be miserable; step over it and you might be more miserable still . . . But anyway, how stupid this is!' he added, annoyed that he'd let himself get carried away. 'All I wanted to say, Mama, is that I'm asking your forgiveness,' he concluded tersely and abruptly.

'That'll do, Rodya, I'm sure that everything you do is quite wonderful!' said his gladdened mother.

'Don't be so sure,' he replied, twisting his mouth into a smile. Silence followed. There was something strained about the whole conversation – the silence, the reconciliation, the forgiveness – and everyone could feel it.

'Maybe they really are afraid of me,' Raskolnikov thought to himself, with a mistrustful glance at his mother and sister. And indeed, the longer Pulkheria Alexandrovna was silent, the more timid she became.

'I seemed to love them so much from a distance,' flashed through his mind.

'You know, Rodya, Marfa Petrovna has died!' Pulkheria Alexandrovna suddenly ventured.

'Who's Marfa Petrovna?'

'Good grief . . . You know, Marfa Petrovna, Svidrigailova! How many times have I written to you about her?'

'Ah yes, I remember . . . So she's died, has she? Has she really?' he asked, as if suddenly rousing himself. 'Of what?'

'Just like that. Can you imagine?' Pulkheria Alexandrovna rattled on, encouraged by his curiosity. 'And just after I sent off that letter to you, on that very same day! The cause of her death seems to have been that dreadful man – can you imagine? He gave her an awful beating by all accounts.'

'Was that really how they lived?' he asked, turning to his sister.

'No, quite the opposite. He was always very patient with her, even courteous. In fact, he was probably much too indulgent, for seven years running . . . His patience must have suddenly snapped.'

'He can hardly be that dreadful, then, if he managed to grin and bear it for seven years. You seem to be standing up for him, Dunechka.'

'No, no, he's dreadful! I can't imagine anyone more dreadful,' Dunya replied, almost with a shudder. She frowned and became pensive.

'It happened at their place in the morning,' Pulkheria Alexandrovna hurried on. 'Afterwards, she immediately had the horses harnessed, so that she could go into town straight after lunch, because she would always go into town on such occasions; she had a very hearty appetite that day, by all accounts . . .'

'After being beaten?'

'. . . Well, she'd always had this . . . habit, and as soon as she'd eaten, so as not to be late setting off, she immediately went off to the bathing hut . . . You see, water was a kind of cure for her. They've got a cold spring there and she'd bathe in it every day, and just as soon as she got in – a stroke!'

'Now there's a surprise!' said Zosimov.

'Did he beat her badly, then?'

'What difference does it make?' answered Dunya.

'A fine topic for conversation, Mama, I must say,' Raskolnikov suddenly snapped, as if without meaning to.

'But my dear, I didn't know what else to talk about,' Pulkheria Alexandrovna blurted out.

'Are you all scared of me, is that it?' he asked with a twisted grin.

'Yes, it's true,' said Dunya, fixing her brother with a stern look. 'Coming up the stairs, Mama even crossed herself from fear.'

His face twisted, as if from a spasm.

'Oh really, Dunya! Please don't get angry, Rodya . . . Dunya, did you have to?' Pulkheria Alexandrovna began in embarrassment. 'I won't deny that I spent the entire train journey dreaming about seeing you again, about all the things we would have to tell each other . . . and I felt so happy I barely noticed the journey! But what am I saying? I'm happy now, too. You shouldn't have, Dunya! Just seeing you, Rodya, is enough to make me happy . . .'

'That'll do, Mama,' he mumbled in embarrassment, squeezing her hand without looking at her. 'We'll have plenty of time to talk!'

Saying this, he suddenly became troubled and pale: once again a dreadful, recent sensation touched his soul with a deathly chill, once again it suddenly became crystal clear to him that he'd just told a dreadful lie, that not only would he never have plenty of time to talk, but that now it had become impossible for him to *talk* about anything, with anyone, ever again. The effect produced on him by this excruciating thought was so powerful that, for a moment, he fell into a kind of trance, got to his feet and, without a glance in anyone's direction, made for the door.

'Now what?' shouted Razumikhin, grabbing him by the arm.

He sat down again and began looking around without speaking. They were all staring at him in bewilderment.

'What on earth's the matter with you all?' he suddenly cried, quite out of the blue. 'Say something! We can't just sit here! Well? Speak! Let's have a conversation . . . seeing as we've got together . . . Anything!'

'Thank goodness for that! For a moment I thought he was back to how he was yesterday,' said Pulkheria Alexandrovna, crossing herself.

'What is it, Rodya?' asked Avdotya Romanovna mistrustfully.

'Oh, nothing, I just remembered something,' he replied, and suddenly burst out laughing.

'Well, nothing wrong with that! I was also beginning to think . . . ,' muttered Zosimov, getting up from the couch. 'Time for me to be off, though. I might drop by again later . . . if I find you in . . .'

He bowed and left.

'What a splendid man!' remarked Pulkheria Alexandrovna.

'Yes, a splendid man, first-rate, educated, intelligent . . . ,' Raskolnikov suddenly began to say at surprising speed and with unusual gusto. 'Can't remember where it was I met him before I fell sick . . . Pretty sure I did meet him somewhere . . . And he's all right, too!' he added, nodding towards Razumikhin. 'How do you like him, Dunya?' he asked her and suddenly, for no apparent reason, burst out laughing.

'Very much,' replied Dunya.

'Ugh, you . . . swine!' said a terribly embarrassed, bright-red

Razumikhin, getting up from his chair. Pulkheria Alexandrovna half-smiled and Raskolnikov roared with laughter.

'Where are you off to?'

'I've also . . . I have to . . .'

'No you don't – stay where you are! Zosimov's left, so you have to go too? Don't go . . . What's the time? Is it twelve yet? What a lovely watch you have, Dunya! Now why have you all gone quiet again? Why's it always me doing the talking?'

'It's a present from Marfa Petrovna,' replied Dunya.

'An extremely expensive one,' added Pulkheria Alexandrovna.

'I see! Look at the size of it – more like a man's watch.'

'I like this kind,' said Dunya.

'So it's not from the fiancé,' thought Razumikhin, rejoicing.

'There was me thinking Luzhin gave it to you,' remarked Raskolnikov.

'No, Dunechka hasn't received any gifts from him yet.'

'I see! And do you remember, Mama, when I was in love and wanted to get married?' he suddenly said, looking at his mother, who was struck by the sudden change of subject and the tone with which he'd broached it.

'Oh yes, my dear, of course I do!'

Pulkheria Alexandrovna exchanged glances with Dunechka and Razumikhin.

'H'm! Yes! But what should I tell you? I don't even remember very much about it. She was always poorly,' he went on, suddenly looking thoughtful again and staring at the floor, 'such a sickly young girl; liked giving alms, always dreaming of the nunnery, and when she started telling me about it once she was in floods of tears. Yes, yes . . . I remember that . . . I remember it very well. She was . . . ugly enough. Heaven knows why I became so fond of her – because she was always ill, I suppose . . . If she'd been lame as well, or a hunchback, I suppose I'd have loved her even more . . .' He smiled pensively. 'The spring must have gone to my head . . .'

'No, it wasn't that,' said Dunechka with feeling.

He looked at his sister closely, intently, but he didn't catch the words, or else he didn't understand them. Then, deep in thought, he got up, went over to his mother, kissed her, returned to his place and sat down.

'You still love her now?' said Pulkheria Alexandrovna, touched.

'Her? Now? Oh, I see . . . you mean her! No. That's a world away now ... and so long ago. Actually, everything seems to be happening somewhere else ...'

He looked at them attentively.

'Take you, for example ... It's as if I were looking at you from a distance of a thousand miles ... But what the devil are we talking about? And why all these questions?' he snapped, then fell silent, biting his nails and sinking into thought once more.

'What a horrid room you have, Rodya – just like a coffin,' said Pulkheria Alexandrovna suddenly, breaking the awkward silence. 'I'm sure that's half the reason you've become such a melancholic.'[8]

'The room?' he replied distractedly. 'Yes, the room had a lot to do with it ... That's occurred to me, too ... But if you only knew, Mama, what a strange thing you've just said,' he suddenly added with a peculiar grin.

A little more, and this group of people, this family, together again after three years, and this familial way of talking despite there being nothing at all to talk about, would have become utterly unbearable for him. There was, however, one urgent matter that had to be resolved today one way or another – or so he'd decided when he woke up. Now he rejoiced at having something *to do*, as if it were a way out.

'Now listen, Dunya,' he began seriously and tersely. 'Please forgive me, of course, for what happened yesterday, but I consider it my duty to remind you again that I won't yield an inch on my main point. It's me or Luzhin. I may be a scoundrel, but you shouldn't do it. One or the other. Marry Luzhin and I'll no longer consider you my sister.'

'Rodya, Rodya! But this is just what you were saying yesterday,' cried Pulkheria Alexandrovna bitterly. 'And why do you keep calling yourself a scoundrel? It's more than I can bear! Yesterday was just the same ...'

'Brother,' Dunya replied firmly, and no less tersely, 'you're making a mistake here. I thought it through overnight and located it. You seem to think that I'm sacrificing myself to someone and for someone. But that's not the case at all. I'm marrying for my own sake, that's all, because life is hard enough for me, too. Naturally, I'll be only too glad if I also manage to be of help to my family, but that's not the main motive for my decision ...'

'She's lying!' he thought to himself, biting his nails from spite. 'Too proud by half! Can't admit she wants to do good! Oh, vile souls! Even their love is like hatred ... Oh, how I ... hate them all!'

'In short, I'm marrying Pyotr Petrovich,' Dunechka continued, 'because it's the lesser of two evils. I intend to be honest in carrying out everything he expects of me, and therefore I am not deceiving him . . . Why did you smile like that just now?'

She also reddened, eyes flashing with anger.

'You'll carry out everything?' he asked, with a poisonous smirk.

'Up to a point. Both the manner and the form of Pyotr Petrovich's proposal showed me right away what it is that he needs. He does not lack self-esteem, of course, and perhaps he has too much of it, but I hope he esteems me, too . . . Now why are you laughing again?'

'And why are you blushing again? You're lying, sister. You're lying on purpose, out of sheer female stubbornness – anything so as not to yield an inch to me . . . You can't respect Luzhin. I've seen him. I've spoken to him. Which means you're selling yourself for money, which means you're behaving despicably and I'm glad that at least you're still capable of blushing!'

'That's not true! I'm not lying!' cried Dunechka, losing all composure. 'I'll only marry him if I'm convinced that he values and prizes me; and I'll only marry him if I am quite convinced that I'm capable of respecting him. Fortunately, I have the opportunity to make absolutely certain of this no later than today. Such a marriage is not shameful. You're wrong! And even if you were right, even if I really had decided to do something shameful – then wouldn't it be heartless of you to speak to me like this? Why demand of me a degree of heroism you may not even possess yourself? That's tyranny, coercion! The only person I run the risk of ruining is myself . . . I haven't killed anyone! Now why are you looking at me like that? Why have you gone so pale? Rodya, what's wrong? Rodya, my dearest! . . .'

'Good grief! You've made him faint!' cried Pulkheria Alexandrovna.

'No, no . . . nonsense . . . It was nothing! . . . Just a bit of dizziness. I certainly didn't faint . . . You've got a thing about fainting! . . . H'm! . . . Now what was I saying? Oh yes: how will you make certain no later than today that you are capable of respecting him and that he . . . esteems you – is that how you put it? It was today, wasn't it? Or did I mishear you?'

'Mama, show Rodya the letter from Pyotr Petrovich,' said Dunechka.

Pulkheria Alexandrovna passed him the letter in her trembling hands. He took it with the greatest curiosity. But before unfolding it he suddenly glanced with a sort of astonishment at Dunechka.

'How strange,' he said slowly, as though suddenly struck by a new thought. 'Why am I getting so involved? Why all this fuss? Marry whoever you like!'

He seemed to be speaking to himself, but he said the words out loud and looked for some time at his sister, as if puzzled by something.

He eventually unfolded the letter, still retaining a look of strange astonishment; then he began reading it through, slowly and attentively, and read it again. Pulkheria Alexandrovna was unusually tense; in fact, everyone was expecting something unusual.

'I'm amazed,' he began after a few moments' reflection, passing the letter back to his mother, but addressing no one in particular. 'I mean, he's a man of business, a lawyer, even speaks with a certain ... swagger – but look, he's barely literate.'

Everyone stirred. This was the last thing they were expecting.

'But they all write like that,' came Razumikhin's curt comment.

'You mean you've read it, too?'

'Yes.'

'We showed it to him, Rodya. We ... talked it over together earlier,' Pulkheria Alexandrovna began.

'It's lawyer-speak, that's all,' Razumikhin interrupted. 'That's the way legal documents have always been written.'

'Legal? Yes, that's right – legal, business-like ... Not exactly illiterate or exactly literary: business-like!'

'Pyotr Petrovich doesn't conceal the fact that he was educated on a shoestring, and even boasts about having made his own way in life,' remarked Avdotya Romanovna, rather offended by her brother's new tone.

'Well, if he's boasting, then he must have something to boast about – I won't argue. You seem to be offended, sister, that the only thing I had to say about the whole letter was this frivolous observation, and you think I deliberately picked up on such petty things because I was annoyed and wanted to show off a bit. On the contrary, as regards style, a very pertinent point occurred to me. There's a certain expression he uses: "You'll have no one to blame but yourselves", very prominently placed; and besides, there's the threat that he'll leave immediately if I come. This threat actually amounts to a threat to abandon you both if you fail to do as he says, and to abandon you now, after he's already summoned you to Petersburg. What do you think? Can such an expression be as offensive coming from Luzhin as if it had been written by, say, him,' (he pointed at Razumikhin) 'or Zosimov or any one of us?'

'N-no,' replied Dunechka, livening up a bit. 'I could see perfectly well that this was very artlessly put and that perhaps he is simply no great writer . . . You put that very well, brother. I wasn't expecting it . . .'

'It's said like a lawyer, and in legal-speak there's no other way of putting it, so it came out sounding more vulgar than perhaps he intended. But I have to disappoint you a little: in this letter there's one other expression, an aspersion cast on me, and a fairly shabby one at that. The money I gave away yesterday went to a widow, a consumptive, devastated widow, and not "on the pretext of the funeral", but for the funeral itself, and I gave it not to the daughter – a girl, as he writes, "of notorious conduct" (whom, by the way, I had never seen before) – but to the widow herself. In all this I see a great haste to sully me and set us against each other. Once again, it's said like a lawyer: the purpose is far too blatant and the haste is artless in the extreme. He's an intelligent man, but to act intelligently you need more than that. It all goes to show what he's like . . . and I doubt he esteems you all that much. I'm telling you this simply for your own edification, because I sincerely want what's best for you . . .'

Dunechka made no reply. She'd already taken her decision earlier, and now she was just waiting for the evening.

'So what have you decided, Rodya?' asked Pulkheria Alexandrovna, even more worried than before by his sudden, new, *business-like* tone.

'What do you mean – "decided"?'

'Well, here's Pyotr Petrovich writing that you mustn't be at ours this evening and that he'll leave . . . if you are. So what have you . . . will you come?'

'That, of course, is not for me to decide, but, firstly, for you, if Pyotr Petrovich's demand does not offend you, and secondly, for Dunya, if she, too, is not offended. And I'll do whatever suits you best,' he added tersely.

'Dunechka has already decided, and I fully agree with her,' Pulkheria Alexandrovna hastened to say.

'I've decided to ask you, Rodya, in the most forceful terms, to be present at our meeting at all costs,' said Dunya. 'Will you come?'

'I will.'

'I'm asking you, too, to be at ours at eight,' she turned to Razumikhin. 'I am inviting the gentleman as well, Mama.'

'Marvellous, Dunechka. Well then, if you've all decided,' said Pulkheria Alexandrovna, 'then that's how it will be. It's a relief for me, too. I don't like pretending and lying. We're better off telling the whole truth . . . Be angry all you like, Pyotr Petrovich!'

IV

At that moment the door opened softly. Looking timidly about her, a girl entered the room. Everyone turned to her in surprise and curiosity. At first, Raskolnikov didn't recognize her. It was Sofya Semyonovna Marmeladova. He'd seen Sonya yesterday for the first time, but at such a moment, in such circumstances and in such an outfit, that the image imprinted on his memory was of a quite different person. Before him now was a modestly, even poorly dressed girl, still very young, much like a child, with a modest and decorous manner and a clear yet somewhat frightened-looking face. She was wearing a very simple little house dress and a worn, old-fashioned little hat; only the parasol in her hands was the same. Seeing the room so unexpectedly full of people, she was not so much disconcerted as utterly lost and girlishly shy; she even made as if to go back out.

'Ah . . . it's you?' said Raskolnikov in the greatest astonishment, and suddenly became embarrassed himself.

It had immediately occurred to him that his mother and sister already knew in passing, from Luzhin's letter, about a certain girl of 'notorious' conduct. Just now he'd objected to Luzhin's slander and mentioned having seen this girl for the first time, when suddenly here she was. He also recalled making no objection at all to the expression 'notorious conduct'. All this passed through his mind in a flash and a blur. But, after a closer look, he saw just how low this lowly creature had been brought, and felt a sudden pity. And when she made as if to run away in terror, something seemed to turn over inside him.

'I wasn't expecting you at all,' he hurried, stopping her with his look. 'Please, kindly take a seat. Katerina Ivanovna sent you, I suppose. Not there, if you don't mind – why not here . . . ?'

When Sonya came in, Razumikhin, who had been sitting on one of Raskolnikov's three chairs right next to the door, had got up to let her pass. At first, Raskolnikov had wanted to seat her on the corner of the couch where Zosimov was sitting, but remembering that this was too *familiar* a place and served as his bed, he rushed to point her towards Razumikhin's chair.

'And you sit here,' he told Razumikhin, seating him in the corner where Zosimov had been sitting.

Sonya sat down, almost trembling with fear, and glanced timidly at both ladies. It was obvious that she herself did not understand how she could ever sit next to them. Realizing this, she had such a fright that she suddenly got up again and turned in complete embarrassment to Raskolnikov.

'I . . . I . . . won't stay long, and I'm very sorry to disturb,' she stammered. 'Katerina Ivanovna sent me. There was no one else . . . Katerina Ivanovna told me to ask you most kindly to attend the funeral service tomorrow, in the morning . . . during the liturgy . . . at Mitrofanievsky Cemetery,⁹ and then come to us . . . to her . . . to eat . . . To do her the honour . . . She told me to ask.'

Sonya broke off and fell silent.

'I'll certainly try . . . certainly . . . ,' replied Raskolnikov, also getting up and also stuttering and not finishing his sentence. 'Kindly take a seat,' he said suddenly, 'I need to have a word with you. Please – I expect you're in a hurry – be so kind, give me two minutes . . .'

He drew up a chair for her. Again Sonya sat down and again, as if lost, shot a timid, hasty glance at the two ladies and suddenly looked down.

Raskolnikov's pale face suddenly flushed; his whole body seemed to convulse; his eyes caught fire.

'Mama,' he said firmly and insistently, 'this is Sofya Semyonovna Marmeladova, the daughter of that same unfortunate Mr Marmeladov, who yesterday was trampled by horses before my very eyes. I've already told you about her . . .'

Pulkheria Alexandrovna glanced at Sonya and narrowed her eyes a little. For all her discomfort beneath Rodya's insistent and defiant gaze, she was simply unable to deny herself this satisfaction. Dunechka stared straight into the poor girl's face, seriously and intently, examining her in bewilderment. On hearing this introduction, Sonya briefly looked up again, but became even more embarrassed than before.

'I wanted to ask you,' Raskolnikov quickly addressed her, 'how it all went today. Did anyone bother you? . . . The police, for example?'

'No sir, everything was fine . . . The cause of death was very clear, and no one bothered us. The tenants are cross, that's all.'

'What about?'

'About the body lying there so long . . . in this heat, smelling . . . So today, before Vespers, they'll move it to the cemetery, until tomorrow, in the chapel. Katerina Ivanovna didn't want to at first, but now she can see for herself it's not . . .'

'Today, then?'

'She asks you to do us the honour of attending the service tomorrow, in the church, and then invites you to her, for the funeral banquet.'[10]

'She's putting on a funeral banquet?'

'Yes, sir, a small one. She gave strict instructions to thank you for helping us yesterday . . . If it wasn't for you we'd have nothing at all for the funeral.' Her lips and chin suddenly began to twitch, but she steeled herself and held firm, quickly lowering her eyes again to the floor.

While they were talking, Raskolnikov studied her closely. She had a terribly thin, terribly pale little face, quite irregular and somehow sharp, with a sharp little nose and chin. You couldn't even call her pretty, but her light-blue eyes were so clear, and her whole expression became so kind and guileless when they lit up, that it was impossible not to be drawn towards her. In addition, her face, and indeed her whole figure, had one special, characteristic trait: despite her eighteen years, she still looked like a little girl, all but a child, and at times there was even something comical about the way her gestures betrayed this.

'But how could Katerina Ivanovna make do with such a small sum – and there'll even be a bite to eat, you say?' asked Raskolnikov, determined to keep the conversation going.

'But the coffin will be simple enough, sir . . . and everything will be simple, so it won't cost much . . . Katerina Ivanovna and I worked it all out yesterday, and there'll be enough left over for the banquet . . . and Katerina Ivanovna badly wants there to be one. After all, sir, one can't just . . . She'll feel better for it . . . You know how she is . . .'

'Yes, I understand . . . of course . . . Why are you studying my room like that? And there's Mama saying it looks like a coffin.'

'But yesterday you gave us all you had!' Sonechka shot back in a loud and rapid whisper, suddenly looking down at the floor again. And again her lips and chin began to twitch. She'd been struck straight away by the poverty of Raskolnikov's circumstances, and now these words suddenly burst from her lips. Silence followed. Dunechka's eyes became somehow brighter, while Pulkheria Alexandrovna looked at Sonya almost with warmth.

'Rodya,' she said, getting up, 'we'll have lunch together, of course. Off we go now, Dunechka ... And you go out, too, Rodya, have a little walk, then a rest and a lie-down, and come as soon as you can ... I fear we've tired you out ...'

'Yes, yes, I'll come,' he replied, getting up in a hurry ... 'Though actually, there's something I have to do ...'

'Don't tell me you're not even going to eat together?' yelled Razumikhin, looking at Raskolnikov in astonishment. 'What are you saying?'

'Yes, yes, I'll come, of course I will ... And you stay here for a minute. After all, you don't need him now, do you, Mama? Or perhaps you do?'

'Oh, no, no! But do come and have lunch, Dmitry Prokofich, won't you?'

'Yes, do come,' asked Dunya.

Razumikhin bowed, beaming all over. For a second, everyone became strangely embarrassed.

'Goodbye, Rodya, till soon, I mean. I don't like the word "goodbye". Goodbye, Nastasya ... Dearie me, I said it again!'

Pulkheria Alexandrovna was about to bow to Sonechka as well, but somehow she didn't quite manage, and hurried out of the room.

Dunya, though, seemed to be waiting her turn and, as she, too, passed Sonya on her way out, she bowed to her attentively and courteously, bending fully. Sonechka was embarrassed and returned the bow in a somewhat rushed, frightened manner; there was even a look of pain on her face, as if Avdotya Romanovna's courtesy and attention were a burden and a torment to her.

'Dunya, goodbye!' shouted Raskolnikov, when they were already by the door. 'Give me your hand, then!'

'But I already did – or have you forgotten?' answered Dunya, turning round to him warmly and awkwardly.

'So give it to me again!'

He gave her little fingers a firm squeeze. Dunechka smiled to him, turned bright red, hurriedly wrenched her hand free and followed her mother out – she, too, for some reason, a picture of happiness.

'Well, isn't that splendid?' he said to Sonya, returning to his room and looking at her brightly. 'May the dead rest in peace and may the living live! Isn't that right? Isn't it? Isn't it?'

Sonya was astonished to see his face brighten so suddenly. For several seconds he studied her in silence: at that moment, everything her late father had said about her suddenly flashed through his mind . . .

'Goodness gracious, Dunechka!' began Pulkheria Alexandrovna the second they were outside. 'Now I'm almost happy we've left – relieved, in a way. Could I ever have thought yesterday, in the train, that such a thing could make me happy?'

'I keep telling you, Mama, he's still very sick. Can't you see that? Perhaps it was our suffering that upset him. We mustn't be too hard on him, and then a great deal can be forgiven.'

'But you *were* hard on him!' Pulkheria Alexandrovna immediately interrupted, hotly and jealously. 'You know, Dunya, I was looking at you both and you're his spitting image, and I don't mean your face so much as your soul: both of you are melancholics, both of you are moody and quick-tempered, both haughty and high-minded . . . After all, it's impossible that he could be selfish, isn't it, Dunechka? Isn't it? . . . And when I think what's going to happen at our place this evening, my heart goes numb!'

'Don't worry, Mama, what has to be will be.'

'Dunechka! Just think about our situation! What if Pyotr Petrovich refuses?' poor Pulkheria Alexandrovna suddenly ventured.

'And what will he be worth after that?' Dunechka snapped back with contempt.

'It's a good thing we left just now,' Pulkheria Alexandrovna hurriedly interrupted. 'He was rushing off somewhere; a walk will do him good . . . some fresh air at least . . . It's dreadfully stuffy up there . . . But where can you find fresh air here? Even the streets are like rooms without windows. Heavens, what a town! . . . Watch out or they'll crush you – they're carrying something! Well I never, it's a piano . . . How they push and shove . . . This young girl scares me as well . . .'

'Which young girl, Mama?'

'That one, you know, Sofya Semyonovna, we saw her just now . . .'

'But why?'

'I have this premonition, Dunya. You won't believe me, but the moment she came in it occurred to me that this is the crux of it all . . .'

'It's not the crux of anything!' Dunya cried in vexation. 'Really,

Mama, you and your premonitions! He's only known her since yesterday and when she came in just now he didn't recognize her.'

'Well, wait and see! . . . She troubles me . . . You'll see, you'll see! I
got such a fright: the way she was looking at me, those eyes of hers – I
nearly fell off my chair – and the way he began introducing her, remember? How strange: Pyotr Petrovich writing all those things about
her, and there he is introducing her to us like that, and even to you! So
she must be dear to him!'

'He can write what he likes! People have said – and even written –
things about us as well, or have you forgotten? But I'm quite sure that
she is a . . . beautiful person and that all this is just nonsense!'

'God help her!'

'And Pyotr Petrovich is a wretched gossip,' Dunechka suddenly
snapped.

At this, Pulkheria Alexandrovna simply wilted. The conversation
broke off.

'Now then, here's what I want to ask you about . . . ,' said Raskolnikov, leading Razumikhin away towards the window . . .

'So I can tell Katerina Ivanovna you'll come . . . ?' Sonya put in,
hastily bowing and preparing to leave.

'Just a minute, Sofya Semyonovna. We've no secrets here and you're
not in the way . . . There's something else I'd like to tell you . . . Now
then,' he said without finishing, turning very abruptly to Razumikhin.
'You know that – what's his name again? – Porfiry Petrovich?'

'Too right I do! We're related. Why do you ask?' he added, bursting
with curiosity.

'Well, he . . . that business, you know, the murder . . . Weren't you
saying yesterday . . . he's in charge?'

'Yes . . . and?' Razumikhin's eyes suddenly bulged from their sockets.

'He wanted to see the pawners and, well, I left pledges there, too –
just junk really, but still: my sister's ring, which she gave me as a memento when I moved here, and my dad's silver watch. The whole lot's
only worth five or six roubles, but it's dear to me, for the memory. So
what should I do now? I don't want the things to disappear, especially
not the watch. I was worried just now that Mother would ask to see
them when Dunechka's watch was mentioned. It's the only thing of
my father's that's survived. She'll take to her bed if it disappears!
Women! So what should I do? Tell me! I suppose I should go down to

the police station and declare them. But wouldn't I be better off going straight to Porfiry? Eh? What d'you think? The sooner I do it, the better. Mama will have asked by lunchtime, you'll see!'

'Forget about the police station and go straight to Porfiry!' shouted Razumikhin, quite unusually excited. 'That's made my day! We may as well go now. It's just round the corner – he's bound to be there!'

'All right . . . let's go . . .'

'He'll be very, very, very pleased to meet you! He's heard a lot about you from me, at various times . . . Yesterday, too. Off we go! . . . So you knew the old crone, eh? Well I never! . . . Isn't it marvellous how it's all turned out? . . . Oh yes . . . Sofya Ivanovna . . .'

'Sofya Semyonovna,' Raskolnikov corrected him. 'Sofya Semyonovna, this is my friend Razumikhin, and a good man, too . . .'

'If you need to be going now . . . ,' Sonya began, without even a glance in Razumikhin's direction, which only made her more embarrassed.

'Off we go, then!' Raskolnikov decided. 'I'll call by later today, Sofya Semyonovna. Just tell me: where do you live?'

The words came out clearly enough, but he seemed to be rushing and avoiding her gaze. Sonya gave her address and blushed as she did so. They all went out together.

'Don't you lock up?' asked Razumikhin, following them down the stairs.

'Never! . . . Though I've been meaning to buy a lock for two years,' he added nonchalantly. 'Happy are those with no need to lock, eh?' he laughed, turning to Sonya.

Outside, they stopped beneath the arch.

'You're turning right here, Sofya Semyonovna? How did you find me, by the way?' he asked, as though wishing to say something completely different to her. All this time he'd been wanting to look into her quiet, clear eyes, but somehow he never quite managed it . . .

'You gave your address to Polechka yesterday.'

'Polya? Ah yes . . . Polechka . . . the little one . . . She's your sister? So I gave her my address?'

'Have you really forgotten?'

'No . . . I remember . . .'

'And I'd already heard about you from the dear departed . . . Only I didn't know your surname yet, and he didn't know either . . . And when I came just now . . . and seeing as I found out your surname yesterday . . . So today I asked: does Mr Raskolnikov live around

here? . . . I didn't know you were sub-renting too . . . Goodbye, sir . . .
I'll let Katerina Ivanovna . . .'

She was terribly relieved to get away at last. She walked off, head
down, hurrying along, anything so as to get out of sight as quickly as
possible, to put these twenty paces behind her, turn right and be alone
at last, and then, walking along quickly, not seeing anyone, not noticing anything, to think, recall, consider every spoken word, every circumstance. Never before had she felt anything like it. A whole new
world – obscurely, out of nowhere – had entered her soul. She suddenly remembered: Raskolnikov wanted to come to see her today, perhaps even this morning, perhaps right now!

'Just not today, please, not today!' she muttered, her heart skipping
a beat, as if she were begging someone, like a frightened child. 'Heavens! Coming . . . to my room . . . He'll see . . . Lord!'

And, of course, there was no chance of her noticing at that moment
a certain gentleman, a stranger, who was watching her closely and
following in her footsteps. He'd been trailing her ever since she'd
turned out of the gates. At that moment, when Razumikhin, Raskolnikov and she had paused for a few words on the pavement, this man,
passing by, happened to catch Sonya's words – 'so I asked: does Mr
Raskolnikov live around here?' – and gave a sudden start. He looked
all three of them over quickly but thoroughly, especially Raskolnikov,
to whom Sonya was speaking; then he glanced at the building and
noted that, too. All this was done in a flash, on the go, and the passer-by,
trying not to draw the slightest attention to himself, carried on, while
slowing his pace, almost expectantly. He was waiting for Sonya. He
saw that they were saying goodbye and that Sonya was about to go
home, wherever that was.

'But where's home for her? I've seen her somewhere before . . . ,' he
thought, recalling Sonya's face. 'I must find out.'

At the turning, he crossed to the opposite side of the street, looked
back and saw that Sonya was following him, going exactly the same
way, not noticing a thing. At the turning, she also took the very same
street. He followed, training his gaze on her from the opposite pavement; after fifty paces or so he crossed back onto the side on which
Sonya was walking and almost caught up with her, keeping five paces
between them.

He was a man of about fifty, above average in height, stout, with
broad, sloping shoulders, which gave him a somewhat stooped

appearance. He was foppishly and affluently dressed, looking every bit the country lord. In his hand was a handsome cane, which he tapped at every step against the pavement, and his gloves looked new. His broad, high-boned face was pleasant enough, with a fresh complexion rarely seen in Petersburg. His hair, still very thick, was blond through and through, with just the merest fleck of grey, and his broad, thick, spade-shaped beard was even fairer than the hair on his head. His eyes were light blue, and their gaze cold, intent and thoughtful; his lips, crimson. On the whole, he was a marvellously well-preserved man, who looked far younger than his years.

When Sonya came out by the Ditch, they found themselves alone on the pavement. Observing her, he had time to note her pensive, distracted air. On reaching her building, Sonya turned into the arch; he followed, as if somewhat surprised. On entering the courtyard, she turned right, towards the corner, where there were stairs leading up to her apartment. 'Ha!' muttered the stranger and began climbing up after her. Only now did Sonya notice him. She carried on up to the third floor, turned off along the gallery and rang at Number 9, on the door of which *Kapernaumov, Tailor* had been written in chalk. 'Ha!' the gentleman repeated, surprised by the peculiar coincidence, and rang at Number 8 next door. The doors were half a dozen paces apart.

'You lodge at Kapernaumov's!' he said, looking at Sonya and laughing. 'He altered a waistcoat for me yesterday. I'm right next door, at Madam Resslich's, Gertruda Karlovna. Fancy that!'

Sonya looked at him closely.

'Neighbours,' he continued, in a particularly cheerful kind of way. 'This is only my third day in the city. Well, goodbye ma'am.'

Sonya did not reply; someone opened the door and she slipped through to her room. She felt ashamed for some reason, almost frightened . . .

Going to see Porfiry, Razumikhin was unusually animated.

'This is splendid, brother,' he said several times. 'I'm so glad! So glad!'

'What have you got to be so glad about?' Raskolnikov thought to himself.

'I'd no idea you were also pawning items with the old woman. So . . . so . . . was that a while ago? I mean, was it a while ago that you last visited her?'

('Naive idiot!')

'When was it?' Raskolnikov stopped for a moment to remember. 'Well, about three days before her death, I suppose. But anyway, I'm not about to try to redeem them now,' he went on with some kind of hasty, emphatic concern for his items. 'I'm down to my last silver rouble again . . . All because of yesterday's damned delirium!'

He laid particular stress on that last phrase.

'Yes, yes, yes,' said Razumikhin, though it was unclear what he was assenting to in such a hurry. 'So that's why you were . . . a bit shocked at the time . . . You know, even when you were raving you kept mentioning rings, chains and what have you! . . . Yes, yes . . . Now it's all clear, perfectly clear.'

('Ha! That idea of theirs has certainly done the rounds! I mean, this man would go to the cross for my sake, but look how glad he is that the reason I kept mentioning the rings has been *cleared up*! None of them can get it out of their heads!')

'Will he be in?' he asked out loud.

'Of course he will. You know, brother, he's a smashing lad . . . You'll see! A bit awkward – not that he's lacking in social graces, but awkward in a different way. He's not stupid, that's for sure – in fact, he's pretty damn clever – but he's got a very particular way of thinking . . . He's mistrustful, sceptical, cynical . . . likes playing tricks on people, or rather, making fools of them . . . Then there's that old, material method of his . . . But he knows what he's doing, that's for sure . . . There was one murder case last year, you should have seen what he dug up – nearly all the trails had gone cold! He's very, very, very eager to meet you!'

'Very? I can't see why.'

'I don't mean . . . Recently, you see, ever since you fell ill, I've had reason to mention you often . . . Well, he'd listen . . . and when he heard that you were reading law and couldn't complete the course, due to your circumstances, he said, "What a shame!" So I came to the conclusion . . . on the basis of everything, not just of that. Yesterday Zametov . . . You see, Rodya, I blurted out something to you yesterday under the influence, when we were walking home . . . and I'm worried you might have made too much of it . . .'

'Of what? That people think I'm mad? Perhaps they're right.'

He forced a grin.

'Yes . . . yes . . . I mean, no, dammit! . . . Whatever I may have said (and about other things too) it was all poppycock, because I was drunk.'

'Why do you keep apologizing? I'm so sick of all this!' shouted Raskolnikov with immense irritation. He was partly putting it on.

'I know, I know. I understand. Rest assured, I understand. I'm even ashamed to say it . . .'

'Then don't!'

Both fell silent. Razumikhin could barely contain his excitement, and this disgusted Raskolnikov. He was also troubled by what Razumikhin had just said about Porfiry.

'I'll have to play Lazarus[11] for him as well,' he thought with a hammering heart, 'and make it look natural. It would be more natural not to pretend anything. Go out of my way not to pretend! No, *going out of my way* wouldn't be natural either . . . Well, let's see how it goes . . . Let's see . . . Right now . . . Am I sure this is such a good idea? A moth making straight for the flame. My heart's thumping – that's bad . . .'

'This grey building here,' said Razumikhin.

('Above all, does Porfiry know that I went to that witch's apartment yesterday, or doesn't he . . . and that I asked about the blood? I have to find out the second I walk in, from his face. Or else . . . I'll find out if it kills me!')

'Know what?' he suddenly said to Razumikhin with a roguish smile. 'I've noticed that you've been unusually restless all day. Haven't you?'

'Restless? I'm not remotely restless,' replied Razumikhin, flinching.

'Really, brother, it's very noticeable. I've never seen you sit on a chair like you were doing before, perched on the edge, your whole body convulsing. Jumping up for no reason. Angry one minute, a face like treacle the next. You even blushed; especially when they invited you to lunch . . . My, how you blushed!'

'Complete rubbish! . . . What's your point?'

'Just look at you – wriggling about like a schoolboy! Damned if you're not blushing again!'

'You really are a swine!'

'What are you so embarrassed about, Romeo? I'll have to find someone to share this with today. Ha-ha-ha! I'll make Mama laugh . . . and not just her . . .'

'Listen, listen, I say, this is serious, this is . . . And then what, dammit?' Razumikhin, cold with fear, could no longer make sense. 'What will you tell them? Brother, I . . . Ugh, what a swine!'

'Like a rose in spring! And how it becomes you, if only you knew: a seven-foot Romeo! Just look how you've scrubbed up today, even cleaned your nails, eh? When was the last time that happened? Goodness me, you've even pomaded your hair! Bend down, then!'

'Swine!!!'

Raskolnikov was laughing so hard he seemed quite out of control, and so it was that they entered Porfiry Petrovich's apartment. It was just what Raskolnikov needed: from inside, they could be heard laughing as they came in and still guffawing in the entrance hall.

'Not another word or I'll . . . smash your face in!' Razumikhin whispered in wild fury, grabbing Raskolnikov by the shoulder.

V

The latter was already entering the main room. He entered with the air of a man doing all he could not to explode with laughter. Following him in, with a thoroughly downcast, scowling countenance, as red as a peony, all lanky and awkward, came a sheepish Razumikhin. There really was, at that moment, something comical about his face and entire appearance that warranted Raskolnikov's laughter. Raskolnikov, yet to be introduced, bowed to their host, who was standing in the middle of the room and looking at them quizzically, then shook the latter's hand while continuing to make apparently desperate efforts to suppress his gaiety and at least string a few words together by way of an introduction. But no sooner did he manage to assume a serious expression and mumble something than suddenly, as if unable to help himself, he glanced at Razumikhin again, and that was that: the suppressed laughter, held in for so long and with such effort, burst out uncontrollably. The ferocity of the scowls which this 'heartfelt' laughter drew from Razumikhin gave to the whole scene an air of the sincerest gaiety and, most importantly, spontaneity. Razumikhin, as if on cue, gave another helping hand.

'Damn you!' he roared with a great swing of his arm, which smacked straight into a little round table bearing an emptied glass of tea. Everything went flying with a clink and a tinkle.

'No need to break the chairs, gentlemen – there's the public purse to think about!'[12] shouted Porfiry Petrovich gaily.

The scene was as follows: Raskolnikov, his hand forgotten in that of his host, was still laughing, but, not wishing to overdo it, was waiting for the right moment to stop. Razumikhin, hopelessly embarrassed by the toppled table and broken glass, glowered at the fragments, spat and turned around sharply to face the window, with his back to his audience and his face all furrowed, looking out of the window and seeing nothing. Porfiry Petrovich was laughing and was eager to do so, but it was also clear that he was waiting for an explanation. On a chair in the corner sat Zametov, who had half-risen when the guests came in and was waiting expectantly, his lips parted to form a smile, though he was looking at the whole scene with bewilderment, not to say scepticism, and at Raskolnikov even with a certain discomfort. Zametov's presence came as an unpleasant shock to Raskolnikov.

'What's he doing here?' went through his mind.

'Please forgive me,' he began, with a great show of embarrassment, 'Raskolnikov . . .'

'Don't mention it. It's my pleasure, sir, and a pleasure to see you make such an entrance . . . But isn't he even going to say hello?' said Porfiry Petrovich, with a nod in the direction of Razumikhin.

'I can't think why he's so mad at me. I merely said to him, on the way over, that he's like Romeo and . . . and proved it, and that's really all there was to it.'

'Swine!' Razumikhin shot back, without turning round.

'He must have had good reason to get so upset about one little word,' laughed Porfiry.

'Look at you – investigator! . . . Well, to hell with you all anyway!' snapped Razumikhin, before he, too, suddenly burst out laughing and, with a cheerful expression, as if nothing had happened, walked up to Porfiry Petrovich.

'Enough of this! We're idiots, the lot of us. Now then: my friend, Rodion Romanovich Raskolnikov, has heard a lot about you and was keen to meet you, that's the first thing; secondly, he's here on a bit of business. Ha! Zametov! What are you doing here? Don't tell me you know each other? When did that happen?'

'Now what?' thought Raskolnikov anxiously.

Zametov seemed embarrassed, though only a little.

'We met yesterday, at your place,' was his nonchalant reply.

'Oh well, that's one less job for me, then. All last week he was pestering me to arrange an introduction with you, Porfiry, but I see you're already in cahoots . . . Now where's your tobacco?'

Porfiry Petrovich was dressed for indoors – a dressing gown, immaculate linen and soft, down-at-heel shoes. He was a man of about
thirty-five, of somewhat less than average height, plump and even
with a bit of a belly, clean-shaven, with neither a moustache nor
whiskers, and with thick cropped hair on a big round head, its round-
ness somehow especially marked from behind. His puffy, round and
slightly snub-nosed face was of a sickly, dark-yellow hue, but lively
enough and with a touch of mockery about it. It might even have been
good-natured, were it not for the expression of the eyes, with their
vaguely watery sheen and lashes that were almost white and kept
blinking, as if winking at someone. This expression was somehow
strangely at odds with his general appearance, which even had something womanish about it, and imparted a far more serious aspect than
might have been expected at first glance.

As soon as Porfiry Petrovich heard that his visitor had come 'on a
bit of business', he immediately offered him a seat on the couch, sat
himself down at the other end and stared at his guest, eagerly waiting
for him to explain what this business was, with that emphatically and
excessively serious attention which can be quite oppressive and dis-
concerting when first encountered, especially in a stranger and especially when what you are explaining is, in your own opinion, completely
incommensurate with the unusual solicitude being shown to you. But
Raskolnikov, in a few brief and coherent sentences, lucidly and precisely explained the matter and was so satisfied with his efforts that
he even managed to take a good look at Porfiry. Nor did Porfiry
Petrovich take his eyes off Raskolnikov, during all this time. Razumikhin, who had sat down opposite them at the same table, was following Raskolnikov's summary with a burning impatience, constantly
shifting his eyes from one to the other and back again, which seemed
a little excessive.

'Idiot!' Raskolnikov swore to himself.

'You ought to submit a statement to the police,' Porfiry responded
with the most business-like air, 'to the effect, sir, that being apprised
of such-and-such an incident – the murder, I mean – you are request-
ing, in your turn, that the investigator entrusted with this matter be
informed that items such-and-such belong to you and that you wish to
redeem them . . . or whatever . . . but they'll write it for you themselves, in any case.'

'The problem is,' said Raskolnikov, with as much embarrassment as he could muster, 'that I'm a bit out of pocket right now . . . and I can't even stump up the petty cash for . . . You see, for the moment all I wish to do is declare that the items are mine, and when the money comes in . . .'

'Makes no odds, sir,' replied Porfiry Petrovich, unmoved by this clarification about the state of his finances, 'but if you prefer you may write directly to me to the same effect, namely, that being apprised of such-and-such and declaring items such-and-such to be mine, I request . . .'

'Ordinary paper[13] will do, I take it?' Raskolnikov hastened to interrupt, expressing his interest once again in the financial side of the matter.

'Oh, as ordinary as you like, sir!' – and Porfiry Petrovich suddenly looked at him with a sort of blatant mockery, narrowing his eyes and even winking at him. Or perhaps this was just Raskolnikov's impression, for it lasted no more than an instant. In any case, something of the sort occurred. Raskolnikov could have sworn he winked at him, the devil only knew why.

'He knows!' flashed through him like lightning.

'Forgive me for bothering you with such trifles,' he went on, somewhat knocked off his stride. 'My items are only worth five roubles, but they're especially dear to me, as a memento of who they came from, and I admit I had a real fright when I heard . . .'

'So that's why you got in such a flap yesterday when I blurted out to Zosimov that Porfiry was questioning the pawners?' Razumikhin put in, with obvious intent.

This was too much to bear and Raskolnikov's black eyes flashed fire in the direction of Razumikhin. But he instantly came to his senses.

'You seem to be making fun of me, brother?' he said to him with artfully affected irritation. 'I understand that in your eyes a bit of junk may not be worth all this fuss, but that's no reason to think me either selfish or greedy, and in my eyes these two paltry little things might not be junk at all. Didn't I tell you just now that the silver watch, which is barely worth a copeck, is the only thing of my father's to have survived? Laugh all you like, but my mother has come to see me' – he suddenly turned to Porfiry – 'and if she were to find out' – he turned back sharply to Razumikhin, trying his best to make his voice tremble – 'that the watch has vanished, she'd be distraught, I swear! Women!'

'No! That's not what I meant at all! Quite the opposite!' cried an aggrieved Razumikhin.

'Any good? Natural enough? Not over the top?' Raskolnikov asked himself anxiously. 'Why did I go and say "women"?'

'So your mother has come to see you, has she?' Porfiry Petrovich enquired for some reason.

'Yes.'

'And she arrived when, sir?'

'Yesterday evening.'

Porfiry fell silent, as if working something out.

'There's no way your items could have vanished, no way at all,' he continued calmly and coldly. 'After all, I've been expecting you here for some time.'

And then, as if nothing had happened, he set about offering an ashtray to Razumikhin, who was scattering ash all over the rug. Raskolnikov flinched, but Porfiry, still preoccupied with Razumikhin's papirosa, appeared not to notice.

'What did you say? Expecting him? But how could you know he'd been pawning things *there* too?' Razumikhin shouted.

Porfiry Petrovich addressed Raskolnikov directly:

'Both your items, the ring and the watch, were found *at hers* wrapped up in the same piece of paper, and your name was clearly marked on the paper in pencil, as was the day of the month when she received them from you . . .'

'How very perceptive of you . . . ,' said Raskolnikov, forcing an awkward grin and trying his best to look him straight in the eye; but he couldn't restrain himself and suddenly added: 'I said that just now because there must have been a great number of pawners . . . and it would have been hard for you to remember them all . . . Yet you remember them all so clearly and . . . and . . .'

('How stupid! How pathetic! Why did I go and say that?')

'Nearly all the pawners have now been identified – you alone did not see fit to visit,' Porfiry replied, with a barely discernible hint of mockery.

'I wasn't entirely well.'

'So I heard, sir. I even heard that you were terribly upset about something. You seem somewhat pale even now?'

'I'm not remotely pale . . . in fact, I'm perfectly well!' Raskolnikov snapped back, suddenly changing his tone. The spite was bubbling up inside him and he couldn't keep it down. 'I'll end up saying something I regret!' flashed through his mind once more. 'But why must they torment me?'

'Perfectly well, did he say?' Razumikhin jumped in. 'Poppycock! Even yesterday you were still raving, almost out of your mind . . . Consider this, Porfiry: he could barely stand, but the second Zosimov and I turned our backs yesterday he got dressed, made off and gadded about somewhere until it was nearly midnight, and all this, let me tell you, when he was completely and utterly delirious. Can you imagine? A most extraordinary case!'

'*Completely and utterly delirious!* Really? Well I never!' said Porfiry, with a womanish shake of the head.

'What nonsense! Don't believe him! Though actually, you don't believe a word of this anyway!' Raskolnikov let slip in his anger. But Porfiry Petrovich appeared not to hear these strange words.

'But how could you have gone out if you weren't delirious?' asked Razumikhin with a sudden rush of excitement. 'Why did you go out? What for? . . . And why so secretly? You can't have been thinking straight, can you? I can be frank with you now the danger's passed!'

'I was sick to death of them yesterday,' Raskolnikov suddenly told Porfiry with an insolent, defiant sneer, 'so I ran off to rent a place where they couldn't find me, and took a pile of money with me. Mr Zametov over there saw the cash. Well, Mr Zametov: was I delirious yesterday or was I clever? You settle the argument.'

He could have strangled Zametov there and then. The way he was looking at him without saying anything was more than he could stand.

'If you ask me, you were speaking perfectly sensibly and even cunningly, sir, only you were much too irritable,' came Zametov's dry response.

'And today,' Porfiry Petrovich put in, 'Nikodim Fomich was telling me that he met you yesterday, at a terribly late hour, in the apartment of a man who'd been trampled by horses, a civil servant . . .'

'There you go – that civil servant!' Razumikhin exclaimed. 'I mean, what was that if not crazy? You gave away your every last copeck to a widow for the funeral! All right, you felt like helping out – so give her fifteen roubles, give her twenty, or at least leave yourself three, but no, you had to fork out all twenty-five!'

'What if I've found a hidden treasure somewhere and you don't know? Wouldn't that explain my fit of generosity yesterday? . . . Mr Zametov over there knows all about it! . . . Please excuse us,' he said to Porfiry, lips trembling, 'for bothering you with half an hour of such silliness. I expect you've had quite enough of us, eh?'

'The very idea, sir! On the contrary, on the contrary! If only you knew how much you intrigue me! How interesting it is to observe you and listen to you . . . and, I must admit, I'm so glad you've seen fit to visit at last . . .'

'You might at least offer us some tea! I'm parched!' cried Razumikhin.

'A splendid idea! Perhaps everyone will have a cup. But how about something a touch . . . more substantial, before the tea, I mean?'

'Get out!'

Porfiry Petrovich went off to order the tea.

Thoughts whirled in Raskolnikov's mind. He was terribly annoyed.

'The main thing is they're not even concealing it. They're not even going to be polite about it! But what cause did you have, seeing as we've never met, to talk to Nikodim Fomich about me? So they can't even be bothered to conceal the fact that they're hounding me like a pack of dogs! Spitting in my face, that's what they're doing!' He was shaking with fury. 'Hit me if you have to, but don't play cat-and-mouse. That's bad form, Porfiry Petrovich, and I may not stand for it, sir! . . . I'll get up and I'll blurt out the whole truth right in your faces; then you'll see how much I despise you!' He could barely catch his breath. 'But what if I'm imagining this? What if this is just a mirage and I've got everything wrong, if I'm angry through lack of experience, too angry to keep up my despicable act? Perhaps there's no intent in any of this. Their words are all ordinary enough, but there's something about them . . . something about these everyday phrases . . . Why did he say "at hers" so bluntly? Why did Zametov add that I was speaking *cunningly*? Why do they take this tone? Yes . . . their tone . . . Razumikhin was sitting right here – why doesn't he sense anything? That harmless dimwit never senses anything! . . . And here's the fever again! . . . Did Porfiry wink at me before or didn't he? What nonsense; why should he wink? Working on my nerves, are they? Or just teasing me? Either this is all a mirage or else *they know*! . . . Even Zametov's got a nerve . . . Hasn't he? . . . Changed his mind overnight. I had a feeling he would! He's quite at home here, though it's his first time. Porfiry doesn't even think of him as his guest and sits with his back to him. They're in cahoots! And all *because of me*, I'm sure of it! I'm sure they were speaking about me before we got here! . . . Do they know about the apartment, then? The sooner the better! . . . When I said I'd run off to rent a place yesterday he let it go, he didn't react . . .

Very clever of me to slip that in: it'll come in handy later on! . . . Delirious, they say! . . . Ha-ha-ha! He knows all about yesterday evening! And didn't know about Mother's arrival! . . . That witch even put the date, with a pencil! . . . Rubbish, you won't catch me so easily! These aren't facts yet – just a mirage! No, you give me facts, if you have any! The apartment's not a fact, either, it's delirium; I know what to say to them . . . Do they know about the apartment? I won't leave till they tell me! Why have I come here? My being angry now – that's a fact, I suppose! Ugh, how irritable I am! But maybe that's good; the sick man's act . . . He's feeling me out. Hoping to confuse me. Why have I come here?'

All this swept through his mind like lightning.

Porfiry Petrovich was back in a flash. He seemed merrier, somehow.

'You know, brother, my head's aching from last night at your place . . . I feel a wreck,' he began in a quite different tone, turning to Razumikhin and laughing.

'You had a good time, then? I left you at the most interesting point, remember? Who won?'

'No one, of course. We alighted on the sempiternal question, our heads in the heavens.'

'Can you imagine, Rodya, what it was they alighted on yesterday: does crime exist or does it not? Didn't I say the devil would have blushed to hear them?'

'What's so surprising about that? Just an ordinary sociological question,' replied Raskolnikov absently.

'That's not how it was formulated,' remarked Porfiry.

'Not exactly, that's true,' Razumikhin hurriedly agreed, as excited as ever. 'Rodion, just listen to this and tell me what you think. I want to know. I was at my wits' end with them yesterday and was just waiting for you. I'd even told them you'd be coming . . . It all began with the socialist position. No surprises there: crime is a protest against the abnormality of the social order – and that's all there is to it! They accept no other causes! Nothing else!'

'Liar!' cried Porfiry Petrovich. He was becoming increasingly animated and laughed whenever he looked at Razumikhin, which only goaded him on.

'Nothing else at all!' Razumikhin interrupted him hotly. 'And I'm not lying! . . . I'll show you the kind of books they write: with them it's always "the environment"[14] that's to blame and nothing else! They love that word! Their conclusion? The proper organization of society would lead to all crime disappearing at once, as there'd be no reason to protest and everyone would become righteous, just like that. Human nature is discounted, banished, surplus to requirements! With them it's not humanity, which, having developed along its historical, *living* path to the end, will eventually turn into a normal society on its own, but rather the social system, which, emerging from some kind of mathematical head, will immediately organize all humanity and make it righteous and sinless, just like that, quicker than any living process, and without the need for any historical, living path! That's why they have such an instinctive dislike of history: "mere chaos and stupidity" – stupidity being the only explanation required. And that's why they have such a dislike of life as a *living* process: a *living soul* is the last thing they want! Living souls demand life; living souls don't obey mechanics; living souls are suspicious; living souls are reactionary! Whereas here – all right, there may be a whiff of carrion about it, and you could make it from rubber if you had to, but at least it's not alive, at least it has no will, at least it's slavish and it won't rebel! So all that's left is to lay bricks for the phalanstery[15] and arrange the corridors and rooms! Well, the phalanstery may be ready, but your nature is not: it wants life; it wants to complete its living process; it's a bit too early for the cemetery! You can't leap over nature by logic alone! Logic foresees three eventualities, but there's a million of them! So cut them all off, the whole million, and boil everything down to just one thing: comfort! The easy solution! Seductively simple! No need to think! That's the main thing – no need to think! All life's mystery reduced to two printer's sheets!'

'Look at him explode! He needs tying down!' laughed Porfiry. 'Just imagine,' he turned to Raskolnikov, 'this is exactly how it was yesterday evening, in a single room, six voices all going at once, after he'd served us some punch for good measure – can you picture that? No, brother, you're lying: the "environment" has a lot to do with crime. I can confirm it.'

'I know that myself, but tell me this: a forty-year-old man abuses a ten-year-old girl – was it the environment, then, that made him do it?'

'Well, strictly speaking, it probably was the environment,' remarked Porfiry with astonishing solemnity. 'A crime committed against a young girl may very easily be explained by the "environment" – very easily indeed.'

Razumikhin was almost beside himself.

'Fine, so allow me to *prove* to you right now,' roared Razumikhin, 'that the only reason you have white eyelashes is that the Ivan the Great Bell Tower[16] is two hundred and forty-five feet high; what's more, I'll prove it clearly, precisely, progressively and even with a touch of liberalism! I'm game! Fancy a bet?'

'You're on! Let's hear it!'

'He's always pretending, damn him!' cried Razumikhin, jumping to his feet and waving him away. 'Is there any point talking to you? He does it all on purpose – you just don't know him yet, Rodion! Yesterday, too, he took their side, with the sole intention of making fools of everyone. The things he was saying – good God! And they loved him for it! . . . He can keep this up for two weeks at a time, believe me. Last year he assured us for some reason that he was set on becoming a monk: he banged on about it for a whole two months! Recently he started assuring us he was getting married, told us everything was already in place. He even had a suit made specially. We were already congratulating him. No bride, nothing: it was all a mirage!'

'Now that's a lie! I'd had the suit made earlier. It was the suit that gave me the idea of making such asses of you all!'

'Is it true you're always pretending?' asked Raskolnikov nonchalantly.

'And you thought it wasn't? Give me a chance and I'll take you in too – ha-ha-ha! No, sir, let me tell you the whole truth. Apropos all these questions, crimes, the environment, young girls, I'm suddenly reminded – though, in fact, it has always intrigued me – of a little article of yours: "On Crime" . . . was that the title? I'm afraid it's slipped my mind. I had the pleasure of reading it two months ago in the *Periodical Review*.'

'An article of mine? In *Periodical Review*?' asked Raskolnikov with surprise. 'It's true that a year and a half ago, after leaving university, I did write an article about some book, but at the time I offered it to the *Weekly Review*, not the *Periodical*.'

'Well, it ended up in the *Periodical*.'

'But the *Weekly Review* has ceased to exist; that's why they never published it . . .'

'True enough, sir; but, ceasing to exist, the *Weekly Review* merged with *Periodical Review*,[17] which is why, two months ago, that little article of yours appeared in the *Periodical*. You mean you didn't know?'

Raskolnikov did not know.

'For pity's sake – you should ask to be paid for it! You are a funny one! You live such an isolated existence that you are ignorant even of things that concern you directly. And that's a fact, sir.'

'Bravo, Rodka! I didn't know either!' cried Razumikhin. 'I'll stop by at the reading room today and call up that issue! Two months ago? What was the date? Never mind, I'll track it down! Well, this is a turn-up! Trust him not to mention it!'

'But how did you know it was mine? It's only signed with an initial.'

'By chance, just the other day. Via the editor, an acquaintance . . . I was most intrigued.'

'I was analysing, as I recall, the psychological condition of a criminal during the entire course of a crime.'

'Exactly, sir, and you insist that the act of carrying out the crime is always accompanied by illness. Very, very original, but . . . speaking for myself, it wasn't this part of your article that intrigued me, but a certain thought which you let slip at the end, but which, unfortunately, is only hinted at and remains rather obscure . . . In short, what is hinted at, as you may recall, is the apparent existence in the world of certain individuals who are able . . . or rather not so much able as fully entitled . . . to commit all manner of outrageous and criminal acts, and that they are, as it were, above the law.'

Raskolnikov sneered at this gross and deliberate distortion of his idea.

'What's that? Come again? Entitled to commit crimes? Surely not because of the effect of "the environment"?' enquired Razumikhin, who looked almost frightened.

'No, no, not exactly,' replied Porfiry. 'In the gentleman's article, you see, everyone is divided into two categories, the "ordinary" and the "extraordinary". Ordinary people should live a life of obedience and do not have the right to overstep the law, because, you see, they are ordinary. But extraordinary people have the right to carry out all manner of crimes and to break the law as they please, all because they are extraordinary.[18] I think that's the gist, or am I mistaken?'

'What on earth? Impossible!' muttered Razumikhin in bewilderment.

Raskolnikov sneered once more. He'd grasped at once what this was all about and why he was being provoked; he remembered his article. He decided to accept the challenge.

'That's not quite it,' he began, simply and unassumingly. 'Your summary is mostly fair, I'll admit; even, one might say, entirely fair . . .'

(Conceding this seemed to give him a kind of pleasure.) 'The only difference is that I am far from insisting that extraordinary people have always, without fail, had a duty and obligation to commit all manner of outrageous acts, as you put it. In fact, I'm inclined to think that such an article would never have even seen the light of day. All I did was hint that an "extraordinary" person has the right . . . not an official right, that is, but a personal one, to permit his conscience to step over . . . certain obstacles, but if and only if the fulfilment of his idea (one that may even bring salvation to all humanity) demands it. You observe that my article is obscure; I am ready to elucidate its meaning to you, as best I can. I am not mistaken, it seems, in assuming that to be your wish; very well, sir. In my view, if, owing to a combination of factors, the discoveries of Kepler and Newton could not have become public knowledge without the lives of one, ten, a hundred or however many people who were interfering with these discoveries, or standing in their way, being sacrificed, then Newton would have had the right and would even have been obliged . . . to *remove* these ten or one hundred people, so as to make his discoveries known to all humanity. In no way, however, does it follow from this that Newton had the right to kill whomsoever he wanted, whenever the mood took him, or to steal every day at the market. Subsequently, as I recall, I develop in my article the thought that . . . well, take, for want of a better example, the legislators and founders of humanity, beginning with the most ancient and continuing with the Lycurguses, Solons, Muhammads, Napoleons and so on – they were criminals to a man, if for no other reason than that, by introducing a new law, they violated the ancient law held sacred by society and handed down from the fathers, and it goes without saying that they did not flinch from bloodshed, so long as this blood (sometimes perfectly innocent blood, shed valiantly for the ancient law) could help them. In fact, it's remarkable how terribly bloodthirsty the majority of these benefactors and founders of humanity have been. In short, I infer that actually all those who, never mind being great, diverge even a little from the beaten path, i.e., are even the slightest bit capable of saying something new, must, by their very nature, be criminals – to a greater or lesser degree, needless to say. Otherwise, how would they ever leave the path, which, of course, they cannot agree to keep to, by their very nature – indeed, I think it is their duty not to agree. In short, as you can see, there's nothing particularly new here up to this point. It's all been published and read a thousand times before. As regards my dividing people into the ordinary and the extraordinary, well this, I agree, is somewhat arbitrary, but I'm hardly insisting on exact numbers. What I believe in is my main idea. It consists precisely in the fact that people, by a law of nature, are divided *in general* into two categories: the lower one (the ordinary), i.e., the material, as it were, that serves solely to generate its own likeness, and actual people, i.e., those with the gift or the talent to utter, within their own environment, *a new word*. Needless to say, the number of subdivisions here is infinite, but the distinctive features of both categories are unmistakable: the first category, i.e., the base material, is made up, generally speaking, of people who are conservative and deferential by nature, who live a life of obedience and enjoy being obedient. In my view, they are simply obliged to be obedient, because that is their purpose, and for them there is absolutely nothing demeaning about it. In the second category, everyone oversteps the law; they are destroyers or they are that way inclined, in accordance with their abilities. The crimes committed by these people are, needless to say, relative and diverse; in the majority of cases they demand, in a great multitude of forms, the destruction of the present in the name of something better. But if such a man needs, for the sake of his idea, to step right over a corpse, over blood, then in my view he may, inside himself, as a matter of conscience, grant himself permission to step over this blood – though this depends, please note, on the idea and its magnitude. Only in this sense do I speak in my article about their right to commit crime.[19] (You'll remember, after all, that we began with a question of law.) There's no great cause for alarm, though: the mass of humanity almost never accepts their right, punishes them and hangs them (more or less) and in so doing fulfils its perfectly reasonable conservative purpose, even if, in subsequent generations, these same masses will place those they've punished on a pedestal and bow down before them (more or less). The first category is always master of the present, the second – master of the future. The first preserves the world and multiplies; the second moves the world and leads it towards a goal. The first and the second have exactly the same right to exist. In short, with me everyone has an equal right, and so – *Vive la guerre éternelle*,[20] until, needless to say, the New Jerusalem!'[21]

'So you do believe in the New Jerusalem?'

'I do,' answered Raskolnikov firmly. While saying this, and

throughout the course of his long tirade, he'd been staring at the floor, having chosen for himself a particular spot on the rug.

'And . . . you believe in God? Please forgive my curiosity.'

'I do,' repeated Raskolnikov, lifting his eyes towards Porfiry.

'And . . . you believe in the raising of Lazarus?'[22]

'I . . . do. But why are you asking?'

'You believe in it literally?'

'Literally.'

'I see, sir . . . Well, I was just being curious. Do forgive me. But with respect – I refer to your earlier remark – they are not *always* punished; in fact, some . . .'

'Are victorious during their lifetime? Oh yes, some get their way even during their lifetime, and then . . .'

'They begin handing out punishments themselves?'

'If necessary, and actually, you know, more often than not. Rather witty of you, I must say.'

'My humble thanks. But tell me, if you would: how exactly are the extraordinary to be distinguished from the ordinary? Should we look out for birthmarks of some kind? The reason I ask is that we could do with some accuracy here, some objective certainty, as it were: please forgive the natural anxiety of a practical and well-intentioned man, but couldn't one introduce some special type of clothing, for example; couldn't they be, I don't know, branded in some way?[23] Because wouldn't you agree that if things got muddled and one person from one category fancied that he belonged to the other, and began to "remove all obstacles", as you so felicitously put it, then . . .'

'Oh, that happens all the time! This observation is even wittier than your previous one . . .'

'My humble thanks . . .'

'Don't mention it, sir. But please bear in mind that such a mistake is possible only on the part of the first category, i.e., "ordinary" people (a rather unfortunate phrase, I'll admit). For despite their innate predisposition towards obedience, a very great number of them, by virtue of a certain natural playfulness, such as even a cow possesses, like to fancy themselves as the vanguard, as "destroyers", to claim their slice of the "new word", and they couldn't be more sincere, sir. And very often they don't even notice those who really are *new*,[24] and even look down on them as people with outmoded and demeaning ways of thinking. But, in my view, there can be no significant danger here, and you really have nothing to worry about, because if they take one step forward they take two steps back. Of course, you could flog them a little every now and again for getting carried away, so as to put them in their place, but no more than that; you don't even need to find someone to do it: being so well-behaved, they'll do it themselves. Some will render this service to their peers, others will even flog themselves ... They'll also submit themselves to various forms of public penance – it's all rather beautiful and edifying, and there's nothing, in short, for you to worry about ... There's a law at work here.'

'Well, on this point, at least, you've reassured me a little. But there's something else that worries me, sir. Tell me, please, are there many such people, "extraordinary ones", I mean, who have the right to butcher others? I don't mind bowing down, of course, but wouldn't you agree that having a lot of them would be rather frightful, sir?'

'Oh, don't you worry about that, either,' Raskolnikov continued in the same tone. 'In general, the number of people born with new ideas, with the ability to say something, anything, even the slightest bit *new*, is extraordinarily small, strangely so, in fact. Only one thing is clear: the pattern according to which these people are born, of these categories and subdivisions, must be very reliably and precisely determined by some law of nature. This law, needless to say, is not currently known, but I believe it exists and that it might become known in due course. The great mass of humanity, the base material, exists only for that reason – so that, in the end, by some special effort, via some hitherto mysterious process, through some intersection of blood and breed, it can make one last push and finally bring into the world that one person in, let's say, a thousand, born with at least some measure of independence. Even broader will be the independence of the one in, say, ten thousand (these are approximate figures, of course). Still broader – the one in a hundred thousand. Geniuses take millions, while the great geniuses who crown human history may require the passing of many thousands of millions of people on this earth. I've not peeked into the retort where all this takes place. But there simply must be a definite law. It can't be chance.'

'Are the pair of you joking?' cried Razumikhin at last. 'Are you pulling each other's legs? Look at them sitting there, laughing at the other's expense! Are you being serious, Rodya?'

Raskolnikov silently lifted towards him his pale, almost sad face and made no reply. And to Razumikhin there seemed something strange, next to this quiet, sad face, about Porfiry's unconcealed, importunate, petulant and *discourteous* sarcasm.

'Well, brother, if you really are serious, then ... Of course, you're right to say that this isn't new and resembles everything we've read and heard a thousand times before; but what is truly *original* about it all – and truly belongs to you alone, to my horror – is that, in the end, you permit bloodshed *as a matter of conscience*, and, if you'll excuse me, you're actually quite fanatical about it ... This, then, must be the main idea of your article. But the permission to shed blood *as a matter of conscience*, well ... it's more terrifying, to my mind, than any official permission, any legal permission ...'

'Spot on, sir, it is more terrifying,' Porfiry chimed in.

'No, you must have got carried away somehow! There's some mistake here. I'll read it ... You just got carried away! You can't really think that ... I'll read it.'

'None of that's in the article, only hints,' said Raskolnikov.

'Yes indeedy,' – Porfiry just couldn't sit still – 'and your views on the subject of crime are by now almost clear to me, sir, but ... do please forgive my persistence (what a nuisance I'm being – I'm quite ashamed of myself!), but you see, sir, you did so much to reassure me before about those erroneous cases in which the two categories are confused, but ... I'm still rather bothered about how it all works in practice! I mean, what if some man or youth were to fancy himself a Muhammad or Lycurgus – of the future, needless to say – and went around removing all the obstacles in his way ... ? He's making preparations for some big crusade, say ... and needs to rustle up some funds ... understand?'

Zametov gave a sudden snort from his corner. Raskolnikov didn't even look round.

'I have to agree with you,' he calmly replied, 'that such cases must indeed occur. Those who are a bit stupid or a bit vain are particularly susceptible; the young, especially.'

'You see, sir. So what about it, sir?'

'What about it?' Raskolnikov sneered. 'It's hardly my fault. That's how it is and always will be. He was saying just now,' (he nodded towards Razumikhin) 'that I permit bloodshed. Well, so what? Society, after all, has more safeguards than it needs – exile, prisons, investigators, penal servitude – so why worry? Catch him if you can!'

'And if we do?'

'Serves him right.'

'You're logical, I'll grant you that. But what about his conscience, sir?'

'Why should you care about that?'

'You know, simply on grounds of humanity.'

'Well, he can suffer if he's got one and if he acknowledges his mistake. That'll be his punishment – besides hard labour.'

'So what about those who really are geniuses,' asked Razumikhin, frowning, 'the ones who've actually been given the right to butcher others – are you saying they shouldn't suffer at all, not even for the blood they've shed?'

'What does the word *should* have to do with it? It's not a matter of permitting something or forbidding something. Let him suffer, if he's sorry for his victim . . . Suffering and pain are always mandatory for broad minds and deep hearts. Truly great people, it seems to me, should feel great sadness on this earth,' he added with sudden pensiveness, in a tone that jarred with the conversation.

He looked up, fixed everyone with a thoughtful gaze, smiled and picked up his cap. He was far too calm compared to how he'd walked in, and he was aware of it. Everyone stood up.

'Well, sir, curse me if you must, be angry if you must, but I just can't help myself,' Porfiry Petrovich piped up once more. 'Just one more tiny question (I know I'm being a nuisance, sir!), just one little idea I wanted to air, purely so as not to forget it later . . .'

'All right, share your little idea with us,' said Raskolnikov, standing expectantly before him, serious and pale.

'Well, here it is, sir . . . though I don't know how best to put it . . . It's a terribly playful little idea . . . a psychological one, sir . . . Well, here it is: when you were composing that little article of yours, well, it's simply inconceivable – heh-heh! – that you didn't also think of yourself as being at least a teeny bit "extraordinary" as well, as also having a *new word* to utter, in your understanding of those terms . . . Wouldn't you say, sir?'

'Quite possibly,' came Raskolnikov's contemptuous reply.

Razumikhin stirred.

'Well if that's the case, then do you really mean to say that you would decide – in view of certain disappointments and hardships in everyday life or in order to assist all humanity in some way – to step right over this or that obstacle? . . . Say, for example, commit murder and robbery?'

And somehow he suddenly winked at him again with his left eye and broke into silent laughter – just like before.

'I'd hardly tell you if I did step over them,' Raskolnikov replied with defiant, haughty contempt.

'No, sir, the only reason I ask, frankly, is to gain a better understanding of your article, in a purely literary respect, sir . . .'

'Ugh, the brazen cheek of it all!' thought Raskolnikov with disgust.

'Permit me to observe,' he replied stiffly, 'that I consider myself neither a Muhammad nor a Napoleon . . . nor any such figure; consequently, I am unable, being none of the above, to give you a satisfactory account of how I'd behave.'

'Come come, which of us in Rus today does not consider himself a Napoleon?'[25] Porfiry suddenly uttered, with terrifying familiarity. This time, there was something blatant even in the tone of his voice.

'What if it was some future Napoleon who bumped off Alyona Ivanovna last week with an axe?' Zametov suddenly blurted out from his corner.

Raskolnikov said nothing, staring hard at Porfiry. Razumikhin was frowning darkly. Even before this, he thought he could sense something. He cast an angry glance round the room. A minute passed in gloomy silence. Raskolnikov turned to leave.

'Don't tell me you're leaving!' said Porfiry warmly, offering his hand with the utmost courtesy. 'So, so glad to have met you. And do put your mind at rest about that request of yours. Just write it the way I told you. Or even better, come and find me there yourself . . . in the next few days . . . even tomorrow, if you like. I expect I'll be there at about eleven. We'll sort everything out . . . have a chat . . . And you, as one of the last people *there*, might even be able to tell us something . . . ,' he added with the kindliest air.

'So you want to question me officially, by the book?' asked Raskolnikov curtly.

'Whatever for, sir? That certainly won't be necessary for now. You misunderstood me. I'm not one to miss an opportunity, you see . . . and I've already spoken to all the pawners . . . taken statements from some . . . and you, as the last . . . Ah, by the way,' he cried, with sudden delight, 'how could I forget?' – he turned to Razumikhin – 'Remember how you gave me an earful that time about that Mikolai . . . I know perfectly well, of course,' – he turned to Raskolnikov – 'that the boy's clean, but it had to be done, and I had to bother Mitka as well . . . but here's the thing, sir, the nub of the matter: climbing the stairs that time, sir . . . between seven and eight, if I'm not mistaken?'

'Correct,' replied Raskolnikov, struck that same second by an unpleasant awareness that he need not have said it.

'So, as I say, climbing the stairs, sir, between seven and eight, sir, did you at least happen to see, on the second floor, I mean, in the apartment with the open door – remember? – two workmen or at least one of the two? They were decorating, perhaps you noticed? It is of the utmost, utmost importance for them!'

'Decorators? No, I didn't . . . ,' Raskolnikov slowly replied, as if rummaging through his memory while tensing every muscle, rigid with the agony of suspense: where was the trap, what was he missing? 'No, I didn't, and I can't say I noticed an open door either . . . but the fourth floor' – he'd mastered the trap and now he could gloat – 'now that I do remember, someone was moving out, a civil servant . . . opposite Alyona Ivanovna . . . I remember that . . . quite clearly, in fact . . . soldiers were carrying out some couch or other, squeezing me against the wall . . . but decorators – no, I don't recall there being any decorators . . . and I'm fairly sure there weren't any open doors. No, there weren't . . .'

'What are you playing at?' Razumikhin yelled, as if suddenly coming to his senses. 'The decorators were painting on the day of the murder, but he was there three days earlier. So what are you on about?'

'Well I never! I got everything mixed up!' cried Porfiry, slapping himself on the forehead. 'This whole business is playing havoc with my mind!' he said to Raskolnikov, almost as if he were apologizing. 'It's so terribly important for us to find out whether anyone saw them, between seven and eight, in that apartment, that I had a sudden fancy just now that you might also be able to tell us something . . . I got it all mixed up!'

'Be a bit more careful next time,' Razumikhin sullenly remarked.

These last words were spoken in the entrance hall. Porfiry Petrovich showed them right to the door, with the utmost courtesy. Both stepped outside with gloomy, scowling expressions, and for a while neither said a word. Raskolnikov slowly caught his breath . . .

VI

'. . . I don't believe it! I can't believe it!' a bewildered Razumikhin kept saying, desperately trying to refute Raskolnikov's arguments. They were already approaching Bakaleyev's rooms, where Pulkheria Alexandrovna and Dunya had long been expecting them. Razumikhin kept stopping on the way, embarrassed and excited by the mere fact that they were talking about *that* openly for the first time.

'Well don't, then!' Raskolnikov replied with a cold and nonchalant sneer. 'You, as usual, didn't notice a thing, but I was weighing up every word.'

'You're suspicious, that's why . . . H'm . . . Porfiry's tone really was rather strange, I agree, and especially that scoundrel Zametov! . . . You're right, there was something about him – but why? Why?'

'Changed his mind overnight.'

'No – just the opposite! If they really did have such a brainless idea, they'd be doing all they could to conceal it, keeping their cards close to their chest before pouncing later . . . But *now* – that would be insolent and reckless!'

'If they had any facts, I mean real facts, or at least serious grounds for suspicion, then yes, they would try to hide their cards, in the hope of doubling their winnings (but in that case they'd have done a search ages ago!). But they have no facts, not a single one – it's all a mirage, all double-edged, an idea plucked from the air – so they're trying to trip me up with their insolence. Or perhaps he himself was angry at the lack of facts and his irritation boiled over. Or perhaps he's got something up his sleeve . . . He looks a clever sort . . . Or perhaps he meant to frighten me with what he knows . . . There's a whole psychology at work here . . . But it disgusts me to explain it. Just leave it!'

'And it's positively insulting! How well I understand you! But . . . seeing as we're talking openly at last (and what a fine thing that is – I'm so pleased!), I'll come straight out with it and admit that I've noticed it all along, this idea of theirs; no more than a sniff of an idea, of course, a worm of an idea, but why even a worm? How dare they? Where are the roots of all this hidden – where? If only you knew how furious I've been! What? All because a poor student, crippled by beggary and hypochondria, on the verge of succumbing to a vicious illness and delirium that (note!) may have been lying dormant in him already, a man who's suspicious, proud, who knows his own worth, who hasn't had anyone visit him in his corner for the last six months and is dressed like a tramp, in boots without soles, has to stand there before a bunch of local coppers and endure their mockery; not to mention a debt that comes out of the blue, an overdue promissory note from court counsellor Chebarov, rotten paint, thirty degrees Réaumur,[26] not a breath of fresh air, a throng of people, a story about the murder of someone he'd visited the day before – and all this on an empty belly! Try not fainting after that! And they base everything on this! Damn it all! I understand what a pain this is, but in your shoes, Rodka, I'd laugh in their faces, or even better I'd spit on them all, gob at them, the thicker the better, dish out several slaps on each cheek – intelligently, of course, that's the only way to do it – then leave it at that. Just spit on them! Pull yourself together! The shame of it!'

'He actually put that rather well!' thought Raskolnikov.

'Spit on them? Then face another grilling tomorrow!' he said bitterly. 'Do I really have to explain myself to them? It's bad enough that I stooped to Zametov's level in the tavern yesterday . . .'

'Damn it all! I'll go and see Porfiry myself! I'll pin him down, *in the family spirit*. I'll drag it out of him, all of it! And as for Zametov . . .'

'The penny's finally dropped!' thought Raskolnikov.

'Wait a minute!' shouted Razumikhin, grabbing him suddenly by the shoulder. 'Wait! You've got it wrong! I've had a think and you've got it all wrong! I mean, how could it be a trick? You say the question about the workmen was a trick? Try this for size: if you had done *that*, would you really have blurted out that you saw the apartment being painted . . . and the workmen? Just the opposite: you'd have seen nothing, even if you had! Who'd ever admit to something so damaging?'

'If I had done *that*, then I'd have been sure to say I saw both the workmen and the apartment,' Raskolnikov replied, with reluctance and obvious disgust.

'But why admit something so damaging?'

'Because only a peasant or the most inexperienced novice simply clams up under questioning. Any man with a bit of brains and experience would have been sure to admit, wherever possible, to every objective and undeniable fact; only he'd find different reasons for them and put his own, unexpected mark on them, thereby lending them an entirely different meaning and showing them in a quite different light. Porfiry could have counted on me replying like that and saying I'd

seen everything, so as to make it sound more convincing, while adding something by way of an explanation . . .'

'But he'd have shot back that the workers couldn't have been there
two days earlier, so you must have been present on the day of the murder, between seven and eight. He'd have caught you out on a petty
detail!'

'That's precisely what he was counting on – that I wouldn't manage
to think it through in time, that I'd hurry to say something convincing
and forget that the workers couldn't have been there two days before.'

'But how could anyone forget that?'

'Quite easily! It's always the silly things that catch sly people out.
The slyer a man is, the less he suspects he'll be caught out by something simple. It's the simplest things that catch out the slyest. Porfiry
is far less stupid than you think . . .'

'A scoundrel's what he is now!'

Raskolnikov couldn't help laughing. But as he did so he felt there
was something strange about his own animation and the enthusiasm
with which he'd just offered this last explanation, when until then
he'd kept the conversation going with sullen disgust, for reasons of his
own, out of sheer necessity.

'I'm getting a taste for some of this!' he thought to himself.

But almost as he did so he suddenly became anxious, as if struck by
an unexpected and alarming thought. His anxiety grew. They'd already reached the entrance to Bakaleyev's rooms.

'You go in,' Raskolnikov suddenly said. 'I'll be right back.'

'Where are you off to? We're here now!'

'There's something I have to do . . . I'll be back in half an hour . . .
You tell them.'

'As you wish, but I'm coming with you!'

'So you want to torment me, too, do you?' he cried, with such bitter vexation, such despair in his gaze, that Razumikhin gave up. For a
while he remained standing on the porch, watching sullenly as Raskolnikov strode off briskly in the direction of the lane in which he
lived. Eventually, clenching his teeth and his fists, swearing there and
then that he would squeeze Porfiry dry, like a lemon, that very same
day, he went up to reassure Pulkheria Alexandrovna, who was already alarmed by their lengthy absence.

When Raskolnikov got home, his temples were damp with sweat
and he was breathing heavily. He hurriedly climbed the stairs, entered

his room, which he'd left unlocked, and immediately put the door on the hook. Next, he rushed over in crazed terror to the corner, to that same hole in the wallpaper where he'd kept the items back then, stuck a hand inside and spent several minutes rummaging about, running his fingers over every nook and cranny, every crease in the wallpaper. Finding nothing, he got to his feet and took long, deep breaths. Walking up to Bakaleyev's porch, he'd had a sudden fancy that one or other of the items, a little chain or cufflink, or even one of the scraps of paper in which they'd been wrapped, with a label in the old woman's hand, might have slipped into some crack or other, only to confront him later as unexpected, irrefutable evidence.

He stood as if lost in thought and a strange, abject, almost senseless smile played on his lips. Eventually he picked up his cap and quietly left the room. His thoughts were all tangled. Still pensive, he came out by the arch.

'There he is!' shouted a booming voice. He lifted his head.

The caretaker was standing by the door to his lodge and was pointing him out to a shortish man, a tradesman in appearance, who was wearing some kind of dressing gown over his waistcoat, and from a distance looked a lot like a woman. His head hung down beneath a soiled cap and there was something hunched about his entire appearance. To judge by his flabby, wrinkled face he was over fifty and his puffy little eyes had a sullen, stern and dissatisfied look.

'What's all this about?' asked Raskolnikov, walking up to the caretaker.

The tradesman looked askance at him from under his brows and measured him with an attentive, unhurried stare; then he slowly turned around and, without saying a word, walked out of the arch into the street.

'What's all this?' cried Raskolnikov.

'Some man asking if this is where the student's living – he gave your name – and who you're renting from. Then you come down, I point you out and he wanders off. Fancy that.'

The caretaker was also a little bewildered, though no more than a little, and after scratching his head about it for another second or two, turned round and went back to his lodge.

Raskolnikov rushed after the tradesman and spotted him immediately, walking on the opposite side of the street with the same steady, unhurried gait, his eyes glued to the ground, as if he were turning something over in his mind. He soon caught up with him, but for a while he kept a few steps behind; eventually he drew level with him and stole a glance at his face. The man immediately noticed him, looked him over and lowered his gaze again, and they walked on like that for a minute or so, one beside the other and not a word between them.

'You asked the caretaker for me?' Raskolnikov eventually said, but his voice was strangely hushed.

The tradesman made no reply and didn't even look up. Silence again.

'What . . . ? You come and ask for me . . . and say nothing . . . I mean, what is this?' Raskolnikov's voice kept breaking off and the words refused to come out clearly.

This time the tradesman lifted his eyes and gave Raskolnikov an ominous, dismal look.

'Killer!' he suddenly said in a soft, but clear and distinct voice . . .

Raskolnikov was walking beside him. His legs suddenly became dreadfully weak, his back felt cold and, for an instant, his heart seemed to stop; then it began pounding again, as if suddenly unhooked. They walked about a hundred paces like that, side by side and again in total silence.

The tradesman did not look at him.

'What is this . . . ? What are you . . . ? Who is a murderer?' mumbled Raskolnikov in a barely audible voice.

'*You're* the killer,'[27] uttered the other, articulating each syllable ever more imposingly and half-smiling with triumph and loathing; then, once again, he looked straight into Raskolnikov's pale face and deadened eyes. By now they'd reached the crossroads. The tradesman turned left along the street, without glancing back. Raskolnikov remained where he was, following him with his eyes. He saw how the other turned round after fifty paces or so and looked at him, still rooted to the spot. It was hard to be sure, but Raskolnikov thought that now, too, the tradesman had smiled at him with his cold, hateful, triumphant smile.

With slow, weak steps, knees trembling, chilled to the bone, Raskolnikov went back to his building and up to his cell. He took off his cap, put it on the table and stood motionless beside it for a good ten minutes. Then he sank feebly on to the couch and stretched out in pain, groaning weakly; his eyes were closed. He lay like that for about half an hour.

He wasn't thinking about anything. There was just the odd random thought or scrap of thought, or the odd image without rhyme or reason: faces seen by him back in his childhood or people he'd met only once and would never have recalled again; the bell tower of V—— Church;[28] a billiard table in a tavern and some officer standing next to it; the smell of cigars in some basement tobacco shop; a drinking den; a back staircase, pitch dark, soaked in slops and spattered with eggshells; and from somewhere or other the ringing of Sunday bells . . . One object replaced another in a constant whirl. There were even some that he liked and he tried to cling on to them, but they faded, and something was pressing on him inside, but only a little. Sometimes it even felt nice . . . The shiveriness did not pass, and that, too, felt almost nice.

He heard Razumikhin's hurried steps and voice, closed his eyes and pretended to be asleep. Razumikhin opened the door and stood for a while on the threshold, as if he were hesitating. Then he stepped softly into the room and tiptoed over to the couch. Nastasya's whisper carried over.

'Let 'im sleep. He'll eat later.'

'All right,' answered Razumikhin.

They tiptoed out and shut the door. Another half hour passed. Raskolnikov opened his eyes and again fell supine, clutching his head . . .

'Who is he? Who is this man from out of the ground? Where was he and what did he see? He saw everything, there's no doubt about that. So where was he standing, then, and from where was he watching? Why has he only come out now? And how could he see – how's that possible? . . . H'm . . . ,' continued Raskolnikov, growing cold and shuddering. 'Or what about the jewellery case that Mikolai found behind the door: how's that possible? Evidence? Miss the hundred-thousandth little mark and there you go: evidence the size of an Egyptian pyramid! A fly flew past – a fly saw! How's it all possible?'

And suddenly, with a sense of loathing, he felt how weak he'd become, how physically weak.

'I should have known it,' he thought with a bitter grin, 'and how did I dare – knowing how I am, *sensing in advance* how I'd be – take an axe and steep myself in blood? I simply must have known beforehand . . . Ha! But I did know beforehand!' he whispered in despair.

Every now and again he paused, rooted to the spot by some thought:

'No, those people are made differently. A true *master*, to whom everything is permitted, sacks Toulon, unleashes slaughter in Paris, *forgets* an army in Egypt, *expends* half a million lives marching on Moscow, then laughs it all off with a quip in Vilno;[29] and he even has idols erected to him after his death – so *everything* really is permitted. Such people are made not of flesh but of bronze!'[30]

A sudden, extraneous thought almost reduced him to laughter:

'Napoleon, the pyramids, Waterloo[31] – and a scraggy, horrid pen-pusher's widow, a hag, a moneylender with a red box beneath her bed; it's a bit much even for the likes of Porfiry Petrovich to digest! . . . Not to mention the rest of them! . . . Aesthetics will intervene: would a Napoleon really go crawling under the bed of some "old hag"! Please!'

For minutes at a time he felt almost delirious, succumbing to a mood of feverish exaltation.

'The hag's neither here nor there!' he thought impetuously. 'Maybe she's the mistake here – maybe it's not about her at all! She was only the sickness . . . I was in such a hurry to step right over . . . I didn't murder a person, I murdered a principle! Yes, I murdered the principle all right, but I didn't step over; I remained on this side . . . All I managed to do was kill. I didn't even manage that, as it turns out . . . Principle? What was Razumikhin, such a silly boy, berating the socialists for just now? Hardworking folk, trading folk; concerned with "general happiness" . . . No, I'm only given one life and that's my lot: I don't want to sit around waiting for "universal happiness". I want to live myself or else I'd rather not live at all. Well? I just didn't feel like walking past a hungry mother, gripping a rouble in my pocket and waiting for "universal happiness". As if to say: "Look at me carrying my little brick for universal happiness[32] – so my heart is at peace." Ha-ha! Why did you have to leave me out, of all people? I've only got one life, after all, and I also want . . . Oh, I'm an aesthetic louse, that's all there is to it,' he suddenly added with a volley of laughter, like a madman. 'Yes, I really am a louse,' he went on, clutching at this thought with grim delight, rummaging around in it, toying and amusing himself with it, 'if for no other reason than because, firstly, here I am talking about it, secondly, because I've been bothering all-gracious Providence this whole month, summoning her as my witness to the fact that I set out on this venture not for my own carnal desires, but with a splendid and pleasing purpose in mind – ha-ha! Thirdly, because I intended to observe in my actions the highest possible degree of justice, to weigh and to measure, to tot it all up; of all the lice in the world I chose the most utterly useless and, having killed her, intended to take from her the precise amount I needed for the first step, no more and no less (so the rest really would have gone to the monastery, in accordance with her will – ha-ha!) . . . Because, because I'm a louse, pure and simple,' he added, gnashing his teeth, 'because I myself may be still fouler and more horrid than the louse I killed, and because I *sensed in advance* that this is what I would tell myself *after* the murder! Can any horror compare to it? So vulgar! So vile! . . . Oh, how I understand the "prophet", with his sword, on horseback. Allah commands, so obey, O "quivering" creature![33] How right the "prophet" is when he lines up a top-notch battery[34] across the street and fires a salvo at the righteous and the guilty, without even deigning to explain himself! Submit, quivering creature, and – *do not desire* . . . for desiring is not your business! . . . Oh, never, never will I forgive the old hag!'

His hair was damp with sweat, his trembling lips caked, his gaze riveted to the ceiling.

'Mother, sister, how I loved them! So why do I hate them now? Yes, I hate them. I physically hate them. I can't bear to have them near me . . . I went up to Mother earlier and kissed her, I remember . . . Embracing her, thinking that if she found out . . . would I really tell her? Wouldn't put it past me . . . H'm! *She* must be just like me,' he added, making an effort to think, as if struggling in the grip of delirium. 'Oh, how I hate the hag now! I expect I'd murder her all over again if she came to! Poor Lizaveta! Why did she have to turn up? . . . Strange, though – why do I almost never think of her, as if I'd never murdered her? . . . Lizaveta! Sonya! Poor things, meek, meek-eyed . . . So sweet! . . . Why don't they cry? Why don't they groan? . . . Always giving . . . and their meek, quiet gaze . . . Sonya, Sonya! Quiet Sonya!'

Oblivion came over him; it seemed strange to him that he couldn't remember how he'd ended up in the street. It was already late evening. The dusk was gathering, the full moon shone ever more brightly, but somehow it felt even more stifling than usual. People thronged the streets; craftsmen and employees were making their way home; others were out for a walk; it smelled of mortar, dust, stagnant water. Raskolnikov walked along, sad and preoccupied. He clearly recalled that he'd left home with the intention of doing something and doing it quickly, but what that was he couldn't remember. Suddenly he stopped and caught sight of a man on the opposite side of the street, on the pavement, standing there, waving to him. He crossed the street towards him, but the man suddenly turned and walked off as if nothing had happened, with his head down and without turning round or giving any sign of having called him over. 'Well maybe he didn't?' thought Raskolnikov, but set off after him all the same. When he was only ten paces away, he suddenly recognized him – and took fright; it was the tradesman from before, with the same dressing gown and the same hunch. Raskolnikov kept his distance; his heart was pounding; they turned into a lane – and still the man did not look round. 'Does he know I'm following him?' Raskolnikov wondered. The tradesman entered the gates of a big building. Raskolnikov hurried up to the gates and stared: would he glance back? Would he call him? And, indeed, after walking right through the archway and coming out into the yard, the man suddenly turned round and seemed to wave to him once more. Raskolnikov immediately followed him into the yard, but the tradesman was no longer there. So he must have taken the first staircase. Raskolnikov rushed after him. And indeed, someone's measured, unhurried footsteps could still be heard from two flights up. Strange: the staircase was somehow familiar! There was the window on the first floor – moonlight streamed through it, sadly and mysteriously – and here was the second floor. Ha! The very same apartment the workmen had been decorating . . . How had he not recognized the place straight away? The footsteps of the man walking ahead of him died away: 'So he must have stopped or found somewhere to hide.' Here was the third floor. Should he carry on? Such silence . . . almost frightening . . . But he went on. The sound of his own footsteps scared and disturbed him. God, how dark! The tradesman was surely hiding in some corner or other. Ah! The apartment was wide open to the stairs. He thought for a moment, and went in. The entrance hall was very dark and empty; not a soul, as though everything had been taken out. Softly-softly, on tiptoe, he went through to the living room: the entire space was flooded in bright moonlight. Nothing had changed: the chairs, the mirror, the yellow couch, the little pictures in their frames. A huge, round, copper-red moon stared through the windows. 'The silence comes from the moon,' thought Raskolnikov, 'and the moon must be posing a riddle.' He stood and waited for a long while, and the quieter the moon, the louder the pounding of his heart, until it even began to hurt. Silence. Suddenly, a short dry crack, like the snapping of a twig, then everything went dead once more. A fly, waking up, suddenly hit a pane in full flight and began buzzing plaintively. At that very same moment, in the corner, between the small cupboard and the window, he noticed what seemed to be a lady's velvet coat hanging on the wall. 'What's that coat doing here?' he wondered. 'Wasn't here before . . .' He stole up to it and sensed there might be someone hiding behind it. He carefully moved the coat to one side with his hand and saw a chair, and on the chair in the corner was the old hag, all curled up with her head bowed down, making it impossible for him to see her face, but it was her. He stood over her. 'She's afraid!' he thought, gently freeing the axe from the loop and striking the old woman on the crown, once, twice. How strange: she didn't even twitch from the blows, as if she were made of wood. Frightened, he bent down and looked closer: but she, too, just bent her head down further. So he bent all the way to the floor and looked up from there into her face, looked up and went as numb as a corpse: the old woman was sitting there laughing – yes, she was almost bursting with soft, inaudible laughter, doing all she could to keep him from hearing. Suddenly he had the impression that the bedroom door had opened a fraction and that laughs and whispers were coming from there as well. He was seized with rage: he began hitting the old woman on the head as hard as he could, but with each blow of the axe the laughter and whispering from the bedroom grew louder still, while the hag simply rocked with mirth. He wanted to run, but the entrance hall was already packed with people, the doors on the staircase were wide open, and on the landing and all the way down the stairs there was nothing but people, a row of heads, all watching – but biding their time in silence . . . His heart clenched, and his legs were rooted to the spot . . . He wanted to scream – and woke up.

He drew deep breaths – but how strange! It was as if the dream still continued: the door was wide open, and there was a complete stranger standing on the threshold, studying him closely.

Raskolnikov hadn't fully opened his eyes yet, and instantly closed them again. He lay prone, without stirring. 'Am I still dreaming?' he wondered, and again raised his eyelids a fraction: the stranger was standing on the same spot, still staring at him. Suddenly he stepped warily over the threshold, closed the door carefully behind him, walked over to the table, waited for a minute or so – his eyes fixed on him throughout – and softly, noiselessly sat down on the chair beside the couch. He placed his hat on its side, on the floor, and leant with both hands on his cane, resting his chin on his hands. Clearly, he was prepared to wait a very long time. Insofar as could be seen through blinking eyelids, this man was no longer young, solidly built and with a thick, light beard that was all but white . . .

Some ten minutes passed. Though it was still light, evening was closing in. In the room there was complete silence. No sounds even from the stairs. Only the buzzing and knocking of some big fly as it struck the pane in mid-flight. Eventually it became unbearable: Raskolnikov suddenly raised himself and sat up on the couch.

'Well, go on: what do you want?'

'Just as I thought: you weren't sleeping, merely pretending,' came the stranger's peculiar reply and easy laugh. 'Allow me to introduce myself: Arkady Ivanovich Svidrigailov . . .'

PART FOUR

I

'Am I really still dreaming?' Raskolnikov wondered once more. Warily and mistrustfully, he examined his unexpected guest.

'Svidrigailov? Nonsense! Impossible!' he finally said out loud, bewildered.

The guest seemed not in the least surprised by this exclamation.

'Two reasons bring me here: in the first place, I was keen to meet you in person, having heard a great deal about you, for some time now, from a most intriguing and favourable source; secondly, I cherish the hope that you will not shrink from assisting me in a venture that bears directly on the interests of your dear sister, Avdotya Romanovna. Without your approval, she may very well refuse to allow me anywhere near her now, owing to a certain prejudice, but with your assistance I may, on the contrary, reckon . . .'

'You reckon wrongly,' interrupted Raskolnikov.

'They arrived only yesterday, did they not, sir?'

Raskolnikov did not reply.

'I know it was yesterday. I only arrived two days ago myself. Well, sir, here's what I'll say to you on this score, Rodion Romanovich. I see no need to explain myself, but permit me to ask: what is there about all this, really, that is so very criminal on my part, if we leave all prejudices to one side and take a sensible view of things?'

Raskolnikov continued to study him in silence.

'The fact, sir, that I persecuted a defenceless girl in my own home and "insulted her with my beastly propositions"? (I'm getting ahead of myself!) But suppose for a moment that I, too, am a man, *et nihil humanum*[1] . . . , in short, that I, too, am apt to be tempted and to fall in love (such things, of course, are beyond our control), then everything may be explained in the most natural way. The only question is this: am I a monster or myself a victim? What's that? A victim? Well, in proposing that my dear *objet* make off with me to America or to Switzerland, I may have been nurturing the most respectful feelings, and even intending to arrange our reciprocal happiness! . . . Is not reason the servant of passion? I dare say I came out of it even worse, for pity's sake!'

'That's hardly the point,' interrupted a disgusted Raskolnikov. 'You're simply repugnant, whether or not you're right, which is why people don't want to have anything to do with you and send you packing – so get out!'

Svidrigailov suddenly roared with laughter.

'Well I never . . . You're not easily flummoxed, are you?' he said with the most candid laugh. 'I had half a mind to trick you, but no, you put your finger on the nub right away!'

'You're still trying to trick me now.'

'Well, what of it? What of it?' repeated Svidrigailov, laughing without inhibition. 'Is this not, as they say, *bonne guerre*?[2] Such tricks are entirely permissible! . . . You rather interrupted me, though, and I'll say it again: there would have been no unpleasantness at all, were it not for the incident in the garden. Marfa Petrovna . . .'

'Oh yes, Marfa Petrovna – another of your victims, I'm told,' Raskolnikov rudely interrupted.

'So you've heard about that as well? Difficult not to, I suppose . . . Regarding your comment – well, I don't know how best to put it, although my personal conscience on this score is entirely untroubled. That is, you really mustn't think I have anything to fear: everything was done by the book and with complete precision. The medical investigation revealed the cause of death to be a stroke brought on by bathing straight after a heavy meal and the consumption of nigh on a bottle of wine, and there was little else it could have revealed . . . No sir, here's what I found myself thinking about for a while, especially en route, in the train: might I have done anything to facilitate this whole . . . misfortune – in a moral sense, through being irritable or something like that? But I concluded that this, too, was positively impossible.'

Raskolnikov laughed.

'A fine way of worrying!'

'Why are you laughing? Consider this: I only struck her twice with a little whip; it didn't even leave any marks . . . Now please don't think me a cynic; I know perfectly well how beastly this was of me, etcetera, etcetera; but I also know full well that Marfa Petrovna probably welcomed this "enthusiasm" of mine. The story about your dear sister had been flogged to death. This was already the third day Marfa Petrovna had had to spend at home; she could hardly show up in town empty-handed and she'd already bored everyone to tears with that letter of hers (you heard about how she went round reading it?). Then, all of a sudden, out of a clear blue sky, these two whippings! Harness the carriage, quick! ... I won't even mention the fact that there are times when women find it very, very pleasurable to be insulted, for all their apparent indignation. That goes for everyone, actually; humankind in general is terribly fond of being insulted, have you noticed? But it's particularly true of women. One might even say it's their sole amusement.'

At one point Raskolnikov was on the verge of getting up and walking out. But a certain curiosity, even a kind of forethought, held him back for a moment.

'Are you fond of fighting?' he asked absently.

'Not particularly, no,' came Svidrigailov's calm reply. 'In fact, Marfa Petrovna and I hardly ever fought. We lived in great harmony and she was always perfectly satisfied with me. As for the whip, throughout our entire seven years together I used it no more than twice (if we exclude a third, highly ambiguous occasion): the first was two months after our wedding, straight after we'd arrived in the country, and now this very recent incident. And I dare say you thought me a monster, a reactionary, a serf-driver? Heh-heh ... By the way, do you happen to recall, Rodion Romanovich, how a few years ago, back in the days of beneficent free speech, a certain nobleman – I've forgotten his surname! – was shamed in every town and journal for giving that German lass a good thrashing in a railway carriage? That was the same year, I believe, of "The Scandal of *The Age*"[3] (you know, the *Egyptian Nights*, that public reading, remember? Those black eyes! O, where are you, golden days of our youth?). Well, sir, here's what I think: towards the gentleman who gave the German lass a thrashing I feel not one whit of sympathy, because, after all, there's ... well, no cause for sympathy! But I must also mention that one occasionally comes across "German lasses" who lead one on to such an extent that, it seems to me, there is not a single apostle of progress who could vouch entirely for his own behaviour. Nobody considered the topic from this perspective at the time, yet it is precisely this perspective that is truly humane. Yes indeed, sir!'

Saying this, Svidrigailov suddenly burst out laughing again. Raskolnikov could see that before him was a man who had set his mind on something and who kept his thoughts to himself.

'It's been several days, I suppose, since you last spoke to anyone?' he asked.

'More or less. Well, you must be surprised to find me so very accommodating.'

'No, I'm surprised to find you so excessively accommodating.'

'Just because I'm not offended by the rudeness of your questions? Is that it? But ... what's there to be offended about? You asked, I answered,' he added with a strikingly ingenuous air. 'After all, there's nothing much that particularly interests me, if truth be told,' he went on with a pensive air. 'Nothing that really occupies me, particularly now ... Still, you're entitled to think I'm currying favour for my own ends, especially as the business in hand relates to your dear sister, as I told you myself. But I'll be frank with you: I'm bored sick! Especially these past three days. In fact, I'm even pleased to see you ... Now don't be angry, Rodion Romanovich, but you yourself strike me as awfully strange somehow. Really, there's something about you; and precisely now, not right this minute, but now in general ... All right, all right, I won't – no need to frown! I'm less of a bear than you think.'

Raskolnikov looked at him sullenly.

'A bear might be the last thing you are,' he said. 'In fact, you look to me like a man of the best society or, at any rate, that you can behave decently enough if you need to.'

'Well, I'm not much interested in anyone's opinion,' replied Svidrigailov dryly, even with a hint of arrogance, 'so why not play the boor every now and again, especially when that costume suits our climate so well and ... and especially if you are naturally inclined that way yourself,' he added with another laugh.

'I heard, though, that you know a lot of people here. You are, as they say, well connected. So what do you need me for, if not for some specific purpose?'

'You're quite right to say that I know people,' Svidrigailov rejoined, leaving the main point unanswered. 'I've met some already. After all, I've been loafing about for three days. There are people I recognize and people who seem to recognize me. Hardly surprising, I suppose: I'm well turned-out and considered a man of means; even the peasant reforms passed us by:[4] all woods and water-meadows, so our income's safe and sound. But ... I won't go there; I was already sick of it then, so I've been walking around for three days without telling anyone ... And just look at this city! How did we ever invent such a thing, tell me that? A city of pen-pushers and seminarians of every stripe! Honestly, there's so much that escaped my attention back then, eight or so years ago, when I was knocking about here . . . Anatomy's my only hope now, honest to God!'

'What anatomy?'

'And as for all these clubs of yours, and Dussots and *pointes*[5] and, for that matter, progress – well, we'll leave that to others,' he went on, ignoring the question again. 'Besides, who wants to be a card sharp?'

'So you were a card sharp too?'

'But of course! There was a whole group of us, utterly respectable, eight or so years ago. It passed the time, and you should have seen how well-mannered we all were, some of us poets, some – capitalists. Actually it's a general rule, in Russian society, that the best-mannered people are the ones who've taken a few beatings – have you noticed? It's only when I moved to the country that I let myself go. Still, some Greek from Nezhin almost landed me in prison back then for my debts. That's when Marfa Petrovna turned up, haggled a bit and ransomed me for thirty thousand pieces of silver. (I owed seventy thousand in all.) We were lawfully wed and she promptly took me off to her place in the country, like some precious jewel. She's five years older than me, after all. Loved me rotten. Seven years I spent cooped up on her estate. And don't forget that she kept those thirty thousand hanging over me for the rest of her life – she had this document against me, signed by a third party; the slightest hint of rebellion and she'd have sprung the trap! She wouldn't have thought twice! Women see no contradiction in such things.'

'Would you have bolted, but for the document?'

'How can I put it? The document scarcely inhibited me. I was in no hurry to go anywhere, and actually it was Marfa Petrovna who, seeing me bored, wanted to take me abroad on a couple of occasions. No thanks! I'd travelled abroad before and I'd always been miserable. It's all right, I suppose, but you look at the sunrise, the Gulf of Naples, the sea, and you can't help feeling sad. And the most disgusting thing is that you really are sad! No, you're better off in the motherland: here, at least, you can always blame everything on someone else. I suppose I might agree to an expedition to the North Pole, because *j'ai le vin mauvais*,[6] and I hate drinking anyway, though wine is all that's left. I've tried. Now tell me: I hear that on Sunday, in the Yusupov Gardens, Berg's[7] going up in a huge balloon and inviting people to join him for a fee – is that true?'

'Why, would you go?'

'Me? No ... I just ...,' muttered Svidrigailov, who really did seem deep in thought.

'Is he serious?' wondered Raskolnikov.

'No, the document didn't inhibit me,' Svidrigailov ruminated, 'and it was my choice to stay cooped up on the estate. Besides, it's almost a year since Marfa Petrovna returned it to me on my name day and gave me a tidy sum while she was at it. She had money, you know. "See how I trust you, Arkady Ivanovich?" – those were her exact words. You don't believe me? Actually, you know, I learned to run the estate pretty well. People know who I am. I started ordering books as well. Marfa Petrovna approved at first, then started worrying that too much studying would do me harm.'

'You miss Marfa Petrovna a great deal, it seems.'

'Me? Perhaps. Perhaps I do. By the way, do you believe in ghosts?'

'What ghosts?'

'Ordinary ghosts, what else?'

'You do, I suppose?'

'I suppose not, *pour vous plaire*[8] ... Or rather ...'

'You've been seeing them?'

Svidrigailov gave him a strange look.

'Marfa Petrovna is fond of paying visits,' he said, twisting his mouth into a peculiar smile.

'How do you mean "is fond of paying visits"?'

'Well, she's already come three times. The first time I saw her was on the day of the funeral, an hour after she was buried. The day before I left to come here. The second was the day before yesterday, en route, at daybreak, Malaya Vishera Station; and the third was a couple of hours ago, in my lodgings, in the main room. I was alone.'

'And awake?'

'Wide awake. All three times. She comes, talks for a minute or so, and leaves through the door; always through the door. There's even a sort of noise.'

'Now why did I think that something like that must be happening to you?' said Raskolnikov suddenly, and was amazed to have said it. He was extremely worked up.

'Well, well! So that's what you thought?' asked Svidrigailov in surprise. 'How extraordinary! But didn't I say we have something in common, eh?'

'No, you never said that!' came Raskolnikov's sharp and heated response.

'I didn't?'

'No!'

'I thought I did. Before, when I walked in and saw you lying there with your eyes closed, pretending, I immediately said to myself, "That's the one!"'

'What do you mean: "the one"? What are you talking about?' cried Raskolnikov.

'What am I talking about? Well, I honestly don't know . . . ,' muttered Svidrigailov frankly, himself in something of a muddle.

For a minute or so they were silent. Each riveted their eyes on the other.

'Nonsense, all of it!' Raskolnikov cried out in vexation. 'So what does she say when she comes?'

'What does she say? Why, the most trivial things, and – funnily enough – that's precisely what makes me so angry. She came in that first time (I was tired: the funeral service, then the hymns and prayers for the deceased, then some food, and at last I was alone in my study, having a smoke and a think), came in through the door and said: "You know, Arkady Ivanovich, what with all the fuss today you forgot to wind the clock in the dining room." I really did wind that clock myself, once a week, all those seven years, and if I ever forgot she'd be sure to remind me. The very next day I left to come here. At daybreak I walked into the station – I'd hardly slept, I was shattered, bleary-eyed – ordered some coffee and look, there's Marfa Petrovna sitting down next to me with a pack of cards in her hands: "A bit of fortune-telling, Arkady Ivanovich, for the road?" She was a dab hand at that. Well, I'll never forgive myself for not taking her up on her offer! I fled in terror and the next thing I knew the bell rang for the train. Then today, I'd just had a lousy lunch from a cook-shop and my stomach was groaning – I was sitting and having a smoke – when in comes Marfa Petrovna again, done up to the nines in a new green silk dress with an extremely long train: "Hallo, Arkady Ivanovich! How do you like my dress? Aniska couldn't make one like this." (Aniska's our local seamstress, her parents were serfs, she was apprenticed in Moscow – a pretty young thing.) There she was, spinning about in front of me. I had a good look at the dress, then peered into her face: "What a thing to come and see me about, Marfa Petrovna!" "Dearie me, how very touchy you've become!" So I said, just to tease her: "I plan to get married, Marfa Petrovna." "I wouldn't put it past you, Arkady Ivanovich. Doesn't do you much credit, though – your wife barely in the grave and you rushing off to get married. What's more, you're bound to make the wrong choice – you'll both be miserable and only make good people laugh." And off she went with a rustle of her train – or so I thought. Such nonsense, eh?'

'But perhaps you're just lying?' said Raskolnikov.

'I rarely lie,' replied Svidrigailov pensively, as if he hadn't even noticed the rudeness of the question.

'And you'd never seen ghosts before?'

'I . . . I did, but only once, six years ago. I had a house-serf called Filka. We'd only just buried him and I yelled, absent-mindedly, "Filka, my pipe!" and in he came and walked straight over to the cabinet where I keep my pipes. I'm sitting there, thinking, "He's come to get his own back," because we'd had an almighty row shortly before he died. "How dare you," I say, "come in here with holes at your elbows? Get out, you rascal!" He turned, walked out and never came back. I didn't tell Marfa Petrovna at the time. I was about to arrange a memorial service for him, but then I thought better of it.'

'You should see a doctor.'

'I don't need you to tell me I'm unwell, though I honestly couldn't tell you what's wrong with me. I expect I'm five times healthier than you are. My question to you was not: do you or do you not believe that people see ghosts? My question was: do you believe that ghosts exist?'

'No, nothing could make me believe that!' cried Raskolnikov, almost bitterly.

'After all, what do people normally say?' muttered Svidrigailov, as if to himself, looking away and bowing his head a little. 'They say, "You're sick, so what you imagine is mere delirium, mere illusion." But that's hardly logical. I agree that only the sick see ghosts, but this merely proves that you have to be sick to see ghosts, not that they don't exist in themselves.'

'Nonsense!' Raskolnikov irritably insisted.

'You really think so?' Svidrigailov went on, slowly turning his eyes on him. 'But what if we try to reason like so (give me a hand, old boy): ghosts are, as it were, shreds and scraps of the other worlds from which they come. A healthy man, needless to say, has no reason to see them, because no one is more earthbound than he; he should live here and here alone, and live a full, well-ordered life. But, at the first sign of sickness, at the first disturbance of the normal, earthbound order in his organism, the possibility of another world instantly comes to the fore, and the sicker he becomes, the greater his contact with this other world, so that when a man dies completely, he crosses over to it right away. I thought this through a long time ago. If you believe in the life to come, then you can believe this, too.'

'I don't believe in the life to come,' said Raskolnikov.

Svidrigailov was deep in thought.

'What if there's nothing but spiders there or something like that?' he suddenly said.

'The man's insane,' thought Raskolnikov.

'We're forever imagining eternity as an idea beyond our under-standing, something vast, vast! But why must it be vast? Just imagine: what if, instead of all that, there'll just be some little room, some sooty bath-hut, say, with spiders in every corner, and that's it, that's eternity? I have such fancies every now and again, you know.'

'And you can't imagine anything more comforting or more just than that!' Raskolnikov cried out with a sickening feeling.

'More just? But who's to say: perhaps that is just – in fact, that's exactly how I'd arrange things myself!' Svidrigailov replied, with an indeterminate smile.

A chill suddenly came over Raskolnikov when he heard this outra-geous reply. Svidrigailov lifted his head, looked straight at him and suddenly roared with laughter.

'This takes some beating, don't you think?' he shouted. 'Half an hour ago we'd never even set eyes on one another; we're meant to be enemies; we've got unfinished business between us; and now look, we've dropped our business and plunged head-first into literature! Well, wasn't I right to say we're birds of a feather?'

'Be so kind,' Raskolnikov persisted irritably, 'as to explain yourself without further delay and tell me why you are honouring me with a visit . . . and . . . and . . . I'm in a hurry, no time to spare, I've got to go out . . .'

'By all means. Your dear sister, Avdotya Romanovna, is marrying Mr Luzhin, Pyotr Petrovich, yes?'

'Could we please avoid all questions concerning my sister and any mention of her name? I fail to understand how you even dare utter her name in my presence – if, that is, you are who you say you are?'

'But it's her I've come to speak about – how can I not mention her?'

'Fine. Just get on with it!'

'I dare say you've already formed an opinion about this Mr Luzhin, to whom I am related through my wife, assuming you've spent even half an hour in his company or heard anything reliable and accurate about him. He's no match for Avdotya Romanovna. As I see it, Avdotya Romanovna is sacrificing herself in this matter very nobly and without forethought, for the sake of . . . of her family. I had the impression from all I'd heard about you that, from your side, you'd be only too glad to see this marriage collapse without anyone's interests being jeopardized. Now that I've met you in person, I'm even quite certain of it.'

'From your side, this is all very naive; sorry, I meant to say insolent,' said Raskolnikov.

'Which is your way of saying that I am only in this for myself. You shouldn't worry, Rodion Romanovich. If this really were the case, I'd hardly be so blunt about it – I'm not a complete fool. In fact, let me share with you a certain psychological quirk of mine. Before, while justifying my love for Avdotya Romanovna, I said that I myself was the victim. Well, you ought to know that I feel no love at all now, none whatsoever – in fact, this seems strange even to me, because I really did feel something before . . .'

'From idleness and depravity,' interrupted Raskolnikov.

'I am indeed a depraved and idle man. But then your dear sister has so many points in her favour that I could hardly fail to be somewhat taken with her. But it's all nonsense, as I can now see for myself.'

'And when did you see this exactly?'

'I've been aware of it for some time, but I became fully convinced only two days ago, almost at the very moment I arrived in Petersburg. Back in Moscow, I still thought I was coming here to win Avdotya Romanovna's hand and to vie with Mr Luzhin.'

'Forgive me for interrupting you, but please be so kind as to turn, without delay, to the purpose of your visit. I'm in a hurry, I have to go out . . .'

'With the greatest pleasure. After arriving here and deciding to undertake a certain . . . voyage, I conceived a desire to make the necessary preliminary arrangements. My children will remain with their aunt; they are rich and have no need of me personally. I'm not much of a father anyway! For myself I've taken only that which Marfa Petrovna gave me a year ago. That's all I need. Forgive me, I'm just about to turn to the business at hand. Before my voyage, which may indeed come to pass, I want to have done with Mr Luzhin. It's not that I dislike him so much, but that, were it not for him, I'd never have had that row with Marfa Petrovna, when I learned about her concocting this marriage. I wish to see Avdotya Romanovna now so that, through your good offices and – why not? – in your presence, I can explain to her, firstly, that not only does she stand to gain nothing from Mr Luzhin, but she will lose out very badly, and that's a fact. Next, having begged her forgiveness for all this recent unpleasantness, I would request that she permit me to offer her ten thousand roubles and thereby alleviate her parting with Mr Luzhin, a parting which, I am sure, she would not mind too much herself, were it only possible.'

'You're properly, properly mad!' cried Raskolnikov, less angry than astonished. 'How dare you speak like that?'

'I knew you'd start yelling. But, firstly, though I may not be rich, these ten thousand roubles are going spare. I've no need of them, no need at all. If Avdotya Romanovna says no, then I dare say I'll find an even more idiotic use for them. That's one thing. Secondly, my conscience is quite untroubled. I'm making this offer without any ulterior motive. You don't have to believe me, but later both you and Avdotya Romanovna will see this for yourselves. The fact of the matter is that I really did cause your much-esteemed sister a certain amount of trouble and unpleasantness; therefore, experiencing sincere remorse, I have a heartfelt wish, not to buy my way out by paying for the unpleasantness, but purely and simply to do something to benefit her, because, after all, it's not as if I've claimed some prerogative only to commit evil. If there were even the tiniest hint of forethought in my offer, I would hardly make it so bluntly; nor would I offer a mere ten thousand, when only five weeks ago I offered her more. Besides, I may be about to marry a certain young girl in the very nearest future, so all suspicions of any possible designs against Avdotya Romanovna ought thereby to be quashed. I will conclude by saying that, in marrying Mr Luzhin, Avdotya Romanovna is taking exactly the same money, only from another hand ... Now don't be angry, Rodion Romanovich – think about it calmly and coolly.'

Saying this, Svidrigailov was himself exceptionally cool and calm.

'Please hurry up and finish,' said Raskolnikov. 'If nothing else, you're being unforgivably rude.'

'Not in the least. If that's the case, then man can do nothing but evil to man, and is actually denied the right to do even a crumb of good, all because of empty formalities. It's absurd. Say, for example, I died and left this sum to your dear sister in my will, are you saying that she would still refuse it then?'

'Very possibly.'

'Not a chance, sir. But have it your way if you must. Only, ten thousand can be a fine thing. In any case, kindly pass on what I've said to Avdotya Romanovna.'

'No, I won't.'

'In that case, Rodion Romanovich, I shall be obliged to seek a personal meeting and, thereby, to make a nuisance of myself.'

'And if I do pass this on, you won't seek a personal meeting?'

'H'm, how should I put it? I'd be very keen to see her once.'

'Don't pin your hopes on it.'

'Shame. Still, you don't know me. We may even become close.'

'You think we might become close?'

'Why ever not?' said Svidrigailov with a smile, getting up and taking his hat. 'After all, I wasn't actually all that keen to disturb you, and, walking over here, I wasn't expecting too much from our meeting, although just this morning I was struck by your features . . .'

'Where did you see me this morning?' asked Raskolnikov anxiously.

'By chance, sir . . . I can't help feeling that you and I are somehow well-matched . . . Now don't worry, I'm really no bother: I've got along with card sharps; and I've stayed the right side of Prince Svirbey, a distant relative of mine and a grandee; and I've scribbled something about Raphael's *Madonna* in Mrs Prilukova's album; and I've spent seven years cooped up with Marfa Petrovna; and I've bedded down in times past at Vyazemsky's house on Haymarket;⁹ and, who knows, I might just go flying in Berg's balloon.'

'All right, sir. Kindly tell me: will you be setting out on your journey soon?'

'What journey?'

'You know, that voyage of yours . . . It was you who mentioned it.'

'Voyage? Oh yes! . . . You're quite right, I did tell you about it . . . Well, that's a broad question . . . If only you knew what you were asking!' he added and suddenly laughed out loud. 'I may end up with a wife, not a voyage; a bride is being sought for me.'

'Here?'

'Yes.'

'When did you find the time for that?'

'But I'd be most eager to have a meeting with Avdotya Romanovna. It's a serious request. Well, goodbye ... Oh, yes! I've remembered! Rodion Romanovich, do tell your dear sister that she's marked down for three thousand in Marfa Petrovna's will. That's a definite fact. Marfa Petrovna made arrangements a week before her death and I was present at the time. Avdotya Romanovna will be able to claim the money in two or three weeks' time.'

'Are you telling the truth?'

'The truth. Tell her. Well, sir, at your service. After all, I live close by.'

Walking out, Svidrigailov bumped into Razumikhin in the doorway.

II

It was almost eight already; both men were in a hurry to get over to Bakaleyev's rooms before Luzhin arrived.

'So who was that?' asked Razumikhin as soon as they were outside.

'Svidrigailov, the landowner at whose home my sister was insulted while employed as their governess. Pestered with his attentions, she left, chased out by his wife, Marfa Petrovna. The same Marfa Petrovna who later begged her forgiveness and has now suddenly died. It was her we were talking about earlier. I don't know why, but I'm very scared of this man. He arrived straight after his wife's funeral. He's very strange and he's set on something ... It's as if he knows something ... Dunya must be protected from him ... that's what I wanted to tell you, do you hear?'

'Protected! What could he ever do to her, to Avdotya Romanovna? Well, I'm grateful to you, Rodya, for speaking to me like this ... We'll protect her, no fear! ... Where does he live?'

'I don't know.'

'Why didn't you ask? What a pity! Never mind, I'll find out!'

'Did you see him?' asked Raskolnikov after a pause.

'Yes, I took good note of him.'

'You're sure you saw him? Saw him clearly?' Raskolnikov persisted.

'I'm sure. I remember him so clearly I could pick him out in a crowd – I have a memory for faces.'

They were silent again.

'H'm ... just as well ...,' muttered Raskolnikov. 'Because, you know ... the thought occurred to me ... and I still can't help feeling ... that this might be a fantasy.'

'Meaning? I don't quite follow.'

'Here you all are,' Raskolnikov went on, twisting his mouth into a smile, 'saying I'm mad. Well, just now I had the impression that perhaps I really am insane and what I saw was only a phantom!'

'What are you on about?'

'Who knows? Maybe I really am mad, and maybe everything that's happened during all these days was just my imagination ...'

'Oh, Rodya! They've upset you again! . . . But what did he say? What was he after?'

Raskolnikov didn't reply. Razumikhin thought for a moment.

'Well, then, here's my report,' he began. 'I called by, you were sleeping. Then we had lunch, then I went to see Porfiry. Zametov's still there. I wanted to broach the subject and couldn't. I just couldn't get going. It's as if they don't understand and can't understand, but they're not in the slightest embarrassed. I led Porfiry over to the window, but again – nothing doing; he looks away, I look away. Finally, I lifted my fist to his face and said I'd beat him to a pulp, in the family spirit. He just looked at me. I spat, walked out, and that's that. All very stupid. Not a word between me and Zametov. But listen: I thought I'd botched it all up, but going down the stairs a certain thought occurred to me – or rather, hit me: why are the two of us going to so much trouble? If you were in danger or anything of the kind, then fine. But why should you care? You're nothing to do with it, so to hell with them! We'll have plenty of time to make fun of them later – in fact, in your shoes I'd try hoaxing them, too. Think how ashamed they'll be afterwards! To hell with them! We can give them a good drubbing later, but for now – let's laugh!'

'Yes, absolutely!' replied Raskolnikov. 'And what will you say tomorrow?' he wondered to himself. How strange that the question 'What will Razumikhin think when he finds out?' had never once occurred to him. Thinking this, Raskolnikov gave him a long hard look. Razumikhin's report about visiting Porfiry was of scant interest to him: so much had been and gone since then!

In the corridor they ran into Luzhin: he'd arrived at eight o'clock sharp and was looking for the room, so all three walked in together, but without exchanging so much as a glance or a bow. The young men went ahead, while Pyotr Petrovich thought it good manners to dawdle a bit in the entrance hall while taking off his coat. Pulkheria Alexandrovna immediately came out to meet him on the threshold. Dunya greeted her brother.

Entering, Pyotr Petrovich bowed to the ladies courteously enough, though with redoubled gravity. He continued to look somewhat disconcerted. Pulkheria Alexandrovna, who also seemed embarrassed, hurriedly sat everyone down at an oval table on which a hot samovar was waiting. Dunya and Luzhin took their places opposite each other at the two ends of the table. Razumikhin and Raskolnikov ended up opposite Pulkheria Alexandrovna – Razumikhin closer to Luzhin, and Raskolnikov next to his sister.

There was a momentary silence. Pyotr Petrovich slowly took out a cambric handkerchief reeking of perfume and blew his nose with the air of a virtuous man who has suffered a wound to his pride and who, moreover, is determined to receive an explanation. While standing in the entrance hall the thought had even occurred to him to keep his coat on and leave, thereby punishing and shaming both ladies with an impressive display of severity. But he didn't go through with it. Besides, this was a man who disliked uncertainty, and clarification was certainly required here: they can't have flouted his order for no reason, so he was better off finding out first; there would always be time to punish them later – it was all in his hands.

'I trust you had a satisfactory journey?' he asked Pulkheria Alexandrovna stiffly.

'Yes, Pyotr Petrovich, God be praised.'

'Very pleased to hear it, ma'am. And Avdotya Romanovna is not too weary, either?'

'I'm young and strong, I don't tire easily – but it was terribly hard for Mama,' replied Dunya.

'Our national railways, alas, are very extensive. How great is so-called "Mother Russia" . . . For my part, I was simply unable, with the best will in the world, to meet you off the train yesterday. I trust, however, that everything passed off smoothly?'

'Far from it, Pyotr Petrovich – we were at a low ebb,' Pulkheria Alexandrovna hastened to declare in a very particular voice, 'and if

God Himself, it seems, had not sent us Dmitry Prokofich yesterday, then I don't know what would have become of us. Here he is, Dmitry Prokofich Razumikhin,' she added, introducing him to Luzhin.

'Why, I had the pleasure . . . yesterday,' muttered Luzhin, with a hostile glance at Razumikhin; then he frowned and fell silent. Pyotr Petrovich, one could safely say, belonged to that category of men who appear exceptionally courteous in society and lay special claim to courtesy, but who, the moment they are crossed, instantly lose all their powers and begin to look more like sacks of flour than happy-go-lucky types who are the soul of any gathering. Everyone fell silent again: Raskolnikov stubbornly refused to speak, Avdotya Romanovna didn't wish to break the silence too soon, Razumikhin had nothing to say, and Pulkheria Alexandrovna began to fret.

'Marfa Petrovna has died – have you heard?' she began, resorting to her trump card.

'How could I not, ma'am? I was among the first to know and, in fact, I am here to tell you that Arkady Ivanovich Svidrigailov, directly after the funeral of his spouse, departed with all due haste for Petersburg. Thus, at any rate, according to the very reliable information at my disposal.'

'For Petersburg? Here?' Dunechka asked in alarm, exchanging glances with her mother.

'Quite so, ma'am, and no doubt with some purpose, taking into account the hasty nature of his departure and, more generally, the preceding circumstances.'

'Good Lord! Won't he leave Dunechka in peace here, either?' shrieked Pulkheria Alexandrovna.

'It seems to me that there is no particular cause for alarm, neither for you nor for Avdotya Romanovna, assuming, of course, that you yourselves do not wish to enter into any kind of relations with him. For my part, I am keeping a close eye on the situation, and trying to find out where he is staying . . .'

'Oh, Pyotr Petrovich, you'll never believe what a fright you've just given me!' Pulkheria Alexandrovna went on. 'I've only ever seen him twice and I found him dreadful, dreadful! I'm sure he was the cause of the late Marfa Petrovna's death.'

'It's impossible to say. I have reliable information at my disposal. I don't deny that he may have expedited the course of events through, as it were, the moral influence of his offensive actions; but as far as the individual's conduct and, more generally, moral profile are concerned, I agree with you. Whether or not he is rich and what exactly Marfa Petrovna has left him, I do not know; I will be apprised of this in the very nearest future; but it goes without saying that here, in Petersburg, with even the most modest funds at his disposal, he will immediately resume his old habits. Of all his kind he is the most depraved and the most far gone in vice! I have significant grounds for assuming that Marfa Petrovna, who had the misfortune of loving him so and paying off his debts eight years ago, was of service to him in a further respect as well: it was solely thanks to her efforts and sacrifices that a criminal case was snuffed out at birth, one with elements of bestial and, as it were, quite fantastical villainy, for which he could have perfectly, perfectly easily have taken a long hike to Siberia. That's the kind of man he is, if you care to know.'

'Good Lord!' cried Pulkheria Alexandrovna. Raskolnikov was listening attentively.

'Do you really have reliable information about him?' asked Dunya, in a tone that brooked no argument.

'I am merely repeating what I heard, in confidence, from the late Marfa Petrovna. It should be noted that from a legal standpoint the case is murky in the extreme. There was – and, I believe, still is – a certain Mrs Resslich living here, a foreigner and, what's worse, a petty moneylender who has other irons in the fire as well. Mr Svidrigailov had long been on the most intimate and mysterious terms with this Resslich woman. She had a distant relative living with her, a niece, I believe, a deaf-and-dumb girl of fifteen or even fourteen, whom Resslich loathed beyond reason and reproached for every crumb; she even beat her brutally. One day the girl was found hanging in the loft. The verdict: suicide. The usual procedure was followed and the case ended there, but subsequently a report was submitted to the effect that the child had been . . . cruelly abused by Svidrigailov. True, it was all very murky: the report came from another German, a notorious woman with scant credibility, and in the end even that went missing, thanks to Marfa Petrovna's efforts and money. Rumour was as far as it went. Still, the rumour was highly indicative. No doubt, Avdotya Romanovna, you heard another story, too, while you were there, about a certain Filipp who was tortured to death, six years or so ago, back in the days of serfdom.'

'On the contrary, I heard that this Filipp hanged himself.'

'Quite so, miss, but it was Mr Svidrigailov's continuous system of persecution and punishment which forced him, or rather disposed him, to take his life.'

'I don't know about that,' replied Dunya, coldly. 'I merely heard some very strange story about this Filipp being some kind of hypochondriac, a home-grown philosopher – "too much reading", people said – and that he hanged himself more from being teased than from Mr Svidrigailov's beatings. From what I saw, he treated people rather well, and people even liked him, although they did blame him for Filipp's death.'

'I see, Avdotya Romanovna, that you are suddenly disposed to excuse him,' Luzhin remarked, twisting his mouth into an ambiguous smile. 'He is indeed a cunning and charming man where ladies are concerned, as the lamentable example of Marfa Petrovna, who died so strangely, attests. I merely wished to offer you and your mama my advice, in view of his latest and no doubt imminent efforts. For myself, I am quite certain that this man is destined for debtor's prison once more. Marfa Petrovna never had the slightest intention of providing him with any security, having the children in mind, and if she did leave him anything, then only what was absolutely essential, ephemeral and of little value, hardly enough to last a man of his habits for even a year.'

'Pyotr Petrovich, please,' said Dunya, 'let's speak no more about Mr Svidrigailov. It depresses me.'

'He came to see me just now,' said Raskolnikov suddenly, breaking his silence for the first time.

Cries went up on all sides; everyone turned towards him. Even Pyotr Petrovich was on edge.

'An hour and a half or so ago, when I was sleeping, he came in, woke me up and introduced himself,' Raskolnikov went on. 'He was quite relaxed and cheerful, and very optimistic about the two of us becoming close. Incidentally, he's desperate to see you, Dunya, and asked me to be the intermediary at this meeting. He wants to make you an offer and told me what it is. What's more, Dunya, he gave me the most definite assurance that a week before she died Marfa Petrovna left you three thousand roubles in her will, and that you can receive this money in the very nearest future.'

'God be praised!' cried Pulkheria Alexandrovna, making the sign of the cross. 'Pray for her, Dunya, pray!'

'That is indeed the case,' Luzhin let slip.

'And what else?' Dunechka pressed him.

'Next he said that he himself is not rich and that the whole estate would go to his children, who are with their aunt. Next, that he's staying somewhere not far from here, but where – I don't know, didn't ask . . .'

'But what is it that he wants to offer Dunechka, what?' asked Pulkheria Alexandrovna, frightened to death. 'Did he tell you?'

'Yes, he did.'

'And?'

'I'll tell you later.' Raskolnikov fell silent and turned his attention to his tea.

Pyotr Petrovich took out his watch and checked it.

'I have urgent business to attend to, so I won't get in your way,' he added, looking somewhat piqued, and began getting up from his chair.

'Stay, Pyotr Petrovich,' said Dunya, 'after all, you were intending to spend the evening with us. Besides, you wrote to say you had something you wished to discuss with Mama.'

'Quite so, Avdotya Romanovna,' said Pyotr Petrovich in an imposing tone, sitting back down, though still holding on to his hat. 'I did indeed have matters to discuss with you, and with your much-esteemed mama, even some of the highest importance. But just as your brother is unable to discuss in my presence certain of Mr Svidrigailov's proposals, so too am I unwilling and unable to discuss . . . in the presence of others . . . certain matters of the highest, highest importance. Besides, my fundamental and most earnest request was not heeded . . .'

Looking most aggrieved, Luzhin lapsed into dignified silence.

'Your request that my brother not attend our meeting has not been heeded solely at my insistence,' said Dunya. 'You wrote that my brother had insulted you. I believe that this must be cleared up immediately and you should make your peace. And if Rodya really did insult you, then he *should* and *shall* apologize.'

This was all the encouragement Pyotr Petrovich needed.

'There are certain insults, Avdotya Romanovna, which, with the best will in the world, cannot be forgotten. There is always a mark which it is too dangerous to overstep, for, once overstepped, there can be no return.'

'That's not what I was getting at, Pyotr Petrovich,' Dunya interrupted a little impatiently. 'Please understand that our whole future now depends on whether or not all this can be cleared up and settled as quickly as possible. I am telling you bluntly, from the outset, that I can take no other view of the matter, and if you prize me at all, then, however hard it may be, this entire episode must end today. I repeat: if my brother is to blame, he will ask your forgiveness.'

'I am astonished to hear you frame the question in this way, Avdotya Romanovna,' Luzhin replied, his irritation mounting with every word. 'While valuing and, as it were, adoring you, I am perfectly, perfectly capable of not liking a member of your family. Aspiring to the happiness of your hand, I am unable at one and the same time to take upon myself incompatible obligations . . .'

'Oh, enough of all this touchiness, Pyotr Petrovich,' Dunya interrupted hotly, 'and be that intelligent and noble man I always considered – and still wish to consider – you to be. I made you a great promise – I am your bride. So trust me in this matter and trust that I shall be able to judge without bias. My role as arbiter is as much of a surprise to my brother as it is to you. When I asked him today, after receiving your letter, to be sure to attend our meeting, I said nothing of my intentions. Please understand that if you do not make your peace I will have to choose between you: either you or him. That is how the question stands, on both his side and yours. I do not wish to make the wrong choice and must not do so. For you I must break off with my brother; for my brother I must break off with you. Now is my chance to find out for sure: is he a brother to me? And as for you: am I dear to you? Do you value me? Are you a husband to me?'

'Avdotya Romanovna,' said Luzhin, taken aback, 'your words are too rich in meaning, I would even say hurtful, in view of the position I am honoured to hold in relation to you. Quite aside from the hurtful and strange decision to put me on a level with . . . an arrogant youth, your words permit the possibility of your breaking the promise you gave me. "Either you or him," you say, thereby showing me how little I mean to you . . . I can hardly allow this in view of the relations and . . . obligations that exist between us.'

'What?' flared Dunya. 'I place your interests alongside everything I have ever held dearest, everything that my *whole life* has consisted of until now, and you suddenly take offence because I hold you too *cheap*!'

Raskolnikov said nothing and sneered; Razumikhin's whole body jerked. But Pyotr Petrovich did not accept the criticism; on the contrary, he became ever more captious and irritable, almost as if he'd begun to enjoy it.

'Love for one's future partner in life, for one's husband, should exceed love for one's brother,' he sententiously began, 'and in any case, I cannot be put on the same level . . . Even though I previously insisted that I did not wish to say what I have come to say in the presence of your brother, and could not do so, nevertheless I now intend to turn to your much-esteemed mother for an essential clarification of one highly fundamental and, to me, offensive point. Your son,' he said, turning to Pulkheria Alexandrovna, 'yesterday, in the presence of Mr Rassudkin (is that your surname? Sorry, it seems to have slipped my mind)' – he said to Razumikhin[10] with a courteous bow – 'offended me by distorting a thought I once shared with you during a private conversation over coffee: namely, that marriage to a poor girl who has already tasted life's woes is, to my mind, of greater profit from the conjugal point of view than marriage to one who has only tasted plenty, being of greater benefit to morality. Your son purposely exaggerated my meaning to the point of absurdity, charging me with malicious intentions and, as far as I can see, basing his remarks on your own correspondence. I will consider myself happy, Pulkheria Alexandrovna, if you can disabuse me to the contrary and thus go some way to reassuring me. So tell me: what were the exact terms in which you conveyed my words in your letter to Rodion Romanovich?'

'I don't remember,' came Pulkheria Alexandrovna's faltering reply. 'I conveyed them as I understood them. I don't know how Rodya conveyed them to you . . . Perhaps he did exaggerate something.'

'He couldn't have exaggerated anything without your prompting.'

'Pyotr Petrovich,' answered Pulkheria Alexandrovna, 'the very fact that we are *here* is proof that Dunya and I did not take your words so amiss.'

'Well said, dear Mama!' remarked Dunya.

'So this is my fault, too?'

'Now listen, Pyotr Petrovich, you keep blaming Rodion, but you yourself wrote an untruth about him in your letter earlier,' added an emboldened Pulkheria Alexandrovna.

'I don't recall writing any untruths, ma'am.'

'You wrote,' said Raskolnikov sharply, without turning towards Luzhin, 'that yesterday I gave the money away not to the widow of the man who'd been trampled, which was what actually happened, but to his daughter (whom I'd never seen before). You wrote that to set me at odds with my family, which is why you added those loathsome words about the behaviour of a girl you do not know. It's all just gossip, despicable gossip.'

'Excuse me, sir,' replied Luzhin, shaking with fury, 'the sole reason I enlarged upon your qualities and actions was to satisfy thereby the request of your sister and mama to describe for them the state in which I found you and the impression you made on me. As regards the aforementioned part of my letter, I challenge you to find in it a single unfair sentence – did you not spend all the money? And in that family, however unfortunate, were there not unworthy persons?'

'You yourself, for all your qualities, are not worth the little finger of the unfortunate girl at whom you are casting stones.'

'So you'd dare bring her into the company of your mother and sister, I suppose?'

'I've already done so, if you must know. Today I sat her down next to Mama and Dunya.'

'Rodya!' cried Pulkheria Alexandrovna.

Dunechka reddened; Razumikhin knit his brows. Luzhin gave a sneering, supercilious smile.

'You may judge for yourself, Avdotya Romanovna,' he said, 'whether there is any scope for agreement here. I trust that this business is now finished and clarified, once and for all. I shall make myself scarce so as not to impede the further enjoyment of your family gathering and the sharing of secrets.' (He rose from his chair and took his hat.) 'But before I leave, I venture to remark that I hope to be spared any more such meetings and, as it were, further compromise. My request is addressed above all to you, much-esteemed Pulkheria Alexandrovna, especially as my letter was also addressed to you and not to any other party.'

Pulkheria Alexandrovna was somewhat offended.

'It seems that you want us completely under your thumb, Pyotr Petrovich. Dunya told you the reason why your wish was not heeded: she acted with the best intentions. And you write to me as if you were giving orders. Must we really consider your every wish an order? If you ask me, you ought to be going out of your way to be sensitive and indulgent towards us, seeing that we've trusted you and dropped everything to come here – we're almost under your thumb as it is.'

'That is not entirely fair, Pulkheria Alexandrovna, and especially at the present moment, following the announcement of the three thousand left by Marfa Petrovna – which appears to have been most timely, to judge by the new tone you've taken towards me,' he added with venom.

'To judge by this remark, one might indeed assume that you were counting on our helplessness,' snapped Dunya.

'That, at any rate, is something I can no longer count on, and I certainly do not wish to impede the communication of the secret proposals with which Arkady Ivanovich Svidrigailov has entrusted your brother and which, I see, are of fundamental and, perhaps, highly agreeable significance to you.'

'Good grief!' shrieked Pulkheria Alexandrovna.

Razumikhin just couldn't sit still.

'And you're not ashamed now, sister?' asked Raskolnikov.

'I am, Rodya,' said Dunya. 'Pyotr Petrovich, get out!' She was white with rage.

Such a conclusion, it seems, was the last thing Pyotr Petrovich had expected. He had too much confidence in himself, in his power and in the helplessness of his victims. He could not believe it even now. He turned pale and his lips began to tremble.

'Avdotya Romanovna, if I leave this room now, with these words ringing in my ears, then make no mistake: I will never come back. So think about it! I mean what I say.'

'The cheek!' cried Dunya, swiftly rising from her seat. 'As if I want you to come back!'

'What? Well, well, we-e-ell!' cried Luzhin, unable to believe, until the very last moment, that such an outcome was possible, and losing his thread entirely as a result. 'Well, well, miss! But you know, Avdotya Romanovna, I may have something to say about this.'

'What right have you to speak to her like that?' Pulkheria Alexandrovna burst in. 'And what on earth can you have to say about it? What are these rights of yours? Do you really think I will give my Dunya to a man like you? Get out and don't come back! We ourselves are to blame for going along with this wrongful business, I more than anyone . . .'

'Nevertheless, Pulkheria Alexandrovna,' raged Luzhin, 'you have bound me with a promise you now renounce . . . not to mention . . . not to mention the fact that I have incurred, as it were, certain expenses . . .'

This final reproof was so characteristic of Pyotr Petrovich that Raskolnikov, who'd gone pale with rage and with the effort of restraining himself, suddenly roared with laughter. But Pulkheria Alexandrovna was beside herself:

'Expenses? And what would they be? You don't mean our trunk, I hope? You got the conductor to take it for free! Good Lord – we bound you, did we? Come to your senses, Pyotr Petrovich – you bound us hand and foot, not the other way round!'

'Enough, dear Mama, enough!' pleaded Avdotya Romanovna. 'Pyotr Petrovich, be so good as to leave!'

'I'm leaving, young lady, but just one last thing!' he said, losing almost all self-control. 'Your mama seems to have quite forgotten that I chose you, as it were, after the rumours concerning your reputation had circulated around town and spread through every house in the neighbourhood. In disregarding public opinion for your sake and restoring your reputation, I surely, surely could have entertained every hope of compensation and even demanded your gratitude . . . Only now have my eyes been opened! I see myself that I may have acted all too hastily – all too hastily – in disregarding the voice of society . . .'

'Is he mad?' shouted Razumikhin, leaping from his chair and preparing to take matters into his own hands.

'You are a despicable and evil man!' said Dunya.

'Silence! Stay right there!' yelled Raskolnikov, restraining Razumikhin; then, walking right up to Luzhin:

'Kindly get out!' he said quietly and distinctly. 'And not another word, or else . . .'

Pyotr Petrovich looked at him for a few seconds, his face white and twisted with fury, then turned and left, and it hardly needs saying that few men can ever have carried away so much spite and hatred in their hearts as this man bore towards Raskolnikov. He blamed him and him alone for everything. And, remarkably enough, even as he was going down the stairs he still imagined that this whole business was by no means lost and, as far as the ladies were concerned, could still 'perfectly, perfectly well' be saved.

III

The main point was that, until the very last moment, such an outcome was the last thing he'd ever expected. He'd blustered all the way to the end, never even recognizing the possibility that two penniless and defenceless women could escape from under his thumb. He was greatly assisted in this certainty by his vanity and that degree of self-confidence which may best be described as narcissism. Pyotr Petrovich, a nobody made good, had a morbid habit of admiring himself, thought highly of his own intelligence and ability, and sometimes, when alone, even admired his own face in the mirror. But what he loved and valued most in the world was his own money, gained by labour and every means available: it made him the equal of whatever was above him.

Reminding Dunya just now, with bitterness, that he'd resolved to take her despite all the bad things said about her, Pyotr Petrovich had spoken with complete sincerity and even felt a deep indignation at such 'rank ingratitude'. And yet, when seeking Dunya's hand in marriage, he'd had no doubt about the absurdity of all this tittle-tattle, which had been publicly refuted by Marfa Petrovna herself and which had long been dismissed by all the townsfolk, who defended Dunya ardently. In fact, even now he would not have denied having already known all this then. Yet still he continued to think highly of his determination to raise Dunya to his level and considered it something of a feat. In telling Dunya about this now, he was giving expression to a secret, cherished thought, which he had found himself admiring more than once; indeed, it was quite beyond him how anyone could fail to admire his exploit. Paying a visit to Raskolnikov that time, he had felt like a benefactor come to reap his harvest and to hear some quite delicious compliments. Now, of course, walking down the stairs, he felt utterly offended and unappreciated.

He simply had to have Dunya; giving her up was unthinkable. He'd been dreaming fondly of marriage for several years already, but all he'd done was save up money and wait. In deepest secrecy, he'd thrilled at the thought of a young maiden who was virtuous and poor (the latter was essential), very young and very pretty, noble and educated, timid to the core, someone with endless misfortunes behind her, who'd prostrate herself before him, consider him her saviour her whole life long, revere him, submit to him, marvel at him – at him alone. How many scenes, how many delightful episodes had he created in his imagination on this alluring and frolicsome theme, while resting from his affairs! And now the dream of so many years had almost come true: Avdotya Romanovna's beauty and education astonished him; her helpless plight excited him beyond measure. Reality was even outstripping his dreams: a proud girl of character and virtue, his superior (so he felt) in education and intellectual maturity – and just such a creature would be slavishly grateful to him all life long for his exploit and abase herself before him in veneration, and he would reign supreme without let or hindrance! . . . Only recently, after much deliberation, as if right on cue, he had finally decided to change career for good and enter a broader sphere of activity, in the hope of working his way up in society, something he'd long been thinking about with voluptuous pleasure . . . In a word, he had made up his mind to try his luck in Petersburg. He knew that it was 'perfectly, perfectly' possible to gain a great deal through women. The charms of an adorable, virtuous and educated woman could smooth his path quite remarkably, attract others to him, create an aura . . . and now the whole thing had collapsed! This sudden, hideous rift hit him like a thunderstroke. A hideous joke, that's what it was. An absurdity! He'd only blustered a little. He hadn't even managed to say all he wanted to say. He'd merely joked, got carried away, and look how it had ended! Not to mention the fact that he'd even come to love Dunya after his own fashion; indeed, he was already reigning over her in his dreams – when suddenly! . . . No! The next day at the very latest all this had to be recovered, healed, put right and, above all – this arrogant mummy's boy who was the cause of it all had to be destroyed. With a sickening sensation he was reminded, somewhat against his will, of Razumikhin . . . but he quickly reassured himself: 'As if I have to measure myself against him as well!' If there was one man he was seriously afraid of, it was not him, but Svidrigailov . . . In short, he had his hands full . . .

'No, the person most to blame here is me, me!' Dunechka was saying, hugging and kissing her mother. 'I was tempted by his money, but I swear, brother, I never imagined him to be such an unworthy man. If only I'd seen through him earlier, I'd never have been tempted! Don't blame me, brother!'

'God has saved us!' Pulkheria Alexandrovna muttered, but almost unconsciously, as if she still hadn't grasped what had just taken place.

Everyone rejoiced. Five minutes later they were even laughing. Only Dunechka would occasionally turn pale and knit her brow, recalling all that had happened. Pulkheria Alexandrovna could never have imagined that she, too, would be happy; only that morning a rift with Luzhin had still seemed a terrible catastrophe. But Razumikhin was ecstatic. He didn't dare show it fully yet, but he was shaking all

over as if in a fever, as if a two-hundred-pound weight had been lifted
from his heart. Now he had the right to give up his whole life to them,
serve them . . . Anything was possible! But he was even warier now of
thinking too far ahead, he was scared of his own imaginings. Raskolnikov, alone, was still sitting in the same place, almost sullen and even
distracted. He, who had insisted more than anyone on getting rid of
Luzhin, now seemed the least interested in what had occurred. Dunya
couldn't help feeling he was still very angry with her, while Pulkheria
Alexandrovna studied him timidly.

'So what did Svidrigailov say to you?' Dunya asked, walking over
to him.

'Oh yes, yes!' cried Pulkheria Alexandrovna.

Raskolnikov lifted his head:

'He's determined to give you ten thousand roubles and expresses
his desire to see you once, in my presence.'

'See you? Not for the world!' cried Pulkheria Alexandrovna. 'And
how dare he offer her money?'

Next, Raskolnikov related (rather stiffly) his conversation with
Svidrigailov, omitting Marfa Petrovna's ghosts so as to avoid digres-
sion and feeling revolted by the thought of any but the most essential
conversation.

'So what did you reply?' asked Dunya.

'First, I said I wouldn't pass any of this on to you. Then he announced he would seek a meeting himself by every means at his disposal. He assured me that his passion for you was merely a whim and
that he feels nothing for you now . . . He doesn't want you to marry
Luzhin . . . In general, he wasn't all that coherent.'

'What do you make of him, Rodya? How did he seem to you?'

'Frankly, none of it makes much sense to me. He's offering ten
thousand, but says he's not rich. Declares a desire to take off somewhere or other, but forgets having said it ten minutes later. Then he
suddenly says he wants to get married and that a bride's already being
arranged . . . He's got his reasons, of course, most likely bad ones. But
then again, it's rather strange to think of him going about it all so
stupidly if he has bad intentions towards you . . . Needless to say, I
refused the money on your behalf, once and for all. On the whole he
struck me as very strange and even . . . in some respects . . . almost
insane. But I may well be mistaken, and it might all just be some kind
of hoax. Marfa Petrovna's death is affecting him, it seems . . .'

'God rest her soul!' exclaimed Pulkheria Alexandrovna. 'I shall never, ever cease praying for her! I mean, what would have become of us now, Dunya, without these three thousand? Good grief – they just fell from the sky! Oh, Rodya, this morning Dunechka and I only had three roubles between us and our only hope was to hurry up and pawn the watch somewhere, so as not to have to ask anything from that man until he worked it out for himself.'

Dunya seemed almost stunned by Svidrigailov's proposal. She stood where she was, plunged in thought.

'He's planning something, something horrid!' she said almost under her breath, all but shuddering.

Raskolnikov noticed her immoderate fear.

'That won't be the last I see of him, I suppose,' he told Dunya.

'We'll follow him! I'll track him down!' shouted Razumikhin with vigour. 'I won't take my eyes off him! Rodya has allowed me to. "Protect my sister!" he told me just now. But will you allow me, Avdotya Romanovna?'

Dunya smiled and held out her hand to him, but her face remained troubled. Pulkheria Alexandrovna stole timid glances at her; she was clearly comforted, though, by the three thousand roubles.

A quarter of an hour later the conversation was at its height. For a while even Raskolnikov, though taking no part, listened attentively. Razumikhin was holding forth, the words pouring out of him with rapturous emotion.

'Why on earth would you leave? And what will you find to do in that provincial town? You're all here together, that's the main thing, and you all need each other, goodness knows how badly – can't you see? For a while, at least . . . Take me as your friend, your partner, and I assure you we'll start an excellent business! Let me set it all out to you in detail – the whole plan! Even this morning, before any of this happened, it was taking shape in my head . . . Here it is: I have an uncle (I'll introduce you – he's an exceedingly obliging and exceedingly respectable old so-and-so) and this uncle of mine has a capital of a thousand roubles – which he doesn't need, as he lives off his pension. This is the second year he's been badgering me to take this thousand off him and pay him six per cent interest. I won't be fooled: he just wants to help me. Last year I had no need of it, but this year I was just waiting for him to arrive and made up my mind to take it. If you put in another thousand, from your three, that's enough to begin with, enough for us to join forces. And what will we be doing exactly?'

Here, Razumikhin started setting out his plan, explaining at great length how ignorant nearly all our booksellers and publishers are about their goods, which is why they usually make bad publishers, while decent editions pay their way and even turn a profit, sometimes a quite considerable one. A career in publishing was Razumikhin's dream. He'd already spent two years working for other people and was competent in three European languages, despite the fact that six days or so before he tried telling Raskolnikov that his German was 'hopeless', in the hope of persuading him to accept half a translating job and three roubles up front; he was lying then, and Raskolnikov knew it.

'Why, I ask you, should we not seize our chance, now that we have that most essential thing – our own money?' Razumikhin went on in the greatest excitement. 'Of course, there's lots to be done, but we'll work hard: you, Avdotya Romanovna, me, Rodion . . . nowadays, some books turn a splendid profit! And we'll base our business on the fact that we know exactly what needs translating. We'll translate and publish and study, all at the same time. With some experience behind me, I can actually make myself useful now. I've been running from one publisher to another for nigh on two years and I know how they work: they're no better than the rest of us, believe you me! And why look a gift horse in the mouth? I already have two or three books up my sleeve: the very thought of translating them is worth a hundred roubles per book, and there's one idea I wouldn't part with if I was offered five hundred. But even if I did tell someone, they'd probably think twice, the idiots! And as for the practical side of things – the printers, paper, sales – you can leave that to me! I know all the ins and outs! We'll start small, we'll grow big – we won't go hungry, that's for sure, and at the very least we'll break even.'

Dunya's eyes were shining.

'I like what you say very much, Dmitry Prokofich,' she remarked.

'I don't know the first thing about it, of course,' Pulkheria Alexandrovna put in. 'Maybe it's a good thing, although, who knows? It's all a bit new, a bit uncertain. Of course, we do have to stay on here, at least for a while . . .'

She looked at Rodya.

'What do you think, brother?' said Dunya.

'I think he's onto a very good thing,' he replied. 'It's much too early to be dreaming of a firm, of course, but five or six books could indeed be published with certain success. I myself know one book that would definitely be suitable. And as for his ability to make it work, there's little doubt about that either: he knows what he's about . . . Anyway, you'll have plenty of time to arrange everything . . .'

'Hurrah!' shouted Razumikhin. 'Now wait: there's an apartment here, in this very building, the very same landlords. It's separate and doesn't connect with this part. It's furnished, moderately priced, three rooms. You should move in there for the time being. I'll pawn the watch for you tomorrow and bring the money, and the rest will take care of itself. The main thing is, the three of you can all live together, with Rodya . . . But where are you off to, Rodya?'

'You're not leaving already, Rodya, are you?' asked Pulkheria Alexandrovna in alarm.

'At such a moment!' shouted Razumikhin.

Dunya looked at her brother with mistrust and amazement. His cap was in his hand; he was ready to leave.

'Anyone would think you were burying me or saying goodbye for good,' he said, rather strangely.

He seemed to smile, though a smile was the last thing it seemed.

'But then – who knows? – perhaps we are seeing each other for the last time,' he added, just like that.

He meant to keep this thought to himself, but somehow it came out of its own accord.

'What on earth's the matter with you?' his mother shrieked.

'Where are you going, Rodya?' asked Dunya, rather strangely.

'I just have to,' came his vague reply, as if he were hesitating about what he wanted to say. But his pale face betrayed a keen resolve. 'I wanted to say . . . coming over here . . . I wanted to tell you, Mama . . . and you, Dunya, that it would be best for us to be apart for a while. I don't feel well, I'm not calm . . . I'll come later, I'll come myself, when . . . I can. You're in my thoughts and I love you . . . Now leave me! Leave me alone! That's what I decided, even before . . . I was quite sure about it . . . Whatever happens to me, whether I sink or swim, I want to be alone. Forget about me. It's for the best . . . Don't ask around about me. When the moment's right, I'll come myself or . . . I'll call for you. Perhaps everything will rise again! . . . But now, if you

love me, give me up . . . Or else I'll start hating you, I can feel it . . .
Goodbye!'

'Lord!' shrieked Pulkheria Alexandrovna.

Mother and sister were horrified; Razumikhin, too.

'Rodya! Rodya! Make peace with us, we'll go back to how we
were!' his poor mother exclaimed.

He turned slowly towards the door and walked slowly out of the
room. Dunya caught up with him.

'Brother! What are you doing to your mother?' she whispered, eyes
burning with indignation.

He gave her a heavy look.

'It's all right. I'll come. I'll visit!' he mumbled under his breath, as
if not fully aware of what he wanted to say, and left the room.

'Callous, spiteful egoist!' shrieked Dunya.

'He's mad, m-a-d, not callous! He's insane! Can't you see that? Then
you're the callous one!' Razumikhin whispered hotly into her ear,
squeezing her hand. 'I'll be right back!' he shouted, turning to Pulkheria Alexandrovna, who was frozen to the spot, and ran out of the room.

Raskolnikov was waiting for him at the end of the corridor.

'I knew you'd come running out,' he said. 'Go back to them and be
with them . . . Be with them tomorrow, too . . . and always. I . . . might
come . . . if I can. Goodbye!'

And, without offering his hand, he walked away.

'But where are you going? Why? What's wrong? How can you?'
muttered Razumikhin, utterly lost.

Raskolnikov stopped once more.

'For the last time: never ask me about anything. I've no answers to
give you . . . Don't come to see me. Perhaps I really will come back
here . . . Leave me and . . . *don't leave them*. Understood?'

It was dark in the corridor; they were standing by a lamp. For a minute or so they looked at each other without speaking. Razumikhin remembered this minute for the rest of his life. Raskolnikov's burning stare
seemed to grow more intense by the second, burrowing into his soul, his
mind. Suddenly, Razumikhin shuddered. Something strange seemed to
pass between them . . . An idea slipped out, almost a hint; something
horrible, something hideous, suddenly grasped on both sides . . . Razumikhin turned white as a corpse.

'Understand now?' said Raskolnikov suddenly, his features painfully twisted. 'Off you go, back to them,' he added and, with a swift turn, walked out of the building . . .

I won't start describing what happened that evening in Pulkheria Alexandrovna's room: how Razumikhin came back, how he calmed them down, how he swore that Rodya was sick and needed rest, swore that Rodya was certain to come, would come every day, that he was very, very distressed, that it wouldn't do to aggravate him; how he, Razumikhin, would keep an eye on him, find him a good doctor, the very best, an entire council . . . In short, from that evening on Razumikhin became their son and their brother.

IV

As for Raskolnikov, he made straight for the house on the Ditch where Sonya lived. It was an old three-storey building painted green. He managed to find the caretaker, who gave him vague directions to Kapernaumov, the tailor. Having eventually located, in a corner of the yard, an entrance to a narrow and dark stairwell, he went up to the second floor, coming out on the gallery that skirted it on the yard-facing side. As he groped about in the dark – he couldn't see an entrance to the Kapernaumovs' anywhere – a door suddenly opened three paces away. He automatically grabbed it.

'Who's there?' asked an anxious female voice.

'It's me . . . come to see you,' Raskolnikov replied, stepping into the tiny entrance hall. There, on a sunken chair, in a twisted copper holder, stood a candle.

'It's you! Goodness!' cried Sonya weakly, rooted to the spot.

'Which way to your place? This way?'

Trying not to look at her, Raskolnikov hurried on through to her room.

A minute later Sonya came in with the candle, set it down and stood before him in utter confusion, lost for words and visibly frightened by his unexpected visit. The colour suddenly rushed to her pale face and tears even appeared in her eyes . . . She felt sick and ashamed, and happy . . . Raskolnikov turned away sharply and sat down on a chair facing the table. With a quick glance he took in the entire room.

The room was large, but exceptionally low, the only one let by the Kapernaumovs, the locked door to whom lay along the left-hand wall. On the opposite side, along the right-hand wall, was yet another door, permanently sealed. That connected with a completely separate apartment, which had a different number. There was something shed-like about Sonya's room, something grotesque about its highly irregular oblong shape. A wall with three windows faced the Ditch and cut across the room at a slant, meaning that one horribly sharp corner tapered off into the distance, barely even visible in the weak light, while the angle of the other corner was monstrously obtuse. This large room was almost entirely unfurnished. In the corner, on the right, was a bed; next to it, nearer the door, a chair. Along the same wall where the bed was, right by the door to the neighbouring apartment, stood a simple plank table covered with a blue cloth; around the table, two wicker chairs. Next, by the opposite wall, not far from the sharp corner, was a small chest of drawers made of ordinary wood, seemingly lost in space. And that was all. The yellowish, glossy, frayed wallpaper had turned black at every corner; it must have been damp and smoky in here during the winter. The poverty was unmistakable; there were no curtains even by the bed.

Sonya looked silently at her guest, who was examining her room so attentively and unceremoniously; in the end, she even began to shake with fear, as though she were standing before the judge who would decide her fate.

'It's late, I know . . . Is it eleven yet?' he asked, still not lifting his eyes to her.

'Yes,' mumbled Sonya. 'Oh yes, it is!' she suddenly rushed, as though for her everything depended on it. 'The landlord's clock struck just now . . . I heard it myself . . . Yes, it is.'

'I've come to you for the last time,' Raskolnikov went on sullenly, though this was only his first. 'I may not see you again . . .'

'You're . . . going somewhere?'

'Don't know . . . tomorrow it'll all . . .'

'So you won't be coming to Katerina Ivanovna's tomorrow?' asked Sonya in a quavering voice.

'Don't know. Tomorrow morning it'll all . . . But that's not why I'm here: I came to say something . . .'

He lifted his pensive gaze to her face and suddenly noticed that he was seated while she was still standing before him.

'But why are you standing? Have a seat,' he said suddenly in a changed voice that was soft and warm.

She sat down. He looked at her for a minute or so with a friendly, almost pitying gaze.

'How skinny you are! Just look at your hand! You can see right through it. A dead woman's fingers.'

He took her hand. Sonya smiled weakly.

'But I've always been like that.'

'Even when you were still at home?'

'Yes.'

'But of course!' he said curtly, and his facial expression and tone of voice suddenly changed again. He took another look round the room.

'So you're renting from Kapernaumov?'

'Yes, sir . . .'

'They're there, behind the door?'

'Yes . . . Their room's just the same.'

'All in one room?'

'Yes, sir.'

'I'd be afraid in your room at night,' he sullenly remarked.

'The landlord's very kind, very warm,' replied Sonya, as if she were still coming to her senses and unable to think straight, 'and all the furniture and everything else . . . it's all theirs. And they're very kind and their children often come round to see me . . .'

'The tongue-tied ones?'

'Yes, sir . . . He's got a stammer and he's lame. And his wife, too . . . Though she doesn't stammer exactly, she just can't seem to get her words out. She's kind, very kind. He used to be a house-serf. Seven children . . . only the eldest stammers, the rest are just sick . . . and don't stammer . . . But how do you know about them?' she added with a certain astonishment.

'Your father told me everything then. He told me everything about you . . . Told me how you went off at six o'clock and were back before nine, told me about Katerina Ivanovna kneeling by your bed.'

Sonya was embarrassed.

'I was sure I saw him today,' she whispered indecisively.

'Who?'

'Father. I was out walking, around there, on the corner of the street, between nine and ten, and thought I saw him walking ahead of me. Looked just like him. I was even about to call on Katerina Ivanovna.'

'You were walking the streets, then?'

'Yes,' Sonya hurriedly whispered, embarrassed again and looking down at the floor.

'Katerina Ivanovna used to beat you, didn't she, at your father's place?'

'No, no! What are you saying? Not at all!'

Sonya glanced up at him with a kind of terror.

'You love her, then?'

'Her? Of course I do!' wailed Sonya, suddenly clasping her hands in pain. 'Oh! You . . . If you only knew. She's just like a child . . . She's almost lost her mind . . . from grief. To think how clever she was . . . how generous . . . how kind! You don't know anything, anything . . . oh!'

Sonya said this in a kind of despair, in turmoil and pain, wringing her hands. Again, her pale cheeks flushed; torment was in her eyes. One could see how deeply everything had affected her, how unbearable was her desire to express something, to speak, to intercede. Some kind of *insatiable* compassion, if one can put it like that, was suddenly etched in every feature of her face.

'Beat me? What are you saying? Beat me, indeed! And even if she did, so what? Well, what? You don't know anything about it, not a thing . . . She's so unhappy, oh, so unhappy! And sick . . . Justice, that's what she seeks . . . She is pure. She really believes there should always be justice. She demands it . . . Torture her if you like, but she won't do anything that's not just. She can't see that it's simply not possible, that there will never be justice among people, so she gets annoyed . . . Like a child, a child! She is just!'

'And what will happen to you?'

Sonya looked mystified.

'They've only got you now. Though it was the same before, of course, and it was you the deceased used to visit for his hair of the dog. So what'll happen now?'

'I don't know,' said Sonya sadly.

'They'll stay there?'

'I don't know, they're behind with their rent. Apparently, the land-lady told her today that she wants her out, and Katerina Ivanovna is saying she won't stay a minute longer either.'

'Why such bravado? Is she counting on you?'

'Oh, no, don't talk like that! . . . We're one, we live as one,' replied Sonya, getting suddenly worked up again and even annoyed, like an angry canary or some other little bird. 'What's she supposed to do? Well, what? What?' she asked, agitated and upset. 'How she cried

today! How she cried! She's unhinged, or haven't you noticed? Yes,
she is. One minute she's fretting like a little girl about getting
everything right for tomorrow, the food and all the rest . . . the next
she's wringing her hands, coughing up blood, crying, suddenly banging her head against the wall, in complete despair. Then she calms
down again and it's you she always counts on: she says you're her
helper now and she'll borrow some money somewhere and go off to
her town, with me, and set up a boarding school for girls of noble
birth and put me in charge, and we'll begin a completely new and
beautiful life; and she kisses me, hugs me and comforts me; and she
truly believes in these fantasies of hers – yes she does! And how could
anyone contradict her? And what did she do today except scrub,
clean, mend, drag the washing tub into the room with her feeble arms,
puff and pant and collapse on her bed? Never mind that we went to
the market in the morning to buy shoes for Polechka and Lenya,[11]
because theirs have fallen apart, only we didn't have enough money
for them, nowhere near enough, and she'd chosen such a sweet pair of
boots – you've no idea what good taste she has . . . She started crying
there and then, in the shop, right in front of the merchants . . . How
pitiful she looked!'

'Well, now it makes sense why you . . . live like this,' said Raskolnikov with a sour grin.

'But don't you pity her, too? Don't you?' Sonya flung back at him.
'After all, you gave away all you had, I know you did, without having
even seen anything. But if you had seen it all – O Lord! And how
many times I've made her cry! How many! Even only last week!
Shame on me! Only a week before his death. How cruel that was!
And how many times have I done that? So many! And how painful it's
been to spend all day remembering!'

Sonya even wrung her hands as she spoke, from the pain of the
recollection.

'You – cruel?'

'Me, me! I'd just come in,' she continued, crying, 'and Father said:
"Read to me, Sonya, I've got a bit of a headache, read to me . . .
There's the book," – he had some book or other, he'd got it from Andrei Semyonych, from Lebezyatnikov, who lives right here and was
always getting these funny little books. And I said, "I have to go" – I
just didn't want to read and I'd come by mainly to show Katerina Ivanovna some collars; Lizaveta, the clothes-dealer, had brought me

some collars and cuffs on the cheap, nice, new embroidered ones. Katerina Ivanovna took a fancy to them, tried them on and looked at
herself in the mirror, and liked them even more: "Give them to me,
Sonya," she said. "Please." *Please*, she said, that's how much she
wanted them. But what would she do with them? She'd remembered
happier days, that's all! There she was looking at herself in the mirror
and admiring herself, but she's not had one dress to call her own, not
a single thing, for how many years now? And you won't catch her
asking anyone for anything. She's proud. She'd sooner give away the
last thing she has, but here she was asking – that's how much she liked
them! But I was sorry to give them away. "What good are they to you,
Katerina Ivanovna?" That's what I said: "What good?" That was the
last thing I should ever have said to her! What a look she gave me;
how miserable she was when I refused her and how pitiful it was to
see her like that! Miserable not because of the collars, but because I'd
refused. I could see. Oh, what I'd do to take all those words back . . .
Shame on me . . . But anyway . . . it's all the same to you!'

'You knew this Lizaveta?'

'Yes . . . Why, did you?' Sonya asked in return, with some surprise.

'Katerina Ivanovna's consumptive – a bad case; she'll be dead
soon,' said Raskolnikov after a pause, ignoring the question.

'Oh, no, no, no!' And Sonya, making an unconscious movement,
grabbed him by both hands, as if pleading that it be no.

'But it's better if she does die.'

'No, not better, not better, not better at all!' she mechanically repeated in horror.

'And what about the children? What will you do with them, unless
you take them in yourself?'

'Oh, how do I know?' cried Sonya in near despair and clutched her
head. Evidently, the thought had already crossed her mind, too, many
a time, and all he'd done was startle it back to life.

'And what if now, while Katerina Ivanovna's still alive, you get sick
and are taken off to hospital, what then?' he persisted mercilessly.

'But what are you saying? That's just not possible!' – and Sonya's
face twisted with terror.

'Why's it not possible?' Raskolnikov went on with a harsh grin.
'You're not insured, are you? So what'll become of them? They'll end
up on the streets together, the whole lot of them; she'll be coughing and
begging and banging her head against a wall somewhere, like today,

and the children will be crying . . . Then she'll collapse, be taken off to
the police station, then the hospital, and die, while the children . . .'

'Oh, no! . . . God won't allow it!' was all that escaped Sonya's constricted chest. She listened, looking at him beseechingly and folding
her arms in dumb entreaty, as if everything depended on him.

Raskolnikov got up and began pacing the room. A minute or so
passed. Sonya stood there with her arms and head hanging down, in
terrible anguish.

'Can't you save a bit? Put something aside for a rainy day?' he
asked, suddenly halting in front of her.

'No,' whispered Sonya.

'Of course not! But have you tried?' he added, almost mockingly.

'Yes.'

'And it didn't last! Well, of course! Why even ask?'

He started pacing the room again. Another minute passed.

'You don't earn every day, I suppose?'

Sonya became even more embarrassed and the colour rushed to her
face once more.

'No,' she whispered with excruciating effort.

'Polechka will go the same way, I expect,' he suddenly said.

'No, no! That's impossible! No!' shrieked Sonya in desperation, as
if she'd been stabbed. 'God would never allow anything so dreadful!'

'But He often does.'

'No, no! God will protect her, God!' she kept saying, beside herself.

'But what if there is no God?' replied Raskolnikov, almost with a
sort of malicious glee, then laughed and looked at her.

An awful change had suddenly come over Sonya's face: it began
twitching convulsively. She glanced at him with unspeakable reproach. She was on the point of saying something, but couldn't get her
words out and merely dissolved into bitter sobs, covering her face
with her hands.

'You say Katerina Ivanovna is unhinged – the same thing's happening to you,' he said after a pause.

Some five minutes passed. He was still walking back and forth, in
silence and without so much as a glance in her direction. Eventually,
he walked up to her, eyes flashing. He grabbed her shoulders with
both hands and looked straight into her weeping face. His gaze was
dry, inflamed, piercing; his lips trembled violently . . . Suddenly he
bent right down and, falling to the floor, kissed her foot. Sonya

recoiled in horror, as from a madman. And, indeed, a madman was just what he resembled.

'Please, what are you doing? Before me?' she muttered, turning white, and her heart clenched with pain.

He immediately got to his feet.

'I bowed not to you, but to all human suffering,' he uttered almost wildly and moved off to the window. 'Listen,' he added, returning to her a minute later, 'I told one offensive individual earlier on that he wasn't worth your little finger . . . and that I did my sister an honour today by seating her next to you.'

'Oh, you shouldn't have said that to him! And she heard it?' Sonya shrieked in fright. 'Sit with me? An honour? But I . . . have no honour . . . I'm a great, great sinner! Oh, you should never have said that!'

'It wasn't your dishonour or your sin that made me say it, but your great suffering. You are a great sinner, it's true,' he added in near ecstasy, 'and above all you are a sinner for having destroyed and betrayed yourself *for nothing*. If that's not a horror, what is? To live in this filth, which you loathe so much, and at the same time to know yourself (if you only open your eyes) that no one is being helped by your actions and no one is being saved! But what I'd really like to know,' he said in near frenzy, 'is how your saintly feelings can abide the contrast of something so shameful and abject? It would be more just, a thousand times more just and more reasonable, to throw yourself off a bridge and end it all!'

'And what will become of them?' asked Sonya feebly, with a look full of suffering, and yet, it seemed, quite unsurprised by his suggestion. Raskolnikov looked at her strangely.

Her eyes alone told him everything. It was true, then: this thought had occurred to her, too. Perhaps, in her despair, she'd considered it many times, how to end it all, and so seriously that now she was barely surprised by his suggestion. She didn't even notice the cruelty of his words (nor, of course, did she notice the meaning of his reproaches or the particular view he took of her shame – he could see that). But he understood perfectly well what monstrous pain the thought of her dishonourable and shameful plight had caused her, and not just now. What on earth, he wondered, could have kept her from ending it all? Only then did he fully grasp what these poor little orphaned children meant to her, and this pitiful, half-crazed, consumptive Katerina Ivanovna, forever banging her head against the wall.

Yet nor could he fail to see that Sonya, with the character she had and with that bit of education she'd somehow received, could never remain as she was. He couldn't help wondering: how, if throwing herself off a bridge was beyond her strength, could she have remained in this plight for so long, far too long, and not gone mad? He understood, of course, that Sonya's plight was a random social phenomenon, albeit, sadly, a far from isolated or exceptional one. But this very randomness, together with her smattering of education and her whole previous life, might well have killed her the moment she set out on this disgusting path. What had sustained her? Not depravity, surely? It was obvious that disgrace had touched her in a purely mechanical way; real depravity had not yet penetrated her heart, not even a drop. He could see it: here she was standing before him . . .

'She can take one of three paths,' he thought. 'She can throw herself into the Ditch, end up in the madhouse or . . . or finally, plunge into the depravity that stupefies the mind and petrifies the heart.' He found this last thought more disgusting than anything, but he was already a sceptic, he was young, theoretical and, by that token, cruel, so it was impossible for him not to believe that the third path – depravity – was the most likely.

'But can this really be true?' he exclaimed to himself. 'Can this creature, who still retains her purity of spirit, eventually allow herself to be sucked into this foul, stinking pit? Can this process really have already begun, and can it be that the only reason she has held out until now is that she no longer finds vice so disgusting? No, no, that's just impossible!' he exclaimed, like Sonya before. 'No, it's the thought of sin that's kept her from the Ditch until now, and *that lot* . . . And if she still hasn't gone mad . . . But who's to say she hasn't? Is she really in her right mind? To talk the way she talks? To reason the way she reasons? To perch above her ruin, right over the stinking pit that's already sucking her in, and wave her hands, and stop up her ears when she's being warned of danger? What is she expecting, a miracle? Yes, that must be it. Aren't these all signs of insanity?'

He paused stubbornly on this thought. This solution pleased him more than any other. He began to study her more closely.

'So you pray to God a lot, Sonya?' he asked.

Sonya said nothing. He stood next to her, waiting for an answer.

'What would I be without God?' she whispered quickly and vigorously, glancing at him with a sudden flash of her eyes, then squeezing his hand firmly in hers.

'Just as I thought!' Raskolnikov said to himself.

'And what does God do for you?' he asked, probing further.

Sonya was silent for a long time, as if unable to reply. Her weak little chest heaved with emotion.

'Be quiet! Don't ask! You aren't worthy!' she suddenly shrieked, with a stern and angry look.

'Just as I thought!' he kept saying to himself.

'He does everything!' she whispered quickly, lowering her eyes once more.

'So that's the solution! And that's how to explain it!' he decided to himself, examining her with avid curiosity.

With a new, strange, almost sick feeling he studied this pale, thin, irregular, angular little face, these meek, pale-blue eyes capable of blazing with such fire, with such stern and vigorous feeling, this little body, still quivering with indignation and anger, and all this struck him as more and more strange, almost impossible. 'Holy fool! Holy fool!'[12] he kept saying to himself.

There was a book lying on the chest of drawers. He noticed it every time he paced the room; now he picked it up and looked at it. It was the New Testament in Russian translation.[13] It was an old book, well-thumbed, bound in leather.

'Where did you get this?' he shouted to her across the room. She was still standing in the same place, three paces away from the table.

'I was brought it,' she replied, with apparent reluctance and without looking at him.

'Who brought it?'

'Lizaveta. I asked her to.'

'Lizaveta? How strange!' he thought. Everything about Sonya was becoming stranger and more wondrous to him with each minute that passed. He brought the book into the candlelight and began leafing through it.

'Where's the bit about Lazarus?' he suddenly asked.

Sonya looked doggedly at the floor and didn't reply. She stood at a slight angle to the table.

'You know, the raising of Lazarus – where is it? Look it up for me, Sonya.'

She glanced at him out of the corner of her eye.

'You're looking in the wrong place ... It's the fourth Gospel ... ,' she whispered sternly, still not moving towards him.

'Find it and read it to me.' He sat down, rested his elbows on the table, propped his head in his hand and sullenly stared off to the side, preparing to listen.

'Another three weeks,' he muttered to himself, 'and they'll be showing her round the asylum! I'll be there, too, if nothing worse happens first.'

Sonya took a hesitant step towards the table, having listened with mistrust to Raskolnikov's strange request. But she still took the book.

'You mean you've never read it?' she asked, glancing at him across the table from beneath her brow. Her voice was becoming sterner and sterner.

'Ages ago . . . back at school! Read it!'

'And you never heard it in church?'

'I . . . didn't go. Do you go often?'

'N-no,' whispered Sonya.

Raskolnikov grinned.

'I see . . . So I suppose you won't be going to bury your father tomorrow?'

'I will. I went last week, too . . . for a memorial service.'

'Whose?'

'Lizaveta's. She was murdered with an axe.'

His nerves were on edge. His head began to spin.

'Were you friendly with Lizaveta?'

'Yes . . . She was a just person . . . She came by . . . not often . . . She couldn't. We read together and . . . talked. She will see God.'[14]

They sounded strange to him, these bookish words, and now another surprise: mysterious meetings with Lizaveta, one holy fool and another.

'Watch you don't become one yourself! It's catching!' he thought. 'Read!' he suddenly exclaimed in an insistent, irritated tone.

Sonya still wavered. Her heart was thumping. Somehow she didn't dare read to him. In near agony he watched the 'wretched lunatic'.

'Why are you asking? You're not a believer, are you?' she whispered softly, even gasping.

'Read! I want you to!'[15] he insisted. 'You read to Lizaveta, didn't you?'

Sonya opened the book and found the place. Her hands were trembling and her voice failing. Twice she began, but not one syllable came out.

'Now a certain man was sick, Lazarus of Bethany . . . ,'[16] she eventually uttered, with great difficulty, but suddenly, from the third word, her voice twanged and then snapped, like a string stretched too far. She couldn't breathe and her chest tightened.

Raskolnikov partly understood why Sonya could not bring herself to read to him, and the more he understood it, the more rudely and irritably he seemed to insist on the reading. He understood far too well how painful it was for her now to disclose and display what was *hers*. He realized that these feelings really did constitute, as it were, her true and perhaps already long-held *secret*, perhaps ever since her girlhood, in that family, with that unhappy father and grief-crazed stepmother, amid hungry children and hideous shouting and scolding. But he had also now learned, beyond any doubt, that though she was distressed and terribly scared of something as she prepared to read, she herself had an excruciating desire to do so, despite all her distress and apprehension, and precisely to *him*, for him to hear *right now* – 'come what may!' . . . He read this in her eyes, understood it from her rapturous excitement . . . She mastered herself, suppressed the guttural spasm that cut her short at the beginning of the verse, and continued reading from John, Chapter 11. Eventually, she reached verse 19:

'And many of the Jews had come to Martha and Mary to console them concerning their brother. When Martha heard that Jesus was coming, she went and met him, while Mary sat in the house. Martha said to Jesus, "Lord, if you had been here, my brother would not have died. And even now I know that whatever you ask from God, God will give you."'

She stopped again at this point, in shame-faced anticipation that her voice might once again quiver and snap . . .

'Jesus said to her, "Your brother will rise again." Martha said to him, "I know that he will rise again in the resurrection at the last day." Jesus said to her, "*I am the resurrection and the life*; he who believes in me, though he die, yet shall he live, and whoever lives and believes in me shall never die. Do you believe this?" She said to him,'

(catching her breath, as if in pain, Sonya read on in a clear and forceful voice, as though confessing her faith for all to hear)

' "Yes, Lord; I believe that you are the Christ, the Son of God, he who is coming into the world."'

She was about to stop and steal a glance *at him*, but hastily pulled herself together and carried on reading. Raskolnikov sat and listened, without moving or turning around, resting his elbows on the table and looking off to the side. She read as far as verse 32.

'Then Mary, when she came where Jesus was and saw him, fell at his feet, saying to him, "Lord, if you had been here, my brother would not have died." When Jesus saw her weeping, and the Jews who came with her also weeping, he was deeply moved in spirit and troubled; and he said, "Where have you laid him?" They said to him, "Lord, come and see." Jesus wept. So the Jews said, "See how he loved him!" But some of them said, "Could not he who opened the eyes of the blind man have kept this man from dying?"'

Raskolnikov turned to face her and looked at her in excitement: yes, just as he thought! She was already shaking all over with real, genuine fever. He'd been expecting this. She was drawing closer to the words describing the very greatest, utterly unprecedented miracle and great rapture had seized her. Her voice rang as clear as metal, strengthened by audible exultation and joy. The lines ran together in front of her – her eyes had gone dark – but she knew it all by heart. On reaching the last verse, 'Could not he who opened the eyes of the blind man. . .', she conveyed, in lowered, fervent, passionate tones, all the doubts, reproaches and abuse of the disbelieving blind Jews, who now, in a minute's time, as if thunder-struck, would fall, start sobbing and believe . . . 'And *he, he* – also blinded and disbelieving – he, too, will now hear, he too will believe, yes, yes! Right here, now,' she dreamt, and shook in joyful anticipation.

'Then Jesus, deeply moved again, came to the tomb; it was a cave and a stone lay upon it. Jesus said, "Take away the stone." Martha, the sister of the dead man, said to him, "Lord, by this time there will be an odour, for he has been dead *four* days."'

She vigorously stressed that word: *four*.

'Jesus said to her, "Did I not tell you that if you would believe you would see the glory of God?" So they took away the stone. And Jesus lifted up his eyes and said, "Father, I thank thee that thou hast heard me. I knew that thou hearest me always, but I have said this on account of the people standing by, that they may believe that thou didst send me." When he had said this, he cried with a loud voice, "Lazarus, come out." *And the dead man came out,*'

(she read loudly and rapturously, and she shook with cold, as if seeing it all with her own eyes) 'his hands and feet bound with bandages, and his face wrapped with a cloth. Jesus said to them, "Unbind him and let him go."

'*Many of the Jews therefore, who had come with Mary and had seen what he did, believed in him.*'

She did not and could not read any further, closed the book and rose swiftly from her chair.

'It's all about the raising of Lazarus,' she whispered curtly and sternly and stood motionless, turning away from him, seemingly ashamed to lift her eyes towards him. Her feverish shaking had still not passed. The candle-end had been guttering for some time in the crooked holder, shedding a dull light, in this beggarly room, on the murderer and the harlot, who'd come together so strangely to read the eternal book. Five minutes passed, if not more.

'I haven't come just to talk,' said Raskolnikov loudly all of a sudden. Frowning, he got to his feet and walked over to Sonya. Silently, she lifted her eyes towards him. His gaze was particularly stern, expressing some wild determination.

'I left my family today,' he said, 'my mother and sister. I won't go back to them now. It's a clean break.'

'But why?' asked Sonya, as though stunned. The recent meeting with his mother and sister had made an extraordinary, if indistinct, impression on her. It was with a kind of horror that she heard the news of the rift.

'Now I have only you,' he added. 'We'll go together ... I've come to you. Together we're damned, together we'll go!'

His eyes blazed. 'Like a madman!' Sonya thought in her turn.

'Go where?' she asked in fright, automatically taking a step back.

'How should I know? All I know is that there's one road before us. One aim!'

She looked at him, understanding nothing. All she understood was that he was dreadfully, infinitely unhappy.

'None of them will understand a thing, if you tell them,' he went on, 'but I understood. I need you, that's why I've come to you.'

'I don't understand ... ,' whispered Sonya.

'You'll understand later. Haven't you done the same thing? You also managed to take that step ... transgress. You've laid hands on yourself, ruined a life ... *your own* (it's all the same!). You could have lived the life of the spirit, the life of reason, yet you'll end up on Haymarket

Square . . . But it's too much for you, and if you're left *alone*, you'll go mad, just like me. There's something crazy about you even now. So we've one road ahead of us. We'll walk it together! Let's go!'

'But why? Why are you saying this?' said Sonya, strangely restless and agitated.

'Why? Because something has to change – that's why! It's time to think about things seriously, head-on, instead of childish crying and yelling about God not allowing it! I mean, what will happen if you really are taken off to hospital tomorrow? She's consumptive and out of her mind, she'll soon die, but the children? You think Polechka won't go to rack and ruin? You mean you haven't seen the children around here, on street corners, sent out by their mothers to beg? I've seen where these mothers live, the conditions they live in. Children can't remain children there, it's impossible. There, a seven-year-old is depraved and a thief. Yet children are the image of Christ: "Theirs is the Kingdom of Heaven."[17] He commanded that they be honoured and loved. They're humanity's future . . .'

'But what's to be done? What?' repeated Sonya, weeping hysterically and wringing her hands.

'What's to be done? Break what must be broken, once and for all, and take suffering upon yourself! You don't understand? You'll understand later . . . Freedom and power, especially power! Over all quivering creatures, over the whole ant heap! . . . This is the aim! Remember that! My parting words! Who knows? I may be speaking to you for the last time. If I don't come tomorrow, you'll hear about everything yourself. When you do, recall these words of mine. And some day, later, years later, as life goes by, perhaps you'll understand what they meant. But if I do come tomorrow, I'll tell you who killed Lizaveta. Goodbye!'

Sonya's whole body shuddered.

'You mean you know who did it?' she asked, frozen with horror and looking at him wildly.

'I know and I'll say . . . To you, only to you! I've chosen you. I won't come to ask your forgiveness, I'll just say it. I chose you a long time ago so as to tell you this, back when your father was talking about you and Lizaveta was still alive, that's when the thought came to me. Goodbye. Don't give me your hand. Tomorrow!'

He left. Sonya had been looking at him as if he were crazy, but she, too, seemed almost mad, and she felt it. Her head was spinning. 'Lord!

How does he know who murdered Lizaveta? What did those words mean? How awful!' But at the same time the *thought* never entered her head. Never! Never! . . . 'Oh, he must be dreadfully unhappy! . . . Left his mother and sister. Why? What happened? And what is he planning?' What was it he'd told her? He'd kissed her foot and said . . . said (yes, he'd said it clearly) that he could no longer live without her . . . O Lord!

Sonya was feverish and delirious all night long. Every now and again she'd leap up in her bed, cry, wring her hands, then lose herself again in a feverish sleep, and she'd dream of Polechka, Katerina Ivanovna, Lizaveta, Gospel readings, and him . . . him, with his pale face, his burning eyes . . . He was kissing her feet, he was crying . . . O Lord!

On the other side of the door – that same door on the right which divided Sonya's apartment from that of Gertruda Karlovna Resslich – there was an in-between room, long empty, which was part of Mrs Resslich's apartment and was rented out by her, hence the little notices on the gates and the bits of paper stuck to the panes of the windows that gave onto the Ditch. Sonya had long assumed that the room was unused. Yet all the while, standing quietly by the door in the empty room, Mr Svidrigailov had been listening in. When Raskolnikov left, he stood and thought for a while, tiptoed off to his own room adjoining the empty one, took a chair and carried it noiselessly right up to the door leading to Sonya's room. He found the conversation both diverting and revealing, and enjoyed it very, very much; in fact, he'd brought the chair in so that in future, say tomorrow, he would no longer have to suffer the inconvenience of spending a whole hour on his feet, but could make himself comfortable and derive every possible pleasure from the experience.

V

When, the next morning at eleven o'clock sharp, Raskolnikov walked into the Criminal Investigations department of ——y District Police Station and asked to be announced to Porfiry Petrovich, he was astonished to be kept waiting so long: at least ten minutes passed before he was called. According to his own calculations someone should have pounced on him straight away. Instead, he just stood there in the reception room, utterly ignored by the people walking past him in both directions. Several clerks were sitting and writing in the next room, which looked like an office, and it was obvious that none of them had even the faintest idea who Raskolnikov was. He scanned the area around him with an anxious, suspicious gaze: wasn't there at least some guard or other, some secret pair of eyes, charged with keeping tabs on him in case he wandered off? But there was nothing of the kind: all he saw were bureaucratic, trivially preoccupied faces, plus a few other people, and no one took the slightest interest in him: he could do what he liked for all they cared. He became ever more convinced that if the mysterious man from yesterday, the phantom from out of the ground, really did know everything, really had seen everything, then would he, Raskolnikov, have been left standing here now, calmly waiting? And would they really have waited for him here until eleven o'clock, when he himself saw fit to drop by? Either that man had not yet reported anything or . . . or he simply didn't know anything either, hadn't seen anything with his own eyes (and how could he have done?), so all of that, from yesterday, was, once again, a phantom, exaggerated by his own, Raskolnikov's, sick and over-wrought imagination. Even yesterday, during the worst of his panic and despair, this conjecture had begun to take root in his mind. Going over it all again now and readying himself for a new fight, he suddenly realized that he was shaking – and even began seething with indignation at the thought that he was shaking with fear before someone as loathsome as Porfiry Petrovich. To meet this man again was for him the most dreadful thing of all: he loathed him beyond measure, infinitely, and was even afraid lest his loathing betray him. So great was his indignation, in fact, that it instantly put a stop to his shaking; he prepared to walk in with a cool and insolent air and promised himself to say as little as possible, to look and listen hard and, at least for this once, to overcome at all costs his morbidly excitable character. At that very moment he was called in to see Porfiry Petrovich.

Porfiry Petrovich, it turned out, was alone. His office was neither large nor small; it contained a big desk in front of an oilcloth-covered couch, a bureau, a cupboard in the corner and several chairs – all government property and made of yellow, polished wood. In the corner, in the far wall – or rather, in a partition – there was a locked door: so over there, beyond the partition, there must have been some other rooms, too. When Raskolnikov entered, Porfiry Petrovich immediately closed the door behind him; the two men were alone. Porfiry received his guest with what seemed to be the most cheerful and cordial of welcomes, and only several minutes later did Raskolnikov detect certain vague signs of embarrassment – as if Porfiry had suddenly been thrown into confusion or surprised in the middle of some particularly private and secret business.

'Ah, my good chap! You too . . . in our neck of the woods . . . ,' Porfiry began, holding out both hands. 'Well, have a seat then, father! Or perhaps you don't like being called good chap and . . . father – just like that, *tout court*? Please don't think I'm being too familiar, sir . . . This way, please, to my little couch.'

Raskolnikov sat down, never taking his eyes off him.

'In our neck of the woods', apologies for excessive familiarity, that bit of French and everything else – they were all characteristic traits. 'Still, he held out both hands, but withdrew them before offering either one,' flashed across his suspicious mind. Each was observing the other, but the moment their eyes met, both averted their gaze with lightning speed.

'I've brought you that little note . . . about the watch . . . Here you go, sir. Will it do or should I rewrite it?'

'What? A little note? Yes indeed . . . worry not, all in order, sir,' said Porfiry Petrovich, as if he were hurrying off somewhere, and only then did he take the document and look it over. 'Yes, all in order. Nothing else needed,' he confirmed, still pattering away, and placed the document on the desk. Then, a minute later, while talking about something else, he picked it up again and transferred it to the bureau.

'I believe you said yesterday that you would like to ask me . . . formally . . . about my acquaintance with that . . . murdered woman?' Raskolnikov began again. 'Why did I say *I believe*?' flashed across his mind like lightning. 'Why am I so worried about having said *I believe*?' came another flash, like lightning.

And he suddenly sensed that his mistrust had, from the very first contact with Porfiry, the first two words, the first two looks, instantly swelled to monstrous dimensions . . . and that this was terribly dangerous: his nerves were on edge, his agitation was mounting. 'Watch out! Watch out! . . . I'll give myself away again.'

'Yes, yes! Worry not! That can wait, sir, that can wait,' muttered Porfiry Petrovich, walking back and forth in the vicinity of the desk, but to no apparent purpose, as if in a hurry to reach the window or the bureau or the desk again, now avoiding Raskolnikov's suspicious gaze, now suddenly stopping in his tracks and staring right at him. As he did so, his tubby, round little figure seemed extraordinarily strange, like a little ball rolling off in various directions before bouncing off every wall or corner.

'Plenty of time for that, sir, plenty of time! . . . Do you smoke? Got your own? Have a papirosa on me . . . ,' he went on, proffering a papirosa to his guest. 'You know, I'm receiving you here, but my own apartment's right there, behind the partition – grace and favour, sir, though I've got my own place, too, for the meantime. There were a few little improvements to be made here first. Now it's nearly ready . . . A grace-and-favour apartment, you know, is a splendid thing – eh? What do you reckon?'

'Yes, a splendid thing,' answered Raskolnikov, looking at him almost mockingly.

'Splendid, splendid . . . ,' Porfiry Petrovich kept saying, as if suddenly absorbed by quite different thoughts. 'Yes! A splendid thing!' he fairly shrieked by the end, suddenly flashing a glance at Raskolnikov and halting just a couple of paces away from him. The silly way he was banging on about a grace-and-favour apartment[18] being a splendid thing contrasted far too much in its petty vulgarity with the serious, thoughtful and enigmatic gaze he was now directing at his guest.

But this merely stoked Raskolnikov's anger even more, and he could not resist throwing down a mocking and fairly reckless challenge.

'You know,' he suddenly said, looking at him almost insolently and deriving a kind of pleasure from his insolence, 'I believe a certain principle exists in legal practice, a certain legal technique – to be used by every conceivable investigator – whereby one begins from a long way off, with trifles or even with something serious, but completely irrelevant, in order, as it were, to reassure, or rather distract, the man being questioned, to lull his vigilance, before all of a sudden, in quite the most unexpected way, clubbing him smack on the crown with the most fateful and dangerous question. Isn't that right? I believe that to this day it receives reverent mention in all the rulebooks and manuals.'

'Yes indeedy . . . So you think that by mentioning the apartment I was . . . eh?' Saying this, Porfiry Petrovich squinted and winked; something merry and sly flitted across his face, the wrinkles on his brow smoothed out, his little eyes narrowed, his features lengthened and he suddenly broke into a bout of nervous, prolonged laughter, his whole body swaying with excitement while he continued to look straight into Raskolnikov's eyes. The latter also began to laugh, not without effort, but when Porfiry, seeing that he, too, was laughing, became so overcome with mirth that he very nearly turned purple, Raskolnikov's disgust suddenly got the better of his caution; he stopped laughing, frowned and looked for a long while and with loathing at Porfiry, keeping his eyes fixed on him for the entire duration of his lengthy and, it seemed, intentionally unceasing laughter. A lack of caution, though, was in evidence on both sides: Porfiry Petrovich seemed to be laughing at his guest quite openly, to the latter's utter disgust, and to be quite unembarrassed by this circumstance. For Raskolnikov, this last point was highly significant: he realized that earlier, too, Porfiry Petrovich had probably not been in the least embarrassed, and he, Raskolnikov, must have fallen into a trap; there was something afoot here of which he was ignorant, some purpose or other; everything, perhaps, was already in place, and any minute now would be unveiled and unleashed . . .

He got straight to the point, rising from his seat and grabbing his cap.

'Porfiry Petrovich,' he began decisively, if rather too irritably, 'yesterday you expressed the wish that I present myself here for some sort of interrogation.' (He laid particular stress on the word *interrogation*.) 'Well, here I am, so if there's anything you need to ask, ask; otherwise please permit me to leave. I've no time, there's something I have to do . . . I need to attend the funeral of the civil servant who was trampled by horses, the very one you . . . also know about . . . ,' he added, and was immediately angry with himself for having done so, which immediately irritated him even more, 'and I'm fed up with all this – do you hear? – and have been for some time . . . and that's partly why I fell ill . . . and, in short,' he all but shrieked, sensing that the phrase about his illness was even more misjudged, 'in short, be so kind either to question me or let me go this minute . . . and if you are going to question me, you had better do so formally, sir. I won't have it any other way. Goodbye for now, then, seeing as we are merely wasting each other's time.'

'Heavens above! What are you saying? Question you about what?' Porfiry Petrovich suddenly cackled, immediately changing both his tone and his appearance and instantly ceasing to laugh. 'Worry not, please,' he fussed, now tearing off again to the four ends of the room, now trying to sit Raskolnikov down. 'That can wait, sir, that can wait, and these are all mere trifles! You know, I'm simply delighted to see you here at last . . . and welcome you as a guest. And as for this wretched laughter of mine, please forgive me, Rodion Romanovich, father. It is Roman, is it not? Your father's name, I mean . . . I'm highly strung, sir, and you had me in fits there with the wittiness of your remark; believe me, there are times when I start quivering like India rubber and I won't stop for half an hour . . . I'm the laughing sort. I even fear a stroke, sir, considering my constitution. Now do take a seat, eh? . . . Please, father, or else I shall think you're cross . . .'

Raskolnikov kept silent, listened and watched, still frowning angrily. Nevertheless, he sat down, but without letting go of his cap.

'I should tell you something about myself, Rodion Romanovich, father, by way of an explanation, as it were, of my character,' Porfiry Petrovich continued, bustling about the room and appearing to avoid, as before, the gaze of his guest. 'I'm a bachelor, you see, no airs or graces, no fame or name, and, as if that's not enough, I'm finished, sir, I've frozen over, I've gone to seed and . . . and . . . Have you noticed, Rodion Romanovich, that here, here in Russia, I mean, and most especially in our Petersburg circles, whenever two intelligent people, who don't yet know each other all that well but, as it were, respect one another, just like you and me, come together, they are quite incapable, for at least half an hour, of finding a single topic of conversation? They just freeze in each other's presence and sit around feeling awkward. Everyone else has things to discuss . . . ladies, say, or high-society types . . . they can always find a topic, *c'est de rigueur*, but middling people like us are awkward and untalkative . . . thinking people, I mean. Now why, father, should this be so? Is there really no topic of public interest for us to discuss, or are we too honest for our own good and unwilling to deceive each other? Eh? What do you think? Do put away that cap, sir, one might think you were about to leave – makes me quite uncomfortable . . . You know, I'm simply delighted . . .'

Raskolnikov put down his cap, keeping silent and continuing to listen with a serious, frowning face to Porfiry's idle and muddled chatter. 'Is he really trying to distract me with his silly talk?'

'I won't offer you coffee, sir, this isn't the place. But where's the harm in sitting down with a friend for five minutes and relaxing a little?' Porfiry prattled on. 'And you know, sir, all these official duties . . . Now, please don't be offended by all my walking around, back and forth. Forgive me, father, the last thing I want to do is offend you, but I just can't get by without regular exercise. I'm always at my desk and

five minutes on my feet is sheer delight . . . Piles, sir . . . I keep meaning
to try gymnastics. I'm told that state counsellors, actual state counsellors and even privy[19] counsellors are fond of the skipping rope, sir; the
wonders of modern science, eh? . . . Yes indeedy . . . And as for duties,
interrogations and all these formalities . . . you yourself, dear man, saw
fit to mention interrogations just now . . . well, let me tell you, Rodion
Romanovich, father, these interrogations sometimes confuse the man
who's asking the questions even more than the man who's answering
them . . . Your witty comment about that just now was spot on, sir.'
(Raskolnikov had made no such comment.) 'You can get tied up in
knots! Really you can! And it's always the same thing, again and
again, like a drum! Now there are reforms afoot,[20] so at least we'll get
different titles, heh-heh-heh! And as for those legal techniques of
ours – as you so wittily put it – well, I couldn't agree with you more,
sir. Just try finding a suspect, even the most rustic peasant, who doesn't
know, for example, that first he'll be lulled with irrelevant questions
(in your felicitous phrase) before being suddenly clubbed smack on the
crown, sir, butt-first, heh-heh-heh! Yes, smack on the crown, in your
felicitous comparison, heh-heh! And you really thought that was why I
mentioned the apartment . . . heh-heh! What an ironical fellow you
are. All right, I'll stop! Oh, yes, while I'm at it, since one word, one
thought beckons another: earlier on you also saw fit to mention matters of form, concerning, you know, interrogations, as it were . . . But
why such a fuss about form? Form, you know, is often just a lot of hot
air, sir. Sometimes a friendly chat gets you a great deal further. There's
no running away from form, don't you worry about that. But ultimately, sir, what is it? An investigation can't be inhibited by form every
step of the way. An investigation needs, so to speak, the freedom of
art, sir, or something like that . . . heh-heh-heh!'

Porfiry Petrovich paused for a moment to catch his breath. On and
on he prattled with his meaningless, empty phrases, occasionally
coming out with a few enigmatic words before immediately lapsing
back into nonsense again. By now he was virtually running around
the room, making his chubby little legs work faster and faster, keeping his eyes to the floor, tucking his right arm behind his back and
continuously waving his left in a variety of gestures, all astonishingly
ill-matched to his words. Raskolnikov suddenly noticed how, running
around the room, he appeared to pause at least twice by the door, as
if he were listening in . . . 'Is he waiting for something?' he wondered.

'I must say, you're absolutely right, sir,' Porfiry set off again, looking cheerfully and with extraordinary frankness at Raskolnikov
(causing the latter to shudder and instantly brace himself), 'absolutely
right to mock these legal formalities of ours with such wit, heh-heh!
These (or at least some of these) profound psychological techniques
are of course quite absurd, sir, and I dare say useless, too, especially
when they are very inhibited by form. Yes, sir . . . I'm back to form
again: imagine that I had deemed or, better, suspected someone –
anyone, anyone at all – to be a criminal, in some case that had been
entrusted to me . . . You're studying to be a lawyer, Rodion Romanovich, are you not?'

'Yes, I was . . .'

'Well, here's a little example, as it were, for the future – although far
be it from me, of course, to teach you anything: just look at those articles you've been publishing on the subject of crime! No, sir, allow me
to put this example to you for its purely factual interest. Say, for example, that I considered someone, anyone, a criminal, why ever, I ask
you, would I trouble him ahead of time, even if I had evidence against
him? There are those, of course, whom I'm obliged to arrest promptly,
but this man may have a quite different character; so why not let him
wander around town a bit? Heh-heh-heh! No, I can see you're not
quite following, so let me illustrate the point more clearly: if, for example, I lock him up too soon, I may end up providing him with, as it
were, moral support, heh-heh! I see you're laughing.' (Laughter was
the last thing on Raskolnikov's mind: he sat tight-lipped, keeping his
inflamed gaze fixed on Porfiry Petrovich's eyes.) 'But that's how it is,
sir, especially with certain individuals, because you get all kinds of
people and only one procedure. You saw fit to mention evidence just
now, but with respect, father, even supposing there is evidence, still,
evidence is a double-edged thing, for the most part anyway, and as you
know I'm an investigator and hence, I admit, a weakling: I'd like to set
out the case with, as it were, mathematical clarity. I'd like a bit of evidence that looks like two times two! Like direct and incontrovertible
proof! But if I lock him up before time – even if I'm quite sure it's *him* –
I may very well end up depriving myself of the chance to get any more
out of him. Why? Because I'll be defining his situation for him, as it
were. I'll be defining him psychologically, so to speak, and reassuring
him, and then he'll withdraw from me into his shell: it'll have finally
got through to him that he's a prisoner. I'm told that down there in

Sebastopol, straight after the Battle of Alma,[21] all the clever folk were
terrified at the prospect of the enemy launching an open attack any
moment and taking Sebastopol there and then; but when they saw that
the enemy had chosen a regular siege instead and was digging the first
line of trenches, why, the clever folk, I'm told, were simply delighted,
sir, and felt quite reassured: it meant that the whole thing would drag
on for at least another two months, because a regular siege might take
forever! Again you're laughing, again you don't believe me. Well, I suppose you have a point, too. Yes, you're right, sir, you're right! These
are all one-offs, I agree. The case I've just described really is a one-off,
sir! But here's what we need to bear in mind, dear sweet Rodion Romanovich: typical cases, the very same ones according to which all the
legal forms and principles are tailored and calculated and written up
in books, simply do not exist, sir, by virtue of the fact that each and
every deed, each and every – for want of a better example – crime, just
as soon as it occurs in reality, immediately becomes a one-off, sir; in
fact, sometimes it's like nothing that's ever gone before. Certain such
cases are utterly comic, sir. But if I leave a gentleman well alone, don't
bring him in, don't disturb him, just let him know, or at least suspect,
every hour and every minute, that I know everything, all the ins and
outs, that I'm following him day and night, keeping him forever in
my sight, just let him feel the constant weight of suspicion and fear,
then, mark my words, he'll become quite dizzy, yes indeed; he'll
come to me himself and he might even go and do something after
which two and two really will make four and it will all look perfectly
mathematical – and very nice that would be, too. Even the most coarse-
cut peasant is quite capable of this sort of thing, to say nothing of our
good friend, brainy modern man, whose development has taken a particular slant! Because, my dear chap, it's terribly important to understand which slant a man's development has taken. And what about
nerves, sir? Nerves, you've forgotten all about them! After all, nowadays everyone's so sick and gaunt and irritable! . . . And what about
bile? They're all bursting with it! This, in its way, is a goldmine, sir, let
me tell you! And why should I worry about him walking freely around
town? Let him wander as much as he likes, for now; after all, I already
know I've got my catch and he can't run away! I mean, where would he
run to? Heh-heh! Abroad? A Pole would run abroad, but *he* never
would, especially when I'm watching him and I've taken certain precautions. Or perhaps he'd run away to the darkest depths of his

homeland? But that's where the peasants live, real, rustic, Russian mu-
zhiks; our advanced modern man would rather be locked up than live
with anyone as foreign as our muzhik, heh-heh! But this is just superfi-
cial nonsense. What does it mean: run away? That's mere form. It's not
the main thing. The reason he won't run away from me isn't just that
he's got nowhere to run away to; it's that he won't run away *psychologically*, heh-heh! What a lovely little phrase! The laws of nature won't
let him run away, even if he did have somewhere to go. Ever seen a
moth near a candle? Well, that's how he'll be, forever circling around
me, like a moth around a candle; freedom will sour, he'll start thinking too much, entangling himself, worrying himself to death! . . . And
if that's not enough, he'll even present me with some mathematical
trick, like two times two – I just need to give him a long enough en-
tr'acte . . . And that's how he'll be, going round and round in circles,
the radius narrowing and narrowing, and – hop! – straight into my
mouth, where I'll swallow him up, sir, and how very nice that will be,
heh-heh-heh! You don't believe me?'

Raskolnikov didn't reply. He sat pale and motionless, staring into
Porfiry's face with the same intensity as before.

'A nice little lesson!' he thought with a chill. 'This isn't even cat-and-
mouse like it was yesterday. And it's not a pointless show of strength,
either . . . He wants me to know he's far too clever for that. There's
some other purpose here. But what? You're wasting your breath, trying
to frighten and fool me! You've no proof and the man from yesterday
doesn't exist! You just want to confuse me, irritate me and, when I'm
good and ready, gobble me up. Only it won't work; you'll come un-
stuck! But why make it so obvious? . . . Counting on my sick nerves, are
we? . . . No, my friend, this won't work, whatever it is you've prepared
over there . . . Well, let's see what that is exactly.'

He summoned all his strength, bracing himself for some dreadful
and unknown catastrophe. There were moments when he felt like
throwing himself on Porfiry and strangling him on the spot. Even as he
was walking in, this anger had frightened him. He could feel how dry
his mouth was, how his heart was thumping, how his lips were caked
with foam. But still he was determined to say nothing for now. He realized that these were the best tactics in his situation, because not only
would he not blurt anything out, but his silence would irritate his ad-
versary, who might himself let something slip. Or so he hoped.

'No, I see you don't believe me, sir. You think these are just my

harmless japes,' Porfiry went on, becoming ever more cheerful, constantly giggling with pleasure and setting off again around the room.
'Well, I suppose you're right, sir. Even my shape was thus arranged by
God Himself merely to arouse comical thoughts in others; a buffoon,
sir. But here's what I'll tell you, father, and I'll say it again: you, Rodion
Romanovich – please excuse an old man – are still young, sir, in the
first flush of youth, as it were, which is why you value the human intellect above all else, like all young people. The play of wit and the
abstract arguments of reason seduce you, sir. And that's just like the
old Austrian Hofkriegsrat, for example, if my limited understanding
of war serves me right: on paper, they'd already crushed Napoleon
and taken him captive – they'd worked it all out so cleverly and tot-
ted everything up at their desks – but lo and behold, General Mack²²
goes and surrenders with his entire army, heh-heh-heh! Yes, I see
you're laughing at me, Rodion Romanovich: here am I, a civilian
through and through, plucking all my examples from military history.
But what can I do? Military science is a weakness of mine. How I love
to read all those communiqués . . . I'm in the wrong job, no two ways
about it. My place is in the military, sir, really it is. I might never have
made a Napoleon, but I'd have risen to the rank of major, heh-heh-
heh! Well then, my dearest, let me tell you the whole truth, in every
detail, about those *one-offs*: reality and human nature, my good sir,
are not to be dismissed – they sometimes play havoc with the most
perspicacious of calculations! Heed the words of an old man, Rodion
Romanovich, I'm being serious,' (saying this, Porfiry Petrovich, all of
thirty-five, really did seem to age: even his voice changed and he became all twisted) 'and what's more, I'm a candid sort of man . . . Am
I candid? What's your opinion? It certainly looks that way: why, I'm
telling you all manner of things without being asked, nor do I expect
any reward, heh-heh! Well, then, I resume. Wit, if you ask me, is a
marvellous thing, sir. It is, so to speak, nature's adornment and life's
consolation, and when you see the sort of tricks it pulls off, why, what
chance, it would seem, does a poor little investigator have against it?
Especially when you consider that he himself gets carried away by his
own fantasies, as is always the case, seeing as he, too, is human! But
human nature, sir, is precisely what saves the poor little investigator,
and there's the rub! That's what never occurs to young people carried
away by their own wit and "striding over every obstacle" (as you so
wittily and cunningly put it). Granted, he may tell a few lies, this man,

I mean, *this one-off*, this incognito, and he'll tell them in a most excellent and cunning way. His victory, it would seem, is assured, and the fruits of his wit stand ready to be plucked, but . . . lo and behold, in the most interesting, most scandalous place, what does he do but faint! Granted, he's sick, and it can get terribly stuffy indoors, but nevertheless! Nevertheless, sir, he's sown a thought! His lies may have been quite superlative, but he failed to make allowances for human nature! There it is, the traitor! On another occasion, caught up in the play of his wit, he'll try to make a fool of the man who suspects him, he'll turn pale as if on purpose, as if he's acting, but the way he does it will be *all too natural*, seem all too true, and once again he'll have planted a thought! Even if he does deceive him at first, overnight the other chap will think it over, if he's no fool himself. And it's like that every step of the way, sir! Trust me, he'll start running ahead, poking his head in where he's not even wanted, talking nineteen to the dozen when he'd be better off saying nothing, coming out with various allegories, heh-heh! He'll turn up unannounced and ask: why's nobody come for me yet? Heh-heh-heh! And, you know, this can happen to the very wittiest men, to psychologists and literary types! Nature is a mirror, sir, a mirror of the most transparent kind! Look and admire! Yes indeed! Now why are you so pale, Rodion Romanovich? Perhaps the room's too stuffy for you. Perhaps I should open a window?'

'Oh, don't you worry about that,' cried Raskolnikov and suddenly guffawed. 'Please don't worry about that!'

Porfiry stopped in front of him, waited a bit and suddenly began to guffaw as well. Raskolnikov rose from the couch, suddenly cutting short his own, perfectly convulsive laughter.

'Porfiry Petrovich!' he said loudly and distinctly, though barely standing on his trembling legs. 'It's finally become quite clear to me that you firmly suspect me of the murder of that old woman and her sister Lizaveta. For my part, I declare to you that I'm completely fed up with all this and have been for some time. If you deem that you have the right to prosecute me in accordance with the law, then prosecute; to arrest, then arrest me. But I won't allow anyone to laugh in my face and torment me.'

Suddenly his lips began to quiver, his eyes flashed with fury and his voice, hitherto restrained, boomed out.

'I won't allow it, sir!' he suddenly yelled, banging his fist on the desk with all his might. 'Do you hear, Porfiry Petrovich? I won't allow it!'

'Good Lord, not again!' cried Porfiry Petrovich, looking thoroughly alarmed. 'Father! Rodion Romanovich! Dearest! What's the matter?'

'I won't allow it!' Raskolnikov started yelling again.

'Hush, father! Or they'll hear you and come. And then what will we tell them? Think about that!' Porfiry Petrovich whispered in horror, bringing his face very close to Raskolnikov's.

'I won't allow it! I won't allow it!' Raskolnikov repeated mechanically, though he, too, was suddenly whispering now.

Porfiry turned away briskly and hurried over to open a window.

'Some fresh air, that's what we need! And you'd better have some water, my dear boy. This is a fit you're having!' He rushed over to the door to order some water, only to find a carafe right there in a corner.

'Have some, father,' he whispered, rushing back over to him with the carafe, 'it might just help . . .' Porfiry Petrovich's alarm and concern were so very natural that Raskolnikov fell silent and began studying him with wild curiosity. He didn't take the water, though.

'Rodion Romanovich! Dear, sweet boy! You'll drive yourself mad if you carry on like this, believe you me! Dear oh dear! Go on, drink some! At least a few sips!'

He more or less forced him to take the glass of water. Mechanically, Raskolnikov started bringing it to his lips, but, coming to his senses, put it down on the table in disgust.

'Yes, sir, that was a little fit you just had! Carry on like this, my dear chap, and your old sickness will come back,' Porfiry Petrovich cackled with amicable concern, though he continued to look somewhat bemused. 'Good heavens! What a way to neglect yourself! You know, I had Razumikhin here as well yesterday. Yes, yes, I agree, I have a poisonous, lousy character, but that's no reason for him to deduce such things! . . . Heavens! He came by yesterday after you left, we had some lunch, he talked and talked and all I could do was throw up my hands. Well I never . . . Good grief! Was it you who sent him? Now do sit down, father, take a seat, for the love of Christ!'

'No, it wasn't me! But I knew he'd gone to see you and why,' replied Raskolnikov sharply.

'You knew?'

'I knew. Well, so what?'

'Simply, Rodion Romanovich, that this is as nothing compared to some of your other exploits. I know about them all, sir! I even know about you going to *rent an apartment*, very late in the day, after dusk; about you ringing the bell and asking about blood, and confusing the workmen and caretakers. I can understand the state of mind you must have been in at the time . . . but still, you'll drive yourself mad like this, mark my words! You'll make yourself quite giddy! You're positively boiling with indignation, sir, with noble indignation, no less, from insults meted out first by fate, then by the local police officers, and that's why you're haring around everywhere, so as to get everyone else to talk and have done with it all as soon as possible, because you're fed up with all this silliness, all these suspicions. Isn't that so? Haven't I guessed your state of mind? . . . Only it's not just yourself you'll make giddy, but Razumikhin, too. He's far too *good* for all this, you know that yourself. You're sick and he's good, so sickness is bound to stick to him . . . Once you've calmed down, dear boy, I'll tell you something . . . Now do sit down, for the love of Christ! Please, have a rest, you look terrible. Take a seat, I say.'

Raskolnikov sat down, shaking less now and feeling hot and feverish. In deep astonishment, he listened intently as Porfiry Petrovich fussed about him like a concerned friend. But he didn't believe a word he said, though he felt a strange inclination to do so. Porfiry's unexpected mention of the apartment had astounded him. 'So he knows about the apartment. How come?' he suddenly thought. 'Then he tells me about it himself!'

'Yes, sir, we had an almost identical case in court, sir, lots of psychology there, too, and illness,' Porfiry pattered on. 'He also tried to slander himself as a murderer and you should have seen how he did it: he came up with a complete hallucination, presented the facts, described the circumstances, succeeded in muddling and confusing everyone, and why? He himself, quite unintentionally, did partly cause the murder, but only partly, and when he discovered that he'd given the murderers a pretext for their crime, he fell into a state of depression and stupor, started seeing things, became completely unhinged and ended up convincing himself that he carried out the murder himself! Eventually, the Governing Senate got to the bottom of it all, and the unfortunate man was acquitted and taken into care. Thank heavens for the Governing Senate! Ay-ay-ay! What are you playing at, father? You'll give yourself a fever by irritating your nerves with these sudden fancies – ringing doorbells at night and asking about blood! I know all this psychology inside out, sir, from practical experience. A man can end up wanting to throw himself from a window or a bell tower – such a tempting sensation. The same goes for doorbells, sir . . . It's an illness, Rodion Romanovich, an illness! You've started neglecting your illness far too much, sir. Try having a word with an experienced doctor, not this fat friend of yours! . . . It's delirium, sir! Everything you're going through is sheer delirium!'

For a moment Raskolnikov felt the room begin to spin.

'Surely, surely,' flashed across his mind, 'he's not still lying even now? Impossible! Impossible!' He pushed the thought away, sensing in advance how furious, how livid it could make him, sensing he might go mad with rage.

'I wasn't delirious. I was fully awake!' he cried, straining all his powers of reasoning to enter into Porfiry's game. 'Fully awake! Do you hear?'

'Yes, I understand, sir. I hear you! Yesterday, too, you said you weren't delirious. You even laid particular emphasis on the fact! Say what you like and I'll understand you, sir! Dearie me! . . . But hear me out, Rodion Romanovich, my benefactor, at least on this one point. Say you really, truly, were a criminal or that you were somehow mixed up in this wretched business, well, for heaven's sake, would you really start emphasizing the fact that you weren't delirious while you did all this, but, on the contrary, in full possession of your faculties? And, what's more, emphasize it in such a particularly obstinate way – I mean, how could such a thing be possible, for heaven's sake? It should be exactly the other way round, if you ask me. I mean, if there were anything bothering you, then you ought to emphasize precisely the fact that yes, absolutely, you were raving! Isn't that so? Isn't it?'

There was something sly about the tone of the question. With a jolt, Raskolnikov shrank back from Porfiry to the very spine of the couch and stared in silent bewilderment at the man leaning over him.

'Or take Mr Razumikhin and the matter of whether it was his idea to come by yesterday or you who prompted him? "His idea" is what you should say, of course, concealing the fact that you prompted him! But no, you don't conceal it at all! You even emphasize the fact that you prompted him!'

Raskolnikov had never emphasized this fact. A chill went down his spine.

'You're still lying,' he said slowly and feebly, his lips twisted into a sickly smile. 'Once again you're trying to prove to me that you know my game inside out, that you know all my replies in advance.' He himself almost knew that he was no longer weighing his words as he should. 'You're trying to frighten me . . . or else you're just laughing at me . . .'

He continued to stare straight at him as he said this, and once again his eyes suddenly flashed with boundless rage.

'You're lying, lying!' he cried. 'You know full well that for any criminal the best dodge in the book is not to conceal what doesn't have to be concealed. I don't believe you!'

'What a wriggler you are!' tittered Porfiry. 'It's hard work getting on with you, father. You've become positively monomaniacal! So you don't believe me? But I say that you do believe me, that you already believe me an inch of the way, and I'll make you go the whole mile, because I am deeply fond of you and truly want what is best for you.'

Raskolnikov's lips began to quiver.

'Yes, sir, I do, so let me tell you once and for all,' he went on, taking Raskolnikov gently, amicably, by the arm, just above the elbow, 'once and for all, sir: attend to your sickness. Especially now that your family has come to visit you. Think about them. You should be putting them at their ease and spoiling them, and instead you're frightening them . . .'

'What business is it of yours? How do you know? Why are you so interested? You want to show me you're on my trail, is that it?'

'Father! It's you who told me all this – you! You don't even notice how, in your excitement, you tell everyone everything in advance, me included. Mr Razumikhin, Dmitry Prokofich, also furnished me with a lot of interesting details yesterday. No, sir, you interrupted me just now but let me tell you that, for all your wit, your suspicious nature has even deprived you of your common sense, of your ability to see things clearly. Take the example I just mentioned, the bells: what a jewel, what a fact (a proper fact, sir) for me, an investigator, to present you with, just like that! And this doesn't tell you anything? Why ever would I have done that if I suspected you even slightly? On the contrary, I ought to have begun by lulling your suspicions and concealing any knowledge of this fact; made you look the other way, as it were, before suddenly clubbing you smack on the crown (to use your own expression): "What, pray, were you doing, sir, in the apartment of the murdered woman at ten o'clock in the evening, in fact almost eleven o'clock? And why did you ring the bell? And why did you ask about blood? And why did you confuse the caretakers and call them over to

the police station, to the district lieutenant?" That's what I ought to
have done if I'd had even the faintest suspicion. I ought to have taken
a formal statement from you, searched you and probably arrested you
as well ... So how can I nurture any suspicions towards you if I acted
otherwise? I repeat, sir, you're not seeing things clearly, you're not
seeing anything at all!'

Raskolnikov gave a violent jerk. Porfiry Petrovich couldn't help but
notice.

'You're still lying!' he cried. 'I don't know what you're up to, but
you're still lying ... You were saying something different before. I
know I'm not mistaken ... You're lying!'

'I'm lying?' Porfiry rejoined, appearing to get worked up while retaining the most jovial and mocking expression, and seemingly quite untroubled by whatever opinion Mr Raskolnikov might hold of him. 'I'm
lying? ... But what about the way I acted with you just now (me, the
investigator!), dropping you hints and giving you every means to defend
yourself, handing you all this psychology on a plate: "Sickness, delirium, mortally offended, depression, local police officers" and all the rest
of it? Eh? Heh-heh-heh! Although it's worth pointing out, in passing,
that all these psychological defence mechanisms, excuses and dodges
are extremely flimsy, not to mention double-edged: "Sickness, delirium,
daydreams – I imagined it – I can't remember" – it's all very well, sir, but
why, dear boy, when sick or delirious, should it be precisely these daydreams that one imagines and not something different? After all, they
could have been different, couldn't they? Eh? Heh-heh-heh-heh!'

Raskolnikov looked at him with proud contempt.

'In short,' he said in a loud, insistent voice, getting up and pushing
Porfiry back a little as he did so, 'this is what I want to know: do you
declare me beyond suspicion, definitively, or do you *not*? Tell me that,
Porfiry Petrovich, tell me firmly and definitively, and tell me now!'

'Look at him – a veritable investigation committee!' cried Porfiry
with a perfectly jovial, sly and untroubled air. 'But why on earth do
you need to know all these things, when nobody has even begun to
trouble you yet? You're like a little child: not happy till he's burned his
fingers! And why are you so anxious? Why this urge to thrust yourself
upon us? What reasons can there be? Eh? Heh-heh-heh!'

'I repeat,' cried Raskolnikov, raging, 'I can no longer endure ...'

'What, sir? Uncertainty?' interrupted Porfiry.

'Don't taunt me! I won't have it! ... I'm telling you, I won't ... I can't and I won't! . . . Do you hear? Do you hear?' he shouted, banging his fist on the table again.

'Not so loud! Quiet, I say! You'll be heard! This is a serious warning: look after yourself. I'm not joking, sir!' Porfiry whispered, but this time the kindly, womanish, alarmed expression of before was nowhere to be seen; on the contrary, now he was giving *orders*, sternly, with knitted brow, as if destroying all secrets and ambiguities at one fell swoop. But this lasted no more than an instant. Briefly bemused, Raskolnikov now flew into a complete frenzy. It was strange, though: once again he obeyed the order to speak quietly, even though he was in the grip of the most violent paroxysm of fury.

'I will not be tortured!' he suddenly whispered in the same voice as before, instantly realizing, with pain and loathing, that he was incapable of not submitting to the order, and becoming even more enraged as a result. 'Arrest me, search me, but kindly observe the correct form. Do not play with me, sir! Don't you dare . . . !'

'Now don't you worry about form,' interrupted Porfiry with the same sly grin as before, observing Raskolnikov admiringly, even delightedly. 'I invited you here, father, as if it were my own home; one friend inviting another, as simple as that!'

'I don't want your friendship – I spit on it! Understand? Look, I'm taking my cap and I'm going. So what do you say to that, if you're still planning to arrest me?'

He grabbed his cap and made for the door.

'What about my little surprise – aren't you interested?' tittered Porfiry, grabbing him again just above the elbow and stopping him by the door. He was becoming ever more jovial and playful, and Raskolnikov could stand it no longer.

'What little surprise? What are you talking about?' he asked, suddenly stopping and staring at Porfiry in alarm.

'Just a little surprise, sir, right there, on the other side of the door, heh-heh-heh!' (He pointed towards the locked door in the partition, which led to his government apartment.) 'I've locked it for the time being, to prevent him escaping.'

'What are you on about? Where? What?' Raskolnikov went over to the door and tried to open it, but it was locked.

'Locked, sir. Here's the key!'

And, indeed, he took a key from his pocket and showed it to him.

'You're still lying!' screeched Raskolnikov, abandoning all self-restraint. 'You're lying, you damned buffoon!' – and he charged at Porfiry, who seemed quite unafraid even as he retreated towards the door.

'I understand everything, everything!' he shouted, leaping towards him. 'You're lying and you're taunting me, until I give myself away . . . !'

'You could hardly give yourself away any more than you have done already, father. Look, you're in a perfect frenzy. Don't yell or I'll call people in, sir!'

'You're lying! Nothing will happen! Call them in! You knew I was sick and you wanted to irritate me, enrage me, until I gave myself away, that's your aim! But where are your facts? I've understood everything! You haven't got any facts, just useless, worthless conjecture borrowed from Zametov! . . . You knew my character. You wanted to drive me into a frenzy, then suddenly club me round the head with priests and deputies[23] . . . Is that who you're waiting for? Eh? Go on then! Where are they? Bring them in!'

'Deputies! What deputies, father? Whatever will he imagine next? We can hardly observe the correct form, as you say, if this is how you're going to be. You don't know how things are done, my dearest . . . There's no running away from form, you'll see,' muttered Porfiry, listening in at the door.

And indeed, at that very moment, from the other side of the door, there came some sort of noise.

'Ah, they're coming!' cried Raskolnikov. 'You sent for them . . . You were waiting for them! You'd counted on . . . Well, bring them all in: deputies, witnesses, the whole lot . . . Go on! I'm ready! Ready!'

But here a strange incident occurred, something so very unexpected, in the normal course of events, that there was simply no way either Raskolnikov or Porfiry Petrovich could ever have anticipated it.

VI

Later, recalling this moment, Raskolnikov would picture it all as follows.

The noise behind the door suddenly grew a great deal louder and the door opened a little.

'What's going on?' snapped Porfiry Petrovich. 'Didn't I tell you . . . ?'

At first there was no reply, but there were clearly several men behind the door, and someone, it seemed, was being pushed aside.

'What's going on out there, I say?' Porfiry Petrovich repeated in alarm.

'We've brought the prisoner, Mikolai,' came someone's voice.

'Not now! Clear off! You'll have to wait! . . . How did he get in here? What a shambles!' yelled Porfiry, rushing towards the door.

'It was him who . . . ,' the same voice began again and suddenly broke off.

There was a second or two, no more, of actual fighting; then, all of a sudden, someone seemed to push someone else forcefully aside, after which a very pale man stepped right into Porfiry Petrovich's office.

This man's appearance, at first glance, was very strange. He looked straight ahead, but it was as if he didn't see anyone. His eyes flashed with determination, yet at the same time a deathly pallor covered his face, as if he were being led to his execution. His lips, now completely white, quivered faintly.

He was still very young, dressed like a commoner, average height, skinny, pudding-bowl hair and fine, somehow dry features. The man who had been unexpectedly shoved aside was the first to chase after him into the room and managed to grab him by the shoulder – he was a guard. But, with a jerk of his arm, Mikolai wrenched himself free once again.

Several curious faces crowded the doorway. Some wanted to get in. It all happened in the blink of an eye.

'Clear off, it's too early! Wait to be called! . . . Why was he brought ahead of time?' Porfiry Petrovich muttered, extremely annoyed, as if knocked off his stride. But Mikolai suddenly dropped to his knees.

'Now what?' shouted Porfiry in amazement.

'I'm guilty! I'm the sinner! I'm the killer!' Mikolai suddenly uttered, fairly loudly, despite seeming short of breath.

The silence lasted ten seconds or so, as if everyone had been struck dumb; even the guard shrank back from Mikolai, retreating mechanically towards the door and standing there without moving.

'What's going on?' cried Porfiry Petrovich, emerging from a momentary stupor.

'I'm . . . the killer . . . ,' Mikolai repeated, after the briefest of pauses.

'How . . . ? You . . . How . . . ? Who have you killed?'

Porfiry Petrovich seemed quite lost.

Again, Mikolai paused briefly.

'Alyona Ivanovna and her sister, Lizaveta Ivanovna. I . . . killed them . . . with an axe. It was like a blackout . . . ,' Mikolai suddenly added and fell silent once more. He was still on his knees.

Porfiry Petrovich stood still for a moment or two, as if deep in thought, then suddenly burst into motion again and began waving his arms at the uninvited witnesses. They vanished in a flash and the door closed. Next Porfiry glanced at Raskolnikov, who was standing in the corner and staring wildly at Mikolai, and made a move towards him, but suddenly stopped, looked at him, immediately transferred his gaze to Mikolai, then back to Raskolnikov, then back to Mikolai and suddenly, as if carried away, went for Mikolai again.

'Why are you trying to get ahead of me?' he yelled at him almost spitefully. 'I don't remember asking you about blackouts . . . So, you killed them?'

'I'm the killer . . . I'm tes . . . testifying . . . ,' uttered Mikolai.

'Dearie me! What did you do it with?'

'An axe. Had one ready.'

'Dearie me, this man's in a hurry! On your own?'

Mikolai failed to grasp the question.

'Did you do it on your own?'

'Yes. And Mitka's innocent and had nothing to do with it.'

'Mitka can wait! Dear oh dear! . . . So – erm – so what on earth were you doing running down the stairs? The caretakers met the pair of you, did they not?'

'That was to . . . distract people . . . me running out with Mitka like that,' Mikolai replied, as if he were hurrying through answers prepared in advance.

'See, just as I thought!' cried Porfiry with spite. 'These aren't his own words!' he muttered, as if to himself, then suddenly noticed Raskolnikov again.

Evidently, he'd got so carried away with Mikolai that he'd forgotten all about Raskolnikov. Now he suddenly came to his senses. He was even embarrassed . . .

'Rodion Romanovich, father! I do apologize,' he said, rushing towards him. 'It's really not on. Please, sir . . . there's no point you . . . I am also . . . So much for surprises! . . . Please, sir . . .'

And, taking him by the arm, he began showing him out.

'You weren't expecting this, it seems?' said Raskolnikov, who was still fairly confused by the whole business, of course, but had perked up considerably.

'You weren't expecting it either, father. My oh my, just look how your hand's shaking! Heh-heh!'

'You're shaking, too, Porfiry Petrovich.'

'So I am, sir. Hadn't expected it, sir!'

They were already at the door. Porfiry was waiting impatiently for Raskolnikov to go through.

'So you won't be showing me your little surprise?' said Raskolnikov suddenly.

'His teeth are chattering, but he's still talking. Heh-heh! You are an ironical man! Well, sir, till next we meet!'

'It's *goodbye*, if you ask me!'

'All in God's hands, sir, all in God's hands!' muttered Porfiry with a rather twisted smile.

Walking through the office, Raskolnikov noticed lots of people staring at him. In the crowded lobby he managed to pick out both of the caretakers from *that* house, the ones he'd been urging to go to the police bureau that night. They were standing there waiting for something. But no sooner had he set foot on the staircase than he suddenly heard Porfiry Petrovich's voice behind him. He turned round to see Porfiry catching up with him, puffing and panting.

'Just one tiny thing, Rodion Romanovich. That's all in God's hands, sir, but still, formally speaking, I will have to ask you one or two questions . . . So we'll see each other again, sir, indeed we will.'

And Porfiry stood still before him, smiling.

'Yes indeedy,' he added.

He seemed to want to say something else, but somehow nothing came out.

'And you forgive me, Porfiry Petrovich, about before . . . I got overexcited,' began Raskolnikov, who'd cheered up so much that he couldn't resist the chance to strike a pose.

'Don't mention it, sir . . . ,' replied Porfiry almost joyfully. 'I, too, sir . . . I've a quite poisonous character, I must admit! So we'll be seeing each other, sir. God permitting, we'll be seeing each other a whole lot more!'

'And we'll get to know each other properly?' rejoined Raskolnikov.

'And we'll get to know each other properly,' echoed Porfiry Petrovich and, screwing up his eyes, gave him an extremely serious look. 'Off to that name-day party, sir?'

'The funeral, sir.'

'Oh yes, the funeral! You take care of your health now, sir, your health . . .'

'I've no idea what I should be wishing *you*!' Raskolnikov replied, suddenly turning round again once he was already on his way down the stairs. 'I'd like to wish you greater success, but look what a comical job you have!'

'But why "comical", sir?'

Porfiry Petrovich, who'd already turned to go back, instantly pricked up his ears.

'Well, what about this poor Mikolka, for example. You must have given him a terrible going over, psychologically, I mean, and in your own particular fashion, until he finally confessed. Day and night you must have been drumming it into him, "You're the murderer, you're the murderer . . ." – and now he's confessed you're stretching him out on the rack again: "Liar, you're not the murderer! You couldn't have been! These aren't your own words!" What's that if not comical?'

'Heh-heh-heh! So you noticed me telling Mikolai just now that those weren't his own words?'

'How could I not?'

'Heh-heh! You're a wit, sir, you really are. Nothing escapes your notice! Such a playful mind, sir! And such a gift for winkling out comedy . . . heh-heh! They say that Gogol, among the writers, had that knack, do they not?'

'That's right, Gogol.'

'Yes, sir, Gogol . . . Well, till next I have the pleasure, sir.'

'Quite so . . .'

Raskolnikov went straight home. He was so muddled and confused that, after returning home and collapsing on his couch, he sat there for a good quarter of an hour, just resting and trying as best he could to collect his thoughts. He didn't even try to make sense of Mikolai: he felt that he was beaten; that Mikolai's confession contained something inexplicable, something astonishing, which for now was utterly beyond his comprehension. But Mikolai's confession was an actual fact. The consequences of this fact instantly became clear to him: it was impossible for the lie to remain uncovered, and then they would be after him once more. But until then, at least, he was free, and he simply had to do something, somehow, to help himself, for the danger was imminent.

But how imminent, exactly? The situation was becoming clearer. Recalling, *in rough*, in its general contours, the whole scene that had just passed between him and Porfiry, he couldn't help shuddering all over again. Of course, he still did not know all of Porfiry's aims, nor could he grasp all of his calculations. But part of the game had been revealed, and he, of course, understood better than anyone the terrifying significance, for him, of this 'move' on Porfiry's part. A little more and he *might* have given himself away completely, as an irreversible fact. Knowing the infirmity of his character, having correctly grasped it and pierced it at first glance, Porfiry had taken excessively drastic, but almost unerring steps. There was no denying that Raskolnikov had already managed, just now, to compromise himself far too much, but there were still no *facts*; everything was still merely relative. On second thoughts, though, perhaps he was missing something? Perhaps he was mistaken? What exactly was Porfiry hoping to achieve today? Had he really prepared anything for him? What exactly? Had he really been waiting for something? How would they have parted today but for the unexpected drama caused by Mikolai?

Porfiry had shown almost his entire hand. He'd taken a risk, of course, but he'd shown it and (so it seemed to Raskolnikov) if he really had had anything more, he'd have shown that, too. What was his 'surprise'? A joke at his expense? Did it mean anything? Could it have contained anything even faintly resembling a fact, a concrete accusation? The man from yesterday? Where had he got to? Where was he today? If Porfiry really did know anything concrete, then it could only be in connection with the man from yesterday . . .

He sat on the couch, his head drooping, his elbows on his knees and his face in his hands. Nervous tremors still coursed through his body. Eventually he got up, took his cap, thought for a moment and made for the door.

Something told him that today, at least, he was almost certainly safe. Suddenly, in his heart, he felt something close to joy: he wanted to get over to Katerina Ivanovna's immediately. It was too late for the funeral, of course, but he'd be in time for the banquet, and there, now, he'd see Sonya.

He stopped, thought for a moment, and his lips forced out a sickly smile.

'Today! Today!' he repeated to himself. 'Yes, today! Has to be . . .'

He was just about to open the door when it suddenly began to open all by itself. He jumped back with a shudder. The door opened slowly and quietly, and there suddenly appeared the figure of yesterday's man *from out of the ground*.

The man paused on the threshold, looked at Raskolnikov without saying anything and took a step into the room. He was no different from yesterday, exactly the same figure, the same clothes, but his face and his gaze had undergone a marked change: there was something doleful about him now and, after standing there a while, he heaved a deep sigh. All it needed was for him to put a palm to his cheek while cocking his head to one side and he could have been taken for a woman.

'What do you want?' asked Raskolnikov, more dead than alive.

The man said nothing, then suddenly made a very low bow, almost to the ground. At the very least, he touched the ground with a finger of his right hand.

'Well?' cried Raskolnikov.

'I'm sorry,' said the man quietly.

'What for?'

'Malicious thoughts.'

Each was looking at the other.

'I felt aggrieved. The way you showed up that time, sir, under the influence, maybe, wanting the caretakers to go down the station and enquiring about blood. Well, I felt aggrieved they let you off and marked you down as a drunk. I was so aggrieved I lost sleep. So, re-calling the address, we came here yesterday and made enquiries . . .'

'Who came?' Raskolnikov interrupted, instantly beginning to re-member.

'I did, I mean. I've done you wrong.'

'So you're from that house?'

'But I was there that time, standing with them under the arch, or have you forgotten? We've even got our own business there, have had for years. We're furriers, tradesmen, we work from home . . . and what aggrieved me most was . . .'

Raskolnikov had a sudden, vivid recollection of the whole scene under the arch two days earlier; it occurred to him that apart from the caretakers there were several other people there, even some women. He remembered one voice suggesting that he be taken straight to the police. He couldn't recall the face of the speaker and didn't recognize him even now, but he did remember making some sort of reply to him then, and turning towards him . . .

So here was the solution to yesterday's dreadful riddle! Most dread-ful of all was to think how very close he'd come to his own, self-inflicted ruin, all on account of such a *paltry* circumstance. So aside from the talk of renting an apartment and of blood, this man had nothing to tell. So Porfiry also had nothing, nothing except that *delirium*, no facts except *psychology*, which is *double-edged*, nothing concrete. So if no more facts emerged (and why on earth should they?), then ... then what could they do with him? How could they expose him definitively, even if they arrested him? So Porfiry had only found out about the apartment now – and had known nothing before.

'Was it you who told Porfiry today ... about me showing up that time?' he cried, struck by an unexpected idea.

'Which Porfiry?'

'The chief investigator.'

'Yes, it was me. The caretakers didn't go, so I went instead.'

'Today?'

'Barely a minute before you. And I heard everything, heard him torture you.'

'Where? What? When?'

'Right there, behind that partition of his. I was sitting there all that time.'

'What? So *you* were the surprise? How on earth did that happen? Incredible!'

'When we saw,' the tradesman began, 'that the caretakers weren't having any of my suggestion, because, they said, it was too late, and anyway he'd probably be angry we hadn't come right away, I was aggrieved and started losing sleep, and began making enquiries. Yesterday I found out and today I went. First time I went he weren't there. Came back an hour later – he couldn't see me; came back a third time – admitted. I started filling him in on everything and he started hopping about the room and beating his chest. "What are you doing to me, you brigands?" he said. "If I'd only known such a thing, I'd have had him brought in under escort!" Then he ran out, called someone and began talking to him in the corner, then back to me again – asking me questions and cursing. He weren't happy with me at all. I told him everything and said that you didn't dare answer me at all yesterday and hadn't recognized me. So he started haring about the room and beating his chest, and getting angry, and running around again, and when you were announced – "All right," he says, "get yourself behind the partition; sit there for the time being and don't budge, whatever you hear," and he brought me a chair himself and locked me in. "I might even ask for you," he says. But when Mikolai was brought in, well, he showed me out, after you. "I'll need you again," he says, "I'll have more questions for you . . ." '

'So were you there when he questioned Mikolai?'

'First he showed you out, then me straight after, and then he began interrogating Mikolai.'

The tradesman paused and suddenly bowed once again, touching the floor with his finger.

'Forgive my slander and malice.'

'God will forgive,' replied Raskolnikov, and no sooner had he said this than the tradesman made another bow, though not to the ground, turned and walked out. 'Everything is double-edged now; yes, everything is double-edged,' Raskolnikov kept saying and left the room in better spirits than ever.

'So the fight goes on,' he said with a spiteful smile as he went down the stairs. His spite was directed at himself, and the memory of his 'petty cowardice' filled him with contempt and shame.

PART FIVE

I

The morning after his fateful conversation with Dunechka and Pulkheria Alexandrovna had a sobering effect on Pyotr Petrovich as well.
He, to his very greatest displeasure, was obliged, little by little, to accept
as an accomplished and irrevocable fact an event that only yesterday
had seemed to him almost fantastical and, though it had already happened, still somehow impossible. All night long the black serpent of
wounded pride had sucked at his heart. Getting out of his bed, Pyotr
Petrovich immediately looked in the mirror. Might he have had an
attack of bile overnight? No, there were no concerns on that score for
the time being, and after a glance at his noble, white and lately somewhat flabby countenance Pyotr Petrovich even cheered up a little,
fully determined to find himself a bride somewhere else and, perhaps,
a rather better one; but he instantly came to his senses and spat vigorously over his shoulder, thereby eliciting a silent but sarcastic smile
from his young friend and room-mate Andrei Semyonovich Lebezyatnikov. Pyotr Petrovich noted the smile and immediately held it against
him. He'd been holding a lot of things against his young friend recently. His spite was redoubled when he suddenly realized how unwise it had been of him yesterday to inform Andrei Semyonovich of
the outcome of the conversation. That had been his second mistake,
made in the heat of the moment, from an excess of candour and irritation . . . And the rest of the morning, as ill luck would have it, was
one unpleasantness after another. There was even a setback waiting
for him in the Senate, on some case he was working on. Especially
irritating was the landlord of the apartment which he'd rented with a
view to his imminent marriage and done up at his own expense: nothing could persuade this landlord, some German craftsman flush with
money, to rescind their freshly signed contract; in fact, he demanded
full payment of the penalty stipulated therein, despite the fact that
Pyotr Petrovich was returning to him an almost entirely redecorated
apartment. Similarly, the furniture shop refused to return a single
rouble of the deposit on the goods that had been bought but not yet

delivered. 'I can hardly get married just for a few tables and chairs!' thought Pyotr Petrovich, grinding his teeth, and as he did so a desperate hope flashed across his mind once more: 'Is the situation really so irretrievable? Is it really all over? Surely I can have one more go?' The delicious thought of Dunechka pricked his heart once more. This moment was sheer agony and if he had only been able, by merely desiring it, to kill Raskolnikov there and then, Pyotr Petrovich would surely have voiced that desire without delay.

'Another mistake was never giving them any money,' he thought, returning sadly to Lebezyatnikov's tiny room. 'Why did I have to make such a Jew of myself? It didn't even make any sense! I thought if I treated them meanly enough they'd end up viewing me as Providence itself – so much for that! . . . Pah! . . . No, if only I'd given them fifteen hundred, say, to tide them over, to spend on the trousseau and on gifts, on nice little boxes, toilet cases, cornelians, fabrics and all that tat from Knop's and the English Shop,[1] everything would have worked out a whole lot better . . . and with far less uncertainty! They wouldn't have found it so easy to refuse me, then! They're just the kind of people who always consider it their duty, in the event of a refusal, to return both the gifts and the money; but they'd have been too sorry to part with them! Plus, their conscience would have bothered them: how can we suddenly turn out a man who's been so generous till now and actually rather considerate? . . . H'm! What a blunder!' Grinding his teeth again, Pyotr Petrovich promptly called himself an idiot – under his breath, needless to say.

Reaching this conclusion, he returned home twice as cross and irritated as when he'd left. The preparations for the funeral banquet in Katerina Ivanovna's room offered some distraction. He'd already heard a little about this banquet yesterday; he even seemed to recall being invited along himself; but with so many worries of his own, he hadn't paid the slightest attention. Now he lost no time in asking Mrs Lippewechsel – she was fussing around the dining table, making preparations in the absence of Katerina Ivanovna (who was at the cemetery) – and learned that the banquet would be a grand affair, that nearly all the tenants were invited, among them some who had never even met the deceased, that even Andrei Semyonovich Lebezyatnikov had been invited, despite his previous row with Katerina Ivanovna, and, finally, that he, Pyotr Petrovich, was not only invited but eagerly awaited, as virtually the most important guest of all the tenants. Mrs Lippewechsel had also been invited with great fanfare, despite all the unpleasant things that had happened, which was why she was now giving orders, fussing about and almost enjoying herself; and though dressed for mourning, she wore brand-new silk from top to toe and wore it proudly. All this information put a thought in Pyotr Petrovich's mind and he went through to his room – which is to say Andrei Semyonovich Lebezyatnikov's room – in a rather pensive mood: for he'd learned that Raskolnikov, too, was invited.

For some reason, Andrei Semyonovich had spent the whole morning at home. The relationship Pyotr Petrovich had established with this gentleman was somewhat strange, though in some ways also quite natural: Pyotr Petrovich despised and loathed him beyond measure, almost from the day he'd moved in, yet at the same time he felt a kind of wariness towards him. A tight wallet wasn't the only reason he'd decided to stay with Andrei Semyonovich on arriving in Petersburg, though it was more or less the main one; there was another reason, too. Even back in the provinces he'd heard Andrei Semyonovich, his former charge, being spoken of as a leading young progressive, even as a major player in certain intriguing and legendary circles. This had come as a shock to Pyotr Petrovich. It was just these circles – powerful, all-knowing, all-despising, all-unmasking – that had long filled Pyotr Petrovich with some special, though utterly obscure, terror. Of course, there was no way that he – in the provinces, to boot – could have formed an accurate notion, even approximately, about anything *of this sort*. Like everyone else he'd heard of the existence, especially in Petersburg, of progressivists, nihilists and so on, but, like many, he'd exaggerated and distorted the meaning and significance of these words to the point of absurdity. What had scared him most, for several years now, was *to be shown up*, and this was the chief cause of his constant, disproportionate anxiety, especially when dreaming of his professional relocation to Petersburg. In this respect he was, as they say, *frightened to bits*, in the way that little children are sometimes *frightened to bits*. Several years earlier, in the country, when his career was only just getting started, he'd encountered two incidents in which fairly important local individuals, to whose patronage he'd clung, were cruelly shown up. One ended in a manner that was quite unusually scandalous for the person in question, while the other almost proved very troublesome indeed. So Pyotr Petrovich had resolved, on arriving in Petersburg, to find out right away what was behind it all and, if necessary, to get ahead of the game just in case by currying favour with 'our young generations'. For this, he relied on Andrei Semyonovich, and by the time he visited Raskolnikov, he'd already learned to get his tongue around a few well-worn, borrowed phrases . . .

Of course, it didn't take him long to identify Andrei Semyonovich as an exceptionally crass and simple-minded individual. But this did nothing to reassure or hearten Pyotr Petrovich. Even if he had managed to convince himself that all progressivists were equally stupid, it would have done nothing to relieve his anxiety. Frankly, he couldn't care less about all the doctrines, philosophies and systems which Andrei Semyonovich was in such a hurry to share with him. He had his own goal in mind. The only thing that mattered to him was to find out right away: what had happened *here* and how had it come about? Were *these people* in the ascendant or were they not? Did he himself have anything to fear or did he not? Would he be shown up if he undertook this or that, or would he not? If yes, then what for exactly? What *were* people shown up for nowadays? And another thing: couldn't he butter them up somehow and then trick them, if they really were in the ascendant? Or maybe he shouldn't? Mightn't he even use them to make some headway in his own career? In short, hundreds of questions confronted him.

This Andrei Semyonovich was an under-nourished, scrofulous little man with a job in some department, peculiarly blond hair and mutton-chop whiskers of which he was very proud. On top of that his eyes were almost always sore. He was soft-hearted enough, but he spoke with great confidence and sometimes exceptional arrogance – the effect of which, given his stature, was almost always comical. Still, Mrs Lippewechsel numbered him among her more distinguished tenants – i.e., he didn't get drunk and he paid on time. For all these qualities Andrei Semyonovich really was rather dense. He'd signed up to progress, together with 'our young generations', out of mere enthusiasm. He was one of that numberless and motley legion of crass, wilting halfwits – half-educated, pig-headed fools – who are always the first to jump on the latest intellectual bandwagon, so as to cheapen every idea right away and reduce to ridicule whatever they venerate, however sincerely.

But Lebezyatnikov, for all his niceness, was also beginning to find his room-mate and former guardian, Pyotr Petrovich, a touch unbearable. On both sides this process had somehow just happened of its own accord. Andrei Semyonovich may have been somewhat simple, but even he had begun, little by little, to see that Pyotr Petrovich was playing him for a fool and secretly despised him; that 'this man is not what he seems'. He'd wanted to introduce him to Fourier's system and Darwin's theory,[2] but Pyotr Petrovich, especially recently, had started listening with a little too much sarcasm, and more recently still, had actually become quite abusive. By instinct more than anything, it was beginning to get through to him that Lebezyatnikov was not just a crass and rather stupid little man but possibly a fibber to boot, and that he had no connections worth talking about at all, not even in his own circle, but merely heard this or that at third hand; not only that: he didn't even seem to be much good at this *propaganda* of his, to judge by all the muddles he kept getting himself into; as if he could show anyone up! We should note in passing that, in the course of these ten days, Pyotr Petrovich had (especially at the beginning) gladly accepted all manner of strange compliments from Andrei Semyonovich, never correcting him or objecting if, say, Andrei Semyonovich ascribed to him a willingness to facilitate the imminent construction of a new *commune* somewhere on Meshchanskaya Street,[3] or a refusal to stand in Dunechka's way if she, in the very first month of marriage, felt like taking a lover, and to have his future children baptized, and so on and so forth – all in the same vein. Pyotr Petrovich, as was his habit, did not object to such qualities being ascribed to him and found even this sort of praise acceptable – indeed, any compliment at all was music to his ears.

Having cashed several five per cent bonds that morning for some purpose or other, Pyotr Petrovich was sitting at the table and counting bundles of banknotes and Treasury notes. Andrei Semyonovich, almost always penniless, was walking around the room pretending (to himself) that he was observing all these bundles with indifference and even disdain. Nothing, of course, would ever have persuaded Pyotr Petrovich that Andrei Semyonovich could observe so much money with indifference; and Andrei Semyonovich, for his part, was reflecting bitterly on the fact that Pyotr Petrovich was more than capable of entertaining such thoughts about him and was probably only too glad to have the chance to tickle and taunt his young friend with this display of banknotes, the better to put him in his place and remind him of the gulf that was meant to lie between them.

On this occasion he found him quite exceptionally irritable and inattentive, despite the fact that he, Andrei Semyonovich, had launched into his favourite topic: the founding of a new and special 'commune'. The terse objections and remarks that escaped Pyotr Petrovich in the intervals between the clinking of abacus beads exuded the most blatant and deliberately discourteous scorn. But Andrei Semyonovich, being so very 'humane', put Pyotr Petrovich's mood down to the effects of yesterday's rift with Dunechka, and had a burning desire to broach this subject as quickly as possible: he had something progressivist and propagandicist to say about it, something that would console his esteemed friend and 'undoubtedly' advance his subsequent development.

'What's all this about some funeral banquet over at that . . . widow's?' Pyotr Petrovich suddenly asked, interrupting Andrei Semyonovich at the most interesting point.

'As if you don't know. Only yesterday I was discussing this very subject with you and gave you my opinion of all these rites and rituals . . . Anyway, she's invited you along, too. I heard as much. You spoke with her yesterday yourself . . .'

'I could never have imagined that this fool of a beggar would go and fritter away all the money she got from that other fool, Raskolnikov, on a banquet. I was quite amazed as I walked past just now: so many preparations, so much wine! Several people have been invited – whatever next?' continued Pyotr Petrovich, who seemed to be driving at something with all his comments and questions. 'What? She's invited me along too, you say?' he suddenly added, lifting his head. 'When was that? Can't say I remember. Anyway, I won't go. Me, there? Yesterday, in passing, I merely mentioned to her the possibility of her receiving, as the destitute widow of a civil servant, a year's salary as a lump-sum payment. Surely that's not why she's inviting me, is it? Heh-heh!'

'I don't intend to go, either,' said Lebezyatnikov.

'I dare say! Not after that pummelling. No wonder you're ashamed, heh-heh-heh!'

'Who pummelled who?' asked Lebezyatnikov, suddenly flustered and even turning red.

'You pummelled Katerina Ivanovna a month or so ago, I believe! I heard about it, sir, just yesterday . . . So much for all those convictions of yours! . . . And so much for the Woman Question, heh-heh-heh!'

Cheering up a bit, Pyotr Petrovich set about clicking his beads again.

'Hogwash and slander, all of it!' flared Lebezyatnikov, always fearful of any allusion to this episode. 'That's not how it was at all! It was quite different . . . You got the wrong end of the stick. Sheer gossip! I was merely defending myself. She was the one who went at me with her claws . . . Barely left a whisker in place . . . All men, I trust, are permitted to defend their person. Moreover, I will not permit anyone to use force against me . . . On principle. Because that's tyranny, more or less. What was I supposed to do, just stand there? All I did was push her away.'

'Heh-heh-heh!' Luzhin continued to scoff.

'You're only picking on me because you're angry and peeved yourself . . . But this is pure hogwash and has nothing whatsoever to do with the Woman Question! You've got it all wrong. I even used to think that if women really are men's equal now, even in strength (as some are already claiming), then there should be equality here as well. Later, of course, I reasoned that, in essence, such a question should not arise, because fights should not arise, and that fights in the society of the future are inconceivable . . . and that it's rather strange, of course, to demand equality in fighting. I'm not that stupid . . . although fighting is . . . I mean, there won't be any later, but as of now there still is . . . Ugh! Dammit! Anyone would get in a muddle talking to you! I'm not not going to the banquet on account of that unpleasantness. I'm not going on principle, simple as that. I want no part in the vile preconception of funeral banquets! Although, I suppose one might go just to laugh . . . A shame there won't be any priests. Otherwise I'd have been there like a shot.'

'So you would enjoy someone's hospitality while insulting it and those who invited you. Is that what you mean?'

'Not insulting – protesting. For a useful cause: I may thereby be of indirect benefit to the cause of enlightenment and propaganda. Every man has a duty to enlighten and propagandize, and the harsher the message, perhaps, the better. I can thereby scatter ideas, seeds . . . From the seed will grow a fact. In what way am I offending them? First they'll take offence, then they'll see for themselves that I've done them a favour. Take Terebyeva (she's in the commune now), only recently she was being criticized for how, when she left her family and . . . gave herself . . . she wrote a letter to her mother and father saying she didn't want to live among preconceptions and was entering into a civil marriage;[4] apparently this was too rude, writing to your parents like that, and she should have spared their feelings and been a little more gentle. Utter hogwash, if you ask me. You shouldn't be gentle, far from it – you should protest. Look at Varents: spent seven

years with her husband, abandoned her two children and fired off a
letter to her husband: "I realized that with you I could never be happy.
I will never forgive you for deceiving me by concealing the fact that a
different social order exists, via the commune. I learned all this recently from a certain high-minded man, to whom I gave myself, and
together we will start a commune. I speak frankly because I think it
dishonourable to deceive you. Carry on as you see fit. Do not hope to
get me back. You are too late for that. I wish you happiness." Now
that's the way to write 'em!'

'This Terebyeva, isn't she the one you said was in her third civil
marriage?'

'Only her second proper one, as it happens! But anyway, fourth,
tenth or fifteenth, so what? And if there was ever a time I regretted the
death of my father and mother, then, of course, it's now. I keep dreaming about how, if only they were still alive, I'd really give it to them
hot! When they were least expecting it . . . Another young man who's
"flown the nest",[5] they'd say. H'm! I'd show them what protest means!
I'd shock them! Such a shame there's no one left!'

'No one left to surprise, you mean? Heh-heh! Well, have it your
way,' Pyotr Petrovich interrupted. 'But tell me this: I believe you know
the daughter of the late departed, that slip of a girl! Well, is it really
true what they say about her, eh?'

'What are you saying? My opinion – my personal conviction, I
mean – is that there can be no more normal state for a woman. And
why not? Well, *distinguons*.[6] In today's society, of course, it is not
quite normal, because it is forced, but in the future it will be entirely
normal, because it will be free. But even now she had the right: she
was suffering and this was her fund, her capital, as it were, which she
had every right to dispose of. In the society of the future, of course,
there'll be no need for funds; but her role will signify a different
significance – it will be elegantly and rationally determined. As for
Sofya Semyonovna, at the present time I view her actions as a vigorous and embodied protest against the social order and I respect her
deeply for it. I am overjoyed just to look at her!'

'But I was told it was you who forced her out of this building!'
Lebezyatnikov went positively berserk.

'More gossip!' he shrieked. 'That's not how it was at all! Not at all!
I mean, really! It was all Katerina Ivanovna's invention – she hadn't
understood a thing! I wasn't making up to Sofya Semyonovna in the

slightest! I was simply enlightening her, without a thought for myself, striving to rouse her to protest . . . That was all I was after! And anyway, Sofya Semyonovna could hardly have stayed on here.'

'Invited her into the commune, did you?'

'These jokes of yours are pretty feeble, if you don't mind my saying so. You don't understand a thing! In the commune, this role does not exist. That's why people found communes in the first place. In the commune, the essence of this role will be completely transformed: what is stupid here will become clever there, and what, in the current circumstances, is unnatural here will be entirely natural there. Everything depends on a man's circumstances and environment. Environment is everything, man is nothing. Sofya Semyonovna and I get on well to this day, which you may take as proof that she never took offence at me or thought me her enemy. Yes! I may be tempting her into the commune, but my grounds for doing so are quite different, quite different! What's so funny? We want to found our own commune, a special commune, on broader grounds than the previous ones. We've gone further in our convictions. We reject even more! Were Dobrolyubov to rise from his grave, I'd argue with him. Not to mention Belinsky[7] – I'd pulverise *him*! But meanwhile I'll carry on enlightening Sofya Semyonovna. She has a beautiful, beautiful character!'

'And you make good use of her beautiful character, I suppose? Heh-heh!'

'No! Goodness, no! On the contrary!'

'On the contrary, my foot! Heh-heh-heh! Well said!'

'Believe me! What reasons could I possibly have to lie to you? Tell me that! On the contrary, I myself find it strange: with me she's somehow even chaster and coyer than usual!'

'And you, needless to say, enlighten her . . . heh-heh . . . and tell her how silly it is to be coy?'

'Not at all! Not at all! Oh, how crudely, how stupidly even – do forgive me – you understand the word "enlightenment"! You don't understand a thing about it! Goodness me, how very . . . immature you are! We want women's freedom, but you have only one thing on your mind . . . Leaving completely to one side the question of chastity and female coyness, as things that are useless in themselves and even preconceived, I fully, fully accept her chastity towards me, because that is her freedom, that is her right. Of course, if she were to say to me, "I want to have you," I'd think myself a very lucky man, because

I like the girl very much: but for now, at the very least, could anyone have treated her more courteously or considerately than I, or with greater respect for her dignity . . . ? I wait and hope – that's all!'

'You'd be better off giving her something. I dare say the thought's never even crossed your mind.'

'You don't understand a thing, I say! Her situation is what it is, but I'm talking about something different here! Quite different! You have nothing but contempt for her. Seeing a fact which you mistakenly deem worthy of contempt, you refuse to view a person with any humanity. You know nothing of her character! Only one thing upsets me: recently, for some reason, she's completely stopped reading and no longer borrows books from me. She certainly used to. And it's also a shame that with all her vigour and determination to protest – which she's proved once already – there still doesn't seem to be quite enough self-sufficiency about her, enough independence, as it were, enough negation, so as to make a clean break with various preconceptions and . . . idiocies. Nevertheless, there are some questions she understands extremely well. She grasped the question of hand-kissing superbly well, for example: how a man insults a woman through the unequal gesture of hand-kissing.[8] We'd had a debate about it and I immediately informed her of what was said. She also listened attentively when I told her about workers' associations in France.[9] Now I'm explaining the question of open doors[10] in the society of the future.'

'And what on earth's that?'

'Recently there was a debate on the question: does a member of a commune have the right to enter another member's room, a man's or a woman's, at any time he or she chooses . . . ? Well, it was decided that yes, the member does . . .'

'And what if he or she happens to be attending to their essential needs? Heh-heh!'

Andrei Semyonovich became positively angry.

'Is that all you can talk about, these blasted "needs"?' he cried with loathing. 'Ugh, I'm so furious and annoyed with myself for mentioning them to you when I was explaining the system that time – I should have waited! Damn it! It's always a sticking point for people like you. Not only that – they don't even know what they're making fun of! And they think they're right! They're even proud of themselves! Ugh! Haven't I stated several times that this whole question should be explained to novices only at the very end, once they are already convinced about the system, once they've already been enlightened and guided? And anyway, pray tell me what you find so shameful and despicable about, say, cess-pits?[11] I'd be the first to clean out any cesspit you care to mention! And without the slightest self-sacrifice! It's just work; a noble, socially useful activity, as good as any other and certainly far better, say, than the activ-ity of some Raphael or Pushkin. Why? Because it's more useful!'[12]

'And noble, nobler – heh-heh-heh!'

'What does "nobler" mean? I don't understand such expressions when applied to human activity. "Nobler", "more high-minded", etcetera – it's all hogwash, mere absurdities, the old preconceived lan-guage which I reject! Whatever is *useful* to humanity is thereby noble![13] That's the only word I understand: *useful*! Snigger all you like, but that's how it is!'

Pyotr Petrovich just couldn't stop laughing. He'd finished counting the money and put it away. Some of it, though, remained on the table. This wasn't the first time that the 'cesspit question', for all its vulgar-ity, had caused rifts and disagreements between Pyotr Petrovich and his young friend. The stupidest thing was that Andrei Semyonovich really did get angry. Pyotr Petrovich found it all a pleasant distraction and right now he had a particular urge to rile his friend.

'You're still cross about yesterday's setback – that's why you're so tetchy,' Lebezyatnikov finally snapped. On the whole, for all his 'inde-pendence' and for all his 'protests', he didn't quite dare stand up to Pyotr Petrovich, and, from long-established habit, continued to treat him with respect.

'Tell you what,' Luzhin interrupted in a haughty, irritated tone, 'would you be able . . . or rather, are you really on close enough terms with the aforementioned young person to ask her to come over, right now, just for a minute, to this room? It seems they're already all back from the cemetery . . . I can hear people walking around . . . I need to see her, the one we mentioned, I mean.'

'You? But why?' Lebezyatnikov asked in amazement.

'I just do, sir. I'll be leaving in the next day or two, which is why I'd like to tell her . . . But why don't you stay here while we're having our talk? That would be even better. Otherwise, God knows what you might think.'

'I wouldn't think anything . . . I was merely asking. Of course I can call her over if you have business with her. I'll go now. And rest as-sured, I won't get in the way.'

Sure enough, some five minutes later Lebezyatnikov came back with Sonechka. She entered the room in complete astonishment, as shy as ever. She was always shy at moments like these and had a great fear of new faces and new acquaintances; she'd always had it, even as a child, but now more than ever . . . Pyotr Petrovich greeted her 'warmly and courteously', though not without a hint of the kind of light-hearted familiarity which he deemed appropriate to such a distinguished and respectable man as himself in relation to such a young and, in a certain sense, *interesting* creature. He hastened to 'reassure' her and sat her opposite him. Sonya sat down and looked around – at Lebezyatnikov, at the money lying on the table, then suddenly back at Pyotr Petrovich again, her eyes never leaving him from that moment on, as if riveted. Lebezyatnikov moved towards the door. Pyotr Petrovich got up, gestured to Sonya to stay seated and stopped Lebezyatnikov in the doorway.

'Is that Raskolnikov there? Has he come?' he asked in a whisper.

'Raskolnikov? Yes. What about him? Yes, yes . . . He arrived just now, I saw . . . What about it?'

'Well in that case I must ask you to stay here, with us, and not leave me alone with this . . . young girl. It's a trivial matter, but God knows what conclusions people may jump to. I don't want Raskolnikov talking about it *over there* . . . Do you follow?'

'Ah yes, yes!' said Lebezyatnikov, suddenly grasping the point. 'Yes, you have every right . . . Your fears may be rather far-fetched, if you ask me, but still . . . you have every right. Very well, I'll stay. I'll stand here by the window and I won't get in your way . . . In my opinion, you have every right . . .'

Pyotr Petrovich returned to the couch, made himself comfortable opposite Sonya, looked at her closely and suddenly assumed a very imposing, even stern, air, as if to say, 'Now don't you go thinking anything, young miss.' Sonya's embarrassment was complete.

'First of all, Sofya Semyonovna, please apologize on my behalf to your much-esteemed mama . . . That's right, isn't it? Katerina Ivanovna is like a mother to you, is she not?' Pyotr Petrovich began imposingly, though not without warmth. It was clear he had the friendliest of intentions.

'Yes, just so, sir. Like a mother, sir,' came Sonya's hurried and timid reply.

'Well, miss, please explain to her that, as a result of circumstances

beyond my control, I am obliged to absent myself and shan't be joining you for the pancakes . . . I mean banquet, despite your mama's
kind invitation.'

'Yes, sir. I will, sir. At once, sir.' Sonechka fairly leapt from her
chair.

'But that's not *all*,' Pyotr Petrovich stopped her, smiling at her
simple-minded ignorance of social niceties. 'You clearly don't know
me very well, Sofya Semyonovna, if you think that such a trivial matter, concerning no one but me, could be enough to induce me to trouble such a person as you. I have a different purpose.'

Sonya hurriedly sat down. The grey and rainbow-coloured banknotes[14] that had not been cleared from the table flashed before her
eyes once more, but she quickly turned her face away and raised it to
Pyotr Petrovich: it suddenly struck her as dreadfully unseemly, especially *for her*, to look at another person's money. She began to fix her
gaze on Pyotr Petrovich's gold lorgnette, which he was holding in his
left hand, and also at the large, hefty, exceptionally beautiful ring
with a yellow stone on the middle finger of this hand – then suddenly
looked away from that, too, and, not knowing what to do with herself, ended up staring straight into Pyotr Petrovich's eyes again. After
an even more imposing silence than before, the latter continued:

'It so happened that yesterday, in passing, I exchanged a few words
with the unfortunate Katerina Ivanovna. These few words were suffi-
cient to ascertain that her current condition is, if one may use the
term, unnatural . . .'

'Yes, sir . . . unnatural, sir,' Sonya hurriedly echoed.

'Or, to put it more simply, she's ill.'

'Yes, sir, to put it . . . Yes, sir, she's ill.'

'Quite. Well then, from a humane and, as it were, compassionate
impulse, so to speak, I would, for my part, like to be of some use, in
anticipation of her inevitable fate. It would seem that this poor, destitute family now depends on you and you alone.'

'May I ask,' said Sonya, suddenly rising, 'what it was you kindly
said to her yesterday about the possibility of a pension? Because she
told me yesterday that you have taken it upon yourself to see to a pension for her. Is that true, sir?'

'Not at all, miss. In fact, that's almost absurd. I merely alluded to
temporary assistance for the widows of civil servants who die while still
in service – assuming, of course, they have a patron – but it appears

that not only did your late parent not serve his time, but recently he wasn't even serving at all. In short, what hope there was has proved highly ephemeral, because, in essence, no grounds for assistance exist in this case. In fact, just the opposite . . . And she's already thinking about a pension, heh-heh-heh! She's a plucky one!'

'Yes, sir, a pension . . . She's gullible and good, you see, so good she believes everything and . . . and . . . and . . . what a mind she has . . . Yes, sir . . . sorry, sir,' said Sonya and again got up to leave.

'That's not all, miss.'

'No, sir, not all, sir,' muttered Sonya.

'Well sit down, then.'

Terribly abashed, Sonya sat down once again, for a third time.

'Seeing the nature of her plight, and her unfortunate infants, I should like – as I have already said – to make myself, insofar as my means permit, useful in some way; as I say, only insofar as my means permit, miss, no more than that. One could, for example, collect contributions for her or, say, organize a lottery . . . or something of the kind – as is always done in such cases by friends and family or by outsiders who simply wish to help. Now that is what I intended to tell you about. It could be done, miss.'

'Yes, sir, very good, sir . . . May God . . . ,' babbled Sonya, staring at Pyotr Petrovich.

'Could be done, miss . . . but that's for later . . . Actually, why don't we make a start today? We could meet this evening, come to an arrangement and establish, as it were, a foundation. Come and find me here at about seven. Andrei Semyonovich, I hope, will also join us . . . But . . . one particular circumstance needs to be mentioned in advance and in detail. Indeed, Sofya Semyonovna, it is for this reason that I have troubled you now. Specifically, miss, it would be unwise, in my view, to give money to Katerina Ivanovna directly; today's banquet is proof of the fact. Without, as it were, one crust of daily food for tomorrow, without . . . well, shoes and all of that, she goes and purchases Jamaican rum for today and even, if I'm not mistaken, Madeira and coffee. I noticed while walking past. But tomorrow it'll be you picking up the pieces, down to the last crumb of bread. It's just absurd, miss. Which is why the contributions, in my personal view, should be collected in such a way that the unfortunate widow, as it were, would not know about the money, and you, for example, would be the only one who did. Am I right?'

'I don't know, sir. It's only today she's like that, sir . . . Just once in all her life . . . She so much wanted to do something in his honour, in his memory . . . and she's so clever, sir. But as you wish, sir, and I will be very, very . . . They will all be very, very . . . And may God . . . and the orphans, sir . . .'

Sonya didn't finish and burst into tears.

'I see. Well, miss, bear that in mind; and now kindly accept, in your relative's interests and as my means permit, this initial sum from me personally. I do most sincerely hope that my name shall not be mentioned in this connection. Here you are, miss . . . Having, as it were, preoccupations of my own, this is as much as I . . .'

With that, Pyotr Petrovich held out a ten-rouble banknote, unfolding it with great care. Sonya took it, flushed, leapt to her feet, muttered something and began hastily taking her leave. Pyotr Petrovich accompanied her solemnly to the door. Eventually she all but ran out of the room, overwhelmed and exhausted, and returned to Katerina Ivanovna in a state of the most extreme confusion.

Andrei Semyonovich spent the duration of the scene either standing by the window or walking around the room, reluctant to interrupt the conversation; but just as soon as Sonya left, he walked up to Pyotr Petrovich and solemnly extended his hand.

'I heard everything and I *saw* everything,' he said, laying particular emphasis on the penultimate word. 'How noble . . . I mean to say, how very humane! You wished to avoid being thanked, I saw! And while I admit that I am unable, on principle, to approve of private charity, which not only fails to eradicate evil at its core but actually provides it with further sustenance, nevertheless I am unable not to admit that it was a pleasure to observe your action – yes indeed, a pleasure.'

'Pah, what nonsense!' muttered Pyotr Petrovich, who was somewhat restless and kept stealing glances at Lebezyatnikov.

'No it isn't! Here you are, a man insulted and exasperated by yesterday's incident, yet still able to consider the misfortune of others – such a man, sir . . . though he may be committing a social error with his actions . . . is, nevertheless, worthy of respect! In fact, you've surprised me, Pyotr Petrovich, especially since your own ideas – oh! How these ideas of yours still hold you back! How upset you are, for example, by yesterday's setback!' exclaimed Andrei Semyonovich with his customary niceness, feeling another surge of goodwill towards Pyotr Petrovich. 'And why, why are you so set on this marriage, on this *lawful* marriage, most noble, most courteous Pyotr Petrovich? Why must you have this *lawfulness* in marriage? Well, punch me if you wish, but I'm so glad it didn't come off, that you're free, that you're not yet entirely lost to humanity. Yes, I'm glad . . . There, I've said my piece!'

'For the simple reason, sir, that I have no wish, in this civil marriage of yours, to wear horns and raise other people's children – that's why I need a lawful marriage,' said Luzhin by way of an answer. He was, for some reason, especially preoccupied and pensive.

'Children? Did I hear you say children?' asked Andrei Semyonovich with a start, like a warhorse hearing the battle trumpet. 'Children are a social question and a question of prime importance, I agree, but this question will have a different solution. Some go so far as to reject children entirely, together with any allusion to family life. We'll talk about children later, but first let's deal with the horns! It's my weak point, I'll admit. This vile, hussarish Pushkinism[15] is inconceivable in the lexicon of the future. What are horns anyway? Oh, what a fallacy! Which horns? Why horns? What nonsense! On the contrary, in a civil marriage there won't be any horns! Horns are merely the natural consequence of any lawful marriage, its corrective, a protest, so in this sense they aren't even remotely demeaning . . . And if I ever – to take an absurd example – find myself in a lawful marriage, I'll be only too glad to wear your sodding horns, and I'll tell my wife: "My dear, before I merely loved you, but now I respect you,[16] because you've managed to protest!" You're laughing? Only because you're unable to abandon your preconceptions! I understand perfectly well how unpleasant it is to be cuckolded in a lawful marriage, dammit; but this is merely the lousy consequence of a lousy fact, whereby both parties are demeaned. When horns are on open display, as they are in a civil marriage, they no longer exist, they're inconceivable and can no longer even be described as horns. On the contrary, your wife will simply be showing you how much she respects you by deeming you incapable of standing in the way of her happiness and enlightened enough not to seek revenge for her new husband. Dammit, I sometimes dream of how, were I to be married off – sorry, I mean were I ever to marry (be it a civil or a lawful marriage) – I'd bring my wife a lover myself, if she were slow to take one. "My dear," I would say to her, "I love you, but on top of that I would like you to respect me – so here you go!" I'm right, am I not?'

Pyotr Petrovich tittered as he listened, but without any great enthusiasm. He wasn't even really listening. He had something else on his mind and even Lebezyatnikov eventually noticed. In fact, Pyotr Petrovich was quite excited about something, rubbing his hands and lost in thought. Only later did Andrei Semyonovich remember this and piece it all together . . .

II

It would be hard to identify with any precision the reasons that gave rise, in the distressed mind of Katerina Ivanovna, to the notion of this idiotic banquet. Nearly half of the twenty-odd roubles received from Raskolnikov and intended for the funeral itself had been thrown at it. Perhaps Katerina Ivanovna felt that she owed it to the deceased to honour his memory by 'doing things properly', in order that all the tenants, and especially Amalia Ivanovna Lippewechsel, understood that not only was Marmeladov 'not one whit worse' than them, but very possibly 'a cut above them', and that none of them had any right to 'turn their nose up' at him. Perhaps the most influential factor here was that particular *pauper's pride*, whereby certain social rituals, deemed obligatory for all and sundry in our country, lead many to stretch their resources to the limit and spend what few copecks they've saved merely in order to be 'no worse than the others' and to prevent any of these others somehow 'finding fault' with them. It also seems more than likely that Katerina Ivanovna, on precisely this occasion, at precisely this moment, when the whole world seemed to have forsaken her, felt like showing all these 'worthless and poxy tenants' that not only did she know 'how to live and how to receive', but also that this was nothing compared to the life she was raised for 'in the noble, one might even say aristocratic house of a colonel', and that the last thing she of all people was brought up to do was sweep floors and wash children's rags by night. Such paroxysms of pride and vanity do sometimes visit the poorest and most browbeaten people, in whom, on occasion, they are transformed into a nervous, irrepressible need. Katerina Ivanovna, moreover, was not the browbeaten sort: she could be beaten to death by circumstances, but for her to be morally beaten, through intimidation and the subordination of her will – that was simply impossible. Sonechka, moreover, had every reason to say that Katerina Ivanovna was unhinged. True, it was still too early to assert this definitively, but there was no doubt that over the past year her poor mind had been through far too much not to have been at least partly affected. The later stages of consumption, the medics say, also lead to the impairment of the mental faculties.

Wines, as such, were not on offer, nor was Madeira: that was an exaggeration. Still, there was Lisbon wine, and there was vodka, and there was rum, making up in quantity what they lacked in quality. In terms of food, apart from the *kutya*,[17] there were three or four dishes (pancakes among them), all from Amalia Ivanovna's kitchen, as well as two samovars on the go for the tea, and punch to follow the meal. Katerina Ivanovna had seen to the purchases herself with the help of a tenant, some sorry little Pole living at Mrs Lippewechsel's for reasons best known to himself, who was immediately recruited as Katerina Ivanovna's errand boy and spent the whole of the previous day and the whole of that morning tearing about at breakneck speed with his tongue hanging out – something he seemed particularly keen to draw attention to. He came running up to Katerina Ivanovna on the merest trifle, even went looking for her in the shops of Gostiny Dvor,[18] and was forever calling her *Pani chorążyna*,[19] until she was heartily sick of the sight of him, although to start with she'd been saying how lost she would have been without this 'obliging and high-minded' man. It was a feature of Katerina Ivanovna's character to paint every random acquaintance in the best and brightest colours, making some of them feel quite uneasy, and, to this end, to invent all manner of circumstances with not the slightest foundation in reality, but which she believed in with complete, open-hearted sincerity, and then, all of sudden, to be disappointed, to cut off, insult and forcibly drive out the same person whom, only a few hours earlier, she had been literally worshipping. By nature she was of a giggly, cheerful and peaceable disposition, but an endless succession of misfortunes and setbacks had made her so very *fierce* in desiring and demanding that everyone live in peace and joy and *dare not* live otherwise that the slightest discordant note, the smallest setback, instantly drove her to a virtual frenzy, and in the blink of an eye, after the brightest possible hopes and fantasies, she began cursing fate, ripping up whatever came to hand, hurling it across the room and bashing her head against the wall. Amalia Ivanovna had also suddenly gained extraordinary significance and respect in Katerina Ivanovna's eyes, for no other reason, perhaps, than the fact that there was a funeral banquet to arrange and

Amalia Ivanovna was putting her heart and soul into preparing it: she'd taken it upon herself to set the table, provide the linen, the crockery and so on, and cook the food in her kitchen. Setting out for the cemetery, Katerina Ivanovna had left her in sole command. And the results were truly impressive: the table was set and looked almost clean; the crockery, forks, knives, cups and glasses for wine and vodka were a jumble of different styles and qualities, gathered from various tenants, but everything was in place on time, and Amalia Ivanovna, sensing that she had excelled at her task, greeted the returning group with a certain pride, all dressed up in a bonnet with new mourning ribbons and a black gown. This pride, however well-earned, was not to Katerina Ivanovna's liking: 'You'd have thought we couldn't set a table without her!' Nor did she like the bonnet with new ribbons: 'I wouldn't put it past this stupid German to take pride in the fact that she's the landlady here and has agreed to help some poor tenants out of the goodness of her heart. I mean, really! There were times when Papa, who was a colonel and very nearly a governor, had the table set for forty and no Amalia Ivanovnas – or perhaps I should say Ludwigovnas – were allowed anywhere near it, nor even the kitchen . . .' Still, Katerina Ivanovna resolved to keep her feelings to herself for the time being, though in her heart she'd decided that today was the day to take Amalia Ivanovna down a peg or two and remind her of her proper place, or else God only knows what airs she might start giving herself, but for now she contented herself with being merely unfriendly. Katerina Ivanovna's irritation was further exacerbated by the fact that almost none of the tenants invited to the funeral showed up at the cemetery, except for the Pole, who seemed to turn up everywhere; the banquet, meanwhile, had drawn only the poorest and most inconsequential lodgers, many looking quite out of sorts – the dregs of society, if ever there were. Those who were a bit older and a bit more respectable had all made themselves scarce, as if by prior agreement. Pyotr Petrovich Luzhin, for example, the most respectable of all the tenants, was nowhere to be seen, yet only the previous evening Katerina Ivanovna had been telling anyone who would listen – namely, Amalia Ivanovna, Polechka, Sonya and the Pole – that he was the noblest and most high-minded of men, that he had vast connections and great wealth, that he'd been a friend of her first husband and was received by her father at home, and that he was promising to do all he could to arrange a sizeable pension for her. We should note at this

point that if Katerina Ivanovna boasted of someone else's connections
and means, she did so without any personal interest or design, entirely selflessly, from the warmth of her heart, as it were, and for no
other reason than the pleasure of ascribing even greater merit to the
object of her praise. 'That toad Lebezyatnikov' hadn't shown up
either – he must have 'taken his cue' from Luzhin. 'Who does he think
he is? We only invited him out of the goodness of our hearts and because he shares a room with Pyotr Petrovich, his acquaintance. It
would have been awkward not to.' Also absent were a lady of fashion
and her 'overripe wench of a daughter' – they'd only been lodging at
Amalia Ivanovna's for two weeks, but they'd already made several
complaints about the hue and cry emanating from the Marmeladovs'
room, especially when the deceased came home drunk, and these,
needless to say, had been conveyed to Katerina Ivanovna by Amalia
Ivanovna herself when she, quarrelling with Katerina Ivanovna and
threatening to throw out the entire family, yelled at the top of her
voice that they were disturbing 'noble tenants whose toes they were
not worth'. So Katerina Ivanovna had made a point of inviting this
lady and her daughter, 'whose toes they were not worth', especially as
the lady was in the habit of turning away from her in disdain whenever they chanced to meet – well, now was the time for her to find out
that around here 'people have a nobler way of thinking and feeling,
and issue invitations without bearing grudges', and for them to see
that this was the least Katerina Ivanovna was accustomed to. Her
plan was to explain this to them during the meal, and to tell them
about the governorship of her late papa, while giving them to understand that there was no need for them to turn away on meeting her
and that nothing could be more silly. Absent, too, was the fat lieutenant colonel (actually, a retired junior captain), who, it turned out, had
been 'the worse for wear' since the previous morning. In short, the
only people present were: the Pole; a shabby, tongue-tied paper-pusher,
wearing a soiled tailcoat, ridden with acne and smelling disgusting;
and a deaf and almost completely blind old man, who'd once worked
in some post office and whom someone, since time immemorial and
for reasons unknown, had been maintaining at Amalia Ivanovna's.
There was also a drunk retired lieutenant – actually, a quartermaster –
who had the loudest and most indecent laugh imaginable and who
appeared ('Fancy that!') without a waistcoat! Some other chap just sat
down at the table without even a bow in Katerina Ivanovna's direction;

and, lastly, one character, lacking the appropriate attire, turned up in his house-gown, but this was simply too indecent and he was shown out through the joint efforts of Amalia Ivanovna and the Pole. The Pole, though, had brought along two more compatriots, who had never once stayed at Amalia Ivanovna's and whom no one had ever seen in her rooms before. Katerina Ivanovna found it all extremely disagreeable and extremely annoying. 'So who have we gone to all this bother for?' To make space, the children were not even at the table, which already took up the whole of the room, but on a trunk in the far corner, where both the little ones were sat on a bench, while Polechka, being the eldest, was charged with watching over them, feeding them and keeping their noses clean, 'like all noble children'. In short, Katerina Ivanovna found herself greeting everyone with redoubled self-importance, even haughtiness. She ran a particularly fierce eye over some of the guests, before condescendingly inviting them to sit down. Convinced for whatever reason that Amalia Ivanovna should be held responsible for all the absentees, she suddenly became exceptionally short with her, which Amalia Ivanovna immediately noticed, becoming exceptionally offended. Such beginnings did not augur well. Eventually, everyone took their places.

Raskolnikov walked in almost at the very moment they got back from the cemetery. Katerina Ivanovna was terribly pleased to see him. Firstly, because he was the only 'educated guest' present and, as everyone knew, was 'in line for a chair at the university here in two years' time', and secondly, because he made an instant and courteous apology to her for having had to miss the funeral, much to his regret. She all but threw herself on him, offered him the seat to her left (Amalia Ivanovna was on her right) and, despite her endless fussing and worrying about how the food was being served and whether everyone had their share, despite the excruciating cough which kept interrupting her and choking her and which seemed to have got a great deal worse during these past two days, constantly engaged him in conversation and, in a half-whisper, poured out to him all her pent-up feelings and all her righteous indignation about the failed banquet; moreover, her indignation frequently gave way to the gayest, most irrepressible ridicule of the assembled company, and of the landlady in particular.

'It's all the fault of that cuckoo over there. You know who I mean. Her! Her!' she told Raskolnikov, nodding in the direction of the landlady. 'Just look at her with those eyes popping out of her head. She senses we're talking about her, but can't understand a thing. A real owl! Ha-ha-ha! . . . Cuh-cuh-cuh! And what's she trying to say with that bonnet of hers? Cuh-cuh-cuh! Have you noticed how desperate she is for everyone to think she's bestowing her favour on me and honouring me with her presence? I asked her nicely enough to invite the right sort of people, by which I mean acquaintances of the dear departed, and look who she's dragged in: clowns and slatterns! Take that one with the filthy face: a real snot-rag! And as for these Polskees . . . Ha-ha-ha! Cuh-cuh-cuh! Nobody, and I mean nobody, has ever seen them here before, and I've never seen them. So why have they come? Tell me that! So solemn, the lot of them. Hey, *Panie!*[20] she suddenly yelled at one of them. 'Had your pancakes yet? Have some seconds! And have some beer! Or perhaps some vodka? Just look at him leaping to his feet and bowing to the floor. They must be starving, poor chaps! Well, let them eat. At least they're not rowdy, although . . . although I fear for the landlady's silver spoons! . . . Amalia Ivanovna!' she suddenly said to her, for almost everyone to hear. 'If they do steal your spoons don't expect me to answer for it! Ha-ha-ha!' she continued, in stitches, before turning to Raskolnikov again and nodding towards the landlady, delighted with her sally. 'She didn't understand. Once again she didn't understand! Look at her sitting there, gawping: an owl, a proper owl, a screech owl in new ribbons – ha-ha-ha!'

Here her laughter turned once more into a violent fit of coughing that lasted a good five minutes. It left blood on her handkerchief and beads of sweat on her forehead. She showed the blood to Raskolnikov in silence and, scarcely pausing to catch her breath, started whispering to him again in the most animated tones, with red blotches all over her cheeks:

'See for yourself: I gave her the extremely delicate task of inviting that lady and her daughter – you know who I mean, don't you? The task called for the greatest subtlety, the greatest refinement, but she went about it in such a way that this silly parvenue, this stuck-up so-and-so, this provincial nobody, simply because she's the widow of some major or other and has come to Petersburg to wear out her skirts begging for a pension in government offices, because, at fifty-five years of age, she slaps on powder and rouge and dyes her hair (everyone knows) . . . well, not only did this so-and-so not deign to show up, she didn't even ask anyone to convey her apologies, as even the most elementary rules of etiquette demand! And why on earth hasn't Pyotr

Petrovich come either? And where's Sonya? Where's she got to? Ah, here she is at last! Well, Sonya, where have you been? Strange that you can't even arrive at your father's funeral on time. Rodion Romanovich, she can sit next to you. There's your place, Sonechka . . . Take whatever you want. Try the aspic – that's the best. Pancakes are on their way. What about the children? Polechka, got everything you need down that end? Cuh-cuh-cuh! Good. Lenya, be a good little girl, and you Kolya, stop swinging your legs; sit like all noble children should sit. What were you saying, Sonechka?'

Sonya breathlessly conveyed to her Pyotr Petrovich's apologies, trying to raise her voice so that everyone might hear and using only the most respectful turns of phrase, specially chosen, in fact, to imitate Pyotr Petrovich, and further embellished by her. She added that Pyotr Petrovich had specifically instructed her to convey that, at the first possible opportunity, he would pay her a visit in order to discuss *some business* in private and agree about what could be done and undertaken in future, and so on and so forth.

Sonya knew that this would appease and assuage Katerina Ivanovna, flatter her, and above all be a sop to her pride. After a hasty bow to Raskolnikov, she sat down next to him and threw him a curious glance. For the rest of the time, though, she managed to avoid both looking at him and talking to him. She even seemed rather distracted, though she barely took her eyes off Katerina Ivanovna's face, the better to please her. Neither she nor Katerina Ivanovna were in mourning, for want of appropriate clothing; Sonya was wearing a sort of darkish brown, while Katerina Ivanovna was in the only dress she had, a dark cotton one with stripes. The news about Pyotr Petrovich went down very well. Gravely hearing Sonya out, Katerina Ivanovna enquired with the same air of importance: how's Pyotr Petrovich's health? Then, instantly and for almost everyone to hear, she *whispered* to Raskolnikov that it really would have been rather strange for such an esteemed and respectable man as Pyotr Petrovich to find himself in such an 'unusual crowd', notwithstanding all his devotion to their family and his old friendship with her papa.

'That is why I am especially grateful to you, Rodion Romanovich, for not shunning my bread and salt,[21] even in such a setting as this,' she added, for almost everyone to hear, 'though I dare say that it is only on account of your special friendship towards my poor late husband that you have kept your word.'

Next, she once again ran a proud and dignified gaze over her guests and, with particular solicitude, loudly asked the deaf old man sitting across the table whether he might like some seconds and whether he'd been served any Lisbon. The man made no reply and struggled for a long time to grasp the meaning of the question, although his neighbours even started shaking him, just for fun. But he merely looked around with his mouth hanging open, which only increased the general merriment.

'What a dolt! Just look at him! What's he doing here? But as for Pyotr Petrovich, I've always had complete confidence in him,' Katerina Ivanovna went on to Raskolnikov, 'and, of course, he has nothing in common . . . ,' she snapped at Amalia Ivanovna, who positively wilted from the exceptional ferocity of her look, 'nothing in common with those overdressed tail-slappers of yours whom Papa wouldn't even have taken on as his cooks, and whom my late husband, needless to say, would have accorded a great honour by receiving, and even then only on account of his inexhaustible kindness.'

'Yes, ma'am, he liked a drink. That he did, ma'am!' the ex-quarter-master suddenly shouted, draining his twelfth vodka.

'My late husband did indeed possess that weakness, as everyone knows,' Katerina Ivanovna suddenly pounced on him, 'but he was a kind and noble man, who loved and respected his family. More's the pity that in his kindness he was far too trusting of all manner of debauchees, and drank with God knows who – people who weren't even worth the sole of his shoe! You know, Rodion Romanovich, they found a gingerbread cockerel in his pocket: he may have been dead drunk, but he hadn't forgotten his children.'

'Cock-er-el? Did I hear you say cock-er-el?' yelled the quartermaster.

Katerina Ivanovna did not dignify him with a reply. She was thinking about something and sighed.

'I expect that you, like everyone else, think I was much too strict with him,' she continued, turning to Raskolnikov. 'But I wasn't! He respected me. He truly, truly respected me! He had a kind soul, that man! And sometimes you couldn't help but pity him! He'd be sitting in the corner looking at me and I'd feel so sorry for him I'd want to be nice to him, but then I'd think: "Be nice to him and he'll only get drunk again." Being strict was the only way of restraining him even a little.'

'Yes, ma'am, there was much tugging of forelocks; more than once, ma'am,' roared the quartermaster again, then sank another vodka.

'Never mind forelocks: a broom would do well enough for dealing with certain idiots. And I don't mean my late husband!' Katerina Ivanovna fired back.

The red blotches on her cheeks burned brighter and brighter; her chest heaved. Another minute of this and she'd be making a scene. There was much tittering among the guests, who were evidently enjoying the show. They started nudging the quartermaster and whispering something to him. They were clearly hoping for a fight.

'Per-permission to ask, ma'am, what you mean,' the quartermaster began. 'I mean which . . . noble . . . individual . . . did you see fit, just now . . . ? Actually, forget it! Rubbish! Widow! Widowed! I forgive . . . I'm out!' – and he dispatched another vodka.

Raskolnikov sat and listened in disgusted silence. Out of courtesy he nibbled at the food which Katerina Ivanovna kept putting on his plate, simply so as not to offend her. He studied Sonya closely. But Sonya was becoming more and more anxious and preoccupied; she, too, had a feeling that the banquet would end badly, and observed Katerina Ivanovna's mounting irritation with dread. She happened to know that the main reason the two ladies from the provinces had given such short shrift to Katerina Ivanovna's invitation was her, Sonya. She'd heard from Amalia Ivanovna herself that the mother had even been offended by the invitation and had posed the question: 'How could she even think of sitting our daughter at the same table as *that girl*?' Sonya sensed that Katerina Ivanovna somehow knew about this already, and an insult directed at her, Sonya, meant more to Katerina Ivanovna than any insult directed at herself, her children, her father; in short, it was a mortal insult, and Sonya knew that nothing could appease Katerina Ivanovna now, not until 'she shows these tail-slappers that they are both' etcetera, etcetera. As if on cue, someone sent a plate down to Sonya from the other end of the table; on it two hearts had been sculpted out of black bread, both pierced by an arrow. Katerina Ivanovna flared up and immediately shouted down the table that whoever had sent it was a 'drunken ass'. Amalia Ivanovna, who also sensed trouble, while being wounded to the depths of her soul by Katerina Ivanovna's disdain, suddenly, in the hope of improving the general mood and, at one and the same time, her own reputation, launched into a story, apropos of nothing, about how some acquaintance of hers, 'Karl of the chemist's', had taken a cab one night and 'the cabbie vanted him to kill und Karl begged und begged him not kill him, und cried, und folded his arms, und frightened, und from terror his heart vas pierced.' Katerina Ivanovna smiled before immediately remarking that Amalia Ivanovna would be well advised not to tell stories in Russian. The landlady took even greater offence at this and objected that her 'Vater aus Berlin[22] vas ferry important man and vent about hands in pockets putting.' This was too much for giggly Katerina Ivanovna and she guffawed outrageously. By now, Amalia Ivanovna was at the very end of her tether and could barely contain herself.

'A real screech-owl!' Katerina Ivanovna whispered to Raskolnikov again, cheering up considerably. 'She meant to say "with his hands in his pockets", but instead made him out to be a pickpocket, cuh-cuh! And wouldn't you agree, Rodion Romanovich, once and for all, that these Petersburg foreigners, mainly Germans, who come here from God knows where, are all so much more stupid than we are? I mean, what a way to tell a story: "Karl of the chemist's with terror heart pierced" and (what a baby!) instead of tying up the cabbie "folded his arms, und cried, und ferry begged". What a birdbrain! And she thinks this is so very touching, and has no idea how stupid she is! If you ask me this sozzled quartermaster is far cleverer than her; at least with him it's obvious he's a soak, that he's drunk himself stupid, but the rest of them are so very solemn and serious . . . Just look at her, with those eyes popping out. She's angry! She's angry! Ha-ha-ha! Cuh-cuh-cuh!'

Brightening up, Katerina Ivanovna got carried away and suddenly started talking about how she would be sure to use the hard-won pension to found a boarding school for noble girls in T——, the town of her birth.[23] Katerina Ivanovna had never spoken to Raskolnikov about this before and she immediately plunged into the most beguiling details. As if from nowhere, there suddenly appeared in her hands that same 'certificate of distinction' which Raskolnikov had first heard about from Marmeladov, the late departed, who had explained to him in the drinking den that Katerina Ivanovna, his spouse, had danced the pas de châle 'in the presence of the governor and other persons' at the school leaving ball. Evidently, this certificate of distinction was now meant to serve as evidence of Katerina Ivanovna's right to found a boarding school herself; above all, though, she was keeping it up her sleeve in order to take 'those overdressed tail-slappers' down a peg or

two once and for all, should they appear at the banquet, and prove to
them that Katerina Ivanovna was 'from the noblest, one might even
say most aristocratic, home, a colonel's daughter and a cut above the
adventure-seekers who are two a penny nowadays'. The certificate of
distinction immediately did the rounds of the drunken guests, something which Katerina Ivanovna did nothing to prevent, for it did indeed spell out, *en toutes lettres*,[24] that she was the daughter of a court
counsellor, one decorated by the state, and that she really was, thereby,
almost a colonel's daughter. Afire with inspiration, Katerina Ivanovna
lost no time in enlarging on every detail of her beautiful and tranquil
future life in T——; about the teachers she would invite to her boarding school from the gymnasium; about a certain estimable old French-
man, Mangot, who had taught French to Katerina Ivanovna herself at
her boarding school, was living out his days in T——, and would almost certainly agree to join her for a very reasonable fee. She eventually got on to Sonya as well, who would accompany her to T—— 'and
help out with everything'. But at this point there was a sudden snort
from the other end of the table. Though Katerina Ivanovna made every
effort to appear oblivious to the laughter, she immediately raised her
voice and began enthusing about Sofya Semyonovna's undoubted abilities to serve as her helper, about 'her meekness, patience, self-sacrifice,
nobility and education'; not only that, she patted Sonya on the cheek
and, half-rising, kissed her twice with great warmth. Sonya blushed,
while Katerina Ivanovna burst into tears, noting to herself as she did
so that she was a 'silly fool who's lost her nerve and gets upset over
nothing, and anyway, this has gone on long enough – they've finished
eating, so let's have tea'. At that very moment Amalia Ivanovna, now
utterly offended by having taken no part at all in the entire conversation and by the fact that nobody had even listened to her, suddenly
made one final sally and, concealing her pain, ventured an eminently
sensible and profound observation to Katerina Ivanovna about how,
at the boarding school, she would need to pay particular attention to
the cleanness of the girls' linen (*die Wäsche*) and that 'there better be
one gut lady keeping eyes on the linen', and secondly that 'all the
young girls better no noffels read under cover'. Katerina Ivanovna,
who really was upset and exhausted and had had quite enough of this
banquet, immediately snapped back that Amalia Ivanovna was 'talking rubbish' and didn't have a clue; that *die Wäsche* was a matter
for the linen-keeper and not the director of a boarding school for the

nobility; and as for novel-reading, well, that was simply indecent of her and could she please shut up. Amalia Ivanovna turned red and spitefully remarked that she 'only vanted to help', that she 'ferry much only vanted to help', and that she was owed 'rent *Geld*[25] for ferry long time'. Katerina Ivanovna immediately 'put her in her place' by telling her that she was lying about 'vanting to help', because even yesterday, with the late departed still laid out on the table, she'd been bothering her about the unpaid rent. To this, Amalia Ivanovna made the entirely logical riposte that she 'invited those ladies, but those ladies not come because those ladies noble and not come to not-noble ladies'. Katerina Ivanovna 'reminded' her that, as a slattern, she was hardly in a position to know about true nobility. This was too much for Amalia Ivanovna, who declared that her '*Vater aus Berlin* vas ferry, ferry important man and vent about hands in pockets putting and everything did *Pouf! Pouf!*' and, the better to impersonate her *Vater*, Amalia Ivanovna leapt from her chair, thrust both hands into her pockets, puffed out her cheeks and started making vague sounds with her mouth resembling *pouf-pouf*, to the loud guffaws of all the tenants, who purposely egged Amalia Ivanovna on with their approval, sensing a fight. But this was more than Katerina Ivanovna could bear and thereupon, for all to hear, she shot back that perhaps Amalia Ivanovna never had a *Vater* at all – she was simply a drunken Balt who probably used to work in a kitchen, if not worse. Amalia Ivanovna turned red as a lobster and screeched that perhaps it was Katerina Ivanovna who 'no *Vater* had', but she, Amalia Ivanovna, had a '*Vater aus Berlin*, and he such long frock coats had and everything did *pouf, pouf, pouf!*' Katerina Ivanovna noted contemptuously that her own origins were well known and that the certificate of distinction spelled out in black and white that her father was a colonel;[26] and that Amalia Ivanovna's father (assuming she even had one) was probably some milk-selling Balt, though in all likelihood there really was no father, because even now no one knew what her patronymic was: Ivanovna or Ludwigovna? At this Amalia Ivanovna, positively livid, banged her fist on the table and set about screeching that she was Ivanovna, not Ludwigovna, that her *Vater* was called Johann and 'a *Bürgermeister*[27] vas', while Katerina Ivanovna's *Vater* 'never *Bürgermeister* vas'. Katerina Ivanovna got up from her chair and in a stern, seemingly calm voice (despite her pallor and heaving chest) remarked that should she dare ever again, even once, put her 'lousy *Vater* on a level with Papa', then she, Katerina Ivanovna, would 'rip off that bonnet and stamp all over it'. On hearing this, Amalia Ivanovna started tearing around the room and yelling at the top of her voice that she was the land-lady and that Katerina Ivanovna should 'vacate the apartment this ferry minute', after which, for some reason, she set about clearing the silver spoons from the table. Uproar ensued; the children began cry-ing. Sonya rushed to restrain Katerina Ivanovna, but when Amalia Ivanovna suddenly shouted something about a yellow ticket, Katerina Ivanovna pushed Sonya aside and made straight for Amalia Ivanovna, to bring her warning about the bonnet into immediate effect. At that moment the door opened and a man suddenly appeared on the threshold: Pyotr Petrovich Luzhin. He stood there casting a stern, at-tentive gaze over the assembled company. Katerina Ivanovna rushed towards him.

III

'Pyotr Petrovich!' she shouted. 'You defend me, at least! Make this stupid creature understand that this is no way to treat a noble lady in distress, that the law exists for a reason . . . I'm going straight to the Governor General . . . She'll answer for this . . . In memory of my fa-ther's bread and salt, protect the orphans.'

'Excuse me, ma'am . . . Do, please, excuse me,' said Pyotr Petrovich dismissively, 'but, as you well know, I never once had the honour of meeting your papa . . . Excuse me, ma'am' – someone gave a roar of laughter – 'but I have not the slightest intention of participating in your endless disputes with Amalia Ivanovna . . . I'm here for my own pur-poses . . . I should like to have words with your stepdaughter, Sofya . . . Ivanovna . . . if I'm not mistaken? Kindly let me pass, ma'am . . .'

And Pyotr Petrovich, edging past Katerina Ivanovna, made for the opposite corner, towards Sonya.

Katerina Ivanovna remained rooted to the spot, as if thunder-struck. She was simply unable to understand how Pyotr Petrovich could renounce her papa's bread and salt. Having once invented this bread and salt, she now held it as a sacred truth. She was also shocked by Pyotr Petrovich's tone: business-like, dry and filled with a kind of contemptuous menace. In fact, everyone gradually went quiet at his appearance. Leaving aside the fact that this 'business-like and serious' man looked utterly out of place in such a crowd, it was obvious that something important had brought him here, that only something out of the ordinary could explain his appearance in such a setting, and that, therefore, something was just about to happen. Raskolnikov, who was standing next to Sonya, made way for him; Pyotr Petrovich seemed not to notice him at all. A minute later Lebezyatnikov also appeared on the threshold. He didn't enter the room, but paused in an attitude of great curiosity, almost surprise. He was listening, but seemed unable to grasp something.

'Forgive me if I am interrupting, but I'm here on rather important business,' Pyotr Petrovich remarked, as if to nobody in particular. 'In fact, I'm glad there's an audience. Amalia Ivanovna, I humbly ask you, in your capacity as landlady, to pay attention to my ensuing conversation with Sofya Ivanovna. Sofya Ivanovna,' he continued, directly addressing a thoroughly astonished and already frightened Sonya, 'immediately after your visit, in the room of my friend, Andrei Semyonovich Lebezyatnikov, a government banknote to the value of one hundred roubles disappeared from my desk. If, for any reason, you happen to know and can tell us where the note may be found, then I give you my word of honour, taking everyone here as my witness, that there the matter shall end. But should this not be the case, I shall be obliged to resort to the most serious measures, and then . . . you'll have no one to blame but yourself!'

Complete silence reigned in the room. Even the crying children fell quiet. Deathly pale, Sonya looked at Luzhin and could say nothing in reply. It was as if she hadn't understood yet. Several seconds passed.

'Well, miss, what do you have to say?' asked Luzhin, staring straight at her.

'I don't know . . . I don't know anything . . . ,' Sonya eventually replied in a faint voice.

'You don't? You don't know?' Luzhin repeated and paused for a few seconds more. 'Think it through, mademoiselle,' he began sternly, though as if he were still trying to persuade her. 'I'm prepared to grant you more time for deliberation. Please understand that if I were not so sure, then, of course, with all my experience, I should hardly risk accusing you so directly; for such a direct and public accusation, if false or even merely erroneous, is one for which I, in a certain sense, must answer. I am only too aware of that, miss. This morning, for my own purposes, I cashed several five per cent bonds for the nominal value of three thousand roubles. I have kept a record of the transaction in my wallet. Arriving home – Andrei Semyonovich is my witness – I began counting the money and, having counted out two thousand three hundred roubles, I put them in my wallet, and my wallet in the side-pocket of my frock coat. About five hundred roubles were left on the table, in notes, among which were three notes of one hundred roubles each. At that moment you appeared (at my summons) and spent the entire duration of your visit in a state of such extreme embarrassment that on no less than three occasions, right in the middle of our conversation, you stood up and, for some reason, were in a hurry to leave, even though we were still talking. Andrei Semyonovich can vouch for it all. I expect, mademoiselle, that you yourself will not refuse to confirm and publicly state that the only reason Andrei Semyonovich invited you on my behalf was in order that I might discuss with you the wretched and helpless plight of your relative, Katerina Ivanovna (whose banquet I was unable to attend), and how useful it would be to organize a collection or a lottery or something of the sort. You thanked me and were even moved to tears (I am relating everything as it happened, in order firstly to remind you, and secondly to show you that my memory has not smoothed out the slightest detail). Next, I took a ten-rouble banknote from the table and gave it to you, as a personal gift to help your mother, by way of an initial contribution. Andrei Semyonovich saw everything. Next, I showed you out – the embarrassment, on your side, had not lessened – after which, remaining alone with Andrei Semyonovich and talking with him for about ten minutes, Andrei Semyonovich went out, while I turned my attention back to the table and the money lying thereupon, with the aim of counting it and then putting it – as I had been planning to do – to one side. To my astonishment one of the hundred-rouble notes was missing. Kindly consider: for me to suspect Andrei Semyonovich is quite out of the question; I am ashamed of the very idea. Nor could I have made a mistake in my calculations, since I had finished counting only a minute before your arrival and found the total to be correct. You will agree that, recalling your embarrassment, your impatience to leave and the fact that your hands had, for a certain amount of time, rested on the table, and taking into consideration, when all's said and done, your social status and the habits it entails, I, however horrified and even reluctant, was, as it were, *compelled* to alight on a suspicion that may be harsh, yet is also just! Let me add and repeat that, for all my *self-evident* certainty, I understand that by making this accusation

I am, nevertheless, running a certain risk. But as you can see, I could not let it go. I reacted, and I will tell you why: solely, miss, on account of your rank ingratitude! I mean, really! I am the one who invites you over for the benefit of your impoverished relative, I am the one who offers you alms, insofar as my means permit, of ten roubles, and look how you set about repaying me! No, miss, this is no way to behave! You must be taught a lesson. Consider this well, and while you do – I'm asking you as a true friend now (for what better friend could you have at this moment?) – bethink yourself! Or else I shall be quite implacable! Well then?'

'I've taken nothing from you,' Sonya whispered in horror. 'You gave me ten roubles – here, have them back.' Sonya took a handkerchief from her pocket, located a small knot in it, untied it, extracted a ten-rouble note and held it out to Luzhin.

'So you won't admit to the other hundred?' he insisted reproachfully, not taking the note.

Sonya looked around. Everyone was staring at her with such dreadful, stern, mocking, hateful expressions. She glanced over at Raskolnikov . . . He was standing by the wall, arms folded, staring at her with eyes of fire.

'O Lord!' broke from Sonya.

'Amalia Ivanovna, we shall have to inform the police, so may I humbly ask you, in the meantime, to send for the caretaker?' said Luzhin in a soft, even affectionate voice.

'*Gott der Barmherzige!*[28] I knew she shtole!' cried Amalia Ivanovna, throwing up her hands.

'You knew?' echoed Luzhin. 'Then even before you must have had grounds to think so. May I request, most esteemed Amalia Ivanovna, that you remember these words, uttered, moreover, before witnesses?'

A loud hum suddenly started up on all sides. Everyone stirred.

'Wha-a-at?' cried Katerina Ivanovna, coming to her senses and rushing at Luzhin with a sudden burst. 'What's that? You're accusing her of stealing? Her? Sonya? Oh, scoundrels! Scoundrels!' And rushing over to Sonya, she hugged her, vice-like, in her withered arms.

'Sonya! How dare you take ten roubles from him? Oh, silly girl! Give it here! Give me those ten roubles right now – there!'

Snatching the note from Sonya, Katerina Ivanovna scrunched it up and flung it hard in Luzhin's face. The pellet hit him in the eye and bounced off onto the floor. Amalia Ivanovna rushed to pick up the money. Pyotr Petrovich flew into a rage.

'Restrain this madwoman!' he yelled.

In the doorway, at that moment, some other people appeared alongside Lebezyatnikov; among those looking in were the two ladies from the provinces.

'What? I'm the mad one am I? Idiot!' screeched Katerina Ivanovna. 'Yes you, you loathsome shyster! As if Sonya would take his money! Her? A thief? She'd sooner give away her own money to you, you idiot!' – and she laughed hysterically. 'Ever seen such an idiot?' she shouted, rushing from one corner of the room to the next, pointing at Luzhin. 'What? You too?' – she'd spotted the landlady – 'You're at it too, are you, you sausage-maker?[29] You poxy Prussian drumstick wrapped in crinoline, claiming "she shtole"! Look at you all! She's been in the room all along – she came back from yours, you scoundrel, and sat straight down next to Rodion Romanovich! . . . Search her! Seeing as she's never been out of the room, the money must still be on her! Go on, search her! Search her! Only if nothing turns up, then I'm terribly sorry, my dear, but you'll have to an-swer for it! I'll go running to His Majesty, His Majesty, to the Tsar him-self, Most Merciful, I'll throw myself at his feet, right now, today! I've no one left! I'll be seen! You think I won't? Rubbish! I'll be seen! I will! You were counting on her meekness, I suppose? Weren't you? But I'm plucky enough for two! You'll get burnt, my friend! Search her! Go on, then, search her!!'

In her frenzy, Katerina Ivanovna kept grabbing at Luzhin, drag-ging him over to Sonya.

'I'm ready to do so and to answer for it . . . but calm down, madam, calm down! Your pluckiness is all too apparent! . . . I mean . . . really . . . whatever next?' muttered Luzhin. 'This is a matter for the police . . . Although, I suppose there are more than enough witnesses here already . . . I'm ready, madam . . . Though in any case this is rather awkward for a man . . . on account of one's sex . . . If Amalia Ivanovna were to assist . . . although this is hardly the way to do things . . . Whatever next, ma'am?'

'Whoever you like! Whoever wants to can search her!' shouted Katerina Ivanovna. 'Sonya, turn your pockets out for them! There, there! Look, you monster, it's empty! The handkerchief was there and now it's empty. See? And here's the other pocket! See! See!'

Katerina Ivanovna did not so much turn the two pockets inside out
as pull them out, one after the other. Suddenly, a note dropped out of
the second, right-hand pocket and, tracing a curve in the air, fell at
Luzhin's feet. Everyone saw it; most shrieked. Pyotr Petrovich bent
down, picked the note up with two fingers from the floor, held it up
for all to see and unfolded it. It was a one-hundred rouble banknote,
folded to an eighth of its size. With a sweep of his arm, Pyotr Petrovich showed everyone the note.

'Thief! Out of my premise, now! Police, police!' shrieked Amalia
Ivanovna. 'Siberia! Exile! Out!'

Shouts went up on all sides. Raskolnikov was silent, keeping his
gaze fixed on Sonya with only the occasional rapid glance at Luzhin.
Sonya was still standing in the same spot, as if dazed: she was barely
even surprised. Suddenly the colour rushed to her face. She gave a cry
and hid herself in her hands.

'No, it's not me! I didn't take it! I don't know!' she cried in a heart-
rending howl and threw herself on Katerina Ivanovna, who grabbed
her and hugged her tight, as if wishing to protect her from everyone
with her bosom.

'Sonya! Sonya! I don't believe it! You see, I don't!' shouted Katerina
Ivanovna (against all the evidence), rocking her vigorously in her
arms, like a baby, kissing her time and again, catching her hands and
almost biting them with her kisses. 'As if you'd take it! How stupid
these people are! Good Lord! You're stupid, stupid!' she cried, addressing everyone, 'and you haven't a clue, not a clue, what sort of a
heart this is, what sort of a girl this is! As if she'd take it! She'd sooner
throw off her last dress, sell it, go barefoot and give away everything
to you, if you needed it – that's the kind of girl she is! She only took
the yellow ticket because my children – mine – were going hungry. It
was for us that she sold herself! . . . Ah, husband, dear departed! See
this? See this? Some funeral banquet you've had! Lord! Well, defend
her then! What are you all waiting for? Rodion Romanovich! Why
aren't you, of all people, standing up for her? So you believe it too, do
you? You're not worth her little finger – none of you, none of you!
Lord! Defend her, for goodness' sake!'

The wailing of poor, consumptive, orphaned Katerina Ivanovna
seemed to have a powerful effect on her listeners. There was so much
pitiful suffering in her pain-racked, withered, consumptive face, in
her dried-up, blood-caked lips, in her hoarse shouting and wailing

sobs so like a child's, in her trusting and childish yet desperate plea for protection, that everyone seemed to take pity on the unfortunate woman. Pyotr Petrovich, at any rate, instantly *took pity.*

'Madam! Madam!' he exclaimed in an imposing voice. 'This fact does not concern you! No one could dare accuse you of plotting or colluding, especially when it was you who made the discovery by turning out her pockets: so you can hardly have entertained any suspicions. I am more than ready to feel pity if, as it were, beggary was the cause of Sofya Semyonovna's action. But why, mademoiselle, did you not wish to admit it? For fear of disgrace? Of taking the first step? Or perhaps you were simply flustered? That's understandable, quite understandable, miss ... But still, why did you have to sink to such propensities? Gentlemen!' he said to all those present. 'Gentlemen! Feeling pity and, as it were, sympathy, I am, I dare say, ready to forgive even now, notwithstanding the personal insults I have received. And may your current shame, mademoiselle, be a lesson to you for the future,' he added, turning to Sonya, 'and for my part, I shall let everything else go and end on that note. Enough!'

Pyotr Petrovich cast a sidelong glance at Raskolnikov. Their eyes met. Raskolnikov's burning gaze was ready to incinerate him. Katerina Ivanovna, meanwhile, no longer seemed to be hearing anything: she kept hugging and kissing Sonya, as if she were mad. The children also wrapped their little arms round Sonya from every side, while Polechka – though she had not fully understood what was going on – seemed to be drowning in her tears, convulsing with sobs and burying her pretty little face, all swollen from crying, in Sonya's shoulder.

'Despicable!' somebody suddenly boomed in the doorway.

Pyotr Petrovich looked round sharply.

'How despicable!' Lebezyatnikov repeated, staring straight into his eyes.

Pyotr Petrovich even seemed to flinch. Everyone noticed. (And recalled it later.) Lebezyatnikov stepped into the room.

'And you had the nerve to put me down as a witness?' he said, walking up to Pyotr Petrovich.

'What's the meaning of this, Andrei Semyonovich? What on earth are you talking about?' mumbled Luzhin.

'The meaning of this is that you ... are a slanderer, that's my meaning!' said Lebezyatnikov hotly, fixing him sternly with his purblind eyes. He was dreadfully cross. Raskolnikov simply sank his eyes

into him, as if hanging on his every word and weighing them all up.
Silence set in again. Pyotr Petrovich was almost flustered, especially at
first.

'If you mean me . . . ,' he began with a stutter. 'But what's wrong
with you? Are you in your right mind?'

'I am indeed, sir, it's you who . . . Oh, you swindler! How despicable! I heard everything. I deliberately waited until I'd understood
everything, because, I admit, it's not entirely logical even now . . . .
But why you did all this – that is beyond me.'

'What did I do exactly? Stop talking in these silly riddles of yours!
Or maybe you've been at the vodka?'

'If anyone's been drinking it's you, you despicable man! I never
touch vodka. It doesn't agree with my convictions! Can you imagine:
it was him, him, who gave this one-hundred rouble note to Sofya Semyonovna with his own hands – I saw it. I witnessed it. I'll take the
oath! Him! Him!' repeated Lebezyatnikov, addressing all and sundry.

'Have you gone completely crazy, you daft child?' shrieked Luzhin.
'Here she is right in front of you. Here she is confirming, in front of
everyone, that apart from the ten roubles she never received anything
from me. So how on earth am I supposed to have given it to her?'

'I saw it! I saw it!' Lebezyatnikov kept shouting. 'And although it's
against my convictions, I am ready, right now, to stand in court and
take any oath you care to mention, because I saw you slipping it to her
on the sly! Only I thought – fool that I am – that you did so as a kindness. In the doorway, saying goodbye, when she turned round and
you were squeezing her hand in yours, with the other hand, the left
one, you slipped the note into her pocket. I saw! I saw!'

Luzhin turned white.

'A pack of lies!' he cried with insolent defiance. 'How could you
have spotted a note if you were standing by the window? You imagined it . . . with those purblind eyes of yours. You're raving!'

'No, I didn't imagine it! And though I was standing far away I saw
everything, everything, and even though it really is difficult to see a
banknote clearly from the window – you're right about that – I, on
account of a particular circumstance, knew for a fact that the note was
worth a hundred roubles, because, when you were giving Sofya Semyonovna the ten-rouble note – I saw this myself – you also took a
hundred-rouble note from the table (I saw this because I was standing
near you at the time, and since a certain thought immediately occurred

to me I did not forget that you had it in your hand). You folded it and held it, clenched in your fist, the whole time. I'd have forgotten about it again except that when you started getting up you transferred it from your right hand to your left and very nearly dropped it; at that point I remembered again, because the very same thought occurred to me again, namely, that you wanted, without my noticing, to do her a kindness. You can imagine how closely I started watching – well, then I saw you slipping it into her pocket. I saw! I saw! I'll take the oath!'

Lebezyatnikov was almost choking. Shouts went up on all sides, most of them signalling surprise; others had a more menacing tone. Everyone crowded around Pyotr Petrovich. Katerina Ivanovna rushed to Lebezyatnikov.

'Andrei Semyonovich! I was wrong about you! Protect her! She's got no one else! She's an orphan! You've been sent by God! Andrei Semyonovich, dear kind Andrei Semyonovich, father!'

Katerina Ivanovna, scarcely aware of what she was doing, fell to her knees before him.

'Madness!' howled Luzhin, raging with fury. 'Sheer madness, sir. "Forgot, remembered, forgot" – what are you talking about? So I planted it on purpose, did I? Why? To what end? What can I have in common with this . . . ?'

'Why? Well, that's beyond me, too, but what I've told you is an honest-to-goodness fact! I'm so far from being wrong – you foul, criminal man – that I remember the exact question that immediately occurred to me, at the very moment I was thanking you and shaking your hand. Why precisely did you put it in her pocket by stealth? What I mean is, why precisely by stealth? Surely not just because you wanted to conceal it from me, knowing of my convictions to the contrary and my rejection of private charity, which never gets to the root of the problem? So I decided you really were ashamed to give her such a princely sum in front of me, and besides, I thought, perhaps he wanted to surprise her when she suddenly found all of one hundred roubles in her pocket. (Certain do-gooders take great pleasure in making a point of their kindnesses.) Then I had another thought: you wanted to test her – would she come and thank you when she found it? Then: that you wished to avoid being thanked and – how does it go? – for the right hand – or is it left? – not to know[30] what the . . . well, something like that . . . Anyway, all manner of thoughts occurred to me then, so I resolved to think it all through later, but in any case I deemed it tactless to let on to you that I knew your secret. But on the other hand, something else immediately occurred to me yet again: that Sofya Semyonovna might well lose the money before she even knew it was there; which was why I decided to come here, to summon her and inform her that someone had put a hundred roubles in her pocket. In passing, I called in on the Kobylyatnikov ladies first, to drop off *The General Conclusion of the Positive Method*,[31] recommending Piderit's article in particular (and Wagner's, too, come to mention it); then I arrived here and just look what I found! I mean, honestly, how, how could I have come up with all these ideas and arguments if I really hadn't seen you put a hundred roubles in her pocket?'

When Andrei Semyonovich reached the end of his long-winded argument, concluded in so logical a fashion, he was dreadfully tired and the sweat was pouring off him. Alas, he wasn't even able to express himself decently in Russian (though it was the only language he knew); all the stuffing had suddenly been knocked out of him, and he even looked thinner after his feat of advocacy. Nevertheless, his speech had an extraordinary effect. He spoke so fearlessly and with such conviction that everyone clearly believed him. Pyotr Petrovich realized he was in trouble.

'What do I care about idiotic questions that may or may not have occurred to you?' he cried. 'What kind of proof is that? You might have dreamt it all up in your sleep for all I know! In fact, sir, you're lying! You're lying and slandering because you're angry with me about something, and I even know what it is you're so cross about: that I wouldn't agree to your free-thinking, godless proposals for society!'

But this ploy did not help Pyotr Petrovich. On the contrary, grumbling could be heard on all sides.

'Nice try!' shouted Lebezyatnikov. 'Liar! Call the police! I'll take an oath! But what I can't understand is: why take the risk of sinking so low? Oh, you pathetic wretch!'

'I can explain why he took such a risk and, if need be, I'll take an oath!' uttered Raskolnikov at last in a firm voice, and stepped forward.

He seemed calm and certain. Somehow everyone realized, just by looking at him, that he really did know what had happened and that the climax was fast approaching.

'It all makes perfect sense to me now,' Raskolnikov went on, addressing Lebezyatnikov directly. 'I suspected foul play right from the start. I suspected it in view of certain particular circumstances known only to me, which I will now explain to everyone: they're the key to it all! And now, Andrei Semyonovich, your priceless testimony has cleared everything up for me once and for all. I ask everyone, everyone to listen closely: this gentleman' (he pointed at Luzhin) 'recently became engaged to a girl, and specifically to my sister, Avdotya Romanovna Raskolnikova. But on arriving in Petersburg he picked an argument with me at our very first meeting, the day before yesterday, and I threw him out, as two witnesses will confirm. This man is terribly angry . . . Two days ago I still didn't know he was lodging here with you, Andrei Semyonovich, and that, therefore, on the very same day of our argument, that is, the day before yesterday, he witnessed how I, as a friend of the late Mr Marmeladov, gave some money to his spouse, Katerina Ivanovna, for the funeral. He immediately dashed off a note to my mother to inform her that I had given all the money away not to Katerina Ivanovna, but to Sofya Semyonovna; not only that, he referred, in the most odious terms to . . . to Sofya Semyonovna's character, or rather, he alluded to the character of my relationship to Sofya Semyonovna. All this, you'll understand, was intended to set my mother and sister against me, by giving them to understand that I was squandering the money they'd sent me, their very last roubles, in the most disgraceful fashion. Yesterday evening, before my mother and sister, and in his presence, I established the truth of the matter, proving that I gave the money to Katerina Ivanovna for the funeral, and not to Sofya Semyonovna, and that the day before yesterday I hadn't even met Sofya Semyonovna and had never even seen her. I also added that he, Pyotr Petrovich Luzhin, for all his qualities, was not worth the little finger of Sofya Semyonovna, whom he spoke of so disapprovingly. As for his question – would I sit Sofya Semyonovna next to my sister? – I replied that I'd already done so, earlier the same day. Angered by the fact that his slanders failed to set my mother and sister against me, he started saying the most outrageous, unforgivable things to them. That was the last straw and he was thrown out for good. All of this happened yesterday evening. Now, please listen closely: imagine for a moment that he'd succeeded just now in proving that Sofya Semyonovna was a thief, then, first of all, he would have proved to my sister and mother that his suspicions were not without foundation; that he had had every reason to be angry at my placing my sister on a level with Sofya Semyonovna; that in attacking me he had thereby defended and protected my sister's – and his fiancée's – honour. In short, he might even have managed to set my family against me again, while hoping, needless to say, to get back in their good books. I haven't even mentioned the fact that he had scores to settle with me personally, because he has grounds to assume that Sofya Semyonovna's honour and happiness are very dear to me. That's what he was after! That's how I understand this business! And that's all there is to it!'

Thus, more or less, did Raskolnikov end his speech, one frequently interrupted by the cries of the public, which, nevertheless, listened very attentively. Despite these interruptions, he spoke tersely, calmly, precisely, clearly, firmly. The terseness of his voice, the conviction in his tone and the severity of his expression had an extraordinary effect on everyone.

'Yes, that's it. That's it!' Lebezyatnikov ecstatically confirmed. 'That must be right, because the moment Sofya Semyonovna entered our room he specifically asked me: "Is he here? Did you see him among Katerina Ivanovna's guests?" He called me over to the window to ask me that, in a hushed voice. So for him it was crucial that you should be here! That's it! That's exactly it!'

Luzhin said nothing, smiling contemptuously. But he was very pale. He looked as if he were trying to think up some ruse to save his skin. He might have been only too pleased to drop everything and leave, but right now that was more or less impossible. It meant openly acknowledging that the charges levelled against him were fair and that he had indeed slandered Sofya Semyonovna. And anyway, the public, which was tipsy enough already, was far too restless. The quartermaster, though a little confused about everything, shouted loudest of all and proposed some highly unpleasant measures for dealing with Luzhin. But not everyone was drunk; people had been pouring in from every room. The three Poles were terribly excited and kept shouting *'Panie łajdak!'*[32] at him and muttering various threats in Polish. Sonya was straining to catch every word, but she, too, seemed to be struggling to understand it all, as though she were waking from a faint. Never once did she take her eyes off Raskolnikov, sensing that only he could protect her. Katerina Ivanovna's breathing was heavy and hoarse; she seemed utterly exhausted. And no one looked more stupid than Amalia Ivanovna, standing there with her mouth open and understanding precisely nothing. All she knew was that Pyotr Petrovich was in a fix. Raskolnikov wanted to speak again, but he wasn't able to finish: everyone was shouting and crowding round Luzhin with curses and threats. But Pyotr Petrovich held his nerve. Seeing that he had lost his case against Sonya hands down, he resorted to insolence.

'Excuse me, gentlemen, excuse me. Don't crowd around. Let me through!' he said, making his way through the throng. 'And kindly desist from your threats. It'll get you nowhere, I assure you – I'm no shrinking violet, while you, gentlemen, shall have to answer for use of violence to cover up a criminal case. The thief has been amply exposed and I will prosecute. Judges are not so blind ... or so drunk, and they won't believe two notorious atheists, disturbers of the peace and free-thinkers, who accuse me for no better reason than personal revenge, which they, in their idiocy, admit themselves ... Now if you'll excuse me!'

'I want no trace of you in my room. Kindly move out this minute – it's over between us! When I think of the tears I sweated, explaining everything to him ... for an entire fortnight!'

'Andrei Semyonovich, I told you myself that I was moving out, and you wouldn't let me leave. Now I shall merely add that you are an idiot, sir. May you succeed in curing your mind and your purblind eyes. Now if you'll excuse me, gentlemen!'

He squeezed past, but the quartermaster was reluctant to let him out just like that, with nothing but curses: he grabbed a glass from the table and hurled it with all his strength at Pyotr Petrovich; but the glass hit Amalia Ivanovna instead. She squealed and the quartermaster, losing his balance from the effort of throwing, collapsed beneath the table. Pyotr Petrovich went to his room and was gone in half an hour. Sonya, timid by nature, had always known that nobody could be destroyed more easily than her and that anyone could insult her with virtual impunity. But still, right until that moment, it seemed to her that disaster could somehow be avoided – by being careful, meek and obedient to all. Her disappointment was overwhelming. Of course, she could endure anything – even this – with patience and barely a murmur. But the first minute was just too painful. She had come out victorious and vindicated, yet, once the initial fright and shock had passed, once she'd understood and grasped everything clearly, an excruciating sense of helplessness and hurt pressed on her heart. She became hysterical. Eventually, she could bear it no longer, rushed from the room and ran off home. Luzhin had walked out just moments before. After being hit by the glass, to the riotous amusement of those present, Amalia Ivanovna had also had enough of being sober at someone else's party. Shrieking, as if possessed, she rushed over to Katerina Ivanovna, holding her responsible for everything:

'Out of my premise! Now! Quick!' Saying this, she began grabbing whichever of Katerina Ivanovna's things came to hand and throwing them on the floor. Katerina Ivanovna, more dead than alive, barely conscious, gasping and pale, leapt from her bed (onto which she'd fallen in exhaustion) and threw herself on Amalia Ivanovna. But the struggle was far too uneven and she was brushed away like a feather.

'What? As if godless slanders weren't enough, this animal's started attacking me too! On the day of my husband's funeral I'm thrown out of our apartment, despite my bread and salt, out onto the streets, with the orphans! And where will I go?' the poor woman howled, sobbing and gasping. 'Lord!' she suddenly shouted, eyes flashing. 'Is there really no justice? Who will you protect, if not us orphans? Well, we'll see! There is judgement and justice on this earth – I'll find them! Just you wait, you godless animal! Polechka, you stay with the children, I'll be back. Wait for me – on the streets if you have to! We'll see if there's justice on this earth!'

Wrapping that same green *drap de dames* shawl around her head – the one the late Marmeladov had mentioned in the drinking den – Katerina Ivanovna squeezed through the drunk and disorderly throng of tenants still crowding the room and ran out, weeping and wailing, into the street, with the vague intention of finding justice somewhere, right now, come what may. Terrified, Polechka shrank into the corner with the children, sat on the trunk and there, hugging the two little ones and shaking all over, began waiting for her mother's return. Amalia Ivanovna stormed around the room, screeching and whining, hurling onto the floor whatever came her way and making a great din as she did so. The tenants became ever more rowdy: some drew what conclusions they could about these events; some argued and swore; others began singing . . .

'Time for me, too!' thought Raskolnikov. 'Well, Sofya Semyonovna, let's see what you say now!'

And he set off to visit Sonya.

IV

Raskolnikov had been energetic and animated in his defence of Sonya against Luzhin, despite the fact that he himself was carrying so much dread and suffering in his soul. But, having been through so much that morning, he'd felt a kind of joy at the chance to experience different impressions, to say nothing of the very personal and heartfelt nature of

his urge to plead Sonya's case. Aside from that, there lay before him
the prospect – which at moments he found quite terrifying – of seeing
Sonya: he *had* to tell her who killed Lizaveta, and sensed in advance
how agonizing this would be; it was as if he were trying to fend it off.
And so, when he exclaimed, on leaving Katerina Ivanovna's, 'What
will you say now, Sofya Semyonovna?', he was still in a state of out-
ward excitement: animated, defiant and flushed with his recent victory
over Luzhin. But something strange came over him. On reaching
Kapernaumov's apartment, he felt within himself a sudden weakening
and fear. He stopped outside the door, hesitating over the strange
question, 'Must I say who killed Lizaveta?' It was a strange question
because he suddenly felt, at one and the same time, that not only did he
have to tell her, but that even to postpone this moment, however
briefly, was impossible. Why it was impossible he still did not know; he
merely *felt* it, and this excruciating awareness of his impotence in the
face of necessity all but crushed him. To cut short his deliberations and
agony, he quickly opened the door and looked at Sonya from the
threshold. She was sitting with her elbows on the table and her face in
her hands, but on seeing Raskolnikov she hurriedly got up and went
over to greet him, almost as if she'd been waiting for him.

'What would have become of me, but for you?' she said in a rush,
meeting him in the middle of the room. Clearly, it was this she'd so
wanted to tell him. It was this she'd been waiting for.

Raskolnikov walked over to the table and sat down on the chair
from which she'd only just got up. She stood facing him, two steps
away, just like yesterday.

'Well, Sonya?' he said and suddenly felt his voice tremble. 'So, you
see, everything hinged on "social status and the habits it implies". Did
you understand that just now?'

Suffering was written on her face.

'Just don't talk to me as you did yesterday!' she interrupted him.
'Please don't start. It's bad enough as it is . . .'

She gave him a hurried smile, frightened he might have taken her
criticism badly.

'How stupid of me to leave. What's happening there now? I was
just about to go, but I kept thinking that you might just . . . come.'

He told her that Amalia Ivanovna was throwing them out of the
apartment and that Katerina Ivanovna had run off somewhere, 'seeking justice'.

'O God!' cried Sonya with a start. 'Quick, off we go . . . !'
She grabbed her cape.

'It's always the same!' Raskolnikov exclaimed in irritation. 'All you ever think about is them! Stay with me a while.'

'What about . . . Katerina Ivanovna?'

'You'll see her soon enough, no doubt. She'll come here herself, seeing as she's already run away from home,' he added peevishly. 'And if she doesn't find you in, you'll be the one to blame . . .'

Sonya sat down, racked with indecision. Raskolnikov said nothing, staring at the floor and mulling something over.

'Let's suppose Luzhin wasn't in the mood for that now,' he began, without a glance in Sonya's direction. 'But if he had been, or if it had been part of his plans, then he'd have had you locked up, but for Lebezyatnikov and me happening to be there! Eh?'

'Yes,' she said in a weak voice. 'Yes!' she repeated, distracted and alarmed.

'But I might very easily not have been there! And as for Lebezyatnikov, it was pure chance that he showed up.'

Sonya said nothing.

'And if prison, then what? Remember what I said yesterday?'

Once again she did not reply. He was waiting.

'And I thought you'd start up again with your, "Oh, don't, please stop!"' laughed Raskolnikov, though not without a strain. 'What, more silence?' he asked a minute later. 'Surely there must be something we can talk about? What I'd really like to know, for example, is how you'd set about solving a certain "question", as Lebezyatnikov likes to say.' (He seemed to be losing his thread). 'No, really, I'm being serious. Just imagine, Sonya, that you knew all Luzhin's intentions in advance, that you knew (for a fact) that they'd be the ruin of Katerina Ivanovna, and the children, too – and of you, into the bargain (*into the bargain* seems about right, seeing as you think so little of yourself). Polechka, too . . . because she'll go the same way. Well, miss, what if it were suddenly left up to you now who should survive? Him or them? I mean, should Luzhin live and commit his abominations or should Katerina Ivanovna die? Well, what would you decide? Which of them would die? I'm asking you.'

Sonya glanced at him anxiously: she caught a peculiar note of something in his uncertain, roundabout words.

'I had a feeling you'd ask a question like that,' she said, with a searching look.

'As you wish. But still, what would you decide?'

'Why do you ask about things that can't happen?' said Sonya with disgust.

'So it's better for Luzhin to live and commit his abominations? You don't dare decide even about that?'

'But how can I know the ways of God . . . ? And why do you ask me what mustn't be asked? Why all these empty questions? How could it ever depend on my decision? And who has made me the judge here about who should live and who shouldn't?'

'Well, if you're bringing the ways of God into it, there's nothing more to be said,' muttered Raskolnikov sullenly.

'Just tell me what it is that you want!' cried Sonya with suffering. 'You're hinting at something again . . . Surely you didn't come here just to torment me!'

She could take it no longer and began sobbing bitterly. He looked at her in dismal anguish. Some five minutes passed.

'I suppose you're right, Sonya,' he said at last, softly. There was a sudden change in him; his tone of affected insolence and feeble defiance was gone. Even his voice had suddenly become weak. 'I told you myself, only yesterday, that I wouldn't come to ask forgiveness, and I've begun by doing almost precisely that, asking forgiveness . . . All that about Luzhin and the ways of God was for myself . . . That was me asking forgiveness, Sonya . . .'

He made as if to smile, but his smile came out pale, feeble, unfinished. He bowed his head and covered his face in his hands.

Suddenly, a strange, unexpected sensation of almost caustic hatred towards Sonya crossed his heart. As though himself astonished and frightened by this sensation, he suddenly raised his head and fixed his eyes upon her; but he met a look of anxiety and tortured concern. There was love here; his hatred vanished, like a phantom. He'd got it wrong; mistaken one feeling for another. All it meant was that *that* moment had come.

Once again he covered his face in his hands and bowed his head. He suddenly turned pale, got up from his chair, looked at Sonya and mechanically, without saying a word, moved over to her bed and sat down.

This moment was dreadfully similar, in sensation, to the moment when he was standing behind the old woman, having freed the axe from the loop, and felt 'there wasn't a second to lose'.

'What's the matter?' asked Sonya with dreadful timidity.

He couldn't say a word. This wasn't how he'd imagined his *declaration*, not at all, and he himself could not understand what was happening to him now. She walked over to him quietly, sat down next to him on the bed and waited, never once taking her eyes off him. Her heart pounded and froze, pounded and froze. It became unbearable: he turned his deathly pale face towards her; his lips twisted feebly, straining to say something. Dread touched Sonya's heart.

'What's the matter?' she repeated, retreating from him slightly.

'Nothing, Sonya. Don't be frightened . . . What rubbish! Really, it's just rubbish when you think about it,' he muttered, with the air of a man losing himself in his delirium. 'But why does it have to be you I've come to torment?' he added suddenly, looking at her. 'Really. Why? This is the question I keep asking myself, Sonya . . .'

Perhaps he really had been asking this question a quarter of an hour earlier, but now he was utterly enfeebled and scarcely aware of himself, his whole body trembling without pause.

'You're in such agony!' she said with suffering, looking at him intently.

'It's all rubbish! . . . Here's what, Sonya,' (for some reason he suddenly smiled, in a pale, feeble kind of way, for a second or two) 'do you remember what I wanted to say to you yesterday?'

Sonya waited anxiously.

'I said as I was leaving that I might be saying goodbye to you forever, but that if I came today I'd tell you . . . who killed Lizaveta.'

Her whole body suddenly began to shake.

'Well, here I am: I've come to tell you.'

'So you really meant it yesterday . . . ,' she whispered with difficulty. 'But why would you know?' she hurriedly asked, as if suddenly coming to her senses.

Sonya's breathing became laboured. Her face turned ever paler.

'I know.'

She was silent for about a minute.

'Has *he* been found then?' she timidly asked.

'No, he hasn't.'

'Then how come you know about *that*?' she asked, again barely audibly, and again after nearly a minute's silence.

He turned towards her and fixed her with a steady, steady stare.

'Guess,' he said, with the same twisted and feeble smile as before.

Convulsions seemed to ripple through her body.

'But you . . . Why . . . ? Why are you . . . frightening me like this?' she said, smiling like a child.

'*He* must be a great friend of mine, then . . . if I know,' Raskolnikov went on, continuing to stare at her unrelentingly, as if he no longer had the strength to avert his gaze. 'That Lizaveta . . . He didn't want . . . to kill her . . . He killed her . . . without meaning to . . . It was the old woman he wanted to kill . . . when she was alone . . . and he came . . . Only for Lizaveta to walk in . . . So then . . . he killed her.'

Another dreadful minute passed. They were both still looking at each other.

'So you can't guess, then?' he suddenly asked with the sensation of a man throwing himself from a bell tower.

'N-no,' whispered Sonya, barely audibly.

'Well, take a good look.'

No sooner had he said this than once again an old, familiar sensation suddenly turned his soul to ice: he was looking at her and suddenly, in her face, he seemed to see the face of Lizaveta. He remembered vividly the expression on Lizaveta's face when he was walking towards her then with the axe and she was retreating towards the wall, putting her arm out in front of her, with a quite childish look of fear on her face, just as little children have when something suddenly begins to frighten them, when they fix their gaze anxiously on the thing that's frightening them, back away and, holding out a little hand, prepare to cry. Almost exactly the same thing happened now to Sonya: she looked at him for a while just as feebly and just as fearfully, then suddenly, putting her left arm out in front of her, slightly, just barely, pressed her fingers into his chest and started rising slowly from the bed, backing away from him, further and further, her stare becoming ever more fixed. Her dread suddenly conveyed itself to him as well: exactly the same fear appeared on his face, too, and he began to look at her in exactly the same way, even with almost the same *childish* smile.

'Guessed?' he whispered at last.

'Lord!' broke with a dreadful howl from her breast. Enfeebled, Sonya collapsed onto the bed, face-down on the pillow. But the very next moment she hurriedly got up and moved towards him, grabbed him by both hands and, squeezing them vice-like in her slender fingers, fixed her gaze on his face once more, as if she were glued to it. With this last, desperate stare she wanted to seek out and catch some last hope for herself, however small. But there was no hope; not the slightest doubt remained. *This* was how it was! Even later, even afterwards, she felt something both strange and wondrous when she recalled this moment: why exactly had she seen *straight away* that no doubts remained? After all, she could hardly claim to have sensed that something of the kind would happen, could she? Yet now, no sooner had he said this than it suddenly seemed to her that *that* was precisely what she'd sensed.

'Enough, Sonya, enough! Don't torment me!' he asked, in a voice full of suffering.

It wasn't how he'd imagined telling her, far from it, but *this* was how it came out.

As if forgetting herself, she leapt to her feet and walked over to the middle of the room, wringing her hands; but she quickly came back and sat down next to him again, almost touching his shoulder with hers. Suddenly, as if transfixed, she shuddered, cried out and, without herself knowing why, fell to her knees before him.

'Oh what have you done to yourself?' she said in despair and, leaping to her feet, threw herself on his neck, hugged him and squeezed him tightly-tightly in her arms.

Raskolnikov drew back and looked at her with a sad smile:

'You're a strange one, Sonya – hugging and kissing me when I've just told you *about that*. You barely know what you're doing.'

'No, no, nobody in the whole world is unhappier than you are now!'[33] she exclaimed in a kind of frenzy, deaf to his remark, and began sobbing out loud, almost hysterically.

A long-unfamiliar feeling burst over his soul like a wave and softened it at once. He did not try to resist it: two tears rolled from his eyes and hung on his lashes.

'So you won't leave me, Sonya?' he said, looking at her almost hopefully.

'No, no. Never, nowhere!' cried Sonya. 'I'll follow you, wherever! O Lord! . . . How unhappy I am! . . . Why, why didn't I know you before? Why didn't you come before? O Lord!'

'Well I've come now.'

'Now! What can be done now? . . . Together! Together!' she repeated as if in a trance and hugged him again. 'I'll walk with you to Siberia!' All of a sudden his body seemed to convulse and his old, hateful and almost haughty smile broke out across his face.

'But I might not want to walk to Siberia yet, Sonya,' he said.

Sonya threw him a quick glance.

Her passionate, excruciating sympathy for the unhappy man gave way, suddenly, to the terrible idea of the murder. In his altered tone she heard the voice of the murderer. She looked at him in astonishment. She didn't know anything yet – why this had happened, how it had happened, for what reason. Now all these questions suddenly took fire in her mind. And again she could not believe it: 'Him – a murderer? How is that possible?'

'What is this? Where am I?' she said in the deepest bewilderment, as if she hadn't quite come round yet. 'How could you, a *man like you* . . . bring yourself to do that? . . . What is all this?'

'To rob her, what else? Don't, Sonya!' came his weary, even irritated reply.

Sonya stood as if stunned, but suddenly she cried:

'You were hungry! You . . . To help your mother. Yes?'

'No, Sonya, no,' he mumbled, turning away and hanging his head. 'I wasn't that hungry . . . I really did want to help my mother, but . . . that's not quite it either . . . Don't torment me, Sonya!'

Sonya threw up her hands.

'How? How can this be true? Lord, what sort of truth is that? Who could believe it? . . . And how – how could you give away your last rouble, but kill to steal? Ah!' she suddenly cried out. 'That money you gave to Katerina Ivanovna . . . that money . . . Lord, surely that wasn't the same . . . ?'

'No, Sonya,' he hastily interrupted, 'that wasn't the same money. Don't worry! That was the money my mother sent me, through a merchant, and I got it when I was sick, the same day I gave it away . . . Razumikhin saw . . . He received it on my behalf . . . That money's mine, it really is.'

Sonya listened to him in bewilderment, desperately trying to work something out.

'As for *that* money . . . actually, I don't even know that there was any,' he added quietly, almost hesitantly. 'I took a purse from her neck, a suede one . . . It was full to bursting . . . but I didn't look inside; there wasn't time, I suppose . . . As for the things, they were all cufflinks, chains and so on – I hid all the items and the purse under a stone in some courtyard, on V—— Prospect, the very next morning . . . They're still there now . . .'

Sonya was all ears.

'In that case, why . . . if you say you did it to steal, did you not take anything?' she hurriedly asked, clutching at a straw.

'I don't know . . . I still haven't decided about taking the money,' he said in the same almost hesitant way, and suddenly, coming to his senses, gave a quick grin. 'What a stupid thing I just came out with, eh?'

The thought flashed across Sonya's mind: 'Is he mad?' But it immediately vanished: no, this was something else. She didn't understand any of it, any of it!

'You know, Sonya,' he said, with sudden inspiration, 'here's what I'll say to you: if I'd killed them just because I was hungry' – he was stressing every word and looking at her with an enigmatic but sincere expression – 'then I'd be . . . *happy* now! You'd better know that!

'And anyway,' he cried out a second later, almost despairingly, 'even if I were to admit now that what I did was wrong, what good is that to you? Well, what? What good is it to you to claim this stupid victory over me? Ah, Sonya, as if that's why I've come to you now!'

Again Sonya wanted to say something, but kept silent.

'That's why I asked you to come with me yesterday – you're all I have left.'

'Come with you where?' asked Sonya timidly.

'Not to steal and not to kill – don't worry, not for that,' he said, with a caustic smile. 'We're chalk and cheese, you and I . . . You know, Sonya, it's only now, just now, that I've understood *where* it was I was asking you to go yesterday! Yesterday, when I asked you, I didn't know myself. I had one reason for asking, one reason for coming: don't leave me. You won't, Sonya, will you?'

She squeezed his hand.

'Why, why did I tell her, open up to her?' he exclaimed in despair a minute later, looking at her with infinite torment. 'Here you are, Sonya, waiting for me to explain myself, sitting and waiting. I can see it, but what can I tell you? It won't make any sense to you anyway – you'll just wear yourself out with suffering . . . because of me! There you go, crying and hugging me again – but why are you hugging me? Because I couldn't bear it any longer and I've come here to unload my burden? "You suffer too and I'll suffer less!" And you can love such a scoundrel?'

'But you're in agony too!' cried Sonya.

Again the same feeling burst like a wave over his soul and again softened it for an instant.

'Sonya, I have an angry heart, remember that: it explains a great deal. That's why I came here – because I'm angry. There are those who wouldn't have come. But I'm a coward and ... a scoundrel! But ... never mind! That's all by the by ... Now's the time for speaking, and I can't even start ...'

He paused, deep in thought.

'Chalk and cheese, that's us!' he cried again. 'And why, why have I come? I'll never forgive myself!'

'No, no, it's good you've come!' exclaimed Sonya. 'It's better that I know! Far better!'

He looked at her in anguish.

'But perhaps that's just it!' he said, as if he'd finally made his mind up. 'That's how it was! Listen: I wanted to become a Napoleon, that's why I killed ... Now do you understand?'

'N-no,' whispered Sonya, guilelessly and timidly, 'but ... speak, speak! I'll understand – I'll understand everything *inside myself*!' she begged him.

'You will? Fine – so let's see!'

He fell silent and had a long think.

'Here's what: I once asked myself the following question: what if, say, Napoleon had found himself in my shoes and had neither Toulon nor Egypt nor the pass at Mont Blanc[34] to get his career going, and instead of all those beautiful, grand things all he had was some ridiculous old hag, some pen-pusher's widow, and what's more he'd have to murder her to get his hands on the money she kept in her box (for his career, understand?); well, could he have brought himself to do that, if he had no other way out? Wouldn't he have been put off by the fact that it was insufficiently grand, to say the least, and ... and a sin? Well then, let me tell you that I agonized over this "question" for such a long time that I was horribly ashamed when it finally got through to me (all of a sudden) that not only would he not have been put off, it wouldn't even have occurred to him that there was nothing grand about it ... he wouldn't even have understood the question: put off by what? And if there really were no other path open to him, he'd have throttled her before she could even squeak, with no second thoughts! ... So I, too ... put second thoughts aside ... and throttled her ... taking him as my authority . . . And that's precisely what happened! You find it funny? Yes, Sonya, and the funniest thing about it is that perhaps this is exactly how it was . . .'

Sonya didn't find it funny in the least.

'Please speak plainly . . . without examples,' she asked even more timidly, barely audibly.

He turned to face her, looked at her sadly and took her hands in his.

'You're right again, Sonya. That's all rubbish; little more than empty talk! You see, my mother, as you know, has almost nothing. By chance, my sister received an education and now she has to go from one governess job to another. They pinned all their hopes on me. I was at university, but I could no longer support myself and had to put my studies on hold. Still, even if things had gone on like that, in ten, maybe twelve years' time (circumstances permitting) I'd have had every chance of finding a job in a school or in the civil service somewhere, on a thousand roubles a year . . .' (He spoke as if he'd learned it all by heart.) 'But by then mother would have wasted away with worry and grief, and there'd have been nothing I could have done to reassure her, while my sister . . . well, her plight might have been even worse! . . . And anyway, who wants to go through life walking past everything, turning your back on everything, forgetting about your mother and, for example, respectfully putting up with insults to your sister? What for? So that once they're dead you can replace them with new ones – a wife and children, and then leave them, too, without a copeck or a crust of bread? So . . . so I decided I'd use the hag's money on my first few years, on supporting myself at university and taking my first steps after that without pestering Mother – and I'd make a real go of it, setting up my new career in such a way that I could hardly fail, and launching myself on a new, independent path . . . And . . . well, that's about it . . . Yes, of course, killing the old woman was a bad thing to do . . . but enough!'

He limped feebly to the end of his story and hung his head.

'Oh, that's not it,' Sonya exclaimed in anguish. 'How could it be . . . ? No, that's not it, it's not!'

'You can see that yourself! . . . But I was being sincere. I was telling the truth!'

'What sort of truth is that? O Lord!'

'I only killed a louse, Sonya, a useless, foul, noxious louse.'

'A human being, not a louse!'

'I know that myself,' he replied, giving her a strange look. 'But I'm lying, Sonya,' he added. 'I've been lying for so long . . . That's not it at all. You're right. The real reasons are quite different – quite different! . . . I haven't talked to anyone for so long, Sonya . . . My head's aching terribly.'

His eyes blazed with fever and fire. He was on the verge of delirium and an anxious smile played on his lips. But his excitement could no longer conceal his complete enfeeblement. Sonya saw his suffering. Her head, too, was beginning to spin. And what a strange way he had of putting things: it almost seemed to make sense, but . . . 'How on earth? How, Lord?' And she wrung her hands in despair.

'No, Sonya, that's not it!' he began again, suddenly lifting his head, as though a sudden, surprising change in the direction of his thoughts had aroused him again. 'That's not it! Better for you . . . to assume (yes! it really is better!) that I'm vain, envious, angry, loathsome, vindictive and . . . and – why not? – prone to madness as well. (Better to get it all out at once! There was talk of madness before – I noticed!) I told you just now that I couldn't support myself at university. But . . . maybe I could. Mother would have sent me enough for my fees, and as for shoes, clothes and meals, I'd have earned what I needed myself. I'm sure of it! There were lessons going, fifty copecks a time. Razumikhin works, doesn't he? But I didn't want to – out of spite. Yes, *out of spite* (a fine phrase!). So I crawled back into my little corner, like a spider. You've been in my hovel, you've seen what it's like . . . Do you have any idea, Sonya, how small rooms and low ceilings cramp the soul and the mind? Oh, how I hated that hovel! But I still didn't want to leave it. On purpose! I was there day and night, didn't want to work, didn't even want to eat, just lay there. If Nastasya brought something, I'd eat a bit; if not – the day would just pass. I wouldn't ask on purpose, from spite! At night, I just lay there in the dark – didn't even want to earn enough for a candle. I should have been studying, but I'd sold my books; even now the dust on my desk, on my papers and notebooks, is half an inch deep. I preferred to lie on the couch and think. Think and think . . . And my dreams were always so strange, no two the same – I can't begin to describe them! But that was when I also began imagining that . . . No, that's not it! I'm still not telling it right! You see, at the time I couldn't stop asking myself: why am I so stupid that even though others are stupid and I know for a fact that they're stupid, I don't want to be any cleverer? Later, Sonya, I discovered that if you wait for everyone else to become cleverer, you'll be waiting a very long time . . . Later still I discovered that this will never happen anyway, that people will never change, and no one can reform them, and there's no point trying! Yes, that's it! That's their law . . . Their law, Sonya! That's it! . . . And now I know, Sonya, that he who is tough in mind and spirit will be their master! For them, he who dares is right. He who cares least is their lawmaker, and he who dares most is most right! It's always been the way and always will be! Only a blind man would fail to see it!'

Though Raskolnikov was looking at Sonya as he said this, he no longer worried whether or not she would understand. The fever had him in its grip. Some dismal ecstasy had overcome him. (Yes, it had been far too long since he'd last spoken to anyone!) Sonya understood that this gloomy catechism had become his creed and law.

'That, Sonya,' he continued rapturously, 'was when I realized that power is given only to the man who dares to stoop and grab. One thing, just one: to dare! A certain thought came to me then, for the first time in my life; one which had never come to anyone, ever! Anyone! It suddenly dawned on me like the sun: how come not a single person, walking past all these absurdities, has ever dared, not now, not ever, to grab everything by the tail and shake it to hell? I . . . I felt like trying . . . I killed *for a dare*, Sonya, and that's the whole reason!'

'Oh, be quiet, be quiet!' cried Sonya, throwing up her arms. 'You walked away from God and God struck you and gave you away to the devil!'

'By the way, Sonya – when I was lying in the dark and all this was dawning on me,[35] was that the devil playing with my mind? Eh?'

'Be quiet! Don't you dare laugh, you blasphemous man. You don't understand a thing, not a thing! O Lord! He'll never understand, never!'

'Hush, Sonya, I'm not laughing at all. I know myself that it was the devil dragging me along. Hush, Sonya, hush!' he repeated dismally and insistently. 'I know everything. I thought and whispered my way through it all while lying on my own in the dark back then . . . Argued my way through every point, down to the last little mark, the last little jot, and I know everything, everything! How sick and tired I was of all this empty talk! I wanted to forget it all and start again, Sonya, and stop wittering! Surely you don't think I went there like some idiot, without a moment's thought? I went there like a man with brains, and that was my downfall! Can't you see that I must have known that if I'd already started asking myself the question, "Do I have a right to power?", then it already meant I didn't. Or that if I asked, "Is a human being a louse?", then man was certainly no louse *for me*, only for someone to whom the question never occurs, and who sets off without asking questions ... And if I'd already tormented myself for so many days wondering, "Would Napoleon have gone or wouldn't he?", then I obviously knew that I was no Napoleon ... I endured all the agony of this empty talk, Sonya, all of it, and now I just wanted to shake it off. I wanted to kill without casuistry, Sonya, to kill for myself, for myself alone! I didn't want to lie about it, not even to myself! It wasn't to help mother that I killed – nonsense! It wasn't to acquire funds and power that I killed, so as to make myself a benefactor of humanity. Nonsense! I just killed. I killed for myself, for myself alone; and whether I'd become anyone's benefactor or spend my entire life as a spider, catching everyone in my web and sucking out their vital juices, shouldn't have mattered to me one jot at that moment! ... And it wasn't so much money I needed, Sonya, when I killed; not so much money as something else ... I know all this now ... Try to understand: taking that same road again, I might never have repeated the murder. There was something else I needed to find out then, something else was nudging me along: what I needed to find out, and find out quickly, was whether I was a louse, like everyone else, or a human being. Could I take that step or couldn't I? Would I dare to stoop and grab or wouldn't I? Was I a quivering creature or did I have *the right* ... ?'

'To murder? The right to murder?' Sonya threw up her arms.

'Oh, Sonya!' he cried out in exasperation. He was about to answer back, but lapsed into scornful silence. 'Don't interrupt me, Sonya! I merely wanted to prove one thing to you: that it was the devil who dragged me along then, and only after did he explain to me that I had no right to go there, because I'm as much of a louse as everyone else! He had a good laugh at me then, so here I am! Make me welcome! Would I have come to you now if I weren't a louse? Listen: when I went to the old woman that time, it was only as a *test* ... You'd better know that!'

'And you killed! You killed!'

'But just look how I did it! Who kills like that? Who goes off to kill the way I went off to kill? One day I'll tell you what that was like ... Was it really the hag I killed? It was myself I killed, not her! I murdered myself in one fell blow, for all time! ... And the hag was killed

by the devil, not me . . . Enough, Sonya. Enough! Enough! Leave me
be!' he suddenly cried, convulsed with anguish. 'Leave me be!'

He rested his elbows on his knees, his head clamped between his
palms.

'Such suffering!' came Sonya's howl of torment.

'So what's to be done? Tell me!' he asked, suddenly lifting his head
and looking at her, his face disfigured by despair.

'What's to be done?' she exclaimed, leaping from her seat, her tearful eyes suddenly ablaze. 'Get up!' (She grabbed him by the shoulder
and he started getting to his feet, looking at her in near amazement.)
'Off you go, right now, this minute, stand at the crossroads and bow
down; kiss the earth you've polluted,[36] then bow down to the whole
world, to all four corners, and tell everyone out loud: "I have killed!"
Then God will send you life once more. Are you going? Are you going?' she asked him, shaking all over as if in a fit, grabbing both his
hands, squeezing them hard in her own and looking at him with fire
in her eyes.

He was amazed and even shocked by this sudden ecstasy.

'Do you mean Siberia, Sonya? What, do I have to turn myself in?'
he asked, dismally.

'Accept suffering and through suffering redeem yourself – that is
what you must do.'

'No! I won't go to them, Sonya.'

'Then how will you live? How on earth will you keep going?' exclaimed Sonya. 'How's that even possible now? How will you ever
speak to your mother? (And what on earth will they do now?) But
what am I saying? You've already abandoned your mother and sister,
haven't you? Of course you have. O Lord!' she cried. 'But he already
knows it all himself! How, how can you live your life without a single
human being? What will become of you now?'

'Don't be a child, Sonya,' he said softly. 'In what way am I guilty before them? Why should I go? What would I say to them? These are all
just phantoms . . . They themselves wipe out millions and think it a virtue. They're swindlers and scoundrels, Sonya! . . . I won't go. What
would I say? That I killed, but didn't dare take the money and hid it
under a stone?' he added with a caustic grin. 'They'll only laugh at me
and say: "You're an idiot for not taking it. A coward and an idiot!" They
won't understand anything, Sonya, anything, and they don't deserve to
understand. Why should I go? I won't go. Don't be a child, Sonya . . .'

'The torment will be too much for you,' she said, holding her arms out towards him in a despairing plea.

'Maybe I'm *still* slandering myself now,' he remarked dismally, in a pensive kind of way. 'Maybe I'm *still* a human being, not a louse, and I was in too much of a hurry to condemn myself . . . Maybe I can *still* fight.'

A haughty smile was forcing itself to his lips.

'To bear such torment! And for a whole lifetime, a whole lifetime!'

'I'll get used to it . . .' he said sullenly, seriously. 'Listen,' he began a minute later, 'enough crying, enough talking. I've come to tell you that they're after me, looking for me . . .'

'Ah!' shrieked Sonya in fright.

'There's no need to shriek! You yourself want me to go to Siberia and now you're frightened? Only I won't let them have their way. I've still got some fight left in me and they won't get anywhere. They've no proper evidence. Yesterday I was in grave danger and thought I was done for; today things are looking up. All their evidence is double-edged. I can turn all their accusations to my advantage – understand? – and that's precisely what I'll do. Now I know how . . . They'll put me away, though, that's for sure. But for one stroke of fortune, they'd probably have done so already today, and they might *still* do so . . . But that's nothing, Sonya. They'll keep me in a bit, then let me out . . . because they haven't a scrap of solid proof and never will, I give you my word. And what they do have isn't enough to lock anyone up. Well, enough of that . . . I just wanted you to know . . . As for my sister and mother, I'll do what I can to put their minds at rest . . . Anyway, my sister seems to be out of harm's way now . . . so mother is, too . . . Well, that's about it. Be careful, though. Will you visit me, once I'm inside?'

'Oh yes! Yes!'

They sat side by side, sad and broken, as if they'd been washed up, after a storm, alone on an empty shore. He looked at Sonya and felt all her love upon him. How strange: he suddenly found it hard and painful to be loved so much. Yes, a strange and dreadful feeling! Walking over to Sonya's he'd felt that she was his one hope, his one way out; he'd expected to cast off at least some of his suffering, and now, all of a sudden, when her whole heart was turned towards him, he suddenly felt and realized that he was infinitely unhappier than before.

'Actually, Sonya,' he said, 'you'd better not visit when I'm inside.'

Sonya did not reply; she was crying. Several minutes passed.

'Are you wearing a cross?' she unexpectedly asked, as if suddenly remembering.

At first, he failed to understand the question.

'You aren't, are you? Here, take this one, a cypress one. I've got another, a copper one, Lizaveta's. Lizaveta and I swapped crosses: she gave me hers, I gave her my little icon. Now I'll start wearing Lizaveta's and you take this one. Take it ... It's mine! Mine!' she begged him. 'Together we'll suffer. Together we'll carry the cross!'

'Give it to me!' said Raskolnikov. He didn't want to upset her. But he immediately withdrew his hand.

'Not now, Sonya. Better later,' he added, to reassure her.

'Yes, yes, better, better,' she echoed enthusiastically. 'When you go away to suffer, that's when you'll wear it. You'll come to me, I'll put it on you, we'll pray and we'll go.'

There and then someone knocked three times on the door.

'Sofya Semyonovna, may I?' came a very familiar, courteous voice.

Sonya rushed to the door in alarm. Mr Lebezyatnikov's blond head poked round it.

V

Lebezyatnikov looked worried.

'I'm here to see you, Sofya Semyonovna. Do forgive me ... I thought I'd find you here,' he suddenly addressed Raskolnikov. 'Now don't get me wrong ... I didn't think anything ... of that kind ... But I did think ... Katerina Ivanovna has gone mad,' he suddenly informed Sonya, abandoning Raskolnikov.

Sonya shrieked.

'Or so, at least, it would appear. Although ... Well, we don't know what to do about it, that's the problem, miss! She's back now ... She was thrown out by someone somewhere, and maybe beaten a bit as well ... or so it would appear ... She'd gone tearing over to see Semyon Zakharych's head of department, but he wasn't at home; some other general had invited him over for lunch ... So – can you imagine? – off she ran ... to this other general and – can you imagine? – simply insisted on being seen by the head, and even, it would appear, while he was still eating. You can guess what happened next. They threw her out, of course; though she says she called him names and even threw something at him. Perfectly plausible, I suppose ... How she got away scot-free I'll

never know! Now she's busy telling everyone about it – Amalia Ivanovna, too – only it's hard to understand her when she's shouting and flailing about ... Oh yes, she's yelling about how – now that everyone's
abandoned her – she'll take to the streets with her children and drag a
barrel-organ around, and the children will sing and dance – her, too –
and collect money and go and stand under the general's window every
day ... "Let them see the noble children of a state official walk the
streets like beggars!" she says. She keeps beating the children – they cry.
She's teaching Lenya to sing "Little Farm" and the little boy to dance,
and Polina Mikhailovna, too; she's ripping up all their clothes and making little hats for them, like actors wear; she wants to carry a basin
around with her and bang on it, instead of a musical instrument ...
Won't listen to a word you say ... Can you imagine? I mean, really!'

Lebezyatnikov would have gone on and on, but Sonya, who
scarcely drew breath as she listened, suddenly grabbed her cape and
hat and ran out of the room, putting them on as she went. Raskolnikov went out after her; Lebezyatnikov followed.

'She's definitely gone crazy!' he said to Raskolnikov as they stepped
outside. 'I just didn't want to scare Sofya Semyonovna, so I said, "It
would appear", but there's no doubt about it. Consumptives get these
tubercles on the brain,[37] I'm told. Shame I know so little about medicine. I tried persuading her of it, but she just won't listen.'

'You told her about the tubercles?'

'Not exactly. She'd never have understood anyway. What I'm saying is: if you persuade a man through logic that, in essence, he has
nothing to cry about, he'll soon stop crying. That much is clear. Why?
Is it your belief that he won't?'

'Life would be too easy then,' replied Raskolnikov.

'I disagree, sir. It's a difficult business understanding Katerina Ivanovna, of course, but are you aware that in Paris serious experiments
have already been conducted with regard to the possibility of curing
the mad through logical persuasion? One professor there, a serious
scholar, recently deceased, came up with this notion. His main idea
was that the mad do not suffer from any particular disturbance of the
organism, but that madness is, as it were, a logical error, an error of
judgement, an incorrect view of things. He gradually refuted his patient's arguments and, I'm told, achieved certain results. Can you imagine? But since he also used shower-baths the results of this treatment
may, of course, be questioned ... Or so it would appear ...'

Raskolnikov had long ceased listening. Drawing level with his building, he nodded to Lebezyatnikov and turned in through the arch. Lebezyatnikov came to, looked about him and hurried on.

Raskolnikov entered his garret and stood in the middle of the room. Why had he come back here? He ran his eye over this yellowish, frayed wallpaper, this dust, his couch ... From the yard there came a loud, constant banging, as if something somewhere were being knocked in, some nail or other ... He went over to the window, stood on tiptoe and, with an exceptionally attentive air, scanned the courtyard for a good long while. But the yard was empty and he couldn't see anyone banging away. To the left, in the side wing, a few windows were open; on the sills were pots with straggly geraniums. Washing hung outside the windows ... He knew it all by heart. He turned away and sat down on the couch.

Never in all his life had he felt so dreadfully alone!

Yes, he felt once again that perhaps he really could come to hate Sonya, and precisely now, after making her more miserable. Why had he gone to beg her tears? Why was it so necessary for him to prey on her? The shame of it!

'I'll stay on my own!' he said with sudden decisiveness. 'And she won't visit me in prison!'

Five minutes later he lifted his head and smiled strangely. A strange thought – 'Perhaps I'll be better off in Siberia' – had suddenly occurred to him.

He couldn't remember how long he sat in his room, his mind crowded with uncertain thoughts. Suddenly the door opened and Avdotya Romanovna walked in. She stopped and looked at him from the threshold, as he had at Sonya before; and only then did she come through and sit down opposite him, on the chair she'd sat in yesterday. He looked at her in silence, as if he weren't even thinking.

'Don't be cross, brother, I'll only stay a minute,' said Dunya. The expression on her face was pensive, but not stern. Her gaze was clear and soft. He saw that this one, too, had come to him with love.

'Brother, I know everything now, *everything*. Dmitry Prokofich explained everything to me. You're being hounded and tormented, all because of some stupid, vile suspicion ... Dmitry Prokofich told me there's no danger whatsoever and you needn't be so horrified by it all. That's not what I think and I *completely understand* that you must be seething inside, and that this indignation may leave a permanent scar.

This is what scares me. I do not and dare not judge you for abandoning us, and forgive me for reproaching you before. I can fully imagine how I would feel if such a terrible misfortune were to befall me: I, too, would turn away from everyone. I won't tell Mother anything *about that*, but I will talk about you constantly and say on your behalf that you will come very soon. Don't torture yourself about her. *I'll* reassure her; but don't torture her, either – come round once, at least. She's your mother, remember that! But the only reason I've come now' (Dunya started getting up) 'is to say that if, by any chance, you should need me for anything or you should need . . . my entire life, or anything . . . just call for me and I'll come. Goodbye!'

She turned round sharply and made towards the door.

'Dunya!' Raskolnikov stopped her, getting up and walking towards her. 'This Razumikhin, Dmitry Prokofich, is a very good man.'

Dunya coloured slightly.

'And?' she asked after waiting a minute or so.

'He's a business-like, hard-working, honest man, capable of great love . . . Goodbye, Dunya.'

She flushed all over, then suddenly panicked:

'Brother, what are you saying? Surely we're not parting for good? Why all these . . . instructions?'

'Never mind . . . Goodbye . . .'

He turned and walked away from her towards the window. She waited a moment, looked at him anxiously and left in great alarm.

No, he hadn't been cold towards her. There'd been a moment (the very last) when he was seized by the urge to hug her close and *take his leave* of her, and even *tell* her, but he couldn't bring himself even to give her his hand.

'She'll only shudder when she remembers how I hugged her just now – she'll say her kiss was stolen!

'Will *this one* be able to cope or won't she?' he added a few minutes later, still thinking to himself. 'No, she won't cope. Not *people like her*! They never can . . .'

And he thought of Sonya.

A fresh breeze came in through the window. Outside it was no longer quite so bright. He grabbed his cap and went out.

He, of course, could not and would not pay any heed to his sick condition. But this continuous anxiety and all this dread in his soul could not pass without consequence. And if he was not yet laid up with a high fever, then perhaps it was only because this inner, continuous anxiety was keeping him on his feet and in his senses, albeit in a somewhat artificial, temporary way.

He wandered aimlessly. The sun was setting. Some particular anguish had begun to communicate itself to him lately. There was nothing particularly caustic or scalding about it; instead, it was somehow constant and eternal, presaging year on year of this cold, deadening anguish, some kind of eternity on 'one square yard'. In the evening this sensation usually began to torment him even more.

'With such idiotic, purely physical ailments that all depend on some sunset or other, how can you avoid doing something stupid? Never mind Sonya, you'll end up going to Dunya!' he muttered with loathing.

Someone called his name. He looked round. Lebezyatnikov rushed towards him.

'I was at your place just now. I've been looking for you. Can you imagine? She's done what she said she'd do and taken the children off with her! Sofya Semyonovna and I had a real job finding them. She's banging away on a frying pan, forcing the children to sing and dance. They're crying. They stop at crossroads and outside shops. Silly commoners run after them. Let's go.'

'And Sonya?' asked Raskolnikov anxiously, hurrying after Lebezyatnikov.

'In a complete frenzy. Not Sofya Semyonovna, I mean, but Katerina Ivanovna; although Sofya Semyonovna is in a frenzy, too. But Katerina Ivanovna is in a perfect frenzy. I'm telling you, she's completely mad. They'll end up at the police station. You can imagine the effect that will have on . . . They're by the Ditch now, near ——sky Bridge, not far at all from Sofya Semyonovna's place. Close by.'

By the Ditch, not far from the bridge and only two buildings before Sonya's, a small throng had gathered – mainly little boys and girls. Katerina Ivanonvna's hoarse, frayed voice was audible even from the bridge. It was indeed a strange spectacle, more than capable of grabbing the interest of the street. Katerina Ivanovna, wearing her old dress, the *drap de dames* shawl and a ruined straw hat scrunched up horribly on one side, really was in a frenzy. She was tired and gasping for breath. Never had her worn-out, consumptive face expressed more suffering (not to mention the fact that outside, in the sun, a consumptive always looks more sickly and disfigured than at home); but her excitement did not abate and she grew more irritable by the minute.

She kept rushing over to the children, shouting at them, urging them on, teaching them right there, in front of everyone, how to dance and what to sing, trying to make them understand why all this was necessary, despairing at their dimness, hitting them ... Then, suddenly abandoning them, she would rush over to the crowd. If she noticed anyone watching who was even remotely well-dressed, she would immediately set about explaining to that person what these children 'from a noble, one might even say aristocratic household' had been driven to. If she heard laughter in the crowd or some pointed remark, she'd immediately pounce on the impudent offenders and give them a piece of her mind. Some really were laughing, others were shaking their heads, and all were curious to have a good look at the crazy woman with the terrified children. The frying pan which Lebezyatnikov had mentioned was nowhere to be seen – Raskolnikov, at least, had not seen it – but instead of banging a pan, Katerina Ivanovna was marking time with her dry palms as she made Polechka sing and Lenya and Kolya dance. Not only that, she even started singing along herself, but every time she did so an excruciating coughing fit would cut her short on the second note and she would plunge into despair once more, cursing her cough and even crying. But nothing infuriated her more than the tears and terror of Kolya and Lenya. Efforts really had been made to dress the children up as street singers. The boy's head was wrapped in a turban of red and white material, to make him resemble a Turk. No such outfit was found for Lenya; all she had was the late Semyon Zakharych's red worsted cap (or rather, nightcap), pierced with a fragment of the white ostrich feather that once belonged to Katerina Ivanovna's grandmother and had been kept until now in the trunk, as a family curiosity. Polechka was wearing her usual little dress. She was looking at her mother timidly, in bewilderment, never leaving her side, gulping back tears, suspecting her mother's derangement and nervously looking about her. The street and the crowd had given her a dreadful fright. Sonya walked after Katerina Ivanovna everywhere, crying and pleading with her again and again to go back home. But Katerina Ivanovna was implacable.

'Stop it, Sonya! Stop it!' she shouted in great haste, gasping and coughing. 'You don't even know what you're asking – just like a child! I've already told you I won't be going back to that woman, that German drunk. Let everyone – all Petersburg – watch the children of a noble father go begging, a father who was a loyal and faithful servant

all his life and who, one might say, died at his post.' (Katerina Ivanovna had already managed to concoct this fantasy for herself and believe
in it blindly.) 'All the better if that useless general sees us. Anyway,
you're being silly, Sonya. What will we eat now, tell me that? We've
tortured you enough – I won't stand for any more! Oh, Rodion Romanych, it's you!' she shrieked, catching sight of Raskolnikov and rushing towards him. 'Please make this fool of a girl understand that this
is the cleverest thing we can do! Even organ-grinders make a living,
and as for us, we'll be singled out straight away – everyone will see
we're a poor noble family of orphans reduced to beggary, and that
poxy general will lose his position, you'll see! We'll stand under the
general's window each day, and when the Tsar goes by in his carriage
I'll fall to my knees, push this lot out in front of me, point at them and
cry: "Protect us, Father!" He is the father of all orphans, he is merciful, he will protect us, you'll see; and as for this lousy general . . .
Lenya! *Tenez-vous droite*![38] And you, Kolya, you'll be dancing again
in a minute. What are you whimpering about? There, he's whimpering again! What are you so scared of, you stupid little boy? Lord!
What am I to do with them, Rodion Romanych? If only you knew
how dim they are! What on earth is one to do with them?'

And, on the verge of tears (which did nothing to stem her relent-
less, unceasing patter), she pointed at the whimpering children. Raskolnikov wanted to convince her to go back and even said, as a sop to
her vanity, that it was unseemly for her to walk the streets like an
organ-grinder, seeing as she was preparing to be headmistress of a
boarding school for girls of the nobility . . .

'A boarding school? Ha-ha-ha! That would be nice!' cried Katerina
Ivanovna, her laughter immediately yielding to a fit of coughing. 'No,
Rodion Romanovich, that dream is gone! Everyone's abandoned
us! . . . And as for that lousy general . . . Do you know, Rodion Romanych, I threw an inkpot at him – there was one on the table, in the
lobby, next to the sheet you have to sign, so I signed, threw it and ran
off. Oh, the scum! But never mind. From now on I'm going to feed
this lot myself – I won't bow down to anyone! We've put her through
enough misery!' (She pointed at Sonya.) 'Polechka, how much have
you all collected? Show me! What? Just two copecks? Oh, the beasts!
They never give anything, just run after us with their tongues hanging
out! Now what's this halfwit got to laugh about?' (She pointed at a
man in the crowd.) 'Kolya's dimness is to blame for all this – he's hard

work, that boy! Yes, Polechka? Speak to me in French, *parlez-moi français*. I taught you, didn't I? I'm sure you remember a few phrases! . . . Otherwise who's to know you're from a noble family, that you're well-brought-up children and nothing like other organ-grinders? This isn't some puppet show we're performing, you know, some *Petrushka*[39] or other! We'll sing something noble – a *romance* . . . Oh yes – so what are we going to sing? You keep interrupting me and we . . . You see, Rodion Romanovich, the reason we stopped here was to choose what to sing – something even Kolya can dance to . . . because, as you can well imagine, we haven't prepared any of this. We need to agree on what we're doing, practise till everything's perfect, then head off to Nevsky Prospect, where the public is far more discerning and we'll be noticed right away. Lenya knows "Little Farm"[40] . . . "Little Farm" and nothing else – they're all at it! We should be singing something far nobler . . . Any ideas, Polya? You, at least, should help me out! My memory's gone, clean gone, or else I'd remember! We can hardly sing "The Hussar Leaning on His Sabre" can we? Oh, let's sing that French song "*Cinq sous*"![41] I taught you, didn't I? The main thing is it's in French, so they'll see straight away that you're gentry children and that will be so much more touching . . . Or even "*Marlborough s'en va-t-en guerre*", as it's perfect for children and is sung as a lullaby in every aristocratic household.

> *Marlborough s'en va-t-en guerre,*
> *Ne sait quand reviendra . . .*[42]

she began singing . . . 'Actually, no – let's have "*Cinq sous!*" Come on, Kolya, hands on hips, look lively, and Lenya, you spin round the other way, while Polechka and I sing along and clap!

> *Cinq sous, cinq sous,*
> *Pour monter notre ménage . . .*[43]

Cuh-cuh-cuh!' (Once again, the coughs came thick and fast.) 'Straighten that dress, Polechka, your shoulders are showing,' she observed between coughs, out of breath. 'Now more than ever you have to look decent and dainty, so that everyone can see you're gentry. Didn't I say that your bodice should have been cut a bit longer and made from two widths? It was you, Sonya, who kept saying, "Shorter,

shorter," and now look, the child's a disgrace . . . But what are you all crying about again? Such stupid children! Come on then, Kolya, I'm waiting – oh, what an insufferable boy!

Cinq sous, cinq sous . . .

Not another soldier! Well, what do you want?'
A policeman really was squeezing through the crowd. But at the very same time a respectable-looking civil servant of about fifty, wearing uniform, a greatcoat and a decoration around his neck (which particularly pleased Katerina Ivanovna and impressed the policeman), came up and silently handed a green, three-rouble banknote to Katerina Ivanovna. His face expressed sincere compassion. Katerina Ivanovna accepted it and made a courteous, even ceremonious, bow.
'I thank you, kind sir,' she began loftily. 'The reasons prompting us to . . . Now take the money, Polechka. See, there are noble, generous souls, ready, at a moment's notice, to help a poor gentlewoman in distress. You see before you, kind sir, well-born orphans with, one might say, the most aristocratic connections . . . Meanwhile, that poxy general just sat there eating hazel grouse . . . and stamping his feet at me for having disturbed him . . . "Your Excellency," I say, "protect the orphans," I say, "knowing the late Semyon Zakharych so very well and bearing in mind the fact that his own daughter was slandered so viciously by that scoundrel, that scum of the earth, on the very day of his death . . ." Not that soldier again! Protect us!' she screamed at the civil servant. 'Why does he have to keep pestering me? We only came here to get away from another one, on Meshchanskaya Street . . . Mind your own business, you stupid man!'
'But this is forbidden in public, ma'am. Please cease this disgraceful behaviour.'
'You're the disgrace! I'm no different from an organ-grinder, so mind your business!'
'Organ-grinders need a licence, since you mention it, but you're making a public nuisance of yourself. Where are you lodging, ma'am?'
'A licence!' yelled Katerina Ivanovna. 'I buried my husband today and you talk about licences!'
'Madam, madam, please calm down,' the civil servant began. 'Let's go – I'll accompany you . . . It's unseemly here, with all this crowd . . . You're not well . . .'

'Kind sir, you know nothing!' shouted Katerina Ivanovna. 'We're off to Nevsky – Sonya, Sonya! Where has she got to? Crying as well! What's wrong with you all? . . . Kolya, Lenya, where are you off to?' she suddenly cried in alarm. 'Oh, stupid children! Kolya, Lenya, where on earth are they going?'

What had happened was that Kolya and Lenya, frightened out of their wits by the crowd and the whims of their crazy mother, and seeing that a soldier was just about to take them off somewhere, suddenly, as if with one mind, grabbed each other by the hand and took to their heels. Poor Katerina Ivanovna set off after them, yelling and weeping. It was a ghastly, pitiful thing to see her running, weeping, gasping. Sonya and Polechka rushed after her.

'Bring them back, Sonya! Bring them back! Oh, stupid, ungrateful children! . . . Polya, catch them! . . . It was for you that I . . .'

At full tilt, she stumbled and fell.

'She's badly hurt – she's bleeding! O Lord!' cried Sonya, bending over her.

Everyone came running, everyone crowded round. Raskolnikov and Lebezyatnikov were among the first to arrive; the civil servant also hurried over, followed by the policeman, grumbling 'My oh my!' and gesturing as if to say – what a nuisance this is going to be.

'Out of the way! Out of the way!' he shouted at the crowd.

'She's dying!' cried a voice.

'She's mad!' came another.

'God save us!' said one woman, crossing herself. 'Did they catch the little mites? Well I never – here they come, the eldest has caught 'em . . . All very peculiar!'

But when Katerina Ivanovna was properly examined, it transpired that she hadn't hurt herself against the stones, as Sonya thought; the blood that was staining the road purple was gushing up from her chest.

'I've seen this before, gentlemen,' the civil servant muttered to Raskolnikov and Lebezyatnikov. 'It's consumption. The blood just gushes up and chokes you. I saw it happen to a woman I know, a relative, just recently – about a pint of it . . . just like that . . . Still, what should we do now? She'll die any minute.'

'This way, this way, to my room!' Sonya pleaded. 'I live right here! . . . That building there, the second one along . . . To my place – quick! Quick!' she begged everyone, rushing from one person to another. 'Send for a doctor . . . O Lord!'

Thanks to the civil servant, this was quickly arranged, and even the policeman helped carry Katerina Ivanovna. She was brought into Sonya's room more dead than alive and placed on the bed. The bleeding continued, but it seemed as if she were beginning to come round. Sonya was immediately followed into her room by Raskolnikov, Lebezyatnikov, the civil servant and the policeman, the latter having first dispersed the crowd, from which a few accompanied them right to the door. Kolya and Lenya, trembling and crying, were led in by Polechka. The Kapernaumovs came over too: there was Kapernaumov himself, lame and crooked, a strange-looking man with unruly, bristly hair and whiskers; his wife, with her permanently frightened look; and several of their children, with faces frozen in perpetual surprise and mouths hanging open. Amidst all these another person suddenly appeared – Svidrigailov. Raskolnikov looked at him in astonishment, wondering how he'd got there and unable to recall his face in the crowd.

There was talk of doctors and priests. The civil servant, while whispering to Raskolnikov that there was little need for a doctor now, instructed that one be sent for. Kapernaumov himself hurried off to fetch him.

Meanwhile, Katerina Ivanovna got her breath back and for a time the bleeding abated. She fixed her sick, though steady and piercing gaze on pale, trembling Sonya, who was wiping beads of sweat from Katerina Ivanovna's brow; eventually, she asked to be lifted up. They sat her up on the bed, supporting her on both sides.

'And the children?' she asked in a weak voice. 'Did you bring them, Polya? Oh, stupid ones! . . . Why did you have to run away? . . . Ahh!'

Her parched lips were still covered in blood. She cast her eyes around her:

'So this is how you live, Sonya! The first time I've ever been here . . . Now of all times . . .'

Her eyes were full of pain as she looked at her:

'We've sucked you dry, Sonya . . . Polya, Lenya, Kolya, come here . . . So, Sonya, here they all are, take them . . . from my hands to yours . . . You'll get no more from me! . . . The dance is over! Ahh! . . . Lower me back down. Let me die in peace, at least . . .'

They lowered her onto the pillow again.

'What's that? A priest? Don't bother . . . As if you've got money for that! . . . There's no sins on me! . . . God should forgive me without all

that . . . He knows how I've suffered! . . . And if he won't forgive me –
fine!'

A restless delirium was steadily gaining hold of her. Now and then
she would startle, cast her eyes around and briefly recognize everyone;
but awareness instantly gave way to delirium. Her breathing was
hoarse and laboured; a kind of gurgle seemed to come from her throat.

' "Your Excellency!" I say to him,' she yelled, stopping for breath
after every word. 'That Amalia Ludwigovna . . . Ah! Lenya, Kolya!
Arms on hips, look lively, *glissé glissé, pas de basque!*[44] Beat those
little feet . . . Look graceful, child!

> *Du hast Diamanten und Perlen . . .*

Then what? Now there's a song . . .

> *Du hast die schönsten Augen,*
> *Mädchen, was willst du mehr?*[45]

How could I forget? *Was willst du mehr?*, indeed! Whatever next? . . .
Oh yes, and this:

> In the midday heat, in a vale in Dagestan . . .[46]

Ah, how I loved that song . . . I simply adored it, Polechka! . . . Your
father, you know . . . sang it when he was courting . . . Oh, days! . . .
Now there's a song for us! But then what? Then what . . . ? I've forgotten again . . . Well, remind me!' She was terribly agitated and kept
trying to lift herself up. Eventually, in a dreadful, hoarse, breaking
voice she began to sing, shrieking and gasping at every word, and
looking ever more frightened:

> 'In the midday heat . . . in a vale . . . in Dagestan!
> With lead in my breast!

Your Excellency!' she suddenly howled with lacerating force, drenched
in tears. 'Protect the orphans! Remember the late Semyon Zakharych's
bread and salt! . . . The aristocratic Semyon Zakharych, one might
even say! . . . Ahh!' she said with a start, regaining her senses and

casting her eyes over everyone with a sort of horror, before suddenly recognizing Sonya. 'Sonya, Sonya!' she said, meekly and tenderly, as if astonished to see her before her. 'Sonya, darling, you're here too?'

They lifted her up again.

'Enough! . . . It's time! . . . Goodbye, poor creature! . . . This nag's been ridden too hard! . . . She's had it!' she cried in despair and hatred, and her head fell back heavily onto the pillow.

She fell unconscious once more, but only briefly. Her pale, yellow, shrivelled face fell right back, her mouth opened wide, and a spasm stretched out her legs. She gave a deep, deep sigh and died.

Sonya fell on her corpse, wrapped her arms around her and froze, pressing her head tight against the dead woman's shrivelled bosom. Polechka fell at her mother's feet and kissed them, sobbing uncontrollably. Kolya and Lenya, still unsure of what exactly had happened, but sensing something quite dreadful, grabbed one another's little shoulders with both hands and, staring into each other's eyes, suddenly opened their mouths together and began to scream. Both were still in their outfits: one wearing a turban, the other a skullcap with an ostrich feather.

And how did this 'certificate of distinction' suddenly materialize on the bed, next to Katerina Ivanovna? It lay right there, by the pillow; Raskolnikov could see it.

He withdrew to the window. Lebezyatnikov hurried over to him.

'Dead!' said Lebezyatnikov.

'Rodion Romanovich, I have two urgent things to tell you,' said Svidrigailov, walking over. Lebezyatnikov immediately made way and faded tactfully into the background. Svidrigailov led the astonished Raskolnikov even further off into the corner.

'I'll take care of all this – the funeral and so on. I told you I had some money going spare – so why not use it? I'll find decent orphanages for those two mites and for Polechka, and put one thousand five hundred aside for each of them, until they come of age, so Sofya Semyonovna won't have the slightest cause for anxiety. And I'll save her from ruin as well, because she's a good girl, is she not? Well then, sir, be so kind as to tell Avdotya Romanovna that this is the use to which her ten thousand have been put.'

'And the purpose of all this charity?' asked Raskolnikov.

'Dear dear! Aren't we mistrustful!' laughed Svidrigailov. 'I told you this money was going spare. What if it's simply for reasons of humanity – can't you accept that? I mean, she was no "louse"' (he jabbed his finger in the general direction of the deceased), 'she wasn't some hag of a moneylender. I mean, really, "should Luzhin live and commit his abominations or should she die?" And, but for my help, "Polechka, say, will go the same way . . ." '

He said this with a sort of *winking*, merrily roguish air, never once taking his eyes off Raskolnikov. Raskolnikov turned white and a chill came over him as he heard his own words once spoken to Sonya. He immediately shrank back and stared wildly at Svidrigailov.

'H-how . . . do you know?' he whispered, scarcely able to breathe.

'Because I live right here, on the other side of the wall, at Madame Resslich's. She's a very old and devoted friend. Neighbours, sir.'

'You?'

'Yes, me,' Svidrigailov went on, swaying with mirth, 'and let me assure you, on my honour, dearest Rodion Romanovich, that I find you quite fascinating, astonishingly so. Didn't I tell you we'd become close? Didn't I predict it? Well, now we have. And you'll see what an accommodating fellow I am. You'll see that I'm not so very hard to get along with . . .'

PART SIX

I

For Raskolnikov a strange time had begun: it was as if a fog had suddenly descended, trapping him in hopeless, oppressive isolation. Recalling this time much later, he surmised that he'd experienced, now and then, a dimming of his consciousness and that this had continued, with a few intervals, right up until the final catastrophe. He was absolutely convinced that he'd been mistaken about many things, such as the duration and timing of certain events. At any rate, when he subsequently recalled what had happened and tried to make sense of it all, he learned a great deal about himself, guided as he now was by external information. He had, for example, mixed up one event with another, and considered a third to be the consequence of something that had happened solely in his imagination. At times, he'd been possessed by morbid, excruciating anxiety, which could even mutate into sheer panic. But he also remembered that minutes, hours and even, perhaps, days had been filled with an apathy that possessed him as if in direct contrast to his previous fear – an apathy that resembled the morbid, indifferent state occasionally experienced by the dying. On the whole, it was as if, during these final days, he himself had been trying to run away from a clear and full understanding of his situation; certain crucial facts that needed to be explained there and then weighed especially heavily upon him; but how glad he would have been to cast off some of his worries and flee – even if to forget them, in such a situation as his, threatened him with total and inevitable ruin.

Svidrigailov made him especially uneasy: he even seemed to get stuck, as it were, on Svidrigailov. It was as if, ever since he heard Svidrigailov say those words, so full of menace for him and so clearly expressed, at Sonya's apartment at the moment of Katerina Ivanovna's death, the usual flow of his thoughts was disrupted. But though this new fact made him exceptionally anxious, he seemed in no hurry to get to the bottom of it. Now and then, suddenly finding himself in a remote and isolated part of the city, alone at a table in some wretched tavern, brooding and barely conscious of how he'd ended up there, he would suddenly think of Svidrigailov: he would suddenly realize all too clearly and uneasily that he had to come to an arrangement with this man at the earliest opportunity and, if possible, settle things for good. Once, wandering off somewhere beyond the city limits, he even imagined that he was expecting Svidrigailov and that they'd fixed a meeting there. Another time, he woke before daybreak on the ground somewhere, in the bushes, unsure of how he'd got there. Although, in fact, in the course of these two or three days since Katerina Ivanovna's death he'd already met Svidrigailov a few times, almost always at Sonya's, where he would wander in as if for no reason and almost always for only a minute. They'd exchange brief remarks, never once touching on the essential point, as if they'd agreed not to mention it for the time being. Katerina Ivanovna's body still lay in the coffin. Svidrigailov was busy seeing to the funeral arrangements. Sonya also had her hands full. At their last meeting, Svidrigailov explained to Raskolnikov that he'd dealt with Katerina Ivanovna's children, and dealt with them successfully; that he'd managed, through certain connections, to find the right people to help him place the three orphans, without delay, in entirely suitable institutions; that the money set aside for them had also been a great help, since it was far easier to place orphans with money than orphans with nothing. He said something about Sonya, too, promised to call on Raskolnikov himself in the next day or two, and mentioned that he wished to ask his advice; that they really needed to have a chat; that they had 'some business to discuss' . . . This conversation took place by the main door, on the stairs. Svidrigailov stared straight into Raskolnikov's eyes and suddenly, pausing and lowering his voice, asked him:

'What's come over you, Rodion Romanych? You're not yourself at all! You look and listen, but it's as if you're not even following. You should cheer up a bit. And we must have a chat: just a shame I've so much on – other people's affairs as well as my own . . . Ah, Rodion Romanych,' he suddenly added, 'every human being needs air – Yes, air, air . . . More than anything!'

He suddenly stepped aside to make way for a priest and a deacon coming up the stairs. They were about to perform the memorial service. Svidrigailov had arranged for this to be done twice a day, on the dot. Svidrigailov went on his way. Raskolnikov stood there, thought for a moment, then followed the priest into Sonya's room.

He stood in the doorway. The service was beginning with quiet, sad decorum. Awareness of death and its presence had always contained for him something oppressive, some mystical dread, ever since childhood; besides, it was a long time since he'd last heard a service for the dead. But there was something else as well, something far too dreadful and disturbing. He was looking at the children: they were all by the coffin, on their knees; Polechka was crying. Behind them, weeping softly and almost shyly, Sonya was praying. The thought, 'She hasn't glanced at me once these past few days, nor spoken a word to me,' suddenly struck him. The room was brightly lit by the sun; puffs of smoke floated up from the censer. 'God rest her soul,' read the priest. Raskolnikov stood for the duration of the service. Giving his blessing and taking his leave, the priest looked about him in a strange kind of way. After the service Raskolnikov walked up to Sonya. Suddenly, she took both his hands in hers and inclined her head towards his shoulder. This brief gesture left Raskolnikov bewildered. In fact, it felt strange. What? Not the slightest disgust? Not the slightest revulsion towards him? Not the slightest tremble in her hand? What was this if not some infinity of self-abasement? That, at any rate, was how he understood it. Sonya said nothing. Raskolnikov squeezed her hand and left. He felt dreadful. Had he only been able to go off somewhere there and then and be entirely alone, even if it were for the rest of his life, he'd have thought himself lucky. But lately, even though he was almost always alone, he never felt alone. He might walk out of the city and out onto the high road or even, on one occasion, to some little wood; but the more isolated the place, the more strongly he seemed to be aware of someone's close and unsettling presence – it wasn't terrifying exactly, just extremely bothersome, so he would hurry back to the city, mix with the crowds, visit the taverns and drinking dens, go to the flea market, to Haymarket. It was as if he somehow felt better there, more isolated. In one eating-house, in the late afternoon, there was singing: he sat and listened for a whole hour and remembered having even enjoyed it. But towards the end he suddenly became anxious again, as if a pang of conscience had suddenly begun to torment him: 'Look at me sitting here, listening to songs – as if there's nothing else I should be doing!' was the kind of thought in his mind. But he soon realized that wasn't the only thing troubling him: there was something that demanded to be resolved at once, but it could neither be grasped nor put into words. As if everything were being wound into a ball. 'No, a fight would be better than this! Porfiry again . . . or

Svidrigailov . . . I need a challenge, someone to attack me . . . Yes! Yes!' He left the eating-house and almost broke into a run. The thought of Dunya and his mother had, for some reason, suddenly thrown him into a kind of panic. That was the night when he woke before dawn in the bushes on Krestovsky Island, shivering to the bone and feverish. He set off home, arriving in the early morning. After several hours' sleep the fever passed, but it was already late when he woke: two in the afternoon.

This, he recalled, was the day fixed for Katerina Ivanovna's funeral, and he was relieved to have missed it. Nastasya brought him some food. He ate and drank with gusto, almost greedily. His mind felt fresher and he himself calmer than at any point in these last three days. He even felt a passing surprise at his earlier surges of panic. The door opened and Razumikhin walked in.

'Ha! He's eating, so he can't be that sick!' said Razumikhin, grabbing a chair and sitting down at the table, opposite Raskolnikov. He was very worried about something and made no attempt to hide the fact. He spoke with evident vexation, but without hurrying and even without raising his voice very much. One might have thought that some special, even all-consuming purpose had taken hold of him. 'Listen,' he began decisively, 'you can all go to hell as far as I'm concerned, but what I see now tells me clearly that I don't understand a thing; but please, don't think I've come here to interrogate you. As if I care! Go ahead and reveal everything, all your secrets, and I might very well not even listen – I'll spit and walk away. I only came to find out in person, once and for all: is it true, first of all, that you're mad? You see, there's this notion about you (among some people, somewhere) that you might be mad or very much that way inclined. I'll admit that I myself was strongly tempted to support this opinion, firstly, on account of your stupid and not infrequently beastly actions (which are beyond explanation), and secondly, on account of your recent behaviour towards your mother and sister. Only a monster and a scoundrel, if not a madman, could have behaved towards them as you did; therefore, you are mad . . .'

'When did you last see them?'

'Just now. So you've not seen them since then? Where do you keep gadding off to, eh? This is the fourth time I've come by. Your mother's been seriously ill since yesterday. She wanted to visit you. Avdotya Romanovna tried to stop her, but she wasn't having any of it: "If he's sick, if he's disturbed, who'll help him if not his mother?" We all came over together – we could hardly let her go on her own. Begged her to calm down all the way to your door. Came in, but you were out. She sat right here. Sat here for ten minutes, with us silently hovering over her. She got up and said: "If he's out and about, which means he must be well and has forgotten all about his mother, then it's unseemly and shameful for me to loiter on the threshold, begging for a kiss as if it were charity." She went back home and took to her bed. Now she's running a fever. "He can find time for *his girl*, I see." By that she means Sofya Semyonovna, your fiancée or lover – don't ask me. I set off straight away to see Sofya Semyonovna, because, brother, I wanted to get to the bottom of it all. I walk in and what do I find? A coffin, children crying. Sofya Semyonovna measuring their mourning dresses. No sign of you. I looked, apologized and left, and reported back to Avdotya Romanovna. So it was all rubbish and there was no *girl*; madness, more likely. But here you are wolfing down beef as if you haven't eaten for three days. Fair enough, the mad have to eat too; but even though you've not said a word to me, you're . . . not mad! I'll swear on it. If there's one thing you're not, it's mad! In short, you can all go to hell, because there's some mystery here, some secret; and I don't intend to rack my brains wondering what you're all hiding. I only came over here to shout and swear,' he concluded, getting up, 'and to get it all off my chest, but I know what I'm going to do next!'

'And what do you want to do next?'

'Why should you care what I want to do next?'

'Mind you stay away from the bottle!'

'How on earth did you guess?'

'Do me a favour!'

Razumikhin fell silent for a minute.

'You've always been a rational sort and you've never, ever been mad,' he suddenly remarked with feeling. 'Yes, I'll hit the bottle! See you!' – and he made as if to leave.

'You know, Razumikhin, I was speaking about you with my sister – must have been the day before yesterday.'

'About me? But . . . where on earth could you have seen her the day before yesterday?' asked Razumikhin, suddenly stopping and even turning a little pale. One look at him was enough to feel the slow, tense thumping of his heart.

'She came here, all alone, sat here and talked to me.'

'She came here?'

'Yes.'

'So what did you say . . . about me, I mean?'

'I told her that you're a very good, honest and hard-working man. I didn't tell her you love her – she already knows.'

'She already knows?'

'Of course she knows! Wherever I go and whatever happens to me, you'll still be their Providence. I am, you might say, handing them over to you, Razumikhin. I say this because I know full well how much you love her and I know your heart is pure. I also know that she can love you and perhaps already does. Now it's for you to decide, whether or not to go boozing.'

'Rodka . . . You see . . . Well . . . Ah, damn it all! And where are you off to anyway? You see, if this is all a secret, fine! But I'll . . . I'll discover this secret . . . And I bet it's something completely idiotic, something dreadfully trivial, and that it's all your own doing. Never mind – you're a smashing lad! A smashing lad!'

'I was just about to add, before you interrupted, that it was very sensible of you to decide earlier on to leave these mysteries and secrets alone. Forget all about them. You'll find everything out in your own time, just when you need to. Yesterday someone was telling me that air is what man needs – air, air! I'm just about to go and see him and find out what he means.'

Razumikhin stood there, pensive and uneasy, trying to work something out.

'He's a political conspirator![1] No doubt about it! And he's on the verge of some drastic step – no doubt about it! And . . . and Dunya knows . . . ,' he suddenly thought to himself.

'So Avdotya Romanovna comes to see you,' he said, enunciating every syllable, 'but the person you want to see is a man who tells you that what you need is air, more air and . . . and so this letter . . . must also have something to do with that,' he concluded, as if talking to himself.

'What letter?'

'She received a letter today; it worried her very much. Too much, in fact. I started talking about you – she asked me to shut up. Then . . . then she said that very soon, perhaps, we'd have to part; then she started thanking me very effusively for something; then she retired to her room and that was that.'

'She received a letter?' repeated Raskolnikov pensively.

'Yes, a letter. You didn't know? H'm.'

They both fell silent.

'Goodbye, Rodion. I ... there was a time, brother ... but never mind. Goodbye ... You see, there was a time ... Well, goodbye! I have to go, too. I won't go drinking. I mustn't now ... See, you're wrong!'

He was in a rush, but, having all but closed the door behind him, he suddenly opened it again and said, looking off to the side:

'By the way, do you remember that murder? You know – Porfiry – the old woman? Well, the murderer's been found. He's confessed and supplied all the proof himself. He was one of those workmen, the decorators – fancy that! Remember how I was defending them here? You'll never believe it. All that fighting and laughing on the stairs with his friend, when the others were on their way up, I mean the caretaker and the two witnesses – well, he set it all up as a blind. Such cunning, such presence of mind – in a puppy like that! It beggars belief. He explained it all himself, admitted everything! And I fell for it! Well, I suppose he's just a genius faker and quick-thinker, a master of the red herring, and there's really nothing to be so surprised about! Why shouldn't such people exist? And as for him bottling it and confessing – well, that only makes me believe him all the more. Truer to life, somehow ... But how I fell for it! What an ass! Sticking my neck out for them like that!'

'But who told you all this? And why are you so interested?' asked Raskolnikov, visibly agitated.

'Do me a favour! Why am I interested! Of all the questions! ... It was Porfiry who told me, and others besides. Actually, he told me pretty much all of it.'

'Porfiry?'

'Porfiry.'

'And ... well?' asked Raskolnikov in fear.

'He explained it to me quite brilliantly. Explained it psychologically, in his own way.'

'He explained it? Explained it to you himself?'

'Yes, yes. Well, goodbye! I've something else to tell you about later, but I have to go. Once ... there was a time when I thought ... But later, later! ... No point getting drunk now. You've already got me drunk without that. I'm drunk, Rodka! Look, I'm drunk without drinking, so goodbye. I'll drop by, very soon.'

He left.

'A political conspirator, no doubt about it!' Razumikhin decided once and for all, walking slowly down the stairs. 'And he's roped his sister in. That's perfectly, perfectly possible given Avdotya Romanovna's character. Regular meetings, it seems . . . She dropped me hints, too, come to think of it. A few things she said . . . little things . . . hints . . . it all adds up! How else to explain this great muddle? H'm! And there was I thinking . . . Good grief, there was I thinking God knows what. Yes, sir, something came over me and I owe him an apology! It was him, in the corridor by the lamp that time, who made me think it. Ugh! What a sordid, coarse, disgraceful thing for me to think! Good on you, Mikolka, for confessing . . . Now everything else, from before, finally makes sense! That sickness of his, all those strange things he'd do, earlier on as well, back at university, always so gloomy and sullen . . . But what about this new letter? What does that mean? Something's up here as well. Who's the letter from? I've got my suspicions . . . H'm. I just have to get to the bottom of it all.'

He recalled everything he knew about Dunechka, put it all together, and his heart froze. He burst into a run.

Just as soon as Razumikhin left, Raskolnikov stood up, turned towards the window, bumped against one corner and then another, as if forgetting how cramped his hovel was, and . . . sat back down on the couch. He seemed as good as new. Another chance to fight! So there was a way out!

'Yes, there is a way out!' Everything had become far too shut-in, sealed-up, stifling – excruciatingly, stupefyingly so. Ever since that scene with Mikolka at Porfiry's he'd been suffocating in some cramped, closed-in space. And after Mikolka, on that very same day, there was that scene at Sonya's. He hadn't managed to carry it off or end it anywhere near as well as he thought he might . . . His strength must have deserted him! All at once! And hadn't he agreed with Sonya then, agreed in his heart, that he couldn't go on like this on his own, carrying a thing like that in his soul? And Svidrigailov? An enigma, that man . . . Svidrigailov troubled him, true enough, but in a different way. Perhaps there was a fight to be had with Svidrigailov, too. Perhaps Svidrigailov also represented a way out, all of his own; but Porfiry was another matter.

So, Porfiry had gone and explained it to Razumikhin himself, explained it to him *psychologically*! Once again he'd started harping on about his damned psychology! Porfiry, really? Porfiry believing, even for one minute, that Mikolka was guilty, after what had happened between them, after that scene, eye to eye, before Mikolka came along, for which no correct interpretation could possibly be found, save *one*? (In the course of these days, bits of that scene with Porfiry had flashed through Raskolnikov's mind more than once; recalling it in its entirety would have been too much to bear.) The words uttered between them then, their movements and gestures, the looks they exchanged, the voices they sometimes spoke in, were such that there could be no way for Mikolka of all people (that same Mikolka whom Porfiry had seen right through the moment he opened his mouth) to shake the very ground of his convictions.

And now this! Even Razumikhin had begun to suspect him! So the scene in the corridor, by the lamp, hadn't passed without consequence. He'd rushed over to Porfiry . . . But why on earth was Porfiry trying to trick him like this? What possible reason could he have for diverting Razumikhin's attention to Mikolka? He must have had something in mind; there was definitely some purpose here, but what? True, a lot of time had passed since that morning – far too much, in fact, and there had been neither sight nor sound of Porfiry. Hardly a good sign . . . Raskolnikov took his cap and walked out, plunged in thought. It was the first day in all this time when he could feel that at least he was thinking straight. 'I have to put an end to this business with Svidrigailov,' he thought, 'and quickly, whatever it takes. He, too, seems to be waiting, waiting for me to go to him.' At that moment, so much hatred surged from his weary heart that he might very well have been able to kill either one of them: Svidrigailov or Porfiry. At least, he sensed he could do so later, if not now. 'We'll see, we'll see,' he kept saying to himself.

But no sooner did he open the door onto the landing than he bumped into Porfiry himself, coming the other way. For a minute, Raskolnikov froze in his tracks. Strangely enough, he wasn't very surprised to see him, and he was barely frightened. He merely shuddered and instantly pulled himself together. 'The dénouement, perhaps! But how did he manage to come up so quietly, like a cat, and I didn't hear a thing? Surely he wasn't listening in?'

'I see you weren't expecting anyone, Rodion Romanych,' cried Porfiry Petrovich, laughing. 'I've been meaning to come by for ages – I was walking past and thought: why not drop in for five minutes? On your way out somewhere? I won't keep you. Just one papirosa, if I may.'

'Sit down, Porfiry Petrovich, sit down,' said Raskolnikov to his guest, with such a contented and friendly air that he would have been quite amazed had he been able to see himself from the outside. The leftovers and dregs were being scraped! So it is that a man may endure half an hour of mortal terror in the company of a brigand, but when the knife is finally placed at his throat, even the terror will pass. He sat directly facing Porfiry and looked at him unblinkingly. Porfiry screwed up his eyes and began lighting up.

'Go on then, out with it, out with it,' all but leapt from Raskolnikov's heart. 'Why, why aren't you speaking?'

II

'Damn these papirosi!' Porfiry Petrovich eventually began, after lighting up and catching his breath. 'They do nothing but harm, but I just can't stop! I'm always coughing, sir, and now I've got a tickle in my throat and I'm short of breath. I'm a cowardly sort, sir, and the other day I went to see B——[2] – he examines every patient for at least half an hour; well, he actually burst out laughing when he looked at me: he tapped, he listened – "Tobacco," he says, "isn't doing you any favours. Your lungs are enlarged." And how am I to give it up? What'll I replace it with? I don't drink, sir, that's the problem, heh-heh-heh. Not drinking, eh? That's the problem! You see, everything's relative, Rodion Romanych, everything's relative!'

'Now what's he up to? Surely not those old tricks of the trade again!' thought Raskolnikov with disgust. The scene of their most recent meeting suddenly came back to him in its entirety, and the feeling he'd had then swept like a wave towards his heart.

'I dropped by to see you just the day before yesterday, in the evening. Or didn't you know?' Porfiry Petrovich went on, surveying the room. 'I came right in, to this very room. I was walking past, just like today, and thought, "Why don't I pay him a little visit?" Up I come and the door's wide open. I had a look around, waited a bit, didn't bother announcing myself to the maid – and left. You don't lock your door?'

Raskolnikov's face grew darker and darker. Porfiry seemed to guess his thoughts.

'I've come to explain myself, Rodion Romanych, my dear chap – to explain myself! I have to. I'm obliged to,' he continued with his little smile, and even patted Raskolnikov lightly on the knee, but then, almost instantly, his face assumed a serious and preoccupied expression;

there was even, to Raskolnikov's surprise, a hint of sadness. He had never seen or imagined such an expression on his face. 'A strange scene took place between us last time, Rodion Romanych. One might say that a strange scene took place between us at our first meeting, too; but at the time . . . Well, never mind that! Now listen: I fear I may have done you a great wrong; I can feel it, sir. Just remember how we parted: your nerves humming and your kneecaps wobbling, and my nerves humming and my kneecaps wobbling. There was even something untoward about it all, unbefitting true gentlemen. But we are true gentlemen. Whatever else we are, we are gentlemen first and foremost. That must be understood, sir. Just remember how it all ended . . . quite unseemly, sir.'

'Now what's he up to – and who does he take me for?' Raskolnikov asked himself in amazement, lifting his head and staring, wide-eyed, at Porfiry.

'I've come to the conclusion that we're better off being open with one another,' Porfiry went on, tipping back his head a little and lowering his eyes, as if reluctant to embarrass his former victim any more with his gaze, and disdaining his old tricks and ruses. 'Yes, sir, we have to put a stop to all these suspicions and all these scenes. Just as well Mikolka came between us then, otherwise who knows what might have happened? I had that damned tradesman sitting behind the partition all the way through – can you imagine? You already know that, of course. Just as I know that he called on you later. But your assumption at the time was mistaken: I hadn't sent for anyone – in fact, I hadn't yet made any arrangements at all. Why not, I hear you ask? How can I put it? It was as if I myself had just been whacked around the head by this whole business. I barely even managed to send for the caretakers. (I take it you noticed them while walking past.) A thought flashed through me then, just one, as swift as lightning. You see, Rodion Romanych, at the time I was utterly convinced. So I thought, "A bird in the hand's worth two in the bush, and at least I'll get what's mine, I won't let it go." You see, you're terribly irritable, Rodion Romanych, by your very nature, sir; too much so, in fact, despite all the other essential aspects of your character and heart, which I am vain enough to think I have at least partly grasped. Of course, even I, even then, could see that you can't always expect a man just to get up and spill all the beans. Sometimes he does, especially when you've got him at the end of his tether, but it's rare. Even I could see that. No, I thought, "I need something, even if it's just some little mark, some little jot or tittle, but something you can actually get your hands on; it needs to be a thing, not mere psychology!" Which is why, I thought, if a man's guilty, the very least you can expect from him is something substantial. You might even be entitled to count on something entirely unexpected. Your character is what I was counting on then, Rodion Romanych. Your character, sir, more than anything else! I'd really pinned my hopes on you.'

'But why . . . ? Why do you keep talking like this, now of all times?' Raskolnikov eventually mumbled, not even sure what he was asking. 'What's he going on about?' he thought to himself in bewilderment. 'Surely he can't really think I'm innocent?'

'Why am I talking like this? I came to explain myself, sir. I consider it, so to speak, my sacred duty. I want to tell you everything, the whole story of that blackout, so to speak. I've put you through a lot, Rodion Romanych. I'm no monster, sir. After all, even I can see what a burden all this must be for a man who's dejected but proud, masterful and impatient – especially the last! At any rate, I consider you the noblest of men and not without signs of magnanimity, though I cannot go along with all your convictions and feel obliged to say so in advance, frankly and quite sincerely, for the last thing I wish to do is deceive you. I developed a fondness for you after we met. Perhaps you find all this rather hilarious? You have every right, sir. I know you disliked me the moment you saw me – and indeed, there's really nothing to like me for. Think what you will, but I want to do all I can to make up for this first impression and prove that even I have a heart and a conscience. I'm being sincere, sir.'

There was a dignified pause. Raskolnikov felt a surge of a new kind of fear. The thought that Porfiry considered him innocent had suddenly begun to frighten him.

'Going through it all from A to Z and describing how it suddenly began back then seems hardly necessary,' Porfiry Petrovich continued. 'In fact, it would be quite redundant. And anyway, I'm probably not up to it, sir. After all, how can this be properly explained? First there were rumours. What kind of rumours, who started them and when . . . and why, to put it bluntly, your name came up – this too, I think, is redundant. For me personally, it began quite fortuitously, from a completely fortuitous fortuity that might very easily have never happened – which? H'm, nothing to be said here either, I think. At the time, all these rumours and fortuities merged in my mind into a single thought.

If you're going to confess, you should confess everything, so I'll be frank and say I was the first to pounce on you. The labels the old woman had scribbled on her items, say, and all the rest of it – well, it's neither here nor there, sir. You could find a hundred things like that. I also happened to learn in detail, then, of the scene in the district police bureau, also quite fortuitously, sir, and not merely in passing, but from a special, first-rate storyteller, who, without knowing it himself, had really mastered this scene. You see, it all adds up, Rodion Romanych, my dear chap, it all adds up! How could I not be swayed in a particular direction? A hundred rabbits never make a horse, and a hundred suspicions never make a proof, as a certain English proverb has it,[3] but that's just the voice of reason. What's one to do about the passions? That's the real question, because even an investigator is human. I was also reminded of that little article of yours in that journal, remember? You spoke about it in some detail during your very first visit. I scoffed at you then, but that was just to provoke you. You are, I repeat, terribly impatient and terribly sick, Rodion Romanych. As for your being daring, arrogant, serious and . . . a man of feeling, a man who's already felt a great deal – well, I've known that all along, sir. All these sensations are not unknown to me and your little article struck a chord when I read it. It was hatched during sleepless nights, at white heat, with a heaving, thumping heart, with suppressed enthusiasm. But it's dangerous, this suppressed, proud enthusiasm of youth! I scoffed at you at the time, but now I can tell you how much I adore – speaking purely as an amateur – these youthful, hot-blooded tests of the pen. Smoke, mist, and in the mist, the plucking of a string.[4] Your article is absurd and fantastical, but contains flashes of pure sincerity, not to mention the incorruptible pride of youth and the audacity of despair; it's a gloomy little article, sir, and a very good thing too. I read it through, put it aside and thought: "I fear for this man!" Now tell me: after a precedent like that, how could I be indifferent about what followed? Heavens above! But what am I actually saying here? Am I really asserting anything? At the time, I merely made a mental note. What have we got here, I wondered? Nothing, precisely nothing, nothing to the nth degree, perhaps. And anyway, it's positively unseemly for an investigator like me to get so excited: I've got Mikolka right here, with facts to boot. Say what you like, but facts are facts! He's at it, too, bringing his own psychology into it. He'll keep me busy, don't you worry. It's a matter of life and death, after all. And why am I explaining all this to you now? Because I want you to know; because I don't want you to blame me, in your heart and mind, for my malicious behaviour back then. There was no malice, sir, honest – heh-heh! What? Do you think I didn't have this room searched? Of course I did, sir, heh-heh, of course I did, while you were laid up sick right here in your bed. Not officially and not in person, but I did. Every last hair in your lodgings was inspected, the trail as fresh as could be; but – *umsonst*![5] I thought, "He'll come himself, this man. He'll come all by himself, and soon, very soon; he's bound to, if he's guilty. Others wouldn't, but this one will." Remember how Mr Razumikhin became so indiscreet with you all of a sudden? We arranged that to get you worried; we started the rumour deliberately, counting on his indiscretion; after all, Mr Razumikhin is the kind of man who can't endure his own indignation. It was your fury and your brazen audacity that leapt out at Mr Zametov most of all: fancy blurting out in the tavern, "I'm the murderer!" Too daring, too bold. "If he's guilty," I thought, "what a fighter he must be!" Yes, that's what I thought. I was waiting, sir. I was on tenterhooks. You'd simply crushed Zametov and . . . well, that's precisely the problem: this damned psychology cuts both ways! I was waiting for you to come, when suddenly – like a gift from God – there you were! My heart just leapt. Good grief! What made you come just then? And that laughter of yours when you came in – remember? It was as if I could see everything through a pane of glass, though if I hadn't been waiting for you like that I wouldn't have noticed a thing, not a thing. Goes to show how everything depends on our state of mind! And when I think of Mr Razumikhin then . . . oh yes! The stone, the stone – remember? – the stone under which the items were hidden? I can almost see it there, in some vegetable patch – you did say vegetable patch, didn't you? To Zametov, I mean, and then again in my office? And then, when we started analysing that article of yours, when you started setting out your argument – well, your every word seemed to have a double meaning, as if there were another word just beneath it! And that, Rodion Romanych, is how I reached the final pillars,[6] banged my head on them and came to my senses. Stop there, I said to myself! After all, you could explain all this, from start to finish, in a completely different way if you wanted to, and it might even come out sounding more natural. Sheer torture, sir! "No," I thought, "I'm better off with some little mark or other!" And then, when I heard about

those little bells, I almost froze on the spot. I even got the shivers.
"Well," I thought, "there's the mark I'm after! Right there!" Not that
I really thought it through at the time – I didn't want to. I'd have given
a thousand roubles of my own money at that moment simply to look
at you *with my own eyes*: to watch you walking a hundred paces side
by side with that tradesman after he said "murderer" straight to your
face, not daring to ask him anything, for the entire one hundred
paces! And that chill in your spine? Those bells, when you were sick,
half-delirious? So you see, Rodion Romanych, can you really be surprised at my playing games with you then? And why did you have to
come right then, at that very moment? It was as if you, too, were being nudged by someone, and if Mikolka hadn't come between us,
well . . . Remember him, Mikolka? Did he stick in your mind? What a
thunderbolt! Out of a great black cloud! A veritable crash of thunder!
So how did I greet him? Well, I didn't fall for it, not for a moment, as
you saw yourself! As if I would! Later on, once you'd left, he started
giving me extremely polished answers on certain points, which astonished even me, and after that I didn't believe a thing he said! Adamant
is the word for it, I believe. "No way," I thought. "Mikolka? Mikolka
Schmikolka!"'

'Razumikhin was telling me just now that you still hold Mikolka
responsible and that you assured Razumikhin of the fact yourself . . .'

He was struggling for breath and couldn't finish. He listened with
indescribable agitation as the man who'd seen right through him disa-
vowed himself. He was scared to believe it, and didn't believe it. In
these still-ambiguous words he hungrily sought something more precise and definitive.

'Mr Razumikhin – ha!' cried Porfiry Petrovich, apparently delighted to
be asked this question by Raskolnikov, silent for so long. 'Heh-heh-heh! I
misled Mr Razumikhin on purpose, and just as well: two's company,
three's a crowd. Mr Razumikhin's got nothing to do with it. Fancy running over to me like that, pale as a sheet . . . Well, God bless him – why
mix him up in all this? But perhaps you'd like to know more about
Mikolka? About the sort of *sujet* we've got here – as I understand it, that
is? First and foremost, he's still a child,[7] still wet behind the ears; not exactly a coward, more like an artist of one kind or another. You mustn't
laugh, sir, at my explaining him like this. Innocent and highly impressionable. With a heart and a lively imagination. He can sing, he can dance and
when he tells stories people come to listen from all over, apparently. He

can go to school, laugh till he drops just from someone holding up a finger, or drink himself senseless, not from debauchery, more like a child, in
spurts, whenever someone offers. He stole that time without even realizing it. "It's finders keepers, ain't it?" And do you know he's a "Raskolnik", a schismatic; actually, not so much a schismatic as simply a sectarian;
there were "Runners" among his ancestors, and not so long ago, out in
the country, he spent two whole years under the wing of a certain Elder.[8]
I learned all this from Mikolka himself and from his Zaraisk chums. He
even wanted to run off into the wilderness! A zealous sort – prayed to
God all night, kept reading the old, "true" books[9] and read himself silly.
Petersburg had a powerful effect on him, especially the fairer sex, and the
drink, of course. Impressionable, sir – forgot all about his Elder and
everything else. A certain artist here took a liking to him, I'm told, and
started visiting him, then this came along! Well, he got scared. "Find me
a noose! Where can I run?" So much for the common folk's opinion of
our legal process! The very word "trial" is enough to put the wind up
some of them. Who's to blame? The new courts[10] will have something to
say about it. Or at least, I hope they will! Anyway, sir, while in jail he
must have remembered about his good old Elder; the Bible's made a reap-
pearance, too. Do you have any idea, Rodion Romanych, what the word
"suffering" means to some people? Not suffering for anyone's sake, but
simply because "I must suffer"? Because one must accept one's suffering,
and if it comes from the authorities so much the better. In my time, there
was a convict, meek as a lamb, who spent a whole year in prison, sat on
the stove all night reading the Bible, and really did read himself silly, to
the point that one day, out of the blue, he picked up a brick and hurled it
at the warden, without the slightest provocation. You should have seen
how he threw it: he missed by a yard so as not to hurt him! We all know
what happens to a convict who attacks an officer with a weapon: well
then, he "accepted his suffering". So my suspicion now is that Mikolka
wants to "accept his suffering" or something of the kind. I'm sure of it,
sir – I've even got the facts to prove it. It's just that he doesn't know that I
know. Why, do you really find it so inconceivable that such fantastical
people should emerge from the common folk? They're two a penny! Now
the Elder's back on the scene, especially after that business with the noose.
Anyway, he'll come and tell me everything himself. You think he'll hold
out? Just you wait: he'll change his tune! I'm waiting for him to come any
moment and go back on his testimony. I've taken a shine to this Mikolka.
I'm making a thorough study of him. And guess what? Heh-heh! On

certain points his answers were very polished indeed – he was clearly well informed and well prepared – but on others he was utterly clueless and completely unaware of his own ignorance! No, Rodion Romanych, Mikolka's not our man! What we've got here, sir, is a fantastical, dark deed, a modern deed, a deed of our time, when the heart of man has clouded over; when there's talk of "renewal" through bloodshed;[11] when people preach about anything and everything from a position of comfort. What we have here are bookish dreams, sir, a heart stirred up by theories, a visible determination to take the first step, but determination of a particular kind – as if he were throwing himself off a cliff or a bell tower, and when he did get to the scene of the crime he hadn't a clue how he'd got there. Forgot to close the door behind him, but still did it, still murdered two people, in accordance with the theory. Murdered, but didn't manage to take the money, and what he did grab he hid beneath a stone. The torment of sitting inside the old woman's apartment while the door was being forced and the bell was ringing wasn't enough for him – no, later on back he came to the empty apartment, half-delirious, to remind himself of that little bell, desperate to experience once again the chill down his spine ... He was sick, you might say, but how about this: he murdered, but thinks himself honest, holds others in contempt, wanders around like a pale-faced angel – no, Rodion Romanych, my dear chap, Mikolka's not our man – not a chance!'

These last words, after all that had gone before, so similar to a recantation, caught him completely by surprise. Raskolnikov started shaking all over, as if he'd been stabbed.

'So ... who did it?' he asked, unable to resist, gasping for air. Porfiry Petrovich all but threw himself back in his chair, as if utterly astounded by the question.

'What do you mean – who did it?' he repeated, as if he couldn't believe his ears. 'Why, *you* did, Rodion Romanych! With respect, sir, the murderer is you ...,' he almost whispered, in a voice of total conviction.

Raskolnikov leapt from the couch, stayed on his feet for a few seconds, then sat back down, not saying a word. Faint convulsions suddenly rippled across his face.

'Your lip's trembling again, just like then,' muttered Porfiry Petrovich, almost with sympathy. 'You seem to have misunderstood me, Rodion Romanych,' he added, after a pause, 'hence your amazement. This is the whole reason I've come here: to leave nothing unsaid and bring everything out into the open.'

'It wasn't me,' Raskolnikov began in a whisper, just like a frightened little child who's been caught red-handed.

'Yes it was, Rodion Romanych. Yes it was, sir – can't be anyone else,' Porfiry whispered, with stern conviction.

They both fell silent and the silence lasted a strangely long time, ten minutes or so. Raskolnikov leant his elbows on the table and silently ruffled his hair with his fingers. Porfiry Petrovich meekly sat and waited. Then, with a sudden, contemptuous glance, Raskolnikov said:

'Up to your old tricks again, Porfiry Petrovich? The same old ruses? Aren't you tired of it all, I wonder?'

'Oh please – what good are tricks to me now? If there were any witnesses here, that would be another matter; but it's just the two of us. You can see for yourself that I haven't come here to chase you around like a hare and trap you. Whether or not you confess means nothing to me at this moment in time. I don't need you to convince me.'

'So why have you come?' asked Raskolnikov irritably. 'I'll ask you again: if you consider me guilty, why not put me inside?'

'Now there's a question! I'll take each point in turn: firstly, arresting you just like that is no use to me.'

'What do you mean, no use? If you're convinced, you should . . .'

'And what if I am convinced? For now, these are mere dreams of mine, sir. What would be the point of my putting you away *to rest in peace*? You must know that yourself if you're encouraging me. Say I bring that tradesman in to prove your guilt. You'll just tell him, "Are you drunk or what? Who saw me with you? I just took you for a drunk, and quite right, too" – well, what will I say to you then? Especially as your story's more likely than his, seeing as his testimony is mere psychology, which hardly suits a mug like his, while you get straight to the point, because he's an old soak, that man, as everyone knows. And haven't I admitted to you openly, more than once, that all this psychology is double-edged and that the second edge cuts deeper than the first and is a whole lot more likely? And I still haven't got anything else on you anyway. And even though I will still arrest you and even though I've come here myself (not the done thing) to tell you about everything in advance, all the same I'm telling you straight (which is not the done thing, either) that this will be no use to me. And secondly, I've come here because . . .'

'Oh yes – and secondly?' (Raskolnikov was still gasping.)

'Because, as I told you before, I think I owe you an explanation. I

don't want you to think me a monster, especially when I'm sincerely
fond of you, believe it or not. As a result of which, thirdly, I've come
here with an open and frank suggestion: that you turn yourself in.
You'll be infinitely better off, and so will I – one less thing to worry
about. Very frank of me, don't you think?'

Raskolnikov thought for a minute.

'Listen, Porfiry Petrovich: you say yourself it's mere psychology
and here you are plunging into mathematics. What if you're the one
who's mistaken now?'

'No, Rodion Romanych, I'm not mistaken. I have this little mark,
you see. I found it back then; a real godsend!'

'What little mark?'

'I'm not saying, Rodion Romanych. In any case, I have no right to
put things off any longer. I'll arrest you, sir. So think about it. It's all
the same to me *now*, which means I'm only thinking of you. It's for
the best, Rodion Romanych – believe me!'

Raskolnikov grinned back at him spitefully.

'You know, this is more than just comical – it's shameful. Imagine
I really was guilty (which I'm not saying for one moment I am), why
on earth would I turn myself in to you, when you're telling me yourself that you'll put me away *to rest in peace*?'

'Now, now, Rodion Romanych, you trust words too much. Who
knows? Maybe you won't exactly *rest in peace*! After all, this is only
a theory, and mine to boot. What sort of an authority am I to you?
Who knows? I may be concealing one or two things from you even
now. I'm hardly going to show you all my cards, am I? Heh-heh! Secondly, what do you mean, what good will it do you? Do you have any
idea what sort of reduction you'll get for that? Just think about the
timing! When the other man's already taken the crime upon himself
and muddied the waters? And I swear to you, in the name of God,
that I will fix and fiddle things *there* in such a way that your confession will come as a bolt from the blue. We'll smash all this psychology
to smithereens, and I'll turn all the suspicions against you to dust,
making your crime look like some kind of mental blackout, because,
in all conscience, a blackout is what it was. I'm an honest man, Rodion
Romanych, and I'll keep my word.'

Raskolnikov fell into a sad silence and hung his head; after a long
think he finally grinned once more, but this time his smile was meek
and sad:

'Oh, don't bother!' he said, as if he were being entirely frank with Porfiry now. 'It's not worth it! I don't want your stupid reduction!'

'Just as I feared!' exclaimed Porfiry with feeling, as if he couldn't help it. 'Just as I feared – you don't want our reduction.'

Raskolnikov threw him a sad, serious look.

'Life's not to be sniffed at, you know!' Porfiry went on. 'You've still got plenty of it ahead of you. What do you mean, you don't want it? How very impatient you are!'

'Plenty of what ahead of me?'

'Life! A prophet, are you? How much do you really know? Seek and ye will find.[12] Perhaps this is where God's been waiting for you. And they're not forever, the shackles . . .'

'Oh yes, the reduction . . . ,' Raskolnikov laughed.

'What are you so frightened of? The bourgeois shame of it all? That might be the case without you even knowing it – you're young, after all! But still, you of all people should not be frightened or ashamed of turning yourself in.'

'What do I care?' Raskolnikov whispered with contemptuous disgust, apparently reluctant even to speak. He was about to get up again, as if he wanted to leave, but sat back down in visible despair.

'There you go! You no longer believe anything and think this is just cheap flattery. But how much of life have you actually seen? How much do you really understand? You came up with a theory, only to feel ashamed when it all collapsed, when it proved so very unoriginal! It turned out pretty badly, that's true, but even so, you're not a lost cause. You're not a complete scoundrel. In fact, you're not a scoundrel at all! At least you didn't agonize about it for long – you made straight for the final pillars. I mean, what kind of a man do I take you for? I take you for the kind of man who, even after he's had his insides ripped out, stands there smiling at his tormentors – assuming he's found something to believe in, or God. Well, find and you will live. A change of air's what you need. Suffering also has a lot to be said for it, you know. So do a bit of that. Mikolka might just be onto something, with his eagerness to suffer. I know belief doesn't come easily – but try not to complicate things. Yield to life without thinking about it. And don't worry – you'll be brought safely to shore and set on your feet. Which shore? How should I know? I just believe you've got plenty of life ahead of you. I know that to you this all sounds like a sermon

I've prepared in advance, but perhaps you'll remember it later and find it useful; that's why I'm saying it. Just as well you only killed the old hag. Had you come up with some other theory, you might have gone and done something a billion times more ghastly! Perhaps it's God we should be thanking. God might just be saving you for something; how can you know? So have a great heart and a bit less fear. What? Are you shying away from the great duty ahead of you? That would be shameful now. Having taken such a step, you'd better steel yourself. There's justice in it. So do what justice demands. I know you lack belief, but life, by heaven, will bring you to shore. You'll get a taste for it in the end. Air is what you need now – air, air!'

Raskolnikov couldn't help shuddering.

'Who are you to speak like this?' he cried. 'A prophet? From what heights of supreme tranquillity do you dispense such oracular wisdom?'

'Who am I? A man whose best days are behind him. A man of feeling and sympathy. A man who may even know a thing or two, but whose day has come and gone. But you – you're a different matter: God has a life in store for you (and – who knows? – perhaps this will all just blow over). So what if you have to cross over into a different category of people? Don't tell me you'll miss the life of comfort – a man with a heart like yours? So what if no one sees you again for a very long time? It's not about time – it's about you. Be a sun and everyone will see you. A sun must be a sun – that's its main job. Why are you smiling again? Because I'm such a Schiller? You think I'm toadying up to you, I dare say! Well, maybe I am, heh-heh-heh! You know, Rodion Romanych, you shouldn't believe my every word. In fact, I expect you should never believe me entirely – I'm quite incorrigible, I agree. All I'll say is this: you, of all people, can judge for yourself how shoddy I am, and how honest!'

'When are you planning to arrest me?'

'Well, I suppose I can let you wander around for another day or two. Think about it, my dear chap, and say a few prayers. It's for the best, by heaven, for the best.'

'And if I run away?' asked Raskolnikov with a strange grin.

'You won't. A peasant would run; and a fashionable religious fanatic – a slave to someone else's thoughts – would run, because you need only show him the tip of your little finger, as happened to that warrant officer[13] in Gogol's play, for him to believe whatever you want for the rest of his life. But you no longer believe in that theory of yours, do you? So what cause would you have to run? Do you really want to? It's a ghastly, difficult business, when what you need above all is life and a well-defined situation, and, of course, the right kind of air. You won't find it there, will you? You'll run away and come back of your own accord. *You can't get by without us.* But if I have you taken into custody – well, give it a month or two, maybe three, and, mark my words, you'll come forward yourself and I expect you'll be amazed at how it all happens. You won't know, even an hour before, that you're about to confess. I even think you'll end up wanting to "accept your suffering"; but don't take my word for it, think it over in your own time. Suffering, Rodion Romanych, is a great thing. Now pay no attention to my waistline and don't laugh: there's an idea in suffering, I know there is. Mikolka's right. No, you won't run away, Rodion Romanych.'

Raskolnikov rose and took his cap. Porfiry Petrovich stood up as well.

'Going out for a walk? Should be a nice evening, unless there's a storm. Although at least that would freshen things up . . .'

He, too, picked up his cap.

'Now please don't go getting the idea, Porfiry Petrovich,' said Raskolnikov with stern insistence, 'that I admitted anything to you today. You're a strange man and I listened to you out of pure curiosity. I didn't admit a thing . . . Do remember that.'

'Yes, yes, I know. I'll remember. My, he's even shaking. Don't you worry, my dear chap, your will shall be done. Have a little walk. Just don't go overboard. In any case, I have one tiny favour to ask, if you don't mind,' he added, lowering his voice. 'It's a bit of a ticklish one, but important: if, by any chance (though I can't believe it and consider you quite incapable of it), if by any chance – by any remote chance – you should feel inclined, in the next forty or fifty hours, to have done with all this in some other way, in some fantastical manner – by, say, taking your own life (a quite ridiculous notion, but I'm sure you'll forgive me) – then please leave a short but comprehensive note. Two lines will do, just two tiny lines, not forgetting to mention the stone: it would be the noble thing to do. Well then, goodbye . . . Here's to good thoughts and fine intentions!'

Porfiry went out, looking rather hunched and, it seemed, trying not to glance in Raskolnikov's direction. Raskolnikov walked over to the window and waited with irritable impatience until, according to his calculations, Porfiry would have left the building and headed off. Then he, too, hurried out of the room.

III

He was hurrying to Svidrigailov. What was he hoping for? He himself did not know. But this man held some hidden power over him. Having once realized this, he could no longer forget it. Now, moreover, the time had come.

On the way he was tormented by one question in particular: had Svidrigailov been to see Porfiry?

As far as he could tell – and he would have sworn to it – no, he hadn't! Again and again he asked himself this question, recalling Porfiry's entire visit, and concluded: no, he hadn't. Of course he hadn't!

But if he hadn't yet been to see Porfiry, might he still go?

It seemed to him now that he wouldn't, not for the time being. Why? He couldn't have answered this question either, and he certainly didn't want to start racking his brains over it now. All this was a torment to him, but at the same time it was as if he couldn't really care less. It was strange – no one, perhaps, would have believed him – but he felt no more than a faint, absent-minded concern about his current, immediate fate. Something else was tormenting him, something far more important, extraordinarily so – about himself and no one else, something different, something crucial. What was more, he felt boundlessly weary at heart, even though his mind was working better that morning than at any time during these recent days.

And was there now any point, after all that had happened, in trying to overcome all these new, paltry obstacles? Was there any point, say, in scheming to stop some Svidrigailov or other from visiting Porfiry; in researching, making enquiries, wasting time on him?

How sick and tired he was of it all!

And yet, here he was hurrying to Svidrigailov. Surely he wasn't expecting anything *new* from him, any pointers, a way out? How people clutch at straws! Or was it fate, some instinct or other, that was bringing them together? Perhaps it was just weariness, despair; perhaps it wasn't Svidrigailov he needed but someone else, and Svidrigailov just happened to be there. Sonya? But why go to Sonya now? To beg her tears again? But Sonya terrified him. Sonya was an implacable sentence, an irrevocable decision. It was her road or his. Now more than ever he was in no condition to see her. Wasn't he better off probing Svidrigailov? He found himself admitting that he really did seem to need that man for something, and had done for some time.

And yet, what could they ever have in common? Even their villainy could not be the same. That man, furthermore, was extremely unpleasant, exceptionally depraved (it was obvious), sly and deceitful (how could he not be?) and, perhaps, downright nasty. There were all sorts of stories about him. True, he was going to great lengths for Katerina Ivanovna's children; but who could say why or what it meant? That man was always plotting.

One other thought kept occurring to Raskolnikov, day in day out, causing him terrible anxiety; so unbearable was it that he even tried to chase it away. He'd think: Svidrigailov was always hovering around him, and was still doing so now; Svidrigailov had learned his secret; Svidrigailov used to have designs on Dunya. What if he still did? It was almost certain that yes, *he did*. And what if now, having learned his secret and thus gained power over him, he decided to use that power as a weapon against Dunya?

This thought tormented him even during his sleep, but never had it struck him so consciously, so vividly, as it did now, on his way to Svidrigailov. This thought alone was enough to plunge him into dark fury. Firstly, that would change everything, his own situation included: he'd have to reveal his secret to Dunechka without delay. He would, perhaps, have to give himself up so as to dissuade Dunechka from taking some reckless step. And the letter? Dunechka had received it only this morning! From whom in Petersburg might she receive a letter? (Surely not Luzhin?) True, he'd left Razumikhin on guard, but Razumikhin didn't know anything. Perhaps he ought to open up to Razumikhin as well? The very thought disgusted him.

'In any case, I have to see Svidrigailov as soon as possible,' he decided definitively. 'Thankfully, it's not the details I need so much as the essence of the thing. But if he really is capable of it, if Svidrigailov really is scheming against Dunya – then . . .'

Raskolnikov had become so weary by now, after this whole month, that he had only one answer to such questions: 'Then I'll kill him,' he thought, in cold despair. A heavy feeling pressed down on his heart. He stopped in the middle of the street and looked around: which road had he taken and where had he ended up? He was on ——sky Prospect,[14] some thirty or forty paces from Haymarket, which he'd crossed just now. A tavern took up the whole of the first floor of the building to his left. All the windows were wide open. Judging by the amount of people he could see moving about in them, the tavern was full to bursting. He could hear a group of professional singers, a clarinet, a violin, the thudding of a Turkish drum, and women shrieking. He was about to turn back, wondering why on earth he'd taken ——sky Prospect, when suddenly, in one of the furthest open windows, at a tea table by the window, with a pipe between his teeth, he spotted Svidrigailov. He was astounded, horrified. Svidrigailov was observing him in silence and, to Raskolnikov's further astonishment, seemed to be on the point of getting up, so as to slip away before being seen. Raskolnikov instantly pretended not to have seen him and to be looking elsewhere, lost in thought, while continuing to observe him out of the corner of his eye. His heart was racing. So he was right: Svidrigailov didn't want to be seen. He'd taken his pipe from his mouth and was just about to hide; but, having got up and moved the table, he must have suddenly noticed that Raskolnikov could see him and was observing him. Something happened between them not unlike the scene of their first encounter in Raskolnikov's room, while he was sleeping. A roguish grin broke out over Svidrigailov's face, growing broader and broader. The two men knew that each was observing the other. Eventually Svidrigailov burst into raucous laughter.

'Well, well! In you come then, if that's what you're after. Here I am!' he shouted from the window.

Raskolnikov went up to the tavern.

He found him in a very small back room with only one window; it adjoined a large saloon, where, seated around twenty little tables and deafened by the desperate singing of the chorus, merchants, civil servants and all sorts were drinking tea. From somewhere there came the clicking of billiard balls. On the little table in front of Svidrigailov stood an open bottle of champagne and a half-filled glass. The room also contained a boy playing a small hand organ, and a strapping, red-cheeked girl wearing a tucked-up, striped skirt and a Tyrolean hat with ribbons – she was a singer, aged eighteen or so, who, despite the chorus in the next room, was performing some maudlin song in a hoarse contralto, accompanied by the young boy on the hand organ . . .

'All right, that'll do,' Svidrigailov interrupted her when Raskolnikov came in.

The girl broke off her song at once and lingered in deferential anticipation. There had been a hint of seriousness and deference in her expression even while she was singing her doggerel rhymes.

'Hey, Filipp, a glass!' shouted Svidrigailov.

'I'm not drinking,' said Raskolnikov.

'As you wish. It's not for you anyway. Have a drink, Katya! I won't be needing you any more today, so off you go!' He poured her a full glass of wine and took out a yellow banknote. Katya drained the glass in one go – without a break, in twenty gulps, as women do – took the note, kissed Svidrigailov's hand, with the latter's gravest consent, and went out, with the little boy in tow. Both had been brought in off the street. Svidrigailov had been in Petersburg for less than a week, yet he was already on a patriarchal footing with all and sundry. He was also on familiar terms with the servant at the tavern, Filipp, who fawned on him. The door to the saloon was kept locked. Svidrigailov was very much at home in this room and probably spent whole days in it. The tavern was filthy and shabby, even by average standards.

'I was looking for you,' Raskolnikov began, 'but why did I suddenly turn into ——sky from Haymarket just now? I never turn off there or take this street. I always turn right from Haymarket. And anyway, this isn't the way to your place. I turned and there you were! How strange!'

'Why don't you call a spade a spade? It's a miracle!'

'Because it might be mere chance.'

'What is it about these people?' Svidrigailov guffawed. 'They'll never admit a miracle, even if it's what they believe inside! I mean, you say yourself it "might" be mere chance. And how very chicken-hearted people are about their opinion – it beggars belief, Rodion Romanych! I don't mean you. You've got your own opinion and you weren't too afraid to have one. That's why I became interested in you.'

'Nothing else?'

'Isn't that enough?'

There was no mistaking Svidrigailov's excitement, however faint (he'd drunk no more than half a glass).

'If you ask me, you came to see me before you discovered that I'm capable of having what you call my own opinion,' Raskolnikov remarked.

'Well, things were different then. We each have our own steps to

take. But as for the miracle – well, what can I say? You must have
slept through the last two or three days. I suggested this tavern to you
myself and there's nothing remotely miraculous about the fact that
you came straight here. I explained the entire route to you, the precise
location and the hours at which I may be found here. Remember?'

'I must have forgotten,' replied Raskolnikov with astonishment.

'I believe you. I told you twice. The address imprinted itself automatically in your memory. You took this turning automatically as
well, unaware that you were heading in exactly the right direction.
Even when I was speaking to you about it, I didn't think you'd understood me. You do give yourself away, Rodion Romanych. And another
thing: I'm convinced that Petersburg is full of people who walk around
talking to themselves. People who are halfway mad. If we had any
scholars worth the name, then doctors, jurists and philosophers could
carry out priceless studies in this city, each according to his specialism.
Where else would you find so many dark, drastic, strange influences
on the soul of man? Consider the influence of the climate alone! And
yet this is the administrative centre of all Russia; the whole country
should reflect its character. But that's not the point now. The point is
that I've observed you on several occasions. You leave your building,
still holding your head up. Twenty or so paces later, you've already
lowered it and clasp your hands behind your back. You're looking but
no longer seeing, whether ahead of you or to the sides. Eventually, you
begin to move your lips and talk to yourself. From time to time you
even free one of your arms and declaim something. And in the end
you stop for an age in the middle of the street. It's simply no good, sir.
You might be noticed by someone else as well, and you wouldn't want
that. In the end, it's all the same to me, and I can't cure you, but you
must understand me.'

'Do you know I'm being followed?' asked Raskolnikov with a
searching look.

'No, I don't know anything,' Svidrigailov replied with apparent
surprise.

'Then let's leave me out of it,' mumbled Raskolnikov, frowning.

'All right then, we'll leave you out of it.'

'Perhaps you should tell me, seeing as you come here to drink and
seeing as you yourself have twice suggested I come to see you here,
why, when I was looking through the window from the street just
now, you hid and wanted to leave? I saw it quite clearly.'

'Heh-heh! And why, when I was standing on your threshold, did you lie on your sofa with your eyes closed and pretend you were sleeping, when you weren't sleeping at all? I saw it quite clearly.'

'I might have had . . . reasons . . . as you know yourself.'

'And I may have had my reasons, though you'll never know them.'

Raskolnikov lowered his right elbow onto the table, supported his chin with the fingers of his right hand and fixed his eyes on Svidrigailov. For about a minute he studied his face, which had always fascinated him, even before. It was a strange sort of face, not unlike a mask: white and bright red, with cherry red lips, a light blond beard and, still, a full head of blond hair. His eyes were a little too blue somehow, and their gaze a little too heavy and static. There was something terribly unpleasant about this beautiful and, for its age, exceptionally youthful face. Svidrigailov was foppishly dressed in light, summery clothes, and sporting especially stylish linen. On one hand he wore an enormous ring with an expensive stone.

'Do I really have to deal with the likes of you as well?' said Raskolnikov, coming out into the open in a sudden fit of impatience. 'You may be the most dangerous person there is, if you put your mind to it, but I refuse to put myself through any more of this. I'll show you right now that I value myself less than you must think. I've come to tell you frankly that if you still harbour your old intentions towards my sister and if, to that end, you're planning to exploit any recent revelations, then I'll kill you before you manage to throw me in jail. I give you my word: you know I'll honour it. Secondly, if you have something you want to tell me – I've had that impression all along – then say it now, because time is precious and very soon, perhaps, it will be too late.'

'But why this great hurry – where do you have to go?' asked Svidrigailov, examining him with some curiosity.

'We each have our own steps to take,' said Raskolnikov, with gloomy impatience.

'Only a minute ago you were urging openness, yet you refuse to answer the first question I ask you,' Svidrigailov remarked with a smile. 'You always think I'm plotting something, hence all these suspicious glances. Well, that's quite understandable in your situation. But however much I want us to become closer, I'm not going to burden myself with the task of trying to persuade you otherwise. The game, by heaven, is not worth the candle, and in any case there was nothing in particular that I was planning to speak to you about.'

'So why did you need me so badly? Why were you always running after me?'

'Simply to observe you – I found you curious. The fantastical nature of your situation, that's what I liked about you! On top of that, you're the brother of a person who interested me greatly, not to mention the fact that this person was always talking about you, from which I concluded that you wield considerable influence over her. Isn't that enough? Heh-heh-heh! Although I admit that I find your question extremely complex and it's hard for me to give you an answer. I'll give you an example. You're not just here on some errand or other, are you? It's because you're after something a little bit new. Isn't that right? Isn't it?' Svidrigailov insisted with a roguish grin. 'So try imagining that I myself, while still on my way to Petersburg, on the train, was counting on you to tell me something *a little bit new* as well and on my managing to borrow something from you! See how rich we are!'

'Borrow what from me?'

'What can I say? How do I know? You see the sort of hole I spend my days in, and I enjoy it; or rather, I don't exactly enjoy it but I have to sit somewhere, don't I? Take poor Katya – I mean, did you see her? . . . If only I were a glutton, say, or a gourmet going from club to club, but I'll eat anything, even this!' (He pointed towards the corner, where, on a tin plate on a small table, lay the remains of some revolting dish of steak and potatoes). 'Have you eaten, by the way? I've had a bite and that's all I want. I never drink wine, for example. Unless it's champagne, and even then only one glass all evening, which is more than enough to give me a headache. I just ordered some now to perk myself up, because I've somewhere to go and you've caught me in a very particular mood. That's why I was hiding like a schoolboy – I thought you'd spoil my plans. But it would seem' – he took out his watch – 'that I have an hour to spend with you; it's half past four now. Believe me, I'd take anything: the life of a landowner, say, or father or uhlan or photographer or journalist . . . but look, I've got nothing, no specialist skills at all! It even gets a bit boring sometimes. I really did think you would have something new to tell me.'

'Who are you anyway and why are you here?'

'Who am I? You know who I am: a nobleman, did two years in the cavalry, then gadded about here in Petersburg, then married Marfa Petrovna and lived in the country. My life in a nutshell!'

'You're a gambler, aren't you?'

'Nonsense. A card sharp, not a gambler.'

'So you were a card sharp?'

'I was.'

'You must have taken a few beatings, I suppose?'

'Occasionally. And?'

'So a duel was always a possibility . . . how invigorating.'

'I won't disagree with you; in any case, philosophizing is not my strong suit. I'll admit: I came here more for the women.'

'With Marfa Petrovna barely in the grave?'

'I suppose,' smiled Svidrigailov with winning candour. 'And? You seem to think there's something wrong with the way I talk about women?'

'You mean, do I think there's anything wrong with depravity?'

'Depravity? So that's what you're getting at! But I'll take your questions in turn and start with the women. I'm in the mood for talking. So tell me: why should I hold back? Why give up on women, when it's about the only thing I enjoy? At least it gives me something to do.'

'So depravity is the only reason you're here?'

'And what if it is? People have a thing about depravity. But I like a straight question. At least there's something constant about depravity, something founded on nature and not subject to fantasy, something that's always afire in the blood, like burning coal, something which may take you a very long time, even with the passing of the years, to put out. Gives people something to do, wouldn't you say?'

'What have you got to be so pleased about? It's a sickness, and a dangerous one.'

'So that's what you're driving at! I agree it's a sickness, like everything that goes too far – and here you simply have to go too far – but actually, everyone's different, that's the first point, and secondly, yes of course, you should always know when enough is enough (even if you're a scoundrel), but what's a man to do? If it weren't for this, you might end up having to shoot yourself. I agree that no decent man can entirely avoid boredom, but still . . .'

'And would you be able to shoot yourself?'

'Well, really!' parried Svidrigailov with disgust. 'Kindly refrain from talking about that,' he continued hastily and without so much as a hint of his previous swagger. Even his face seemed to change. 'It's an unforgivable weakness of mine, I'll admit, but what can I do? I fear

death and I don't like to hear it discussed. Did you know that I'm a bit
of a mystic?'

'Ah! The ghosts of Marfa Petrovna! Still visiting, are they?'

'Don't mention them, please. Haven't seen any yet in Petersburg
and to hell with them anyway!' he cried with an air of irritation. 'No,
I'd rather we talked about . . . although . . . H'm! Shame there's so
little time and I can't stay with you longer! I could have told you a
thing or two.'

'A woman, is it?'

'Yes, a woman, just a random case . . . but I don't mean that.'

'So the loathsomeness of all this no longer affects you? You no
longer have the strength to stop?'

'Laying claim to strength as well, are you? Heh-heh-heh! This time
you've really surprised me, Rodion Romanych, although I knew this
would happen. And there you are telling me about depravity and aesthetics! You're a Schiller, an idealist! That's just as it should be, of
course, and it would be a surprise if it were any different, but still,
there's something strange about it all when it actually happens . . . Ah,
what a shame there's so little time – you're an exceptionally intriguing
individual! Do you like Schiller, by the way? I simply adore him.'

'What a show-off you are!' said Raskolnikov, with a certain disgust.

'Whatever next?' replied Svidrigailov, roaring with laughter. 'Well
all right, if you must. But what's wrong with a bit of showing off if it's
not doing anyone any harm? I've lived at Marfa Petrovna's in the
country for seven long years, so when I manage to collar an intelligent
man like you – intelligent and highly intriguing – I'm only too glad to
have the chance to talk. Besides, I've drunk half a glass of this stuff
and it's already slightly gone to my head. But the main thing is a certain circumstance, which has really put the wind in my sails, but
about which I will say . . . nothing. But where are you off to?' Svidrigailov suddenly asked in alarm.

Raskolnikov was about to get up. He felt oppressed, stifled and
somehow embarrassed about having come here. He'd satisfied himself
that Svidrigailov was the shallowest and most contemptible villain in
the world.

'Dear oh dear! You must stay a bit longer,' Svidrigailov implored
him. 'Order yourself some tea at least. Really, sit down and I'll stop
talking rubbish – about myself I mean. I'll tell you a story. Wouldn't

you like me to tell you the story of how I was once "saved" (as you
might put it) by a woman? In fact, it'll be a reply to your first question, because the individual in question is your sister. May I? It'll kill
the time.'

　　'All right, but I hope you'll . . .'

　　'Oh, don't you worry! Not to mention the fact that even a man as
abominable and shallow as me can feel only the deepest respect for
Avdotya Romanovna.'

IV

'You perhaps know (in fact, I told you myself),' Svidrigailov began,
'that I did some time in debtor's prison here, for an enormous sum,
without the slightest prospect of being able to pay. I won't bore you
with the details of how Marfa Petrovna bought me out. Are you aware
of the degree of stupefaction to which a woman can be brought by
love? She was an honest woman and far from stupid (though completely uneducated). Just imagine: this same, jealous, honest woman
decided to condescend, after many dreadful outbursts and reproaches,
to a sort of contract with me, one she upheld for the duration of our
marriage. You see, she was significantly older than me, and besides,
she was forever sucking on cloves. I was enough of a pig at heart, and
honest enough in my own way, to tell her frankly that I could never be
entirely faithful. This admission worked her up into a frenzy, but
something about my rough candour seemed to appeal to her: "He
doesn't want to deceive me himself, then, if he's telling me this now" –
for a jealous woman, nothing could be more important. After many
tearful scenes, a kind of unwritten contract was established between
us: first, I would never leave Marfa Petrovna and would always remain
her husband; second, I would never wander off without her permission; third, I would never take a regular mistress; fourth, Marfa Petrovna would permit me, in exchange, to look in on the housemaids every
now and again, though never without her secret knowledge; fifth,
God forbid that I should ever love a woman of our own class; sixth, if,
God forbid, I should succumb to some great and serious passion, I
should reveal it to Marfa Petrovna. This last point, however, never
caused Marfa Petrovna undue concern. She was an intelligent woman,
so she could hardly see me as anything but a depraved skirt-chaser

incapable of true love. But an intelligent woman and a jealous woman are two very different entities – and therein lies the problem. Still, with some people, in order to judge them without bias, one must begin by renouncing various preconceptions and one's habitual attitude towards the people and objects that ordinarily surround us. I'm entitled to count on your judgement more than that of anyone else. I expect you've already heard a great many absurd and ridiculous things about Marfa Petrovna. She did indeed possess some quite ridiculous habits. But I will tell you frankly that I sincerely regret the countless sorrows of which I was the cause. Well, that ought to do as a perfectly acceptable *oraison funèbre* from a dear-beloved husband to his dear-beloved wife. In the event of an argument between us, I would tend to say nothing and avoid becoming irritated, and this gentlemanly conduct almost always attained its purpose; it had an effect on her – in fact, she liked it; and there were occasions when she was even proud of me. Nevertheless, your dear sister proved too much for her. Why oh why did she risk welcoming such a beauty into her home – as a governess! My explanation is that Marfa Petrovna was a fiery and impressionable woman and she herself simply fell in love – literally fell in love – with Avdotya Romanovna. But your sister's a fine one, too! I had no doubt, from the moment I saw her, that there was trouble ahead and – can you imagine? – decided that I wouldn't so much as look at her. But Avdotya Romanovna took the first step herself – can you believe it? And can you believe that Marfa Petrovna even chastised me at first for never saying a word about your dear sister, for being so indifferent to her own incessant, besotted praise of Avdotya Romanovna? God knows what she was after! Well, you won't be surprised to hear that Marfa Petrovna told Avdotya Romanovna everything there is to know about me. She had the most unfortunate trait of telling the world all our family secrets and constantly complaining about me to all and sundry; a new and beautiful friend like Avdotya Romanovna was too good an opportunity to miss! I suspect that they spoke of nothing but me, and there can be little doubt that Avdotya Romanovna became acquainted with all those dark, mysterious tales that people associate me with . . . You, I dare say, will also have heard something in this line?'

'I have. Luzhin even accused you of being responsible for the death of a child. Is that true?'

'Kindly avoid such vulgar topics,' Svidrigailov snapped back with peevish disgust. 'If you are so very desperate to find out about all this nonsense, I'll tell you about it another time, but now . . .'

'There was also talk about a servant of yours in the country – you were responsible for something there, too, apparently.'

'Please – enough!' Svidrigailov interrupted with obvious impatience.

'I don't suppose that's the same servant who came to fill your pipe after he died . . . the one you told me about yourself?' asked Raskolnikov with mounting irritation.

Svidrigailov looked closely at Raskolnikov, who thought he caught in this glance the briefest flash of malicious mockery, but Svidrigailov managed to restrain himself and replied with great courtesy:

'The very same. I see that you, too, are unusually interested in all this, and I'll consider it my duty, at the first available opportunity, to satisfy your curiosity on all counts. Damn it all! I see that I really could be taken for some character from a novel. Judge for yourself how grateful I should be to the late Marfa Petrovna for telling your dear sister so many mysterious and intriguing things about me. I dare not judge what impression this must have made on her, but it was certainly to my advantage. For all Avdotya Romanovna's natural disgust towards me, and despite my habitually dismal and repulsive appearance, she ended up taking pity on me, a washed-up man. And when a girl's heart is moved to *pity*, she thereby puts herself, as everyone knows, in the gravest possible danger. We all know what comes next: she'll want to "save" him and knock some sense into him, and resurrect him and exhort him towards more noble goals, and restore him to new life and activity – the usual fantasies. I immediately twigged that the bird was flying into the net all by herself and prepared myself accordingly. You seem to be frowning, Rodion Romanych? Not to worry, sir. As you know, it all blew over. (Damn it, I'm drinking a lot today!) You know, it's always been a source of regret to me, right from the beginning, that fate did not allow your sister to be born in the second or third century AD, as the daughter of a ruling prince or governor, or of some proconsul or other in Asia Minor. She would, no doubt, have been among the martyrs; and she would, no doubt, have smiled at having her breast burned with white-hot tongs. She'd have sought this out herself, while in the fourth or fifth century she'd have retreated into the Egyptian desert for thirty years, living off roots, raptures and visions. She craves nothing else and demands to suffer some agony or other for someone or other, and if you don't give her this agony quickly she'll probably throw herself out of the window. I've heard about a certain Mr Razumikhin. A sensible sort, I'm told (as his name suggests – must be a seminarian).[15] Let him take care of your sister. In short, I think I've understood her and I'm rather proud of the fact. But back then ... well, as you know yourself, one is always a bit more frivolous at the beginning of an acquaintance, a bit more foolish, liable to get things wrong, not to see them as they really are. Why does she have to be so pretty, damn it? It's hardly my fault! In short, for me it all began with the most irrepressible surge of lust. Avdotya Romanovna is appallingly chaste – it's unheard of, unprecedented. (Note that I am telling you this simply as a fact. Your sister is almost morbidly chaste, for all her breadth of mind, and it'll do her nothing but harm.) At this point a girl turned up on the estate, Parasha, black-eyed Parasha, a housemaid newly brought in from another village. I'd never seen her before – a very pretty little thing, but incredibly stupid: she made a terrible racket with her sobbing and wailing, and ended up causing a scene. Once, after lunch, Avdotya Romanovna caught me alone on one of the paths in the garden and, eyes flashing, *demanded* that I leave poor Parasha alone. It was virtually our first tête-à-tête. I, needless to say, considered it an honour to satisfy her wish, tried my best to look stricken and abashed, and, in short, carried it off rather well. A relationship began: mysterious conversations, admonitions, exhortations, supplications, entreaties, even tears – can you believe it? – even tears! The things a passion for propaganda can do to a girl! I, of course, blamed everything on my fate, affected a terrible thirst for enlightenment and, finally, deployed the greatest and surest method for conquering a woman's heart, a method which never lets you down and works on absolutely everyone, without exception. The method is well known: flattery. Nothing in the world is harder than candour, and nothing easier than flattery. Candour that contains even the faintest false note results in immediate dissonance and a scene is sure to follow. Flattery, even if it contains false notes and nothing else, is always welcome and heard with pleasure; a vulgar kind of pleasure, perhaps, but pleasure nonetheless. And however crude this flattery may be, at least half of it will always seem true. This holds for all social groups, whatever their level of education. Even vestal virgins can be seduced by flattery – to say nothing of ordinary people. I can't help laughing when I recall how I once seduced a certain lady who was deeply devoted to her husband, her children and her own virtue. What fun that was – and how easily done! She really was a lady of virtue, at least in her own way. My tactics were simple enough: to appear crushed by her chastity and prostrate myself before it at every turn. I flattered her shamelessly and no sooner would I win a squeeze of her hand or even a glance than I'd immediately berate myself that I'd taken it from her by force while she'd resisted, resisted to such a degree that she would never have granted me anything had I myself not been so ridden with vice; she, in her innocence, hadn't seen it coming and had yielded without meaning to, unaware of having done so, etcetera, etcetera. In short, I had my way, while my lady remained perfectly convinced that she was blameless and chaste, that she was performing all her duties and obligations, and that her ruin had come about quite inadvertently. How very angry she was with me when I eventually told her that, in my sincere opinion, she'd been seeking pleasure no less than I had. Poor Marfa Petrovna also yielded to flattery all too easily, and had I but wanted to I could, of course, have transferred her entire estate to myself while she was still alive. (Dear me! I'm drinking and talking far too much.) I trust you won't be angry if I now mention that this method was beginning to have the same effect on Avdotya Romanovna. But I went and ruined everything through my own stupidity and impatience. Even before then (I remember one occasion in particular) she'd taken a violent dislike to the expression of my eyes – can you believe that? In short, they'd begun to burn, ever more intensely and ever more recklessly, with a fire that frightened her and that she eventually came to detest. I won't go into the details; we went our separate ways. Then I committed another stupidity. I set about mocking all this propaganda and oratory in the most vulgar way imaginable. Parasha came back into the picture, and not just her. Sodom, in a nutshell. Oh, if you could but see, Rodion Romanych, at least once in your life, your dear sister's eyes flash as only they know how! Never mind that I'm drunk now and that I've had a whole glass of champagne – I'm telling the truth. I used to dream of that look, I assure you. By the end, even the rustling of her dress was too much for me. Really, I thought an epileptic fit was just around the corner. I'd never imagined reaching such a state of frenzy. In short, I needed to resign myself, but this was no longer possible. So can you imagine what I went and did then? The idiocy to which a man can be

reduced by rage! Never undertake anything in a rage, Rodion Romanych. Calculating that Avdotya Romanovna was more or less a beggar (oh dear, I'm sorry, not what I meant to . . . but doesn't it all come
to the same thing?), in short, that she was living by the fruits of her
own labour and supporting both her mother and you (damn it, you're
frowning again . . .), I made up my mind to offer her all the money I
had (even then, that came to about thirty thousand) in the hope that
she would elope with me, if only to Petersburg. Naturally I'd have
sworn eternal love, bliss, etcetera. Believe it or not, I was so besotted
by that point that if she'd said, "Cut Marfa Petrovna's throat or poison
her and marry me," I'd have done so without a second thought! But the
upshot of it all was the catastrophe you already know about, and you
can judge for yourself how furious I must have been on learning that
Marfa Petrovna had found that scum of a clerk, Luzhin, and all but
fixed up a wedding – one that, in the end, would have come to the
same thing as what I was proposing. Would it not? Would it not, I say?
I can't help noticing that you've started listening very attentively . . .
What an interesting young man . . .'

Svidrigailov impatiently banged his fist on the table. He'd gone red
in the face. Raskolnikov could see quite clearly that the glass or glass
and a half of champagne which he'd been quietly sipping had affected
him for the worse – and decided to take advantage. He found Svidrigailov's behaviour very suspicious.

'Well, you've left me in no doubt that my sister is the reason you've
come here,' he told Svidrigailov plainly, without concealing anything,
so as to irritate him all the more.

'Oh, enough of that,' said Svidrigailov, as if suddenly checking
himself. 'Didn't I tell you . . . ? And anyway, your sister can't bear the
sight of me.'

'I've no doubt about that either, but that's not the point.'

'You've no doubt, eh?' (Svidrigailov narrowed his eyes and smiled
derisively.) 'You're right, she doesn't love me, but you should never
vouch for what goes on between a husband and wife or a pair of lovers. There's always one little corner closed off to the rest of the world,
known only to the two of them. Are you quite sure that Avdotya Romanovna looked at me with disgust?'

'Judging by some of the words and phrases you've been using in the
course of your account, I notice that even now you have the most
pressing designs on Dunya – shameful ones, needless to say.'

'Really? I came out with words and phrases like that, did I?' asked Svidrigailov with the most artless alarm, paying not the faintest attention to Raskolnikov's description of his intentions.

'You're still coming out with them now. I mean, what are you so scared of? What was it that suddenly frightened you just now?'

'Me? Scared and frightened? Frightened of you? If anything, it's you who should be scared of me, *cher ami*.[16] Can we really not find anything better to talk about . . . ? But I must be a bit tipsy. I almost said something careless again. Damn this wine! Hey, bring me some water!'

He grabbed the bottle and unceremoniously tossed it out of the window. Filipp brought some water.

'Such nonsense,' said Svidrigailov, soaking a towel and applying it to his head. 'I can silence you with a single word and smash all your suspicions to smithereens. Are you aware, for example, that I'm getting married?'

'You've told me that before.'

'I have? I'd forgotten. But at the time I couldn't say for sure, never having seen my fiancée. It was merely an intention. Now my fiancée is already in hand – the deal's been done – and were it not for a piece of urgent business I'd take you over there right now, as I need your advice about something. Damn it all! Only ten minutes left. See, look at the clock. But I'll still tell you this story, because it's a rather curious thing, my marriage, in its own way . . . Now where are you off to? Leaving again?'

'No, I won't be leaving now.'

'You won't be leaving at all? We'll see about that! I really will take you over there and show her to you, only not now – you'll have to go soon. You to the left, me to the right. Do you know that Resslich woman? That same Resslich I'm renting a room from – eh? Are you listening? No, what are you . . . ? I mean that woman whose little girl is said to have, you know, in the water, in winter – well, are you listening? Are you? So she's the one who cooked all this up for me. "You must be bored," she says. "Have some fun." I really am a gloomy, dull sort. You think I'm cheerful? I'm not, I'm gloomy. I just sit harmlessly in the corner and three days might pass before you get a word out of me. That Resslich's a handful, I can tell you. Can you believe it? She thinks I'll get bored, drop my wife and go away, so she'll get the wife and put her into circulation; among our class, that is – the posher the better. There's this invalid father, she says, a retired civil servant, sits in his armchair and hasn't moved his legs in three years. There's also a mother, she says, a sensible lady. The son's got a position somewhere out in the sticks – no help from him. One daughter's married and stays away, then there's two little nephews to take care of (as if they didn't have enough on their plate already), plus the girl they've taken out of school before finishing, their last daughter, just sixteen next month, which, as it happens, is also the date she can be given away. To me. So off we went. It's simply hilarious over there. I introduce myself: landowner, widower, bearer of a well-known surname, well-connected, moneyed . . . So what if I'm fifty and she's only fifteen? Who cares about that? All rather tempting, isn't it? Rather tempting, eh? Ha-ha! You should have seen me chatting away to Papa and Mama! The very sight of me would have been worth good money. Out she comes, curtseying and wearing – can you imagine? – a short little frock, like a bud still waiting to open; and blushes and lights up like the dawn (they'd told her, of course). I don't know whether women's faces do much for you, but for me, these sixteen years, these still-childish eyes, this shyness and these bashful tears – for me, that's better than any beauty, not to mention the fact that she herself is simply exquisite. That lovely fair hair of hers, done up in those sweet little lamb's curls, those chubby little lips, those little legs – just adorable! . . . Well, we were introduced. I announced I was in a hurry on account of certain domestic circumstances and the very next day – that is, the day before yesterday – we were blessed. Now, as soon as I arrive, I sit her on my knees and just keep her there . . . So there she is, lighting up like the dawn, and there am I, showering her with kisses. Mama, needless to say, keeps telling her that this is your husband and this is the done thing. In short, bliss! And actually, being a fiancé, as I am now, is probably even better than being a husband! *La nature et la vérité*,[17] you might call it! Ha-ha! We've talked a couple of times and she's certainly not stupid. Sometimes she'll steal a glance at me – and it burns like fire. You know, her sweet little face is like Raphael's *Madonna*. The *Sistine Madonna*,[18] after all, has a quite fantastical face, the face of a sorrowing holy fool – don't you think? Well, it's a bit like that. No sooner were we blessed than I lavished fifteen hundred roubles on her the very next day: a set of diamonds and another of pearls, as well as a silver beauty case – about this size, containing all sorts of goodies. It was enough to make even the Madonna's face glow. Yesterday, when I sat her on my knees – without so much as a by-your-leave – she flushed bright red and out spurted little tears, which she tried to hide, though she was burning inside. Everyone went out for a moment and we were left to our own devices; suddenly she threw herself on my neck (the first time she'd done so), wrapped her two little arms around me, kissed me and vowed to be an obedient, faithful and loving wife, to make me happy, to devote her whole life to me, every single minute, to sacrifice everything, everything, and in return desired *my respect and nothing more.* "Nothing else," she said. "No presents, nothing!" Wouldn't you agree that to hear such an intimate confession from a sixteen-year-old angel like her, wearing a little tulle dress and her hair done up in curls, blushing with girlish shame and weeping with enthusiasm – wouldn't you agree that it's all rather tempting? Not to be sneezed at, eh? So . . . so listen to me . . . Let's go and see my fiancée . . . Only not now!'

'In short, it's the monstrous difference in age and education that excites your lust! Are you really going ahead with this marriage?'

'Why on earth not? Most definitely. Every man must look after himself and no one has more fun than the man who deceives himself best. Ha-ha! What are you doing charging at virtue with a battering ram? Be merciful, father. I'm just a sinner. Heh-heh-heh!'

'And yet, you've taken care of Katerina Ivanovna's children. Although . . . although, you had your own reasons for doing so . . . It all makes sense now.'

'I've always been fond of children, very fond of them,' Svidrigailov laughed. 'In fact, I can tell you a particularly interesting story on precisely this topic, one still unfolding now. On the very first day after my arrival I did a tour of the local dives – after waiting a whole seven years I just plunged straight in. I expect you've noticed that I'm in no hurry to take up with my usual crowd – my old friends and acquaintances. In fact, I'll get by without them for as long as I can. In the country, you know, at Marfa Petrovna's, it was sheer agony remembering all these mysterious nooks and crannies where you can find whatever you want if you know your way around. Damn it all! The masses get drunk; the educated youth, having nothing to do, burns itself out with unfeasible dreams and fantasies, and deforms itself with theories; the Yids have poured in from God knows where and are hiding the money; and the rest is debauchery. From the moment I arrived the city breathed all over me with its familiar smell. One evening I went along to a so-called dance – a quite disgusting dive (for me, the filthier the better) – and there was cancan dancing, of course, like nothing I'd ever seen; in my day it didn't even exist. Progress, I suppose. Suddenly, I see a young girl, thirteen or so, in the prettiest outfit, dancing with a virtuoso, face to face. And her mother's right there, sitting on a chair by the wall. Just imagine the kind of cancan they do there! The girl's embarrassed, blushes, eventually takes offence and starts crying. The virtuoso sweeps her up and starts spinning her about and posing in front of her. All around people are laughing loudly – I love our public at such moments, even the cancan sort – laughing and shouting, "Good on you! That's the way! It's no place for a child!" Well, what do I care whether their attempts to put their own minds at rest make the least bit of sense? I immediately chose my spot, sat down near the mother and began going on about how I'm not from here either and what boors people are in this town: not a clue how to distinguish true qualities and nurture respect where respect is due. I let it be known that I have plenty of money, offered them a lift in my carriage, took them home and became acquainted (they're sub-renting a tiny room somewhere – they've only just arrived). I was solemnly informed that both she and her daughter could consider it nothing but an honour to count me their acquaintance; learned they hadn't two roubles to rub together and had come to petition for something in some department; offered my services and my money; learned they'd gone to that dive under the misapprehension that they really did teach dancing there; offered, for my part, to assist with the young maiden's upbringing, with learning French and dancing. They were overjoyed, considered it an honour, and we're still on friendly terms now . . . Let's go if you like . . . Only not now.'

'Enough! Enough of your vile anecdotes, you depraved, lecherous man!'

'What a Schiller we have here – our very own Schiller! *Où va-t-elle la vertu se nicher?*[19] You know, I'm going to have to tell you more stories like this, just to hear you squeal. Such fun!'

'I'm sure. Don't you think I find myself ridiculous at this moment?' muttered Raskolnikov spitefully.

Svidrigailov roared with laughter. Eventually, he called Filipp, paid and began getting up.

'Drunk, that's what I am. Well, *assez causé!*[20] he said. 'What fun!'

'I'm sure – for you of all people,' shrieked Raskolnikov, also getting up. 'Who if not a clapped-out lecher like you would enjoy relating such adventures, while intending to do something equally monstrous – especially in circumstances like these and speaking to a man like me . . . ? Stirs the blood.'

'Well, if that's the case,' Svidrigailov replied, examining Raskolnikov with a certain astonishment, 'if that's the case, then you yourself are a cynic to reckon with. Your potential, at any rate, is immense. You may apprehend a great deal . . . and do a great deal, for that matter. Well, there we are. I'm truly sorry not to have had a longer chat with you, though you won't get away from me . . . Just wait a little . . .'

Svidrigailov left the tavern. Raskolnikov followed. Svidrigailov wasn't actually all that tipsy; it had gone to his head for no more than an instant, and the effects were fading by the minute. He was very worried about something, something terribly important, and he was frowning. The anticipation of something was clearly troubling and disturbing him. In the last few minutes his behaviour towards Raskolnikov had suddenly changed, and with every moment that passed he became ruder and more derisive. Raskolnikov noted all this and also became anxious. He'd begun to find Svidrigailov very suspicious and decided to follow him.

They stepped out onto the pavement.

'You to the right, me to the left, or vice versa, but in any case – *adieu, mon plaisir,*[21] till next we meet!'

And, turning right, he walked off towards Haymarket.

V

Raskolnikov followed him.

'Now what?' cried Svidrigailov, turning round. 'Didn't I say . . . ?'

'You won't shake me off now – that's what.'

'Wha-a-at?'

The two men stopped and for a minute or so each looked at the other, as if sizing him up.

'All these half-drunken stories of yours,' Raskolnikov snapped, 'leave me in no doubt *whatsoever* that not only have you not abandoned your disgraceful designs on my sister – you're more wrapped up in them than ever. I know that my sister received a letter this morning. All through our meeting you couldn't sit still ... Even if you have managed to unearth a wife along the way, it doesn't mean a thing. I should like to ascertain for myself ...'

Raskolnikov himself could scarcely have said what it was that he wanted now and what it was that he needed to ascertain.

'Well I never! And if I call the police?'

'Go on!'

Once again, they stood facing each other for a minute or so. Eventually a change came over Svidrigailov's face. Assured that Raskolnikov was not frightened by his threat, he suddenly assumed the most cheerful and friendly air.

'Aren't you a character? I deliberately avoided mentioning that business of yours, although, needless to say, I'm consumed with curiosity. A quite fantastical business. I was going to leave it for next time, but really – even a dead man would lose his composure talking to you ... Off we go then, but let me warn you: I'm only going home for a minute, to grab some money; then I'm locking up the apartment and taking a cab to the Islands for the whole evening. Do you still want to follow me?'

'Only as far as the apartment, and not to yours, but Sofya Semyonovna's, to apologize for missing the funeral.'

'As you like, but Sofya Semyonovna isn't in. She's taken all the children off to a certain lady, a distinguished old woman and an acquaintance of mine from times past, who runs a few orphanages[22] here and there. I charmed this lady by bringing her money for Katerina Ivanovna's three mites. Not only that, I donated further funds to her institutions. Lastly, I told her Sofya Semyonovna's story in every detail, concealing nothing. The effect was indescribable. That's why Sofya Semyonovna was asked to come immediately, today, directly to ——aya Hotel, where my lady is temporarily residing before returning to her dacha.'

'Never mind – I'll still call by.'

'As you wish, but count me out. Anyway, what's it to me? Ah, we're already home. I'm convinced you look at me so suspiciously because I was so very tactful and I still haven't troubled you with any questions ... Is that right? It struck you as rather extraordinary. I'm sure of it! Fancy being tactful after that!'

'And listening in at doors!'

'Ah, I see!' laughed Svidrigailov. 'Yes, it would have been rather surprising if, after everything, you'd let that pass without comment. Ha-ha! I do have some idea of the sort of pranks you got up to then . . . over there . . . and which you told Sofya Semyonovna about yourself. But still, what am I to make of it? Perhaps I'm hopelessly behind the times and no longer capable of understanding anything. Explain, my dear boy, for the love of God! Enlighten me about the latest principles.'

'You couldn't have heard a thing – these are all lies!'

'Oh, I don't mean that (although I did hear something). No, I mean the way you never stop sighing! As if you've got Schiller squirming about inside you. And then they tell us not to listen in at doors. In that case, go and tell the authorities that look, a peculiar thing's happened to me: something went a bit wrong with the theory. If you're convinced one mustn't listen in at doors, but it's all right to bash old hags with whatever comes to hand, whenever the mood takes you, then you'd better get yourself off to America[23] or somewhere! Run, run, young man! There might still be time. I'm being sincere. No money, is that it? I'll give you some for the journey.'

'That's the last thing on my mind,' interrupted Raskolnikov with disgust.

'I understand (still, you mustn't overexert yourself: no need to talk too much if you don't want to). I understand what kind of problems are in vogue now: moral problems, I suppose? Problems to do with being a citizen, a man? Forget about them. What good are they to you now? Heh-heh! Because you're still a citizen and a man?[24] But if that's the case, there was no need to poke your nose in. You should have stuck to what you know. So shoot yourself – or don't you want to?'

'You seem to be taunting me on purpose, to shake me off . . .'

'What a funny man you are. Well, here's our staircase already – make yourself at home! Here's Sofya Semyonovna's door, and look – no one in! Don't believe me? Ask the Kapernaumovs; she leaves them the key. And here's Madame de Kapernaumov herself. What? (She's a bit deaf.) She's gone out? Where? There, do you see now? She's not in and she might not be back until late evening. So let's go to mine. You wanted to go to my place, too, didn't you? Well, here we are. Madame Resslich's out. That woman's always got her hands full, but she's a good sort, I assure you . . . She could be of real use to you if only you were a little more sensible. So, see for yourself: I'm taking this five per cent bond from the bureau (look how many I've got!) – it's going straight to the money changer. See that? Right, enough time-wasting. I'm locking the writing desk, locking the apartment, and here we are on the stairs again. Why don't we hire a cab? I'm off to the Islands, after all. What do you say to a ride? Take this carriage right here and go to Yelagin, eh? You're refusing? All a bit too much for you? Come on, it's just a ride. Is that rain on its way? Never mind, we'll raise the hood . . .'

Svidrigailov was already seated in the carriage. Raskolnikov decided that, for the moment at least, his suspicions were unfounded. Without saying a word in reply, he turned and walked back in the direction of Haymarket. Had he looked back even once, he would have seen Svidrigailov, after travelling no more than a hundred yards, settle his fare and step back onto the pavement. But he no longer could: he'd already turned the corner. A wave of deep disgust had borne him away from Svidrigailov. 'To think that I could ever, even for one second, have expected something from this crude and evil man, from this lecherous scoundrel!' came his involuntary cry. In truth, Raskolnikov delivered his verdict all too hastily and lightly. There was something about Svidrigailov which, at the very least, gave him a certain originality, if not mystery. And as for the place of his sister in all this, Raskolnikov remained utterly convinced that Svidrigailov would not leave her in peace. But it was becoming far too painful to keep thinking about it all, to keep turning it over in his mind!

As was his habit, he, once left alone, fell deep in thought after about twenty paces. Stepping onto the bridge, he paused by the railings and began staring at the water. Standing right over him, meanwhile, was Avdotya Romanovna.

Their paths had crossed at the beginning of the bridge, but he'd walked straight past her without noticing. It was the first time Dunechka had seen him walking the streets in this state and she took a bad fright. She stopped, unsure whether to call out to him or not. Suddenly, she noticed Svidrigailov hurrying over from the general direction of Haymarket.

But there was something secretive and wary about his approach. He didn't step onto the bridge, but stayed off to one side on the pavement, making every effort not to be seen by Raskolnikov. He'd noticed

Dunya long before and began gesturing to her. She thought he was entreating her not to call out to her brother, but to leave him in peace and go over to him.

Dunya did just that. She slipped past her brother and came up to Svidrigailov.

'Quick, off we go,' Svidrigailov whispered to her. 'I don't want Rodion Romanych to know of our meeting. I should warn you: I've just been with him not far from here, in a tavern – he found me there himself and I had a job getting rid of him. Somehow he knows about my letter to you and suspects something. Surely it can't have been you who told him? And if not you, who?'

'All right, we've turned the corner,' Dunya interrupted, 'my brother won't see us now. I'll go no further with you. Tell me everything here. It can all be said outside.'

'Firstly, this certainly cannot be said outside. Secondly, you ought to hear what Sofya Semyonovna has to say as well. Thirdly, I have one or two papers to show you ... Oh yes, and last of all, if you don't agree to come up to mine, I'll refuse to say anything more and I'll walk away right now. What's more, please bear in mind that one particularly intriguing secret of your dear beloved brother lies entirely in my hands.'

Dunya hesitated and looked piercingly at Svidrigailov.

'Now what are you so afraid of?' he calmly remarked. 'This is the city not the countryside. And even in the country you did me more harm than I did you, while here ...'

'Has Sofya Semyonovna been warned?'

'No, I didn't say a word to her and I'm not even sure she's home now. Though I expect she is. She buried a close relation of hers today: hardly a day for paying social calls. I don't want to tell anyone about this for the time being and I even rather regret telling you. Here, the slightest indiscretion is equivalent to a tip-off. I live right here, in this building; we're approaching it now. Here's our caretaker; knows me very well; there, he's bowing to me. He sees I'm walking with a lady and, needless to say, he's taken note of your face – you'll be glad to know that if you're very scared and suspicious of me. Forgive me for speaking so crudely. I'm sub-renting a room. Sofya Semyonovna and I live wall to wall – she's sub-renting, too. The whole floor's rented out. So why are you so scared, like a child? Or am I really so terrifying?'

Svidrigailov's face twisted into a patronizing smile; but he was in no mood for smiling. His heart was thumping and his breath felt trapped in his chest. He was deliberately talking louder to hide his mounting agitation; but Dunya hadn't yet noticed this special excitement; she was far too annoyed by his remark about her being scared of him, like a child, and finding him so terrifying.

'Even though I know you to be a man . . . without honour, I'm not frightened of you in the least. You go first,' she said calmly enough, though her face was very pale. Svidrigailov paused outside Sonya's apartment.

'Let me check if she's home. She's not. Curses! But I know she may be back any moment. If she's gone out, then it's only to see a certain lady about her orphans. Their mother's died. I got involved in that, too, and made a few arrangements. If Sofya Semyonovna doesn't return in the next ten minutes, I'll send her over to you, today if you wish; and here's me. My two rooms. My landlady, Mrs Resslich, lives the other side of the door. Now take a look here, I'll show you my chief documents: the door you see here connects my bedroom with two completely empty rooms that are rented out. Here they are . . . You need to look at this a bit more attentively . . .'

Svidrigailov occupied two furnished and fairly spacious rooms. Dunechka looked around mistrustfully, but she didn't notice anything special about either the decor or the arrangement of the rooms, even though there were one or two things that might have been noticed, such as the fact that Svidrigailov's apartment somehow nestled between two almost uninhabited apartments. It was entered not directly from the corridor but through two of the landlady's rooms, both virtually empty. In his bedroom, Svidrigailov unlocked a door and showed Dunechka another almost empty apartment. Dunechka hesitated on the threshold, failing to understand why she was being asked to look, but Svidrigailov hurried to explain:

'Here, take a look over here, the second of the large rooms. Note the door: it's locked. Next to the door there's a chair, just one chair for both rooms. I brought it over from my rooms, so I could listen in comfort. On the other side of the door, right now, is Sofya Semyonovna's table. That's where she and Rodion Romanych sat and talked. And I was listening in, sitting right here on the chair, two evenings in a row, a couple of hours each time. I must have learned a thing or two, wouldn't you say?'

'You were listening in?'

'Yes, I was listening in. Now back to mine – there's nowhere to sit here.'

He led Avdotya Romanovna back into his first room, which he used as a drawing room, and offered her a chair. He himself sat down at the other end of the table some three or four paces away, but the same flame that had once given Dunechka such a fright must already have been flickering in his eyes. She shuddered and cast another mistrustful look around the room. She did so without meaning to – she evidently wished to keep her mistrust to herself. But the isolation of Svidrigailov's apartment eventually struck home. She felt like asking whether his landlady was in or not, but she didn't . . . out of pride. Besides, there was another, immeasurably greater source of pain in her heart than fear for herself. Her torment was too much to bear.

'Here's your letter,' she began, placing it on the table. 'Is what you write really possible? You hint at a crime supposedly committed by my brother. Your hints are all too obvious – and don't you dare deny it. You may as well know that I'd already heard about this idiotic tale and I don't believe a word of it. What a foul and ridiculous thing to suspect. I know the story, how and why it was invented. You haven't a shred of proof. It's impossible. You promised to prove it. Well? Speak! But know in advance that I don't believe you! I don't!'

Dunechka said this in a breathless hurry and for an instant the colour rushed to her face.

'If you didn't believe it, would you really ever risk coming here alone? Then why have you come? Out of mere curiosity?'

'Don't torment me – just speak!'

'You're gutsy, no doubt about that. Honest to God, I thought you'd ask Mr Razumikhin to accompany you here. But I couldn't see him anywhere near you. How brave! Means you wanted to spare Rodion Romanych. Although everything about you is divine . . . As for your brother, well, what can I say? You've just seen him yourself. How did he seem?'

'And is that all you have to go on?'

'No, I have his own words to go on. This is where he came two evenings in a row to see Sofya Semyonovna. I showed you where they sat. He confessed everything to her. He's a murderer. He murdered a civil servant's old widow, a moneylender he used to pawn things with. He killed her sister, too, a clothes-dealer, Lizaveta by name, who happened to walk in during her sister's murder. He murdered them both with an axe he brought with him. He murdered them in order to rob them, and rob them he did; he took the money and some items . . . He said this in so many words to Sofya Semyonovna, who alone knows the secret, though she had no part in the murder in word or deed – on the contrary, she was as appalled as you are now. Don't worry: she won't betray him.'

'It can't be true!' mumbled Dunechka through pale, numb lips; she was gasping. 'It can't. There's not the slightest reason, not the slightest cause . . . Lies! Lies!'

'Robbery – that's the whole reason. He took the money and the items. True, by his own account he made no use of the money or the things and buried them under a stone somewhere – they're still there now. But that's because he didn't dare to.'

'Is that likely? That he stole, robbed? That he could even have such an idea?' cried Dunya, leaping from her chair. 'You know him. You've seen him. How could he ever be a thief?'

She was almost imploring Svidrigailov; her fear was quite forgotten.

'The combinations and possibilities here are endless, Avdotya Romanovna. A thief goes thieving but knows in his own mind he's a scoundrel. I've even heard of one fine gentleman who robbed a mail coach.[25] Who knows? He probably thought it was a perfectly respectable thing to do! Needless to say, I wouldn't have believed it either, just like you, if I'd heard it at second hand. But I believed my own ears. He even gave all his reasons to Sofya Semyonovna. She wouldn't believe her own ears at first, but eventually she believed her own eyes. After all, he was telling her himself.'

'Reasons . . . ? What reasons?'

'It's a long story, Avdotya Romanovna. What we have here is – how can I put it? – a kind of theory, the kind of business where I might decide, for example, that a single wicked deed can be permitted if the overall aim is good. One evil deed for a hundred good ones! Not to mention, of course, that it's rather galling for a gifted young man with an exceptionally high opinion of himself to know that three thousand roubles or so would be enough to change the direction of his entire career, his entire future and purpose in life – only he hasn't got these three thousand roubles. Add to this the irritation caused by hunger, cramped lodgings, rags and tatters, a vivid awareness of his social status, in all its beauty, and that of his mother and sister. And above all, vanity, pride and vanity, although, who's to say there aren't some good traits mixed in as well . . . ? So please don't think I'm blaming him. It's none of my business anyway. There was also a theory at work – nothing special, as theories go – according to which people may be divided – don't you know? – into human material and those who are somehow exceptional; that's to say, people who, on account of their lofty status, are outside the law, and not only that, who them-selves write the law for the others – for the material, I mean . . . the rubbish. Nothing special, as mini-theories go; *une théorie comme une autre.*[26] Napoleon really turned his head; or rather, the fact that a great many men of genius have turned a blind eye to isolated acts of evil, stepping right over them without a second thought. He seems to have fancied that he, too, is a man of genius – or at least, he was sure of it for a time. He was greatly pained – and still is – by the thought that he may have managed to come up with a theory, but as for taking that step without a second thought – that was beyond him. So how can he be a man of genius? What could be more demeaning for a young man with a high opinion of himself, especially in our day and age . . . ?'

'And the voice of conscience? Are you denying him all moral sense? Is he really like that?'

'Ah, Avdotya Romanovna, nowadays all the waters are muddied; al-though, come to think of it, things were never terribly orderly. Russians are a broad people, Avdotya Romanovna, as broad as their land, and they have an exceptional propensity for the fantastical and the disor-derly; but breadth without genius is a recipe for disaster. Do you remem-ber how often the two of us talked like this, on this very subject, out on the terrace in the evenings, after dinner? In fact, it was precisely this breadth you reproached me with. Who knows, while we were talking he may have been lying on his bed here, thinking his thoughts. After all, Avdotya Romanovna, our educated society has no truly sacred tradi-tions to call its own: not unless someone cobbles something together from books . . . or digs something out of the Chronicles.[27] But that's just scholars, fools in their own way, and it's all rather embarrassing for a man of society. But anyway, you know my views. I've no intention of accusing anyone. I prefer to keep my hands clean. But we've discussed this more than once. I even had the good fortune of interesting you in my opinions . . . You're very pale, Avdotya Romanovna!'

'I know this theory of his. I read his article in the journal about people to whom all is permitted . . . Razumikhin brought it to me . . .'

'Mr Razumikhin? An article by your brother? In a journal? Such an article exists? I didn't know. Well, well, that must be interesting! But where are you off to, Avdotya Romanovna?'

'I want to see Sofya Semyonovna,' said Dunechka faintly. 'Which way to her room? She may be back already. I just have to see her now. Maybe she can . . .'

Avdotya Romanovna couldn't finish; she literally ran out of breath.

'Sofya Semyonovna won't be back before dark. That's my guess. She should have come by now, or else not until very late . . .'

'Ah, so you're a liar, a fibber! Damn you! You were lying all along! I don't believe you! I don't! I don't!' shouted Dunechka hysterically, losing all self-control.

She dropped almost unconscious into the chair hurriedly provided by Svidrigailov.

'Avdotya Romanovna, whatever's the matter? Wake up! Here's some water. Take a sip at least . . .'

He splashed her with water. Dunechka started and came round.

'Well that shook her up!' Svidrigailov muttered to himself with a frown. 'Avdotya Romanovna, you mustn't worry! He has friends, you know. We'll save him. We'll rescue him. Shall I take him abroad? I have money and I can get a passport certificate within three days. And as for his murder, well, there's plenty of time for him to make amends and smooth everything over. You mustn't worry. He may still turn out a great man. But what's the matter? How are you feeling now?'

'You wicked man! And you even have the nerve to laugh at me. Let me go . . .'

'But where are you off to?'

'To see him. Where is he? Do you know? Why's this door locked? We came in by this door and now it's locked. When did you manage to lock it?'

'I couldn't let the entire floor hear what we were saying. I'm not laughing at you in the slightest. I'm just sick of talking like this. Where will you go in such a state? Or do you want to give him up? You'll work him up into a rage, then he'll do it himself. He's being followed, you know; they're already onto him. You'll merely end up betraying him. Just have patience. I saw him and spoke to him only moments ago. He can still be saved. Have a seat and we'll think it through. That's why I brought you here – to talk this over in private and think it through. Just sit down, I say!'

'How on earth can you save him? How can he be saved?'

Dunya sat down. Svidrigailov sat next to her.

'That all depends on you, on you alone,' he began, eyes flashing, almost in a whisper, stuttering and even swallowing some of his words in his emotion.

Dunya shrank back in alarm. He, too, was shaking all over.

'You . . . One word from you and he is saved! I . . . I will save him. I have money and friends. I'll pack him off right away and I myself will get a passport, two passports. One for him, one for me. I have friends, people who can get things done . . . Well? I'll get you a passport, too . . . and one for your mother . . . What do you need Razumikhin for? I love you just as much . . . I love you boundlessly. Let me kiss the hem of your dress! Please! Please! I can't bear to hear it rustle. Say "Do that" and I'll do it! I'll do everything. I'll do what can't be done. Whatever you believe in, I'll believe in. I'll do everything, everything! Just don't look at me like that, don't! You're killing me, do you know that . . . ?'

He'd even started raving. Something had suddenly come over him, like a rush to the head. Dunya leapt to her feet and ran to the door.

'Open up! Open up!' she shouted through the door, calling out to anyone who would hear and shaking the door. 'Open up! There must be someone!'

Svidrigailov got to his feet and pulled himself together. His still-quivering lips slowly forced out a malicious, mocking smile.

'There's no one at home,' he said softly and slowly. 'The landlady's gone out and you're wasting your breath, getting worked up for no reason.'

'Where's the key? Open the door. Open it now, you vile man.'

'I've lost it and can't find it anywhere.'

'Ha! So this is assault!' cried Dunya, turning pale as death and running over to a corner, where she shielded herself with a little table lying close by. She didn't shout, but she fastened her eyes on her tormentor and followed his every move. Svidrigailov also stood motionless, facing her from the other end of the room. He'd even managed to regain his self-control, or so at least it seemed. But his face was as pale as before. The mocking smile had not left it.

'You said "assault" just now, Avdotya Romanovna. If it's assault, then you can see for yourself that I've taken precautions. Sofya Semyonovna's out; the Kapernaumovs are far away – five locked rooms between us. Lastly, I'm at least twice as strong as you, and besides, I've nothing to fear, because you can hardly go and complain about it later. You wouldn't really want to betray your brother, would you? No one would believe you anyway: what was she doing visiting a man who lives on his own? So even if you do sacrifice your brother you won't prove a thing: assault is very hard to prove, Avdotya Romanovna.'

'Scoundrel!' whispered Dunya indignantly.

'As you please, but note that everything I've said was purely hypothetical. My personal conviction is that you are absolutely right: assault is a loathsome thing. All I was trying to say was that you would have nothing at all on your conscience, even if . . . even if you felt like saving your brother of your own free will, in the way I'm suggesting. It would simply mean that you had yielded to circumstance, or, I suppose, to force, if we really have to use such words. Think about it: the fate of your brother and mother is in your hands. I'll be your slave . . . my whole life long . . . I'll be waiting right here . . .'

Svidrigailov sat down on the couch, about eight paces away. Dunya no longer had the slightest doubt: he was utterly determined. Besides, she knew him . . .

Suddenly, she took a revolver from her pocket, cocked it and rested her hand with the revolver on the little table. Svidrigailov leapt to his feet.

'Aha! I see!' he cried in astonishment, but grinning with malice. 'Well, that changes everything! You're making this a great deal easier for me, Avdotya Romanovna! And where did you find the revolver? Don't tell me it's from Mr Razumikhin? Ha! That revolver's mine! An old friend! I was looking high and low for it! Our shooting lessons in the country, which I was so honoured to give you, weren't wasted after all.'

'The revolver doesn't belong to you – it belonged to Marfa Petrovna, the woman you murdered, you wicked man! There was nothing you could call your own in her house. I took it when I began to suspect what you're capable of. Take one step towards me and I'll kill you, I swear!'

Dunya was in a frenzy. She held the revolver at the ready.

'And your brother? I'm just curious,' asked Svidrigailov, still motionless.

'Report him if you want! Stay right there! Don't move! I'll shoot! You poisoned your wife, I know you did. You're a murderer yourself!'

'Are you quite sure I poisoned Marfa Petrovna?'

'It was you! You hinted as much yourself. You told me about the poison . . . I know you made a trip to get it . . . You had it ready . . . It must have been you . . . you wretch!'

'Even if this were true, then only because of you . . . You would have been the cause in any case.'

'Liar! I've always hated you, always . . .'

'Now now, Avdotya Romanovna! You must have forgotten how, in the midst of all your lecturing, you were already bending and softening . . . I could tell by your eyes. Don't you remember, that evening, that moon, the piping of the nightingale?'

'Liar!' (Fury flashed in Dunya's eyes.) 'Liar, slanderer!'

'I'm lying? Well, perhaps I am. Or I did. Women aren't to be reminded of this sort of thing.' (He grinned.) 'You'll shoot, I know it, my pretty little beast! So shoot!'

Dunya raised the revolver and stared at him, deathly pale, her lower lip white and trembling, her big black eyes flashing like fire, her mind made up; taking aim, she waited for his first move. Never had he seen her so beautiful. The fire that blazed from her eyes as she raised the revolver seemed to scorch him, and his heart clenched with pain. He took one step. A shot rang out. The bullet grazed his hair and struck the wall behind him. He stopped and gave a quiet laugh:

'Stung by a wasp! Went straight for the head . . . What's this? Blood!' He took out a handkerchief to wipe away the blood trickling down his right temple; the bullet must have brushed against the skin of his skull. Dunya lowered the revolver and looked at Svidrigailov less in fear than in crazed bewilderment. She herself no longer seemed to understand what on earth she'd done or what on earth was happening!

'Oh well, you missed! Have another go, I'm waiting,' said Svidrigailov softly, still grinning, though in a dismal sort of way. 'Carry on like this and I'll grab you before you cock the gun!'

Dunechka shuddered and hurriedly cocked and lifted the revolver.

'Keep away from me!' she said in despair. 'I'll shoot again, I swear . . . I'll . . . kill you!'

'Oh well . . . hard not to kill at three paces. And if you don't kill me . . . then . . .' His eyes flashed, and he took another two steps.

Dunecka shot – a misfire!

'You didn't load it properly. Never mind! You've got another percussion cap there. Load it – I can wait.'

He was standing two paces away, waiting and looking at her with wild determination, with inflamed, passionate, heavy eyes. Dunya realized that he would sooner die than let her go. And . . . and, of course, she couldn't fail to kill him, not now, not at two paces!

Suddenly, she threw the revolver aside.

'She's thrown it down!' said Svidrigailov in astonishment, drawing a deep breath. He seemed to feel a weight instantly lift from his heart, and not merely, perhaps, the burden of mortal fear – if he could sense any such thing at that moment. It was a release from some other, more sorrowful and dismal feeling, which he himself could not have named.

He came up to Dunya and gently wrapped his arm around her waist. She didn't resist but, trembling from top to toe, looked at him with imploring eyes. He was about to say something, but succeeded only in twisting his lips.

'Let me go!' Dunya implored.

Svidrigailov shuddered: something in her tone had suddenly changed.

'So you don't love me?' he asked quietly.

Dunya shook her head.

'And . . . you can't? Ever?' he whispered despairingly.

'Never!' whispered Dunya.

There followed a moment of dreadful, dumb struggle in Svidrigailov's soul. The look he gave her was indescribable. Suddenly, he withdrew his hand, turned aside, quickly walked away to the window and stood before it.

Another moment passed.

'Here's the key!' (He took it from the left pocket of his coat and placed it on the table behind him, without looking at Dunya or turning towards her.) 'Take it and go, now!'

He stared stubbornly out of the window.

Dunya walked up to the table to take the key.

'Now! Now!' repeated Svidrigailov, still not moving or turning round. But there must have been something dreadful in the way he said it.

Dunya heard it, grabbed the key, rushed to the door, quickly unlocked it and fled from the room. A minute later, half-crazed, beside herself, she was running along the Ditch in the direction of ——y Bridge.

Svidrigailov stood by the window for another three minutes or so; eventually, he turned round slowly, looked about him and passed his palm gently across his forehead. A strange smile twisted his face, a pitiful, sad, feeble smile, a smile of despair. The blood, already dry, stained his palm. He looked at it angrily. Then he wetted a towel and cleaned his temple. The gun, which Dunya had thrown aside and which had ended up by the door, suddenly entered his field of vision. He picked it up and examined it. It was a small, old-fashioned three-shot revolver. There were two charges left in it and one cap. Fine for one more shot. He thought for a moment, thrust the revolver into his pocket, took his hat and went out.

VI

He spent that entire evening until ten o'clock going from one tavern, one den, to another. Katya turned up again, too, singing another maudlin song about how some man, 'a wretch and a bully',

> Started kissing Katya.

Svidrigailov saw to it that Katya and the organ-grinder and the chorus singers and the waiters, as well as a pair of clerks, all had plenty to drink. He'd got mixed up with the clerks for no better reason than their crooked noses: one man's curved to the right, the other's to the left. This made a great impression on Svidrigailov. Eventually, they dragged him off to a pleasure garden, where he paid for their admission and drinks. The garden contained a slender, three-year-old fir tree and three little bushes. In addition a 'Vauxhall'[28] had been set up – essentially a drinking den, though it served tea as well, and there were also several green tables and chairs. A chorus of atrocious singers and a German drunk from Munich – a kind of clown, with a red nose, though for some reason utterly miserable – were entertaining the public. The clerks got into an argument with some other clerks and were about to start a fight. They'd chosen Svidrigailov to arbitrate. He'd been doing so for about a quarter of an hour already, but there was so much shouting that it was impossible to make head or tail of it all. The likeliest thing was that one of them had stolen something and had even managed to palm it off on one of the Jews knocking around; but, having sold it, was in no hurry to share the spoils with his friend. The stolen object, it transpired, was a teaspoon belonging to the Vauxhall. Its absence was noticed and the whole business was rapidly getting out of hand. Svidrigailov paid for the spoon, got up and left the garden. It was around ten. He hadn't touched a drop all this time and had only ordered tea, for the sake of form more than anything. It was a stifling, gloomy evening. By ten o'clock terrible storm clouds had gathered from all sides; there was a clap of thunder and the rain gushed forth like a waterfall. It fell not in drops but in jets, lashing the ground. One flash of lightning followed another and you could count to five before the afterglows faded. Soaked to the skin, he arrived home, locked the door, opened his bureau, took out all his money and ripped up two or three sheets of paper. Then, having pocketed the money, he was on the point of changing his clothes, but, after looking out of the window and bending an ear to the thunder and rain, he dismissed the idea, took his hat and walked out, leaving the apartment unlocked. He went straight over to Sonya's. She was at home.

Sonya wasn't alone; all around her were Kapernaumov's four little children. She'd made them tea. She welcomed Svidrigailov in respectful silence, looking in astonishment at his dripping clothes, but not saying a word. The children fled the room in complete horror.

Svidrigailov sat down at the table and asked Sonya to sit next to him. Timidly, she prepared to listen.

'You know, Sofya Semyonovna, I may be leaving for America,' said Svidrigailov, 'and as this is probably the last time we'll see each other I've come to make one or two arrangements. You saw that lady today, didn't you? I know what she said to you. No need to repeat it.' (Sonya almost reacted, then blushed.) 'There's more to people like that than meets the eye. As far as your little sisters and brother are concerned, their future really is settled and I've given the money due to each of them to the appropriate person for safe keeping. But I'll give you the receipts in any case. There you go! Well, that's that dealt with. Here are three five per cent bonds, worth three thousand all told. They're for you, for you and no one else, and do let's keep it between ourselves, whatever anyone else may say to you. You'll need them, Sofya Semyonovna. You can't carry on with that sordid life, and anyway, you no longer have to.'

'You're my benefactor, sir, and I'm so very indebted to you, as are the orphans, and the deceased,' Sonya hastily put in, 'and if I have not yet thanked you enough, then . . . don't think me . . .'

'That'll do, that'll do.'

'And as for this money, Arkady Ivanovich, I'm very grateful to you, but really, I've no need of it now. Don't think me ungrateful, but I will always be able to support myself. If you are so very kind, sir, this money . . .'

'It's for you, for you, Sofya Semyonovna, and please, the less said the better – I've no time. You'll need it. There are two paths open to Rodion Romanovich: a bullet to the head or the Vladimirka²⁹ to Siberia.' (Sonya gave him a wild look and started shaking.) 'Don't worry, I know everything – I heard it all from him – and I'm the soul of discretion. I won't tell anyone. That was good advice you gave him to go and give himself up. He'll be much better off that way. And if it's the Vladimirka – you'll follow him, I suppose? Won't you? Won't you? Well in that case you'll be needing this money. You'll need it for him, understand? Giving it to you is the same as giving it to him. Besides, haven't you just promised Amalia Ivanovna to pay off the debt? I heard you. What on earth are you doing, Sofya Semyonovna, taking on all these contracts and obligations without a moment's thought? After all, it was Katerina Ivanovna who owed that German, not you, so why should you care? You won't last long if you carry on like that. Well, miss, if anyone asks you – tomorrow, say, or the day after – anything at all about me (and I'm sure they will), don't mention this visit of mine and, whatever you do, don't show the money to anyone or say I gave it to you. Well, goodbye.' (He got up from his chair.) 'My compliments to Rodion Romanych. By the way, why not give that money to Mr Razumikhin for the time being? Do you know Mr Razumikhin? Of course you do. He's all right, that boy. Take it over to him tomorrow or . . . whenever the time comes. Until then, keep it well out of sight.'

Sonya also jumped up from her chair and looked at him in alarm. She was desperate to say something, to ask something, but for the first few minutes she didn't dare, and anyway, she didn't know how to begin.

'But sir . . . it's pouring. How can you go anywhere now, sir?'

'Well that would be a fine thing: leaving for America and being scared of the rain! Heh-heh! Goodbye, Sofya Semyonovna, dear girl!

Live and live long. There'll be others who need you. By the way . . .
tell Mr Razumikhin I bow to him. Use those exact words: "Arkady
Ivanovich Svidrigailov bows to you." Just so.'

He went out, leaving Sonya astonished, alarmed and filled with
obscure, oppressive misgivings.

It later transpired that on that same evening, not long before midnight, he paid one more highly eccentric and unexpected visit. It was
still pouring. At twenty past eleven, drenched to the skin, he entered
the cramped apartment of his fiancée's parents, on Maly Prospect,
Third Line, Vasilyevsky Island. He had to knock a long time before
they opened and at first his appearance caused considerable embarrassment; but Arkady Ivanovich could be very charming when the
mood took him, so the initial (and extremely perspicacious) conclusion drawn by his fiancée's prudent parents, that Arkady Ivanovich
must have got so drunk somewhere that he could no longer think
straight, was instantly dismissed. The invalid father was wheeled out
in a chair by the tender-hearted and prudent mother, who began, in
her usual fashion, with some very far-fetched questions. (This woman
never asked anything directly, preferring to limber up with smiles and
much rubbing of hands, after which, if concrete information was ur-
gently required, such as "When would Arkady Ivanovich care to hold
the wedding?", she would begin by asking, with the keenest curiosity,
about Paris and life at the Parisian court, and only then, if at all, turn
to life on the Third Line of Vasilyevsky Island.) On another day, all
this would no doubt have inspired the greatest respect, but on this
particular occasion Arkady Ivanovich was unusually impatient and
adamant that he wanted to see his fiancée at all costs, despite having
been informed right away that she was already in bed. Needless to
say, the fiancée appeared. Arkady Ivanovich told her straight out that
he had to leave Petersburg for a while on a matter of the gravest importance, which was why he'd brought her fifteen thousand roubles in
silver, in various denominations, asking her to accept these notes as a
gift, seeing as it had long been his intention to give her this trifle before their wedding. A logical connection between the gift, his imminent departure and his urgent need to come visiting in the rain, at
midnight, did not thereby emerge, but nonetheless it all went off without a hitch. Even the inevitable oohs and aahs, interrogations and in-
terjections suddenly became unusually moderate and restrained; instead,

there followed expressions of the most ardent gratitude, reinforced by the tears of a prudent mother. Arkady Ivanovich got up, laughed, kissed his fiancée, patted her cheek, confirmed he would soon be back and, glimpsing in her eyes a mute, serious question that exceeded purely childish curiosity, thought for a moment, kissed her again and inwardly cursed the fact that his gift would immediately be stowed away under lock and key by this most prudent of mothers. He departed, leaving everyone in a state of extraordinary excitement. But tender-hearted mama, pattering away in a whisper, immediately resolved some of the most pressing uncertainties: 'Arkady Ivanovich, you see, is an important man, much in demand and well connected, a man of means – who's to say what goes through his mind or why he should suddenly up and leave and part with his money? So there's really no cause for wonder. It is rather odd to see him soaking wet, but the English, for example, are even more eccentric, and actually all these sophisticated types are quite indifferent to other people's opinions and they never stand on ceremony. Perhaps he goes about like that on purpose, to show that no one can scare him. But the main thing is, don't breathe a word about this to anyone, because God knows where it'll all end, and do let's put that money away, and thank goodness Feodosya was in the kitchen – isn't that a relief? – and the main thing is, not a word about this, any of it, to that scheming Resslich woman,' and so on and so forth. They sat up whispering until two o'clock. The fiancée, though, went to sleep much earlier, surprised and a little saddened.

Meanwhile, on the dot of midnight, Svidrigailov was crossing —— kov Bridge[30] onto Petersburg Side. The rain had stopped, but the wind was gusting. He started to shiver, and for a minute or so he looked with particular curiosity – almost questioningly – at the black water of the Lesser Neva. But he quickly began to feel very cold standing there above the water; he turned and set off down ——oy Prospect.[31] He'd been walking along that dark, endless street for ages, almost half an hour, and had lost his footing more than once on the wooden pavement, but he still carried on looking for something on the right side of street. It was somewhere here, near the end of the street, that he'd recently noticed, while travelling past one day, a wooden, yet very sizeable hotel, and its name, as far as he could remember, was Adrianopolis[32] or something of the kind. He wasn't mistaken: in this

back of beyond the hotel stood out so prominently that it couldn't be
missed, even in the dark. It was a long, blackened building in which,
despite the late hour, windows were still lit and there were still signs
of life. He went in and asked a ragamuffin he met in the corridor for a
room. After a quick glance at Svidrigailov, the ragamuffin perked up
and immediately showed him to a distant room, stuffy and cramped,
right at the very end of the corridor, in a corner, beneath the stairs. It
was the only one still going. The ragamuffin looked at him inquiringly.

'Any tea?' asked Svidrigailov.

'That there is, sir.'

'What else?'

'Veal, sir. Vodka, sir. Snacks.'

'Bring me some veal and tea.'

'Sir won't be wanting anything else, then?' the ragamuffin asked
with a kind of bewilderment.

'No, nothing!'

The ragamuffin went off, deeply disappointed.

'A fine place this must be,' thought Svidrigailov. 'Amazed I never
knew about it before. I suppose I must also look like a man who's just
back from some *café-chantant* or other,[33] having had an adventure
along the way. Wonder what kind of person spends the night here?'

He lit a candle and inspected the room more closely. It was a cell so
small that Svidrigailov almost had to bow his head, with just one window; a filthy bed, a simple painted table and a chair took up nearly all
the space. The walls looked as if they had been knocked together from
planks, and the wallpaper was so dusty and frayed that only its colour
(yellow) could still be discerned: the pattern was utterly obscured. One
part of the wall and ceiling were cut at a slant, as in a loft, to make
room for the staircase. Svidrigailov put down the candle, sat on the bed
and sank into thought. But the strange, continuous whispers from the
adjoining cell – at times, they were more like shouts – eventually captured his attention. The whispering hadn't ceased from the moment he
entered. He listened in closely: a man, almost in tears, was cursing and
reproaching another, but only one voice could be heard. Svidrigailov
got up, shielded the candle with his hand, and immediately saw a glint
in the wall; he went over and began looking through the gap. In a room
slightly larger than his own were two guests. One, with unusually curly

hair and a red, swollen face, had struck a declamatory pose, his frock coat off and his feet wide apart so as to keep his balance. Beating his chest, he was reproaching the other in histrionic fashion for being a beggar with no rank at all; having plucked him from the gutter, he could throw him out at a moment's notice, and the only witness to it all would be the finger of the Almighty. His friend sat in a chair, with the look of a man who desperately wanted to sneeze but couldn't. Every now and then he turned his dull, sheep-like gaze on the orator, but it was clear that he hadn't the faintest idea what he was talking about and probably wasn't even listening. A candle was guttering out on the table, where there was a flask of vodka, now almost empty, shot glasses, bread, tumblers, slices of pickled cucumber, and glasses from which the tea had long been drunk. After giving this scene his careful attention, Svidrigailov stepped back, unmoved, and sat back down on the bed.

The ragamuffin, returning with the tea and the veal, could not refrain from asking once more, 'You won't be needing anything else?' and, receiving another negative reply, retired for good. Svidrigailov had a glassful of tea straight away, to warm himself up, but couldn't eat a thing, having lost all appetite. He clearly had a fever coming on. He took off his coat and jacket, wrapped himself in a blanket and lay down on the bed. He was annoyed. 'Now of all times I'd have preferred to be well,' he thought with a grin. The room was stuffy, the candle gave a dim light, the wind was gusting outside and somewhere in the corner a mouse was scratching away; in fact, the whole room smelled of mice and something leathery. He lay there in a kind of daydream: one thought gave way to another. If only, it seemed, he could hold on to a mental picture of something, anything. 'That must be a garden down there, beneath the window,' he thought. 'I can hear the trees in the wind. How I hate the sound trees make at night when it's stormy and dark – such a disgusting feeling!' And he remembered how, walking past Petrovsky Park earlier, he'd been overcome by revulsion just thinking about it. He also remembered ——kov Bridge and the Lesser Neva, and once again he felt almost cold, just like before, as he stood over the water. 'I've never liked water, not even in paintings,' he reflected, before a strange thought suddenly brought another grin to his lips: 'You might have thought I wouldn't care less about aesthetics or comfort now, but just look how fastidious I've suddenly become, like an animal bent on choosing a nice spot for itself . . . on just such an occasion. I should have gone back to the park! It must have seemed

too dark in there, too cold – heh-heh! As if pleasant sensations were
what I needed! . . . And why haven't I snuffed out the candle?' (He
blew it out.) 'The neighbours have turned in,' he thought, seeing no
light through the gap. 'Just the time, Marfa Petrovna, just the time for
you to pay me a visit: dark, the right kind of setting, a moment like no
other. But now, of all times, you won't come . . .'

For some reason he suddenly remembered how, earlier on, an hour
before carrying out his designs on Dunechka, he'd advised Raskolnikov to entrust her to Razumikhin's care. 'I suppose I really did say
that to taunt myself, as Raskolnikov guessed. What a little rascal he
is, that Raskolnikov! What a weight he's carried. He could be a proper
rascal with time, once all this silliness is knocked out of him, but for
now he still wants to live a bit *too much*! They're all like that, these
scoundrels. But to hell with him – he can do what he likes.'

He couldn't sleep. Bit by bit the image of Dunechka, from earlier on,
started appearing before him and a shiver suddenly ran down his body.
'No, this has to stop,' he thought, coming to his senses. 'I have to find
something else to think about. How strange, and ridiculous: I've never
felt any great hatred towards anyone, never even had any particular
desire for revenge, and that's a bad sign, a bad sign! And I've never
liked arguing, never got worked up – another bad sign! But to think of
all the things I was promising her just now – good God! Chances are
she'd have ground me to dust . . .' He fell silent again and clenched his
teeth: once again the image of Dunechka came before him exactly as
she was after firing her first shot, when she'd taken a dreadful fright,
lowered the revolver and looked at him numbly: he could have grabbed
her twice over and she wouldn't have lifted an arm to defend herself,
unless he'd told her to. He recalled feeling at that instant a kind of pity
for her, as if his heart were being squeezed . . . 'Damn it! Those thoughts
again . . . This has to stop, it really does!'

He was dozing off; the feverish shiver was subsiding. Suddenly, under the blanket, something seemed to run down his arm and his leg.
He shuddered: 'Ugh, damn it! Must be a mouse!' he thought. 'Shouldn't
have left the veal on the table . . .' The last thing he felt like doing was
to uncover himself, get up and freeze, but suddenly something scuttled
unpleasantly along his leg again; he threw off the blanket and lit the
candle. Shivering with feverish cold, he bent down to inspect the bed –
nothing; he gave the blanket a shake and a mouse suddenly fell out
onto the sheet. He lunged towards it, but the mouse, instead of

running off the bed, darted around from side to side, slipped out from under his fingers, ran up and down his arm and suddenly dived under the pillow; he threw the pillow to the floor, but in the space of an instant felt something jump onto his chest and scuttle round his body, under his shirt. He shuddered and woke. It was dark and he was lying in the bed as before, wrapped in a blanket, the wind howling beneath the window. 'How disgusting!' he thought in annoyance.

He got up and sat on the edge of the bed, his back to the window. 'Better not to sleep at all,' he decided. But there was a cold, damp draught from the window. Without getting up, he pulled the blanket and wrapped it round him. He didn't light the candle. He wasn't thinking about anything, nor did he want to think; but one dream-vision followed another, and scraps of thought came and went, without beginning or end, without any connection. As if he were falling into a slumber. Whether it was the cold, the gloom, the damp or the wind howling beneath the window and shaking the trees that aroused in him some sort of stubbornly fantastical mood and desire – but all he could think of was flowers. A charming scene came to him; a bright, warm, almost hot day, a holiday, Trinity Day.[34] A splendid, sumptuous country cottage in the English style, overgrown with fragrant flowers planted in rows on all sides; a porch wreathed with creepers and crammed with roses; a bright, cool, sumptuously carpeted staircase, decorated with rare flowers in Chinese pots. In particular he noticed, in water-filled pots on the windowsills, bouquets of white and tender narcissus bending on their stout, tall, bright-green stems and exuding a powerful scent. Dragging himself away from them with the greatest reluctance, he went up the stairs and entered a large, high-ceilinged drawing room, and here too – by the windows, near the doors that opened onto the terrace, on the terrace itself – there were flowers everywhere. The floors were strewn with freshly mown, fragrant grass, the windows were open, a fresh, light, cool breeze entered the room, birds chirruped beneath the windows, and in the centre, on tables covered with white satin cloths, was a coffin. The coffin was lined with white *gros de Naples* and trimmed with thick, white ruche. Garlands of flowers wound around it on all sides. Submerged in flowers, a young girl lay inside, wearing a white tulle dress, her arms folded tight against her chest, as if they were chiselled from marble. But her flowing, light-blond hair was wet, and her head was wreathed in roses. The severe and already rigid profile of her face also seemed cut from marble, but the smile on her pale lips expressed unchildlike, boundless sorrow, a great, great grievance. Svidrigailov knew this girl. There was neither an icon nor a single lighted candle by her coffin, and no prayers could be heard. The girl was a suicide – she'd drowned.[35] She was only four-teen, but her heart had already been broken and it destroyed itself, outraged by an insult that appalled and astonished this young child's mind, that flooded her angelically pure soul with unmerited shame and wrung from her one last cry of despair, unheard and even mocked in the dark of the night, in the gloom and the cold, the damp and the thaw, to the howling of the wind . . .

Svidrigailov snapped awake, rose from the bed and went over to the window. He felt for the catch and opened it. The wind burst vio-lently into his cramped cell and something like rime soon formed on his face and chest, covered only by a shirt. There really did seem to be some kind of garden beneath the window, another pleasure garden by the look of it; during the day there were probably choruses singing there, too, with tea brought out to the tables. But now drops of water sprayed in through the window from the trees and the bushes and it was as dark as a cellar; the most that could be made out was an occa-sional dark smudge representing one object or another. Svidrigailov, leaning out and resting his elbows on the windowsill, had been star-ing fixedly into this murk for five minutes or more. Suddenly, from the gloom and the night, a cannon fired once, then twice.

'Ah, a warning! The water's rising,'[36] he thought. 'By morning it'll have surged onto the streets down there, on lower ground, and flooded the basements and cellars; the cellar rats will swim up, and in the wind and the rain, dripping and cursing, people will start lugging their worthless stuff up the stairs . . . But what time is it now?' No sooner had he thought this than, somewhere close by, ticking away in a kind of frantic hurry, a clock struck three. 'Ha, it'll be light in an hour! What am I waiting for? I'll leave right now and walk straight over to Petrovsky Park. I'll choose some big bush or other, all drenched in rain – one brush of my shoulder and a million drops will spray my head . . .' He moved away from the window, closed it, lit a candle, put on his waistcoat, coat and hat, and went out into the corridor with the candle, hoping to find the ragamuffin asleep in some box room filled with junk and candle stubs, pay him for the room and leave. 'The best moment for it – couldn't have chosen a better one!'

He walked up and down the endless, narrow corridor for a long

time without finding anyone, and he was about to call out when suddenly, in a dark corner between an old cupboard and a door, he spotted a strange object, seemingly alive. He bent over with the candle
and saw a child – a girl of about five, at most, wearing a little dress as
wet as a floor mop, shivering and crying. Svidrigailov didn't even
seem to frighten her. She looked at him in dull astonishment with her
big black eyes and let out an occasional sob, like children who, after a
good long cry, are finally beginning to cheer up, but could easily start
sobbing again at a moment's notice. The girl's little face was pale and
exhausted; she was rigid with cold. 'But how did she get here? She
must have been hiding here. Can't have slept a wink.' He started interrogating her. The girl suddenly came alive and began babbling something in her childish tongue. Something about 'Mumsie' and 'Mumsie
thmacking me', about some cup she'd 'breaked'. The girl barely paused
for breath, and it wasn't too hard to work out from all her stories that
here was an unloved child who'd been thrashed and terrorized by her
mother, some cook never seen sober, probably from this same hotel;
that the girl had broken Mummy's cup and taken such a fright she'd
run away earlier that evening; that she'd probably been keeping out of
sight somewhere outside, in the rain, before eventually making her
way here, hiding behind the cupboard and spending the whole night
in the corner, crying, shivering from the damp and the dark and the
fear that she was due another painful beating. He picked her up, took
her to his room, sat her on the bed and began undressing her. Her
little shoes, full of holes and worn on bare feet, were so wet they
might have been lying all night in a puddle. After undressing her, he
laid her on the bed and covered her, wrapping her up from head to toe
in the blanket. She fell asleep at once. Having done all this, he sank
once more into sullen thought.

'There was no need to get involved!' he suddenly decided with an
oppressive, spiteful feeling. 'How stupid!' Annoyed, he took the candle, so as to find the ragamuffin come what may and get out of there
as soon as possible. 'Ah, silly girl!' he thought with a silent curse, his
hand already on the doorknob, but he went back to take one more
look at her: was she sleeping, and was she sleeping well? He carefully
lifted the blanket. She was fast asleep, blissfully so. She'd warmed up
beneath the blanket and the colour was already returning to her pale
cheeks. But how strange: this colour now seemed somehow brighter

and deeper than one would expect of a child. 'Feverish,' thought Svidrigailov. 'It's the kind of flush you get from drinking, as if someone had given her a whole glass of wine.' Her scarlet lips seemed to be burning, blazing. But what was this? He had the sudden impression that her long black eyelashes were quivering and blinking, even lifting, and from beneath there peeked a sly, sharp, winking and unchildlike eye, as if she were only pretending to sleep. Yes, that was it: her lips were parting in a smile, the edges quivering, as if still holding back. But now she wasn't even trying to restrain herself; this was laughter, unconcealed laughter; something brazen, provocative shone in this thoroughly unchildlike face; here was depravity, the face of a 'camellia',[37] the brazen face of one of those French ladies of the night. And now, both eyes were opening: they were appraising him with a fiery and shameless gaze, they were calling to him, laughing . . . There was something infinitely hideous and offensive about this laughter, about these eyes, about this vileness in the face of a child. 'What? A five-year-old?' whispered Svidrigailov in genuine horror. 'What . . . ? What on earth?' But now she was turning right round to face him, her little cheeks ablaze, her arms stretched out . . . 'Damn you!' cried Svidrigailov in horror, raising his arm over her . . . But at that very moment he woke.

He was in the same bed, still wrapped up in the blanket, the candle unlit, white daylight already pouring through the windows.

'One nightmare after another, all night long!' He lifted himself up, angry, broken; his bones were aching. Outside in the thick fog nothing was visible. Nearly five already. He'd overslept! He got up and put on his jacket and coat, both still damp. Feeling in his pocket for the revolver, he took it out and adjusted the cap. Then he sat down, took a notebook from his pocket and wrote several lines in a large hand on the first, most conspicuous page. He reread them and sank into thought, resting his elbows on the table. The revolver and notebook lay right there, at his elbow. Waking up, flies attached themselves to the untouched portion of veal on the table next to him. He looked at them for a long time and eventually began trying to catch one with his free right hand. He tried and tried, but with no success. Finally, catching himself at this peculiar task, he came to his senses, shuddered, got up and walked straight out of the room. A minute later he was already outside.

A milky thick fog covered the city. Svidrigailov set off along the slippery, dirty wooden pavement in the direction of the Lesser Neva. He had visions of the now swollen waters of the Lesser Neva, of Petrovsky Island, of wet paths, wet grass, wet trees and bushes and, finally, that very bush . . . Annoyed, he began studying the buildings, just to distract himself. He met not a single pedestrian or cab along the avenue. There was something dismal and dirty about the bright-yellow wooden houses with their closed shutters. The cold and the damp got into his bones and he started to shiver. Occasionally, he passed a shop sign and diligently read each one. But the wooden pavement was already coming to an end. He was drawing level with a large stone house. A dirty dog, shivering to the bone, its tail between its legs, crossed the road in front of him. A man, dead drunk, lay face down in his greatcoat across the pavement. He glanced at him and walked on. To his left, he glimpsed a tall watch tower.[38] 'Ha!' he thought. 'Just the place! Why go to Petrovsky? At least here there'll be an official witness . . .' He almost grinned at his new idea and turned into ——skaya Street. The big building with the tower was on this very street. Leaning against the big closed gates stood a short man huddled up in a grey soldier's coat, with a bronze 'Achilles' helmet. He cast a sleepy, cold glance at the approaching Svidrigailov. His face betrayed that sempiternal, peevish sorrow which has left such a sour trace on each and every face of the Jewish tribe. For a while, both men, Svidrigailov and Achilles, silently studied each other. Eventually, Achilles felt there was something amiss: the man was sober and standing three paces away, staring at him and not saying a word.

'Vat you vant here, s-sir?' he said, still not moving or changing his position.

'Nothing much, brother. Good morning to you!' Svidrigailov replied.

'Dis is not de place.'

'I'm off to foreign lands, brother.'

'Foreign lands?'

'America.'

'America?'

Svidrigailov took out the revolver and cocked it. Achilles raised his eyebrows.

'Dis is not de place for choking [joking]!'

'But why's it not the place?'

'Vai, because dis is not.'

'Well, brother, never mind that. It's a nice place, and if someone asks you, tell them I've gone to America.'[39]

He put the revolver to his right temple.

'Stop, dis is not de place!' Achilles suddenly roused himself, his pupils opening wider and wider.

Svidrigailov pulled the trigger.

VII

That same day, only later on, in the evening, some time after six, Raskolnikov was approaching the building where his mother and sister were staying – the apartment in Bakaleyev's house, which Razumikhin had found for them. The staircase was reached directly from the street. As he approached, Raskolnikov checked his step, hesitating whether or not to go in. But nothing would have made him turn back now; he'd taken his decision. 'Besides, they still don't know anything,' he thought, 'and they're used to thinking me a bit odd . . .' His clothes were in a dreadful state: filthy after a whole night in the rain, tattered and frayed. His face was almost disfigured by tiredness, foul weather, physical exhaustion and almost twenty-four hours of inner struggle. He'd spent this whole night alone, God knows where. But at least he'd made his mind up.

He knocked at the door; it was opened by his mother. Dunechka was out. Even the maid was not around. At first, Pulkheria Alexandrovna was speechless with joy and amazement, then she seized him by the hand and pulled him into the room.

'So it's you!' she rejoiced, stutteringly. 'Don't be cross with me, Rodya, for greeting you in this silly way, with tears in my eyes: I'm laughing, not crying. You think I'm crying? No, I'm rejoicing and this is just a silly habit of mine – this tearfulness. Ever since your father died everything makes me cry. Sit down, my darling. You must be tired. I can see. But look how filthy you are!'

'Yesterday I got caught in the rain, Mama . . . ,' Raskolnikov began.

'No, no, no!' Pulkheria Alexandrovna broke in. 'Don't worry, I'm not about to start asking endless questions like I used to in that silly, womanish way of mine. I understand everything, everything. Now I've learned how things are done here and I can see myself it makes more sense. I've finally realized: who am I to understand your reasons or hold you to account? God knows you must have plenty on your mind, plans for the future, new thoughts taking shape. Is it for me to keep nagging you, asking what you're thinking? You know, I . . . Good heavens! What on earth am I doing, pacing around like a lunatic . . . ? You know, Rodya, I've been reading your article in the journal, for the third time already – Dmitry Prokofich brought it to me. I just gasped when I saw it. "You silly woman," I thought to myself. "So this is what he gets up to! This explains everything! I expect he's mulling over some new ideas and here am I tormenting and bothering him." I read, my darling, and there's plenty I don't understand, but that's just how it should be: who am I to understand?'

'Show me, Mama.'

Raskolnikov took the journal and cast a cursory glance at his article. Ill-matched though it was with his situation and his state of mind, he experienced that strange and caustically sweet sensation which every author feels on seeing himself published for the first time, especially at only twenty-three years of age. It was gone in a flash. After reading several lines he frowned and a terrible anguish gripped his heart. All the struggles of his soul in these past few months came back to him at once. Disgusted and annoyed, he threw the article down on the table.

'All I'll say, Rodya, is this: I may be silly, but I can see that in the very near future you'll become one of our foremost scholars, if not our first and foremost. And people had the nerve to think you'd gone crazy. Ha-ha-ha! You're not to know, but that's what they thought! Ah, the pathetic worms – who are they to understand what real intelligence is? Even Dunechka was on the verge of believing it . . . Whatever next? Your father, when he was still alive, twice tried sending work to the journals: first some poems (I still have the notebook – I'll show it to you one day), then a whole novella (I begged him to let me copy it out for him), and you should have seen how we prayed for them to be accepted . . . They weren't! A week or so ago, Rodya, I was simply devastated to see how you live, what you eat, what you wear. But now I realize I was just being silly again: with your mind and your talent you can get whatever you want, whenever you want. You just don't want to yet, that's all, and you've far more important things to worry about . . .'

'Is Dunya out, Mama?'

'Yes, Rodya. She's been going out a lot and leaves me here on my own. Thank goodness for Dmitry Prokofich. He comes by to see me and tells me everything about you. He loves and respects you, my darling. As for your sister, I can't say that she's particularly disrespectful towards me. I'm not complaining. She has her character, I have mine. She has her secrets, too, all of a sudden. Well, I don't keep any secrets from either of you. Of course, I'm quite convinced that Dunya is far too intelligent, and besides, she loves us both . . . but I've no idea where all this will end. You've made me so happy, Rodya, by coming here now, but trust her to waltz off somewhere. When she comes, I'll tell her, "You know, you missed your brother while you were out, and where were you, may I ask?" There's no need to spoil me, Rodya: come by if you can, but if you can't, don't worry – I'll wait. After all, I know you love me and that's enough for me. I'll read what you write, hear about you from all and sundry, and every so often you'll visit me yourself – what could be better? After all, haven't you come over now to comfort your mother? I can see you have . . .'

Here, Pulkheria Alexandrovna suddenly burst into tears.

'Here I go again! What a fool! Just ignore me! But look at me sitting here,' she cried, leaping to her feet, 'without even offering you some coffee! The selfishness of old age, as they say! Won't be a minute!'

'Mama, never mind that – I'll be off in a second. That's not why I came. Please, hear what I have to say.'

Pulkheria Alexandrovna timidly walked over to him.

'Mama, whatever happens, whatever you hear about me, whatever you're told about me, will you still love me as you do now?' he suddenly asked, his heart bursting, as if he were speaking without thinking and without weighing his words.

'Rodya, Rodya, what's the matter? How can you even ask such a thing? And who could ever tell me anything bad about you? I won't believe anyone, whoever they are – I'll just throw them out.'

'I came to assure you that I have always loved you, and I'm glad we're alone now, glad even that Dunechka is out,' he continued with the same surge of feeling. 'I came to tell you frankly that, unhappy though you will be, you ought to know that your son loves you now more than he loves himself, and that everything you thought about me – that I'm cruel and don't love you – is untrue, all of it. I'll never stop loving you . . . Well, that'll do. I felt I had to do this, begin with this . . .'

Without a word, Pulkeria Alexandrovna embraced him, pressed him to her bosom and softly wept.

'If only I knew what the matter was, Rodya,' she said at last. 'All this time I thought you were simply fed up with us, but now everything tells me that a great woe lies in store for you – and that's why you're miserable. I've seen it coming for a while now, Rodya. Forgive me for talking about it now. I keep thinking about it and can't sleep at night. And your sister, too: all last night she was raving in her sleep, and it was you she kept mentioning. I caught the odd word, but couldn't understand a thing. All morning long it was as if I were preparing to face my punishment, my death. I was expecting something, had a feeling – and now look! Rodya, Rodya, where are you off to? Are you going away somewhere?'

'Yes.'

'Just as I thought! But I can go with you, too, if you need me. And Dunya. She loves you, loves you very much. And Sofya Semyonovna, she can come with us, too, if you need her. Look, I'm even prepared to take her instead of my daughter. Dmitry Prokofich will help us get ready . . . but . . . where . . . will you be going?'

'Goodbye, Mama.'

'What? Today!' she shrieked, as if losing him forever.

'I can't . . . I have to go now, I really do . . .'

'And I can't go with you?'

'No. You should kneel and pray to God for me. Your prayer, perhaps, will be heard.'

'Let me bless you with the sign of the cross! There. O God, what are we doing?'

Yes, he was glad, very glad, that there was no one else, that he was alone with his mother. As if, after this long and dreadful time, his heart had suddenly softened, all at once. He fell before her and kissed her feet; embracing, they wept. And she wasn't surprised and she asked no questions. She had long understood that something dreadful was happening to her son, and now the terrible moment, whatever it was, had come.

'Rodya, darling, my first-born child,' she said through her sobs, 'now you're just as you were as a little boy, when you came to me and hugged and kissed me just like now; back when your father and I hadn't a rouble between us, you comforted us just by being there; and then, when your father died, how often, hugging each other like this, did we weep together by his grave? And if I've been crying all this time, it's because a mother's heart can sense misfortune. The minute I saw you that first evening – remember? – when we'd just arrived, I could tell everything just from your eyes, and my heart jumped; and then today, when I opened the door and took one look at you, I thought: "So, the hour of destiny has come." Rodya, Rodya, you're not going away right now are you?'

'No.'

'You'll come again?'

'Yes . . . I will.'

'Rodya, please don't be cross. I won't ask too many questions. I don't dare. Just one little thing: is it far away, this place?'

'Very.'

'What is it? A posting somewhere, your career?'

'Whatever God sends . . . Just pray for me . . .'

Raskolnikov made for the door, but she grabbed him and looked despairingly into his eyes. Her face was disfigured with dread.

'That'll do, Mama,' said Raskolnikov, deeply sorry he'd come.

'It's not forever? I mean, it's not forever yet, is it? I mean, you'll come again, tomorrow?'

'I'll come, I'll come. Goodbye.'

Finally, he escaped.

The evening was fresh, warm and bright; the sun had been out since the morning. Raskolnikov was on his way to his room; he was hurrying. He wanted to get it all over and done with by sunset. And in the meantime, he didn't want to meet anyone. Going up to his garret he noticed that Nastasya, having torn herself away from the samovar, was watching him intently, following him with her eyes. 'Is there someone in my room?' he wondered. With disgust, he imagined Porfiry. But on reaching his room and opening the door he saw Dunechka. She was sitting there all alone, deep in thought, and looked like she'd been waiting for some time. He stopped on the threshold. Startled, she rose from the couch and straightened up before him. Her unwavering gaze expressed horror and unassuageable sorrow. And from her gaze alone he instantly realized she knew everything.

'Well, should I come in or should I go?' he asked, mistrustfully.

'I've been at Sofya Semyonovna's all day. We were both waiting for you there. We thought you'd be bound to come by.'

Raskolnikov entered the room and sat down, exhausted, on a chair.

'I feel weak, Dunya, and very tired, but now, of all times, I want to be in full control of myself.'

He glanced at her with mistrust.

'But where were you all night?'

'I don't really remember. You see, sister, I wanted to take that final step and kept coming back to the Neva, again and again – that much I remember. I wanted to end it all there, but . . . I didn't take it . . . ,' he whispered, stealing another mistrustful glance at Dunya.

'And thank God! That's exactly what we feared most, Sofya Semyonovna and I! So you still believe in life. Thank God! Thank God!'

Raskolnikov gave a bitter grin.

'I didn't believe, but just now Mother and I were hugging and crying; I don't believe, but I asked her to pray for me. I suppose only God can explain that, Dunechka. I don't understand a thing about it.'

'You went to see Mother? You mean you told her?' Dunya exclaimed in horror. 'Could you really bring yourself to tell her?'

'No, I didn't tell her . . . in words; but she understood a great deal. She heard you raving at night. I'm sure she already understands at least half of it. Perhaps I shouldn't have gone. I don't even know why I went. I'm despicable, Dunya.'

'Despicable, but ready to go and suffer! You are going, aren't you?'

'I am. Now. Yes, it was to avoid such disgrace that I wanted to drown myself, Dunya, but then, when I was already standing over the water, I thought: "If I've always considered myself strong, even disgrace should hold no fear for me now,"' he said, running ahead. 'Is that pride, Dunya?'

'Yes, Rodya.'

Fire seemed to flash in his faded eyes, as if he were pleased at still being proud.

'You don't think I was just scared of the water, sister?' he asked with a hideous grin, peering into her face.

'Oh, Rodya, that's enough!' came Dunya's bitter cry.

For a couple of minutes neither spoke. He sat there, staring at the floor. Dunya stood at the other end of the table, looking at him with anguish. Suddenly, he got up:

'It's late. Time to go. I'm off to give myself up. But why I'm going off to give myself up I do not know.'

Large tears ran down her cheeks.

'You're crying, sister, but can you give me your hand?'

'How could you doubt it?'

She hugged him close.

'And by going off to suffer are you not already washing away half your crime?' she cried, squeezing him in her arms and kissing him.

'Crime? What crime?' he cried in a sudden surge of fury. 'I murdered a vile, noxious louse, some hag of a moneylender of no use to anyone, whose murder makes up for forty sins,[40] who sucked the juice from the poor, and that's a crime? I don't even think about it. I don't even think about washing it away. I don't care that you're all prodding me with your "Crime! Crime!" Only now do I see the full absurdity of my petty cowardice. Now, when I've already decided to accept this pointless disgrace! I'm despicable and talentless, that's the only reason I've decided, and maybe also because it's in my own interests, as that man suggested . . . that Porfiry!'

'Brother, brother, what are you saying? You shed blood!' cried Dunya in despair.

'Which everyone sheds,' he rejoined in a kind of frenzy, 'which has always poured like a waterfall, which people pour like champagne, and for which they're crowned in the Capitol[41] and remembered as benefactors of humanity. Look closer, you'll see! I, too, wanted to do good. I'd have done hundreds, thousands of good deeds in exchange for this single stupidity, which in any case was more cack-handedness than it was stupidity, because this whole idea was nowhere near as stupid as it now seems, in the light of failure . . . (Everything seems stupid in the light of failure!) All I wanted was to ensure my independence, to take the first step, to get what I needed and let the immeasurable benefits, relatively speaking, smooth everything over . . . But even the first step was too much for me to cope with . . . because I'm scum! And that's all there is to it! And I refuse to look at it your way: if I'd pulled it off, I'd have been crowned; instead, I'm trapped!'

'But that's all wrong! Brother, what are you saying?'

'The wrong form, you mean – the aesthetics aren't right! I just can't understand it: why is raining down bombs on people, during a regular siege,[42] a more honourable way of doing things? Fear of aesthetics is the first sign of weakness! Never, never have I understood this as clearly as now, and never have I understood my crime less! Never, never have I been stronger and more convinced than now!'

The colour even rushed to his pale, haggard face. But as he uttered this final cry his eyes happened to meet Dunya's and there was such torment for him in her gaze, such pain, that he came to his senses despite himself. If nothing else, he felt, he'd made these two poor women unhappy. He was the cause . . .

'Dunya, dearest! If I'm guilty, forgive me (although if I'm guilty, I cannot be forgiven). Goodbye! Let's not argue! I can't stay a moment longer. Don't come after me, I beg you. I've another visit to make . . . Go now and be with mother. Please, I beg you! It's the last and biggest thing I ask you. Don't leave her for a moment. I've left her too worried to cope: she'll either die or go mad. Stay with her! You'll have Razumikhin with you. I told him . . . Don't weep for me: I'll try to be a man, and honest, for the rest of my life, even though I'm a murderer. One day, perhaps, you'll hear my name. I won't shame you, you'll see. I'll still prove . . . but for the time being, goodbye,' he hurriedly concluded, noticing once again a strange expression in Dunya's eyes at these final words and promises. 'Why are you crying like that? Don't cry, don't! We're not parting forever . . . Oh yes, wait! I forgot!'

He went over to the table, picked up a fat, dusty book, opened it and took out from between its pages a small little portrait, done in watercolour on ivory. It was a portrait of the landlady's daughter, to whom he'd once been engaged and who died of fever, that same strange girl who wanted to be a nun. He spent a minute or so studying this expressive and sickly face, kissed the portrait and passed it to Dunechka.

'You know, I talked to her a lot *about this*, to her and no one else,' he mused. 'All those hideous things that happened later I'd already confided to her heart. Don't worry,' he said, turning to Dunya, 'she didn't go along with it any more than you do and I'm glad she's not alive now. What really matters is that now everything will start afresh, everything will snap in two,' he suddenly cried, returning once more to his own pain, 'everything, everything, and am I ready for that? Is that what I want? They say it's a test I have to endure! But what's the point of all these senseless tests? What? Am I really going to understand any of this any better after twenty years' hard labour, when I'm old and feeble, crushed by suffering and idiocy, than I do now? And what would I be living for then? And why am I agreeing to live like this now? Oh, I knew I was scum today, at dawn, standing there over the Neva!'

Finally, they both went out. It was hard for Dunya, but she loved him! She set off, but, having gone some fifty paces, turned back to take one more look at him. She could still see him. Reaching the corner, he turned back, too, and their eyes met for the last time; but seeing that she was looking at him, he waved her on her way with impatience, even anger, and turned sharply around the corner.

'I'm being spiteful, I can see it myself,' he thought a minute later, ashamed of his petulant gesture towards Dunya. 'But why must they love me so much if I don't deserve it? Oh, if only I'd been on my own and no one had loved me and I'd never loved anyone! *None of this would have happened!* It's a curious thing, though: will these fifteen or twenty years ahead of me really humble me to such an extent that I'll go round bowing and scraping, calling myself a criminal at the first opportunity? Yes, that's exactly what'll happen! That's why they're banishing me; that's what they want from me . . . Just look at them all scurrying around, every one of them a scoundrel and a criminal by his very nature; worse – an idiot! Try not banishing me and they'll go wild with righteous indignation! Oh, how I hate them!'

One thought absorbed him: 'What kind of process will be needed for me to end up humbling myself before them, without a single objection, with total conviction? But then, why not? That's exactly how it should be. As if twenty years beneath the yoke won't finish you off! Water wears out stone. So why live? Why? Why am I going there now, when I know myself that this is exactly how it will be, as it is writ?'

It was probably the hundredth time he'd asked himself this question since the previous evening, but he was going all the same.

VIII

By the time he entered Sonya's room, dusk was already falling. Sonya had been waiting for him all day in a quite dreadful state. Dunya had waited with her. She'd come in the morning, remembering Svidrigailov's words from the day before: that Sonya 'knows about it'. We won't convey the details of their conversation or the tears of both women or how close they became. From this meeting, at any rate, Dunya drew the one consolation that her brother would not be alone: it was to her, to Sonya, that he first brought his confession; in her that he sought a human being when a human being was what he needed; and it was she who would follow him, wherever fate took him. She didn't have to ask: she knew it would be so. She even looked at Sonya with a kind of reverence, and at first this reverential attitude, and the feeling behind it, almost embarrassed Sonya. In fact, Sonya was almost ready to burst into tears: it was she who felt unworthy even to look at Dunya. The image of Dunya bowing to her so attentively and so respectfully during their first meeting at Raskolnikov's had imprinted itself on her soul for all time as one of the most beautiful and unattainable visions in her life.

Eventually, Dunechka could bear it no longer and left Sonya, so as to wait for her brother in his room; she couldn't help thinking he'd go there first. Left alone, Sonya immediately began tormenting herself with the fear that he really might go and kill himself. Dunya was scared of exactly the same thing. But they'd spent the whole day vying to persuade each other that this was impossible, using every available argument, and for as long as they were together they felt calmer. Now that they were apart, neither could think of anything else. Sonya remembered Svidrigailov telling her the day before that Raskolnikov had two roads open to him – the Vladimirka or . . . She also knew all about his vanity, arrogance, self-regard and lack of faith. 'Surely cowardice and fear of death can't be the only two things that keep him alive?' she wondered at last, in despair. The sun, meanwhile, was already setting. She stood sadly in front of the window and stared out – but all that could be seen through the glass was the unpainted wall of the neighbouring building. Eventually, once she'd already convinced herself of his certain death, in he came.

A shriek of joy broke from her chest. But after a closer look at his face, she suddenly went pale.

'That's right!' said Raskolnikov, with a grin. 'I've come for your crosses, Sonya. Wasn't it you who sent me to the crossroads? But now it's time to do the deed you get cold feet?'

Sonya stared at him in amazement. His tone struck her as very peculiar. Cold shivers ran down her body, but it took only a minute to realize he was putting it on – the tone, the words, everything. Even while talking to her he seemed to be looking off into the corner, trying not to look straight at her.

'You see, Sonya, I decided that this was probably in my own best interests. There's a certain consideration here . . . But it's a long story and what's the point? Do you know what really makes me furious?

It's that now I'll have all these idiotic, brutish mugs crowding round, gawking at me, asking me idiotic questions which I have to answer, pointing at me . . . Ugh! You know, it's not Porfiry I'm going to. I'm sick of him. I'd rather go to my good friend Powder Keg – now that'll be a surprise, that'll make an impression. Some composure would help, though. Recently I've become far too irritable. Can you believe it? I was almost threatening to punch my sister just now simply for turning round to take one last look at me. What a pig! To reach such a state! Well, where are those crosses?'

He seemed out of control. He couldn't stay still for even a minute, couldn't focus his attention on a single object; thoughts skipped over each other; his tongue ran away with him; there was a faint tremor in his hands.

In silence, Sonya took two crosses, one cypress, one copper, from a box, made the sign of the cross over herself and over him, and hung the small cypress cross around his neck.

'A symbol, I suppose, of me taking up my cross – heh-heh! Suppose I haven't suffered enough yet! Cypress wood – a peasant's cross; copper – Lizaveta's, which you're taking for yourself. Show it to me! So that was on her . . . then? I know two other crosses like that, a silver one and a little icon. I dropped them on the old hag's breast. Come to think of it, it's probably those I should be wearing now . . . But I'm blathering again. I'll forget what I'm doing. Why am I so distracted? You see, Sonya, the reason I'm here is to warn you, for you to know . . . And that's about it, really . . . That's the only reason I came. (H'm, thought I'd have a bit more to say.) You yourself wanted me to go, so now I'll do my time and your wish will come true. Now why are you crying? You too? Stop! That's enough! I can't take any more of this!'

Still, a feeling was born in him. His heart clenched as he looked at her. 'Her, why her?' he thought to himself. 'What am I to her? Why's she crying? Why's she getting me ready, like mother or Dunya? My nanny – that's who she'll be!'

'Cross yourself and pray, at least this once,' asked Sonya in a trembling, timid voice.

'Oh, by all means, as much as you like! And with a pure heart, Sonya, a pure heart . . .'

It wasn't what he meant to say.

He crossed himself several times. Sonya grabbed her shawl and tied

it round her head. It was a green *drap de dames* shawl, probably the
same one Marmeladov had mentioned that time, the 'family' one. The
thought flashed through Raskolnikov's mind, but he didn't ask. He'd
begun to sense for himself how dreadfully distracted he was, how
horribly nervous. It frightened him. Sonya's desire to go with him also
came as a sudden shock.

'Where are you off to? Stay here, stay here! I'll go on my own,' he
cried with petty irritation, almost hostility, and made for the door. 'I
never asked for a retinue!' he muttered, walking out.

He left Sonya standing in the middle of the room. He hadn't even
said goodbye and he'd already forgotten all about her; a venomous,
mutinous doubt seethed in his soul.

'Can this really be right? Can this be it?' he asked himself again as he
went down the stairs. 'Is it really too late to stop and patch everything
up again . . . and not go?'

But he was going all the same. He suddenly felt, once and for all,
that asking himself questions was pointless. Coming out into the
street, he remembered he hadn't said goodbye to Sonya, that he'd left
her standing in the middle of the room, in her green shawl, too scared
to move, and for an instant he paused. At that very second he was
dazzled by a sudden thought – as though it had been lying in wait for
him, to stagger him once and for all.

'So why did I go and see her just now – why? Time to do the deed, I
told her. What deed? There was no deed! Just to tell her *I'm going* and
that's it? All this just for that? Or because I love her? But I don't, do I?
Didn't I shoo her away like a dog just now? Or was it really her crosses
I needed? How low I've fallen! No – it was her tears I needed, the fear
on her face, the sight of her heart in pain and torment! I needed to grab
hold of something, anything; to buy myself some time; to see a human
being before me! And I dared put so much faith in myself, so many
dreams . . . I'm a beggar. I'm nobody. Just scum. Scum!'

He was walking along the bank of the Ditch, and hadn't much further to go. But, reaching the bridge, he paused, suddenly stepped onto
it and went to Haymarket instead.

Greedily, he looked to his left and to his right, fastened on each and
every object, and couldn't focus his attention on a single one; everything
slipped away from him. 'A week from now, a month from now, when
I'm being taken God knows where in one of those convict wagons over

this very bridge, how will I look at the Ditch then? Should I try to remember all this?' flashed through his mind. 'Or this sign: how will I
read these same letters then? Someone's written "Campany" – I should
remember this first *a*, the letter *a*, and look at it a month from now, at
that same *a*: how will I see it then? What will I be thinking and feeling? . . . God, how pathetic all this must seem, all these . . . worries of
mine! Of course, it must all be quite curious . . . in its way . . . (Ha-ha-ha!
What the hell am I thinking about?) . . . I'm turning into a child, showing off to myself. But why am I so ashamed? Ugh, all this pushing and
shoving! Just look at this fat German. Does he know who he's shoving? Some woman begging with a child; curious that she thinks I'm
happier than she is. How about giving her something, for the fun of it?
Ha! A five-copeck piece! How did I keep hold of that? Here you go,
mother!'

'God bless you!' came the beggar woman's doleful voice.

He entered Haymarket. He found it unpleasant, very unpleasant,
to come face to face with commoners, but he was heading right into
the thick of them. He'd have given anything to be left alone; but he
wouldn't last a minute on his own, he could feel it himself. A drunk
was misbehaving in the crowd: he kept trying to dance and kept falling over. People gathered round. Raskolnikov squeezed through the
throng, watched the drunk for a minute or two, and suddenly,
abruptly, laughed out loud. A minute later he'd forgotten all about
him and didn't even see him, though he was staring straight at him.
Eventually he moved off, no longer even remembering where he was.
But when he reached the middle of the square a sudden impulse, a
sudden sensation, took hold of him and gripped him from top to toe,
body and mind.

He suddenly recalled Sonya's words: 'Go to the crossroads, bow to
the people, kiss the earth, because you have sinned before the earth as
well, and say out loud to the entire world: "I am a murderer!"' Remembering this, he began shaking all over. The anguish and anxiety
of all this time, but especially the last few hours, had suffocated him
to such a point that he simply hurled himself into the possibility of
this sensation of wholeness, of newness and fullness. It came upon
him suddenly, like a fit; from a single spark, it caught fire in his soul
and swept all over him. Everything softened in him at once and the
tears gushed out. His legs gave way beneath him . . .

He kneeled in the middle of the square, bowed right down to the ground and kissed the dirty earth, with pleasure and happiness. He got to his feet and bowed once more.

'He's completely smashed!' observed a lad standing next to him.

Roars of laughter.

'He's on his way to Jerusalem, lads. He's leaving his children, his country, he's bowing to the whole world, kissing our capital city of Saint Petersburg and its soil,' added a tipsy tradesman.

'He's only young!' a third put in.

'Gentry, too!' observed another in an imposing voice.

'There's no telling anymore who's gentry and who's not.'

All this banter and talk deterred Raskolnikov, and the words 'I have killed!', which may have been on the very tip of his tongue, froze inside him. Still, he bore the comments calmly and, without looking round, set off down a side street in the direction of the bureau. A vision flashed before him, but it caused him no surprise; he'd already sensed that this was how it should be. Bowing down to the earth on Haymarket for the second time, he turned his head to the left and there, some fifty paces away, saw Sonya. She was hiding from him behind one of the wooden huts on the square; so she'd accompanied him all along his walk of sorrows! At that moment Raskolnikov felt and understood, once and for all, that Sonya would never leave him, that she'd follow him to the very ends of the earth, wherever fate sent him. His heart turned over inside him . . . but – here he was already, at the place of destiny . . .

There was a spring in his step as he entered the courtyard. He had to go up to the third floor. 'All these stairs to climb first,' he thought. The moment of destiny still seemed a long way off; still plenty of time to think things over.

Once again, the same rubbish, the same eggshells on the spiral staircase; once again, the doors to the apartments flung wide open; once again, the rank fumes and stench from the kitchens. Raskolnikov hadn't been back since then. His legs were numb and buckling, but still they moved. He paused for a moment to get his breath back, to tidy himself up, to enter *like a human being*. 'But why? What's the point?' he suddenly wondered, catching himself at this task. 'If I have to drink this cup anyway, what difference can it make? The fouler the better.' At that instant the image of Ilya Petrovich Powder Keg came briefly before him. 'Must it really be him I go to? Can't it be someone else?

Nikodim Fomich, say? Can't I turn back now and visit the district superintendent at home? It would be a lot less formal . . . No, no! Lieutenant Powder Keg it is! Better to drink it all in one go . . .'

Turning cold and barely conscious of his actions, he opened the door to the bureau. This time there was hardly anyone there, just a caretaker and some other commoner. The guard didn't even poke his head out from behind his screen. Raskolnikov walked through to the next room. 'Perhaps I won't have to say it now either,' flashed through him. Here, some scribe or other, casually dressed, was getting down to some work at a desk. In a corner another clerk was also settling down. No sign of Zametov. Nor, needless to say, of Nikodim Fomich.

'No one in?' Raskolnikov asked the man at the desk.

'Who d'you want?'

'Aha! Years may pass, no sight, no sound,[43] yet the Russian spirit . . . How does it go again, that fairy tale? . . . I've forgotten! My compliments, sir!' a familiar voice suddenly boomed.

Raskolnikov started to shake. Before him stood Powder Keg. He'd emerged suddenly from the third room.

'Must be fate,' thought Raskolnikov. 'Why's he here?'

'And what brings you here, old boy?' exclaimed Ilya Petrovich. (He was evidently in a splendid mood and even a little overexcited.) 'If it's business, you're a touch on the early side. It's pure chance I'm . . . But anyway, how may I . . . ? I must admit, Mr . . . Mr . . . I beg your pardon . . .'

'Raskolnikov.'

'Too right: Raskolnikov! And you thought I'd forgotten! Please don't take me for some . . . Rodion Ro . . . Ro . . . Rodionych, I believe?'

'Rodion Romanych.'

'Yes, yes-yes! Rodion Romanych, Rodion Romanych! *That's* what I was after. I even asked around about it. I must admit, ever since that day I've truly mourned the fact that we . . . later I had it all explained to me: a young literary type, a scholar no less . . . The first steps, as it were . . . Good Lord! Hasn't every literary type or scholar begun by taking an original step or two? My wife and I, we both respect literature, but for her it's a passion! . . . Literature and artistry! Be honourable and all the rest can be acquired by talents, learning, reasoning, genius! A hat, say – now what's the meaning of a hat? A hat's a pancake, I can buy it at Zimmerman's;[44] but as for what's kept under the hat, what's kept hidden by the hat – well, I can't buy that, sir! . . . I must admit, I had half a mind to pay you a visit and clear the air, but then I thought, perhaps you . . . But I haven't even asked: is there anything we can actually do for you? I hear your family has come to see you?'

'Yes, my mother and sister.'

'I've even had the honour and pleasure of meeting your sister – an educated and delightful young lady. I must admit, I regretted the way you and I got so carried away. Won't happen again! And as for my giving you a funny look on account of you fainting – well, a most brilliant explanation was soon found for all that! Zealotry and fanaticism! I understand your indignation. Perhaps you're changing address on account of your family's arrival?'

'N-no, I just . . . I came to ask . . . I thought I'd find Zametov here.'

'Oh yes! The two of you hit it off, I hear. Well, Zametov's not here – you're out of luck. Yes, sir, we've lost Alexander Grigoryevich! Absent since yesterday; moved on . . . and, while moving, fell out with just about everyone . . . Wasn't even civil about it . . . A flighty little boy, no two ways about it. Promising enough at one time; but that's what they're like, our brilliant youth! Seems he wants to take some exam or other, but you don't get a diploma for chatting and bragging. Not a bit like you, say, or your friend Mr Razumikhin! Yours is the career of a scholar, no misfortune will throw you off course! For you, one might say, life's fripperies – *nihil est*; you're an ascetic, a monk, a hermit! . . . A book, a pen behind your ear, scholarly publications – only there does your spirit soar! I myself . . . perhaps you've read Livingstone's journals?'[45]

'No.'

'Well I have. But there's so many nihilists about nowadays. Quite understandable, I suppose; just think of the times we're living in! Although you and I . . . Well, I'm sure you're not a nihilist! Answer me frankly now, frankly!'

'N-no . . .'

'Really, be frank with me, don't hold back – talk as if you were the only person in the room! Public service is one thing, quite another is . . . Ha, you thought I was going to say *friendship*! No sir, not friendship, but the sense of being a citizen and a man,[46] the sense of one's humanity and love for the Almighty. I may be a state official, I may be at my post, but I am forever obliged to sense the citizen within me, to stand up and be counted . . . You saw fit to mention Zametov just now. You know, Zametov's just the type to do something disgraceful, something French, in some seedy establishment, over a glass of champagne or Russian wine – that's Zametov for you! Whereas I, so to speak, burn with loyalty and fine feelings; not only that, I am a man of consequence and rank, with a certain position! Married, with children. Fulfilling my duty as citizen and man. And who's he, pray tell? I speak to you as to a man ennobled by education. Or take these new midwives: there's far too many of them about.'

Raskolnikov raised his eyebrows. For the most part, the words uttered by Ilya Petrovich, evidently just up from the dinner table, rained down on him like empty sounds. Some of them, though, made a kind of sense. He gave him a questioning glance and wondered where it would all end.

'I mean those short-haired wenches,' the loquacious Ilya Petrovich went on. 'Midwives is my own little nickname, and I find the description more than satisfactory. Heh-heh! There they are, sneaking into the medical academy to study anatomy.[47] But tell me, when I get sick am I really going to ask a young lady to treat me? Heh-heh!'

Ilya Petrovich guffawed, savouring his wit.

'An immoderate thirst for enlightenment, I suppose, but one must know when to stop. Why abuse one's privilege? Why insult honourable people, as that scoundrel Zametov likes to do? Why did he insult me, I ask you? Or take all these suicides – you can't imagine how common it's become. Spending their last roubles, then doing themselves in. Young girls, young boys, old men . . . Only this morning a report came in about some gentleman, a recent arrival. Nil Pavlych? Hey, Nil Pavlych! What was his name again, that well-mannered gent who shot himself yesterday on Petersburg Side?'

'Svidrigailov,' came a hoarse, indifferent voice from the other room.

Raskolnikov shuddered.

'Svidrigailov! Svidrigailov's shot himself!' he cried.

'You mean you know Svidrigailov?!'

'Yes . . . I know him . . . He arrived not long ago.'

'That's right, arrived not long ago, recently widowed, a rake if ever there was, and suddenly shot himself in the most scandalous way imaginable . . . Left a few lines in his notebook to say he was sound of mind and to ask that no one be blamed for his death. Had money, I hear. But how do you know him?'

'We're . . . acquainted . . . My sister was their governess . . .'

'Well, well, well . . . Then there must be things you can tell us about him. And you didn't suspect anything?'

'I saw him only yesterday . . . He . . . was drinking wine . . . I didn't know.'

Raskolnikov felt as though something had fallen on him, crushed him.

'You seem to be turning pale again. There's never enough air in here . . .'

'Yes, sir, time for me to be off,' mumbled Raskolnikov. 'Sorry for disturbing . . .'

'Not at all, not at all. Always a pleasure! And I'm glad to declare . . .'

Ilya Petrovich even offered him his hand.

'I simply wanted . . . It was Zametov I . . .'

'I understand, I understand. Always a pleasure!'

'I'm . . . very glad . . . Goodbye, sir,' smiled Raskolnikov.

He walked out, swaying. His head was spinning. He couldn't even feel his legs. He started down the stairs, supporting himself against the wall with his right arm. He had the impression that some caretaker, with a register in his hand, shoved him on his way up to the bureau; that a dog was barking away furiously on a floor below and that a woman had thrown a rolling pin at it and yelled. He reached the bottom and stepped outside. There in the yard, not far from the door, numb and deathly pale, stood Sonya, looking at him wild-eyed. He stopped in front of her. There was something sick and haggard about her expression, something desperate. She threw up her hands. His lips forced out a hideous, bewildered smile. He stood, grinned and went back upstairs, back to the bureau.

Ilya Petrovich had sat down and was rummaging through some papers. Before him stood the same man who'd just shoved Raskolnikov on his way up the stairs.

'Eh? You again? Left something, did you? Whatever's the matter?'

Raskolnikov, lips white, eyes fixed, advanced slowly towards him, went right up to the desk, leant on it, tried to say something, but couldn't; nothing came out except a few incoherent sounds.

'You're having a bad turn! A chair! Here, sit down on this chair! Sit! Some water!'

Raskolnikov lowered himself into the chair, without taking his eyes off the face of the very unpleasantly astonished Ilya Petrovich. They looked at each other for a minute or so, waiting. The water arrived.

'It was me . . . ,' Raskolnikov began.

'Have some water.'

Raskolnikov moved the water aside and said quietly yet distinctly, with pauses between the words:

'*It was me who murdered that civil servant's old widow and her sister Lizaveta with an axe, and robbed them.*'

Ilya Petrovich opened his mouth. People ran in from all sides.

Raskolnikov repeated his statement.

EPILOGUE

I

Siberia. On the bank of a broad, deserted river there stands a town, one of Russia's administrative centres; in the town, a fortress; in the fortress, a prison.[1] In the prison, having already served nine months of his sentence, is the exiled convict of the second category[2] Rodion Raskolnikov. Since the date of his crime almost eighteen months have passed.

His trial went smoothly enough. The criminal backed up his statement firmly, precisely and clearly, without muddling the circumstances, without mitigating them to his own advantage, without distorting the facts, without forgetting the slightest detail. He described the entire process of the murder, to the very end: explained the mystery of the *pledge* (the small bit of wood with a metal strip), which was found in the hands of the murdered old woman; gave a detailed account of how he took the victim's keys, described those keys, described the box and what was in it; even enumerated some of the objects it contained; explained the mystery of Lizaveta's murder; described how Kokh, and then the student, came and knocked, and repeated everything they said to each other; how he, the criminal, then ran downstairs and heard Mikolka's and Mitka's squeals; how he hid in an empty apartment and got back home; and in conclusion identified the stone in the yard, on Voznesensky Prospect, by the gates, beneath which the items and the purse were found. The case, in short, could hardly have been clearer. The investigators and the judges were very surprised, though, to learn that he had hidden the purse and items beneath the stone without availing himself of them and, even more so, that not only could he not recall in any detail all the items he himself had stolen, but even misremembered how many there were. The simple fact that he had never once opened the purse and did not even know how much money there was inside seemed improbable (the purse was found to contain three hundred and seventeen roubles in silver and three twenty-copeck pieces; after being kept so long beneath the stone, some of the largest notes at the top were severely damaged). They struggled long and hard to find out why exactly the accused was lying about this one particular circumstance, while voluntarily and truthfully pleading guilty to everything else. In the end, some (especially the psychologists among them) went so far as to admit the possibility that he really had not looked inside the purse, which was why he did not know what was in it, and, in his ignorance, had gone and buried it beneath a stone; but this immediately led them to conclude that the crime itself could only have been committed in a state of temporary insanity, as a result, so to speak, of a monomaniacal obsession with murder and robbery, with no further aims in mind or expectation of profit. Here, incidentally, they were helped by the latest fashionable theory of temporary insanity,[3] which is so frequently cited nowadays to explain certain crimes. What was more, the long history of Raskolnikov's hypochondriac condition was attested in meticulous detail by numerous witnesses, by Doctor Zosimov, his former friends, his landlady, his maid. All this greatly facilitated the conclusion that Raskolnikov did not really resemble an ordinary murderer, felon and robber: this was something else. To the intense irritation of all who defended this point of view, the criminal made almost no attempt to defend himself; to the crucial questions 'What exactly could have induced him to commit homicide?' and 'What prompted him to carry out the robbery?' he gave the very lucid reply, positively rude in its precision, that the cause of it all had been the squalor of his circumstances; his beggary and helplessness; his desire to secure the first steps in his career with the help of the three thousand roubles, if not more, that he had expected to find at the victim's home. He had managed to go through with the murder thanks to his frivolous and craven character, which, moreover, had been irritated by hardship and failure. In reply to the question of what exactly had prompted him to turn himself in, he answered frankly: heartfelt remorse. There was something almost rude about it all . . .

The sentence, however, proved more lenient than might have been expected, given the nature of the crime, perhaps precisely because the criminal not only did not wish to justify himself, but even evinced a desire to incriminate himself further. All the strange and specific circumstances of the case were taken into account. Not a single doubt was cast on the criminal's sick and desperate condition before the perpetration of the crime. The fact that he had not availed himself of the stolen goods was partly ascribed to the effect of awakened remorse, partly to the imperfect state of his mental faculties during the perpetration of the crime. The unplanned murder of Lizaveta only served to reinforce the latter hypothesis: a man commits two murders while leaving the door open! Lastly, the timing of the confession, just when the case had become exceptionally muddled as a result of the false self-accusations of a disheartened zealot (Mikolai) and when, moreover, there was a near total absence not only of clear evidence concerning the actual offender, but even of any suspicion (Porfiry Petrovich had been as good as his word) – all this did much to ease the lot of the accused.

Quite unexpectedly, other circumstances also emerged that greatly favoured the defendant. The former student Razumikhin managed to exhume some information enabling him to prove that the criminal Raskolnikov, during his time at university, spent all he had on helping a poor, consumptive fellow student and supported him almost single-handedly for half a year. When his friend died, Raskolnikov took care of his old invalid father (whom his friend had supported and fed, by his own labour, ever since his early teens), eventually placed the old man in a hospital and, when he died too, arranged his burial. All this had a favourable influence on how Raskolnikov's fate was decided. Meanwhile, the widow Zarnitsyna, Raskolnikov's former landlady and the mother of his dead fiancée, testified that when they were still living at the previous address, at the Five Corners, Raskolnikov had pulled two small children out of a burning apartment, at night, and was himself burned in the process. This fact was thoroughly investigated and reasonably well attested by numerous witnesses. In short, it all ended with the criminal being sentenced to only eight years hard labour, second category, in view of his voluntary confession and other mitigating circumstances.

Raskolnikov's mother fell ill at the very beginning of the trial. Dunya and Razumikhin deemed it appropriate to take her away from Petersburg until it was over. Razumikhin chose a town on the railway line, a short distance away, in order to keep a close eye on all the developments at the trial, while seeing Avdotya Romanovna as often as possible. Pulkheria Alexandrovna was suffering from a rather strange, nervous sickness, accompanied by something resembling insanity, at least in part. When Dunya returned from seeing her brother for the last time, she found her mother very ill indeed, feverish and delirious. That same evening she and Razumikhin agreed what they would say to her when she asked about Raskolnikov, and even concocted a long story about how Raskolnikov had left for some far-flung place, near the Russian border, on a private mission that would finally bring him both fame and fortune. But they were shocked that Pulkheria Alexandrovna never asked about any of this, neither then nor later. On the contrary, she herself came out with a long story about her son's sudden departure, tearfully describing how he had come to say goodbye to her and hinting as she did so that she alone was privy to many very important and mysterious circumstances and that Rodya had many very powerful enemies, to the point that he had been forced into hiding. As for his future career, she was certain it would prove quite brilliant, once certain hostile circumstances had passed; she assured Razumikhin that with time her son would even become a statesman, as his article and brilliant literary gifts indicated so clearly. She could barely put the article down; she even read it out loud and all but slept with it. Yet the question 'Where's Rodya?' hardly ever escaped her lips, though it was perfectly obvious that everyone was avoiding the subject in her presence – which in itself should have aroused her suspicions. Eventually, Pulkheria Alexandrovna's peculiar silence on certain points began to frighten the others. For example, she wouldn't even complain that he hadn't sent a single letter, whereas before, in her little town, it was the hope that a letter from darling Rodya might be on its way that kept her going. This last circumstance was simply inexplicable and worried Dunya deeply; her mother, it occurred to her, probably had some dreadful foreboding about Rodya's fate and feared to ask too many questions, lest she learn something even more dreadful. In any case, Dunya could see quite clearly that Pulkheria Alexandrovna was not in her right mind.

Once or twice, though, she herself broached topics that made it impossible, when replying, not to mention Rodya's exact whereabouts; and when these replies inevitably proved unsatisfactory and suspicious, she would suddenly become extraordinarily sad, sullen and silent, and would remain in that state for a very long time. Dunya finally realized how hard it was to keep lying and making things up, and decided it would be better simply to say nothing at all on certain points; but it was becoming ever more obvious that her poor mother suspected something dreadful. Dunya remembered her brother saying that Mother had heard her raving the night before that last, fateful day, after her row with Svidrigailov: might she have caught something? Often, sometimes after several days and even weeks of sullen, gloomy

silence and wordless tears, the ailing woman would become almost
hysterically animated and suddenly start talking, with barely a pause,
about her son, her hopes, the future . . . Her fantasies could be very
strange indeed. They humoured her and encouraged her, and she herself, perhaps, could see very well that she was being encouraged and
merely humoured, but still she went on talking . . .

The sentence followed five months after the criminal's confession.
Razumikhin went to see him in prison whenever he could. Sonya did
the same. Then, finally, came the hour of parting. Dunya swore to her
brother that it was not forever; Razumikhin did the same. A plan had
lodged itself firmly in Razumikhin's hot, young head: to try, over the
next three to four years, to lay at least the foundations of their future
income, to put at least a certain amount of money aside and move to
Siberia, where the soil was rich in every sense of the word, and where
workers, people and capital were in short supply; to set up home there,
in the very same town where Rodya would be, and . . . to begin a new
life all together. Saying goodbye, they were all in tears. During the
last few days Raskolnikov had been very pensive, kept asking about
his mother and worried about her constantly. In fact, he tormented
himself so much about her that Dunya became alarmed. Learning in
detail about his mother's morbid mood, he became very gloomy. For
some reason he was always especially untalkative with Sonya. With
the help of the money left to her by Svidrigailov, Sonya had been ready
and waiting, for some time now, to follow the party of convicts with
which he would be sent. Not a word had been said about this between
herself and Raskolnikov; but both knew that this was how it would
be. At the final leave-taking he smiled strangely at the passionate as-
surances given by his sister and Razumikhin about the happy life
ahead of them after his release, and predicted that his mother's illness
would soon end in disaster. Finally, he and Sonya left.

Two months later, Dunechka and Razumikhin were married. The
wedding was a sad, quiet affair. Among the guests were Porfiry Petrovich and Zosimov. Throughout this period Razumikhin bore a look
of unshakeable resolve. Dunya was unquestioning in her faith that he
would carry out all his intentions, and how could she not be? There
was no mistaking his iron will. He also began attending university
lectures again, so as to complete his studies. Both were constantly
hatching plans for the future, and both were set on moving to Siberia
in five years' time. Until then, they were counting on Sonya . . .

Pulkheria Alexandrovna gladly gave her blessing to her daughter's marriage; but after the wedding she seemed to become even sadder and more preoccupied. To offer her at least a moment's relief, Razumikhin told her, among other things, about the student and his decrepit father, about how Rodya was burned and even fell ill after rescuing two infants the previous year. Both these facts brought Pulkheria Alexandrovna's already unsettled mind to a pitch of near ecstasy. She couldn't stop talking about them, even with strangers in the street (though Dunya accompanied her everywhere). On the omnibus, in shops, wherever she could grab anyone's attention, she would steer the conversation to her son, to his article, to how he helped a student, was burned in a fire, etcetera. Dunechka couldn't think how to restrain her. Leaving aside all the dangers of such an ecstatic, morbid state of mind, there was the disastrous possibility of someone mentioning the name Raskolnikov in connection with the trial and talking about it. Pulkheria Alexandrovna even found out the address of the mother of the two infants rescued in the fire and was determined to go and see her. Eventually, her anxiety reached extreme proportions. Sometimes she would suddenly start crying, often she would fall ill and start raving. One morning she announced that, according to her calculations, Rodya should soon be arriving; that she remembered how, when saying goodbye to her, he himself mentioned that they should expect him back in precisely nine months' time. She began tidying up the apartment and preparing for the reunion, decorating the room set aside for him (her own), dusting off the furniture, washing and hanging new curtains, etcetera. Dunya was alarmed, but said nothing and even helped her prepare the room for her brother. After a restless day of ceaseless fantasies, joyous daydreams and tears, she fell ill overnight; the next morning she was already running a fever and raving, began shaking and shivering. Two weeks later she died. In her delirium, words slipped out to suggest that she suspected far more about her son's dreadful fate than they had even thought possible.

Raskolnikov did not learn about his mother's death for some time, even though correspondence with Petersburg had been established from the very beginning of his confinement in Siberia. It was arranged through Sonya, who wrote a punctual letter to Petersburg once a month, addressing it to Razumikhin, and once a month received a punctual reply. At first her letters struck Dunya and Razumikhin as a little dry and unsatisfactory; but in the end both came to the conclusion that there could be no better way of writing them, because from them the fullest and most precise picture began to emerge of the fate of their unfortunate brother. Sonya's letters were filled with the most ordinary reality, with the simplest and clearest description of all the conditions of Raskolnikov's life in penal servitude. There was nothing here about her hopes, no conjectures about the future, no account of her own feelings. Instead of attempts to explain his mental state and his whole inner life, there were facts and facts alone: his own words, detailed reports about the state of his health, accounts of what he wanted at their last meeting, what he asked for, what instructions he gave her, and so on. All these reports were set out in the minutest detail. In the end, the image of the unfortunate brother emerged all by itself, precisely and clearly delineated; here, there could be no scope for error: just one true fact after another.

But Dunya and her husband could draw scant comfort from these reports, especially at the beginning. Sonya kept writing that he was always sullen, untalkative and barely interested in the news she passed on to him whenever she received a letter; that he would sometimes ask about Mother; and that when, seeing that he was already guessing the truth, she finally told him about her death, she found, to her astonishment, that even this did not appear to affect him greatly, or so it seemed from the outside. She wrote, among other things, that however self-absorbed he might have become and however much he might have closed himself off from everyone, his attitude towards his new life was straightforward and simple; he understood his situation perfectly well, expected no sudden improvements, entertained no frivolous hopes (as others in his situation are so prone to do) and found almost nothing to surprise him about his new surroundings, which were so different from anything he had known before. His health, she wrote, was satisfactory. He would go out to work without trying to shirk it and without going out of his way to find more. He barely noticed the food, but it was so bad, except on Sundays and holidays, that in the end he willingly took some money from Sonya to make his own tea once a day; as for everything else, he asked her not to go to any trouble, assuring her that all this concern for him only served to annoy him. Sonya added that he lived in a dormitory with everyone else; that she had not seen the barracks from the inside, but inferred that they were cramped, horrid and unhealthy; that he slept on a plank bed, spreading thick felt beneath him, and refused to try anything else. But it was not on account of any preconceived plan or intention that he lived in this coarse and beggarly way; no, it was simply because of his inattentive, indifferent attitude to his own fate. Sonya wrote quite bluntly that not only did he show no interest in her visits, especially at the beginning, he even became almost annoyed with her, was untalkative and even rude; in the end, though, these meetings became a habit for him and almost a need, to the point that he became quite despondent when she was taken ill for a few days and was unable to visit. They saw each other on rest days at the prison gates or in the guardhouse, where he would be summoned to her for a few minutes; on weekdays, when he was out working, she would come to find him in the workshops or at the brick factories or in the sheds on the bank of the Irtysh. As for her own news, Sonya informed them that she had even managed to make some acquaintances and patrons in the town; that she had taken up sewing and that since there was barely a single seamstress in the whole town she had become indispensable in many homes; the only thing she omitted was that through her Raskolnikov, too, had come under the authorities' protection, his workload had been lightened, and so on. Eventually (after Dunya detected a particular note of anxiety and alarm in Sonya's most recent letters), news arrived that he was shunning everyone, that the convicts in the prison had not taken kindly to him, that he was silent for days at a time and was becoming very pale. Suddenly, in her last letter, Sonya wrote that he had fallen very seriously ill and was laid up in hospital, in the convict ward . . .

II

He'd been sick for some time; but it wasn't the horror of convict life, the forced labour, the food, the shaven head or the patched-together clothes that broke him: oh, what were all these torments and hardships to him? In fact, he was glad to have work to do: exhausting himself physically, he at least earned himself a few hours' untroubled sleep. And what did the food matter to him – this cabbage soup without meat, only cockroaches? Many times as a student, in his previous life, he hadn't even had that. His clothing was warm and well suited to his way of life. He couldn't even feel his shackles. Was he to be ashamed of his shaven head and his half-and-half jacket?[4] Before whom? Before Sonya? Sonya was afraid of him. Was he to feel ashamed before *her*?

And why not? He felt ashamed even before Sonya, whom he tormented in return with his rudeness and disdain. But it wasn't his shaven head and his shackles he was ashamed of: it was his pride that had been badly wounded; it was this that had made him ill. Oh, if only he could have blamed himself, how happy he would have been! He could have put up with anything then, even shame and disgrace. But he judged himself harshly, and his hardened conscience failed to find any especially dreadful guilt in his past, except perhaps for the kind of simple *blunder* that might have happened to anyone. What shamed him was precisely the fact that he, Raskolnikov, had come to grief so blindly, so hopelessly, so stupidly, by some decree of blind fate, and now he had to submit and resign himself to the 'absurdity' of such a decree, if he wanted to give himself any peace at all.

In the present: pointless, purposeless anxiety; in the future: an endless sacrifice by which nothing was to be gained – this was what the world had in store for him. And what did it matter that in eight years' time he'd only be thirty-two and life could begin again? Why live? What would he have to live for? To aim for? Live to exist? But hadn't he been prepared even before, on a thousand occasions, to give up his existence for an idea, a hope, even a fantasy? Existence alone had never been enough for him; he'd always wanted more. And perhaps the only reason he'd considered himself a man to whom more was permitted than to others was the very strength of his desires.

If only fate could bring him remorse – burning remorse that breaks the heart into pieces, that drives away sleep; the kind of remorse whose dreadful torments yield visions of the noose, the whirlpool! Oh, how glad he would have been! Torments and tears – that, too, is life. But he felt no remorse about his crime.

At least then he could have raged at his own stupidity, just as before he had raged at the hideous, idiotic deeds that brought him to prison. But now that he was here, in prison, *at liberty*, he reconsidered all his previous deeds, all over again, and found them not nearly as stupid and hideous as they had seemed to him during that fateful time, before.

'How, how,' he thought, 'was my idea any more stupid than all the other ideas and theories that have swarmed around, colliding with one another, since the beginning of time? You need only take an independent, broad view of things, free from the usual influences, and my idea, needless to say, won't seem remotely . . . strange. Oh, men of wisdom, who deny everything[5] except money – why do you stop halfway?

'Really, what is it about my deed that they find so hideous?' he asked himself. 'That it was evil? What does that mean – an "evil deed"? My conscience is untroubled. Yes, of course, a criminal act has been committed; yes, of course, the letter of the law has been violated and blood's been shed – so take my head for the letter of the law . . . and that's your lot! And, of course, plenty of humanity's benefactors, who never inherited power but grabbed it for themselves, should also have been executed after taking their very first step. But those people coped with the step that they took, which is why *they are right*, but I couldn't cope with mine, so I had no right to take it.'

That was the only crime he acknowledged: that he hadn't coped and had turned himself in.

Another thought also brought him pain: why hadn't he killed himself back then? Why had he stood over the river and preferred to turn himself in? Was the desire to live really so strong, was it really so hard to overcome? Hadn't Svidrigailov overcome it, despite his fear of death?

He tormented himself with this question, incapable of understanding that even then, standing over the river, he might already have sensed a deep falsehood in himself and his convictions. He couldn't understand that this premonition might have been the herald of a future breaking point in his existence, his future resurrection, his future view of life.

He was more inclined to see in all this only the dull yoke of instinct, which it was not for him to break, and over which he, yet again, was unable to step (being weak and worthless). Observing his fellow prisoners he was astonished at how much they, too, loved life, how they all cherished it! In fact, he had the impression that in prison life is loved, valued and cherished even more than at liberty. What dreadful hardships and torments some of them had endured – for instance, the tramps! Could one single ray of sunshine really mean so much to them, or a thick forest, or a cold spring in the back of beyond, which the tramp spotted some two years before and which, like a lover, he yearns to see again and dreams about, with green grass all around, a bird singing in the bush? Looking deeper, he saw instances yet harder to explain.

In the prison, in his immediate surroundings, there was, of course, much that he failed to notice, and didn't even wish to notice. He lived with eyes lowered: looking up seemed loathsome, unbearable. In the end, though, much began to astonish him, and almost against his will he began to notice things that previously he hadn't even suspected. In general, what astonished him most was the dreadful, unbridgeable gulf that lay between him and all these commoners. He and they seemed to belong to different nations. He and they looked at each other with mistrust and hostility. He knew and understood the general causes of this separation; but never before had he acknowledged that these causes might really be so deep, so potent. There were Polish convicts,[6] too; political criminals. They considered the commoners to be nothing more than ignoramuses and slaves, and looked down on them with contempt; but Raskolnikov could not: to him it was clear that these ignoramuses were in many ways far more intelligent than those very same Poles. There were Russians, too, whose contempt for the peasants knew no bounds – one former officer and two seminarians; their error did not escape Raskolnikov either.

He himself was disliked and shunned by everyone. Eventually, he even began to be hated. Why? He did not know. The ones who looked down on him, who mocked him and mocked his crime, were far more criminal than he.

'You're gentry!' they'd say to him. 'What was a gentry boy like you doing with an axe?'[7]

In the second week of Lent his turn came to prepare for the Sacraments, along with everyone else in his barracks. They all went to the church together to pray.[8] One day an argument flared up. Why? He himself did not know. But they fell on him all at once in a frenzy.

'Atheist! You don't believe in God!' they shouted at him. 'You should be killed!'

He'd never spoken with them about God or faith, but they wanted to kill him for his atheism; he said nothing in reply. One convict was on the point of throwing himself on him in sheer fury; Raskolnikov waited for him calmly and in silence: his eyebrows did not stir; not one muscle twitched on his face. A guard managed to put himself between him and the murderer just in time – or blood would have been shed.

There was one other question to which he could find no answer: why had they all become so fond of Sonya? She never sought their approval and they saw her rarely, sometimes only when they were out working, when she came to him for no more than a minute. And yet they all already knew her, knew that she'd *followed him*, knew how she lived and where she lived. She gave them no money, did them no special favours. Only once, at Christmas, did she bring alms for the entire prison: pies and white buns. But little by little closer ties began to form between them and Sonya: she wrote letters for them to their families and posted them. At their request these relatives, on arriving in town, would leave things for them with Sonya, even money. Their wives and lovers knew her and called on her. And whenever she appeared at the place where Raskolnikov was working or met a party of convicts going out to work they all doffed their caps and bowed. 'Dear Sofya Semyonovna, dear mother, gentle, merciful mother!' these coarse, branded convicts would say to this skinny little creature. She smiled and returned their bows and they all liked it when she smiled at them. They even liked her gait, turned around to watch her walk away and praised her; they even praised her for being so little, and could never praise her enough. Some even went to her to be treated when they were sick.

He spent the whole of the last period of Lent and Easter Sunday laid up in hospital. Recovering, he recalled what he'd dreamt while feverish and delirious. In his sickness he'd imagined the entire world condemned to some terrible, unheard-of pestilence, advancing on Europe from deepest Asia. Everyone was to die, apart from the few, very few, who'd been chosen. New trichinae[9] had appeared, microscopic beings that were entering human bodies. But these beings were spirits, endowed with intelligence and will. People who took them into their bodies immediately became possessed and went mad. But never, ever had people thought themselves as intelligent and as certain of the truth as those who had been infected. Never had they considered their verdicts, their scientific conclusions, their moral convictions and beliefs more unshakeable. Entire villages, entire towns and peoples were being infected and driven to madness. Everyone was panicking and no one could understand anyone else; each man thought that he and he alone possessed the truth, and found the sight of others a torment; he beat his breast, wept and wrung his hands. No one knew whom to bring to justice and how, couldn't agree what was bad and what was good, whom to charge and whom to acquit. People were killing one another out of meaningless spite. They mobilized entire armies, but no sooner did these armies set out than they began to tear themselves to pieces; breaking rank, the soldiers attacked, hacked, stabbed, bit and ate each other. In towns, the tocsin was sounded from dawn till dusk: everyone was summoned, but who was doing the summoning and why? No one knew and everyone was panicking. The most ordinary trades were abandoned, because every man had his own ideas, his own solutions, and agreement was impossible; agriculture ceased. Here and there people gathered in groups, agreed on something, swore not to split up – then immediately embarked on something completely different from what they themselves had just proposed, began blaming, fighting and killing each other. Fires broke out; famine broke out. Everyone and everything was perishing. The pestilence[10] grew and spread, further and further. In the whole world there were only a few survivors; these were the pure and the chosen, those destined to begin a new race of people and a new life, to renew and purify the earth, but no one, anywhere, had seen these people, nor heard their words and voices.

Raskolnikov was tormented by the fact that this meaningless delirium echoed so sadly and so agonizingly in his memory; that the impression left by these fevered daydreams was taking so long to pass. It was already the second week after Easter, spring, the days warm and clear; in the prisoners' ward the windows (barred, with a guard below them) stood open. For the entire duration of his illness, Sonya had only been able to visit him twice; each time she'd had to beg for permission. Nevertheless, she came often to the hospital courtyard, especially towards evening, sometimes just to stand in the yard for a minute or two and look up at the windows of the ward, if only from afar. Once, towards evening, when he'd almost completely recovered, Raskolnikov fell asleep; waking up, he happened to go to the window and suddenly caught sight of Sonya in the distance, by the hospital gates. She was standing there as though she were waiting for something. At that moment, something seemed to pierce his heart; he shuddered and hastily retreated from the window. Sonya did not come the next day, or the day after that. He noticed how anxiously he was waiting for her. Finally, he was discharged. Entering the prison, he learned from the convicts that Sofya Semyonovna had fallen ill and was staying at home.

Deeply worried, he sent someone to find out how she was. Her illness, he was soon told, was not dangerous. Learning in her turn of his concern and distress, Sonya sent him a note in pencil, telling him that she felt a great deal better, that it was just a bit of cold and that she would come to see him at work very, very soon. When he read this note, his heart throbbed with pain.

Another clear, warm day. Early that morning, at about six, he went out to work on the river bank, in a shed where a kiln was set up for baking and pounding alabaster. Only two other workers went out with him. One of the convicts took a guard and went back with him to the fortress to fetch a tool; the other began preparing firewood and loading the kiln. Raskolnikov went outside, sat down on the logs stacked up by the shed and looked out at the broad, deserted river. A wide vista opened up from the tall bank. The sound of singing just reached him from the other side. Over there, on the sun-drenched, boundless steppe, the black dots of nomadic yurts were faintly visible. Over there was freedom; over there lived people quite unlike the ones living here; over there time itself seemed to have stopped, as if the ages of Abraham and his flocks had not yet passed. Raskolnikov sat and watched, neither moving nor looking away; his thoughts shaded into daydreams and contemplation; he wasn't thinking about anything, yet something troubled and tormented him.

Suddenly, there was Sonya beside him. She'd approached with barely a sound and sat down next to him. It was still very early; the morning chill had not yet softened. She was wearing her wretched, old burnous and the green shawl.[11] Her face – thin, pale, pinched – still bore the signs of her illness. She gave him a warm, joyful smile but, as usual, offered her hand to him timidly.

She always offered her hand to him timidly and sometimes wouldn't offer it at all, as if scared he might reject it. He always took it with a kind of disgust, always greeted her with a kind of annoyance, and sometimes he remained stubbornly silent all the while she was with him. On occasions, she trembled before him and left in deep sorrow. But now their hands did not part; he cast her a quick, fleeting glance, said nothing and lowered his eyes to the ground. They were alone; no one could see them. The guard had turned away.

How it happened he himself did not know, but suddenly something swept him up and hurled him at her feet. He wept, hugging her knees. At first she was terrified and her whole face went numb. She leapt to her feet and looked at him, shaking all over. But there and then, in that same instant, she understood everything. Her eyes lit up with endless happiness; she'd understood, and could no longer doubt, that he loved her, loved her endlessly, and that the moment had finally come . . .

They wanted to talk, but could not. Tears were in their eyes. They were pale and thin; but in these sick, pale faces there already shone the dawn of a renewed future, of full resurrection into new life. Love had resurrected them, and the heart of each contained inexhaustible springs of life for the heart of the other.

They resolved to wait and be patient. There were seven more years to go. How much unbearable torment still lay ahead of them? How much endless happiness? But he'd been raised to life and he knew it. He felt it fully with his whole renewed being, while she – well, what was her life but his?

That evening, when the barracks had been locked for the night, Raskolnikov lay on his bunk and thought of her. During the day he even had the impression that all the convicts, his former enemies, were already looking at him differently. He even began talking to them himself, and they responded with affection. He recalled this now, but actually, wasn't it all as it should be? Shouldn't everything be different now?

It was her he thought of. He remembered how he'd kept tearing and rending her heart; remembered her pale, thin face; yet now even these memories barely tormented him: he knew with what endless love he would now redeem all her sufferings.

And anyway, what were they, all these torments of the past? Yes, *all* of them! Everything, even his crime, even his sentence and exile, now seemed, in this first surge, somehow alien and strange, as if it were not even him they had happened to. But he was unable, that evening, to think long and hard, to focus his mind on any one thing; besides, he couldn't have resolved anything now by conscious effort; he could only feel. Dialectics had given way to life, and something quite different had to work itself out in his conscious mind.

Under his pillow lay the Gospels.[12] He picked the book up without thinking. It belonged to her, the very same book from which she had read to him about the raising of Lazarus. During his first days in prison he thought she would torture him with religion, keep on about the Gospels and ply him with books. But to his utter astonishment she hadn't once mentioned it, hadn't even offered him the Gospels. It was he who had asked her for the book not long before he fell sick, and she brought it to him without saying a word. He still had not opened it.

He didn't open it now, either, but a thought flashed through him: 'How can her beliefs not be my beliefs too now? Or at least her feelings, her strivings . . .'

She, too, had felt restless all day and she even fell ill again overnight. But she was so happy she was almost scared. Seven years, *only* seven years! At the beginning of their happiness, at certain moments, both were ready to see these seven years as seven days.[13] He didn't even know that his new life was not being given to him for free, that it would still cost him dear, that it would have to be paid for with a great, future deed . . .

But here a new story begins: the story of a man's gradual renewal and gradual rebirth, of his gradual crossing from one world to another, of his acquaintance with a new, as yet unknown reality. That could be a subject for another tale – our present one has ended.

Preface to the Notes

The following abbreviations are used for the sources cited most often:

BT   Boris Tikhomirov, *'Lazar'! Gryadi von': Roman F. M. Dostoevskogo 'Prestuplenie i nakazanie' v sovremennom
prochtenii: Kniga-kommentarii* ['Lazarus! Come Forth':
F. M. Dostoyevsky's novel *Crime and Punishment* Read in
the Light of Its Time: A Commentary] (St Petersburg: Serebryanyi vek, 2006).

KL   Kenneth Lantz, *The Dostoevsky Encyclopedia* (Westport,
CT: Greenwood, 2004).

PSS   The annotations to *Crime and Punishment* supplied in
Volume 7 of the Soviet-era Academy of Sciences edition of
Dostoyevsky's complete works: F. M. Dostoyevsky, *Polnoe
sobranie sochinenii v tridtsati tomakh* (Leningrad: Nauka, 1972–90), vol. 7 (1973).

SB   S. V. Belov, *Roman F. M. Dostoevskogo 'Prestuplenie i nakazanie': Kommentarii* [F. M. Dostoyevsky's Novel *Crime
and Punishment*: A Commentary] (Moscow: Prosvesh-
chenie, 1979; rev. edn. 1985).

All biblical quotations in the Notes are given in the King James Version.

Notes

PART ONE

1. *S——y Lane ... K——n Bridge*: The partial or total concealment of place names, characteristic of much Russian nineteenth-century fiction, is employed inconsistently and enigmatically in *Crime and Punishment*. In these notes only the most important (and least ambiguous) of these concealed locations will be deciphered. According to Dostoyevsky's second wife, Anna Grigoryevna, the locations in question here are Stolyarnyi Lane and Kokushkin Bridge in the crowded district of St Petersburg around Haymarket Square (on the topography of *Crime and Punishment*, see Introduction, II). Indeed, it is possible that Dostoyevsky imagined his protagonist living in the same building where he himself rented an apartment while working on the novel, on the corner of Stolyarnyi Lane and what is now Kaznacheiskaya Street. Another strong possibility is the building at the corner of Stolyarnyi and Grazhdanskaya Street. Vistors to St Petersburg will find memorial plaques at both these addresses (*BT*).

2. *hypochondria*: Closely allied with melancholia in the medical discourse of the time; indeed, Dostoyevsky diagnosed himself as having been 'melancholic and hypochondriac' as a young man. 'The two basic symptoms of melancholia were exaggeration of simple events into singular and ominous occurrences, and episodes of unfounded fear', while 'hypochondria was generally based on real physical complaints, with effects greatly exaggerated by the patient', wrote the late James L. Rice. 'Today Dostoevsky's hypochondria and melancholia might be diagnosed as different degrees of depression', Rice, *Dostoevsky and the Healing Art* (Ann Arbor, Michigan: Ardis, 1985), pp. 114–15.

3. *a new word*: The Russian expression *skazat' novoe slovo*, meaning 'to say something new' (in, for example, a branch of science), is more

idiomatic than its literal English equivalent ('to utter a new word'), which has been retained here and throughout the text for its various connotations, especially as regards the prevalent contrast between 'words' and 'deeds'. Dostoyevsky himself was of the view that Russia had produced three indisputable geniuses who had said 'a new word': Mikhail Lomonosov (1711–65), Alexander Pushkin (1799–1837) and, 'in part', Nikolai Gogol (1809–52); see the entry on Pushkin in *KL*.

4. *King Pea*: Tsar Gorokh (literally, 'Tsar Pea') has his wife's head chopped off in a famous folktale, though he is also remembered as the 'Good Tsar Gorokh' who reigned over an idealized Russia. A striking oxymoron, 'Tsar Pea' eventually came to stand for something silly or nonsensical (*SB*); yet, as often in Dostoyevsky, the use of a familiar image or phrase hides depths of meaning and allusion. In an article of 1981 J. L. Rice noted that the very name 'Tsar Gorokh' is 'a perfect, ironic representation of Raskolnikov's grandiosely unbalanced Napoleonic ambition'; the essay is collected in Rice, *Who Was Dostoevsky?* (Oakland, California: Berkeley Slavic Specialties, 2011).

5. *a top hat, a Zimmerman*: The merchant Karl Zimmerman owned a hat factory as well as a shop on the fashionable Nevsky Prospect (*BT*). This episode introduces for the first time the voice of the 'common people' (*narod*), whose interventions will offer a chorus-like commentary on Raskolnikov's actions and fate.

6. *the Ditch . . . ——a Street*: On all but one occasion throughout the novel the Yekaterinsky (Catherine) Canal, known since 1923 as the Griboyedov Canal, is referred to not by the impressive, foreign-sounding word *kanal*, but by the pejorative *kanava* (ditch). A filthy, sewer-like waterway at the time of the novel's composition, the Ditch is at the heart of its topography; ——a Street is probably Srednyaya Podyacheskaya Street. Here and throughout I follow Boris Tikhomirov's decoding of the novel's topography.

7. *courtyards*: The easily accessible, communicating courtyards characteristic of St Petersburg have arch-like gateways at both ends – well-suited for criminal purposes. Raskolnikov's own courtyard, by contrast, appears to be an example of the high, self-enclosed yard commonly compared by Petersburgers to a 'well'.

8. *caretakers*: In Tsarist Russia the *dvornik* (literally, 'yard-man') was responsible not just for keeping courtyards swept and tidy, but for maintaining order in the buildings themselves and reporting any malfeasance to the police.

9. *father*: The word *batyushka*, a now old-fashioned term of address that is both respectful and familiar, literally means 'little father' and has a broad scope of reference that includes priests and tsars. In view of the centrality of the theme of paternity (and family ties in general) to *Crime and Punishment*, the literal meaning has been retained, here and subsequently.

10. *two nice little notes*: Two one-rouble banknotes, yellow in colour.

11. *ten copecks a rouble each month*: Until 1864 a strict limit was imposed on the interest that could be charged on loans, but from 1865, when Dostoyevsky began work on the novel, this no longer applied, and the writer was quick to seize on this further symptom of a new capitalist order. 'The usurer Alyona Ivanovna [. . .] was an essentially new phenomenon of Petersburg life' (*BT*).

12. *tradesman*: The 'tradesmen' – also sometimes translated, with etymological accuracy, as 'townsmen' (*meshchane*) – were the lowest urban estate, later famous as the 'petty bourgeoisie'.

13. *All year long . . . love of old*: A variation of a popular song about the adventures of a village lad in the capital, transposed from Nevsky Prospect to the less glamorous district in which *Crime and Punishment* unfolds (*BT*).

14. *titular counsellor*: A lowly position in the civil service, ninth in the fourteen-grade 'Table of Ranks' instituted by Peter the Great.

15. *former student*: This phrase, unusual in English, defined the bearer's official status until he found employment.

16. *political economy*: A reference to the theories of Adam Smith (1723–90), Thomas Malthus (1766–1834) and others. Protracted polemics were waged on this issue in the Russian literary journals in 1862, not least in *Time*, the journal run by Dostoyevsky and his brother (*BT*). In his *Letters from France and Italy* (1855) the exile Alexander Herzen (1812–70) described political economy as an 'abstract science of wealth' that treated people as 'organic machines' and society as a 'factory'. Dostoyevsky would have agreed, though here, as often, he appears to be criticizing not just foreign ideas themselves but their caricatured reception on Russian soil.

17. *yellow ticket*: The medical certificate given to prostitutes in exchange for their passport was commonly referred to as the 'yellow ticket', owing to its colour. This certificate gave prostitutes the right to work, while also enabling the state to track their changes of address and state of health. (*BT*)

18. *Behold the Man!*: The words of Pontius Pilate when Jesus came before him wearing a crown of thorns (John 19:5). In addition to direct quotation, Marmeladov's speech throughout this chapter is littered with

biblical allusions, sometimes couched in the high style of Old Church Slavonic. The 'wagging of heads', for example, occurs in both the Psalms and Matthew's Gospel, while the phrase 'all that was hidden is made manifest' is closely modelled on verses in Mark (4:22) and Luke (8:17).

19. *chilly little corner*: The letting of 'corners' rather than entire rooms to impecunious tenants was a characteristic feature of mid-nineteenth-century St Petersburg. It was also the subject of a memorable sketch by the celebrated poet Nikolai Nekrasov (1821–78) entitled 'The Petersburg Corners' and included in Nekrasov's anthology *The Physiology of St Petersburg* (1845, in two volumes), recently translated by Thomas Gaiton Marullo. The sketch begins with a notice pinned to the gate of a house: 'FER [*sic*] RENT: KORNER [*sic*] TO LET, SECOND YARD, CELLAR'. The narrator goes in to find a cellar room crowded with colourful tenants, including new arrivals from the villages looking for work and a disgraced former teacher in a green coat, dismissed from his job for excessive drinking. The teacher bears a striking resemblance in biography, appearance and gestures to Dostoyevsky's Marmeladov: 'the green man presented a sharp picture to the eye. He was not unlike an actor who has carried some favourite and well-learned role into life. His movements were comic to the point of caricature, inevitable for a man unsteady on his legs. There was also something staid about them, though, akin to a feeling of personal dignity and worth. [. . .] There was a certain incoherence in the green man that made him extremely funny'; quoted from *Petersburg: The Physiology of a City*, trans. Thomas Gaiton Marullo (Evanston, Illinois: Northwestern University Press, 2009), pp. 131, 145.

20. *the pas de châle*: According to R. M. Kirsanova, a historian of dress, the 'dance with the shawl became popular in Russian schools for young ladies at the beginning of the nineteenth century, coinciding with the fashion for Persian shawls; its popularity, as a demonstration of grace and elegance, continued for some time thereafter' (*BT*).

21. *Cyrus the Great*: King of Persia in the sixth century BC. Cyrus's conquests included the Median, Lydian and Neo-Babylonian empires.

22. *Lewes's Physiology*: George Henry Lewes's *Physiology of Common Life* (1859) appeared in Russian translation in 1861–2 and rapidly gained popularity among young readers of a materialist bent and young female nihilists in particular (*PSS*). This reference was found provocative by one *nigilistka*, who saw in it an attempt on the author's part to blame 'liberal ideas and the natural sciences' for Sonya's descent into prostitu-

tion. Dostoyevsky had Lewes's book in his library in the early 1860s and later bought a second copy after he lost the first (*BT*).

23. *drap de dames*: 'A very fine type of fabric, which is only half-milled', according to the *Bibliothèque universelle des sciences, belles-lettres et arts* (Volume 11, 1826, p. 30).

24. *as wax melteth*: A compliment that becomes decidedly equivocal when set against its biblical origin (Psalm 68:2): 'As smoke is driven away, so drive them away: as wax melteth before the fire, so let the wicked perish at the presence of God' (*BT*).

25. *'Little Farm'*: Based on a poem (1839) by Alexei Koltsov (1809–42), this song became especially popular in the 1860s (*SB*). Performed here by a child, the poem treats, in a seemingly naive way, the bawdy theme of a young widow being visited by three admirers: a fisherman, a merchant and a dashing young gallant, who, it seems, burns down the farm in a fit of jealousy.

26. *like a thief in the night*: Another double-edged biblical allusion: 'But the day of the Lord will come as a thief in the night; in the which the heavens shall pass away with a great noise, and the elements shall melt with fervent heat, the earth also and the works that are therein shall be burned up' (2 Peter 3:10).

27. *immaculate*: Prostitutes on the 'yellow ticket' had to present themselves for weekly medical check-ups (*BT*).

28. *Thy kingdom come*: This invocation of the Lord's Prayer follows echoes of starkly contrasting biblical passages, notably Jesus' comments about a fallen woman saved by her faith ('Wherefore I say unto thee, Her sins, which are many, are forgiven; for she loved much', Luke 7:47) and Revelation 14:9–10: 'And the third angel followed them, saying with a loud voice, If any man worship the beast and his image, and receive his mark in his forehead, or in his hand, The same shall drink of the wine of the wrath of God, which is poured out without mixture into the cup of his indignation; and he shall be tormented with fire and brimstone in the presence of the holy angels, and in the presence of the Lamb'. The latter quotation suggests some of the rich symbolism of alcohol in this chapter.

29. *papirosi*: The humble *papirosa* (plural, *papirosi*) appears in the *OED* as, accurately enough, 'A type of Russian unfiltered cigarette consisting of a tube of paper or cardboard, a short section at one end of which is filled with tobacco.' I have kept the word throughout this translation.

30. *monomaniacs*: Monomania, writes J. L. Rice, was seen at the time as 'a fluctuating disorder, equivalent to manic psychosis in the present terminology'

(*Dostoevsky and the Healing Art*, p. 116). It was of great interest to the French school of psychiatry with whose ideas Dostoyevsky would have been familiar. 'Esquirol wrote that in monomania the ill person might suffer from loss of will, perhaps only briefly, perhaps under the intermittent influence of hallucinatory voices. Persons thus afflicted became "the *homo duplex* of Saint Paul and Buffon: impelled to evil by one motive and restrained by another"' (ibid., pp. 115–16). Jacques-Joseph Moreau (1804–84), a student of Jean-Étienne Dominique Esquirol (1772–1840), 'saw the monomaniac as the most salient modern type [. . .] because in monomania the individual retains consciousness of the mental disorder' (ibid., p. 157).

31. *R—— province*: The province of Ryazan, located about one hundred miles south-east of Moscow. M. S. Altman argued that this must be Ryazan Province, 'not only because there was no other province in Russia at the time beginning with R, but also because Dostoyevsky had particular grounds for linking Raskolnikov's original place of residence with a province teeming with *raskolniki* [religious dissenters; see List of Characters]' (*SB*). The relevance of this connection will grow in the course of the novel.

32. *unable to support yourself*: University students were expected to pay fees of fifty roubles a year (*BT*).

33. *smearing . . . with tar*: According to the ethnographer Pavel Melnikov (1818–83; pen name Andrei Pechersky), 'this was considered the greatest insult for the whole family and for the girl in particular. A girl whose gates had been tarred would never be taken in marriage' (*BT*).

34. *convictions of our newest generations*: A reference to the 'nihilists' of the time who denied the soul, God and traditional values, hence the contrast with Luzhin's 'positive' features. The sentence might suggest an endemic paradox: 'nihilism' could also be referred to as 'positivism', on account of its allegedly scientific method and principles. In a letter to his publisher Katkov of April 1866 (during work on this novel, and in the wake of the repressions following Dmitry Karakozov's failed attempt to assassinate the Tsar), Dostoyevsky wrote: 'if they, the Nihilists, were given freedom of speech . . . they would make all Russia laugh by the *positive* explanation of their teachings. While now they are given the appearance of sphinxes'; see the discussion in Joseph Frank, *Dostoevsky: A Writer in His Time* (Princeton: Princeton University Press, 2010), pp. 464–7.

35. *private attorney*: An entirely new profession in Russia, made possible by the legal reforms of 1864. It is characteristic of Luzhin, a man on the make with modest education, to want to take advantage of this opportunity without delay.

36. *the Senate*: The Governing Senate in St Petersburg was Imperial Russia's highest judicial body, supervising the activity of all legal institutions and serving as the highest court of appeal (*SB*).

37. *the Feast of Our Lady*: The popular term for the Feast of the Dormition of the Mother of God (15 August), preceded in the Orthodox calendar by two weeks of fasting.

38. *V—— Prospect*: Voznesensky Prospect.

39. *Avdotya Romanovna*: A strikingly formal use of his sister Dunya's full first name and patronymic. See Note on Names.

40. *beautiful souls steeped in Schiller*: Schillerian idealism is a constant butt of irony in Dostoyevsky's fiction, yet the German Romantic Johann Schiller (1759–1805) was a writer of the first importance to him. Aged ten, Dostoyevsky was overwhelmed by a performance in Moscow of *Die Raüber* (*The Robbers*, 1781), a play that would loom large fifty years later in his last novel *The Brothers Karamazov* (1879–80). In his *Letters on the Aesthetic Education of Man* (1795) Schiller claimed that 'it is through beauty that we arrive at freedom' (*KL*).

41. *St Anna in his buttonhole*: A decoration given for service to the state in military or civil employment. The Order of St Anna, First Class, was worn on a ribbon over the shoulder; Second Class on the neck (hence the title of Chekhov's short story 'Anna Around the Neck'); Third Class, as in this case, on a small ribbon on the chest. It was a fairly modest decoration, in keeping with Luzhin's rank as 'court counsellor' (seventh in the Table of Ranks).

42. *Schleswig-Holstein*: Disputed by Prussia, Denmark and Austria, these duchies were much in the news at the time of the novel's composition, before being eventually annexed by Prussia following the Austro-Prussian War (1866).

43. *Negroes ... Latvians*: American Negroes and Latvian peasants were widely discussed in Russia in the late 1850s and early 1860s, and in both cases analogies were drawn with Russian serfs. In 1862 the Dostoyevsky brothers published, as an appendix to their journal *Time*, a translation of Richard Hildreth's anti-slavery novel *The White Slave; or, Memoirs of a Fugitive* (1852); also that year an article due to appear in the same journal was censored for expressing the thought 'that the plight of free Baltic peasants is even worse, and even less tolerable, than the life of our own [Russian] serfs' (*PSS*).

44. *lessons from the Jesuits*: Referring to the allegedly relativistic morality of the Roman Catholic order of the Society of Jesus (associated with the

maxim that 'the end justifies the means'), this continues the theme of
moral adaptation to circumstance that so preoccupies Raskolnikov (see
also Part Five, note 2). Dostoyevsky's own anti-Catholicism was by now
well known, especially following the Polish uprising of 1863–4.

45. *K—— Boulevard*: Konnogvardeisky (Horse Guard) Boulevard.

46. *Svidrigailov*: As well as being the name of the employers of Raskolnikov's sister (see Part One, Chapter III), Svidrigailov was a surname
familiar to Russian readers of the 1860s from the journal *The Spark*,
where the 'Svidrigailov' type was satirically presented as a provincial
'man of obscure origin with a filthy past and a repulsive personality that
is sickening to any fresh, honest gaze and worms its way into your soul'
(*BT*). In addition, according to Richard Peace, 'Svidrigaylov evokes
Svidrigaylo, a Lithuanian prince who was active during the fifteenth
century – so fateful for the Orthodox world. He may be taken as the
barbarian par excellence, the perpetrator of cynical sacrilege for the goal
of self-interest'; see *Fyodor Dostoevsky's Crime and Punishment: A
Casebook*, ed. Richard Peace (Oxford: Oxford University Press, 2006),
pp. 86, 100. Dostoyevsky's own family was descended from Lithuanian
nobility (on his father's side).

47. *Percentage*: A reference to the excitement caused in Russian intellectual
life by the publication in 1865 of a translation of *Sur l'homme et le
développement de ses facultés* (1835) by the Belgian 'father of statistics'
Adolphe Quetelet (1796–1874), and to the success of his German popu-
larizer Adolph Wagner (1835–1917), who thought that the quantity and
distribution of crimes, suicides, marriages and divorces in society could
be scientifically predicted with very high precision (*PSS*). It is also worth
noting the Russian word for moneylender occasionally used for Alyona
Ivanovna: *protsentshchitsa* (literally, 'percentage woman').

48. *the Islands*: The green 'Islands', still famous as a place for relaxation and
walks, are a small archipelago in the northern part of the Neva delta,
reached from the south by crossing Tuchkov Bridge and Petrovsky Island.

49. *kutya . . . a cross*: Brought to churches and graveyards on commemora-
tive occasions. Boris Tikhomirov notes Raskolnikov's 'astonishing [. . .]
childhood memory of the "sweetness of the cross"' (*BT*).

50. *horned headdress*: The *kichka* was a traditional form of headdress worn
by married Russian women on religious holidays (*SB*). It often had a
horn-like point on either side.

51. *clinging to every object they pass*: The first close echo of passages from a
novel of great importance to Dostoyevsky (and translated by his brother

at his initiative in 1860): *Le Dernier Jour d'un condamné* (*The Last Day of a Condemned Man*, 1829) by Victor Hugo (1802–85). Of relevance to Dostoyevsky's own experience in December 1849, as he prepared to face his imminent execution, the plight of Hugo's narrator is given paradoxical significance for Raskolnikov, who appears not to distinguish between his crime and his punishment (*PSS, BT*). Had Dostoyevsky persevered with his first drafts and published *Crime and Punishment* as a first-person narrative, the echoes of the notes of Hugo's 'condemned man' would have been even more striking.

52. *examining magistrate*: A new career possibility in Russia, following the legal reforms of 1864; modelled on the French *juge d'instruction*.

PART TWO

1. *bureau*: Each of St Petersburg's administrative units had one main 'police station' (*chast'*) and several smaller bureaus or offices (*kontory*).

2. *Laviza Ivanovna*: The lieutenant evidently finds the German lady's first name, Luiza, unbearably pretentious, given her profession and status, and rechristens her with a name that sounds both mocking and 'common' to the Russian ear. It will be repeated by other characters.

3. *Catherine Canal . . . Ditch*: One and the same waterway: see Part One, note 6.

4. *tomes on natural science*: In Russia the 1860s witnessed a publishing boom in the natural sciences, with many foreign books in the field translated for the first time and typically put out by publishers linked to the socialists and 'nihilists' with whom Dostoyevsky so often polemicized.

5. *is a woman a human being*: The craze for the natural sciences in the 1860s was related to the prominence of the 'Woman Question' (female emancipation, the relative status of women compared to men, the biology of women) as a bone of contention between the radical and conservative camps. Razumikhin's reference here is to G. Z. Yeliseyev's feuilleton 'Diverse Opinions: Are Women Human? Opinions Ancient and Modern', published in *The Contemporary* in 1861 (*PSS, BT*).

6. *the Radishchev of Geneva*: Alexander Radishchev (1749–1802), author of *A Journey from St Petersburg to Moscow*, critic of serfdom and autocracy and celebrated Siberian exile, was more 'the Rousseau of Russia' than Jean-Jacques Rousseau (1712–78), Radishchev's elder, was 'the Radishchev of Geneva', but the context of this inaccurate formulation is strictly commercial: an attempt to pitch a new title to the bookseller

Cherubimov. Rousseau had been praised by Nikolai Chernyshevsky (1828–89), Dostoyevsky's favourite intellectual target among the socialists, as a 'revolutionary democrat' in an article of 1860, and Rousseau's *Confessions* (1781–8) were republished in Russian translation in 1865, when Dostoyevsky began writing this novel (*BT*, *PSS*).

7. *the First Line*: Parallel streets ('Lines') are a topographic feature of Vasilyevsky Island, where Razumikhin lives (and where the university is still located today). The Lines stretch from the south to the north of the Island, crossing the three main avenues going east to west.

8. *Palace . . . cathedral's dome . . . chapel*: The sites mentioned in this passage are readily identifiable as the Winter Palace (home to the tsars and now to the Hermitage Museum), St Isaac's Cathedral off Nevsky Prospect, and a chapel named after Nicholas the Wonderworker on Nikolayevsky Bridge, which was St Petersburg's first permanent, cast-iron bridge over the Neva. The marble chapel was demolished in 1930 and the bridge rebuilt in 1936–8 (*BT*, *SB*).

9. *dumb, deaf spirit*: An allusion to an episode in Mark's Gospel. A father brings a possessed child to Jesus: 'And they brought him unto him: and when he saw him, straightway the spirit tare him; and he fell on the ground, and wallowed foaming. [. . .] When Jesus saw that the people came running together, he rebuked the foul spirit, saying unto him, Thou dumb and deaf spirit, I charge thee, come out of him, and enter no more into him. And the spirit cried, and rent him sore, and came out of him: and he was as one dead; insomuch that many said, He is dead. But Jesus took him by the hand, and lifted him up; and he arose.' (Mark 9:20, 25–7). The phrase 'dumb and deaf spirit' is marked in quotation marks in an early draft of the novel (*BT*).

10. *your blood yelling inside you*: A possible allusion to God's words to Cain: 'What hast thou done? the voice of thy brother's blood crieth unto me from the ground' (Genesis 4: 10). According to M. S. Altman, 'Artless Nastasya uses the word "blood" in the popular understanding of "illness, fever" [. . .] but once again speech proves wiser than the speaker, and for Raskolnikov the words of this simple woman [. . .] are the accusatory voice of the common people' (*BT*).

11. *Vrazumikhin*: Razumikhin's name – roughly, Mr Reasonable (*razum*: reason, intellect) – would have been a characteristic example of the often ironic names invented by teachers at religious seminaries in mid-nineteenth-century Russia and inspired by the qualities of their pupils (*BT*). The addition of the prefix 'v', however, makes him sound, to a

Russian ear, like a man desperate to make others see reason, by whatever means necessary. See also Note on Names.

12. *through the sugar lump*: The sugar lump was held in the teeth, thus saving sugar.

13. *a stream of electricity*: A Russian dictionary of foreign words published in 1865 described electricity as a 'weightless liquid, found in every organism on earth' (*BT*).

14. *avenante-ish*: *Avenante* (French) means 'comely'.

15. *the countess*: Almost certainly an allusion to the greatest short story by Alexander Pushkin (1799–1837), 'The Queen of Spades' (1834), described by Dostoyevsky as 'the epitome of the art of the fantastic'. Pushkin's protagonist, Hermann, is determined to learn the three-card formula known only to the old countess Anna Fedotovna, who dies when he confronts her. Parallels and contrasts between Hermann and Raskolnikov are a staple of scholarly literature on *Crime and Punishment*.

16. *Palmerston*: Typically used to refer to long, close-fitting men's coats, so named in honour of the English prime minister (1855–65). Various reasons have been given for Razumikhin's characteristically idiosyncratic usage of the term, one of the more convincing being that of Sergei Belov: 'In the early 1860s these coats started going out of fashion, which may be why Razumikhin calls Raskolnikov's decrepit hat a "Palmerston"' (*SB*).

17. *Charmeur's*: E. F. Charmeur was one of the best and most expensive tailors in St Petersburg; Dostoyevsky himself, according to his second wife, Anna Grigoryevna, used to order suits from him (*BT*).

18. *studied law*: The Russian word used here (*pravoved*) indicates that Porfiry studied at the highly prestigious Imperial College of Jurisprudence in St Petersburg, an institution founded in 1835 and open only to sons of the nobility. The course lasted six years. To judge by the reactions of early critics, such an education was unusual for a police investigator like Porfiry, adding to the complexity of his characterization (*BT*).

19. *Ryazan*: See above, Part One, note 31.

20. *The Sands*: An area stretching between Nevsky Prospect and the Smolny Institute, so called because of the character of its soil (*BT*).

21. *Jouvin gloves*: Xavier Jouvin (1801–44) of Grenoble, France, invented and patented the cutting die that enabled the mass production of close-fitting gloves.

22. *Go after several hares ... a single one*: Compare with the Russian (and English) folk saying, 'If you run after two hares, you will catch neither,' which Luzhin characteristically mangles. His speech also makes ironic

allusion to famous passages in the Gospels: Jesus' commandment to 'love thy neighbour as thyself' (Matthew 22:39) and an exchange between John the Baptist and the crowds that come to be baptized by him: 'And the people asked him, saying, What shall we do then? He answereth and saith unto them, He that hath two coats, let him impart to him that hath none; and he that hath meat, let him do likewise' (Luke 3:10–11). Luzhin's argument resembles the teachings and style of the 'rational egoists' and radical 'social democrats' of the time, notably Chernyshevsky and Dmitry Pisarev (1840–68), as well as the utilitarianism of Jeremy Bentham (1748–1832), whose ideas proved influential in 1860s Russia, along with those of J. S. Mill (1806–73) (*BT*, *PSS*).

23. *robbed . . . counterfeiting . . . murdered*: All these episodes relate to stories reported in the press in 1865 or to Dostoyevsky directly by word of mouth. The first episode refers to a student expelled from university, who, as Dostoyevsky wrote to his publisher Katkov, 'decided to rob the mail and kill the postman'; such accounts helped convince him that the plot of his novel was 'far from eccentric' (*BT*).

24. *economic changes . . . when the great hour struck*: Apparent references to the social and economic consequences of the abolition of serfdom in 1861, and in particular to the rapid impoverishment of educated but minor representatives of the nobility. The words of the 'lecturer' echo the actual testimony, as reported by the *Moscow Gazette*, of his real-life prototype A. T. Neofitov, who claimed to have committed his crime 'in order to provide for himself and his mother's family' – words echoed in turn by some of Dostoyevsky's comments on Raskolnikov in his notebooks and letters (*PSS*, *SB*).

25. *a tavern . . . and princesses*: The notorious building in question, on the corner of Haymarket Square and Konnyi Lane, was known as the *Malinnik* ('raspberry bushes'). The first two floors were for eating and drinking, while the third was given over to 'thirteen haunts of the darkest, most appalling debauchery', as described by Vsevolod Krestovsky (1840–95), whose novel of St Petersburg low life, *Petersburg Slums* (1864–6), makes for an illuminating comparison with the depictions of prostitution and poverty in *Crime and Punishment*: 'Each of these [thirteen] burrows contained within itself several more nooks, separated one from the other by thin wooden partitions [. . .] And in these burrows and little wooden cells there huddle between eighty and a hundred of the most pitiful, outcast creatures, who have surrendered themselves to the most ruinous depravity.' According to the historians N. B. Lebina and

M. V. Shkarovsky, 'These women never charged more than fifty copecks for their services. On holidays, a prostitute at the *Malinnik* might see up to fifty men. The clothing worn by girls in these establishments was not just poor, it was indecently primitive. Sometimes it consisted merely of a dirty towel wrapped around the hips' (*BT*).

26. *V——y*: Voznesensky Prospect.

27. *short little lane*: Tairov Lane, since renamed Brinko Lane.

28. *one square yard . . . just live!*: A 'contamination', Tikhomirov convincingly argues, of passages from Victor Hugo's novels *Notre-Dame de Paris* (1831, published in *Time* in 1862) and *Le Dernier Jour d'un condamné* (see above, Part One, note 51).

29. *'Crystal Palace'*: Referred to earlier by Razumikhin in French. In reality, there was no such tavern in St Petersburg at the time, in any language, though there was a hotel by that name, in the same part of town. More importantly, the name alludes to the Crystal Palace erected in Hyde Park at the Great Exhibition of 1851. This had struck Dostoyevsky, during his visit to London in 1862, as some kind of 'biblical scene, like something about Babylon, some prophecy from Revelations taking shape before your eyes'. The Crystal Palace became a motif in Dostoyevsky's polemics with Chernyshevsky and the other socialist radicals of the time; the narrator of *Notes from Underground* (1864) saw in it the model of the rationalist utopia against which he felt compelled to rebel. In Tikhomirov's view: 'The "Crystal Palace" of the Utopianist dreamers turns out, in *Crime and Punishment*, to be a third-rate tavern [. . .] which casts a dark shadow on the radiant image of the New Jerusalem, the route to which, according to Raskolnikov's theory, lies through blood and violence. It is relevant, in this connection, that in one of the drafts Raskolnikov was meant to set out his "idea" precisely there, in the "Crystal Palace" ' (*BT*).

30. *Aztecs – Izler*: The merchant Ivan Izler owned the suburban 'Artificial Mineral Water Gardens' (or simply 'Izler's Gardens'), which opened in the 1840s. By the time Dostoyevsky visited in the 1860s the Gardens had become very popular for their firework displays, theatre shows, giants, gypsies and other attractions. Izler tried to bring Massimo and Bartola, of Liliputian height and putatively Aztec origin, to the gardens, but failed; they were exhibited elsewhere (*BT*).

31. *that chap went to the bank*: This account of a nervous criminal, which continues the story of the forged lottery tickets first mentioned in the previous chapter, cleaves closely to a contemporaneous account published

in the *Moscow Gazette* of 10 September 1865 about a young man who, like Raskolnikov – and the mail-robber mentioned earlier – was a 'former student' who hadn't completed his course (*BT*).

32. *Assez causé!*: 'Enough talk!' (French). A phrase much used by Balzac and, following his example, Dostoyevsky.

33. *Spermaceti*: 'A wax-like substance that results from processing the liquid animal wax obtained from the skull of the sperm whale. In the nineteenth century spermaceti was taken to be a sperm whale's semen (hence its name). It would seem that Razumikhin's surprising image is linked to the notions of medieval alchemists, who used sperm in their experiments to create an artificial man or homunculus' (*BT*).

34. *Since that evening*: As Tikhomirov points out, this is 'a memory slip either by Raskolnikov or Dostoyevsky: the hero walks past *that* house on the way to the police bureau on the morning after the murder' (*BT*).

35. *meloning and lemoning*: An example (freely translated) of the many phrases transposed to *Crime and Punishment* from Dostoyevsky's 'Siberian Notebook' in which he collected colourful examples of the language of his fellow convicts.

36. *A drunk can't hold a candle*: Another unusual idiom recorded by Dostoyevsky while in exile in Siberia.

37. *kammerjunker*: An honorary rank at court typically granted to young noblemen, most famously to Alexander Pushkin. 'Groom of the Chamber' is the approximate English equivalent.

38. *The prince*: Between 1861 and 1866 the Military Governor General of St Petersburg (the administrative head of the city) was Prince A. A. Suvorov, grandson of Generalissimo Alexander Suvorov (1730?–1800), famed for never losing a battle during his illustrious career (*BT*).

39. *a feather the colour of fire*: Viktor Shklovsky compared this to the 'feather of an angel', a point developed by Tikhomirov, who invokes the Orthodox iconography of Sophia (Sofya/Sonya) as angel-like, with face and hands 'the colour of fire'. The iconic significance of this detail contrasts strikingly with Sonya's dress with its 'ridiculously long train', which would have been suitable only for high-society occasions (*BT*).

PART THREE

1. *A complete lack of personality*: In this chapter Razumikhin's defence of personality and cultural difference has much in common with aspects of the 'native soil' philosophy (*pochvennichestvo*) that Dostoyevsky, his

brother and fellow contributors had been elaborating in the pages of
Time and *Epoch* between 1861 and 1865. 'The term derives from *poch-
va* (soil, native soil, "roots") and in its most basic sense as a doctrine it
called for a return to their native soil by Russia's educated classes, who,
since the reforms of Peter I in the early eighteenth century, had evolved
as a Westernized elite split away from their Russian heritage and from
the majority of their fellow Russians' (*KL*). Optimistically conceived by
Dostoyevsky as a philosophy that might reconcile the Slavophiles and
the Westernizers, *pochvennichestvo* was opposed directly to the position of the socialists and of the radical journal *The Contemporary*. The
latter's ideal, Dostoyevsky claimed in 1862, was complete impersonality
and a kind of identikit man 'who would be exactly the same wherever he
was – in Germany, England or France – and who would embody the
general human type that had been manufactured in the West' (*BT*).

2. *monomania*: See Part One, note 30.

3. *a Rubinstein*: Anton Rubinstein (1829–94), the celebrated virtuoso pia-
    nist and founder of the St Petersburg Conservatory; he taught Dos-
    toyevsky's niece and met Dostoyevsky himself at least once (*BT*).

4. *Prussian House of Lords*: The Upper House of the Prussian parliament,
    which between 1862 and 1866 was at loggerheads with Bismarck's gov-
    ernment (*BT*).

5. *hypochondriac*: See Part One, note 2.

6. *The queen . . . who darned her own stockings*: A reference to Marie An-
    toinette (1755–93), imprisoned in 1792 and guillotined the following
    year. Various historians of the French Revolution (1789) mention this
    scene, in which she typically uses toothpicks instead of knitting needles
    (*BT, SB*).

7. *Crevez, chiens, si vous n'êtes pas contents!*: 'Drop dead, dogs, if you
    aren't satisfied!' (French): an almost exact quotation from Victor Hugo's
    novel *Les Misérables*, which Dostoyevsky read on its appearance in
    1862. See Book Eight, Chapter Four ('A Rose in Misery'), in which the
    young student, Marius, receives a visit from the young and appallingly
    emaciated daughter of his neighbour Jondrette. In the course of their
    conversation, she tells him: 'Do you know what it will mean if we get a
    breakfast today? It will mean that we shall have had our breakfast of the
    day before yesterday, our breakfast of yesterday, our dinner of today,
    and all that at once, and this morning. Come! Parbleu! if you are not
    satisfied, dogs, burst!' (trans. Isabel Hapgood).

8. *such a melancholic*: See Part One, note 2.

9. *Mitrofanievsky Cemetery*: A large cemetery in the south of St Petersburg, dismantled in the early Soviet decades. Favoured at the time by poor and middling families, it contained two functioning churches and a chapel by the entrance (*BT*).

10. *funeral banquet*: In Russia, a memorial meal for the dead usually takes place immediately after the funeral, but also forty-nine days after death. A solemn occasion, marked by various rituals, the funeral banquet (*pominki*) can also be a marker of social status and wealth; see, for example, Firs Zhuravlyov's painting *A Merchant's Funeral Banquet* (1876).

11. *play Lazarus*: A reference to the Lazarus laid at the gates of a wealthy man's house, hungry and 'full of sores' (Luke 16:20). His legend inspired a spiritual folk song in Russia, often sung by beggars. In turn, the song gave rise to the Russian idiom used here – *'pet' Lazarya'* (literally, 'to sing Lazarus') – with the meaning of-exhibiting and even exaggerating one's poverty or misfortune and playing for sympathy. Raskolnikov's allusion to the beggar Lazarus closely precedes mention in the next chapter of the more famous biblical Lazarus, who was raised from the dead by Christ and becomes a motif of the novel. As Boris Tikhomirov notes, the two biblical Lazaruses have often been fused, whether in the popular imagination or in Ernest Renan's *Vie de Jésus* (1863), a book well known to Dostoyevsky. On the importance of the spiritual songs for Dostoyevsky, and of the Russian folk heritage in general, see Faith Wigzell's fine contribution to *The Cambridge Companion to Dostoevskii* (Cambridge: Cambridge University Press, 2002), pp. 21–46.

12. *No need to break the chairs . . . to think about!*: An almost verbatim quotation from Nikolai Gogol's great comedy *The Government Inspector* (1836) and the first of many references to Gogol by Porfiry Petrovich.

13. *Ordinary paper*: All official documents had to be written on special stamped paper issued by the Ministry of Finances; such paper came in three varieties, 'ordinary' being the cheapest. This category was itself divided into four further types, 'the most ordinary' costing only twenty copecks a sheet (*BT*).

14. *'the environment'*: The cliché at issue here is the phrase *sreda zayela* ('the environment [that] eats away' at the individual). For Russian radicals of the 1860s the 'environment' was so decisive a factor that it lessened or entirely eradicated the moral responsibility of the individual. *Crime and Punishment* is, among other things, a trenchant response to such theories, particularly as articulated by Nikolai Chernyshevsky. As such, it continues the critique of Chernyshevskian rationalism and

determinism begun in Dostoyevsky's novella *Notes from Underground* (1864).

15. *mathematical head . . . phalanstery*: The utopian socialist François Marie Charles Fourier (1772–1837) conceived of 'phalansteries' as enormous, palace-like buildings congenial to new forms of cooperative life. Eventually, the world would be divided into precisely 2,985,984 such communities. In a letter to his publisher Katkov, written while he was working on this part of the novel, Dostoyevsky noted: 'Fourier was convinced that it needed only one phalanstery to be built and the entire world would immediately be covered with them'. As a young man Dostoyevsky had himself been close to the Fourierists of the 'Petrashevsky circle' in St Petersburg, involvement with which led directly to his imprisonment and exile in Siberia. In a written deposition before his sentencing, Dostoyevsky expressed sympathy with Fourier's 'love of humanity', but called his system the most unrealistic of utopias (*BT, KL*).

16. *Ivan the Great Bell Tower*: The tallest of the towers in the Kremlin, it is, in fact, some twenty-five feet higher than is suggested here. Razumikhin appears to be parodying the determinist arguments of Chernyshevsky's characters in his novel *What Is to Be Done?* (1863) (*BT*).

17. *Weekly Review . . . Periodical Review*: Journals appeared and disappeared with alarming speed in 1860s Russia; the Dostoyevsky brothers' *Time* was shut down by the censor in 1863, only to re-emerge as *Epoch* eight months later (*SB, KL*).

18. *all because they are extraordinary*: The originality of Raskolnikov's argument about the moral rights of extraordinary men continues to exercise scholars; Tikhomirov calls it 'the *Russian version* of a certain pan-European archetype'. In his epic biography Joseph Frank mentions numerous literary precursors – including Schiller, Byron, Balzac and Pushkin – but gives pride of place to the radical critic Dmitry Pisarev's interpretation of Ivan Turgenev's nihilist hero Bazarov in *Fathers and Sons* (1862). Where others saw Bazarov in a satirical light, Pisarev exalted him as a solitary figure who rises above the mass of humanity and the fetters of his own conscience: 'Neither above him, nor outside him, nor inside him does he recognize any regulator, any moral law, any principle.' Dostoyevsky's colleague and friend Nikolai Strakhov (1828–96) observed (in Frank's words) 'that Pisarev had gone farther than other radicals along the path of total negation' and Dostoyevsky appeared to share this view. See Derek Offord, '*Crime and Punishment* and Contemporary Radical Thought' in *Fyodor Dostoevsky's Crime and Punishment : A Casebook*;

Joseph Frank, *Dostoevsky: The Miraculous Years, 1865–1871* (London: Robson Books, 1995), pp. 70–75; and Introduction. A more immediate source of Raskolnikov's emphasis on 'extraordinary' people appears to have been Louis-Napoléon Bonaparte's *Histoire de Jules César*, translated into Russian in 1865 and interpreted as a defence of Napoleon more than of Caesar. Perhaps this is the 'book' to which Raskolnikov's 'article' putatively responded. Ideas about rare individuals were in any case already in the air: twenty-five years earlier Thomas Carlyle's *On Heroes, Hero-Worship and the Heroic in History* (1841) had greatly impressed Russian educated society (*BT*, *SB*).

19. *everyone oversteps the law . . . to commit crime*: The Russian word for 'crime', *prestuplenie*, is literally a 'stepping over', comparable etymologically to the less commonly used English word 'transgression'. See also Introduction, V.

20. *Vive la guerre éternelle*: 'Long live eternal war' (French). A possible allusion to a passage in *La Guerre et la Paix* (1861) by the socialist and self-professed 'anarchist' Pierre-Joseph Proudhon (1809–65): '*la guerre . . . est éternelle. Salut à la guerre*' ('war . . . is eternal. Welcome, war'). In this treatise, published in Russian translation in 1864, Proudhon sought 'to understand war in its innermost idea, its reasoning, its conscience, and even, to put it more boldly, its high morality'. Tikhomirov comments on the 'fundamental proximity of Raskolnikov's theory and Proudhon's doctrine, which paradoxically couples blood and conscience, war and morality' (*BT*).

21. *the New Jerusalem*: A reference to the image of the world without death or sorrow that would follow Christ's Second Coming and the Day of Judgement: 'And I saw a new heaven and a new earth: for the first heaven and the first earth were passed away; and there was no more sea. And I John saw the holy city, new Jerusalem, coming down from God out of heaven, prepared as a bride adorned for her husband' (Revelation 21:1–2). In line with the characteristic ambivalence of Dostoyevsky's method, however, Raskolnikov may equally be referring to the kind of socialist utopia envisaged by the 'new Christianity' of Henri de Saint-Simon (1760–1825) and his many followers, who reinterpreted such biblical imagery in a strictly secular key. For them, paradise would be achieved on earth by human efforts, without any need for God.

22. *the raising of Lazarus*: The story of the dead man brought back to life by Christ, as told in John 11:1–45. See note 11 above.

23. *branded in some way*: Here, as elsewhere, the allusive scope of Porfiry's comments is considerable, from stories of the signs that allegedly marked the birth of Muhammad and other historical figures to the 'Tsar signs' (marks on the body) mentioned in Russian folklore, by which a true ruler or heir to the throne might be identified (*BT*). Of striking relevance to Raskolnikov's drama throughout the novel is a review of Louis-Napoléon Bonaparte's *Histoire de Jules César* (see note 18 above) translated from the English press for a Russian newspaper in 1865. The English critic asks how the French emperor would identify 'who among us is Caesar, Charlemagne, Napoleon?', and concludes that if Napoleon III were to answer honestly, he would say 'that there is no sign to distinguish a prophet from a false prophet, other than the ungainsayable logic of success. Whoever wins, executing his ideas and achieving success through his genius, is right. From this it follows that humanity can do nothing but wait for events to unfold and obey' (cited in Russian translation in *SB*).

24. *who really are new*: Most likely an ironic reference to the 'new people' envisaged by Chernyshevsky (*SB*).

25. *Rus . . . Napoleon*: For Russian readers an obvious allusion to Pushkin's novel in verse *Eugene Onegin* (1823–31), Chapter 2, Stanza 14. The mention of *Rus*, conjuring an image of a pre-modern and 'spiritual' Russia, is also noteworthy, and Tikhomirov aptly teases out the target of Porfiry's irony: 'the ambition of a *Russian* hero "to become a Napoleon" and the impossibility of Western, European principles ("Napoleonism") taking root in Russian soil ("in Rus")' (*BT*).

26. *thirty degrees Réaumur*: The equivalent of 37.5° Celsius and nearly 100° Fahrenheit.

27. *You're the killer*: A particularly striking example of a sudden, unexpected switch to the familiar, second-person singular form of address, especially flagrant given the lowly rank of any 'tradesman'.

28. *V—— Church*: The Church of the Ascension (*Voznesenskaya*), which was located by Voznesensky Bridge and was demolished in 1936. Its bell tower dominated the surrounding area (*BT*).

29. *Toulon . . . Vilno*: Highlights from the military career of Napoleon: his successful orchestration of the siege of Toulon, held by royalists, in December 1793; his violent suppression of a royalist uprising in Paris in October 1795; his desertion of his army in Egypt in August 1799 to return to France (the army suffered great losses and eventually capitulated in 1801); the March on Moscow in 1812 that cost the French about half

a million soldiers, according to François-René de Chateaubriand (1768–1848), whose *Mémoires d'outre-tombe* (1849–50) Dostoyevsky kept in his library, in Russian translation; and the quip attributed to Napoleon in Warsaw (not Vilno) on his retreat from Russia: *'Du sublime au ridicule il n'y a qu'un pas'* ('From the sublime to the ridiculous is but a step') (*PSS, BT*).

30. *idols . . . bronze*: The unusual word chosen by Dostoyevsky to signify monuments (*kumiry*: idols), together with the mention of bronze, sends the reader back to Pushkin and the image in his great narrative poem *The Bronze Horseman* (1833) of Peter the Great (1672–1725) as 'The idol on a bronze horse', thus suggesting a parallel between Napoleon and Peter. Dostoyevsky saw Peter the Great as a 'man of iron, cruel', who 'as a genius, had just one aim: reform and a new order', sacrificing all moral qualms in the process (cited from *BT*).

31. *the pyramids, Waterloo*: References to the so-called Battle of the Pyramids in July 1798, when Napoleon defeated the Mamluks in Egypt, having told his forces: 'Men! Forty centuries look down upon you from the height of those pyramids'; and to Napoleon's defeat at Waterloo in 1815, after which, according to legends cultivated by Romantic writers, Napoleon 'rejected the chance to flee to America and intentionally gave himself into the hands of the English, so that, assuming "the martyr's crown", he could bring his career, the career of "an extraordinary man", to its "ideal" conclusion' (cited from *BT*).

32. *carrying my little brick for universal happiness*: A reworking of the expression *'apporter sa pierre à l'édifice nouveau'* ('to bring one's stone for the new building'), used by Fourier's follower Victor Considerant (1808–93). Having sympathized with the ideals of utopian socialism in his youth, Dostoyevsky was much more critical by the 1860s, especially in his polemics with Chernyshevsky and other Russian socialists and radicals (*PSS, BT*). Tatyana Kasatkina has suggested that the substitution of 'brick' for 'stone' may allude to the building of the Tower of Babel ('And they said one to another, Go to, let us make brick, and burn them throughly. And they had brick for stone, and slime had they for mortar' (Genesis 11:3).

33. *O 'quivering' creature!*: An allusion to Pushkin's cycle 'Imitations of the Koran' (1824), the first poem of which ends with Allah addressing the Prophet Muhammad as follows: 'Be strong, despise deceit / Vigorously follow the path of truth /Love orphans, and teach / My Koran to every

quivering creature.' As Sergei Bocharov has pointed out, Pushkin was translating 'into the language of the Koran the Gospel verse addressed by the risen Christ to the apostles: "Go ye into all the world, and preach the gospel to every creature"' (Mark 16:15). In Raskolnikov's citation, the phrase 'quivering creature' becomes negatively marked and, as such, a motif of Raskolnikov's perception of others and of himself (see *BT*).

34. *lines up a top-notch battery*: Raskolnikov appears to be eliding two of his 'extraordinary' men – Muhammad and Napoleon – with particular reference to Napoleon's violent suppression of the royalist uprising in Paris in October 1795 (*BT*).

PART FOUR

1. *et nihil humanum*: The common misrendering of part of a celebrated quotation from the Roman poet Terence's comedy *Heauton Timorumenos* (*The Self-Tormentor*): '*Homo sum: humani nihil a me alienum puto*' ('I am a man: nothing human is alien to me').

2. *bonne guerre*: Literally, 'good war' (French), but in idiomatic usage signifying something like the English 'All's fair in love and war', or simply 'Fair enough' (*c'est de bonne guerre*').

3. *beneficent free speech . . . German lass . . . 'The Scandal of The Age'*: The context of these comments is the relaxation of censorship in the early 1860s as part of the reforming agenda of Alexander II (1818–81). 'Beneficent *glasnost*', as it was sometimes called, brought with it a litany of public shamings and scandals much debated in the press. In 1860 a landowner, A. P. Kozlyainov, beat a German woman in a train; a correspondent in the *Northern Bee* spoke out against the consensus (as Svidrigailov will do), defending the landowner and citing the provocative behaviour of the possibly drunken woman, who had been pestering Kozlyainov's sister. 'The Scandal of *The Age*' (more literally, 'The Abominable Act of *The Age*') was the title of an attack in the *St Petersburg Gazette* against a feuilleton published in the weekly journal *The Age*, which objected to an allegedly immoral public reading by Yevgenia Tolmachova, the wife of a prominent provincial official, of an episode from Pushkin's unfinished 'Egyptian Nights' (1835), an improvisation in verse on the theme of 'Cleopatra and her lovers'. The scandal caused by the reading was a vivid illustration of the ongoing debate on female emancipation (*PSS*, *BT*). Dostoyevsky wrote two essays defending Tolmachova's

reading and Pushkin's text, and appealing to the transformation of sexual material in the artistic process; see Susanne Fusso, *Discovering Sexuality in Dostoevsky* (Evanston, Illinois: Northwestern University Press, 2006), pp. 3–9.

4. *the peasant reforms passed us by*: A reference to the Emancipation of the Serfs in 1861, when forests and meadows were retained by the old landed gentry.

5. *Dussots and pointes*: Dussot's was a high-class restaurant just off the Moika Canal; by *pointe* Svidrigailov probably means the spit at the western end of Yelagin Island, a fashionable leisure spot (*PSS*).

6. *North Pole . . . vin mauvais*: In 1865 the St Petersburg press frequently reported discussions under way in the Royal Geographic Society in London about preparations for an expedition to reach and explore the North Pole (*PSS, BT*). The French idiom *avoir le vin mauvais* (literally, 'to have bad wine') is typically said of someone who becomes aggressive when drunk.

7. *Berg's*: Wilhelm Berg, a well-known fairground showman and entrepreneur who organized risky and spectacular hot-air balloon rides in the Yusupov Gardens (*BT*).

8. *pour vous plaire*: 'Just to please you' (French).

9. *Vyazemsky's House on Haymarket*: Located just off Haymarket Square, this enormous building was described by Krestovsky in *Petersburg Slums* as 'thirty houses in one': 'inhabited by swindlers, thieves, passportless tramps and other such types, whose existence is considered an inconvenience in a well-ordered town' (*BT*).

10. *Rassudkin . . . Razumikhin*: A confusion arising from the fact that the words *rassudok* and *razum* have broadly similar meanings to do with reason, intellect and sense.

11. *Polechka and Lenya*: The younger sister, Lenya, was referred to in Part Two as Lida. Here, as elsewhere, Dostoyevsky's inconsistencies have not been corrected.

12. *Holy fool*: By Dostoyevsky's time, the Russian word *yurodivyi* had acquired two fundamental, but closely related meanings. One was broadly positive, deriving from the form of eccentric religious behaviour known as *yurodstvo Khrista radi* ('folly for Christ's sake') and finding biblical sanction in Paul's First Letter to the Corinthians. A *yurodivyi* in this sense was a profoundly holy person whose saintliness was expressed in a paradoxical way, whether through provocative 'madness', aggression or godly simplicity. The other meaning, engendered partly by scepticism

towards 'false holy fools' who wished to claim unearned privileges, was
sharply negative: a halfwit or madman, without any redeeming features.
Dostoyevsky often toyed with both of these meanings at once; see Har-
riet Murav, *Holy Foolishness: Dostoevsky's Novels & the Poetics of
Cultural Critique* (Stanford: Stanford University Press, 1992).

13. *the New Testament in Russian translation*: On his way to prison camp
in the Siberian town of Omsk in 1850, Dostoyevsky was given just such
a book by the wives of men punished for their participation in the Decembrist uprising of 1825. Published in 1823, it gave the first full translation of the New Testament into modern Russian, rather than Church
Slavonic (*PSS, BT*). Its publication, though authorized by Tsar Alexander I, met with immediate resistance on the part of some ministers and
prelates, thereby endowing it with subversive, revolutionary force. Ministers and prelates feared, as Victoria Frede has recently written, that the
new translations published by the Russian Bible Society between 1819
and 1824 'would "destroy Orthodoxy", because individuals who sought
to interpret scripture on their own would inevitably reach false conclusions. Not only would translations "destroy the true faith", but they
would also "disrupt the fatherland and produce strife and rebellion"
[. . .] It would be another forty years before church and state authorized
the publication of a Russian Bible' – thus bringing us up to the time of
the writing of *Crime and Punishment*. Quoted from Frede, *Doubt,
Atheism, and the Nineteenth-Century Russian Intelligentsia* (Madison:
University of Wisconsin Press, 2011), p. 34.

14. *She will see God*: See the Sermon on the Mount: 'Blessed are the pure in
heart: for they shall see God' (Matthew 5:8).

15. *Read! I want you to!*: Boris Tikhomirov offers an absorbing account of
the way this passage evolved during work on the novel. Originally (to
judge from his preparatory notes), Dostoyevsky intended Sonya to take
the lead: to thrust the Gospels on Raskolnikov and to compare herself to
the resurrected Lazarus. The first version of the chapter which Dostoyevsky
sent to his publisher, Katkov, has been lost, but was presumably based on
this plan. Katkov and his fellow editor rejected it, seeing in it 'traces of
nihilism'. The revised version we now have (work on which cost Dostoyevsky, by his own account, the equivalent of 'three new chapters') represents, as Tikhomirov argues, an artistic advance on the preliminary
notes: Sonya, no longer a didactic figure, becomes exemplary, here and
throughout, for her presence rather than her words (*BT*). See also Joseph
Frank, *Dostoevsky: The Miraculous Years, 1865–1871*, pp. 93–5.

16. *Now a certain man was sick, Lazarus of Bethany* ...: Here, and throughout the chapter, Sonya's selected reading from the story of the raising of Lazarus (John 11:1–45) is cited in the Revised Standard Version, though I have replaced 'ill' with 'sick'.

17. *Theirs is the Kingdom of Heaven*: A reference to a famous passage in the Gospel of Mark: 'And they brought young children to him, that he should touch them: and his disciples rebuked those that brought them. But when Jesus saw it, he was much displeased, and said unto them, Suffer the little children to come unto me, and forbid them not: for of such is the kingdom of God. Verily I say unto you, Whosoever shall not receive the kingdom of God as a little child, he shall not enter therein' (Mark 10:13–15).

18. *grace-and-favour apartment*: The Russian phrase *kazyonnaya kvartira* ('an apartment at public expense') could also be used idiomatically to mean a prison (*BT*) – a further example of Porfiry's 'double-edged' wit.

19. *state ... actual state ... privy*: Corresponding to grades 5, 4 and 3 in the Table of Ranks.

20. *reforms afoot*: The judicial reforms announced in Russia in 1864 had as one of their aims the separation of the judicial system from the civil service: examining magistrates would replace state officials in carrying out preliminary investigation of criminal offences. However, owing to a lack of qualified examining magistrates (equivalents of the *juge d'instruction* in France) many of the old guard from the civil service, like Porfiry Petrovich, stayed on, but under a different title (*BT*).

21. *straight after the Battle of Alma*: After being defeated at the Battle of Alma in September 1854, during the Crimean War, the Russian army retreated to Sebastopol, where the Allied forces began a siege that lasted almost a year. Sebastopol eventually fell, after heavy casualties on both sides.

22. *Hofkriegsrat ... General Mack*: The war council of the Austrian Empire, the Hofkriegsrat, was responsible for managing the permanent army. General Mack, commander of the Austrian forces, surrendered with 23,000 men to Napoleon at the Battle of Ulm in October 1805, during the War of the Third Coalition (1803–6). Napoleon was now free to advance on the Russian army (commanded by Kutuzov), leading to victory at Austerlitz in December. These events – and the ironies of Mack's failure, despite initial optimism and detailed planning – are reflected in Volume One (Part Two, Chapter III) of Leo Tolstoy's *War and*

Peace (1865–9), which had recently appeared in *The Russian Messenger*, the same journal in which *Crime and Punishment* was being serially published.

23. *deputies*: A reference to the pre-Reform practice whereby 'deputies' were chosen from the same social estate to which the accused belonged (in this case, the nobility) and tasked with monitoring judicial proceedings *(BT)*.

PART FIVE

1. *Knop's and the English Shop*: Two fancy goods shops on Nevsky Prospect *(BT)*.

2. *Fourier's system and Darwin's theory*: The utopian socialist ideas of François Fourier and the evolutionary theories of Charles Darwin (1809–82) both found many unreliable disciples among the Russian 'social democrats', atheists and 'progressivists' with whom Dostoyevsky so often polemicized, and whose ideas are slavishly recycled by Lebezyatnikov in this chapter. Highly sceptical of the practical application of Fourierist ideas to Russia, Dostoyevsky was even more hostile towards the crude application by some Russian radicals of Darwin's *The Origin of Species* (1859) to modern society. The spectre of 'social Darwinism' – of a society in which oppression, moral adaptation and rampant egoism might all be justified – haunts Raskolnikov's thinking throughout the novel.

3. *a new commune somewhere on Meshchanskaya Street*: Young Russian radicals – women as much as men – had begun to establish 'communes' in St Petersburg in the mid-1860s, encouraged in particular by Chernyshevsky's novel *What Is to Be Done?*. It was hoped that a loosely structured communal life, based on the model of ordinary urban dormitories, would ultimately develop into full-blown Fourierist phalansteries. Communes soon acquired notoriety for free love and staunch opposition to Church and law *(BT)*. A commune of nihilists (including some charged in connection with Dmitry Karakozov's failed attempt to assassinate Alexander II in April 1866) did indeed move to Middle Meshchanskaya Street, very close to Raskolnikov's address, though it is unclear whether or not they had already done so by the time this part of the novel was being written *(BT, PSS)*.

4. *Take Terebyeva . . . civil marriage*: Lebezyatnikov's confused attempts to stand up for women's emancipation and the equality of the sexes echo

the ideological concerns of *What Is to Be Done?*, to which Lebezyatnikov unwittingly provides a 'parodic commentary', in the words of Leonid Grossman (cited in *SB*). At the same time, they reflect genuine
changes in the morals of young, anti-religious intellectuals of the time,
among whom so-called 'civil marriages' (which Russian law of the time
did not acknowledge) were rife – the term often being used in a rather
euphemistic sense (*BT*).

5. *Another young man who's 'flown the nest'*: An allusion to comments by
the mother of Bazarov, the nihilist hero of Ivan Turgenev's *Fathers and
Sons* (1862), about her independent and free-thinking son. The Russian
idiom is more graphic: literally, 'a broken-off chunk' (of bread), playing
on the Russian saying that 'a broken-off chunk can't be stuck back on
the loaf'. The context of the quotation perhaps justifies the attenuated
translation given here. The mother says to her husband: 'Well, what can
we do, Vasya? Our son's flown the nest. He's like a falcon: flies in when
he wants to, flies off when he wants to; while you and I never budge'
(Chapter 21).

6. *distinguons*: 'Let's distinguish' (French).

7. *Environment is everything . . . Not to mention Belinsky*: On the environment, see Part Three, note 14. The extent to which the environment
shapes (and consumes) the individual had been a theme of Russian literature since the 1840s, when Vissarion Belinsky (1811–48), the supremely
influential critic and champion of socially minded art, was still alive.
The theme was discussed at length in a long essay of 1860 by Nikolai
Dobrolyubov (1836–61), whose utilitarian aesthetics are a target of Dostoyevsky's own essay 'Mr ——bov and the Question of Art' (1861).

8. *the unequal gesture of hand-kissing*: Further parroting by Lebezyatnikov of *What Is to Be Done?*, in which Chernyshevsky's heroine, Vera
Pavlovna, explains why women find it offensive to have their hands
kissed by men: 'it means that they [men] don't consider women as people
like them, they think that [. . .] however much a man may abase himself
before her, he is still not her equal, but far superior' (Chapter 2, XVIII).

9. *workers' associations in France*: A theme often championed by the *Contemporary* , with which Dostoyevsky's own journals often crossed swords.
One contributor to the *Contemporary*, writing in 1864, saw in the Parisian workers' associations founded by French socialists not just 'liberation'
in a material sense, but 'a moral improvement in the working class' (*PSS*).

10. *open doors*: In *What Is to Be Done?* rules are established for communal
living in which a man and a woman each have one room in which they

cannot be disturbed, as well as one 'neutral' room in which they take tea and meals together. Here Lebezyatnikov appears to suggest that contemporary commune-dwellers have even 'gone beyond' Chernyshevsky (*BT*).

11. *cesspits*: The question of who would attend to the 'cesspits' in a Fourier-style community was a familiar one in journalistic debate of the time. Fourier said that this chore would be carried out by 'cohorts of self-sacrificing' adolescents (*BT*); here, too, Lebezyatnikov and his mentors have gone one step further ('no self-sacrifice would be involved').

12. *more useful*: Dostoyevsky and his journal *Epoch* often scorned the utilitarianism of a rival journal, the *Russian Word*, mocking its contributors for making out that 'a pair of boots are even better than Pushkin' (*PSS*). Their prime target was the talented young critic Dmitry Pisarev, to whom the remark is now commonly attributed. In fact, Pisarev understood 'usefulness' in a much broader sense, asking, in his essay 'The Realists' (1864), for poets to be useful 'as poets'.

13. *Whatever is useful . . . is thereby noble!*: Echoing Chernyshevsky's claim in his essay 'The Anthropological Principle in Philosophy' (1860) that 'only that which is useful for man in general can be considered a true good'.

14. *grey and rainbow-coloured banknotes*: Worth, respectively, 50 and 100 roubles.

15. *vile, hussarish Pushkinism*: A schoolboy poem attributed to Pushkin in the *Contemporary* in 1863 contains a couplet specifically linking 'horns' with Hussars: 'But Hussars are not to blame / For the length of a husband's horns' (*BT*).

16. *but now I respect you*: Again Lebezyatnikov takes his cue from Chernyshevsky's *What Is to Be Done?*, in which a similar sentiment is expressed by Vera Pavlovna's husband Lopukhov when she tells him she has fallen in love with another man (Chapter 3, XXV).

17. *kutya*: A dish of rice, raisins and honey or sugar, usually eaten at funeral banquets; previously mentioned in Part One, Chapter V.

18. *Gostiny Dvor*: A further allusion to the luxurious shops of Nevsky Prospect, glimpsed in the background of the novel from the poverty of its primary setting. The neoclassical Great Gostiny Dvor, one of the world's oldest shopping arcades, still thrives today.

19. *Pani chorążyna*: 'Madame Ensign' (Polish).

20. *Panie!*: 'Mister!' (Polish, vocative case).

21. *bread and salt*: The phrase *khleb-sol'* (bread-salt) is found in a variety of idiomatic expressions in Russian, most commonly to signify hospitality.

In Katerina Ivanovna's repeated usage it gains a proud ring, despite its humble literal meaning (an example of the 'pauper's pride' mentioned earlier).

22. *Vater aus Berlin*: 'Father from Berlin' (German).

23. *T——, the town of her birth*: Almost certainly a covert allusion to Katerina Ivanovna's real-life prototype Maria Dmitrievna, Dostoyevsky's first wife, with whom he had a difficult marriage (1857–64) cut short by her death, also from 'consumption'. Maria Dmitrievna was born in Taganrog and graduated from Taganrog boarding school with a certificate of distinction (*BT*). Compare the descriptions of the ailing Katerina Ivanovna (and her attitude towards her husband, Marmeladov) with the description of Maria Dmitrievna left by Baron Wrangel, a friend of Dostoyevsky's: 'very thin, with a passionate and excitable nature. Even then the ominous flush played over her pale face and a few years later consumption did carry her off to the grave. She was well read, quite well educated, inquisitive, kind-hearted and extraordinarily vivacious and impressionable. She had an ardent concern for Fyodor Mikhailovich and was very kind to him; I don't believe that she held him in very high esteem – it was more a matter of pity for an unfortunate man crushed by fate' (cited in *KL*).

24. *en toutes lettres*: 'Quite explicitly' (French).

25. *Geld*: 'Money' (German).

26. *her father was a colonel*: In the space of two pages, Katerina Ivanovna has upgraded her father's status from 'court counsellor' (whose military equivalent in the Table of Ranks was lieutenant colonel) to colonel (*BT*).

27. *Bürgermeister*: 'Town mayor' (German).

28. *Gott der Barmherzige!*: 'Merciful Lord!' (German).

29. *sausage-maker*: A pejorative nickname for German women in Russia at the time, when most sausage shops in St Petersburg were run by Germans (*SB*).

30. *for the right hand . . . not to know*: See Matthew 6:3: 'But when thou doest alms, let not thy left hand know what thy right hand doeth.' Tikhomirov aptly comments that Lebezyatnikov's 'forgetfulness in this situation is far from accidental, since he renounces alms-giving on principle' (*BT*).

31. *The General Conclusion of the Positive Method*: A collection of articles, edited and translated from French and German by N. Neklyudov and published in St Petersburg in 1866; it included 'Brain and Spirit. A Survey of Physiological Psychology for All Thinking Readers' by the German doctor and writer Theodor Piderit (1826–1912), and 'The Regularity of

Apparently Voluntary Human Actions from the Point of View of Statistics' by the economist Adolph Wagner (see Part One, note 47). A review in the Russian press bewailed the book's incoherence, but singled out Piderit's and Wagner's articles for praise; it seems likely that here, too, Lebezyatnikov is merely parroting someone else's opinion (*BT, PSS*).

32. *Panie łajdak!*: 'Mr Scoundrel!' (Polish).

33. *unhappier than you are now*: An abrupt change in the Russian text: from the respectful, second-person plural form with which Sonya has addressed Raskolnikov until now, she switches to the familiar singular form with which he has long been addressing her. From this point on she will switch between the two forms.

34. *neither Toulon nor Egypt nor the pass at Mont Blanc*: References to two of Napoleon Bonaparte's celebrated triumphs (see Part Three, notes 29 and 31) and to his audacious crossing of Mont Blanc in 1800 with 40,000 men and heavy artillery in order to strike at the rear of the Austrian army in Italy.

35. *all this was dawning on me*: Tikhomirov traces this ambivalent image of sudden revelation, 'like the sun', to the appearance of devils, masked as angels, in the cave of the eleventh-century hermit Isaac of Kiev. St Isaac's hagiographer repeatedly compares their appearance to a sudden burst of illumination, 'like the sun' (*BT*).

36. *kiss the earth you've polluted*: The image may be traced to the Old Testament and to Russian folk culture, with its ancient practice of kissing and even eating the earth on making a vow, and its mythological image of *Mat'-Syra Zemlya* or Mother Damp Earth (*BT*). The latter, following the Christianization of Russia, became popularly linked with the image of the Virgin Mary. Dostoyevsky's readers might also have been reminded of the 'native soil' philosophy (*pochvennichestvo*) that he and fellow-minded writers had been elaborating since 1861 (see Part Three, note 1).

37. *tubercles on the brain*: Tikhomirov argues that Lebezyatnikov's comment probably reflects 'superficially understood information about "tubercular inflammation of the membranes of the brain" (i.e., tubercular meningitis)', which he has misapplied to Katerina Ivanovna (*BT*).

38. *Tenez-vous droite*: 'Straighten up' (French).

39. *Petrushka*: The Russian version of Punch and Judy. A staple of fairgrounds, Petrushka had begun to flourish on city streets as well. Dostoyevsky, who took a great interest in street theatre and music, once described the character of Petrushka as 'a kind of Sancho Panza or Leporello, but a completely Russified, popular character'. As Boris Tikhomirov

notes, it is precisely the popular quality of *Petrushka* that Katerina Ivanovna, with her aristocratic taste, wishes to distance herself from (and also,
perhaps, the fact that the roguish Petrushka is given to mocking seekers of
justice and truth).

40. *'Little Farm'*: See Part One, note 25.

41. *'The Hussar . . . 'Cinq sous'*: 'The Hussar Leaning on his Sabre', based
    on words from Konstantin Batyushkov's poem 'Separation' (1814), is
    sung by prostitutes in Krestovsky's *Petersburg Slums* (*BT*). *'Cinq sous'*
    ('Five pennies') is the refrain from a beggars' song in *Grâce de Dieu*, a
    melodrama known to theatregoers in Moscow and St Petersburg from
    the 1840s onwards (*PSS, BT*).

42. *Marlborough . . . reviendra*: The first lines of a popular French folk song
    ('Marlborough is off to war / And doesn't know when he'll return'). The
    song mockingly describes a page giving (mistaken) news of the death in
    battle of the Duke of Marlborough (1650–1722) to his widow. It gained
    particular popularity in Russia after 1812, 'since its ironic story of Marl-
    borough's unsuccessful campaign [in the War of the Spanish Succession]
    was taken as an allusion to the defeat of Napoleon' (*BT*).

43. *Cinq sous . . . ménage*: 'Five pennies, five pennies / To set up our home'
    (French).

44. *pas de basque*: A ballet step performed either close to the floor (*glissé*) or
    with a jump (*sauté*).

45. *Du hast Diamanten . . . du mehr?*: 'You have diamonds and pearls [. . .]
    You have the most beautiful eyes, / Girl, what more could you want?'
    (German). Lines from a poem by Heinrich Heine (1797–1856), though
    the original has *Mein Liebchen* ('My darling') where Dostoyevsky has
    Mädchen ('Girl').

46. *In the midday heat . . . Dagestan*: The opening words of Mikhail Lermontov's
    poem 'Dream' (1841), set to music many times by Russian composers.

PART SIX

1. *political conspirator*: Work on this part of *Crime and Punishment*, in
   the latter part of 1866, coincided with the public hanging in St Petersburg of Dmitry Karakozov (1840–66), who had tried to shoot Tsar Alexander II in April that year. Also due for public execution was Nikolai
   Ishutin (1840–79), to whose revolutionary circle Karakozov had belonged; Ishutin was spared at the last moment by an unexpected pardon

from the Tsar – as Dostoyevsky himself had been seventeen years earlier
(*BT*). On Karakozov and his significance for Dostoyevsky see Claudia
Verhoeven, *The Odd Man Karakozov: Imperial Russia, Modernity and
the Birth of Terrorism* (Ithaca, NY: Cornell University Press, 2009).

2. *I went to see B——*: The illustrious physician Sergei Botkin (1832–89),
who diagnosed Dostoyevsky's own pulmonary malady as he was beginning work on *Crime and Punishment* (*BT*).

3. *A hundred rabbits . . . English proverb has it*: A characteristic piece of
mystification and misquotation on Porfiry's part, for no such English
proverb exists. A 'French proverb' quoted in one of Ivan Turgenev's letters has been cited as one inspiration (*SB*), but there appears to be a
common source: the *Procès de Madame Lafarge* (Pagnerre: Paris, 1840),
an account of the trial of Marie Lafarge (1816–52), who was eventually
convicted for the murder of her husband by arsenic. The pioneering trial
hinged on forensic evidence and chemical tests, and '*l'affaire Lafarge*'
was followed in the daily press by a gripped and divided French society.
One of the defendant's lawyers, Maître Paillet, criticized the preference
of the Ministère Publique for generalities rather than hard facts. In support of his position, he invoked the words of the Attorney-General at the
Court of Appeal, Monsieur Dupin, who had recently made the following
'picturesque' criticism of the Ministère Publique: '*avec vos trente-six pe-
tits lapins blancs vous ne ferez jamais un cheval blanc*' ('your thirty-six
little white rabbits will never make a white horse'); *Procès de Madame
Lafarge*, p. 433. The case furnishes an interesting and complex precedent
for both Porfiry and Dostoyevsky, given the latter's suspicion of any legal system in which only 'hard facts' – or white horses – hold sway.

4. *the plucking of a string*: An allusion to the delirious final paragraph of
Nikolai Gogol's story 'Notes of a Madman' (1835): 'a bluish mist spreads
itself out beneath my feet; in the mist, the plucking of a string'. Noting the
possible parallel between Raskolnikov, a would-be Napoleon, and Gogol's
'mad' narrator Poprishchin, who fancies himself the King of Spain, Tikhomirov also cites a letter Dostoyevsky wrote to Ivan Turgenev in December 1863, where he employs this motif, endowing it with his own meaning
and artistic credo. After criticizing utilitarian currents in contemporary
culture, Dostoyevsky observes that Turgenev's fantastical tale 'Phantoms'
paradoxically expresses the *real* condition of the soul of contemporary
man: 'This reality *is the anguish of an educated and conscious creature of
our times* [. . .] It's "a string being plucked in the mist", and thank

goodness for that.' According to Tikhomirov, 'it is precisely "the anguish of an educated and conscious creature" [. . .] that is the source of everything that happens to the hero of Dostoyevsky's novel' (*BT*).

5. *umsonst!*: 'To no avail!' (German).

6. *the final pillars*: An unusual idiom inspired by the labours of Hercules, meaning 'to reach the limit', 'the furthest point' (*BT*).

7. *a child*: Mikolka is, in fact, twenty-two (see Part Two, Chapter IV).

8. *schismatic . . . 'Runners' . . . Elder*: The causes and effects of the mid-seventeenth-century schism (*raskol*) in Russian Orthodoxy, between those who accepted the reforms introduced by Patriarch Nikon (1605–81) and those who would henceforth be known as the Old Believers or schismatics, preoccupied Dostoyevsky throughout his life, as reflected in the name he gave to the hero of this novel. One of the most radical sects attached to the Old Belief was that of the Runners (*beguny*), for whom the earth was already in the grip of the Antichrist, and who 'ran' from all worldly authority into forests and remote places. Their tendency to admit to crimes they hadn't committed and to seek out suffering for themselves as a path to holiness was much discussed in the Russian journals of the mid-1860s (*PSS*). The symbolic relationship – in terms both of contrast and of possible affinity – between Raskolnikov and the *raskolnik* Mikolka is further underlined by the fact that both men seem to hail from the province of Ryazan (where the district of Zaraisk is located) and are of similar age (twenty-three and twenty-two). The *starets* (Elder) is a charismatic, often controversial holy man who offers spiritual direction and ministry to Orthodox believers, as depicted most famously in the character of Zosima in Dostoyevsky's *Brothers Karamazov*.

9. *old, 'true' books*: Religious books that were especially valued by the Old Believers and contained, for example, the sayings of St John Chrysostom (347–407). Published before the Schism, in the mid-seventeenth century, they were republished in Poland at the end of the eighteenth century and circulated among Old Believers throughout the nineteenth century (*BT*).

10. *new courts*: A reference to the legal reforms of 1864, not yet implemented at the time in which the novel is set (summer 1865).

11. *'renewal' through bloodshed*: A possible reference to the ideas expounded in Proudhon's *La Guerre et la Paix* (see Part Three, note 20), as well as to those putatively set out in Raskolnikov's article on crime (*BT*).

12. *Seek and ye will find*: See Matthew 7:7: 'Ask, and it shall be given you; seek, and ye shall find; knock, and it shall be opened unto you.'

13. *warrant officer*: A reference to a character in Gogol's play *Marriage* (1842) – called Petukhov, though misremembered by Porfiry (or Dostoyevsky) as the offstage warrant officer Dyrka – who, 'even if you just show him a finger will suddenly laugh out loud, by God, and laugh till the cows come home' (*BT*). The reference echoes Porfiry's characterization of Mikolka earlier in the chapter.

14. ——*sky Prospect*: Obukhovsky (now Moskovsky) Prospect.

15. *must be a seminarian*: See Part Two, note 11.

16. *cher ami*: 'Dear friend' (French).

17. *La nature et la vérité*: A variation of Heinrich Heine's description of Rousseau as '*L'homme de la vérité et de la nature*' ('The man of truth and nature'), which, in turn, paraphrased Rousseau's pledge in the first book of his *Confessions* to show man 'in all the truth of his nature'. In a notebook entry written shortly before he began work on *Crime and Punishment* Dostoyevsky described the ideal of 'the man of truth and nature' as nothing but 'a puppet that doesn't exist' (*BT*). Through Svidrigailov, *la nature* receives an even more critical (and cynical) interpretation.

18. *Sistine Madonna*: According to the memoirs of Dostoyevsky's second wife, Anna Grigoryevna, Dostoyevsky spoke of the 'sorrow in the smile' of the *Sistine Madonna*, which he considered 'the greatest manifestation of human genius' (*BT*). The comparison with a 'holy fool' drawn by Svidrigailov is more fanciful, though it continues a motif of the novel, linking the Virgin Mary with Lizaveta and Sonya, both compared to holy fools earlier in the novel; see Part Four, note 14.

19. *Où va-t-elle la vertu se nicher?*: 'Where does virtue make its nest?' (French). An almost exact quotation from Voltaire's *Vie de Molière*: 'He [Molière] had just given alms to a beggar; the next moment, the beggar ran after him and said: "Sir, perhaps you did not intend to give me a gold coin: here, have it back." "Keep it, my friend," said Molière, "and have another"; then he exclaimed: "See where virtue makes its nest!" '

20. *assez causé!*: 'Enough talk!' (French); see Part Two, note 32.

21. *adieu, mon plaisir*: 'Farewell, the pleasure was all my mine' (French).

22. *orphanages*: Dating to the times of Catherine the Great (1729–96), such orphanages took in children aged seven to eleven, after which they were handed over to schools or factories, or to be apprenticed to private individuals (*SB*).

23. *get yourself off to America*: In Chernyshevsky's novel *What Is to Be Done?* one of the characters, the medical student and 'rational egoist' Lopukhov,

emigrates to America in order not to impede his wife's new romantic attachment. There is also a historical backdrop to Svidrigailov's injunction: the emigration of Russians to America was frequently reported and debated in the Russian press of the 1860s and 1870s, as was the exile of convicts to North America by the British Empire (*SB, PSS*). Furthermore, Napoleon was said to have rejected the chance to flee to America after his defeat at Waterloo (see Part Three, note 31).

24. *a citizen and a man*: 'A man and a citizen' was a stock phrase in nineteenth-century Russian discourse, which Tikhomirov traces to the translated title of a school textbook on morals and civic duty by the educational reformer Johann Ignaz von Felbiger (1724–88), used from the era of Catherine the Great onwards. Variations on the formula make numerous ironic appearances in Dostoyevsky's fiction and the phrase will reappear in a later chapter (see *BT*, p. 417).

25. *robbed a mail coach*: See Part Two, note 23.

26. *une théorie comme une autre*: 'A theory like any other' (French).

27. *no truly sacred traditions ... Chronicles*: Svidrigailov's comments on the lack of strong traditions and memories in Russian civilized society echo the thoughts expressed in the 'First Philosophical Letter' (1836) of Pyotr Chaadayev (1794–1856) (*BT*). In this letter, for which he was declared insane, Chaadayev lambasted Russian culture's dependence on foreign models and ideas, and wrote of how, in consequence, Russian civilization failed to develop a sense of a past. The Russian chronicles, dating back as far as the ninth century, began to be collected and published in the mid-nineteenth century, with the first ten volumes appearing between 1841 and 1863; this scholarly labour continues today.

28. *a 'Vauxhall'*: Taking its name from the famous pleasure gardens on the south bank of the Thames, the first *vokzal* opened in St Petersburg in 1793 on the site apparently described here (and known in the mid-nineteenth century as Demidov Gardens). This and other 'Vauxhalls' in the city hosted concerts, dances, masquerades, circuses and other entertainments (*BT*). In modern usage, a *vokzal* is a railway station.

29. *the Vladimirka*: The dirt road leading from Moscow to the ancient city of Vladimir, 110 miles to the east, along which convoys of shackled prisoners began their long journey to penal exile. It was later portrayed by Isaak Levitan (1860–1900) in a celebrated landscape painting of the same name.

30. ——*kov Bridge*: Tuchkov Bridge.

31. ——*oy Prospect*: Bolshoi Prospect on Petersburg (now Petrograd) Side.

32. *Adrianopolis*: Noting that there was no such hotel in 1860s St Petersburg, Boris Tikhomirov seeks the symbolic significance of this name in the figure of Hadrian, the Roman Emperor (AD 117–38). Paganism and the eventual 'collapse of the pagan, anti-Christian idea', Tikhomirov argues, is thereby associated with Svidrigailov and his subsequent fate (*BT*).

33. *some café-chantant or other*: The *café-chantant* was a new phenomenon in Moscow and St Petersburg, offering not just music but also magicians, gymnasts and cancan dancing (*BT*).

34. *Trinity Day*: Celebrated on Pentecost Sunday (fifty days after Easter), this religious holiday marks the descent of the Holy Spirit to Christ's disciples and followers, and the miracle of the divine Trinity. An important date in the Russian Orthodox calendar, it is also known as the 'green' holiday and is accompanied by popular and pagan customs that include the decoration of homes and churches with branches, flowers and grass. (The reflection of this and other popular traditions in Svidrigailov's dream stands in ironic counterpoint to his previous comment to Dunya about the lack of native traditions in Russia.)

35. *The girl was a suicide – she'd drowned*: Tikhomirov notes that in popular tradition Trinity Sunday comes at the end of a series of designated days for burying and remembering those who have died an unnatural death (suicides, victims of violence and drowning, and so forth). It coincides with the 'week of the *rusalki*', the *rusalka* of Slavic mythology being a water nymph, ghost or mermaid-like creature, often imagined as the soul of a stillborn or unbaptized child or of an unmarried girl who met a watery grave by suicide or otherwise. Many other features of the girl in Svidrigailov's dream recall the *rusalki*, such as the white clothes and wreath of roses. Tikhomirov interprets the vision as a kind of belated funeral rite for the girl Svidrigailov once violated, an attempt 'somehow to mitigate his guilt'. The absence of candles and prayers reflects the Church's view of suicide as a sin on a par with murder; voluntary suicides were denied church burial and kept outside the cemetery (*BT*).

36. *a cannon fired once . . . The water's rising*: A sophisticated signalling system warned residents of St Petersburg about the imminent threat of flooding and the degree of severity; two cannon shots every quarter of an hour from both the Admiralty and the Peter and Paul Fortress indicated that the Neva had risen by a whole seven feet. The Neva reached a comparable height on the night of 29–30 June 1865, shortly before Dostoyevsky started work on the novel (*BT*).

37. *the face of a 'camellia'*: Following the success of *La Dame aux camélias* (1848) by Alexandre Dumas *fils* (1824–95), 'camellia' became a byword, in Russia as elsewhere, for women of the demi-monde – and, more broadly, prostitutes (*BT*). The heroine of Dumas's novel, later adapted for the stage, acquires her nickname because of the camellias that decorate her box at the theatre; perhaps it is the girl's 'scarlet lips' that suggest this particular euphemism to Svidrigailov here.

38. *tall watch tower*: In her notes to the novel, Anna Grigoryevna identified this as the 'Police station on Petersburg Side (Fire-fighting Department). On the corner of Syezzhinskaya Street and Bolshoi Prospect' (*PSS*).

39. *tell them I've gone to America*: This scene completes the reworking of the American motif in *What Is to Be Done?* (see note 23 above); if, in Chernyshevsky's novel, Lopukhov, 'the rational egoist', merely stages his suicide and really does leave for America after the end of his relationship with Vera Pavlovna, Svidrigailov does the precise opposite (*BT*) – offering, one might add, a different model of 'rational' and godless behaviour.

40. *makes up for forty sins*: On the one hand, the phrase is a variation of the notion in Slavonic cultures that the killing of a spider makes amends for forty sins (in a folkloric context where the spider is opposed to the Mother of God in particular); on the other, it echoes the popular Russian legend 'Sin and Penance' (*Grekh i pokayanie*) and its many variants, in which the killing of an oppressor and 'blood-sucker', far from being a sin, proves to be the only atonement possible for the murderer's previous sins (*BT*).

41. *crowned in the Capitol*: A reference to Julius Caesar (100–44 BC) in particular, perhaps in the light of Louis-Napoléon Bonaparte's newly published book on the Roman emperor (see Part Three, note 18).

42. *raining down bombs . . . during a regular siege*: Another reference to Napoleon's successful siege of Toulon in December 1793 (*BT*).

43. *no sight, no sound*: A formula often used in the much-loved collection of folktales by Alexander Afanasyev (1826–71) (*BT*).

44. *Zimmerman's*: See Part One, note 5.

45. *Livingstone's journals*: Almost certainly a reference to the Russian translation of *A Popular Account of Dr Livingstone's Expedition to the Zambesi and Its Tributaries and of the Discovery of the Lakes Shirwa and Nyassa (1858–1864)* (1865). The translation, edited by Dostoyevsky's friend Nikolai Strakhov, had been approved by the Russian censor in late 1866, just as Dostoyevsky was working on this part of the novel. The legendary expeditions of David Livingstone (1813–73) to explore

Africa in the mid-nineteenth century were well known in Russia even
before the publication of this translation (*SB, BT*).

46. *a citizen and a man*: See note 24 above.

47. *short-haired wenches . . . to study anatomy*: A further allusion to the
Great Reforms of the late 1850s and early 1860s, when higher education
was (to a limited extent) opened up to women. The decision to allow
women to attend lectures at St Petersburg University, and then at the
Medical-Surgical Academy (referred to here), caused consternation in
society. As with other reforms, the authorities soon backtracked. The
phrase 'short-haired wenches' was firmly associated at the time with
radically minded, *papirosa*-smoking female 'nihilists'. The passage also
alludes to Chernyshevsky's *What Is to Be Done?*, whose socialist heroine Vera Pavlovna also studied medicine (*BT*).

EPILOGUE

1. *there stands a town . . . a prison*: The model appears to be the town of
Omsk, in Western Siberia, on the banks of the Irtysh. Dostoyevsky was
confined in Omsk Prison from 1850 to 1854. 'Located some 1,500 miles
east of Moscow, this military prison was housed in an eighteenth-century
fortress originally built as protection against the steppe nomads. The
prison itself was surrounded by a high stockade in the form of a hexagon'
(*KL*). Dostoyevsky's experiences there had already been amply reflected
in one of his masterpieces, *Notes from the Dead House* (1860–2), and in
his correspondence. In a letter to his brother Mikhail, written a week
after his release from Omsk Prison, Dostoyevsky wrote: 'Things were
very bad for us. A military prison is much worse than a civilian one. [. . .]
We lived on top of each other, all together in one barrack [. . .] In summer, intolerable closeness; in winter, unendurable cold. All the floors
were rotten. Filth on the floors an inch thick; one could slip and fall';
quoted in Joseph Frank, *Dostoevsky: A Writer in His Time*, p. 189. Also
alluded to in this sentence, not without irony, is the opening of Alexander
Pushkin's narrative poem *The Bronze Horseman* (1833), describing Peter
the Great looking out from the site of his future city, St Petersburg, to the
West: 'On the banks of the deserted waves / Stood he, full of great
thoughts, / And gazed afar. Broadly before him / The river raced past.'

2. *second category*: Convicts were divided into three categories, according
to the gravity of their crime: convicts of the first category worked in the

pits; of the second, in fortresses; of the third, mainly in saltworks and distilleries. Like his protagonist, Dostoyevsky had also been a convict of the second category (SB).

3. *theory of temporary insanity*: Tikhomirov notes that Dostoyevsky may have familiarized himself with this theory in an article by the Austro-German psychiatrist Richard von Krafft-Ebing (1840–1902), which had just appeared in Russian at the time of writing: 'The Doctrine of Temporary or Transitory Insanity (*mania transitoria*), Expounded for Doctors and Jurists' listed a number of symptoms of this condition reminiscent of Raskolnikov's behaviour during the murder. According to Krafft-Ebing, *mania transitoria* lasts only a few hours, 'mainly strikes young people [. . .] aged between twenty and thirty' and is most commonly found in men. 'Temporary insanity,' the psychiatrist concludes, 'is becoming all the more important in court practice, because it evidently represents an entirely unfree state: during a fit of temporary insanity a man is not aware of himself, nor of the meaning of what he does, its consequences, punishability; the place of actions controlled by the will is taken by au-tomatic movements instigated by spurious notions, a false emotional sensation of anguish and an unconscious urge' (*BT*). The theory was not new to Russia, however, having been cited, for example, in the early 1840s by the Ministry of the Interior's Medical Council, which conclud-ed that a peasant who had killed her nine-month-old baby had done so 'during an attack of temporary insanity'; see Rice, *Dostoevsky and the Healing Art*, p. 179.

4. *his shaven head and his half-and-half jacket*: As Dostoyevsky explained in *Notes from the Dead House*, each category of convict had its own dress code. Exiled civilian convicts of the second category wore jackets that were half-grey and half-black. Other categories might have jackets all of one colour except for the sleeves; right and left trouser legs could also be of different colours. Heads, too, were shaved 'half-and-half', ei-ther from one end of the skull to the other or across. Raskolnikov's head, like Dostoyevsky's, would have been shaved 'across' (*BT*).

5. *Oh, men of wisdom, who deny everything*: An unmistakable reference to the 'nihilists', notably Dmitry Pisarev, who were in the ascendant in the 1860s, denying spiritual and cultural values.

6. *Polish convicts*: Participants, presumably, in the uprising against Impe-rial Russia in the former Polish-Lithuanian Commonwealth from 1863 to 1864, many thousands of whom were deported to Siberia. Some of Dos-toyevsky's co-prisoners in Omsk in the 1850s were also Polish noblemen,

punished for their involvement in the movement for national liberation (*BT*). Dostoyevsky wrote warmly of them in *Notes from the Dead House*, though their relations were soured both by the Russian writer's conviction that Poland, Lithuania and other nations all belonged under the rule of the Tsar, and by the Poles' contempt for the Russian peasant convicts; see Frank, *Dostoevsky: A Writer in His Time*, pp. 206–7.

7. *an axe*: No object could be more characteristic of archaic peasant Russia; see, for example, James H. Billington's classic study *The Icon and the Axe: An Interpretive History of Russian Culture* (1966).

8. *his turn came . . . to pray*: During Great Lent, which begins seven weeks before Easter, Orthodox believers devote several days to preparing for the sacraments of Confession and Holy Communion, during which they fast (avoiding animal products in particular), pray intensively and attend every church service. In Omsk, as Dostoyevsky wrote in *Notes from the Dead House*, the prisoners took turns to prepare (thirty at a time) and were let off work. In Part Two, Chapter V of that book, he describes the week of preparation in detail, reflecting on the pleasurable memories it evoked of his childhood. Here, Dostoyevsky is much more restrained, though one is reminded of the association of churches and childhood in Raskolnikov's dream much earlier in the novel (Part One, Chapter V).

9. *New trichinae*: The ability of trichinae – minute parasitic worms – to spread from pigs to humans caused a panic that began in Western Europe in 1863 and reached Russia by the time Dostoyevsky set to work on *Crime and Punishment*. The term had already been used in a metaphorical sense by Krestovsky in his novel *Petersburg Slums*, and would be reworked again by Dostoyevsky in 'The Dream of a Ridiculous Man' (1877) (*BT*).

10. *The pestilence*: Dostoyevsky uses the archaic word 'pestilence' (*morovaya yazva*) in preference to 'plague' (*chuma*), calling to mind passages in the Old Testament where the image is frequently used to express God's anger and punishment (see especially Jeremiah 29:17–19 and Ezekiel 14:21), and in the New Testament (especially Matthew 24:7, Luke 21:11); equally relevant is the use of the term as a metaphor for the moral corruption caused by 'temptation' in the writings of Tikhon of Zadonsk (1724–83), a saint much loved by Dostoyevsky: 'The pestilence begins at first in a single person, then the whole house, and from that the whole town or village, and later the whole country too, is infected and perishes' (*BT, SB*).

11. *old burnous and the green shawl*: According to Tatyana Kasatkina, the *burnous* ('a cloak and outer garment of various types . . . ostensibly based

on an Arab model') 'most resembles the traditional clothing of Mary – the *Maforiy* (the dress of married Palestinian women)'; while *green*, 'as the colour of life on earth, is directly linked to the image of the Madonna' and 'is constantly present even in icons'. See her article on the Epilogue in *Fyodor Dostoevsky's Crime and Punishment: A Casebook* (p. 175).

12. *the Gospels*: See Part Four, note 13. Dostoyevsky later wrote of his brief meeting with the wives of the Decembrists, who gave him the Gospels on his way to prison: 'The meeting lasted an hour. They blessed us on our new journey, made the sign of the cross over us, and gave each of us a copy of the Gospels – the only book allowed in prison. For four years of penal servitude it lay beneath my pillow. I sometimes read it and read it to others. With it, I taught another convict to read' (from his *Diary of a Writer*, 1873).

13. *seven days*: See Genesis 29:20: 'And Jacob served seven years for Rachel; and they seemed unto him but a few days, for the love he had to her' (*SB*).